Lynda Page was born and brought up in Leicester. The eldest of four daughters, she left home at seventeen and has had a wide variety of office jobs. She lives in a village near Leicester. Her previous sagas are also available from Headline, and have been highly praised:

'Filled with lively characters and compelling action' *Books*

'A nostalgic background for its mix of colourful characters fronted by the delightfully strong leading lady' *Lincolnshire Echo*

'It's a story to grip you from the first page to the last' *Coventry Evening Telegraph*

'You'll be hooked from page one' *Woman's Realm*

'A cracking good yarn' *Lancashire Evening Post*

'An enjoyable read with lots going on to keep you hooked until the very end' *Wiltshire Times*

'Lynda Page creates strong characters and is a clever and careful storyteller ... She has the stamina not to alienate you as a reader and to keep the story going on a constant flow of purpose and energy ... A great writer who gives an authentic voice to Leicester ... A formidable talent' *LE1*

'A gripping t   magazine

Also by Lynda Page

Evie
Annie
Josie
Peggie
And One For Luck
Just By Chance
At The Toss Of A Sixpence
Any Old Iron
Now Or Never
In For A Penny
All Or Nothing
A Cut Above
Out With The Old
Against The Odds
No Going Back
Whatever It Takes
A Lucky Break
Onwards And Upwards

FOR WHAT IT'S WORTH

Lynda Page

First published in 2006
by HEADLINE BOOK PUBLISHING

First published in paperback in 2006
by HEADLINE BOOK PUBLISHING

1

0 7553 0885 9 (ISBN-10)
978 0 7553 0885 9 (ISBN-13)

Typeset in Stempel Garamond by
Palimpsest Book Production Limited, Polmont, Stirlingshire
Printed and bound in Great Britain by
Clays Ltd, St Ives plc

Headline's policy is to use papers that are natural, renewable and
recyclable products and made from wood grown in
sustainable forests. The logging and manufacturing processes
are expected to conform to the environmental
regulations of the country of origin.

HEADLINE BOOK PUBLISHING
A division of Hodder Headline
338 Euston Road
LONDON NW1 3BH

www.headline.co.uk
www.hodderheadline.com

For Mary Inchley

I thought it was about time to acknowledge what a truly wonderful friend – in every sense of the word – you are to me.

To describe your qualities and what a good impact you have had on my life would take more words than in this book, so all I'll say now is that if you were a man I would marry you without hesitation!

With all my love
Lynda x

For John Chaplin

In grateful appreciation for the time you spent with me reliving your experiences and imparting information from your forty years in the taxi business.

CHAPTER ONE

Charles Tyme froze rigid as the length of cheese wire throttling him tightened round his neck, cutting into his flesh. He could feel the warm trickle of blood running down to pool in the well of his throat. The nauseating stench of foul breath assailed him as a low throaty voice in his ear warned: 'Hand over yer takings! And no funny business or it's a six-foot hole they'll be digging for you.'

His assailant left Chas in no doubt he meant business. He hadn't liked the look of the scruffily dressed man when he'd appeared out of the shadows and before Chas could stop him, slipped into the back of his vehicle. He'd just dropped off his last fare in a deserted, dimly lit street on the outskirts of the city. The new fare had gruffly indicated 'town' as his destination.

Chas had been earning his living by taxi-driving barely a month, was still in fact a novice compared to the old stalwarts who'd been in the game for years and knew all the tricks of the trade inside out. Nevertheless he was well aware that it was illegal for private-hire taxi companies to pick fares up off the side of the road unless they'd previously booked

1

through the firm's office – a fare accepted off the street was known as a flimp or flimping in the trade. This law, and many more besides, was flouted shamelessly by most other private-hire drivers. Chas, though, was the conscientious sort. To him the law was the law, made for a purpose and to be abided by regardless of the cost in lost business.

He'd informed the man twice that he wasn't for hire but it was obvious the passenger was not going to budge. His response on both occasions had been a curt, 'I said, town.'

As Chas saw it he was faced with two options. Either he dragged the man bodily from the vehicle or else he turned a blind eye to the law and delivered him to his destination. Chas struggled with his conscience. He didn't like the thought of knowingly breaking the law but balancing that was his reluctance to leave anyone in an area of Leicester that was known to be a criminal haunt. Should any ill befall the man there, Chas would never forgive himself. His better nature gave him no option but to take the unwelcome fare where he demanded to go. As a sop to his conscience about breaking the law, Chas decided that he would put his cut of the fare in the box for the blind in his local corner shop and those unfortunate people would receive the benefit of it.

'All right, mate,' he'd eventually agreed. 'I'll make an exception just this once, but next time – no official booking through the office, no ride. Not in my car.'

He'd tried to appraise the man huddled in the back seat through his rear-view mirror as he'd driven along but the night was a dark one, a blanket of thick cloud masking the moon. Besides that the man had kept his head down. In his present dire predicament Chas realised why: to avoid any possible later identification.

Chas hadn't been fazed initially when a few minutes after they'd set off the man had suddenly demanded he should stop, having apparently changed his mind about his destination. Chas had been told on his sketchy induction to the job that people frequently did this and most were disgruntled that, regardless, they still had to pay for the distance already travelled. But Chas hadn't been given the time to calculate what was owed him. Immediately he'd stopped the thin length of wire was slid around his neck, the man issuing his murderous threat to make sure Chas complied with his demand.

When he had decided to take this job, it had never crossed his mind that he'd one day find himself having his life threatened for a meagre amount of money. Making matters even worse for Chas was the fact that the money in the takings bag belonged to his employer, so in truth was not his to hand over to the thief.

In an effort to reason with his attacker he began, 'If you'd let me explain that the . . .'

The wire was yanked tighter and a fresh trickle of blood ran down his neck. 'I said, hand over yer takings. And mek it quick, I ain't got all night. Any more shilly-shallying and I'll finish you off here and now and help meself to 'em.'

Despite Chas's own aversion to violence in any form,

he felt that in this case he was being given no other option.

Despite the pounding of his heart and his restricted breathing, he managed to say matter-of-factly, 'Me takings bag is under me seat. You'll have to release me if yer want me to pass it over.'

Silence prevailed for several long seconds before Chas felt the tension on the wire relax enough for him to lean as far forward as he needed to. 'Don't try 'ote stupid 'cos I meant what I said,' the man snarled, 'I will finish you off.'

Chas felt under his seat for the canvas takings bag. Grabbing the end of it and gripping it tightly, he then sat upright again and, taking a deep breath while praying his aim would be accurate, with a quick flick of his wrist he brought the bulky bag of coins back to land forcefully smack against his attacker's temple. A surprised yelp rent the air as the man let go of the cheese wire, slapping his hands to his head. Simultaneously, Chas made a grab for the car door, levered the handle open and leaped out. Next he yanked the back door open and hauled out his still-stunned assailant. Thrusting him forcibly away, Chas snatched up the length of wire that had fallen out of the taxi. He twisted the ends around his huge hands, flexing it in a threatening gesture. 'You picked the wrong cabby to fleece tonight,' he hissed. 'Now, unless you want a taste of yer own medicine, I'd make a run for it while you can if I was you.'

Sprawled across the pavement, the gash on his head pouring blood, the man stared up at Chas wild-eyed, stunned senseless by this sudden reversal of roles. Chas could tell his mind was flailing around, seeking for a way to turn the situation back in his own favour. As Chas stared down, wondering if the man was going to risk another attack and preparing to defend himself, he felt a sudden rush of pity. He wondered what had brought about this situation where a man would threaten grievous bodily harm on another human being for the sake of a few pounds? Any number of things could have caused him to become desperate enough to resort to such measures. A hungry wife and children perhaps? A sick relative needing expensive care? Being the man he was Chas could not help but extend a show of compassion.

'Look . . . er . . . I don't condone what you've just tried but if you're that desperate for money, desperate enough to threaten murder, I could give you a few shillings. It's not much but, you see, the money in the takings bag isn't mine. If you did try to relieve me of it again, well, I'd have to try and stop you and one of us would come off the worse. I have to tell you straight that I would do my damnedest to make sure it wasn't me.'

The man looked up at him, stupefied, wondering if he had heard right.

Chas smiled kindly. 'Would a few shillings help? Enough to buy you a hot meal at any rate.'

The mugger scrambled up to stand staring at Chas as though he was mad. 'Er . . . you on the level, Gov?'

Chas untwisted the wire and thrust one of his hands into his pocket, pulling out a half-crown which he held out towards the man. 'I should march you down to the police station as any other cabby would after what you tried. Just count yourself lucky it was me you picked on and not one of my colleagues 'cos, I can assure you, they wouldn't have let you off anywhere near so lightly. Now take this and scarper before I change my mind. Oh, and . . . er . . . I'd get that cut on your head seen to urgently in case it turns nasty.'

The man made a sudden snatch for the money then, spinning on his heels, stumbled off into the night.

Chas stared after him until the sound of his footsteps had died away. Forming the wire into a tight ball, he shoved it deep into his trouser pocket then rubbed his big hands wearily over his face. He had just had a close call. If that desperado had carried out his murderous threat, Chas could now be well on his way to whatever lay in store for him in the after-life. He hoped vehemently that his attacker had learned his lesson and in future would choose more legitimate ways in which to earn a living. He also knew that should this incident become common knowledge amongst his fellow workers they would never understand why he had chosen to act the way he had and he would be mercilessly berated. So as far as Chas was concerned, no one else needed to know. No harm had come to him, well, no serious harm, and it was he himself who was out of pocket and not his employer.

A crackling sound over the car radio alerted him. Slipping back into the driver's seat, he unhooked the hand-mic and pressed down the receiver button. 'Romeo with you.' How uncomfortable his call handle made him feel! If he had been Adonis-like then it might have been apt, but as it was he was more the unremarkable, gentle giant sort. He hadn't been given any choice, though. It was the boss who had allotted his call handle to him when his employment began so Chas was stuck with it.

A shrill response in the thick Leicester accent of Marlene Cox, evening-shift radio operator back in the firm's office on Blackbird Road at the other side of town, sounded like gobbledegook to Chas.

'Repeat, base?' he requested.

Irritated, she responded, 'Oh, yer should wash yer lug 'oles out, Chas Tyme, then you'd hear me proper! I asked if you were free to do a pick up on Beaumont Leys? Bloke needs ter get to the station to catch the six-twenty to Nottingham.'

Her disrespectful attitude towards him was not lost on Chas but now was not the time to reproach her for it. He flashed a quick look at his watch. It was a minute to six, in actual fact his knocking off time. Even in a speeding car with no traffic on the road, he'd still be hard pushed to collect the client and get him to the station in time to catch the train. 'I'm at the top of Welford Road at the moment. Traffic permitting, it'd take me fifteen minutes at least to get to the Beaumont Leys. The train would be halfway to Nottingham by the time I got the customer to the station.' If Marlene took more interest in her job instead of forever preening herself to attract the eye of any man who came through the firm's door, or of one driver in particular, then she should have known exactly where Chas was and that he couldn't possibly do the job to the satisfaction of the customer.

'Eh? Wha' did yer say?'

Taking a deep breath, Chas slowly repeated himself.

'So yer won't do it then?' came her shrill reply.

He groaned. After what he'd just been through tonight he was in no mood for dealing with the likes of Marlene who only exhibited a spark of intelligence when the mood took her. In fact, it was Chas's private opinion that she didn't actually have any as he hadn't witnessed any evidence of it so far during the two weeks she'd been at Black's Taxis. He knew from the grumbling of the other drivers too that although they appreciated her physical attributes, they were not at all impressed by her radio-operating skills He snapped down the switch on the mic. 'I didn't say I wouldn't do it,' he sighed. 'Only that it's not humanly possible for me to do it in time. What about one of the other drivers?'

She whined, 'Can't gerrold of no one else. Bloody ignorant sods are ignoring me!'

Regardless of the fact that she had had it explained to her several times, Marlene still didn't seem to appreciate that the radio didn't work in some areas of the city if in the vicinity of tall buildings and, depending on the terrain outside the city boundaries, only sporadically over a ten-mile radius. Meanwhile, Chas was aware that a customer was awaiting his arrival and that precious time was being wasted. 'Tell the bloke I'll be there as soon as I can and I'll do me best to get him to the station on time, but I ain't making any promises.'

'Eh? Wha' did yer say?'

His mind already fixing on the best possible route through the back streets of Leicester to help him achieve this seemingly impossible task, he uncharacteristically snapped: 'I said, I'll do me bloody best!' Replacing the mic in its cradle, Chas roared off.

CHAPTER TWO

In the snug back room of a two-up, two-down rented terraced house a few minutes' walk from the premises of Black's Taxis, a sprightly, neat seventy year old with iron-grey hair, Iris Imelda Tyme, dropped her darning and got to her feet as soon as she heard the back door open. Arriving in the kitchen she smiled, relieved to see her son home safe and sound.

'Yer very late tonight,' she said, moving towards the stove. She picked up a worn tea towel then bent over to open the door and remove a piping hot chipped enamel dish. 'I was starting to worry you'd met with an accident or summat.' Straightening up, she smiled warmly at Chas. 'Well, yer dinner's all ready for yer and it's nice and hot.'

Hanging his working jacket over his arm, he looked quickly into the dish. The contents, whatever they were, were so shrivelled it was hard to tell what she'd cooked but he loved and respected his mother far too much to say anything that would hurt her feelings. 'Looks great, Mam,' he said enthusiastically. Sniffing appreciatively he added, 'Smells good too.'

Iris looked up fondly at the huge man who dwarfed her. At thirty years old, six foot two and a well-muscled fifteen stone, no would ever guess what a struggle for life her son had had when he'd arrived in the world six weeks' premature. He'd been a scrap of humanity, not expected to live by the medical profession. The first few weeks of his existence had been touch and go as his underdeveloped body fought to cope. His survival was like a miracle to Iris. By the time she had learned of her pregnancy – a 'change-of-life baby' the doctors had termed him – she had long ago resigned herself to the fact that the large family her beloved husband Charles and she had longed for was not going to materialise. They had reluctantly resigned themselves to remaining childless.

Then, at the age of forty, in the space of a week Iris had lost her soul-mate in an accident – on his way to work a runaway horse and cart had ploughed into Charles's push bike, killing him instantly – and while still coping with the trauma of her devastating loss, had discovered to her utter shock that she was expecting their much longed-for child. During a time of otherwise desperate sadness, the life growing inside her had become a source of deep comfort and Iris had vowed to her dead husband that she would raise their child as best she could, labour hard not to let it suffer from the loss of the loving father he would have been.

All these years later she still shuddered at the memory of her vigil by her son's hospital cot, willing the tiny scrap within to fight to live, constantly terrified she would lose him. Her gratitude towards the hospital staff when her six-week-old son was finally pronounced to be out of danger knew no bounds, but deep down and despite others possibly labelling her a crank Iris was convinced it was the spirit of her dead husband that had helped their son through his first difficult weeks. From the hereafter Charles had reached out and given her the one thing she desired most in the world, the one thing he had known would help her through the rest of her days without her husband by her side. Thirty years later, every night before she settled down to sleep, Iris thanked him for what she was convinced was his last bequest to her.

With her love and determination to help him on his way, the scrawny child she'd named after his father grew into a strapping lad, possessing a kind and caring nature, eager to help his mother in any way he could to bring money into the house. Iris herself took any work open to her – mostly cleaning for ungrateful people who treated her like a slave, rewarding her labours with as little as they could get away with. Chas run errands for the neighbours, and as soon as he was old enough took a Saturday job with the local garage cleaning cars, despite her protests, always insisting every penny he earned was hers to spend.

Much to her regret, Iris became aware that due to his concern for her and his naturally shy nature, her son had been labelled by the other local children of his age group as a 'mummy's boy'. He was ostracised and ridiculed mercilessly by them at every opportunity. Iris knew that this state of affairs had resulted in her beloved boy finding it difficult even now to trust anyone long enough to forge a close friendship with them. That hadn't stopped him from taking up interests of his own, though. Listening to the wireless as a child had developed his great love of music. He owned an ever-increasing record collection and many people would have envied his selection of rare imports, Chas having a penchant for songs by the likes of Sam Cooke, Harry Belafonte, Nat King Cole, and a variety of black American Rhythm and Blues artists. An avid reader also, the bookcase in his bedroom groaned under the weight of the paper-backs he had amassed over the years, both fiction and non-fiction. He had taught himself the basics of plumbing, electrics and motor mechanics, something the neighbours were well aware of. They often called upon him to help them out in emergencies. Chas always obliged, never accepting payment for his time, just glad to be of help. He enjoyed speedway too, and when the mood took him would pay a visit to the local stadium for a night at the track when certain riders he favoured were appearing.

Her son was handsome in Iris's eyes though she was clear-sighted enough to realise that, pitted against other men, he did not possess the kind of physical attributes that turned women's heads. That in itself, she felt, was not the real reason why he'd never plucked up the courage to ask a girl out. His crippling lack of self-confidence was. It saddened her to think of the missed opportunities he'd suffered because of the constant barrage of unwarranted callous remarks and nasty tricks, some of them potentially dangerous, that he'd suffered at the hands of his tormentors. Iris knew what a wonderful husband and father he would have made, and for Iris herself having a daughter-in-law's compan-ionship would have been a delight. She lived in hope, though, that one day a good woman would present herself, manage somehow to break though her son's reserve, and then when the time came Iris could join her beloved husband, happy in the knowledge that she hadn't left their child alone in the world.

'Yer just like yer dad was, God rest him. He loved my cooking too. Ate 'ote I put before him and never complained once. I should apply to be one of those chefs on the telly, shouldn't I? Show the women of Britain how it's really done. It was yer grandmother, God rest her, that I've to thank because she taught me all I know. "Never be afraid to use yer imagination in the kitchen, Iris," she constantly used to say to me as I stood beside her, watching her throw this and that into a bowl and mixing it all up. "Always make sure all yer meat is cooked well through so it's no germs left in it." So I always have and I've never poisoned yer, son, have I? Or yer dad neither.'

Chas pressed his lips together. In truth her cooking skills left much to be desired. She couldn't follow a recipe to save her life. If the directions said three ounces of flour, Iris would add another 'just in case'. She thought nothing of substituting something else if she hadn't got the exact ingredient the recipe stated, such as nutmeg for cinammon in a cake. She liked to make up her own concoctions too. Chas had often finished a meal with no idea of what exactly he'd just eaten. Regardless, he would never hurt her feelings by making even the slightest complaint, eating everything she put before him with relish and complimenting her after for her efforts, whether he had enjoyed it or not. His mother always made sure he'd a hot meal waiting for him when he came home, and what she produced, she produced with love.

Iris was just about to tell him she'd serve up while he went to change out of his working attire when she spotted dried blood on his shirt collar and then the thin red weal circling his thick neck. Her face creased with worry. 'What on earth happened to you?'

Chas looked at her blankly. In his desire to get his last passenger to the station on time to catch his train, which he'd achieved with only seconds to spare, he'd forgotten about his encounter with the thief and subsequent injuries. The office had been empty when he'd gone in to sign off his shift, apart from Marlene, varnishing her nails, and if she had noticed, she certainly hadn't bothered herself to enquire about it. Considering the circumstances of his father's death on his way to work, he couldn't risk alarming Iris with the truth. As far as he was aware his mother had no inkling of some of the types he encountered during his working hours, was under the impression all his passengers were polite, nice people who were thoroughly appreciative of the service he was doing them. He wanted to keep it that way. Covering the weal on his neck with his hand, he said lightly, 'Oh, I ... er ... walked into a washing line. It looks worse than it is.'

She scowled disbelievingly. 'Do I look as though I was born yesterday? That cut was caused by summat thin like ... like ... wire. It looks to me like someone tried to throttle yer!'

Chas stopped himself from laughing out loud. He should have known his lame excuse would not fool his mother. She might be in her twilight years, not quite as nimble on her feet as she once used to be, but there was nothing wrong with her faculties. 'Yeah, yer right,

Mam. It was a thin wire-type washing line. I . . . er . . . couldn't make a customer hear I'd arrived at the front so I went round the back. The idiots who lived there had hung their washing line across the yard instead of down the length of it like most people do and, well, before I knew it I'd walked into it and it somehow got wrapped around my neck.' Before she could question him further, Chas added, 'I'd better get changed before my dinner goes cold.'

With that he hurried off to his bedroom.

A while later, his injury having been bathed using cold water from the jug on the stand in his room and now concealed by a black polo-necked sweater, he pushed away his empty plate and smiled appreciatively over at his mother. 'That were grand, Mam, thanks.'

She looked pleased as she gathered up the dirty dishes. 'Glad you enjoyed it. I've fruit pie for yer pudding.'

Fruit pie? Now that could mean anything. Apple. Blackberry. Pear. Blackcurrant. Apricot. Tinned fruit salad. Pineapple. Peaches. A mixture of two or three or even the whole lot.

Putting the overflowing dish of pie in front of him, smothered in thick custard so he was unable to determine just what fruit it contained, Iris sat down opposite nursing a cup of tea and looked at Chas hard. 'Yer look tired, son. I thought the idea of you changing yer job was to make it a lot easier on yerself? You worked all hours driving that lorry around all over the country. Now it seems yer working even longer hours, ferrying folks in and around Leicestershire. I suppose the only good side to yer changing yer job is that yer home every night so I can at least be certain you've had a home-cooked meal and can sleep in yer own clean bed.'

'Tired' wasn't the word for what Chas was feeling. His close brush with death was just beginning to register with him. What he'd gone through wasn't uppermost in his mind, it was what his mother could have been facing should the worst have happened to him at the hands of that mindless thief. When his father had had his life cut short through a senseless accident it was only the arrival of her son that had given Iris something to live for. If he had met his end tonight, she would have been left all on her own in the world in her twilight years, when love and help from her family were of paramount importance. Iris would never admit it but everyday tasks she once used to take in her stride, such as shopping and getting in the coal, took their toll on her now. Chas did his best to make sure he tackled this heavy work while endeavouring to make sure her pride was not dented.

From the best of intentions he had not been entirely honest with his mother about his decision to change his job. In fact, he hadn't been honest at all. He had loved his job as a lorry driver, delivering loads around the shires and up and down the country for a boss who was a decent man to work for and who had been sorry to lose such a conscientious worker. The only down-side of that job had been spending several nights on the trot away from home every other week. But after his mother suffered a tumble in the street several weeks previously, turning her ankle on slippery cobbles while she was struggling with heavy bags of shopping, Chas was forced to acknowledge that the years were telling on Iris and he needed to be constantly on hand to avoid anything similar happening again.

At the age of thirty and with no experience of anything else but driving for a living, most local occupations paying a liveable wage were closed to Chas. Just about resigned to the fact that his only option was to take a labouring job in a factory, something he would have detested doing, after his years on the open road, he chanced to overhear a conversation in the pub. A local firm was on the lookout for a taxi driver, apparently. Vacancies for such jobs were few and far between, very much sought after, in fact. Surely he wouldn't stand a chance of securing it, matched against those with experience who were bound to apply. A job such as that, though, would suit Chas perfectly. It was driving which he liked, local which meant it was near at hand to where he lived, but more importantly it meant no nights away from home so he'd be able to do all the heavy chores for his mother. He wasted no time in making an application and couldn't believe his luck when Jack Black, the owner of Black's Taxis, liked the sound of what Chas had to offer and took him on.

Knowing his mother realised how much he had loved his lorry driving, Chas had fobbed Iris off with a tale that slack orders at work meant a cut in the workforce and he had felt morally obliged to put himself forward as one of the first to be let go, since he'd no wife and children as dependants like all the other drivers had. Iris had balked at his reasoning, pointing out that his wage was as important to him as it was to any of his workmates, but Chas had stuck firmly to his story and she had had no choice but to accept his decision. His mother, Chas knew, would have been mortified had she ever found out the real truth. He just prayed she never did.

Now, his filled spoon poised in mid-air, he smiled at her. 'A couple of the part-time drivers called in sick so we were short-handed. It would've been daft of me to turn down the chance of earning a bit extra to put in the house-buying fund, wouldn't it? And besides, with what's going on at work, the least I can do for the boss is pull my weight as hard as I can to keep his business going until ... well ... hopefully he returns.'

Iris gave a disdainful click of her tongue. 'I see the need to do what you can for your boss but, oh, you and this house-buying lark! I keep telling yer, I've lived here all me married life and I've me friends round-abouts ...'

'Yes, Mam, I know that,' Chas cut in. 'But a modern house would be so much easier for you.'

'The way you talk, you make it sound like this new house you want to move me into when yer've saved up enough will just look after itself.'

'Oh, Mam, you know it won't. But don't tell me you don't like the thought of modern conveniences helping to make your life easier? Think about it seriously, Mam. A water heater would mean no more boiling up pans for a wash. And having a proper bathroom ... well, if *you* don't like the thought of that, *I* most certainly do. For a man my size, sitting in the tin bath ain't no fun, Mam. And look how the twin-tub and the Hoover changed your life. You went mad at first when I got you those, saying I should have spent the money of meself.' He looked at her tenderly. 'I just want to make life easier for you. You worked yourself half to death raising me on your own. Now you should be gracious enough to let me return the favour by doing what I can for you. Dad would have wanted that, I know he would. Forgive me for saying it but you're not so young as you were and I want you around for many years to come. If what I do to make your life easier helps achieve that, then it makes me happy.'

Iris pulled a shamed expression. She knew she was a fortunate woman to have a son who possessed such a generous nature. Chas could easily have turned out like so many of her neighbours' offspring whose priorities were strictly centred on themselves, the possible needs of their aging parents not figuring at all in their scheme of things. They even begrudged paying over their board money which in reality was not enough actually to keep them. The rest they earned went on entertainment and sporadic repayments of hire purchase agreements for clothes, cars and other frivolities they in truth couldn't afford and would take years to pay off.

Not that she was ungrateful for all Chas did for her and would do in the future, Iris just felt strongly that his efforts were all centred on what he could do for her, with little or no thought for his own well-being. She realised he was talking to her. 'Eh, what did yer say, lovey?'

'I'm just saying, I'm sorry I never got a chance to get the heavy shopping for you today but I'll make sure I do it tomorrow.'

She leaned over and patted his hand. 'I did gather

that as yer came in empty-handed. Look, if yer can't manage tomorrow . . .'

'I will manage tomorrow,' he cut in, knowing what she was about to suggest. 'I'm not having you lugging bags of heavy groceries up the street at your age.'

'Oh, that's it, lad, remind me how old I am.' It was a scolding tone Iris used but her eyes were twinkling mischievously.

He laughed. 'Your body might be failing you a bit, but inside you're still a young girl. Isn't that right, Mam?'

She chuckled. 'That's about the size of it. Getting old is no fun, son. I wouldn't wish it on anyone. Mind you, I suppose it could be a lot worse. At least I ain't crippled with arthritis and I've n'ote wrong with me hearing or eyesight.' Her eyes settled on him tenderly. 'And I never forget what a lucky woman I am, having the likes of you for a son.'

'It's me that's the lucky one, having you for a mam.'

Although delighted by his compliment, she said dryly, 'Ah, well, I agree with yer there seeing's you could have ended up with one like Clarice Dewhurst.'

Chas shuddered at the very thought. Clarice Dewhurst lived next-door-but-one. Whether she was a widow or her husband had deserted her was not known, but either way it was the opinion of the rest of the neighbours roundabouts that her spouse had had a lucky escape. Clarice and her three threadbare children, two boys and a girl, six, five and four respectively, had arrived in the neighbourhood on one balmy evening twenty years previously, their assortment of shabby belongings carried between them since there wasn't a penny to spare for a cart or barrow. The children immediately took it upon themselves to shatter the peace of the street, becoming personally responsible for causing as much trouble as they possibly could, and no one ever dared complain for fear of a foul tongue-lashing or possible black eye from their hard-faced mother who, as far as she was concerned, was not responsible for what her offspring got up to outside her four walls. How exactly Clarice afforded to pay her way had never been fathomed, but it wasn't from respectable work. It was the general opinion of the neighbours that she lived off the proceeds of her own and her children's misdemeanours.

Of all the other children in the street it was Chas who had suffered worst at the hands of the Dewhursts. Immediately they'd moved in, they had decided this pleasant-natured boy with the widowed mother would be a prime candidate for their own particular brand of fun and had made it their business to make sure all the other local children followed their lead – or risked the nasty consequences.

After years of their torment, much to Chas's relief adulthood saw the Dewhurst children turn their attention further afield. As a result the eldest son met his end falling off a roof while in the process of robbing a factory; the other was serving a life sentence for holding up a bank with a sawn-off shotgun, killing a bank clerk who refused to open the vault for him; the girl, now twenty-five, had married an unsavoury sort who saw providing for his family as an optional extra and she was now living in worse squalor than she had with her mother, four children of her own hanging on her skirts.

Clarice herself was housebound, suffering from the degenerative disease of elephantiasis, dependent for the most part on the long-suffering home help who came in daily to see to her needs. Local rumour had it recently that Nadine, Clarice's daughter, had left her husband, and she and her children were now back with her mother. Chas fervently hoped this rumour had no substance to it. If Nadine's children were anything like she had been when young, then he pitied all the other youngsters in the vicinity.

Iris was looking at her son with concern. 'Any news on Jack Black? Bad luck that state of affairs, ain't it? A fortnight into your new place and the boss suffers a heart attack. Now everything's up in the air about yer job, depending on the outcome.'

Chas had to admit it was but unlike Iris, who saw the bad luck as her own son's, his sympathies lay with Jack himself. From what he had gleaned of the sixty-four-year-old man during the two weeks he had worked under him, Jack had come across as a thoroughly decent man, very focused on keeping his business profitable against constant competition, not only so as to keep a roof over his own head but to keep his workforce employed as well. Trouble was, in doing so he'd worked eighteen hours a day and taken no holidays for the last twenty years. That practice had taken a heavy toll on his health from which he was now suffering.

Chas heaved a sigh. 'I've not heard anything one way or the other, Mam.'

She pulled a face. 'So he's still in hospital then?'

'As far as I know.'

Iris sighed. 'Doesn't look so good for him then, does

24

it? No mild heart attack that wasn't, not if he's still in hospital. My heart goes out to his wife, it really does. Just at a time when she could start looking forward to her husband retiring and to seeing more of him, this has to go and happen. Still, it's my opinion Mrs Black is lucky insomuch as there's still a chance her man could pull through, whereas . . .' Her voice trailed off as she remembered that terrible morning thirty years ago when she was left with no hope of ever seeing her husband again. She mentally shook herself and added, 'Still, that's life, ain't it, son? How's the new day operator panning out?'

Chas put his spoon back in the dish and loudly sighed. 'Ralph Widcombe is doing his best. As a retired driver himself, he at least has a good idea of what the job entails, but as he's never operated the radio before it's all new to him. He's very forgetful too so he gets us drivers in a right pickle sometimes, giving us wrong addresses, etcetera. But after all, he is in his eighties. When all's said and done it's good of him to come out of retirement to help out Mrs Black in her time of need. As for Marlene Cox, the evening girl, well, she's not a clue, Mam, and the trouble is, I don't think she's really that interested. I can only think that when she was interviewed she blagged her way through it as I can't see any other reason why the boss's wife would take her on. Mind you, in fairness to her, Mrs Black did have other things on her mind at the time.'

'Mmm, rather a lot, I'd say,' mouthed Iris sympathetically. 'I suppose she was just glad to find someone who'd work such unsocial hours at short notice so she could get on with caring for her husband. My heart goes out to her, it really does.' A look of sadness filled her face. 'Such a shame about Jack Black. From what you told me about him he seemed to be the rough-around-the-edges sort, but also a fair-minded man.' She smiled warmly at her son. 'A man like yerself, in fact. I'm praying he recovers and that hopefully this has delivered a warning to him to take things easier in future 'cos no one is immortal, however much we might think we are.' She pursed her lips thoughtfully. 'If he doesn't make it . . . well, I wonder what Muriel Black will do about the business?'

'That's something that's concerning quite a few of the drivers. Some of them are putting out feelers for work with other companies should Mrs Black decide to close us down. But getting work with other outfits is touch and go, depending how many, if any, plates they have free at the time.'

Iris looked aghast, thinking of her son's job. 'Oh, surely she wouldn't close the business down?'

Chas gave a shrug. 'As far as I understand it she's never before had anything to do with running the firm so it's not like she's equipped to take over. They have no children so there's no son or daughter to assume the reins. She could appoint a manager, I suppose, and keep it running that way. Or she could decide to cash in on all the plates. Most cabbies who own their own plates look on them as their retirement fund. That might be what Jack Black had it in mind to do when the time came. Black's have fifteen private-hire plates acquired over the years. Between them ABC Taxis, Highfield's and Swift's have the rest of the eighty the council issued. I overheard one of the drivers debating whether he could raise the money to buy one should Mrs Black decide to sell them off and then go into business for himself. But then, it's like he said. Where does someone like him get a spare couple of hundred or so quid at the drop of a hat when on a good week he only earns about thirty-five to forty? 'Course, should ABC, Highfield's or Swift's want the plates by way of expanding their own businesses then they'd be in a position to offer stupid money just to get their hands on them. Anyway, this is all speculation, Mam. Hopefully, Mr Black will pull through.'

Iris vigorously nodded her head. 'Oh, yes, let's hope so, son.' Then something he had said struck her and she frowned quizzically. 'You said that cabby who was wishing he could afford to buy a plate earns about forty quid on a good week? You don't earn that much. Not that what you earn is my business, even though I am yer mother, but you've never hidden yer pay slip from me so that's how I know.'

'Mam, some cabbies can earn that much because of what they're prepared to do for it.'

'Prepared to do? What do you mean, son?'

He took a deep breath. 'Let's put it this way. I don't fancy a term in jail, and neither do I feel it right to blatantly fleece the boss. I know I'm still a greenhorn as far as the drivers' scams go. After all, I've only been in the job a short time. Haven't really had the chance to find out all they get up to so as to boost their pay packet, but one thing I do know is that although it's against the law for private-hire cabbies to pick up straight off the street same as Hackney cabbies, they still do it.'

Iris looked perplexed. 'But I don't understand how they make extra money by doing that?'

'Well, the company hasn't any record of the fare as it's not been booked through the office. That way the cabby can pocket all of it.' Chas could tell his mother still didn't understand so he added, 'Look, Mam, say I have to take a chap to the station, and when I drop him a man coming off the train asks me to take him back into town. Well, I'm going back through town anyway on my way to the office to wait for my next job, or even if I'm radioed through with my next job, I can still detour through town on my way to pick up my next fare so as to cover my mileage that way. As long as a copper doesn't spot you, or a beady-eyed member of the public, then a few of these daily adds up over the week to a nice tidy sum and no one back at the office is any the wiser.'

'Oh, I see what you mean. I hadn't a clue that it was illegal for private-hire firms like you work for to pick up off the street. But then, I suppose I wouldn't as I've never had cause to flag down a taxi. I've always wanted to, just to know what it feels like, but my money would never stretch farther than the bus fare or Shanks's pony. Mmm, well, yes, I'm glad you don't condone such practices as I'd sooner live on fresh air than have to visit you in prison.' She gave a laugh and added, 'Mind you, a slice of my bread pudding would make a handy tool for helping you dig your way out, wouldn't it? You nearly broke your teeth on the last one I made.'

An idea suddenly struck Iris and she grew silent for a moment while she pondered it. It was a good idea, she reckoned. Chas might scoff at it at first but even he would see the wisdom of it when he thought long and hard. 'It's just a thought, son, but should the worst happen to Mr Black and Mrs Black decide to sell up then . . .' She was interrupted by a knock on the back door and a voice calling out, 'It's only me.' She turned her head towards the door leading into the kitchen. 'In here, Freda.'

A tall, thin, shabby but scrupulously clean elderly lady entered. 'Oh, just the person I was hoping to see,' she said, addressing Chas.

'Oh, and yer didn't want to see me?' Ivy asked her, feigning a hurt expression before the woman who had been her friend and next-door neighbour for so many years now both women had lost count.

Freda's aged face looking serious, she replied, 'Unless you've suddenly found yer've a talent with a spanner like your son possesses, then it was him I was hoping was at home rather than you.' She gave a sudden grin, showing tombstone-like, badly fitting dentures. 'Though as you make a better cuppa than yer son, I will let you mash one for me while I ask him me favour.'

'Yer a cheeky beggar, so you are, Freda Lumley. What's this favour yer want from my Chas?'

'You want me to have a look at your mangle, don't you, Mrs Lumley?' Chas piped up.

She looked at him, startled. 'How did you know that? Soothsayer now, are yer?'

He laughed. 'I heard you swearing at it as I went down the yard on me way to work this morning.'

She looked indignant. 'Swearing! I might have been cussing at it but I wasn't swearing.'

'"Bugger" is swearing, Freda, in anyone's language,' said Iris.

Freda flashed her a disparaging look. 'I thought you was mashing a cuppa?' She turned her full attention to Chas. 'So will you look at it for me, ducky? The rollers are jammed.'

'I don't know why you didn't take up your Rita's offer to buy you a twin-tub like the one my Chas got me. I know I hummed and hah-ed for ages before he finally had one delivered but, my goodness, it almost makes me weep now when I think of all those hours I used to spend boiling up the copper! Then after that the backbreaking work of washing it all and mangling it after, 'specially sheets and towels. I couldn't do without my twin-tub now, I really couldn't. It's cut my wash day down to less than half which means I have more time to spend having a cuppa and a natter with you.'

Folding her arms under her flat chest, Freda said haughtily, 'I like me things washed proper.'

'They are washed proper,' Iris scoffed. 'The machine does it for yer instead of you doing it, yer daft ha'p'orth. And I hope you're not insinuating my whites ain't as white since I started using me twin-tub?'

''Course I ain't. It's just that I don't trust motorised things. Vi Newly got a terrible shock off her electric iron.'

'That's 'cos her clot of a son-in-law wired the plug up wrong.'

Freda looked thoughtful. 'Yes, and I have my suspicions about him proclaiming it was an accident. It was rather coincidental that only the week before Vi had confided in me she was going to ask her daughter if they'd consider letting her move in with them as she was finding it difficult managing on her own since her husband died. Funny how after her brush with death she suddenly found she could manage on her own, in't it? Anyway, a copper and a mangle was good enough for me mother so it's good enough for me. I don't like those Hoover contraptions neither. They make such a racket. And ain't you feared yours'll blow up on yer, Iris?'

She had been for a while after Chas had presented the labour-saving device to her a couple of years back, having saved for it to help ease her work load. She had been very grateful for the sentiment behind his generous gesture, but all the same these machines had represented a step into the unknown for her. Chas had patiently maintained that both were safe if used properly and would cut down her housework time dramatically, as well as the aches and pains she suffered as a result. She felt the least she could do was to try them out and, within a short space of time, should anyone have dared try to take these machines away from her, they would not have done so without one hell of a fight.

'Well, if it did blow me to kingdom come, to me it'd be a better way to go than lingering painfully in bed for years, having the embarrassment of yer nearest and dearest attending to yer personal needs. Oh, I couldn't go back to the old ways, not now I've got used to me machines. I'm sure you'd be the same, Freda, if yer'd just get off yer high horse and give 'em a try out. I've offered, I don't know how many times, for you to try out mine.'

'Yes, I know, and I'm grateful. But as I said, I prefer to stick to what I know.'

Chas scraped back his chair. 'I'll go and get me tool box.'

'What about yer apple pie?' asked his mother.

Oh, so it was plain apple? No guessing what the filling was tonight then, like he'd to do most times. 'Keep it hot for me, Mam, and I'll look forward to it when I get back. Hopefully I won't be long. Oh, and on me way back I'll fill the coal buckets for tomorrow.' This offer was meant as a warning for her not even to consider tackling the job while he was gone.

'He's a good lad,' mused Freda as Chas departed for her house next-door. 'Pity my Rita was so much older than him as it's my opinion she'd be a darn' sight happier married to a man like him sooner than the one she did plump for. Oh, not that she's miserable by some standards, and not that Kelvin's a bad lad as men go, but he could help a lot more with the kids and around the house.' She looked at Iris enquiringly. 'Any sign . . .'

Pre-empting what Freda was going to say as she asked the same question every other day, Iris cut in, 'Chas will bring a nice girl home when he's ready to and not before. You'll be the first to know when he does. After me, of course.'

'Huh, well, for all the size and age of him, he's too shy to ask a gel out, that's his problem.'

'Yes, well, I'd sooner me son be of the temperament he is than like some I could name around these parts. Nancy's son treats women like they've been put on this earth just to do his bidding, and he treats her no better.'

'And worse still, those silly women let him.'

'Mmm,' agreed Iris. 'I looked after my husband like he was a king but, bless him, he never took advantage of me.'

'Nor Henry of me neither. We were lucky with our men, weren't we, Iris? God bless 'em.'

She smiled and sighed. 'I can't believe it's thirty years since my Charles passed on. There ain't a minute goes by that I don't miss him. It's my lad I feel most for, though. That 'oss and cart denied him a chance of ever knowing his father and those two would have liked each other so much and got on well, that I know for a fact. Still, it's no good brooding on the past, is it, me old ducky? It's the future we have to get on with.' Iris smiled warmly at her friend. 'Make yerself comfy and I'll get yer that cuppa.'

CHAPTER THREE

An extremely good-looking bleached blonde, wearing a shabby short skirt and tight blouse over her voluptuous curves, was leaning against her back door-frame, smoking a Park Drive cigarette. Her mouth formed a sneer as she spotted Chas enter through the back gate of the house next-door. She silently watched as he located the mangle beside the wash house, put his tool box down beside it, lit a paraffin lamp which he placed on top of the crumbling garden wall so it cast light over the area he was working in, then proceeded to open his tool box to select the ones he needed.

'Still at yer do-gooding I see, Quasimodo,' she called across, her voice heavy with sarcasm.

Not having noticed her presence, his head jerked in surprise as he looked up. 'Oh, hello, Nadine,' he said finally. She looked very much at home on her mother's dilapidated doorstep in the cluttered, weed-filled yard and he wondered if the rumour about her return was indeed true. 'How are you?' he asked automatically, out of politeness.

'D'yer think I'm stupid enough to think you really care how I am after all me and me brothers did to you when we were young? But then, you're that nice a bloke you'd ask Hitler how he was if yer bumped into him in the street,' she snorted sardonically. 'So what has the old duck got you doing for her now? I bet she ain't paying yer. Always was a sucker, weren't yer, Quassie? And it's obvious age ain't wised you up none.'

His back stiffened at this use of the derogatory nickname given to him by the Dewhurst children years ago. This reference to the Hunchback of Notre Dame had caused him much inward grief, though in truth he knew it was unfair. He was definitely not ugly and neither did he have a hump on his back. He would not, though, give Nadine the satisfaction of letting her see that her reminder about his old nickname still managed to upset him all these years later. She was a very good-looking woman but her nasty attitude and cynical view of life badly let her down. 'We all need a helping hand now and again, Nadine, and I'm only too happy to oblige when I can,' Chas replied evenly.

'Yeah, but what you don't seem to realise, Quassie, is that a helping hand now and again in dire emergencies is one thing. Allowing yerself to become the local odd job man without payment for your services is called *the neighbours taking the piss*.'

He smiled tightly at her. 'You may see it that way, Nadine, but I happen to know Mrs Lumley hasn't the money to pay for her mangle to be fixed by a proper tradesman who'd more than likely charge her well over the odds. I receive ample payment for what I do for other people.'

She looked quizzical. 'How? They give yer goods in return you can sell on?'

He looked reproachfully at her. 'Have you never heard the saying, "You don't give to receive"?'

Nadine pulled a scornful face as she took a long drag from her cigarette. Smoke billowing from her mouth, she said, 'Eh, and have you ever heard the saying, "No one helps those that don't help themselves"?' Flicking the butt of her cigarette over on to a pile of discarded rusting objects by the dividing wall, she added, 'I much prefer that one meself.'

'Nadine!' a voice bellowed.

She swivelled her head to look back inside the house. 'What?' she snapped.

'Get yer arse back in here and get yer bleddy kids ter bed, they're driving me daft.'

Childish squabbling could be heard and Nadine turned back to lean wearily against the door-frame. 'Pity my mother's illness affects her legs and not her big gob.' Then she shouted back, 'Just coming.' She made to go back inside then stopped as a thought struck her. She looked expectantly over at Chas. 'You being such a Good Samaritan to the neighbours, yer don't fancy a bit of babysitting so I can escape for a couple of hours and restore me sanity down the local? The kids wouldn't be no bother to yer, honest. Yer can have 'em round your house and it'll give yer mam a taster of what having grandkids is like. Well, a taster's all she's going to get, ain't it, as it ain't likely you're ever going to give her any.'

Her mother's bellowing voice cut through the air like a fog horn on full volume. 'Nadine, get the fuck in here – now, I said! I might be slow on me pins but I can still walk, yer know, and if I have to come and get yer, you'll be paying a visit to the hospital and it won't be to visit *me*.'

Face scowling darkly, Nadine bellowed back, 'Hold yer horses, Mother, I'm bloody coming.' She looked back at Chas. 'I musta bin mad coming back here thinking it'd be better than where I was. So you up for it then?'

He stood staring her, frozen. He would help anyone out if it was in his power to do so but the thought of entertaining Nadine's children for one minute, let alone a couple of hours, terrified him. Plus the fact that his mother, although very fond of most children, would surely draw the line at having Nadine's four rampaging through her house. 'Sorry, Nadine, I'm . . . er . . ., well, it could take me a while to fix Mrs Lumley's mangle and we're short-staffed at work so I could get called in to help out.'

She looked disappointed. 'Oh, another night then.' As her mother bellowed for her again she screamed back, 'All right, Mother, I'm fucking coming!'

With that she turned abruptly and stormed back inside the house, slamming the door behind her.

Chas sighed with relief as he resumed his task, knowing that was the second lucky escape he had had that day.

Back inside the Dewhurst house, Nadine grabbed her children by the scruff of the neck and pushed them in the direction of the stairs, warning them she would be up shortly to check they were in bed, and leaving them all in no doubt what she'd do if they were not. They were all well aware of what their mam could be like in a temper, even the youngest at two years old, and without further ado they scarpered.

Nadine raised her children in the same way her mother had raised hers. For the most part they fended for themselves.

'Your young 'un's got ringworm on his bum,' Clarice told her daughter as she flopped down into the manky armchair opposite.

Nadine's eyes were already glued to an episode of *Emergency Ward 10* which was showing on the flickering, scuffed and dirt-smeared black-and-white television set.

Clarice picked up a filthy threadbare cushion and threw it at her daughter. 'Oi, you ignorant bleeder! I said, yer youngest needs some boracic powder slapping on his arse before it gets any worse.'

Dragging her eyes away from the television set, Nadine gave her a scathing look. 'Oh, and you're suddenly the doting gran, are yer?'

'Ringworm's catching and I don't want to get infected. I've got enough ailing me without having to cope with 'ote else.'

'Well, I don't see how you could catch anything from me kids, being's yer don't exactly show much grandmotherly affection towards 'em. Mind you, you was never much of a mother to yer own so what else can I expect?'

'You done all right,' Clarice hissed through clenched teeth, insulted even though she knew her daughter spoke the truth.

'No thanks to you though, eh, Mother? Many a night we'd have starved if it wasn't for what we managed to find in the neighbours' dustbins or else nicked from the corner shop.'

'A mother's job is to mek her kids resourceful,' Clarice snapped defensively.

'Well, don't bother congratulating yerself that you achieved that, Mother, 'cos if you had then our Simon wouldn't be dead, nor our Jamie serving a life sentence for murder, nor me in the predicament I'm in.'

'Yer can't blame me for what you all got up to outside my four walls. I never asked Simon to rob that factory, or our Jamie to blast that bloke to kingdom come, or you to marry the slimy toad yer did and be stupid enough to have four kids by him, one after the other. What's happened to you all is yer own fault. When are you and yer brood going home anyway?'

'Don't get yer hopes up, Mother, 'cos I ain't. The punching that fucker gave me the other night for catching him in the act was the last one I'll put up with. Yer might as well get used to the fact we're here for a while until summat better comes along.' Nadine cast a sardonic glance around the room. 'Mind you, anywhere is better than here, ain't it?' Bringing her eyes back to rest on her mother, she added, 'Steptoe and Son's scrapyard is a palace compared to this.'

Clarice snatched up her walking stick, thrusting it out to whack it down on her daughter's arm, but it fell short, hitting the arm of the chair instead.

Nadine laughed. 'Your illness has at least done me a favour, 'cos yer can't beat us like you used to anymore, can yer, Mam? Yer've never done much for me so it won't hurt to make up for it by letting us stay for a while.'

Clarice knew that her illness had rendered her powerless to throw her daughter and her brats out bodily so until Nadine decided to move herself she had little choice but to accept their presence. That didn't mean to say she had to give her daughter an easy time of it. 'If yer staying, then keep yer kids quiet. Their screaming and yelling is driving me daft. Eh, and yer can pay yer way. I ain't feeding you all on what bit I get from the Social. And I want something towards the gas. It's not like I can earn 'ote meself any longer, is it?'

Nadine gave her mother a glare. 'How am I supposed to earn a living with four kids to look after? Tell me that, eh?'

'You should have thought of it before you upped and left that excuse of a husband of yours. I told yer the day yer married him he'd lead you a merry dance and it wouldn't be long before you rued the day you wed him.' Clarice gave a sneer before adding gloatingly, 'But would you listen?'

'Oh, and I'm expected to take advice from the woman who married a man like me dad, am I? Some father he was, scarpering, leaving you with three youngsters and not a brass farthing to yer name, and not one word from him since. Mind you, I can't say as I blame him after it hit home just what he'd married. Lucky escape me dad had, didn't he?'

Clarice's face darkened thunderously. 'Shut yer fucking trap! I *am* yer mother.'

'My bad luck, that.'

'Well, I didn't exactly win the top prize landing up with you for a daughter, did I? Let's say we're quits.

I heard yer talking when you was outside. Who was yer talking to?'

'Oh, and 'cos I'm back living with you for the duration I ain't allowed to talk to no one, Mother, unless you give me the go ahead?'

A murderous light flared in Clarice's eyes. 'If I was more able you wouldn't dare speak to me like this, for fear of yer life. I only asked who you was talking to. I know what a gob you've got on yer and I don't want none of the neighbours knowing our business.'

'We ain't got any business no more for the neighbours to gossip over. If yer must know, I was talking to Quasimodo.'

'Eh? Who?'

'Him next-door-but-one. He's fixing Ma Lumley's mangle.'

Clarice realised who her daughter was referring to. 'Oh, Lady Tyme's son. I forgot you called him that.' She looked at her daughter through narrowed eyes. 'Now if you'd half the brains you were born with and learned by yer mother's mistakes, you would have gone after a man like Chas Tyme instead of the cretin you did saddle yerself with.'

'Oh, yer admitting you do make mistakes then, are yer, Mam? And there was me thinking you was under the impression you was perfect.'

'Yer sarky cow,' Clarice spat at her. Then gave a haughty sniff. 'Yes, I do admit I made the biggest mistake of my life in marrying yer dad. The second biggest mistake I made was giving birth to *you*.' She leaned over in her chair, picking up one swollen leg, then another, and settling them as comfortably as her illness allowed on a threadbare low stool whose greying stuffing was protruding in parts. Settling back in her chair again, she folded her arms under her skinny chest and looked at her daughter snidely. 'If I had my time over again, I'd do things very differently, very differently indeed. When I met yer dad I had several lads after me who all wanted to marry me, let me tell yer,' she boasted.

Nadine let out a bellowing laugh. 'Pull the other one, Mother! As if I'd believe that.'

'It's bleddy true, I tell yer. You can scoff all yer like but I was a looker in my day. I could name at least five men who were falling over themselves to win my affections, including a chap called Harry Ingles. Worshipped the ground I walked on, did Harry. No matter how I treated him, he always bounced back. Harry wasn't a looker by any means, not set against someone like yer dad he wasn't. He wore glasses, didn't dress in what we called fashion back then and he was on the beefy side. We used to call him Billy Bunter. He could have been the last man on earth, I still wouldn't have been seen dead with him because of how much me mates would've ridiculed me. But if only I'd had me brains in gear, I would have snapped him up. He might have been shy and had a boring job as a clerk for a man who owned several off-licences, but I was daft enough to judge a book by its cover. I never bothered to find out that Harry had ambitions.

'Yer dad now, he wouldn't have known what the word "ambition" meant, let alone how to spell it. Nowadays Henry owns those off-licences he once clerked in, and more besides, and him and his wife live in a big house up Lutterworth Road and have two cars and holidays abroad. I could have had all that if I'd not been so blinded by yer dad's handsome face and fallen for his gift of the gab, which in fact turned out to be empty words.

'You, my girl, could have had the life of Riley married to someone like Chas Tyme if yer was half as clever as yer try and mek out you are. I hear he's not lorry driving any more but works for Black's Taxis on Blackbird Road. Taxi drivers earn quite a good living, I understand, good enough to pay the bills each week and afford a few luxuries anyway. I bet him and his mam don't have Echo marge on their bread but best butter.' A smug expression spread across Clarice's lined face and her spiteful piggy eyes were fixed stolidly on her daughter. 'Still, you made yer choices ... wrong 'uns as it turns out, like I did. So, like I did, now you have to get on with it. Turn that telly up, I can't hear it.'

Nadine sat staring at her mother. It wasn't often she said anything worth listening to but this latest announcement had set Nadine's brain into overdrive.

When she had set her own sights on Phil Rider he'd been the local heart throb, swaggering around in his trendy Beatles jacket and tight-fitting trousers, and she'd been beside herself that he'd chosen her above all the other women fighting to claim his attention. Her mother was spot on, Nadine hadn't thought to consider what kind of life she could expect when they had been forced up the aisle because she was expecting their first child. She'd thought she had landed on her feet, not only in snaring Phil himself but also in moving into the tiny one-bedroomed flat over a fishmonger's on Fosse Road. It might have been damp and direly in need of renovation, the windows never opened to help stem the fishy stench filtering up from below, but it was still a damned sight better than the home she had come from.

At first it had been fun playing the housewife, but the rot had very quickly set in when it became apparent to Nadine that Phil begrudged handing over any more than a few shillings of his building labourer's pay towards keeping his wife and new baby, much preferring still to play the part of the single man with his mates. Nadine soon had no choice but to resort to her old ways of shoplifting in order to pay the bills and keep herself and her baby fed and clothed. Regardless of not wanting a husband's responsibilities, Phil still expected his conjugal rights and another three children followed in quick succession, although the way he ranted when each pregnancy was revealed to him it appeared he thought Nadine had created their children completely by herself.

Life as a single woman living under her mother's roof had been far from cosy. As a married woman with four constantly hungry children and mounting bills, it was living hell for Nadine. The final straw had come several evenings previously when she found herself with not a bean in her purse, nor even a dry crust in the flat to give her children for their tea. Their hungry misery grating on her already fraught nerves, knowing Phil called into the local on his way home from work every night, she had bundled all the children inside a huge rusting coach pram and gone around to shame him into handing over some money to enable her to buy food. Being a known tea leaf in the area, she was banned from the local corner shop and larger Co-op Society unless she could prove to them as she entered the shop that she had money to pay for what she wanted. It was too late in the evening now for her to find someone to watch her kids while she went further afield to lift what she needed.

She had found her husband all right. Plate of meat pie, chips and peas growing cold on the table in front of him, he'd been draped over a tartily dressed, heavily made-up woman seated beside him, very obviously encouraging his attentions. Nursing suspicions of what her husband got up to were one thing, but having the confirmation staring her in the face was another. Nadine's temper mounting to volcanic proportions, she had flung herself on him, hammering her fists into him, yelling what a bastard he was to be filling his own stomach while his children went hungry and forni- cating with another woman when he was a married man. In the ensuing fight tables had been knocked over, plates of food and beer glasses sent flying. The woman with Phil received a hefty punch from Nadine which knocked her out cold. When he had managed to restrain his wife, Phil had retaliated by dragging her outside by the hair. In front of their children and passers-by who stared agog, he had blacked her eye and split her lip with his fists for humiliating him in front of his drinking companions. Then, leaving Nadine slumped on the dirty pavement, blood pouring from her cuts and bruises blackening rapidly, heedless of his chil- dren's screams of terror at what they had seen, he had stormed back inside the pub, but not before warning her that if she ever did anything like this again she would not live to regret it.

With her children still wailing and distraught, she had dragged herself back to their tiny flat. As far as Nadine was concerned, her tempestuous marriage was over. Phil could do what he liked with whom he liked in future, she didn't care any longer. In fact, truth be told, she hadn't cared for her husband as a man for as long as she could remember.

Collecting what little she possessed of her own and her children's belongings which she stuffed inside brown carrier bags, she slammed the door shut on her marital home, vowing that under no circumstances would she ever return, and headed straight for her mother's house. That place, as bad as it was, was preferable to the accommodation the council offered homeless mothers and their children.

Since the moment of their arrival back in Nadine's childhood home, something Clarice had made very clear she did not welcome, Nadine had worried that somehow she had to find a way of supporting herself and her children. She realised it was no good hoping that Phil would stump up even a paltry amount towards their keep. She knew without asking also that her mother would balk at babysitting while she went out to work, but then Clarice really wasn't in a position to mind four lively youngsters while suffering the debilitating illness that had claimed her, and paying for childcare was out of the question. Nadine wasn't skilled at anything that would pay anywhere near a liveable wage. She'd only been a shop assistant in a grocery store when she had married Phil, and had been on the verge of losing that job because it had only been a matter of time before the owner discovered how much of his profits went missing via her quick-fingered hands. She received her Family Allowance but the bit that there was would only cover a couple of days' worth of food a week and then only if she was careful with it.

As she had stood on the doorstep, tonight, smoking a cigarette she had stolen out of her mother's packet, she had been so at a loss to know what to do that she had come to the reluctant conclusion that she had no choice but to return to her former life, such as it was, until such time as the kids were old enough to fend for themselves, leaving her free to follow her own pursuits. Resigned to her fate, she had returned back inside to shut her mother up by sending her kids to bed.

Now Clarice's ramblings had given her an answer to her problems, one she would never have thought of for herself. Despite the fact that physical contact in any form with her mother made her stomach churn, Nadine could have kissed her for it.

Her mother broke into her thoughts. 'What?' Nadine snapped.

'You bloody deaf cow! I said, you could always dump yer kids on the Social and let them do-gooders tek care of them. Leave you free to pursue whatever yer wanted, wouldn't it?'

Nadine couldn't deny that thought had crossed her mind, but despite her lack of parenting skills she did have a certain affection for her children and the thought of never seeing them again should she hand them over for adoption was hard to take. She sneered her disgust at her mother for suggesting this option. 'Like you wish you had done with us, yer mean, when me dad left you high and dry? Mind you, Mother, it's my guess you never 'cos we kids were useful to yer in what we brought home. And of course yer couldn't queue down at the Parish Office without a pram full of kids to beg handouts for, could yer?' She cast her a mocking smile. 'Pity I can't hand *you* over to the Social and that way have some peace from your constant earache.' Nadine smiled secretively. 'If it'll put yer mind at rest, we won't be here for long 'cos I've a plan that's gonna give me and my kids a comfortable future.'

'A plan!' Clarice scoffed. 'You couldn't plan yer escape out of a brown paper bag. So what is this brilliant plan that's gonna bring you fame and fortune then, eh?'

'If yer think I'm telling you so you can ruin it, you've got enough think coming. You'll just have to be content knowing that I want out of here much more than you want me out, so I'll be putting me plan into operation as soon as possible.' Nadine settled her eyes back on the television set but her mind was not on the programme, it was fixed firmly on her scheme. Her next husband would be Chas Tyme. With him providing for her and her kids she could live the life of Riley because his sort was too soft-hearted ever to retaliate. Smugness filled her. Poor Chas, she thought. As he laboured next-door fixing old Ma Lumley's mangle out of the good-ness of his heart, little did he know what lay in store for him. But then, he should be grateful for what she was about to offer him. After all, a big oaf like him was never going to be given the chance by anyone else in his lifetime to become a husband and father.

CHAPTER FOUR

The next afternoon, as Chas delivered customers to their destinations, totally oblivious to the future Nadine was plotting for him in order to ensure a meal ticket for herself and her children, over in a plush solicitor's office on New Walk in the centre of town, Harriet Harris, an extremely striking twenty-five-year-old with a mane of thick titian hair flowing past her shoulders and blessed with an eye-catching figure which showed off to perfection the short fitted fashions of the day, was saying to her fiancé: 'Jeremy, I know this isn't the time or the place to mention such matters, but with only eight weeks to go to our wedding you still haven't asked me to go and view anywhere suitable for us to live. I'm not worried whether it's a house or a flat but I'll need time to sort out curtains and such like, and we'll need to look for furniture. I haven't mentioned it before because when we got engaged you told me not to worry about our living arrangements, to leave all that to you, but with time wearing on and nothing being said . . . Jeremy, you are doing something about finding us somewhere to live, aren't you?'

His mind fixed firmly on work-related matters, Jeremy Franklin, a boyishly good-looking, blond-haired, smartly suited junior solicitor, lifted his head and looked at his fiancée distractedly. 'Pardon? Oh, yes, everything is in hand regarding our living arrangements, Harriet. There's no need for you to concern yourself. Mother is having my room redecorated and moving an extra wardrobe in for your clothes. She's sure you'll like the colour scheme she's chosen.'

This news stunned Harrie rigid. 'We're ... we're moving in with your mother when we get married?' she mouthed, aghast. 'But ... oh, but I assumed we'd have a place of our own, Jeremy.'

Still distracted he said, 'I told you, didn't I, that we'd be living with my mother for ... well, the foreseeable future? I'm so sorry if I didn't but I really did think I had. It makes sense for us to live with her. The house is certainly big enough.' He raised his head, revealing the arresting deep blue eyes that always had the ability to turn Harrie's legs to jelly, and smiled briefly at her before returning his attention to his work. 'Mother is so looking forward to your moving in and to having a daughter-in-law to share her interests.' He slapped shut a leather-bound, sectioned binder and pushed it across his desk towards her. 'All those letters want sending in the evening post, and can you make sure Mr Podger's file is passed back to me when you have done the necessary as I have one or two things to clarify before his appearance in court next week? He's guilty as sin, of course, but I'm positive I can get him off.'

Harrie's mouth was gaping even wider in astonishment. She was positive no suggestion of living in his mother's house had been made before and wasn't at all sure that she liked the idea. Having a mother-in-law at a distance was one thing; living under the same roof, constantly under her watchful eye, was another. And it wasn't as though she knew Jeremy's mother that well, if at all in fact. She wasn't sure what to make of Daphne Franklin. Admittedly she had been politeness itself to Harrie on the occasions they had been in each other's company, but without being able to pinpoint exactly why Harrie strongly suspected that Daphne only pretended to approve of her in front of her son while in private she saw her future daughter-in-law as not nearly good enough for him.

The truth was Harrie wasn't naturally in her fiancé's social circle. Her own father's occupation before his retirement had been that of foreman in an engineering factory, while Jeremy's had been a prominent solicitor. Jeremy's family had always owned their own home and the one they lived in now was an imposing four-storey double bay-fronted detached house in a highly regarded area of the city. Inside it was tastefully arranged with very nice furniture, most of it antique, that you dare not touch or sit back on for fear of damaging it somehow. Harrie's widowed father had always paid rent on their two-bedroomed single bay-fronted terraced house with its small slabbed yard in the not-so-salubrious Blackbird Road area. Much of their furniture had been acquired from long-dead relatives or via second-hand shops.

Harrie hadn't attended a private school but a state one, gaining her secretarial qualifications at night school, while Jeremy was university-qualified and his mother had articled him to a small but respectable legal practice, fully expecting her son to follow his father and eventually open his own. Jeremy's father had died prematurely when he had been in his early-teens and the business had been sold, leaving his wife comfortably able to finance the life-style she was accustomed to for the rest of her days along with a separate fund to cover their son's education.

Harrie had started her working career as an office junior for the firm of Chatterley and Bigson on leaving school at the age of fifteen, progressing by way of hard work and dedication to senior secretarial level. Nine months ago she had fallen head over heels for Jeremy Franklin the minute she had been introduced to the new junior partner and told she was to be his secretary. Despite her attraction to him, which she had carefully kept hidden, she had never for one moment thought a man like him would look in her direction. She was wrong and got the shock of her life when, not long into his employment, Jeremy had asked her to accompany him to the theatre one evening.

Despite her busy social life and several boyfriends to her credit, Harrie had never been to the theatre before and never had a date with such a well-spoken, handsome escort. Nervous was hardly the word to describe her inward state when she turned up to meet him outside the De Montfort Hall, wondering if she was suitably dressed for such a venue in her cream suit with a pleated mini-skirt, navy blue platform shoes and matching leather shoulder bag. She was terrified she would not be able to converse with Jeremy on his own level in such a setting.

She need not have worried. Jeremy did not turn out to be a chatty sort of man though, despite lengthy lulls in conversation while they were having drinks during the interval and as he drove her home afterwards in his immaculate Rover 2000, he had proved pleasant company and was indeed very gentlemanly and attentive towards her. It was plain to her that he liked her but nevertheless Harrie was surprised when he asked to see her again, considering the difference in their backgrounds.

From then on it seemed she was swept along by his sophisticated pursuit of her which made a welcome change from the kind of relationships she was used to, those having mostly been conducted in noisy pubs and dance halls, usually surrounded by very animated friends, with Harrie having to fend off a young man's groping hands at the end of the evening. Jeremy did not have a large circle of friends, only three or four who she got on well with and who appeared to accept her. Nevertheless when he proposed marriage to her over dinner three months into their courtship, although stunned by the suddenness of it, Harrie was by then deeply in love and readily accepted him.

Moving in with his mother after their marriage had never entered her head, though. The thought did not appeal to her one iota. After all, she was marrying Jeremy, not his mother.

'Is it really the right thing for us to start our married life living with your mother, Jeremy?' she asked now.

He looked at her, bemused. 'Why, yes, of course.' Then scraping a hand through his hair, added, 'Well, of course, it's not ideal, I do admit. I would prefer it if we were starting our life together in a home of our own, but I'm not in a situation financially to afford the type of house a man in my position is expected to live in. Won't be until I receive promotion to full partner. Besides, Mother has no one else in the world apart from me and I cannot simply abandon her to rattle around in that big house by herself.'

But Harrie was having to leave her father all by himself.

'Mother is so looking forward to having your companionship after we're married,' Jeremy was saying to her as he flicked through paperwork to find the report he was looking for. 'She's going to introduce you to her afternoon Bridge Club and get you involved in her women's groups.'

Harrie didn't at all fancy playing bridge. She wasn't a fan of card games. It also sounded very stuffy, not her way of passing an afternoon at all. 'But I work, Jeremy, so . . .'

'Darling, solicitors' wives don't work. Anyway, you'll have more than enough to keep you occupied looking after your new husband and his mother. And, of course, there's all the entertaining I'll be starting to do to consolidate my position in the firm. I intend to become a full partner sooner rather than later before owning my own practice eventually like my father did. As soon as I'm married I'll be considered seriously for such a position by the hierarchy here. In this day and age it really is ludicrous that single men aren't considered for promotion! Can't understand why myself. Just because you're married doesn't mean you're going to do your job any better. Still, that's the way it is and to get on you have to play by the rules.

'I've already interviewed for your replacement as

my secretary, by the way. I've decided on a Miss Abberington. She's not as pretty as you but she seems very capable. I've asked her to start at the beginning of next month so you can get her up to speed before finishing work yourself a week before the wedding. I thought you would need that time free to pack before moving and for any last-minute things you need to arrange before our big day.' He smiled winningly at her. 'See, I do think of you, dear. Now, was there anything else you needed to see me about? I must get on as my next client is due shortly and I've a couple of things to do before he arrives.'

She didn't want to leave her job. Her work situation on marrying had never been broached and Harrie had automatically assumed she would continue until such time as children came along. After all, she loved her job, deriving great satisfaction from her contribution towards solving the problems of the various clients who walked through the busy law firm's doors. But then she supposed she was marrying a solicitor and Jeremy had told her that their wives did not work. She had no choice but to get used to the idea that she wouldn't after she was married; in fact, it was remiss of her not to have realised this for herself. She was marrying a professional man and, like he said, legal practices still abided by the rules and regulations set down centuries ago. Hadn't she herself complained in private to her friends about some of the more anti-quated systems and equipment she had to work with when she heard of the modern conveniences their work-places boasted?

She would have liked a bit more warning so she

could get used to the idea of her husband providing for her in the future and having no money at her disposal that she had earned herself. She supposed, though, that she would have a housekeeping allowance and some of that would be for her own use. Then a question posed itself. If they were to be living with Jeremy's mother, as it was her house, would Harrie herself actually be designated as being in charge of the household or would she have to take a back seat to Mrs Franklin while they were living with her?

Leaving her job to become a full-time housewife and seemingly companion to her future mother-in-law was not all that was bothering Harrie, though. 'Er . . . well . . . yes, Jeremy, there is something I need to discuss that's of concern to me. Where you live, well, it's two bus rides away from my house so me living there when we're married . . . well, I won't be able to pop in and see my father as regularly as I'd like to. I'd thought, you see . . . well, assumed . . . wrongly as it turns out now . . .'

He lifted his head and looked at her in exasperation. 'Harriet darling, could you get to the point? I've already told you that my next client is due any minute and I've a couple of things to do before he arrives.'

'Yes, I'm sorry, I'm rambling, aren't I?' She took a deep breath. 'Jeremy, I was under the impression that you'd be buying a place for us in an area that was between both our parents. Convenient for us to visit them and for them both to visit us. If we can't afford to buy a house at the moment, couldn't we consider renting one?'

'Renting?' He looked appalled at the thought. 'Rather

a waste of money, don't you think, when Mother has so much space?' He frowned at her quizzically. 'How regularly do you propose to visit your father after we're married?'

'I had hoped daily.'

'Daily? That's a bit much, don't you think, darling? Your father isn't going to get used to living on his own if you're constantly on his doorstep, is he? It's not like he's infirm, is it? He can fend for himself.'

'But he's never had to look after himself before, Jeremy. After my mother died five years ago, I took over his care and suddenly to be on his own ... it's going to be a big change for him. He has just turned seventy. He's never actually cooked a meal for himself, and until he gets used to doing things like that I would like to keep a regular check on him, to satisfy myself that he's faring all right.'

'I know you've no other relatives but he's neighbours and friends, hasn't he?'

'Yes.'

'Well, then, they'll pop in and see to him so stop worrying. Lots of people his age live on their own and are perfectly all right. If it puts your mind at rest we can always slip a few shillings weekly to a neighbour to cook him his dinner each day and do his washing, just until he's fully competent himself. Mother entertains her old friends to tea on a Tuesday afternoon so that would be a good time for you to visit your father each week. Oh, that reminds me, Mother is expecting you for dinner tonight. Please don't be late. She does get herself worked up if dinner is held up for any reason, as you've seen for yourself.'

'Well, I did apologise to her. It wasn't my fault the bus never turned up and I had to wait for the next! Anyway, I'm sorry, I can't make dinner tonight. I've already arranged to spend this evening with my father. I haven't spent much time with him recently, what with my dress fittings and all the other running around I've had to do towards the wedding, and he's so looking forward to me helping him with a new puzzle . . .'

'Mother really would like you to come, Harriet,' her fiancé cut in. 'She wants to update you on the table arrangements for the reception at the Belmont. She's also hoping you've finalised your guest list so she can decide where best to sit them.'

'The Belmont? But I thought we'd decided on the Assembly Rooms? My father's already paid a deposit and sorted out the music for the dancing.'

Jeremy looked shocked. 'Oh, gosh, didn't I tell you? I thought I had. I do apologise if not. Mother paid a visit to the Assembly Rooms the other day to go over her instructions with them and wasn't much struck by the standard of the decor or what they had to offer for the wedding breakfast. She would have discussed this with us but there really wasn't time, what with the wedding date being so close and her concern someone else would book the Belmont and then she'd have a real job to find somewhere else suitable, so she had to make a snap decision. We'll get your father's deposit back. And before you start worrying, Mother told me she will settle the difference in cost as she's conscious your father might not be able to stretch to the extra. She just wants to do her bit towards giving us the perfect day, Harriet.'

The Belmont was a hotel frequented by the type of person who earned far more than her father had before he'd retired. Daphne Franklin might see it as a much more fitting place than the Assembly Rooms in which to entertain her family and friends at a wedding reception, but Harrie knew her father and their respective friends and close neighbours would not feel relaxed enough in a place like that to let their hair down and properly enjoy the proceedings. Besides that, Harrie knew her father saw it as his responsibility to finance her wedding day and she didn't know how he would take the news of all the arrangements he had made being cancelled and rearranged without his even being consulted, regardless of the reason behind it.

She made to voice her concerns but was stopped by the intercom sounding on Jeremy's desk and the receptionist announcing in her nasal tones the arrival of the next client.

As she left Jeremy's office Harrie felt a tight knot of apprehension forming in her stomach. She had been so excited at the prospect of her forthcoming marriage ten minutes ago. Now, after the bombshells Jeremy had dropped on her, she was beginning to feel very uneasy about it.

Percy Harris's face lit up when his daughter walked through the back door at just after six that evening. 'Hello, me old duck,' he said, going over to kiss her cheek. 'Get yer coat off and sit yerself down at the table.' He then announced proudly, 'I've cooked you dinner.'

Midway through taking off her coat she stopped to stare at him, stunned. 'You've cooked dinner, Dad?'

Eyes bright, he nodded. 'Well, with you getting wed and leaving home very shortly, I have to start fending for meself. You'll have enough on yer plate looking after your husband without worrying whether I'm eating properly, I know you will, so I thought I ought to get some practice in. Then, if I go wrong, you'll be here to put me right and so hopefully by the time yer big day dawns I'll be an expert.' His gaze grew tender and he said huskily, 'I shall miss you, yer know.' Percy sniffed away a tear and shook himself. 'Still, I should count meself lucky that you ain't left home before this, a pretty gel like you who could pick and choose who she settled for. I know you'll visit yer old dad often and I can always visit you, can't I?'

His eyes grew misty again and he said distractedly, 'I just hope you don't settle for a house too far away.' He coughed to clear his throat. 'When are you going to start house hunting, by the way? I mean, time is wearing on, isn't it? I could always help you out by visiting the agents and seeing what's for sale in your price range roundabout. Or maybe it's a rented place to start? Either way, I'll help if I can, you just have to say the word. I expect with a job like Jeremy has he can afford a nice place for you both.' Percy lapsed back into melancholy again. 'I do hope what you do settle for isn't too far away so I can come over regular and see to any odd jobs you might need doing. Well, Jeremy being a busy man like he is, he'll surely welcome someone giving him a hand with any repairs or whatnot that need doing around the place. That's the trouble with houses, there's always something wanting repairing . . .

'Oh, dear, hark at me, sticking me oar in! Wherever

you decide to live, I don't care as long as yer happy. Just as happy as me and yer mother were, God rest her.' He gazed at Harrie tenderly again, the love he held for his precious daughter unashamedly obvious. 'Yer mother would have been so proud of you, yer know, lovey. Can you imagine what she'd have bin like if she was here now? Fussing and worrying over making sure yer big day was perfect . . . driving us all mad. Well, she can rest easy 'cos she's knows I'll do me best to send our daughter off proper.'

He realised he ought to get off this subject before he broke down altogether and begged his beloved daughter not to leave him, which was what he really wanted to do. 'Anyway, I looked through yer mother's old cookbooks and found a recipe for sausage casserole. It's been in the oven the amount of time the book said so it should be done by now. I've just got to mash the spuds. So, go on then, get yer coat off and settle yerself at the table and I'll bring it through.'

Harrie was choking back a lump in her throat. Her father loved her so much and was having great trouble coming to terms with the fact that very shortly he would be handing over the care and protection of her to another man. Bundling her coat on to the hook on the back door, she rushed over to him and hugged him fiercely. 'You won't have time to miss me when I'm married, Dad. I'll be popping round to check on you as often as I can.' She pulled away to look up at him with a wide grin splitting her face. 'I know how much you loved Mam, but, you never know, with me off your hands you might take up with some other nice woman.'

He gave a scornful grunt. 'And who'd d'yer reckon is going to want to take up with an old fossil like me?'

She slapped him playfully on his arm. 'Old fossil indeed! You're still a very handsome man, and you leave me behind puffed when we run to catch the bus.'

'Ah, well, that's because you will insist on wearing those silly platform shoes. It's a wonder you ain't broke yer neck before now. And them short skirts . . . well, if yer mother was here I know for a fact she would insist you wore woolly drawers underneath to keep out the wind. Mini-skirts don't afford much by way of protection from the elements, do they? Mind you, you always look a picture in whatever you wear, in fashion or not. Right, let's get this dinner dished up before it's cremated. You are hungry, I trust?'

Harrie inwardly groaned. It was bad enough having to tell him that their planned evening together wasn't going to happen, she hadn't the heart to say her future mother-in-law was expecting her for dinner as well. She was so proud of him for making this attempt at independence and under no circumstances was she going to hurt his feelings. Harrie would have to eat two dinners tonight.

'I'll mash the spuds, Dad. It's the least I can do, being's you've gone to all the trouble to cook the actual meal. It smells absolutely delicious.'

He sniffed the air. 'Yes, it does, doesn't it? Hope it tastes as good,' he added a mite worriedly.

When Harrie tested the potatoes to check they were cooked she was dismayed to find that most of them had disintegrated into the water, obviously having been boiled for far longer than was required. She would do

64

her best, though, to resurrect what she could. As she strained them off she said casually, 'Dad, potatoes this size only need to be boiled for twenty minutes at the most.'

Arriving back in the kitchen after putting plates and cutlery on the gate-legged table in the back room, Percy pulled a face and said, 'Oh, I put those on over an hour ago. That's too long, is it? Oh dear, are they ruined, lovey?'

She smiled warmly at him. 'They're just a little over-cooked but I'm sure I can salvage them.'

He looked relieved. 'I'll not boil them so long next time.'

Seated at the table, filled plate in front of him, knife and fork raised, Percy said, 'Well, it looks good if I say so meself. Tuck in then.' With that he scooped up a forkful of the sausage casserole and put it in his mouth. Immediately his face contorted in disgust and, whipping his handkerchief from out of his cardigan pocket, he emptied the contents of his mouth into it. He then leaped up, knocking away the filled fork Harrie was just about to put in her mouth.

As food splattered over the table cloth, she looked at him in bewilderment. 'What on earth . . .'

'Yer can't eat that, lovey, it tastes horrible.' He looked perplexed. 'I don't know what I've done to it, I followed the recipe.'

'I'm sure it's not that bad . . .'

'Oh, it is, ducky. It . . . well, it's so peppery.'

'How much pepper did you put in, Dad?'

'Just like the recipe said. A tablespoon. And I added a bit extra just to be on the safe side.'

'How much!' Then as giggles exploded from her and tears of mirth spurted from her eyes, she spluttered, 'Oh, Dad, I think you'll find the recipe said a teaspoon, not a tablespoon.'

'Oh, really?' he exclaimed. 'I thought the abbreviation tsp stood for tablespoon. It never twigged with me it meant teaspoon. Oh, dear, no wonder it tastes so peppery.'

'Were you wearing your reading glasses?'

He shook his head. 'I had the house upside down but couldn't find them so I had to manage as best I could without them. Oh, I'm sorry, me darling,' he said remorsefully. 'I so wanted to prove to you I can cope by meself.'

'No need to apologise, Dad. You tried, that's the main thing. You were always telling me when I was a little girl that we must learn by our mistakes. Next time you definitely will be much easier on the pepper, won't you? By the way, your reading glasses are on top of your head.'

He took them off and tutted disdainfully. 'Well, would you credit it? There they were all the time.'

'We've a couple of sausages left over in the pantry. Shall I fry them up and do some chips for you?' she said as she scraped up the food from the table then rose to gather the plates.

'What will you have, lovey?' he asked her.

'Oh . . . er . . . well . . . I might have something later.' She decided to disguise the truth a little. 'I hope you won't be too upset, Dad, but I've to pop over to Jeremy's as his mother . . .' She just couldn't bring herself to tell him right this minute that Daphne had ridden rough-shod over all his arrangements for the wedding. She had no idea how much the reception at the Belmont was going to cost but knew without a doubt it would be out of her father's price range and, regardless of the fact that Mrs Franklin had offered to pay the difference, he was going to be insulted, deeply hurt that she had taken it upon herself to do what she had without consulting him. Doubtless he'd still insist on paying the full cost and on a state pension there was no easy way he could raise that sort of money. In Mrs Franklin's endeavours to secure the very best for her son, she hadn't taken the time to consider the impact her change of venue for the reception would have on the bride's family. Harrie needed to think of a way to resolve this situation to the satisfaction of all concerned but at the moment the answer eluded her. Hopefully, it would come to her soon.

'. . . well, Mrs Franklin just wants to go over something to do with the wedding. I'll try and be as quick as I can. I'm looking forward to doing your puzzle with you.'

He smiled warmly at her. 'Harrie lovey, it takes you over an hour to get to Jeremy's house, that's if the buses are running on time and there's no traffic on the road. My puzzle isn't as important as dealing with your wedding arrangements. We want your day to go smoothly, don't we? We'll have a night in together another time.' His face suddenly lit up. 'Talking of yer wedding, the payment for the cashed insurance policy came through today so I can start to settle all the bills. That was a good decision of yer mother's to take out the sixpence-a-week policy when you were born to cover this eventuality. A hundred and forty-nine pounds the maturity figure came to! That amount should pay for a wedding fit for a queen,' he announced proudly. 'No front-room reception for you, me darlin', but a proper sit-down do with waitresses serving us. Might even be a little left over to put towards some furniture for your new place.'

Percy gazed at his daughter tenderly. He and Dora, his beloved late wife, had long given up hope of ever having the large family they'd both wished for when at the age of forty-four Dora discovered to her utter shock that she was expecting a baby – a 'change-of-life baby', the doctors had termed it. They had both worried that they were too old to be running after a youngster, but they needn't have. Harriet, or Harrie as she was affectionately known by them, had brought such joy into their lives. She had been a happy child, very content, and never caused either of them a moment's worry. It was such a pity that Dora had not lived long enough to witness her beloved daughter's success not only at work but also in landing herself a future husband with such good prospects. Married to a solicitor, Percy knew his daughter would never want for anything and he himself could join his dear, very much missed wife when the time came, content in the knowledge that their girl was well provided for.

He had been anxious when the time came to meet Harrie's future mother-in-law. Hadn't felt at all comfortable in the lounge of the Bell Hotel, dressed in his best suit and with a stiffly starched shirt itching his neck, them being served lunch by formal waiters addressing him as 'Sir' and bowing courteously, himself striving to make a good impression for the sake of his daughter, watching his Ps and Qs, remembering to use his napkin, and overpoweringly thankful when it was over and as far as he was aware had all gone well.

Privately, he was surprised by his daughter's choice of future husband. Oh, Jeremy Franklin seemed a nice enough man, very well-mannered and obviously very taken by Harrie. But Percy had found him too stiff for his liking, and he didn't seem to have much of a sense of humour. His Harrie liked to laugh. Still, she seemed set on marrying the man so she must know what she was doing.

He wasn't sure either what to make of Daphne Franklin. He hadn't been able to understand half what she was saying because of her posh accent, sounding very like the Queen's in her Christmas Day speech. He couldn't pinpoint exactly why, after all it was nothing she had specifically said or in the way she had acted, but he could not shake the feeling that beneath her bright smile and words of welcome to Harriet, as she and her son called his girl, the truth was that she was not at all happy with her son's choice of future wife.

His own assumption was that Daphne Franklin viewed the Harrises as being of a lower social standing. But then, according to Harrie, Jeremy had told her his mother had been a tailor's daughter working alongside her own father in his shop as a seamstress when she had met her husband, so in truth it was only through her good fortune in marrying a professional man and his hard work in building up his business, leaving her well provided for on his death, that she had risen in the world.

If it was indeed the case that she was looking down on the Harrises, then she had no right to. She should be glad her son had landed himself such a pretty, bright woman as Harrie, one any man would be proud to have as his wife and who would prove herself more than adequate to the role of solicitor's wife. Still, the most important thing to Percy was that his daughter was happy, and she did seem to be.

'I can see to me own dinner, lovey. You go and get ready and get yerself off.'

'Are you sure, Dad?'

'Eh, surely even I can't make two disasters in one day. There's n'ote to frying a couple of sausages. I've seen yer mam and you do it enough times.' He then added with a twinkle in his eyes, 'If you return home to find the house burned down, I'll be next door having a cuppa with Albert and Nell.'

CHAPTER FIVE

Harrie had just finished putting the finishing touches to her make-up when a tap sounded on her bedroom door and her best friend Marion Allcott came in. She was a tall, slim, attractive young woman of the same age as Harrie and they had been friends forever, it seemed to them both, having teamed up as youngsters playing in the street then attended school together and started their working lives on the very same day, Marion as a wages clerk in a shoe factory, Harrie as a junior for a solicitor's. They had supported each other through their daily ups and downs and each felt that a friendship such as they shared was indeed very special. Neither would relish the prospect of losing it.

'Your dad sent me up,' Marion said, shutting the bedroom door behind her. 'Oh, you do look nice,' she complimented Harrie who was wearing a dark grey maxi-skirt, split to her knees, with a silver-grey, short-sleeved jumper. 'I gather from what he said that you're in a rush to get to Jeremy's to discuss wedding details so I won't keep you a minute.'

Harrie beamed with delight on seeing her. 'Oh, sit yerself down, I can spare two minutes being's it's you.'

Sitting on the edge of Harrie's bed, Marion asked, 'What happened to you last night? I was worried, thought you might be ill or summat.'

Replacing her mascara brush in its case, Harrie snapped it shut and responded, 'Why would you think that?' She swivelled around on her stool, giving her friend her full attention. Then she slapped her hand to her forehead and exclaimed in remorse, 'Oh, goodness, Marion! I was going to come around after my dress fitting and have a catch up with you, wasn't I? I'm so sorry, I completely forgot. You see . . .'

'It's all right, I've been through it all, remember?' Marion cut in, grinning good-humouredly. 'The dress-maker kept you hanging around, pinning and tucking, and what should have taken ten minutes took three hours?'

'That's about the size of it.' Harrie gave a sigh. 'The dress I'm going to end up with isn't the design I originally asked her to make, but after all her expert advice on what she feels will suit me and what won't . . . Oh, I do hope the end result is going to look all right,' she added worriedly.

'You're going to look the biz whatever you wear, Harrie.'

'I just hope Jeremy likes what I'm wearing.'

'He will,' Marion said with conviction. 'You'll take his breath away when he sees you walking down the aisle to meet him. He'll be thinking you're the most beautiful woman he's ever clapped eyes on. Present company excluded,' she added with a giggle. 'I suppose we're lucky the know-all dressmaker hasn't tried to change the style of the bridesmaid's dress we decided upon. Mind you, I haven't told you this before. She *did* attempt to. I soon put her straight. "Oi," I said, "me and Harrie went to great lengths to choose this style and we want it kept this way." She muttered something under her breath but I couldn't make out what it was. I gather she felt insulted but I wasn't willing to listen to her opinions on what suits me and what doesn't – as if I didn't know well enough meself! Why do dressmakers always think they know better than their clients, eh, Harrie? I know I'm going to look smashing in my dress and Allen's going to want to marry me all over again when he sees me in it. Well, he'd better. Do you remember my wedding day, Harrie? Despite all the planning, what a disaster it turned into.'

'Oh, it wasn't. Everything was great.'

Marion gave a disdainful click of her tongue. 'Yes, it was, if that's what you call the bride having to walk to church because the hire firm forgot to send her car, half the guests ending up with stomach cramps because the fish course at the reception was off, and the icing on the wedding cake setting that hard that not only was it inedible unless you risked broken teeth, we had to smash the top with a hammer so we could at least have the cake bit inside to hand around – and that was dry. My mother wouldn't stop crying and my father disappeared during the afternoon for a couple of hours to listen to the football match on the radio back home. Yes, it all went great, didn't it?' she said sardonically. 'You're not having a fish course served at your reception, are you? I won't touch it if you are. I still have fond memories of spending most of my wedding night with my head down the toilet. Mind you, one consolation is the The

Regency Rooms were closed down not long after our reception because of how many complaints the Health Department received about the standard of their cooking. Pity no one bothered to tell me *before* we had our reception there. Still, the Assembly Rooms have a good reputation so you should be all right.' She noticed the look on Harrie's face and frowned. 'Have I said summat wrong?'

'No, it's just that . . . well, it seems my reception isn't going to be at the Assembly Rooms any longer, Marion.'

'It isn't? But why? I thought your dad had arranged it all. He's booked that DJ I recommended to him who played at my cousin's twenty-first birthday do and he's ever so good. He's always booked solid, so yer dad was lucky to get him.'

'Dad had arranged it all but it seems it's now all been unarranged.'

Marion looked bemused. 'Unarranged? By who?'

Harrie gave a deep sigh. 'Look, you must promise to keep this to yourself because I haven't spoken to my dad about it yet and anyway I only found out myself late this afternoon, and then when I got home Dad was going on about the money arriving from the insurance policy that him and my mam took out when I was little to pay for my wedding, and he's so chuffed and thinking he's giving me just the best send off, which he was, and I was so happy with everything . . .'

'Oi,' Marion interjected. 'You're rambling on and not getting to the crux of the matter. Just who changed all your arrangements for the reception?'

'It was Jeremy's mother.'

'Jeremy's mother! But what business is it of hers? It's the bride's parents' privilege to arrange the wedding. 'Course, the poor sods get landed with the bill for the do but that's the joy of having daughters, ain't it? If we have any then we'd better get saving now as weddings ain't cheap, are they? By the time our kids get married, the way prices are rising it's a king's ransom we'll be looking at. Oh, sorry, now I've just done what I accused you of and that's rambling on. It's not Jeremy's mother's place to change the arrangements so why did she take it upon herself to do that?'

Harrie shrugged. 'Whether it is or isn't her place, she has. Jeremy said that she visited the Assembly Rooms and wasn't impressed . . .'

'What do you mean, she wasn't impressed?' Marion sharply interjected. 'There's nothing wrong with the Assembly Rooms. My Allen's firm had their Christmas do there last year and the food was great and plenty of it. The beer and spirits were cheaper than down the pub and plenty of staff on hand to serve so we weren't kept waiting, like what usually happens at these kind of occasions. Couldn't wish for better than that, could you?'

'No, you couldn't,' Harrie agreed. 'They don't charge extortionate rates either so the likes of us can afford to have a do there.' She looked worried. 'I dread to think what having the reception at the Belmont is going to cost, Marion.'

'The Belmont? Where's that?'

'It's a hotel on De Montfort Street.'

'But that's miles away across town. How the hell is your side going to get there after the church service?

Jeremy's side might all have cars but we don't. What's this Belmont Hotel place like anyway?

'It's very nice but . . .'

'But what?'

'Well, it's a bit . . . let's put it this way, I don't think Mrs Brown will feel free to do her can-can when she gets drunk like she usually does, showing off her old-fashioned bloomers. I think if she did attempt it she'd pretty quickly be marched off the premises for un-becoming behaviour.'

'Oh, it's that sort of place, is it? Only waltzing allowed to a string quartet kinda place, where you sip Bristol Cream from schooner glasses with your little finger stuck out, served by stiff waiters who look at you like they've a bad smell under their nose 'cos they know you can't really afford to be in a place like that, and they have never heard of chicken in the basket, and they definitely don't serve pints of beer only bottles and all drinks at double the price of even the poshest pub 'cos yer paying for the privilege of being in their grand surroundings?'

'Mmm, yes, it is that sort of place. We're all going to be sitting looking at each other, not daring to move in case we show ourselves up by our ignorance of etiquette.'

Marion looked at her friend knowingly. 'Well, you're choosing to marry a man like Jeremy so you'll have to get used to places like that in future. No more sawdust and spittoon dives for you, gel. Eh, but your wedding day is your choice. You need to speak to Jeremy, get him to tell his mother she had no business going over your head like this and to change it all back to what you'd originally arranged.'

Harrie looked bothered. 'Yes, I know I'm going to have to do something. Oh, Marion, I just want everyone to feel comfortable at my reception and I thought they all would, but now I know that if it's in the Assembly Rooms then Jeremy's lot are going to feel uncomfortable and if it's at the Belmont our side is going to feel uncomfortable. And as for me . . . Well, how can I enjoy my day, knowing half the guests aren't enjoying themselves?'

'Surely there must be a place that would suit everyone that your dad can afford?' She paused for a moment, looking at Harrie searchingly before adding, 'But then there's always the other option.'

'Oh, and what's that?'

'You could elope.'

Harrie flashed her a wan smile. 'That idea does sound very tempting at the moment, Marion, but I could never get married without my dad and my best friend being present at the very least.'

'I must admit I would feel upset if I wasn't there for your big day. You must speak to Jeremy and sort this out, sooner rather than later as time is wearing on. Oh, listen, I was offered a pair of curtains this morning at a good price. A friend at work bought them for her living room, only they're miles too big and she can't take them back because she got them in a sale. They're really nice. Top quality. Any good to you?' Then Marion frowned quizzically. 'Have you somewhere to live yet? You haven't mentioned even looking so what's going on in that respect? I can't wait to help you arrange your furniture and make the place look homely. You are going to let me help you, ain't yer?'

'I really don't want to talk about that.'

'Why not?' Marion glanced at her friend suspiciously. 'What's bothering you, Harrie? I know you better than I know meself and you've something on your mind that you're not happy about as well as this reception business, so come on, what is it?'

She sighed again and looked at her friend questioningly. 'You know when you were getting married, would it have bothered you if you'd been living with your mother-in-law for a while to start with, Marion?'

'No, not in the least. Allen's mother is a dear, you've met her and know for yourself I've been lucky in that respect. I get on with my mother-in-law better than I do my own mother. In fact, having been married to Mrs Allcott's son for four years and putting up with his habits, I wish I'd married *her* now,' Marion added, laughing. 'Oh!' she exclaimed as the penny dropped. 'So you're not moving into a place of your own but in with his mother. I'm right, ain't I?'

Harrie nodded.

'Oh, I see.' Marion's face clouded over. 'Oh, Harrie, Jeremy lives two bus rides away. I won't see much of you after you're married, will I? I won't be able to pop in for a cuppa and a chat like I do now, or you to me.' Then she looked remorseful. 'Oh, I'm sorry, I'm being selfish. I'm glad for you, really I am. Jeremy's house sounds lovely from what you've told me about it. And lots of people live with their folks until they can afford a place of their own.' She pulled a face. 'I would have thought, though, that with Jeremy being a solicitor he'd be able to afford a place for you both.'

'He says he can't afford the type of place that a man

in his position is expected to live in until he gets promoted to full partner.'

'Oh, I see. Well, which of us can afford what we feel we ought to live in when we first start out? Look at the pokey flat Allen and me rented for the first year of our married life. You could hardly swing a mouse it in, let alone a cat. Even the little terraced place we have at the moment isn't the house I intend to live in for the rest of my life, but it does us for now. Huh, sounds to me like you're marrying a bloody snob!' She looked remorseful. 'Oh, I didn't mean that, Harrie. Jeremy's not the type I thought for a minute you'd settle for but I'm happy for you as long as you're happy. He loves you, anyone can see that, and you're mad about him. Mind you, they do say love's blind.'

'Does that mean you don't like him?'

''Course I like him, you daft clot! Well ... I've only met him a couple of times, but what I know of him I like.' Marion paused and looked for a moment at Harrie, then giving a deep sigh said, 'Now yer asking, I have to say I wasn't exactly relaxed in his company the couple of occasions we went out in a foursome. Look, it wasn't Jeremy who made me feel uncomfortable, it was just the fact that with me knowing he's a solicitor and what kind of background he comes from, well, I felt like I'd to watch my Ps and Qs. So did Allen. We had to make sure we sipped our drinks, not knocked them back, that sort of thing, and the sort of things we talk about ... well, he didn't seem to have much idea what we were going on about. And then when he asked what classics were our favourite, the look on his face when Allen said an open-topped Triumph TR sports and went into great detail about his dream of driving one around the Italian countryside! Well, of course, now I realise Jeremy meant books not classic cars but I felt so stupid at the time. I suppose I can't really blame him for thinking what ignorant friends you've got.' She tilted her head and looked questioningly at Harrie. 'I have wondered if you've ever sat back and really thought what marriage to a man like him is going to be like for you?'

Harrie stared at her, taken aback. 'What do you mean?'

Marion leaned forward, clasping her hands and looking at her friend intently. 'Look, Harrie, I love you and wouldn't want to hurt you for the world. I've wanted to talk to you about all this before but you seemed so . . . well . . . amazed by the fact you'd managed to land a man like Jeremy and so wrapped up in it all . . . I'm not putting this very well, but what I'm trying to say is that he's introduced you to things that you've never experienced before, like the theatre and going to nice restaurants for dinner, eating with silver knives and forks at his house on posh furniture with proper napkins to wipe yer mouth on, and I just think you've got swept up in the glamour of it all. I mean, it's all very well being wined and dined and going to nice places but I just wonder if you'll feel really comfortable when you're actually living that life day to day?'

Harrie was staring at her, open-mouthed. 'You mean . . . I'm not good enough for Jeremy, is that it?' she asked softly.

'You're joking! Far from it,' her friend responded with conviction.

'Well, what are you getting at then, Marion?'

She took a deep breath. 'I'm just concerned you don't know the man you're marrying as well as you should do before you marry him, if you understand what I mean?'

'But I do know him . . .'

'No, you don't, Harrie, not properly you don't,' her friend interjected. 'You've only been going out with him all told for nine months and for six of those you've been planning this wedding. You can't know someone well enough to judge if you can live with them just by going for evenings at the theatre or out for a meal or dinner at his mam's. You can't really talk personally with yer fella's mother sitting opposite, listening to everything you say. Harrie, you know me and Allen went on holiday to Great Yarmouth in that caravan together? Oh, bloody hell, what an experience that was,' she sidetracked as memories of that time blasted to the surface. 'Remember I told you what a pokey little tin can it turned out to be after we were expecting . . . well, something that at least had enough head room to stand up in and somewhere comfortable to lie on and a stove to cook our meals. Good job we had the foresight to take along sleeping bags we'd borrowed off friends and a primus stove or we'd not have had a night's sleep or a hot meal all week. We couldn't afford to eat out, and besides we were stuck in the middle of a field miles from anywhere so going out was an expedition.'

Harrie was giggling now. 'You both had fun that week, though, didn't you?'

'We certainly did. And besides that holiday, Allen and me spent loads of days together just doing things that couples do and really got to know each other before we were married. So although no marriage is without its off days – well, ours certainly isn't as you know because you're the one I turn to and have a good moan with when he's driving me daft – at least we both knew in advance we got on well enough for our marriage to have a chance of working out. Look, I could be wrong but Jeremy doesn't strike me as the type to sit cuddled up with on an evening, both watching the telly and giggling together like me and Allen do over jokes cracked by comedians like Tommy Cooper.' She paused and looked earnestly at her friend. 'Harrie, have you ever spent an evening like that with Jeremy?'

A worried expression clouding her face, Harrie slowly shook her head. 'No, I haven't.'

'Well, don't you think you ought to?'

'Well, it's not like I haven't wanted him to spend an evening at my house, it's just that . . . well . . .'

'You've been too embarrassed to ask Jeremy because your house can't compare with his?' Marion jumped in.

'No, that's not it,' Harrie responded sharply. 'I'm not ashamed of where I come from. It's not like I've hidden my background from Jeremy, and he has been to my house when he asked Dad for my hand in marriage so it's not as if he doesn't know what it's like. It's just that . . . well . . . it's always Jeremy who's decided what we're doing and when we're seeing each other.'

'He doesn't ask you what you'd like to do?'

'Not in the way you mean. It's always "*I'd like to take you for dinner tonight if you're free*" or "*I have tickets for the theatre if you'd like to go*" or "*Mother has asked us to eat with her tonight if you haven't other arrangements*", that sort of thing. It's not like he takes me for granted, Marion, but going out with him hasn't been the same as going out with other boyfriends I've had. Jeremy is a busy man and lots of evenings he's tied up working on cases he's dealing with. He's explained to me he has to do that to prove his worth to his bosses, so that he's considered for promotion when the time comes. I have to have the patience to wait for him to tell me he's free, if you understand me.'

'Mmm, yes, I suppose I do. So when you're married and he's tied up in the evenings working, you'll be doing . . . what?'

Harrie frowned thoughtfully. Keeping his mother company, she supposed. They'd watch the television together. But then, come to think of it, she could not remember seeing a television set on the occasions she had visited Jeremy's house. There was a radiogram in the lounge, a very grand-looking piece of furniture that housed a radio inside as well as the record deck and racks for keeping a selection of records which Mrs Franklin had proudly showed to Harrie. None of the records had been to her own particular taste although she had been too polite to speak out. Would Mrs Franklin let her play her own records in the evening while Jeremy was otherwise occupied? She did not seem the type who would appreciate the likes of the black American artists Harrie had a weakness for as well as Cat Stevens, Bob Dylan and anything by the Rolling Stones.

She flashed Marion a brief smile. 'There's lots I can do in the evenings when Jeremy's working. I love reading and I can . . . can . . . Look, I realise life's going to change for me when I marry him and I have to be prepared for that if I want to be a good wife to him. And I do, Marion, I really do.' She flashed a glance at the alarm clock on her bedside cabinet. 'Oh, goodness, is that the time? I'd better hurry. Jeremy's mother doesn't like lateness at dinner and I want to avoid getting on the wrong side of her before I become a full-time housewife.'

'A full-time housewife! You're giving up work when you get married?'

'Solicitors' wives don't work, Marion.'

She looked affronted. 'Huh! Wives of lowly factory workers like my Allen do though, don't they?'

'Oh, don't be like that. I'm only repeating what Jeremy told me today.'

Her friend's face softened and she said graciously, 'Well, I suppose if we could afford for me to stay at home, I'd jump at the chance. What bliss that would be! I'd skim around my housework in the morning and have all afternoon to do whatever I wanted. Allen would be thrilled to have a proper cooked meal every night instead of some of the slapped together affairs I manage when we both get home 'cos I'm too knackered after a hard day's work to be bothered spending two hours cooking, and anyway Allen's usually that starving he can't wait long for his dinner. Mind you, unless I'd kids to look after, I think I'd soon get bored just being a housewife. I presume someone like Mrs Franklin has a char going in daily and maybe a cook, so while you're living with her you won't exactly be getting your hands dirty, will you? What will you be doing all day?'

'I'll have lots to do such as . . . such as . . . well, lots of things. Mrs Franklin is keen for me to learn to play bridge and join her women's groups.'

Marion laughed. 'Playing bridge?' she scoffed. 'That's an old fogey's game. And it's always fussy middle-aged ladies who go to these women's groups 'cos they've n'ote better to do with their time. Well, marriage is going to be a lot of fun for you, ain't it?' She looked seriously at her friend. 'If you're happy with what you're getting into, then all well and good. I know you're going to make Jeremy a smashing wife, Harrie, and he's lucky to have landed you in my opinion, but upsetting yer dad over this reception business is not really on, is it? You're going to have to at least get that sorted with Jeremy.'

'Yes, I know. I'm sure Mrs Franklin will understand when I talk to her about it and will be willing to change the arrangements back.'

Marion stood up, buttoning her coat and picking up her shoulder bag which she slung over her shoulder. 'I'll love you and leave you. See you soon, yeah?'

'I'm definitely having a night in with Dad tomorrow night to make up for tonight, and if Jeremy wants to see me he'll have to understand why I can't. I know he's got a Round Table meeting on Thursday so I won't be seeing him then. How are you fixed for me coming round to you and making up for not coming last night?'

Marion beamed. 'Suits me. It's Allen's darts evening down at the pub so me and you will have the house to ourselves. See you about eightish.'

CHAPTER SIX

All the way to Jeremy's house, Harrie worried how best to raise the matter of the rearranged reception without hurting Daphne Franklin's feelings. She wished she knew her future mother-in-law better so she'd have a clearer idea of how best to approach the subject, but she didn't. Finally she decided it would be best to speak to Jeremy about it first and take her lead from him.

'I was getting worried you weren't going to arrive in time, darling, it's just coming up for eight,' he said as he affectionately kissed her cheek then helped her off with her coat.

'I did mean to arrive earlier,' Harrie said lightly, kissing him back. 'But by the time I got home from work and got myself ready, and then of course I had two buses to catch ...'

'Very soon you won't have all this travelling back and forth,' he interjected, smiling lovingly down at her. 'You'll be here waiting for me when I get home from work. It can't come soon enough for me.'

'Nor me,' she said sincerely. Then something Marion said came to mind and she asked, 'Jeremy, when we're married and at home together in the evening, will you sit with me cuddled up on the sofa watching the television?'

He looked surprised by her question for a moment before responding. 'We haven't got a television. Mother and I have always been far too busy with other things to have time to watch, that's why we've never bothered. I suppose we could see about getting a set and finding somewhere to put it so you can watch it if there is something of interest you really are keen to view.'

'And you'll sit with me and watch it, cuddled up on the sofa?'

'Darling, we're adults, not silly teenagers anymore to be cuddling on sofas.'

'Oh, well, yes, I suppose we are,' she said with mixed feelings. Disappointed to find he felt that she at twenty-five and he at thirty were too old to be having a cuddle on the settee.

Jeremy glanced appreciatively at her. 'You look lovely.'

'Thank you,' she said graciously.

He circled his arms around her, pulling her close. 'The moment I set eyes on you in the office, I knew you were the one for me. Mother was beginning to despair of my ever meeting anyone suitable I'd want to settle down with. She thinks you're perfect for me.'

A warm glow filled Harrie then. 'I'm glad to hear that. I wasn't sure what your mother thought of me.'

'She thinks you've got great potential, Harriet.'

Locked in his arms, her head resting on his chest, she frowned. What did he mean by 'great potential'?

She wanted to ask him but before she could he had

released her, hooked her arm through his and was saying, 'Shall we go through? Mother is waiting for us.'

'Yes . . . er . . . no. Er . . . Jeremy, could I have a word before we join your mother?'

'Can't it wait, darling, as dinner is about to be served? It's Mrs Rogers' day off today so Mother has cooked it herself. She's done her special in your honour, chicken in white wine sauce.'

'Yes, I suppose it can wait. Er . . . no, it can't, Jeremy. In case the subject is raised during dinner.'

He looked puzzled. 'What subject?'

She took a deep breath. 'This matter of the rearranged reception. My dad is going to be so hurt about this, I can't bring myself to tell him. I was hoping I wouldn't have to.'

'Hurt? Why?'

'Because he wants to give me the best send off his money can buy. He won't be able to hold his head up, knowing he didn't pay for that send off but his daughter's mother-in-law did.'

'Well, yes, I can appreciate that. My mother, though, wants the best for us too. Surely she has a right to contribute as she is my mother?'

'But shouldn't she have consulted my dad first before she went ahead with cancelling all his arrangements?'

Jeremy looked thoughtful for a moment then sighed. 'Yes, I agree she should have, but as I explained this afternoon at the office, we could have risked losing the date at the Belmont.'

'I was happy with the Assembly Rooms, Jeremy, and I thought you were too?'

'Well, yes, I said I was . . .'

'You weren't?' she cut in, shocked.

'Well, if you want me to be truthful, the Assembly Rooms didn't offer exactly the kind of venue I had thought to have when I got married. I didn't say anything as I didn't want to hurt your father's feelings.'

She eyed him, confused. 'But you're prepared to hurt them now?'

'I've no choice, Harriet.'

'What do you mean, no choice?'

'I simply can't hurt my mother's feelings after she's gone to all this trouble to do her best for us.'

'And I can't have my father hurt, Jeremy. I just can't, I'm sorry. I'm sure your mother will understand . . .'

'I'm sure your father will when he learns what the Belmont has to offer against the Assembly Rooms,' he cut in. 'And it's not as if Mother is expecting your father to fork out for the difference in cost, is it? She is being very generous, Harriet.'

'Yes, I know she is, but my father is a proud man and he's been putting money aside in an insurance policy each week since I was born to pay for this day for me. I'm happy with what he's arranged and . . .' She looked at her fiancé pleadingly. 'I really want to have our reception rearranged as it was, Jeremy. Will you please speak to your mother about it? I just hope the Assembly Rooms haven't filled that slot because if they have I don't know what I'm going to tell my dad.' And while she was at it she might as well take this opportunity of addressing another matter that was bothering her. 'I have to tell you, Jeremy, that I'm not happy about moving so far away from him. I won't be able to see him regularly until I'm happy he's coping on his own. I know you said we could pay a neighbour to do for him but he won't like that, Jeremy, I know he'll feel demeaned. Couldn't we rent a house near enough for me to see him regularly, and your mother too, of course, just until we can afford a suitable place to buy?'

'I've told you, I can't see the point when Mother has all this room. And besides, I've already explained that I can't leave her on her own. She has no one else but me.'

'But, Jeremy, you're expecting me to leave my dad on his own and *he* has no one else but me.' It came out in an accusing manner which was not what Harrie had intended.

Jeremy was looking at her askance. 'It seems you're suddenly not happy with a lot of things, Harriet. Why haven't you spoken up about any of this before?'

'But how could I when you only told me about them yourself today?'

'I've already told you that I thought I had, and apologised for my oversight if I hadn't. Now, please, let's go in to dinner.'

He started to guide her through into the dining room to join his mother but Harrie pulled him to a stop. 'Jeremy, you are going to ask your mother to change the reception arrangements back to what they were, aren't you?'

His answer was blunt. 'No.'

She stared at him aghast. 'No?'

'I've told you, Harriet, I can't hurt her feelings. And I really do think you're being most unreasonable about this.'

She wrenched her arm from his, stunned by his refusal. 'You think *I'm* being unreasonable? You don't think you're being unreasonable, Jeremy?'

Just then Daphne Franklin appeared. She was dressed for dinner in a long, loose aqua-green silk kaftan, a string of large pale pink freshwater pearls around her neck and matching drops in her ears. 'What on earth are you both standing out here for?' The large woman smiled warmly at Harriet. 'How nice to see you, dear. You have brought along your completed guest list?' She glanced enquiringly at her son. 'You did ask Harriet to, didn't you, dear? I know how consumed you become by your work and then you forget to do things I've asked you to do. The Belmont want our seating arrangements handed in to them as soon as possible so they can have the place cards printed up.

'Anyway, let's go through and get dinner over with. We have so much to discuss tonight, not only regarding the wedding preparations but also when you propose to start moving your belongings in, Harriet. Then when you return from honeymoon everything here will all be shipshape and Bristol fashion, ready for you to get on with your new life here with us.'

She clasped her large hands together, a smile lighting up her heavily jowled face. 'Oh, the three of us are going to be one big happy family, I just know we are.' She smiled warmly at Harriet again. 'You and I between us are going to be behind Jeremy's rise to great heights. It's true what they say, you know. Behind every great man is a great woman. Or in Jeremy's case, two. You are a lucky man, darling,' she said, beaming at him proudly before returning her attention to Harrie. 'By the time I've smoothed your rough edges, you are going to make a first-class solicitor's wife. I have great faith in Jeremy's judgement, my dear. Come along then,' she ordered them both as she headed back into the dining room. 'You know I'm not amused when food gets cold, Jeremy.'

Harrie's thoughts were whirling frantically. What did Daphne Franklin mean by saying she was looking forward to smoothing her rough edges? But beyond that was another glaring factor. Harrie had received the distinct impression that her future mother-in-law did not see their living with her on first marrying as purely an interim measure, until Jeremy's promotion afforded him the means to buy a house of his own. Harrie was positive that Daphne saw them living with her for good. Trouble was, did Jeremy also?

She looked up at her fiancé quizzically. 'Jeremy, how long do you think we'll be living with your mother after we're married?'

He gave a shrug. 'I don't know. How do you expect me to answer a question like that? It depends how long my superiors take to recognise my potential and offer me a full partnership.'

'Well, do you think that will be in six months? A year? Two?'

A flash of irritation glinted in his eyes. 'Oh, Harriet, for goodness' sake! I've already told you I can't be precise about the timing of my possible promotion.'

'But when you are promoted, you will be buying a house for just the two of us?'

'What on earth makes you ask that?'

She eyed him worriedly. 'Jeremy, I need to ask you

a question. Am I marrying you or you and your mother?'

'What? Oh, now you're just being silly.'

'I don't think I am, Jeremy. I got the distinct impression just now that your mother thinks we will be living with her for good and that we'll be looking after you between us.'

'Harriet, what on earth has come over you? My mother was just trying her best to welcome you into our family and extend the hand of friendship to you.'

Harrie couldn't deny that Daphne Franklin had been very nice to her and appeared to be very welcoming. It was true that she would need help in learning to be a good hostess at all the dinner parties Jeremy had warned her he would be having in order to gain his promotion, and who better to teach her than a woman who'd had plenty of experience during her own marriage to a solicitor? There was, though, still the problem of the reception that needed resolving to Harrie's satisfaction.

'Jeremy, I apologise. It's very nice of your mother to offer her wealth of experience to me and I welcome it, I really do.' She paused, taking a deep breath before adding, 'But I have to make a stand about the reception. It's the bride's family's prerogative to take care of that. You have to allow my father to do this for me. Please will you speak to your mother about putting it all back the way my dad arranged it all? Please, Jeremy?'

His face set tight. 'I've told you, I can't hurt Mother's feelings, Harriet.'

She couldn't believe that the man she was about to vow to love and cherish for the rest of her life was showing such unwillingness even to approach his mother about reversing the results of her interference.

Blinking back the flood of tears that threatened, Harrie asked him, 'Is it always going to be like this, Jeremy?'

He looked at her blankly. 'Like what exactly?'

'Your mother coming first, before me?'

'That's a very selfish attitude, Harriet. I've never seen this in you before.'

'I've never seen you like this before either, Jeremy.'

Suddenly something Marion had said to Harrie earlier that evening flooded back to her full force. Marion was right. Harrie did not really know the man she was marrying. She had been so swept up by his romancing of her that she hadn't stopped to consider whether he was actually offering her the kind of marriage she'd envisaged for herself. She did want someone who would sit with her in the evening, cuddled up on the settee, and Jeremy had shown her that she couldn't expect that from him. She agreed with him that they were adults, but just because they were it didn't mean they had to act grown-up all the time, even in the privacy of their own home. What else had she taken for granted about her marriage without spending lengthy periods of time with Jeremy just doing normal things together, to discover if they were compatible, as Marion and Allen had had the sense to do before theirs? She suddenly knew that if this marriage was going to be the long-lasting happy one she wanted it to be then they needed to spend plenty more time together getting to know each other better. A lot better.

Gnawing her bottom lip anxiously, she took a steadying breath and said, 'Do you think we've jumped into arranging our marriage a little too soon, Jeremy? Maybe it would be a good idea to postpone it for a while, until we get to know each other better.'

'What!' He looked at her, astounded. 'I know quite enough about you to be sure I want to marry you. Just what is it you feel you don't know about me?'

'Well . . . lots of things, Jeremy.'

'Such as? You know I've got good prospects. You know I'm offering you a fine home to live in. You know I love you. What more do you want to know about me?' His face suddenly filled with a knowing look and he said, 'I know what the matter is, darling. You have pre-wedding nerves. The big day's drawing close, it's all overwhelming you, isn't it? I'm sure Mother will know of a tonic that will help calm you. Come on, let's go through and ask her.'

She was looking at him, flabbergasted. 'Jeremy, did you listen to what I said?'

He looked hurt. 'Yes, of course I did, darling, and I've given you my response.'

'That I need a tonic?'

'Yes.'

She gave an exasperated sigh. How on earth did she get it through to him that she was serious about their spending more time together before they became man and wife? She didn't really want to postpone their wedding for long, just enough for them to spend some time together, doing things that she wanted to do as well as the things he liked. That way they'd have a better understanding of each other and could give their marriage the best possible start and chance of lasting. When it came to rearranging their big day again, maybe by that time a place to hold the reception could be found that Jeremy's mother approved of and which was also affordable for her father. And it would give her time to make sure her father was better able to care for himself, and also a chance to adjust to the fact that she would be sharing Jeremy with his mother until they could afford a place of their own, which she had a terrible feeling would be later rather than sooner if Daphne Franklin had any say in it.

Harrie slipped her arm out of his, stepped across to the coat stand and unhooked her coat which she placed over her arm.

'Where are you going?' Jeremy asked her, frowning in bewilderment.

'I need you to think seriously about what I've suggested so I'm leaving you to mull it over.'

Before he could respond, Harrie had unlatched the front door and hurried through it.

CHAPTER SEVEN

The next morning, looking far calmer than she inwardly felt and armed with the post for his attention, Harrie tapped lightly on Jeremy's office door and entered when she heard his response.

Her father had been most surprised the previous evening when she had returned home far earlier than he had expected. He'd had no reason not to accept her explanation that she was tired and wanted an early night, but was delighted that before she retired to bed she had spent over an hour with him, both of them sipping cups of drinking chocolate while attempting to find the right places for some pieces of the complicated two-thousand-piece jigsaw she had bought him for his last birthday. Harrie had enjoyed working alongside her father and this only reaffirmed for her that not only did she want a husband who was also her lover and friend, she wanted this sort of companionship with him, not necessarily spent jigsaw-making but to share the pleasure of joint pastimes.

Despite the way she had left Jeremy, she had slept surprisingly well, confident that her suggestion of delaying their nuptials was right and that leaving Jeremy to think about it would make him see that too.

As she laid the post on his desk, he raised his head to look at her. Locking his eyes on hers, he said, 'Well, I'm waiting.'

She was confused by this cool greeting. 'Er . . . waiting for what, Jeremy?'

He gave an exasperated sigh. 'Your apology.'

She stared at him, stunned. 'My apology?'

'It's the least I deserve after what you did last night. It really was unforgivable of you, walking out like that when Mother was waiting for us to join her for dinner, and especially after she had taken great pains to choose the menu and cook the meal herself.'

The last thing Harrie had been expecting was a demand for an apology, but she supposed he did have a point. She shuffled her feet uncomfortably. 'Yes, I suppose I should not have left without making my excuses to her. I am sorry for that, Jeremy.'

'She was upset but I managed to cover your behaviour by telling her you had a sudden migraine and it was best you went home to take care of it. She's expecting you for dinner tonight so we can sort out the issues we were going to tackle last night. Please remember to bring your completed guest list with you.'

'But, Jeremy, did you not listen to what I suggested last night? That we postpone the wedding until . . .'

'Darling, it's as I told you then. You're suffering from a bout of pre-wedding nerves. It's too late in the day to cancel all the arrangements just on a whim that a simple dose of medication will resolve.'

'A whim!' She scraped her hand despairingly through her neatly styled titian hair, making it stick out wildly in places. Jeremy really was not listening to her. A rush of frustration washed through her and she snapped, 'It's not too late to cancel the arrangements and rearrange them after we've spent some more time getting to know each other better.' And added before she could check herself, 'Your mother has already proved that, hasn't she, by what she did?'

His eyes narrowed in annoyance. 'I will ignore that remark, Harriet, and put it down to your emotional state at the moment.'

He picked up the telephone and started to dial.

'What are you doing?' she asked him.

'I'm calling Mother to ask her to arrange a visit to our doctor so he can prescribe something for you. It seems to me that it's urgently needed.'

She couldn't believe he was totally dismissing her request to delay the wedding as if he was at a loss to understand why she had requested it, without even discussing it with her further, and instead diagnosing her as suffering from an ailment she definitely wasn't prey to. A tonic was not the answer. Getting to know each other better was.

Taking a deep breath, she clasped her hands tightly in front of her and announced, 'Until you take me seriously, Jeremy, I think . . .' She realised that he needed strong words to make him sit up and take notice of her as nothing else seemed to have that effect '. . . well, I think it's best we don't see each other.'

He was staring at her. 'You're calling off our wedding?'

'No, Jeremy, I'm not calling it off. I'm saying we should postpone it for a while and I've already told you why.'

'And I gave you my response last night.'

She gave a deep sigh of exasperation. 'We're getting nowhere, Jeremy. You're not listening to me. You're not even offering to make any sort of compromise . . .'

'How can I compromise? I want us to get married on the day we have arranged.'

'Well . . . well . . . you could offer to take us for a weekend away together before the wedding, and we could spend evenings doing . . .'

Before she could finish he jumped in. 'That's not compromising, Harriet, that's putting you in a compromising position by asking you to go away with me.'

She smiled. 'This is the Swinging Sixties, Jeremy. We haven't . . . well, done anything intimate together so far except kiss, so how do we know whether we are compatible in that department?'

He was looking completely shocked. 'Are you telling me you're not pure?'

'Pure!' She fought not to laugh at his old-fashioned terminology. 'Jeremy, I had other boyfriends before I met you and . . . I'm not a virgin, if that's what you mean. This is what I meant about us not knowing each other as well as we should before we commit ourselves to each other for life.'

He was looking at her as though she had a dreadful social disease. 'This admission from you has come as a great shock to me, Harriet. You should have told me that I wouldn't be your first.'

'But you never asked me. We've never discussed anything like this.'

'I was wrong to take it for granted then, wasn't I?

I don't know how I feel now about introducing you as my wife to my colleagues while wondering if you've been with any of them.'

She was gazing at him, horrified. 'What! Oh, Jeremy, how could you insinuate that I've slept around? It was with one boy who I was very fond of but things didn't work out between us, that's all. I know girls who have slept with several men before they settled for their husbands.'

'Their husbands might not have minded that fact, I do. I don't know how I feel about getting into bed with you on our wedding night while knowing I'm not your first. Would you even have told me about this if it hadn't come out in conversation just now? What else about your past have you been keeping secret from me?'

Her face filled with hurt. 'Nothing, Jeremy.'

'Can I trust that you're telling me the truth?'

'Oh, Jeremy,' she uttered, 'how can you ask me such a thing?'

'Well, after all, it's not every day a man like me comes along for someone like you, is it? Perhaps you're not to blame for keeping secret from me something you had an idea I wouldn't like.'

She gasped at the implied slight. 'Oh, Jeremy, how can you accuse me of being a gold-digger?'

'I wasn't . . . or maybe I was . . . Oh, I don't know. You're right. I don't know you, do I?'

'Have you had girlfriends before me that you were close to, Jeremy? Ones you haven't told me about?'

'Yes, of course I have. I'm a man, and a man has the right to sow his wild oats before he settles down to marriage.' He stared at her thoughtfully. 'I'm wondering if I can overlook your indiscretion as long as I have your assurance there are no other skeletons in your closet?'

Her mouth dropped open at the audacity of his double standards. She knew then that he was not the one for her. This knowledge hit her so hard she actually took a step backwards and gasped. She knew more about Kate Lane's husband who lived next-door than she did about the man she was planning to marry. The Jeremy she loved was only the part of him he had allowed her to see. The side he was showing her now she certainly did not like. What else did she not know about him that would be just as unwelcome? It struck her that the equal partnership she had thought to have with him would never have been possible.

It was glaringly obvious to her now that Jeremy was the type who would see himself as the master in his own home and her as the little woman he expected to jump to attention at the click of his fingers. She hadn't seen this before because they had never been in any domestic situations for it to show itself. When he had ordered food in restaurants for her, she had seen this as a gentlemanly act on his part, an attentiveness she'd never received from a boyfriend before, and she had found it romantic. Now she realised that in actual fact it was Jeremy's way of taking charge, that he automatically considered himself the principal in this relationship, assumed he knew better than she did even down to what food she chose to eat or wine to drink when out dining. He would dominate any marriage, she had no doubt of it, and for it to be an amicable relationship his wife would have to become a woman who jumped unquestioningly whenever he clicked his fingers.

A sudden wave of sadness washed through Harrie. She felt bereft of what she'd thought she had, not the way things had really been. Thank goodness Marion had opened her eyes so she was able to see it clearly or else she dreaded to think what kind of subservience she would blindly have entered into.

With tears in her eyes, voice thick with emotion, Harrie said, 'I don't want you to overlook my indiscretion, as you called it, Jeremy.'

He looked taken aback. 'I beg your pardon?'

'You heard what I said. You accused me of not being the woman you thought I was. Well, you certainly aren't the man I thought you were. I can't marry you now I know your true character. What you really want, Jeremy, is a hostess for your dinner parties and a companion for your mother. A lapdog, in fact. I would have been a good wife to you. I would have done my best to make you happy. But a lapdog I'm not. I'm sorry if I gave you the impression I was something you and your mother could mould into the perfect little wife for you.' She flashed him a wan smile. 'I hope you eventually find what you're looking for, Jeremy, I really do.'

With that she spun on her heels and rushed from the office, leaving him staring after her confounded.

As Harrie arrived back at her desk a colleague sitting nearby stopped what she was doing to look across at her. 'You all right, Harrie? Only yer look like you've just been told a relative has died.'

'Pardon? Oh, yes, I'm fine, thank you. Just . . . er . . . have a lot on my mind, that's all.'

Resuming her task, the office assistant said, 'Well, yer bound to, what with the wedding looming so close. All us girls here are so envious of you, landing Mr Franklin. What a catch he is! I bet you pinch yourself every night, don't yer, Harrie, to make sure you ain't dreaming? Oh, you've never mentioned your hen night. Have you arranged that yet? I will be invited, won't I?'

Harrie stared at her, frozen. Oh, this was awful. All the staff knew of the forthcoming wedding, some of the senior staff even expecting invitations, and would have to be told it was off. What explanation could be given so as not to demean a man in Jeremy's position in front of the staff or, worse still, damage his promotion prospects in the eyes of the fuddy-duddy partners? Then a more worrying question presented itself. How could she continue working so closely with him now she had broken off their engagement? It was going to be extremely difficult for them both. Despite knowing without a doubt that he couldn't be the kind of husband she wanted, Harrie still had deep feelings for him and was in no doubt that he did love the part of her he had known and understood.

She knew then that the only fair thing for her to do was to resign from her job, leaving Jeremy free to decide what information about their break-up he divulged so as to save his own face. She refused to allow herself to think what effect leaving the job she enjoyed so much would have on her. Jeremy would not suffer through lack of secretarial support due to her departure. After all, he'd already chosen a replacement for her on their marriage so all that was needed was to ask Miss Abberington to bring forward her starting date.

Without saying a word to her colleague, very aware the woman was still looking at her, bewildered by her lack of response, Harrie quickly put a piece of paper into her typewriter and expertly tapped out a letter. After signing it, she folded it up to put in an envelope. She then hurriedly swept her desk of personal belongings and put them into her handbag. Grabbing her coat, she handed the envelope containing her resignation to her colleague.

'Would you please give that to Miss Rayner for me, Colleen?' Miss Rayner being the office manager in charge of all the secretaries and clerks.

The other girl frowned. 'What is it?' she asked, taking the letter.

Harrie flashed her the briefest of smiles. 'Please excuse me, Colleen, I have to dash.' She spun round to depart, then stopped to say, 'It's been great working with you all. I shall miss you.'

'But . . . but . . .' a bewildered Colleen stammered.

Harrie, though, had left.

CHAPTER EIGHT

Percy was most surprised to see his daughter walk through the back gate an hour later but he didn't need to ask if there was anything amiss. He instinctively knew there was, and something serious.

After hurriedly laying aside the brush he'd been using to sweep the yard, he rushed across to her. 'Oh, me ducky, what's wrong?' he demanded, taking her arm. 'Are you ill or summat?'

During the bus ride home Harrie had managed to keep her emotions under control. Now, safe in the confines of their back yard with her beloved father by her side, the dam broke and tears welled up to pour down her face. She fell into his arms. 'Oh, Dad ... Dad,' she blubbered. 'I'm so sorry, I really am.'

The sight of his beloved daughter breaking her heart, the reason as yet a mystery to him, sent a chill of fear through Percy. 'Let's get you inside.'

Seating a still sobbing Harrie on a dining chair, he sat down next to her to take her hands protectively in his. His face creased in deep concern, he asked, 'What on earth are you sorry for, ducky?'

'Letting you down, Dad.'

'Now how could you ever let me down?'

She wiped her runny nose with the back of her hand before she answered, 'All the money it's cost you.'

He frowned. 'Harrie ducky, what are you going on about?'

'Oh, Dad, I can't bear to think that you've been putting by money every week all these years and now I've made you lose it! Do you think it's too late to get the deposits back if we tell them we're sorry we have to cancel?'

The penny dropped then and he looked stunned. 'Harrie, are you telling me the wedding's off?'

She nodded.

His face hardened in anger. 'He can't do this to you! It's that mother of his, it's her what's behind this, I bet. I had an inkling she thought you weren't good enough for her son. Well, we'll see about this.'

He made to rise but she stopped him. 'It's me that's called the wedding off, Dad.'

He lowered himself back on to the chair. '*You* have!'

She nodded. 'Please don't think badly of me, Dad. I couldn't marry Jeremy when I realised he wasn't the one for me.'

'Oh, I see. Well, in that case, I'm glad you've been sensible before it's too late.'

'You are, Dad?'

'Of course, me darlin',' he replied with conviction. 'Yer don't think I want you to marry someone you know isn't right for you, just to keep me happy, do yer? As for the money we might have lost, I'd sooner that than find out you married the wrong chap.' He patted her hand and looked at her, at a loss as to quite what to say and do for the best. It was upsetting him greatly to see his daughter so distressed. It was at times like this he really missed his wife. Times of crisis were when women came into their own. He hoped he was handling this catastrophe as well as Harrie's dear late mother would have done. His mind sought to identify what she would do if she was here now. Then the answer came. She would have done what all women do in situations like this: make a cup of sweet tea and offer a sympathetic ear.

A while later Percy gave a deep sigh. 'You've done the right thing, Harrie.'

'I did love him, Dad, or the Jeremy I knew I did. I'm missing that man so much. You don't think I could have been too hasty and . . .' Harrie's voice trailed off. She had seen Jeremy for what he truly was and it was no good thinking she could somehow change herself or him just to ease the pain of the loss she was feeling at the moment. 'Yes, I have done the right thing, haven't I, Dad?' she whispered.

'Oh, ducky, most certainly. When I married yer mam, God bless her, neither of us had any doubts at all. When you finally get married you mustn't have the slightest doubt either. Too many people have gone through with weddings knowing they were doing the wrong thing just because they felt they couldn't upset their families. And then lived the rest of their lives in misery.' He held out his arms to her. 'Come and give your dad a hug.'

She fell into his arms and he embraced her tightly. 'I know this is the last thing you'll want to hear just now, but there's someone else out there for you, a man just right for you. It's best you left yer job. Clean break all round. You'll get another one easily with your skills. And, Harrie, we ain't that hard up yer can't take a little time to get yourself over this properly before you start working again.' In an effort to lighten the mood he said, 'Eh, there's one good thing come outta this.'

She pulled away from him and with tear-blurred eyes smiled and asked, 'What's that?'

'Well, call me selfish, me old ducky, but with you not leaving me so soon I can take a while longer to learn this cooking and washing for meself lark, can't I?'

Despite how wretched she was feeling, she couldn't help but giggle. She'd get through this, she knew she would. She had her wonderful father to help her. She did worry how Jeremy was feeling, mortally sorry for the fact that she must have hurt him as well as leaving him with the task of explaining to his mother that their relationship was over, but once he got over the initial shock and thought clearly, she felt sure he would appreciate that what she had done was for the best in the long run. One thing she had learned from this episode in her life: the next time she met a man and felt like getting serious with him, she would make sure she knew him well enough, and he her, to know without a shadow of a doubt that their relationship offered each of them what they were seeking.

CHAPTER NINE

While Harrie was being consoled by her father, at the front door of a smart residential property in an affluent suburb of the city Chas was depositing bags of shopping where his passenger indicated. He accepted the money the expensively dressed, middle-aged woman handed him.

'Keep the change,' she said in regal tones.

He respectfully tipped his forelock. 'Thank you. I hope you had a pleasant journey and Black's Taxis can be of service to you again.'

As he walked down the drive lined with neatly trimmed laurels he checked the money in his hand and didn't know whether to laugh or cry when he quickly calculated that his tip for this trip was the grand sum of twopence. He'd never become rich at this rate, he thought. Tips made up a good proportion of his wage and he was determined to save as much as he could towards the eventual purchase of a new house.

The boom of a voice over the radio alerted Chas. He made a dash for the car, quickly unlocked the door and leaned inside to unhook the hand-mic from its cradle. Snapping down the button, he spoke clearly into it: 'Romeo receiving.' As usual he cringed inwardly as he always did when having to announce himself by his call handle which he felt had been inappropriately assigned to a man of his plain looks.

Ralph Widcombe's gruff tones came back to him. 'Pick up for you from the Royal Infirmary to Wingate Drive. A Mr Chapman is waiting outside the main entrance on Welford Road. And as soon as you've dropped him off yer'd better come straight to the office. Mrs Black is here dishing out the wages and she's wanting to get back up the hospital as soon as she can to be with Mr Black.'

'Right you are, Ralph. Any news on the boss?'

'No . . .'

Ralph's voice was suddenly replaced by a loud crackle of interference then a second authoritative voice came over the air. Chas knew this was the police whose radio transmissions often broke into taxi operators' as the wave bands used were so close together. It seemed by what was being relayed over the air that a motor accident had occurred on the Narborough Road and the sergeant operating the police radio was summoning all available officers to the area. There was more interference and then Ralph's voice filtered back again. 'You there, Romeo?'

'You'll have to repeat, base, had police interference.'

'I said, no change as far as I know in Mr Black's condition.'

'Oh, dear. Thanks, Ralph. I'll do that pick up and see you back at base in about half an hour, give or take.'

As he put the mic back in its cradle and started the engine Chas grimaced, unsure whether no change in his boss's condition was good news or bad.

A while later, as he waited for his next fare, Chas was taking a break in the drivers' rest area. Most unusually there was no one else present and he was enjoying his own company – for the short time he knew it would last. The once-white walls of the rest room were now stained khaki-yellow by cigarette smoke and the red Formica-topped table was faded, cracked and stained. The end of one of its legs had broken off and was held up by a tatty old telephone book. The matching red plastic-covered chairs had seen better days too. Old newspapers lay in toppling heaps, being added to on a daily basis by drivers chucking theirs on top when they'd finished with them; rows of dirty milk bottles, their contents in varying stages of rancidness, were stacked six deep under the table which held a gas ring, blackened kettle and three grubby plastic containers holding tea, instant coffee powder and sugar, all clogged into lumps from having wet spoons dipped into them.

Taking a sip of stewed tea, Chas slit open his wage packet and counted the contents. Frowning, he pulled out his wage slip and studied it. Something was wrong. The money in his hand did not tally with the net figure on his wage slip. He'd a fiver too much.

He made his way to Jack Black's office which was next-door to the rest room. Tapping on the door, he walked inside. The decor of this room was no better than the drivers' refuge. Three overflowing filing cabinets filled one wall, above them two shelves crammed with bulging ring binders and other paraphernalia to do with the business that Jack Black had never got around to clearing out over the years. The window looking out on to a small yard behind was filthy, preventing much light from filtering through.

Chas smiled politely at Muriel Black who was sitting at her husband's cluttered desk, a tray containing several brown wages envelopes in front of her.

The middle-aged woman looked harassed and distracted. 'Oh, it's you again, Chas. I thought it was one of the other drivers come to collect their pay. I hope the others hurry up as I really need to dish these out then get back to the hospital. Er . . . did you want to see me about something?'

'It's my pay, Mrs Black.'

'Oh?'

'It's not right?'

'Oh!'

'You've given me too much money.'

'I have?'

'A fiver too much according to my wage slip.'

'Oh . . . oh, I see. Oh, dear, you're the third one I've had back today because something wasn't right with their pay and not all the drivers have collected theirs yet so how many others are wrong?' She rubbed her hands wearily over her face, looking defeated. 'Oh, I'm no good at this making up wages lark. Jack saw to all that, you see. I've never had any office experience. Since he took ill I've had to battle through as best I can with just a bit of help from the daughter of a neighbour who works as a wages clerk at the British Shoe Corporation.' She gave a sigh and shook her head ruefully. 'To me the tax and National Insurance books Her Majesty's Tax Inspectors issue might as well be written in Chinese. I can't make head nor tail of them.'

She smiled at him. 'I appreciate your honesty, Chas. Keep the fiver and get yerself drunk on it tonight – my treat.'

'Oh, I couldn't take advantage, Mrs Black.'

'Keeping quiet about the extra fiver in your pay packet would have been taking advantage of me, Chas.' She gave a resigned sigh. 'This has brought home to me that I'm on a fool's errand trying to keep the office side of the business ticking over 'til Jack's better again. I haven't touched any of the bookwork at all since he took ill 'cos in truth I ain't a clue how. If I don't want to end up bankrupting the business, I need to be sensible. I must get someone in to do the office work temporarily 'til Jack's back on his feet again.

'To be honest, I'm about on my knees with popping in here daily to make sure no disasters have happened, though God knows if something had I wouldn't know how to put it right, and then spending the rest of my time at the hospital sitting by Jack's bed willing him to get better. I haven't slept a wink hardly since he had his attack. If I carry on like this I'll end up in the bed next to him.' She gave a rueful shake of her head. 'I kept telling him this place'd be the death of him if he went on working the hours he did with no let up. I just hope to God I ain't proved right, Chas. I pray with all my might I ain't.'

He saw tears glisten in her eyes when she added, 'I'd be lost without that silly old bugger. We've been together forty years. We've only got each other 'cos we weren't blessed with family. It was always a dream of Jack's to own his own business and he scrimped and saved, begged, borrowed and . . . well, he never lowered himself to steal to my knowledge, although between you and me I wouldn't have put it past him if it meant he'd fulfil his dream. He got his first licence plate by paying over the odds for it from a taxi driver friend of the family who was forced to give up 'cos he lost his leg in an accident when he was driving home drunk from the pub one night and met up with a lamp-post.

'For Jack, getting that plate was like being given the crown jewels. From then on he's lived and breathed this business, but then I can't complain 'cos it's bought me a nice house and stuff inside it and put good food on the table. But I was so looking forward to him retiring and us doing all the things we haven't done together since he started up the business over twenty years ago. A week away would be nice. I ain't fussy where. We haven't had a holiday since . . . well, I can't remember when.'

Muriel gave a sigh. 'Mind you, I've always known it's wishful thinking on my part that Jack will ever retire. He couldn't bear to part with this place. It's like his baby. He gave birth to it and since then he's nurtured it carefully. I suppose the most I can hope for is what's happened to him will bring home to him that he needs to slow down a bit.' Muriel gave a sniff and mentally shook herself. 'Forgive me, Chas, this is no way for the boss's wife to carry on in front of the staff, is it? It's just that . . . well, there's something about you that makes you very easy to talk to and that's a rarity in a man.' She looked at him hopefully. 'You don't know anyone who's looking for a job in the office line, do you? Someone who'd take all this lot off me hands so I can devote myself to being with

Jack full-time? I dread the thought of him coming round in a strange hospital bed and me not being there. And of course I'll need to be on hand all the time when he's at home convalescing.'

He shook his head. 'No, sorry, Mrs Black.' Feeling he could not leave her without any hope of having her burdens alleviated, he added, 'I'm sure that there's someone somewhere who'd be willing.'

Muriel looked doubtful. 'Mmm. It's a case of finding them, ain't it? I mean, this ain't the most salubrious of places to work in, is it?' she said, casting her eyes around the room and wrinkling her nose in disgust. 'Any decent temp is going to turn their nose up at working here all day, and I can't say as I blame them. I got a big shock when I saw how bad it is, especially that rest room. Well, it's just a pig sty. Yer can tell no woman works here, they'd never have allowed it to get like that. I shall nag Jack to tidy this place up until I'm blue in the face when he gets better 'cos if the hours he works don't eventually kill him, the germs rife in here certainly will. But even finding office help is difficult for me. The time I have to spend doing it is time I could spend with him. Plus I wouldn't know the first thing about interviewing anyway.' She rubbed her hands over her face again. 'I'll just have to keep battling through as best I can, and hope that at the end of it all my Jack has a business to come back to.'

Just then Ralph's voice was heard outside shouting, 'Got a pick up for yer, Chas.'

He flashed a smile at Muriel Black. 'I'd best go. Er . . . please give my best to Mr Black. Everyone's best wishes, in fact.'

Before he turned and left he put the five pounds she had overpaid him before her on the desk and Muriel Black knew by the look he gave her that despite her offer to let him keep it he was not comfortable about doing so. Jack certainly had chosen well when he had recruited Charles Tyme, she thought. Whether his boss was around or not, his type would carry out his job to the best of his ability and be scrupulously honest into the bargain. She had a feeling, now she had met the drivers, that not all of them were in the same mould as Chas Tyme. She worried some might be taking advantage of their boss's absence. Still, there was nothing she could do about that. If they were up to anything untoward behind Jack's back, she was too inexperienced to do anything about it.

Later that evening, as Chas tucked into an overcooked pork chop and lumpy mashed potatoes, he said to his mother, 'I do feel for Mrs Black, Mam. She's having a tough time of it just now, trying to do what she can for the business while spending as much time as she can at her husband's bedside. She looks frazzled to say the least. She told me herself how much of a struggle the office side is for her, with her having no experience. She really needs help running it, but I fear it's like she said, she'd be hard pressed to find someone to do it temporarily with the facilities our office offers. It's not exactly posh.'

'Oh, I'm sure there's someone who'd cope, but she won't find 'em 'til she starts looking, will she? Is your pork chop tough?' Iris asked him, looking dubiously at the one on her own plate.

It was but only because his mother had fried it in far too hot a pan, for too long. 'It's fine, Mam, just how I like it,' said Chas diplomatically.

'Huh, well, it must just be mine then. I shall be having words with the bucher when I next go in.'

Just then a knock sounded on the back door.

Iris tutted crossly. 'Who can that be, just when we're having our dinner?'

'I'll get it, Mam,' Chas offered, making to lay down his knife and fork.

'You sit where yer are,' she ordered him. 'I don't want yer dinner getting cold.'

She went off to answer the door and Chas could hear the murmur of voices before his mother returned tight-faced to announce, 'It's Nadine Dewhurst, or Rider as she is now, for you.'

Chas looked surprised. 'Me? What does she want with me?'

'She wouldn't say. I told her you was having yer dinner but she said it was urgent.'

A horrifying thought struck him. Nadine couldn't be calling to ask him to watch her four children while she went to the pub, could she? He supposed there was only one way to find out.

'Oh, Quas . . . Chas,' Nadine quickly corrected herself when he went into the kitchen. 'I'm so sorry to bother you, yer mam said you was having yer dinner, but . . . well . . . yer the only one around here I could think of to call on, you always being so helpful to the neighbours like. *It* could go away I suppose, but if *it* doesn't and *it* bit one of me kids . . .'

'If *what* bit one of your children, Nadine?'

'The rat. Bloody great big black thing it is. I saw it with me own eyes shooting across the yard when I went to put some rubbish in the dustbin just now.' Tilting her head, she ran her tongue over her lips and pouted at him. 'Oh, Chas, you will come and see if you can catch it, won't yer? I'd be ever so grateful.'

The suggestive undercurrent in her voice made him squirm uncomfortably. All his wiser instincts told him he'd be best off telling her he was extremely busy and shutting the door on her, but his good nature dictated that he could not turn down anyone's request for help, and especially not when children could be in danger. 'I ... er ... think we've a trap somewhere in the outhouse that we bought a few years back when the dustmen were last on strike, just in case we had a problem like that. I'll dig it out and bring it round and set it for you. It's a case of waiting and hoping then. Best keep your children out of the yard meantime, though. I'll just finish my dinner and I'll be round.'

She smiled charmingly at him. 'Thanks. Proper knight in shining armour you are, Chas Tyme.'

'What did the likes of her want with you?' Iris asked when Chas took his place back at the table.

Tucking into his dinner, he said, 'Apparently they've a rat running amok in their yard.'

'Huh, and why ain't I surprised? All that junk they have stacked in there. Rats' paradise the Dewhursts' yard is. I hope you told her to get the council in?' She saw the look on her son's face. 'Oh, yer never offered to go and try and catch it?' Iris clicked her tongue. 'You don't know the word "no", do yer, son? Still, I suppose I wouldn't have you any other way. But I don't need to tell you, do I, that them Dewhursts are n'ote but trouble so when yer've done what yer have to, make sure that Nadine knows you ain't at her beck and call or she'll be around here asking yer help all hours of the day and night. Them's the type that, given a yard of 'lastic, they'll not be happy until they've stretched it the length of a mile.'

'Don't worry, Mam. I'll be setting the trap and that's all I'll be doing.'

Nadine was leaning on her mother's open back door smoking a cigarette when Chas entered via the yard gate twenty minutes later, armed with the trap he had unearthed from the outhouse.

He was surprised to see her there. He would have thought she would be inside, the back door firmly shut, to stop the rat getting into the house.

Nadine smiled winningly at him, smoothing one hand down her short, tight-fitting skirt and flicking the other through her long blonde tresses. 'You really are a gem, Chas. I was just saying to Mother what a relief it was to be able to call on you.'

Just then a voice from inside boomed, 'Who you talking to, Nadine?'

She hurriedly pulled the back door to. 'As I was saying, it's really good of you to come and help us.'

'Where did you say you saw the rat running to?'

Nadine looked blank. 'Eh? Oh . . . er . . . in there somewhere,' she said, pointing to the outhouse whose rotting door was hanging off its hinges. It was packed full with an array of discarded items in varying stages of decay.

Chas blew out his cheeks. Several nests of rats could be thriving inside that little haven. 'Well, I'll set the trap near the entrance and then hopefully Bob's yer uncle.'

'Oh, I'm sure it will be. I have faith in you, Chas.'

He was very conscious she was watching his every move as he set the trap. When he'd finished, she said, 'You must let me buy you a pint down the pub by way of a thank you.'

'Oh, there's no need really.'

'But I insist. I'll see you there sometime, yeah?'

He gulped. 'Just make sure your children don't come into this yard until you're certain one way or the other whether you have a rat. If you have and the trap doesn't work you'd best get the council in. They're the experts at getting rid of vermin. I'll be getting back now as my mother is waiting to dish up pudding.'

As he hurried off back to his own house, a curl of satisfaction played around Nadine's lips. The first stage of her plan was off to a good start.

CHAPTER TEN

A few streets away in an identical style of terraced house to that where Chas and Iris lived, Marion was giving her best friend a comforting hug. 'Oh, Harrie, you and Jeremy breaking up? Well, it's the last thing I was expecting.' She pulled away and looked sympathetically at her. 'From what yer've told me yer've done the best thing, gel. It's nice for a woman to feel protected by her man, but dominated by him is another thing. Before long yer'd have felt stifled, Harrie, and deeply regretted tying yerself to him for life – and 'is mother too by the sound of it. I'm not saying Jeremy's a bad man, Harrie, I've no doubt he loves you, but it seems he's not the one to make you happy in the long run.'

Harrie issued a deep sigh as she sank down on a well-used chair by the drop-leaf table. 'If you hadn't come round last night and said what you did, I'd still be going ahead with the wedding, too wrapped up in it all to see what I was actually heading for.'

Marion's face filled with horror. 'Oh, Harrie, are you saying you deciding not to marry Jeremy is all my fault?'

'Yes, it is, but in a good way. You opened my eyes

to the type of man he really is. Oh, Marion, I feel so stupid. I shan't ever be so blind again. I've no doubt, though, that Jeremy will find someone else who wants a man just like him and will enjoy the kind of life he's offering.'

'The doormat kind, you mean? You might be some things, Harrie, but the doormat type you ain't.' Marion sat down on a chair beside her. 'Have you told yer dad?'

She nodded.

'And how did he take it?'

Harrie gave a wan smile. 'He was great, Marion. As supportive as he always is. I couldn't wish for a better dad than mine. I could do with my mother, though, at the moment,' she added softly, her voice thick with emotion.

'You never grow too old not to need yer mam, do yer, Harrie? My mam drives me insane sometimes 'cos she's an argumentative old sod but I'd be lost without her.' It was very evident to Marion that her friend was fighting back an emotional outburst. She thought it would be a good idea if she tried to keep Harrie's mind on more positive matters, to give her a breathing space until she got into bed tonight and cried herself to sleep as Marion knew she would. 'So it's job hunting for you then?' she said brightly.

'Mmm, seems so, doesn't it?'

'I got the *Mercury* tonight on my way home from work if you fancy a look down the Jobs column?'

'Thanks, Marion, but I'm not in the mood just now. I haven't given my job situation much thought because as I'm sure you can appreciate I've had other things on my mind, but I thought I might try temping for a bit. I fancy a change from a solicitor's office and I expect you can see why.'

'Yes, I can. Until you're fully over this it's best you avoid as many reminders as you can. Er . . . just a thought, Harrie. Do you think yer've seen the last of Jeremy?'

'What? You mean, you think he'll sue me for breach of promise, Marion? You can't do that any more.'

'No, I mean . . . well, men don't think the way we do. I should know, I've been married to one for long enough. You might think you've made it clear it's best you go your separate ways, but what I'm getting at is that he might not have accepted what you've told him and . . . well, think you're still suffering from pre-wedding jitters and didn't really mean what you said.'

'Well, I *did* mean what I said. He'll know I mean it too after he's found out I've left the firm, which he's bound to have done by now. I don't like the thought of him suffering, I really don't, but Jeremy's an intelligent man. I'm sure in time he'll thank me for what I did.'

Marion wasn't at all sure he was going to take Harrie's rejection of him as quietly as she thought he would, but decided not to voice her thoughts.

Harrie stood up. 'I'd better let you get on with making Allen's dinner. I just thought I'd come round and tell you what was going on.'

Marion smiled warmly. 'Look, don't go. Stay and have dinner with us. I've a chicken pie that Allen's mam made us, it'll stretch to three. I'll send him down the pub after and I'll pop down the offie and get us a bottle of cider. Help you drown your sorrows.'

'That's a nice offer, Marion, but I'll give it a miss, if you don't mind. Dad's fussing around me. I've left him peeling spuds for chips to go with the bit of frying steak he got from the butcher's this afternoon in an effort to cheer me up. He knows steak and chips is usually my favourite dinner. Actually I'm afraid any food will choke me at the moment but I'll have to force it down somehow or I'll hurt his feelings'

'Ah, bless him,' said Marion. 'Yes, I understand, you must get home.' She rose to put her arms around Harrie and gave her a bear hug. 'Remember, no matter what time of day or night, if you need a shoulder to cry on or just a chat, I'm here for yer, gel.'

Harrie smiled appreciatively. 'Yes, I know you are, and thank you, Marion.

CHAPTER ELEVEN

The following Monday morning Harrie found it strange that she needn't leap out of bed to ready herself for work. As well as losing Jeremy it seemed she'd lost the familiar routines of a job she'd loved, and the comradeship of her workmates.

Percy, who was in the process of mashing his daughter a cup of tea, having heard her moving around upstairs, took one look at her when she came down and suggested she go straight back to bed as it didn't look to him like she'd had much sleep.

'I did sleep well, Dad,' Harrie fibbed. 'It's just I'm not quite awake yet, and no woman exactly looks her best when she's just rolled out of bed, does she?'

'You look to me like yer've been rolling around it all night. Darlin', you don't have to cover things up, I know you haven't slept. Go back to bed and I'll bring you up a cuppa.'

'No, Dad. I've spent all weekend wallowing in self-pity and even you must be fed up by now with all the pots of tea you've mashed me and the wet patches on your shirt where I've been crying on your shoulder. I have to start getting my life back together, and the best way I can do that is by getting myself back to work. I'm going to throw some clothes on now and pop down to the telephone box to make an appointment with a temp agency. Chatterley and Bigson used a firm called Ace Employment. The girls they sent along to help us out always seemed to be up to the job so I'm going to approach them first. Hopefully they'll see me soon and be able to get me something for next Monday.'

Percy smiled warmly at her as he put a pot of tea on the table. 'I'm glad to see you're thinking positively, lovey. But before you start on this new episode in yer life, will you at least have a cuppa and slice of toast to keep yer stamina up? Just to please yer old dad.'

Meanwhile, a few streets away in the Tyme household Iris was frowning as she scanned the contents of the pantry, wondering what she could do Chas for his dinner that evening. Left over from the weekend was a slice of corned beef, a noggin of cheese, a couple of potatoes sprouting eyes, one rasher of streaky bacon and one sausage which had burst its skin. There was also a small piece of dried up-looking beef from the Sunday joint which was supposed to have been big enough to provide leftovers for today but had shrunk so much while cooking – possibly because Iris had the oven set too high – it had just about been enough to feed them for the one meal.

She sighed. It seemed she had a bit of everything and not enough of anything. She needed to provide a substantial meal to satisfy her son's healthy appetite when he came home this evening. Chas deserved a good meal after labouring all day and she would have to be on her death bed not to provide him with one. She hadn't done liver and onions for a while. If she hurried she'd catch the butcher before he shut for lunch.

Then a sudden desire to go into town overwhelmed her. Since her tumble in the street a few weeks ago and the resulting injury she had honoured Chas's request for her not to venture too far without someone, preferably himself, accompanying her, just to be on the safe side. Since her accident she had felt redundant to a certain extent as Chas now did the heavy shopping each week on his way home from work at the large branch of the Co-op on the bottom of the Groby Road. The other bits and pieces she might need during the week were obtainable just a short distance away from the local shops and he'd reluctantly conceded after a sharp exchange with his mother that she could manage to get those herself. But Iris missed her window shopping in the big stores and her bargains from the market; a milky frothy coffee and sticky bun from Brucciana's café on Horsefare Street; the hustle and bustle a visit to town afforded her.

A mischievous twinkle lit her eyes. Well, what Chas didn't know wouldn't hurt him.

All ready for the off, she was just about to leave when a tap sounded on the back door. As it opened Freda's voice called out, 'Cooee, it's only me! Got the kettle on, I hope, 'cos I'm parched.' She was fully inside now and immediately spotted her friend dressed for outdoors. 'Oh, you off out? Where yer going?'

'Er . . . just up the shops.'

Freda cocked an eyebrow at her. 'No, you ain't.'

'What do you mean, no I ain't? If I say I'm going to shops then that's where I'm going.'

Her brow still cocked, Freda folded her arms under her skinny chest and took a stance. 'No, you ain't.'

Iris scowled at her. 'You calling me a liar?'

'Yes, I am. You're off up the town, ain't yer.' That was not a question, more a statement.

Her friend looked shocked. 'How the hell did you know?'

''Cos yer wearing yer best coat, which you always do when yer going to town. When you go to the shops you just throw on yer old gabardine mac. And yer've got yer best shopping bag on your arm. For the local shops you just take your old string bag.'

'Bloody Sherlock Holmes you, ain't yer?' Iris hissed at her accusingly.

'I just know yer, Iris. I should do, we've been friends long enough. Anyway, I can't let you go up the town.'

'You can't? You can't bleddy stop me!'

'Oh, I can. I promised Chas that when he wasn't here I'd keep me eye on you and make sure you didn't do 'ote daft like what yer trying to do now. He said if I ever caught you, I was to barricade you in and get him fetched from work.'

'Oh, so you're me jailer now, are you? And as for that son of mine . . .'

'Now get off yer high horse, Iris,' Freda cut in. 'Chas only has yer best interests at heart. We both have. I'd come with you if I'd time but I've not as I've our Rita and me grandkids coming for tea tonight so I've baking to do this afternoon. If you're hell-bent on going to town, I can go with you tomorrow.'

'I am quite capable of getting meself up the town and back. I had one silly accident a few months back and my Chas and you seem to think that from now on 'til the end of me days I'm to be reined like a toddler. I'm as fit as a fiddle and raring to go. Now listen, Freda, and listen good – I'm going up the town and I'm going right now.'

'Your Chas won't like it, Iris.'

'He's my son. It's me that tells him what to do, not the other way around. Anyway, I'll be back long before he gets home from work so he'll be none the wiser. Now do you want me to bring you 'ote back?'

'Well, if yer going through Lewis's you could get me a pound of their loose assorted biscuits.'

'Yes, 'course I will. Now I'd best get off or I'll miss the eleven-forty-seven bus.'

Back in the Harrises' house, Harrie was checking her appearance in the mirror hanging above the 1930s tiled fireplace in the back room.

Her father eyed her appreciatively. 'You look the business, me duck. The top-notch secretary that you are. If that agency don't snap you up, then they ain't what they're cracked up to be.'

Harrie turned and smiled at him. 'Thanks, Dad.' She glanced at the mantel-clock. 'Oh, I'd best hurry or I'll miss the eleven-forty-seven into town.'

'What time is your appointment with the agency?'

'Twelve-forty-five. I was quite surprised when they said they'd like to see me this morning. I got the impression they've lots of temp work in at the moment and not enough staff to cope with it.'

'Have you got your typing certificates to show them?'

She patted her handbag. 'All in here. I still have to do a typing and shorthand test for them, though.'

'And you'll pass with flying colours,' Percy said with conviction. 'I'll walk with you to the bus stop, lovey. I could do with a blow of fresh air. And I'll get a Lyon's sponge from the shop and we can have a slice of that and a cuppa when you get back while you tell me all about the new job the agency has offered you.'

Harrie smiled at him tenderly. The encouragement he was giving her was just what she needed to keep her mind focused, not dwelling on what might have been but only what could be in the future.

The three people waiting at the bus stop were glad to see a bus approaching in the distance.

Iris was relieved it was on its way because Black's Taxis' office was just across the way and the last thing she wanted was for her son to spot her waiting. He'd immediately know what she was up to and challenge her, and she didn't want an altercation in the street with him regardless of his concern for her welfare.

Harrie was relieved to see the bus on its way because it was eight minutes late and she was cutting it fine to get to the agency. The last thing she wanted was to arrive late. That wouldn't create the right impression at all.

Her attention was fixed too firmly on the bus, willing it to hurry, for her to notice the car that overtook it and passed the bus stop only to come careering to a stop a little further down the street. The driver leaped out and came striding towards the bus stop.

Harrie jumped and spun around as she heard her name being called, immediately recognising the voice. 'Jeremy!' she exclaimed.

He was advancing on her with a most annoyed expression on his face. 'I've just been round to your house and was surprised to find no one in,' he said, heedless of the interested onlookers. 'Are you on your way to see me?'

She shook her head. 'No.'

'Oh! I trust you're on your way to see the doctor then?'

She shook her head again. 'No, I'm not.'

'Well, where are you off to?'

'Where I'm going is really none of your business any more, Jeremy.'

'Not my business! Of course what you do is my business, I'm about to become your husband, Harriet.' He gave an aggrieved sigh. 'This has gone on long enough. After your display of dramatics in the office last Friday I thought it best to leave you alone for a couple of days, let you come to your senses. I did think you'd have paid me a visit by now to offer an apology, though. Obviously your condition isn't getting any better. I really must insist you see a doctor and get medical help.' He took her arm and made to guide her towards his car as he continued speaking. 'I have an hour before my next client is due so I have time to take you to my family GP and . . .'

'I'd be obliged if yer'd take your hands off my daughter.'

Jeremy turned his head to look at Percy in surprise, not having noticed his presence. 'Oh, er . . . Mr Harris. Good morning. I didn't see you, I do apologise. Please excuse us but I must get Harriet to the doctor.'

She pulled her arm free. 'I do not need to see a doctor, Jeremy, I'm not ill.'

'Oh, but darling, you are,' he insisted, retaking her arm. 'There's no other explanation for the way you're acting.'

She tugged her arm free again. 'Jeremy, for the last time, I am not ill. If anyone has a problem it's you.'

He looked stunned. 'Me?'

She sighed. 'You have to accept that it's over between us. We're not right for each other. I can't make you the sort of wife you want, and you won't make the sort of husband I want for myself. That's why I thought it best to hand in my notice at work and leave immediately, give us both a clean break.'

'We *are* right for each other. I won't accept that you think we're not. I knew you didn't really mean to give in your notice. You just did it in the heat of the moment because you weren't thinking straight due to pre-wedding nerves, so I retrieved it and explained to Miss Rayner that you're sick.'

'You did what? Jeremy, you had no right to hold back my notice or tell Miss Rayner that I'm ill when I'm not.'

'Listen here, lad,' piped up Percy, stepping between Jeremy and Harrie, 'I know it must be a shock for you, Harrie calling the wedding off, but you're going to have to accept my daughter's decision that it's over between yer.'

'I will never accept that,' he said resolutely. 'I love Harriet and I know she loves me. As far as I am concerned we're still getting married as we planned to do in seven weeks. Once she's been given the right medication by the doctor she'll soon be back to her normal self, you see if I'm not right.'

He made to step round Percy and take Harrie's arm again but his shoulder caught the older man a glancing blow, sending him tumbling backwards to land against the concrete post of the stop.

Iris, who hadn't been able to stop herself from taking an interest in this saga being played out before her, couldn't believe her eyes at what she had just witnessed. Before she could help herself, she'd swung back her handbag and launched it at Jeremy, shouting as she thrashed her bag repeatedly against his arm, 'Oi! And just who the hell are you to be pushing an old gent about? Shame on you! Shame on you, you hear? And trying to drag this young lady off to the doctor when she doesn't want to go . . . well, that's kidnapping, that is.'

Jeremy, shocked himself to realise what he had done to Harriet's father, albeit accidentally, was holding up his hands, trying to fend off the blows from the handbag of his mysterious assailant. 'I didn't mean to do it. It was an accident. Now stop hitting me, will you? Stop it, I said.'

Harrie was over by her father now, arm around him protectively. 'You all right, Dad?' she demanded urgently.

'I'm fine, me ducky.' He could tell she wasn't convinced and added, 'I'm fine, really. I was just taken off guard, that's all. I need to catch me wind.'

Fatigue getting the better of her, Iris finally stopped her attack and stood with hands on hips, glaring at Jeremy. 'Bloody bully, that's what you are, a bloody bully.'

Rubbing his throbbing arm, Jeremy was glaring back at her. 'How dare you accuse me of being a bully?' he snapped at her, outraged.

'Well, from your performance just now there's no other way I or anyone else could describe yer,' she answered him back. 'I heard that poor gel say it was over between yer, but just 'cos you don't want it to be, then as far as you're concerned it ain't. If that ain't bullyboy tactics I don't know what is. Look, lad, you might think that you can browbeat this young lady into doing what you want, but do you really think by forcing her to be with you it'll all end up happy ever after? If yer do, then yer want yer brains seeing to. You'd be best to put this down to experience and find a woman who wants you for who and what you are. Leave this gel here free to do what she wants.'

'This lady is right, Jeremy,' chipped in Percy. 'My daughter knows her own mind and she's made it up that you and she ain't right for each other. Best you say your goodbyes before this turns nasty.'

Jeremy was staring at them both, opening and closing his mouth fish-like. He looked at Harrie and she could plainly see the hurt he was suffering. 'Are you sure you want to call the wedding off? Really sure, Harriet?'

She nodded. 'It's for the best, Jeremy, really. We wouldn't make each other happy, I know we wouldn't. If it's any consolation, I do still care for you very much.'

He heaved a long resigned sigh and his shoulders sagged. 'Mother is going to be so upset when I break this news to her. She really liked you, Harriet, and was so looking forward to having you as her daughter-in-law.' He leaned over and kissed her cheek. 'I hope you find what you're looking for. I'm just sorry it wasn't me. Goodbye, Harriet.'

With his head hanging, he walked back to his car and drove away without a backward glance.

Harrie watched him go, her bottom lip trembling, then a trickle of tears ran down her face. 'Oh, Dad,' she faltered. 'I'm so sorry I hurt Jeremy, I really am.'

'Better this way, ducky, than living for years trapped in a marriage you didn't want to be in,' said Iris, putting a comforting hand on her arm.

'You know, this lady is right. That's why you finished with Jeremy in the first place,' said Percy, sliding his arm around his daughter's shoulders and giving her a comforting hug.

'Are you all right?' Iris asked him.

He flashed a smile at her. 'I feel a bit foolish having a lady come to my rescue but I'd like to thank you all the same.'

Iris was just grateful not to be accused of inter-fering in something that was nothing to do with her, which in truth was what she had done. 'Your daughter needs a cup of sweet tea,' she suggested. 'Best tonic for an upset.'

'That's what my dear late wife would have prescribed. I'll take her into the café over there and get her one. Er . . . would you care to join us?' Percy asked out of courtesy.

Iris looked down the street to see the bus disappearing into the distance. In the excitement of the scene at the bus stop, none of the onlookers had thought to wake it to a halt. There was at least another fifteen minutes to wait for the next, longer if it was late which was usually the case. The incident had fatigued her and a sit down with a welcome cup of tea to revive her before her trip to town would be a good idea. She would also like to satisfy herself that this lovely young girl, who was still clearly upset, was none the worse for her ordeal.

'I'd love to,' she replied, smiling warmly.

Later that evening Iris put Chas's plate of dinner before him and sat down opposite. 'Sorry it's such a mishmash of leftovers, son, but I never got to the shops 'cos I . . . er . . . was busy today.'

From under her lashes she cast a quick glance at her son. Despite the fact that she would dearly have loved to divulge her escapade of today and the promising results, she sincerely hoped he did not ask her just what she had been busy doing because then her intended trip into town would come out. He would not be happy to learn about that despite the fact that in the end she had never actually made it, nor would he like to hear of the way his mother had acted like a fishwife in the street, launching an attack on a perfect stranger, albeit coming to the defence of someone else.

Chas had had a day of it himself. It had seemed to him that everyone suddenly needed a taxi and it had been non-stop. He hadn't even managed to snatch a lunch break but had had to eat the sandwiches his mother had packed him up that morning as he'd driven between jobs.

Now he scanned the contents of his plate. Heaped on it was a mound of cheesy, lumpy mashed potato, a more than well-done burst sausage, slice of corned beef, the remains of the over-cooked roast from yesterday, all swimming in a sea of baked beans. Considering that this was a woman who had once decided to make a chicken and leek pie, but not having chicken thought chunks of belly pork would do the job just as well, and leeks being out of season substituted Brussels spouts, today's offering looked fine to him.

'I hope you haven't been overdoing things, Mam?' he said as he piled his fork with food.

'Oh, no, definitely not,' she said lightly, and thinking it best she change the subject before she told him any more lies to cover up her misdemeanours, asked the first thing that came to mind. 'Fancy a stroll with me down the pub after dinner?'

He looked across at her in surprise. 'I've never known you ask me to accompany you down the pub, it's usually the other way round.'

'Well, yes, but . . . you never went last Friday,' she babbled. 'You're not one for going out but you do like a couple of pints on a Friday after work, and being's you never went last week 'cos you said you was too tired and there was summat good on the telly you wanted to watch, well, I thought you might fancy going tonight instead? And if so I would go with you 'cos I'd quite like a half meself . . .' and she added before she could check herself '. . . after the afternoon I've had.'

He eyed her sharply. 'Why, what happened this afternoon?'

'Oh, nothing, nothing, son, just a turn of phrase, that's all. I had a boring afternoon, if you must know. Yes, extremely boring. So boring in fact it's not worth talking about. Well, eat up before yer dinner gets cold and afterwards I'll wash up while you get changed to go out.'

Chas inwardly groaned. He'd not been entirely truthful with his mother about his reluctance to partake of his weekly two pints down at the local last Friday evening. He'd feigned tiredness and a desire to watch a programme on the television just in case Nadine happened to be there and forced him to accept the drink she had promised him for laying the rat trap. He'd worried that any further conversation between them might lead to her abusing his good nature, thinking she could call on him for anything and everything at any time of the day or night, as his mother had warned him there was a good possibility she would do. Still, Monday wasn't a popular night for a visit to the pub as most people hadn't the spare money for drinking after the weekend. More than likely Nadine would not be in there tonight so he felt safe to go. He quite fancied a pint to wash the day's dust out of his throat and it would do his mother good to have a natter over a glass of stout with any of her old cronies who happened to be in there.

A while later, having washed and changed, Chas arrived in the back room to find his mother settled in her armchair by the fire, engrossed in a programme on the television.

'You ready then, Mam?' he asked her.

She looked at him blankly. 'Eh?'

'You wanted to go to the pub.'

Despite the excitement of the day having taken its toll on her, Iris had never had any intention of accompanying her son. 'Oh, er . . . I've changed me mind, son. I'm all settled now. I forgot *Take Your Pick* was on tonight. Now off you go. It will do you good to get out and socialise instead of sitting here of an evening with yer old mam. I'll see you when you get back.'

Fred Bales, the portly landlord of The Blackbird, greeted Chas with a friendly smile when he arrived at the bar. 'Not your usual night. Everything all right with you and yer mam, is it?'

'Yeah, fine, thanks, Fred. Yourself?'

'Oh, can't grumble, ta. Although maybe I can. There's rumours in the trade that the Government intend sticking another penny on the price of beer and fourpence on a bottle of spirits in the next budget, and of course we landlords will bear the brunt of it with the punters. But apart from that my main worry is this new money that's coming in next year. What's it called . . . decimication?'

'I think you mean decimalisation.'

'Do I? Oh, well, whatever it's called, it's still gonna cause chaos. We've had pounds, shillings and pence since the year dot. Why do we need to suddenly go

143

all foreign? I'm gonna have a job getting my head around it myself as well as keeping an eye on my bar staff to make sure they're giving the right change. If it's too much they'll eventually bankrupt me. Too little and I'll have the punters threatening murder 'cos we're fleecing them. My work is going to be more than cut out for me when it comes in, ain't it? But it's the old dears I really feel sorry for, I fear they'll never get the hang of it. At their time of life they're starting to forget things as it is. How the hell are they gonna learn summat as mind-boggling as this new money lark? Usual?'

Chas nodded. He felt Fred was right to be concerned about the new coinage that was being introduced the following year. It was going to cause pandemonium while people got used to it. Regardless, though, it was coming in whether they liked it or not so they'd better get used to it. It would be a sad day, he thought, when the old coins that had been a part of British life forever, it seemed, disappeared in aid of the country's becoming part of what was known as the Common Market. Whether this was a good thing or not, and whether the change of coinage was a prelude to other changes they would have to endure in future, remained to be seen.

As Fred poured out his pint of bitter, Chas glanced around. 'Not very busy tonight.'

'Never usually are on a Monday, Chas. Get a few in just after ten when the twilight shift finishes at the Marconi factory.' He put a frothy pint of Everard's best bitter in front of Chas and took his money. After putting it in the till, he picked up a cloth and as he dried glasses asked Chas, 'Any news on Jack Black yet?'

'He's still very poorly, his wife says.'

Fred pursed his lips. 'Shame to be cut down like that at his age. I have to say I don't think it looks good for him. Jack wasn't what I could call one of me regulars so I don't know him as well as I do some of me punters but personally I found him a pleasant sort of man. I admire the way he built his business up from nothing, working all the hours he did to make it what it is now. All right, so Black's Taxis ain't in what yer'd call the big league compared to the firms based in town, running twice as many cars as Black's, but it's my guess Jack's profits are enough to keep his wife in stockings. When yer see Mrs Black next please tell her that all of us at the pub are rooting for her husband. Yes, mate?' he said to a man who had just arrived at the bar.

Leaning on it, sipping on his pint, Chas did not see the outer door open and a woman pop her head inside to scan the drinkers. When she spotted her quarry she gave a satisfied smile before stepping in and trotting over to the bar.

'Why, Chas,' said Nadine, arriving to stand beside him. 'How nice to see yer. I've just popped in to buy some ciggies, but while we're both here let me buy you that drink to say thanks for helping me out the other night.'

It seemed to Chas that she was more dressed up for a night out dancing than popping out quickly to get a packet of cigarettes, and he wondered why she hadn't gone to the corner shop to buy them as it was much nearer and considerably cheaper than Fred's pub prices.

'Oh . . . er . . . Nadine . . . How . . . yes, how nice to see you too. I've got a drink, thanks.'

'Which is nearly finished,' she said, observing his near-empty glass. 'I'll get a refill for you.'

'Nadine, there's no need to repay me for what I did the other night. It was my pleasure and I don't expect any recompense.'

She looked at him coyly. 'Oh, Chas, I can assure you the pleasure was all mine.'

The way she was looking at him made him feel mortally uncomfortable. 'Er . . . did . . . you catch anything?'

She looked at him blankly. 'Eh?'

'In the trap?'

'Oh, I dunno, I ain't looked. I was wondering if you would come around and do that for me? I'm scared of rats, living or dead. They wouldn't scare a man like you though, eh, Chas? So you will, won't yer?'

'Er . . . yes, sure. I'll pop round when I get a minute.'

She tilted her head. After running her tongue over her top lip, she said suggestively, 'I'll look forward to it.' Then she clicked her fingers at the landlord. 'Another of what Chas is drinking and I'll have a vodka and black.'

'No drink for me, Fred. Nadine, thanks for the offer but I was just going.'

'Oh, yer can't,' she cried urgently, then hurriedly added, 'I mean, you must let me honour me commitment to say thanks.'

He sighed. 'All right, but just a half.'

She slapped him playfully on his arm. 'Oh, a proper man like you doesn't drink halves. Chas will have that pint, Fred,' she called across to him.

She put her handbag on the counter, opened it and rummaged around for her purse. 'Oh,' she finally exclaimed as Fred put the drinks in front of them. 'Would you believe, silly bugger me has come out without me purse. Oh, what am I like? I hope I didn't forget to put on me drawers,' she added, laughing raucously.

Chas was already fishing in his pocket for his wallet. 'I'll get them. How much, Fred?'

'Oh, you are a proper gent, Chas Tyme, you really are,' said Nadine, batting her eyelashes at him. 'That'll be another favour I owe you. We'll have to have a chat about how I can pay yer back. Maybe . . .'

'No need, really,' he cut her short. 'It's my pleasure, honestly it is.' In a way he was relieved that Nadine had forgotten her purse as he did not feel at all comfortable about a woman buying him a drink, whether it was repaying a favour or not.

'One good deed deserves another, Chas. Er . . . would yer stretch to getting me a packet of Woodbines?'

Chas obliged, then picked up his pint and downed it in one. 'Well, I really must be going.'

'Oh, but won't you have another?' she said, disappointed. 'It's still early.'

'I have an early start in the morning. Well, good night, Nadine. 'Night, Fred,' he called to the landlord.

Nadine snatched up her glass and knocked back its contents. 'Hold up, Chas, I'll walk back with yer.'

He had no way of refusing.

Outside on the pavement she linked her arm through his. 'Oh, a nice big man like you does make a woman feel protected,' she said as they began to make for home, Chas striding and she tottering on her high heels to keep up with him. 'Oh, slow down, will you, Chas? Anyone would think you was in a rush to get home and be rid of me.'

That was exactly what he was trying to do. Never having had a girlfriend, he had never walked down the street before with a woman on his arm and understandably it felt strange to him, but especially strange when it was Nadine whose arm was linked with his, a woman who until very recently had never missed an opportunity to show her scorn of him.

Chas was relieved when they arrived at his entry. He unhooked his arm from hers and said, 'Goodnight, Nadine.'

'Oh, ain't yer going to see me to me door, Chas?'

'Pardon? Oh, well, it's only just there.'

'It might be but it's dark and anything can happen to a woman on her own in the dark.'

She had a point, he supposed. 'Come on then.'

He stepped the several paces with her to her entry then made to take his leave but she got in first with, 'Thanks for tonight, Chas. I really enjoyed it. We must do it again, I'll look forward to it. Oh, don't forget you're going to pop round and check the trap. See yer.'

With that she disappeared off down the entry.

As Chas made his way home, a happy Nadine let herself in by the back door of her mother's house. She

148

had been disappointed every night since she'd first put her plan into operation not to have caught Chas down at the pub, but patience had paid off and tonight she had.

It was a mystified Chas who let himself back inside his house to join his mother. He couldn't understand why Nadine was suddenly acting the way she was with him. She didn't have to be so familiar to get him to help her with the alleged infestation of her yard, she knew enough about him to know that. He would check the trap, he decided. Hopefully it had done its job and that would be the end of it.

CHAPTER TWELVE

The next day, just after twelve-thirty, Chas was making his way into the drivers' rest room to eat his lunch while he waited for his next fare when he stopped short, spotting a young woman backing out of the boss's office, pulling along a bulky sacking bag.

Having no idea who she was but regardless about to offer to help her with the bag – whatever she was doing with it – he was stunned suddenly to be shoved aside by three other drivers charging out of the rest room and across to the woman, all proclaiming, 'I'll help yer with that bag.'

Chas heard her say, 'Thanks, very much appreciated. It's rubbish to go in the dustbin.' Still with her back to Chas she watched the men vying with one another to do the job for her. She suddenly seemed to sense his presence and turned to look across at him. Her face broke into a bright smile. 'Hello, I'm Harriet Harris. My friends call me Harrie though,' she said as she stepped across to him, holding out her hand. 'I'm the temporary office help.'

He smiled back at her. 'I'm Charles Tyme. Chas. Another of the drivers.'

As their hands clasped and their eyes locked, Chas

experienced a peculiar sensation shooting through him. His heart started to race, a rushing sound filled his ears. Time suddenly seemed to stop. Nothing else around him existed but this woman whose hand he was clasping, whose magnetic emerald-green eyes his own unremarkable blue were staring into.

Simultaneously Harrie was thinking that there was something about this big man whose bear-like hand was clasping hers that seemed very familiar to her, but there couldn't be as she had never met him before. Then suddenly she had the overwhelming feeling that he was important to her, that this meeting was a significant milestone in her life, but she had no idea why or what part he was going to play or how she could know this. Then one reason why he was familiar to her registered. His mother had talked so much about him yesterday in the café that in truth Chas Tyme wasn't a stranger. Then she realised he was looking at her strangely and seemed to be frozen to the spot. Besides that he was holding her hand so tight he was cutting off the blood supply and it was beginning to hurt her.

'Are you all right?' she asked in concern.

Through the wind-like rushing that was filling his ears, Chas heard her voice and was jerked out of his trancelike state. 'Sorry,' he blurted.

'I asked if you were okay?' Harrie repeated.

'Eh? Oh, yes, I'm fine. Absolutely fine. Couldn't be better.'

She looked relieved. 'Good. Er . . . do you think I could have my hand back, only you're crushing it.'

'What!' he exclaimed, mortified. He dropped her hand as if it was suddenly burning him. 'I . . . er . . .

sometimes don't know my own strength, I'm so sorry. I haven't hurt you, have I?' he asked worriedly.

Thankfully feeling was returning and she smiled. 'No damage done. It's nice when a man's got a firm handshake, shows he's got strength of character.'

The loud commotion the men were making as they vied with one another to help attracted Chas and Harrie's attention then. Harrie chuckled as Darren, the victor of the three, slung the sacking bag over his shoulder and gave her the thumbs up sign as he made his way towards the back door that led into the yard, the losers making their way back into the drivers' rest room.

'As payment for me help, I'll settle for a drink with yer down the pub tonight,' Darren called out to her.

'You'll settle for a cuppa here in the office and like it,' she bantered back. Harrie then turned her attention back to Chas. 'How's your mum?' she asked him.

He looked taken aback. 'My mum?'

'She did seem fine when she left us yesterday but ... well ... no disrespect to her, she's not as young as she used to be and after what she did ... well, I was concerned it could have an adverse effect on her. I must find some way of repaying her for coming to our rescue – more than the cup of tea in the café we had afterwards. After all, if it wasn't for your mother I would never have found out that Mrs Black needed temporary help here and gone round to see her to apply. I just thank goodness your mum decided to catch the same bus as I did yesterday. Apart from the fact that the situation with Jeremy might have become worse than it did without your mother's intervention, I'd never have found out about this job here and could be starting one I might not be as happy in. I know I'm going to like being here while Mr Black gets better.

'I am sorry, though, that because of what your mother did and the amount of time we spent talking in the café afterwards it was too late for her to go into town, but she did say I wasn't to worry about that as she could go another day. Oh, does Mrs Tyme like chocolates?'

Chas was feeling decidedly hot under the collar. The feelings he had experienced on their initial meeting were returning, doing things to his insides that he'd never experienced before. His heart was thudding in his chest again and he felt light-headed and couldn't think straight. What Harrie was saying to him wasn't quite registering. He stuttered, 'Me mother ... er ... well ... er ... yes, she is my mother. Er ... I mean, I think she likes chocolates.'

Harrie frowned at him. 'You don't know for sure?'

'Er ... yes, of course I do. Yes, she loves roast beef. Er ... chocolates.' Oh, God, what must this woman be thinking of him? He was making a fool of himself. He needed to get away from her before he made even more of an idiot of himself in front of her. Just then the voice of Ralph taking details of a pick up from a customer on the telephone filtered through to him. 'I'll do that,' Chas called across.

'But you're just starting your lunch ...'

'No matter, Ralph. Not hungry. I'll do it.'

Without even excusing himself to Harrie he leaped over to Ralph and waved his hand in front of him for the slip with the details of the job.

Ralph gave him a grin and a wink and in a low voice

said, 'Well, Miss Harris is certainly gonna ruffle a few feathers, ain't she, and one person's in particular methinks. Marlene ain't gonna like competing for Darren's attentions, no siree, she ain't.' His grin broadened. 'You liked her an' all, didn't yer, Chas? An old veteran like me can tell.'

'Just give me the details of the pick up, Ralph,' he demanded, snatching the note on which they were scribbled. Before Ralph could pass further comment Chas had gone.

As he set off, part of the conversation he'd just had with Harrie flooded back to him. She had told him she'd met his mother at the bus stop yesterday. Why had his mother been waiting for a bus? Then the rest of what Harrie had relayed to him came back. His mother had told him last night that she had spent a very boring afternoon, so boring in fact that it wasn't worth repeating. Now it seemed her afternoon had been anything but boring. In fact, distinctly eventful. Oh, Mam, he inwardly groaned. Was that trip into town more important than the possible risk to your health? Well, he'd make sure she didn't attempt anything so stupid again after he'd had strong words with her tonight when he got home.

For the rest of the day Chas was thankfully kept busy on the road and had no reason to return to the office except at clocking off time. Before he went inside to sign off, hoping that Harrie had left for the evening, he spent longer than usual tidying the inside of his vehicle ready for work the next morning. It was kept in the compound at the back where taxis not in use on the night shift were kept secure and Terry Bragg, the maintenance mechanic-cum-night security guard, carried out his work.

Having finished his task, Chas was just locking the car securely when he heard a noise close by and turned his head to see Terry lifting the bonnet of the car he'd parked next to.

Terry's job was to deal with any mechanical problem the firm's vehicles were suffering from. He worked during the night in order to keep cars off the road for as short a time as possible. Problems beyond Terry's abilities to cope with on site were dealt with by the local garage just down the road, quickly and satisfactorily. If not too busy with his maintenance duties he would valet the cars inside and wash them outside for which the driver of that particular vehicle gave him a backhander for his trouble. The appearance of their car was in actual fact their responsibility. The drivers were well aware that Terry's promise to share with them any loose change he found down the back of the seats was a hollow one, but if they'd had a good day they didn't begrudge him the chance of making a little extra for himself.

Terry secretly held a deep-seated rancour against the latest driver employed at Black's. Life had been far from fair to him so far, he felt. Having lost both his parents thanks to the German bomb that landed on the Freeman, Hardy and Willis factory during the war, the young boy had been grudgingly taken in by his widowed grandmother, a sour-faced old woman who had not hidden her resentment at having to take in her only grandchild and never ceased to remind him at every oportunity how grateful he should be to her for her benevolence.

Thanks to her lack of encouragement Terry had left school barely able to read and write, and as a result the only work he could secure was low-paid unskilled labouring on building sites. Most of what he earned his grandmother took from him as her attitude was that now she was too old to work any longer as a cleaner, he should be responsible for paying the bills on the damp one-bedroomed flat they shared over a baker's shop next to the notorious Robin Hood pub on the Woodgate. His sleeping quarters there were in the recess in the grimy kitchen-cum-living room, on an ancient flock mattress that stank disgustingly from when he used to wet himself as a child. There was nothing Terry could do about this. Despite his being desperate to escape, the money he was earning did not afford him the means to get a place of his own so he was stuck.

Thirty-year-old Terry was neither short nor tall, fat nor thin. His hair was fine and mousey, features arranged pleasantly enough but not the sort to set girls looking twice – he was thoroughly mediocre, in fact. Regardless, he'd had several girlfriends but once they learned of the existence of his grandmother, and viewed for themselves what possibly lay in store for them in any permanent relationship with her grandson, they had soon beaten a hasty retreat.

His only saving grace was that at the age of eighteen he'd learned about a job cleaning cars at a garage on Frog Island. Thinking it had to be better than what he was doing, he went along to apply for it, despite his grandmother's ridiculing him, saying that he was wasting his time. The owner's limited choice being between Terry or an elderly man who appeared very much on his last legs, a jubilant Terry was set on. During the course of his ten years' employment there, Terry picked up the rudiments of car maintenance by watching the skilled mechanics as they went about their work. Eventually he was trusted by them to carry out some of the easier tasks when the apprentice was otherwise occupied. This gave Terry the necessary skills to apply for the job at Black's just over a year ago when he heard through local gossip that the maintenance mechanic who'd been in the job since Jack had started had finally succumbed to retirement at the grand old age of seventy-five.

Thanks to the unsocial hours it was only Terry who applied for the position. He was eager to get the job not only because the remuneration was a pound a week better than he was getting before, but more importantly because it gave him the excuse to be far less in his cantankerous grandmother's company, listening to her constant nagging. He could sleep through the day and was out at work from six in the evening until six in the morning.

When the driver's job had become vacant just over a month ago, Terry had been desperate to get it, seeing it as his only means of escaping his grandmother's clutches and leaving his miserable existence with her far behind him. In fairness to Jack Black, he had given the application due consideration before explaining to Terry that the person he had picked brought with him years of driving experience which Terry hadn't got. Despite understanding the wisdom of Jack's choice, nevertheless Terry could not help but view big kindly

Chas as being solely responsible for locking the door to his escape. His resentment against Chas was not helped by the fact that vacancies for cabbies did not come up very often and it could be years before he got another chance to apply for the job that would give him his only opportunity of bettering himself.

'Nothing serious, I hope?' Chas said to him now.

Terry cast him a nonchalant glance. 'Don't know 'til I have a gander,' he said shortly.

Chas could not understand Terry's brusque attitude towards him. As far as he was aware he'd given the maintenance man no reason to treat him in such an off-hand way. From what he had observed Terry wasn't like this with any of the other drivers. Chas, though, saw an opportunity here of building bridges between this man and himself. Despite his need to get home, he offered, 'Want a hand?'

To Chas's surprise Terry cast him a scathing glance and said, 'Oh, want to do me out of this job too?'

'Sorry?'

'I can manage, ta,' he muttered, pulling out a dipstick and giving it a wipe with an oily rag he'd taken out of his grubby working overalls.

'Oh! Oh, right you are. Good night then.'

Chas received no reply.

Marlene, who had by now taken over from Ralph for the evening shift from six to ten, appeared not to hear the telephone ringing and was thumbing through a magazine when Chas walked in. She glanced up momentarily to see who had come in. As it was no one she considered important, she returned to her magazine.

As he put his car keys into the key box on the wall at the back of her desk Chas said to her, 'Aren't you going to answer the telephone, Marlene? Marlene, I said, aren't you going to answer that phone?' Just then it stopped ringing. 'Marlene, that customer will have gone elsewhere now and Black's has lost a fare.'

She lifted her head and looked at him blankly. 'Couldn't do whatever run they wanted anyway as the three night-shift drivers are already out.'

'I'm still here and I would have done it,' Chas said.

'Oh, well, it's too late now. They've rang off, ain't they?'

Chas couldn't believe her attitude and wondered if Mrs Black had any idea that the evening-shift operator was losing the business money. The poor woman, though, had enough to cope with already without more worry heaped on her. As he walked around the desk to leave he noticed a bulky brown paper bag with a note on top with his name written on it.

'Oh, is this for me?' he said, picking it up and wondering what it was.

'Has your name on it so it must be,' she said dismissively and added in a bored voice, 'That new office woman asked me if I saw you to tell you it was for your mother.' Marlene gave a haughty sniff and flicked back her head. 'She thinks she's summat, she does, telling me to make sure I log in all the jobs properly tonight so she can update the books tomorrow. Bloody cheek! Saying I didn't write down the jobs I handled clearly, and insinuating I can't spell proper. And another thing ... I saw the way all the drivers went in to say good night to her before they left. Fucking tart, she is!

Well, she needn't think she's gonna get her claws into Darren by flashing her eyelashes at him 'cos I saw him first and he's *mine*. He's the only reason I stay in this poxy job. As soon as I finally get him to ask me out, I'm off to summat better than this.'

Just then the telephone started ringing and she snatched it up, announcing bluntly into it, 'Black's. We've no vehicles available at the moment,' then slamming the telephone back down in its cradle. Finally she noticed the way Chas was looking at her. 'What you staring at?' she demanded. 'Shouldn't you be getting off home if yer shift's finished?' Her eyes narrowed then and a nasty smirk played round her lips. 'Oh, I get it, you've got the hots for me, ain't yer? Well, sorry to disappoint yer, but I'm keeping meself for Darren, so piss off and leave me alone.'

Chas couldn't be bothered to point out to this conceited woman that she possessed nothing whatsoever that evoked within him any feelings other than pity. Turning from her, he left the office to make his way home.

Iris greeted him in her usual enthusiastic way, glad to see him home safe and sound. After kissing his cheek, she ordered him to sit at the table and said she would bring his dinner through. It was liver and onions tonight. As usual Chas was ravenous and was glad of anything his mother had taken the trouble to cook him.

They were halfway through the meal, the liver being surprisingly tender for a change and the gravy not too thick or thin, just right in fact, albeit the potatoes sported the usual lumps. They'd been chatting away happily until Iris spotted the brown paper parcel Chas had laid on the table when he arrived home.

'What's in the bag?' she asked.

'What bag?'

'The one you brought home with yer. That one,' she said, pointing to it.

'Oh, yes, I'd forgotten about that.'

Before he could explain how he had acquired it an impatient Iris had leaned over to pick it up, untwist the top of the paper bag and taken a peek inside. 'Oh, it's a half-pound box of Cadbury's Milk Tray. Oh, Chas, thank you, what a lovely thought.' Then she frowned quizzically. 'What are these in aid of? It ain't me birthday, is it?' She looked suspicious. 'These are a peace offering, ain't they? What you been up to, son?'

The reason behind the giving of this box of chocolates came flooding back to the forefront of his mind. Laying down his knife and fork, Chas looked at her meaningfully. 'It's not me who's been up to something I shouldn't, but you certainly have, haven't you, Mam?'

She suddenly realised who the chocolates were from and how Chas must have come by them. 'Oh, she got the job then, did she?' Iris exclaimed, pleased. 'And these are by way of thanks for the part I played? Well, I wasn't expecting any reward, I'm just glad she's got set on after the way she was made to miss her appointment with that agency yesterday. I'm so glad Mrs Black liked her enough to take her on, but then I knew she would. I'm a good judge of character and I found Harrie such a nice girl . . .'

'I want to know what Harrie meant by saying you'd come to her dad's rescue, Mam?'

'Eh?' She looked alarmed for a second before she gave a nonchalant shrug and said, 'Oh, I don't know what she's going on about, I'm sure. Eh, what do you think of Harrie yerself, Chas? She's a nice girl . . .'

'Quit the matchmaking, Mam.'

'I'm not . . .'

'Don't try and deny that you are,' he interjected. 'Even if I did find her attractive, which I don't,' he added hurriedly before continuing, 'I'm not stupid enough to think that a woman like Harrie is going to look twice at a man like me.'

'Oh, don't be silly,' his mother scolded him. 'It's only you who thinks that because you don't see what a good catch you are. There's gels out there that'd give their eye teeth for a man like you, if only you'd give 'em the chance. I know this is all down to them Dewhurst kids and how they made you the butt of their jokes for all those years you was growing up. I hope they're proud of 'emselves, I really do. But then, folks like them have no conscience.'

His mother was right. It was due to one of the wicked pranks the Dewhursts had played on him that Chas had lost any last shred of confidence he might have had about approaching suitable girls.

He'd just turned sixteen, was starting to notice girls properly for the first time, and earning just about enough money from his job as a lorry driver's assistant to take a date to the pictures and treat her to a bag of popcorn. A new family called the Vines had taken over the corner shop and Sylvia was the younger of their two daughters, the same age as Chas himself. She was not the prettiest of girls roundabouts, quite ordinary-looking and reserved in fact, like himself, but he thought her beautiful. Immediately they met, when she served him with a packet of Bird's custard powder his mother had sent him to fetch, Chas was smitten. It was obvious to him that she returned his feelings from the way she acted towards him whenever their paths crossed.

How the Dewhursts found out about this budding relationship Chas had no idea but they most certainly did.

After weeks of building up his courage he finally made a decision to ask Sylvia out before his chance passed him by.

Making sure he went into the shop at a time when he knew she'd be helping to serve, and fighting down a bout of nerves, he asked if he could have a private word with her. It was obvious to him that she had a good idea what he wanted to see her about from the way her eyes lit with excitement. She said she would meet him in an hour just inside the entrance to the jetty at the side of the shop, under the lamp-post. Fifty minutes later he was there waiting for her, nervously pacing up and down. When she arrived they stood staring at each other for several long moments.

'Well, what did you want to ask me, Chas?' Sylvia finally prompted him.

'Oh, yes, er . . . well . . .' Then he blurted out, 'I wondered if you'd go to the flicks with me on Friday night? I'd really like that, Sylvia.'

Her reply froze him rigid.

With a look of scorn on her face she said, 'Me go

to the flicks with you? Why, you've got to be joking, ain't yer? I wouldn't be seen dead out with you, Chas Tyme.'

With that she spun on her heels and ran off.

It was then he heard sniggering coming from behind a yard wall close by. Bewildered, he went across and stood on tiptoe to look over it. Crouched behind it were all three Dewhursts along with their teenage cronies, convulsed with laughter.

It was Jamie who spotted Chas looking down at them. 'Oh, Quassie, that's the best laugh I've ever had! Ain't it, you lot? Just the best laugh ever. Fancy you thinking any gel is ever gonna be seen out with the Hunchback of Blackbird Road.'

'Yeah,' one of the others piped up, wiping tears from his face with the back of his hand. 'Worth waiting for that was.'

It was then Chas knew he'd been set up for this. He couldn't believe he'd been so wrong about Sylvia. Consumed by humiliation and devastating hurt, the sound of cruel laughter ringing in his ears, he ran for home. In the safety of his bedroom he vowed that he'd never put himself in a situation like that again, and he never had. He never went into that shop again either, but whenever his mother wanted anything made a detour to a shop several streets away instead.

'Mam, the reason I haven't had a girlfriend is because I've never yet met one I fancy enough to take out,' he fibbed to her. 'Now, stop avoiding my question. What did Harrie mean by saying you came to her dad's rescue?'

'It was nothing,' his mother said evasively. Despite

the fact he'd only half eaten his plate of dinner, she asked, 'Ready for your pudding?'

'Mam?'

She stared at him. Chas was not going to give up until she had come clean, she could see. Iris sighed and explained, 'There was a bit of an altercation between Harrie and her fiancé . . . well, ex-fiancé as that was what the altercation was about. The fact that he couldn't accept it was over between them. Things got a bit out of hand and I just stepped in to calm them down before it all turned really nasty, that's all.'

Chas wasn't surprised to hear that an attractive woman like Harriet Harris had been engaged. Her sort could pick and choose who they wanted. He wondered what had caused her to want to break off the engagement? Then he wondered if she'd already got someone lined up to replace her ex-fiancé? He realised with a sense of shock that he hoped she hadn't. Then mentally checked himself. It was no good his even thinking a woman like her would look in his direction, and even if by any remote chance she did, he would never summon the courage to take any action. His only concern should be that while she was covering temporarily for Mr Black, their working relationship was a harmonious one. Unlike the one he shared with the lazy and conceited evening-shift radio operator.

'What do you mean by "stepping in", Mam?' Chas asked her.

'Just . . . er . . . offered some advice like we old ladies are renowned for doing. Now can we drop this subject?'

'We will after you tell me what you were doing at

the bus stop in the first place. Don't bother, I already know. You were going up the town, weren't you?'

Iris's face set defiantly. 'Now look here, son. I appreciate that you worry about me, and look out for me more than any mother could expect a son to do. I had a silly accident a few weeks ago which could have happened to anyone and which I'm fully recovered from now. If you expect me to live the rest of me life going no further than the corner shop unless I've got someone holding me hand, then you can think again. I'm quite capable of catching a bus into town and taking care of meself while I'm there or anywhere else I choose to go. It's me that will know when the day comes that I ain't. All right, Chas?'

He looked at her hard for several long moments. Suddenly it struck him that in his need to protect her after her accident he was actually treating her like a child, insisting she was accompanied everywhere she went. His mother was not a stupid woman and was well aware of the limitations her advancing years placed on her. She would not have risked going into town unaccompanied if she didn't think she was up to it. There would come a time in the future when she would need much more from him but that time was not here yet, despite a silly accident making him think it was. One thing he dare not divulge to her was that he had actually changed his job to make sure he was close to her, only a telephone call away and not the vast distances he'd been when a lorry driver. But then he was still glad that he had done what he had, despite knowing she would be most annoyed should she find out. The real reasons for his job change would remain Chas's secret.

'I'm sorry, Mam,' he said sincerely. 'I have been treating you like a child and it was wrong of me. I know we've all got to go someday. It's just that I want you around for as long as possible, not to lose you through some silly avoidable accident.'

She smiled warmly at him. 'I know it's what happened to yer dad that's behind this. But you can't let fear ruin your life. Anyway, I intend leaving this world from the comfort of me own bed at least another twenty years in the future. Now finish yer dinner and I'll get yer pudding then afterwards we can settle down to watch the telly.' A wicked twinkle in her eyes she added, 'If yer a good boy I'll let you choose the first chocolate out of the box Harrie kindly bought me. So long as it's not the orange cream.'

An hour later a few streets away Marion was staring at Harrie agog. 'No? No . . .' she was interjecting now and again as Harrie relayed the events of the last two days to her. 'No . . . Really? . . . Well, I never.'

When Harrie had finally brought her up to date she sucked in her cheeks then exhaled loudly. 'Life certainly is eventful for you, ain't it, gel? Must be the star sign you were born under.' Her face creased into a broad grin. 'Oh, what I'd have given to be there when that old lady launched herself at Jeremy. I bet he got such a shock.'

'I don't actually think Jeremy meant to push my dad. After realising what he'd done, he was probably more shocked by that than by Mrs Tyme battering him with her handbag.'

'Well, I did try and warn you that I had a feeling

he might not have accepted you finishing with him and you should be prepared for some backlash. At least he knows now, so he can get on with his life and you with yours.' Marion's eyes lit keenly. 'So this new job. That was a turn up for the books how you got that. Well, you wouldn't have known about it without . . . what was her name . . . the old duck anyway, telling you about it. That's what I call fate. It was meant to happen, you going to Black's Taxis.' She gave a thoughtful frown. 'I wonder what the reason is?'

'Couldn't it simply be that Mrs Black needs someone to take over the office duties until her husband recovers enough to return, and I'm in need of a job?' Harrie tutted. 'You've never been the same since you had a sitting with that gypsy on the front in Skeggie when you went there for the day with Allen a few months ago.'

'Ah, well, are you forgetting that she told me then I had a friend who was going to meet the love of her life through the break-up of one relationship being responsible for bringing about another?'

Harrie pulled a knowing face. 'That could be aimed at any of your friends, Marion.'

'The gypsy said close friend, and I've only got one close friend and that's you. So have you met all the drivers yet 'cos it could be one of them?'

'Most of them I have, and most are already married. The ones that aren't didn't exactly sweep me off my feet.'

'That old lady who came to your rescue . . . She told you about her son who works there, that's how she knew Mrs Black was looking for someone temporary in the office. Did you meet him?'

'Yes.'

'And?'

'And what?'

'Was he handsome?'

'Not what you'd call handsome, but he's certainly not ugly.'

'Athletic body?'

Harrie shook her head. 'More the cuddly bear type.'

'What, small and fat?'

'No, tall and well-made. I meant the grizzly bear type not the teddy bear. But then not a nasty grizzly bear but a gentle one, that type. I'm sure you know what I mean.'

'Not your sort then?'

'I don't know what my sort is, Marion.'

'I'm sure you'll know when you meet him. I did immediately I met my Allen. Well, maybe not immediately but I soon realised he had possibilities as I got to know him better.'

Harrie looked at Marion thoughtfully. 'When you first met Allen, did you feel funny inside?'

'Not inside I never, but my foot certainly hurt me! He stood on it when he was pushing past me to get to the bar. You should remember, you were there when I met him. Anyway, why did you ask me that?'

'Oh, no reason,' Harrie replied evasively.

'I don't believe you. Tell me?'

She sighed. 'When I first met Jeremy, quite honestly it was his looks that attracted me to him. I was shocked to find out he fancied me too and, well, you know what happened next. When I met Chas . . . that's Mrs Tyme's son's name, well . . .' Her voice trailed off and she fought for words to describe how she had felt when they shook hands.

'Well, what?' snapped Marion.

'It's hard to describe, Marion, but it was like I already knew him. I just have this feeling that somehow he's going to be important in my life though I have no idea why. What would make me feel like that? I've never met him before, I know I haven't.'

'What was he like with you then?'

Harrie pulled a face. 'Well, I have to say I got the impression he wasn't very comfortable with me but I can't think what I did to make him feel like that.'

'Is he married? Engaged? Courting?'

'Not according to his mother. Actually, now I come to think on it, she was rather going on about all his good points to me.'

Marion laughed. 'Seeing you as a possible daughter-in-law, do you think?'

'Well, if she is then she's wasting her time because whether Chas is my type or not, judging by the way he was with me I don't think I'm his cup of tea. Anyway, Marion, I'm still getting used to what's happened between me and Jeremy so men aren't my top priority at the moment. I do like my new job, though, and feel I'm going to be happy there.'

'Well, it'll give you a breathing space until you find something you want to take on permanently.' A thought struck Marion then and her face lit up. 'Eh, maybe it's through Chas introducing you to someone he knows that you'll meet the great love of your life, and that's why you got the feeling he was going to be important to you when you met him.'

'Oh, yes, maybe that explains it. But I hope he doesn't introduce me for a while. It's as I said, I'm not in the mood to meet any new man yet, great love of my life or not.'

Just then Allen popped his head round the door. 'Is it safe to come in?'

'What do you mean, is it safe?' his wife shot at him.

'Well, I didn't know whether you were talking about me,' he said, a cheeky grin splitting his face.

A look of scorn filled his wife's. 'As if we haven't got better things to talk about than you. What's so important you need to disturb us?'

'Well, being's I know you two well enough to realise that you'll be sitting in here gossiping for hours, I thought I'd pop down the pub . . .'

'And you haven't any money,' Marion pre-empted him. 'Help yerself to the loose change in me purse. That's if you don't mind pot luck tomorrow night instead of the pork chop I was going to get you.'

He looked at Harrie, feigning sorrow. 'I get pot luck every night, Harrie. My wife saying she was going to get me a pork chop tomorrow is for your benefit only so you'll be under the false impression she feeds me proper.'

Allen laughed as he dodged the teaspoon that was thrown at him by Marion, which clattered against the wall.

'Keep some of that change back and bring us home a bag of chips,' she told him.

After he had left and Marion had made them both a cup of Nescafe and opened a packet of custard creams for them to munch on, she asked Harrie, 'This job at the taxi place – what does it involve?'

'Keeping the office running smoothly, I hope. There is something I need your help with though, Marion.'

'Oh?'

'Well, the office work itself doesn't pose me any problems as such. Of course, from the mess I've been wading through today I'd say Mr Black doesn't seem to have a very structured system so I'm going to have my work cut out sorting through it all and trying to make sense of it. I'm very glad now that when I did my secretarial course, I also did book-keeping. Although I wasn't all that keen on doing it at the time it will serve me in good stead now.' She paused and looked at her friend expectantly. 'I do need to ask you a favour, though. Rather a big one.'

'Oh?'

'Will you teach me how to do wages, Marion? I've never done that before. Well, you being a wages clerk, who better to ask for help? I need to learn before Friday as that's when I have to make the wages up. It can't be that hard, can it? I thought if you could spare me an hour for the next three nights then I should be able to cope all right by myself on Friday.'

Marion was gawping at her. 'You're asking me to teach you in three hours what it's taken me years to learn?' She shook her head in disbelief. 'Oh, Harrie, you never cease to amaze me. Did you tell Mrs Black you hadn't done wages when she interviewed you?'

She nodded. 'Yes, 'course I did, but all she said was that I can't make any more mistakes than she has since she's been trying to do them. I did tell her I had a friend who would show me all I needed to know and

I can't tell you how relieved she looked when I said that.'

'Then all I can say is, it's a good job you have me as your friend then, ain't it?' Marion said sardonically.

CHAPTER THIRTEEN

A few streets away from where Marion lived, Clarice was looking at her daughter suspiciously. 'Are you hoping your prat of a husband is gonna come round and proclaim himself a changed man – beg you and the kids to go back to him?' Which was what she herself was secretly hoping.

From her position by the kitchen window where she was keeping watch, Nadine turned to look across at her mother, framed in the back-room doorway, leaning heavily on her walking stick. 'Not on your nelly! I wouldn't care if that man turned himself into the Angel Gabriel, me and him are over.'

'Huh! Well, what are you up to then?'

'Wadda yer mean?'

'Eh, don't treat me like I'm the village idiot. No sane woman dolls herself up to stand staring out the kitchen window. You're waiting for somebody,' Clarice said accusingly.

Nadine was, and this waiting game was frustrating the hell out of her. Chas had said he would come round to check if anything had been caught in the trap. Two nights later he still had not shown. What was the matter with the man? Was he too thick to notice she was taking a great interest in him and now it was up to him to move matters on?

Nadine wanted the new life she had planned for herself and wasn't prepared to play the normal courting game, months passing while the relationship deepened. Her aim was to pass on all the preliminaries, going straight to the final stage. She needed to come up with something else to give that dim-witted idiot Chas Tyme a shove in the right direction. The rat idea had been a great one, knowing how helpful Chas was. She knew he would eventually come round to check it like he'd said he would but he obviously didn't think there was any great urgency. She was fed up with dolling herself up just in case he should show. She'd already used the pub as an excuse to bump into him, couldn't use that again so soon. Besides, he didn't go down there that often and she herself hadn't the money to spend on drinks in the hope that he would.

Trouble was, she knew, Chas didn't believe someone as good-looking as her would glance at the likes of him twice when she could have any man she wanted. After all the years she had spent convincing him at every opportunity that he was worth no more than something she'd scrape off her shoes, her task wasn't going to be easy, that she did know. Nadine was angry with herself now for siding with her brothers to make him the butt of their cruel fun. She hadn't had the foresight then to see the likes of Chas as her eventual saviour. Still wouldn't have unless her mother had pointed it out to her. She realised it was more than likely he was not going to ask her out on a date so it was up to her to manipulate him into taking her out. But how?

She realised her mother was shouting at her. 'Eh?' Nadine snapped back, irritated.

'Fucking deaf cow, you are. For the third time, who are yer waiting for?'

'Oh, Mam, give it a rest, will yer? You're getting on me nerves.'

Her mother's face darkened thunderously. 'Don't you speak to me like that, you nasty-tongued bleeder!' She raised her stick and stepped forward, meaning to strike her daughter with it, but forgot she was standing on the step that led down into the kitchen. Before she could stop herself she had toppled forward to land with her head thudding against the hard floor.

Nadine stared frozen at the still figure of her mother sprawled before her, her grotesque legs looking like thick gnarled tree trunks. Oh, God, she's dead, she thought. Next part of her thought, Thank God. Then panic reared. Whether she liked the woman or not this was her mother after all, and although Nadine was desperate to get herself from under Clarice's roof she didn't wish her dead. She bent down and put her ear to her mother's mouth. She was still breathing. She really ought to get medical help. The kids were all in bed upstairs but they'd be all right while she ran to fetch a doctor. Then a thought struck her and Nadine smiled. God had answered her prayer and sent her this golden opportunity to call on Chas. What better excuse could she have than this? As she rushed around to the Tyme house, she was muttering under her breath, 'Don't you dare be out, Chas Tyme. Don't you dare be.'

She almost hugged him with relief when he answered the door to her. Before he could ask what she wanted, she cried, 'Oh, Chas, Chas, thank God you're at home! It's me mam.'

'Your mother? What about her, Nadine?'

'She's had an accident. She fell and bashed her head in the kitchen and she's out cold. I thought she was dead but she's still breathing. I don't know what to do. Can you help me, Chas, please?'

Iris appeared in the doorway then, squeezing herself in beside the bulk of her son. She did not look pleased to see who their caller was. 'What can we do for you, Nadine?' she asked stiltedly.

Nadine's eyes narrowed darkly. Chas's mother interfering was the last thing she wanted. 'It's Chas whose help I need, Mrs Tyme.'

'It's Mrs Dewhurst,' explained Chas. 'She's had a fall in the kitchen and knocked herself out.'

Iris was not at all happy that this young woman had started to call on her son for help. Nadine and her brothers had caused him much grief in the past, the effects of which he was still suffering. Just because this woman seemed to have forgotten her own appalling past behaviour didn't mean that Iris could. 'I don't see how my Chas can help as he's not a doctor,' she said stiffly. 'Do what we'd do in the circumstances and call an ambulance.'

Chas shot a look at his mother, shocked by her uncharacteristic sharpness and reluctance to help, though also appreciating why she was acting as she was. Pulling her out of earshot of Nadine, he said to her, 'Mam, I know the Dewhursts aren't your favourite people, they're not mine for that matter, but Mrs Dewhurst needs help.'

'There's other neighbours they can ask, so why us?'

'Now's not the time to argue the toss, Mam. Mrs Dewhurst could be in serious trouble and we need to act.'

She looked shamefaced. 'Yer right, son. You go with Nadine and see what's what and I'll pop over to Fran Parker and ask if I can use her telephone to call an ambulance. She's funny about people using it but in the circumstances I'm sure she'll let me if I bung her the pennies to pay for the call.'

Nadine clung to Chas's arm all the way back to her house where they found Clarice in a dazed state, struggling to sit up.

'What the fuck happened?' she said, voice slurred as though she was drunk.

Chas squatted down on his haunches beside her, putting his arm around her back to help her sit up. 'How do you feel, Mrs Dewhurst?'

She looked at him, befuddled. 'What the hell are you doing in my kitchen?'

'You've had a fall, Mrs Dewhurst. Nadine fetched me to help. My mam's telephoning for an ambulance.'

'Fall? I had a fall?' Her face screwed up as she tried to remember. She looked past Chas to Nadine hovering behind him. 'Did you push me?'

'No, I never bleddy pushed yer,' she cried indignantly. 'You was standing on the kitchen doorstep and went to hit me with yer bleddy walking stick and lost yer balance.'

Clarice looked unconvinced. 'Huh! You sure you never tried to do me in?'

'You wouldn't still be breathing if I had, I can assure you.'

'All right, ladies, that's enough,' said Chas, sensing World War Three about to erupt. 'Do you feel all right, Mrs Dewhurst?'

'Oh, fucking great,' she sneered. 'Ready to dance the Gay Gordons.'

'Mother,' Nadine scolded her.

'Well, what a stupid question! This bloody kitchen floor is hard and me head feels as though me brains are pouring out where I bashed it.'

'Well, the ambulance men should be here soon and they'll advise us what to do now. I don't think it's advisable to move you until they've checked you over, Mrs Dewhurst,' said Chas politely.

'I don't need no ambulance. I think we should call the police and have her questioned,' she said, glaring up at Nadine.

'Give it a rest, will yer, Mam? I won't tell you again, I never tried to kill you.'

Chas stood up and went across to Nadine. 'The ambulance shouldn't be long.'

'You're not going?' she cried, grabbing his arm.

'Well, I don't see what more I can do . . .'

A miracle had happened to get him here and Nadine had no intention of letting him leave until she had at least furthered her plan a little. 'Oh, please don't leave me! What if the knock to me mam's head is more serious than it looks and . . . well, I don't know. I can't cope, not on me own with her. Please stay 'til the ambulance men get here, Chas . . . please?' she begged.

He sighed. 'All right, I'll stay. I'll put the kettle on and mash you a cuppa,' he offered, glancing around the cluttered, filthy kitchen for a sign of any clean cups. Clean anything, in fact.

'I could murder a gin,' piped up Clarice, hands cradling her head where she had hit it on the floor.

'I don't think that's advisable, Mrs Dewhurst,' said Chas, looking worried.

'Listen here, Sonny Jim, if I say I want a gin then I want one.'

'We ain't got no gin, Mam, so you can't,' Nadine told her.

Just then a tap sounded on the back door and an ambulance man appeared.

'See, I told yer I didn't need no ambulance fetching,' snarled Clarice ten minutes later, now sitting in her shabby armchair in the back room, swollen legs resting on the stool. She glared suspiciously at her daughter. 'But I still ain't convinced it was an accident I had.'

Chas was desperate to make his escape. He said to Nadine, 'Your mother needs peace and quiet so I'd better be off. Oh, by the way, I popped over and checked that trap on my way to work this morning and it's empty. I let myself in by the back gate as quietly as I could so as not to disturb you all. If you have got a rat it's a clever one. I will keep my eye out, though.'

So Nadine's vigil at the kitchen window every evening since he'd laid it, all dressed up and hoping to catch him, had been a total waste of time. She couldn't let him go tonight without making some sort of arrangement for him to take her out. Her mind was working feverishly as she followed him to the back door to see him out. As they passed through the kitchen her eyes caught the stack of dirty dinner plates piled in the sink and an answer miraculously presented itself.

As she opened the door for him she said, 'Thanks, Chas.' And before he knew what was happening she had reached up and kissed his cheek. 'You really are Mr Wonderful, ain't yer?' she huskily uttered, batting her eyelashes at him. 'I don't know what I'd have done tonight without yer.'

'Oh, er . . . it was the least I could do for a neighbour,' a mortally uncomfortable Chas blustered back.

'We're more than neighbours now, ain't we, Chas? Things like this happening bring people close together.'

He swallowed hard. 'Well . . . er . . . best you get your mam to bed like the ambulance man suggested.'

Nadine purposely waited until he had walked through the back door and was halfway down the yard before she called after him, 'Oi, Chas, I could thank you by taking you for a curry one night down that new Indian place that's opened on Woodgate. I'll book a table for us and let you know when for. Goodnight.'

He froze in his tracks and spun back to face her, mind racing for an excuse to refuse her unwelcome invitation, but she had already closed the door.

Standing with her back to it Nadine was smiling, very pleased with herself. This was the second time since returning home she'd had cause to thank her mother. First for opening her eyes to Chas's potential, and now due to her accident tonight in pushing forward her plan to entrap him a little more. All she had to do was get him to the restaurant. Friday night would be best, she felt, only two nights away. She was confident that with a few pints and hot curry down him, a quick shag in a dark corner of the jetty afterwards, they'd practically be engaged. She really ought to start proceedings to get out of her marriage to Phil as quickly as possible because she wanted to be free to marry Chas as soon as she'd manipulated him into asking her.

CHAPTER FOURTEEN

The next evening a weary Chas was driving back to the office after dropping off his last fare – hopefully his last anyway if he wasn't radioed to cover a job the night-shift drivers could not tackle because they were late clocking in. One driver in particular of the three employed to cover nights had taken to doing that since their boss had been ill, and no one was actually monitoring their arrival times at the moment or their actual finishing times either.

The night itself was promising to be a cold one. Frost was already forming on the damp pavements. Winter always proved a trial for anyone connected to the transport business. As a lorry driver, sitting for the most part of his working day in a freezing, draughty cab, constantly scraping the icy windscreen, Chas had found it no fun. Now he'd have the task of scraping down a car on frosty mornings ready for use as well as keeping his windscreen ice-free as he drove around, something he was not looking forward to. He wished someone would invent some sort of heating system that worked inside cars rather than merely requiring the driver to open a vent in the dashboard to allow warm air to filter up from the engine. It was a very feeble heating system and didn't really make that much difference. When it rained – and Leicester and the Shires were renowned for their frequent winter deluges – his car's inadequate window wipers struggled to cope and often the motor failed under the pressure. It was constantly in need of repair. It was common practice amongst the taxi drivers at Black's to steal each other's blades in the event that they needed a new one. It was not unusual to arrive for work in a morning and find one or both missing, leaving that unfortunate driver with the task of helping himself to another car's blades or else managing without until the mechanic dealt with the problem.

A brightly lit festive display in a chemist's shop window caught his attention as Chas was driving past. There was an assortment of gift-boxed soap and bath-cube sets, perfumes and men's aftershave. He started wondering what to buy his mother for Christmas which would be upon them in several weeks. He usually bought her slippers and a pound box of Terry's All Gold chocolates, but having spotted the gift sets thought she'd like one of those too. There was a particular brand of soap Iris was fond of. He couldn't quite recollect its name but knew her favourite fragrance was Lily of the Valley. He could ask Freda Lumley the next time he saw her, she would know.

Chas didn't need to wonder what he would receive from his mother. There was always a knitted pullover she'd spent the months between the previous Christmas and the one they were celebrating making up; a box of handkerchiefs with the initial C embroidered in one corner; a pair of slippers; two pairs of socks in black and brown; and a box of Blue Bird assorted toffees. Despite being very grateful for what his mother put together for him, and knowing everything was chosen with love, he would have liked a change, something to surprise him. Realising that made him see that his mother might like a surprise too. Well, this year he would make sure she got one.

As he sat at a junction waiting for a line of cars to pass he glanced quickly at his watch. It was just after six. Hopefully Harrie would have left the office by the time he arrived to sign out. He still wasn't ready to face her after what he felt had been his own idiotic behaviour yesterday. Today he had thankfully been kept busy with a continual run of fares and hadn't needed to find an excuse not to go into the office. He knew he couldn't avoid coming into contact with her for much longer, though, as come Friday he would have to go and collect his wages.

He was vehemently hoping that Harrie hadn't noticed his reaction to meeting her, but should she have, then hopefully by Friday other matters would have taken her attention and she would have forgotten all about it. Chas considered himself nothing special so there was no reason why she should remember him in particular anyway.

The traffic thinned enough for him to manoeuvre safely into the road ahead but as he turned he spotted a hold-up further down where a stream of vehicles was queuing to pass what seemed to be a broken-down lorry, almost blocking the road. He quickly indicated to turn down the next road on the right which would lead him through a maze of backstreets but regardless save him the wait while the lorry was dealt with to allow the traffic through.

He was halfway down a dimly lit, deserted street when something ahead caught his attention. A large object was lying in the gutter. As he got closer he realised it was a person, a man judging by the huddled shape. It was probably a drunken vagrant. But drunk or not, the man was a human being and would freeze to death if he stayed where he was all night. Maybe Chas could rouse him and persuade him to get himself along to a shelter for the homeless, give him the couple of shillings for a bed for the night. Take him there himself if necessary.

As he stopped the car opposite the bundle in the gutter, to his absolute horror a man approaching from the opposite direction thrust out his foot as he passed the tramp, giving him a weighty kick. The tramp issued a low groan.

Chas leaped out of the car, shouting at the attacker, 'Oi, what do you think you're doing?'

The man stared over at him. 'Fucking filthy vermin littering our streets,' he shouted back. 'We don't want that sort round here.' Then, sticking two fingers up at Chas, he strode off.

Chas hurried over to the tramp and knelt down beside him. It immediately struck him that this wasn't the normal kind of vagrant. His clothes, although caked in mud, were far from the rags he'd expect a man of any fallen station in life to be wearing. Nor was there the stench emanating from him that Chas had expected either.

'Hello, mate,' he said kindly, gently shaking the

man's shoulder. 'You can't stay here all night, you'll freeze to death.' He gently shook the shoulder again. 'Come on, mate, let me help you up and we can decide what's best for you to do.'

The man gave a soft groan and as Chas looked closer at him he saw bruises forming on his clean-shaven face. It was then he realised with a sense of shock that this was no tramp he was trying to help but a man who had had some sort of accident.

The man's eyes flickered open. After moaning a little he asked painfully, 'Did he get . . . my wallet?'

Chas was horrified to realise that this was an elderly man who'd been attacked and robbed, not the drunken vagrant he'd assumed. 'Can you sit up?' he asked.

'I . . . I think so.'

With Chas's help he sat up. Cradling his head in his hands, he uttered, 'Thanks.'

'Do you need help getting to the hospital?'

The man lowered his hands and shook his head. 'No, I'll be fine in a minute.'

Chas took a closer look at the abrasions on his face. Thankfully they didn't seem serious. 'Is there somewhere I can take you?' he asked. 'I've a car, I can drive you.'

The old man looked at him appreciatively. 'I'd be obliged if you could take me to me daughter's, if it's not too much trouble. She will see to me. It's just a few streets away. I was on my way there as she's expecting me for me dinner. I was taking a short cut when a man jumped out of the alley and set about me. It all happened so fast.'

'You'd better check your wallet,' Chas told him.

The man felt in his breast pocket and, sighing heavily, nodded.

'Oh, dear,' said Chas, aggrieved that a mindless thug could attack an old man who it was readily apparent wasn't the well-off sort. Immediately his own impulse to help the underdog asserted itself. 'I could help with a few shilling to tide you over?'

The man gratefully patted his hand. 'Thank you, son, you're very kind, but I've a bit put past at home so I'll manage. Thankfully I didn't have that much on me, just a couple of shillings to treat my grandkids with.'

Chas carefully helped him up and over to the car, settling him comfortably inside. The man's daughter was distraught at hearing what had happened to her father and thanked Chas profusely for coming to his aid and getting him to her so she could see to him. Happy in the knowledge that the old man was safe and his injuries only superficial, he politely refused the cup of tea that was being pressed on him. He needed to get home himself before his mother starting worrying about his whereabouts.

He forbore to mention the incident to her on arriving home as he did not want her worrying unnecessarily about her own safety when out and about. She only rarely ventured out alone when it was dark so the chances of something like this happening to Iris were very remote.

CHAPTER FIFTEEN

Friday afternoon found Harrie feeling pleased with herself. All but a couple of the day-shift employees had collected their pay, and none had returned with any queries so far. Hopefully that meant she had worked them all out correctly, and that was thanks to Marion for patiently explaining to her over the last two nights how to calculate the stoppages on each individual's earnings, taking into account their tax codes and marital status using the books issued by the Inland Revenue. Harrie was still far from fully adept, and as she had beavered over her task that morning, had constantly had to refer to the notes she had made during Marion's tutorials. One thing this had brought home to her was that she had never before fully appreciated her friend's responsibilities in her job as payroll clerk. Along with the payroll supervisor, between them they made up the weekly dues for nearly a thousand factory employees and dealt with all the associated problems that arose along the way. Harrie had only twenty-three employees, including herself, to deal with and their pay had seemed to be straightforward, or she hoped she hadn't overlooked anything.

Unlike Marion, though, making up wages was only

part of her duties at Black's Taxis. Harrie's eyes fell on the open ledger book in front of her and the piles of paperwork she needed to enter to bring it up to date, making sure that what she entered was in the right column. The book-keeping had fallen behind since Mr Black had been taken ill, and been left undone. As she had gone over the books, though, it had become glaringly obvious that Jack Black himself was haphazard in his book-keeping. She was constantly finding mistakes he'd made which she had to put right in order for her own figures to tally. It seemed to her from what she had uncovered that when Jack Black couldn't get his columns to balance, he just altered figures willy-nilly to achieve it. To Harrie that was no way to run a business.

Her job as secretary to a busy solicitor had not been easy. She'd been constantly on the hop as she had dealt with all the queries and problems that arose, along with all the administration associated with individual clients' problems. Managing the office of a busy taxi firm was no cushy number either and she was having to draw on all her skills and quickly find some she hadn't yet acquired so as to carry out her work to the high standard she always set herself. She was confident, though, that what she had done so far would confirm to Mrs Black that she hadn't made a mistake in taking her on. And when Mr Black did return to take over the reins, Harrie felt she would hand over to him properly accounted books, showing a true picture of how his business was doing and not how he thought it should be doing.

Before she set about the ledger books again, a cup

of tea was called for. Harrie picked up her mug and made her way to the drivers' rest room to make herself one. As she passed Ralph at the radio-operator's desk, she asked him, 'Want a cuppa?'

He looked at her appreciatively. Jack had been a very good boss to work alongside but he'd drawn the line at mashing tea for the employees, expecting them to furnish him with one when they brewed up for themselves. 'Oh, ta, ducky, I could murder one. I've been too busy to do the honours.'

Having noticed they were getting low on tea and sugar and making a mental note to add them to her list, Harrie made her way back to her office, stopping en route to give Ralph his mug of tea.

He thanked her, adding, 'You're a breath of fresh air in here, Harrie ducky. Judging by the way the other lads are around yer I'm not the only one that thinks . . .' He was cut short by the telephone ringing and, after excusing himself, started to answer it.

She was just about to enter her office when the outside door opened and she saw a pleasant-faced, middle-aged woman approach the counter. Knowing Ralph was busy and not wanting to keep a potential customer waiting, Harrie went over to see what she could do.

'Hello, welcome to Black's Taxis. Where would you like to go?' she asked the woman, smiling welcomingly at her.

'Well, actually, I don't need a taxi. I'm after one of your drivers. Unfortunately I never got his name but thankfully my dad remembered the name of your firm. It was painted on the side of the car. The driver I'm after is a big man, a very pleasant sort. Obviously a very kind man too after what he did. Sorry I can't be more helpful but do you know which of your drivers I'm referring to?'

To Harrie, there was only one driver this description fitted. She wondered what it was he had done. 'The driver you're after is Chas Tyme. I don't think he's in at the moment. Well, I know he's not, none of the drivers is. Can I give him a message?'

The woman looked terribly disappointed. 'Oh, I'm sorry I've missed him personally as I would like to have thanked him more than I did at the time, but if you could give him this,' she said, handing Harrie an envelope in which she could tell there were coins. 'I just hope it's enough to cover the fare, and also for a pint.' She noticed the quizzical expression on Harrie's face. 'I'd better explain. A couple of nights ago my father was robbed in the street and left in the gutter. Mr Tyme came to his aid.

'I dread to think what would have happened to my dad if your driver hadn't done what he did. My father isn't a young man and the evening was a very cold one. Mr Tyme kindly drove Dad to my house, and when I realised he was a taxi driver and offered him the fare he wouldn't take it, said it was the least he could do and he was just glad my dad was all right. After he'd gone and I'd seen to Dad, I realised that Mr Tyme must have covered the fare himself out of the goodness of his heart. I didn't think it fair he should be out of pocket from coming to my dad's rescue. And Dad wanted to show his appreciation for what Mr Tyme did by buying him a drink, which we hope he'll accept.'

As the woman's tale unfolded, Harrie was thinking that Iris Tyme's fulsome praise of her son was not as exaggerated as she herself had thought. Harrie had worked at Black's for not quite four days but already she knew from what she had overheard the drivers saying that they relished nothing more than telling stories to each other about incidents that happened to them while out on jobs. She had not heard one mention of this, either from Chas's own mouth or via any of the other drivers, so that meant Chas had kept it to himself. There was something special about a man who did not court praise from others for the good deeds he had done. Chas Tyme really was a very nice man, she thought.

'I will make sure Mr Tyme gets this,' she said to the woman. 'I have an elderly father myself so I can imagine how upsetting this was for you. I hope your father has recovered from his ordeal?'

The woman smiled. 'Yes, thank goodness. My dad's attitude is that it's nothing to what he faced on the battlefields in France during the First World War.' She ruefully shook her head. 'I can't think what this country is coming to, though, when old people are being attacked in the street for what bit they have on them.'

Neither could Harrie.

The woman took her leave and Harrie made to return to her office but was stopped by another woman coming through the outer door. Ralph was busy on the radio relaying instructions to a driver about the fare he'd just taken so Harrie asked if she could help the new arrival.

'Is Chas Tyme in?'

She shook her head. 'No, I'm sorry, he isn't.'

Nadine already knew Chas was not because she had checked before she had come in to make sure the car he drove was not parked outside. The last thing she wanted was to ask Chas directly to meet her and for him to find an excuse not to accept her invitation. Knowing the sort of man he was, she realised he would never be able to leave a woman sitting waiting for him. She put a disappointed expression on her face. 'Oh, I was hoping to catch him.' She then noticed Harrie properly for the first time. In a male-dominated environment she had not expected to find a good-looking, smartly dressed woman. For a moment she worried that she could have competition for Chas's affections here, but her fears quickly vanished as it struck her that a woman like this one would not look in Chas's direction so Nadine herself had nothing to fear from her.

Harrie meanwhile was wondering if this was another woman Chas had helped in some way who had come in to thank him. 'Can I give Mr Tyme a message for you?' she asked politely.

Nadine smoothed her hands down her tight short skirt and flicked back her long bleached white-blonde hair. 'Yeah, yer can. Tell him Nadine is expecting him at the Rajah's Palace tonight at eight. I've booked a table for us.'

Harrie fought not to show her surprise. She would never have put a man like Chas and this woman together as a couple. She wondered if people had thought the same of herself and Jeremy when they had learned they were together. But what was more of a surprise to her was the fact that she actually felt a stab of jealousy for the fact Chas was spoken for.

'Yes, of course I'll tell him for you.'

Nadine fixed her with her eyes. 'Make sure yer do,' were her parting words.

Harrie stared after her as she flounced out. There had been no please or thank you and Harrie did not like rudeness in any guise. That woman was mannerless. She wondered what a man like Chas was doing with someone like her. Love was indeed blind, she thought.

Returning to her office, she immersed herself in her work. An hour later there was a tap on the door and Chas entered. She smiled at him warmly. 'You've come for your wages then?'

Prior to coming in Chas had given himself a stiff talking to reminding himself that Harrie would have forgotten all about his making a fool of himself on their introduction. She probably hadn't even noticed. Why would she? He was nothing to a woman like her. He returned her smile. 'Yes, I have.'

She handed them to him. 'I hope they're all correct but I'm sure you'll let me know if not.'

'I'm sure they're fine. Thank you.'

He made to depart but she stopped him. 'Oh, a lady came in and asked me to give you that,' she said, picking up an envelope and holding it out to him.

Chas looked puzzled. 'Oh?'

'She told me you helped her father and they wanted to make sure you weren't out of pocket for the fare, and also to buy you a drink to say thank you.'

Chas looked embarrassed and shuffled his feet uncomfortably. 'Oh, they needn't have done that.'

'People like to say thank you when someone has helped them. Your mother helped me and it gave me pleasure to repay her with a box of chocolates.'

'Yes, well, I suppose so.' Then he remembered a message his mother had given him which he hadn't been able to pass on yet since he'd been avoiding the office.

'Er . . . my mother asked me to thank you only I haven't seen you since.'

Harrie beamed, delighted. 'She enjoyed them, did she?'

He laughed. 'I'll say she did! The way to my mum's heart is through chocolates.'

'Me too, I have to say.'

Harrie suddenly realised that on the occasions Jeremy had bought her chocolates they had been the expensive hand-made kind. They had been very nice and she had felt spoiled by the extravagance of the gift but in truth she would have been happier with a box of Rowntree Dairy Milk. Jeremy hadn't known her preference because he hadn't asked her, had just assumed her taste. It was a little thing, she knew, but this realisation only reaffirmed to her that breaking off their engagement had been the right thing to do.

It also struck her what a refreshing change it was to be having a conversation with a man who wasn't chatting her up. Even the conversations she'd had with Jeremy before he'd asked her out had been peppered with insinuations that left her in no doubt how attractive he found her. Despite being flattered by these, nevertheless they'd had a tendency to make Harrie feel uncomfortable. She also realised that she wanted to know more about this man in front of her. There was something about Chas Tyme that was drawing her to him. She was seeing past his plain looks, his burly build, to the real man who lay underneath, and she found herself liking what she was discovering about him.

From under her lashes Harrie glanced at him, up and down. He was very well presented. He might not dress exactly in the latest fashion but what he was wearing was smart, the colours of shirt, jacket and trousers co-ordinating. Most of the drivers seemed to throw on anything to wear for work, heedless of the fact that they were representing the company in the eyes of the general public, and to Harrie a scruffy appearance didn't make for the kind of impression Black's should be striving for. She wondered if this lapse in dress code had come about since Mr Black had been off ill or if it hadn't crossed his mind that he could be losing business by not insisting his drivers presented themselves smartly for work, as Chas Tyme obviously did.

'I noticed from the wages records that you've only worked with Black's a month. What did you do before that?' Harrie asked, interested. Then added hurriedly, 'Oh, I hope you don't think I'm being nosey?'

He hadn't felt she was prying into his private life at all. The way she had asked the question had left Chas in no doubt that she was genuinely curious about what had brought him to Black's Taxis. He smiled at her. 'Not at all. I was a lorry driver. I did some local runs but a lot of my job was deliveries and pick-ups all around the country.'

'Oh, really?' She rested her chin on her hand before

adding, 'I've hardly been out of Leicester myself so I do envy you, having visited all those different places.'

'Unfortunately most of what I saw of each town I visited was their goods yards. The firm I worked for operated to tight schedules so there was no time for sight-seeing.'

'Oh, that's a shame. I suppose, though, you didn't like it that much, considering you left it to take this job as a taxi driver.'

'Oh, I did enjoy it, very much.'

'Really? But you still left that job to come here?'

'Oh, well . . . I was worried about leaving my mother on her own for days on end. She won't admit it, but she's not getting any younger and can't do as much as she used to.'

So he'd given up a job he enjoyed to be on hand should his aging mother need him. Only a man of great integrity would do something so unselfish. Harrie wondered if Jeremy would have. But then she hadn't known Jeremy well enough to be able to answer that question. Yet she had been on the verge of marrying him.

Chas was realising that his initial awkwardness had gone. Instead he was feeling very much at ease in Harrie's company and enjoying chatting to her. In the short time he'd been talking to her he'd revealed more about himself than he ever had before to a woman. Harrie was different from any one he had come into contact with. The feelings he had experienced on their first introduction began to manifest themselves again and he hurriedly pushed them away. He must not read too much into this. Harrie was just being pleasant to another work colleague. More than likely she chatted to all the other drivers like she was doing to him.

Just then Darren breezed in to sit on the edge of her desk. 'Hello, gorgeous,' he said suggestively, looking her in the eye. 'I've come to collect me wages and I can't think of anyone I'd sooner be collecting them from. So what do yer fancy doing tonight then?'

Chas politely excused himself, not wanting to get in the way of them making arrangements with each other to go out this evening. He didn't like the stab of jealousy he was experiencing at the thought either.

As Harrie watched him leave the office she felt annoyed by the way Darren's rude interruption had cut short her conversation with Chas. She fixed Darren with her eyes and said lightly, 'The same as I told you I was when you asked me the same question yesterday.'

He looked downcast. 'Can't you wash your hair another night?'

'No, unfortunately I can't. I've other arrangements every night.'

'He's a lucky fella,' said a disappointed Darren as he stood up. 'You know where I am when you get fed up with him. I can assure you, you'll not want another man after being with me.'

As she watched him saunter out Harrie was very aware Darren wasn't the type who was used to being turned down by women and realised he wouldn't give up on her, certain his charms would eventually win her over. More than likely he felt she was just playing hard to get. Oh, well, she thought, he would eventually get the message. Darren might be good-looking but he didn't appeal to her in the slightest. Neither did he possess the qualities that she now realised she wanted in a man.

She immersed herself in her work and so engrossed did she become in it that it was with a shock that she looked at her watch, expecting the time to be around four o'clock, only to see that it was in fact approaching six. She hurriedly began to tidy her desk. Her father would have been expecting her by now and would be starting to worry where she had got to.

Ready for home, she was just leaving the office when she remembered the message from Nadine that she hadn't given to Chas.

She made her way across to the radio-operator's desk to find that Ralph had gone home and his place had been taken by Marlene for the evening shift.

'Good evening, Marlene,' Harrie said politely. 'Has Chas signed out for the night yet?'

Marlene was not in the best of moods. She had come in early to catch Darren before he signed out for the night, having dressed herself very alluringly she felt in a short white smocked dress, matching white tights and white ankle boots. She had been pleased to see that Darren was still on the premises, in the drivers' rest room chatting to one of the other men, but despite her going in and making a great show of making herself a cup of coffee and endeavouring her best to get herself included in their conversation, which had been about football, she'd only received blank stares in return. It wasn't what she had aimed for and she knew she had made herself look stupid in Darren's eyes.

Without lifting her head from the magazine she was reading, she replied off-handedly, 'How should I know?

I've only just come in. Check for yerself in the comings and goings book.'

Marlene's attitude towards her was not lost on Harrie. She hadn't been long in this job and their hours of work had not brought them much into contact with each other, but she had not formed a favourable opinion of the evening-shift operator.

Going over to the table that held the book in question, Harrie was just looking through it when Darren came out of the rest room. On spotting her he sauntered across. 'So what do you think of how City performed last night, Harrie?'

She gave a shrug. 'Have no idea. I know nothing about football.'

'Well, I'd take great pleasure in teaching you all you need to know,' he said meaningfully.

Both of them were unaware of Marlene glaring murderously at Harrie.

She smiled graciously at Darren. 'Thanks for the offer but football doesn't interest me in the slightest.' She walked back to the radio-operator's desk. 'Chas hasn't signed out, Marlene, and I have an urgent message for him which I'd be obliged if you would give him when he comes in.'

The girl scowled darkly at her. As far as she was concerned this temporary office upstart was blatantly flirting with the object of her own desire and Marlene was not in the slightest bit amused. An idea of how to get back at her then presented itself. The message was urgent, was it? Well, if it was that urgent Harrie should have made sure she passed it on personally instead of landing others with the problem. When the message wasn't received by its intended recipient Harrie's reputation would be blackened and Marlene would make sure her lapse was known to the other drivers who all thought her Miss Wonderful.

Smiling sweetly she said, 'Write it down and I'll do my best to make sure he gets it.'

'Thanks, Marlene.'

Harrie said her goodnights and left. Much to Marlene's displeasure Darren followed moments later, not even saying goodnight to her.

Chas arrived back soon after. 'Good evening, Marlene,' he said cheerily as he signed out from his shift in the book. 'I'll be glad to get home today. It's been a long one.'

She didn't bother to acknowledge him.

Realising his attempt at polite conversation was totally wasted, Chas hung his keys on the key board and left.

He was surprised when he arrived home to find his mother dozing in her armchair by a dying fire. He couldn't ever remember returning home to find her sleeping.

His arrival roused her and, yawning, Iris struggled to sit up, then gawped when she realised the time. 'Oh, goodness, son. Oh, dear, I haven't dinner started yet.'

'Sit where you are, Mam, I can see to dinner.'

'Oh, but you shouldn't have to, being out at work all day.'

'It won't hurt me for once.' Having taken off his top coat which he temporarily draped over the back of a dining chair he crossed over to her, looking down at her with concern. 'You all right, Mam?'

'Yes, why shouldn't I be? An old duck like me is allowed a nap in an afternoon, isn't she?'

Her defensive tone was not lost on Chas. It wasn't the afternoon, though, it was getting on for seven in the evening. 'Yes, of course you are. It's unusual, that's all.'

'Ah, well, maybe it is. I've had a busy day, that's why.' Before he could ask busy doing what, she levered herself out of her chair, saying, 'Right, let's get the dinner cracking. You must be starving. See to the fire, will you, lovey?'

As she bustled off to the kitchen Chas stared after her. His mother had been up to something, and wasn't prepared to tell him about it. Then he knew. She'd been into town and obviously on her own. He stopped himself from having a go at her, remembering her scolding him for treating her like a child. She was home safe and sound, and as long as she had enjoyed herself Chas should be glad.

'You off for a pint tonight being's it's Friday?' Ivy called out to him from the kitchen.

He was kneeling by the hearth now replenishing the fire. A pint after dinner sounded good to him. A vision of Nadine danced before him then and her announcement that she was booking a table for them as a thank you rang in his ears like a threat. Despite appreciating her intentions he nevertheless couldn't understand her insistence on repaying him in such a way when he had told her a simple thank you was more than enough. The thought of them staring at each other across a table in a restaurant for hours on end did not appeal to him at all. What would they talk about? They had nothing in common. And what if she was waiting to pounce on him in the pub tonight to make the arrangements? How could he refuse her invitation without hurting her feelings? Best he avoided the pub tonight just in case. Hopefully, as other things in her life took over, her offer to him would be forgotten about by next Friday and he could resume the weekly ritual he enjoyed. He was tired anyway and what he would be far better doing was fetching a bottle of stout for his mother and beer for himself from the off-licence, and having a cosy evening by the fire with her as they watched television. An early night would see him refreshed for work in the morning as Saturday was always the busiest day of the week for Black's Taxis.

Harrie arrived home that evening to find her father bustling around the kitchen in the process of preparing a meal for them both. The fact that he was cooking was not what struck her most as he'd taken to doing this frequently when the menu was one he felt capable of tackling. Harrie might not be leaving him for Jeremy but someday she would want to marry and move out. Percy intended to be prepared for that. It was the seeming vigour with which he was going about things that had Harrie looking at her father quizzically. He seemed to have an air of excitement about him that she had never noticed before. She wondered what the cause of that excitement was.

'You won the pools, Dad?' she asked him as she went over to kiss his cheek.

'I wish,' he replied. Then asked, 'What made you say that?'

'You seem to be cock-a-hoop about something,' she replied, stripping off her coat and hanging it on the peg on the back door.

Percy gave a disdainful tut. 'People my age don't get excited, Harrie ducky. There's n'ote left in life we ain't experienced to excite us.'

'That I don't believe. There must be lots of things you haven't done but would love to.'

He turned and grinned at her. 'Yes, there are. Like cook an edible meal for once.' He pulled a face. 'I think you'd better look at this gravy. It's got big lumps swimming around in it.'

She went across to inspect it. There were huge lumps in it and Harrie had a suspicion it was actually on the verge of setting like custard as he'd obviously added too much cornflower. Adding boiling water and whisking vigorously with a fork in an effort to resurrect the gravy, she asked him, 'So are you going to tell me what's put this spring in your step?

He had his back to her, was mashing the potatoes at the kitchen table. 'Don't know what yer getting at, lovey, I'm sure. Maybe I'm just glad to be alive. When yer've done that can yer set the table, dear, as it won't be long? I put the faggots in the oven for the length of time you said, I've now mashed the spuds, so all I need to do is heat the tin of garden peas and Bob's yer uncle.'

Her father was being evasive with her. Something had tickled his fancy, of that Harrie was positive. Whatever it was he was keeping it to himself. They didn't usually keep secrets from each other, being the close father and daughter they were, so she supposed he would tell her what had happened when he was good and ready.

They had not long cleared the dinner away when Marion arrived.

'Allen's working overtime tonight so I've popped around for a natter with you,' she told Harrie as she took off her coat and settled herself at the kitchen table. 'I'm miffed 'cos he was taking me out for a drink, but then I suppose we could more than do with the extra money for Christmas. If you're wondering what to buy me this year, Harrie, then I wouldn't mind the latest Walker Brothers LP. I heard a track from it on the radio at lunchtime in the factory canteen and it's ever so good. That Scott Walker is some good-looking man, ain't he?'

Harrie flashed her a look as she shook the kettle to check for water and put it on the stove, lighting the gas underneath. 'Who said I was thinking of buying you a present for Christmas?'

'Well, you usually do. And besides, you owe me an extra big one this year considering all the help I've given you this week out of the goodness of me heart. How did you get on, by the way?'

She was putting leaves in the pot. 'All right, I think. Well, no one returned with any queries. My wages money balanced.'

'Did it? That's great, Harrie. More than I can say I managed the first time I did the wages on my own, when my manager was off on holiday and I was left in charge. You wait, though, when it doesn't balance and you have to go through all the packets to find out where you made the mistake. Or when you start having to change tax codes or calculate rebates when someone gets married. I could go on, but that's when all the fun starts.' She saw the look on Harrie's face and giggled. 'Don't worry, I'll always be there for you to pick me brains.' Her eyes sparkled keenly. 'Did you see your bear man today?'

As she put the pot of tea on the table Harrie looked at her blankly. 'Pardon?'

'You know, the rescue biddy's son?'

'Oh, you mean Chas?'

'Yeah, that's him, I just forgot his name. I'm still intrigued to know all about the important part he's going to play in your life.'

Having put two mugs and milk and sugar beside the tea pot, Harrie sat down opposite Marion. 'Well, he's not going to do it in the way you think he is.'

'What do you mean by that?'

She began pouring out the tea. 'I'm sorry to disappoint you but there isn't going to be any romance. He's already got a girlfriend.' And pushing Marion's filled mug towards her, Harrie added tartly, 'At this very moment they're about to have a romantic meal together at that new Indian place on Woodgate.'

'Oh! Oh, I see.' Her friend looked at Harrie enquiringly. 'I didn't hear a hint of jealousy in your voice when you told me that, did I?'

'Jealousy? Don't be silly,' she replied scornfully.

'I ain't stupid, Harrie, and there's something you ain't happy about.' Marion eyed her friend knowingly. 'You've taken a fancy to this Chas, haven't you? Go on, admit it?'

'I like him as a person, Marion, that's all.' She proceeded to relate to her friend the story of his coming to the aid of the old man who had been attacked in the street and ended by saying how commendable she felt it was of him not to have broadcast his good deed in order to heap praise on himself. Didn't Marion agree that there was something special about a man who didn't feel the need to do that?

It was very obvious to Marion by the way Harrie's eyes had sparkled, and her tone of voice when relating this tale, that Chas Tyme had made a big impression on her.

'You sure you just *like* this man and it's nothing else, Harrie?'

Harrie stared at her, taken aback. Was it just *liking* she felt? Why did the thought of Chas being spoken for disappoint her? Why had she felt rankled when Darren had cut their conversation short that afternoon? Oh, this was absurd, she hardly knew the man. 'Yes, I'm sure, Marion. How can I be fancying someone else when only a week ago I was in love with Jeremy, on the verge of spending the rest of my life with him?'

'You were in love with the side of Jeremy you knew, Harrie,' Marion reminded her. 'You now know a marriage between you two would never have worked. You would have ended up as miserable as sin, playing the part of the dutiful solicitor's wife and companion to his mother, cut off in that house miles away from your dad and your friends until such time as you got a place of your own, and that could have been years in the happening. There's women out there ripe for that kind of role but not you. I just thank God you realised and did something about it before it was too late. I admire you, Harrie, 'cos lots of women would have just put up and shut up, too cowardly to speak up for themselves.'

She smiled warmly at her friend. 'Thanks for being so supportive, Marion.'

'That's what friends are for, Harrie. I do n'ote for you that you don't do for me. Do I need to remind you that it's thanks to you that me and Allen are happy together now. I was prepared never to see him again after that stupid row we had when I sent him packing. I can't even remember what it was about now, but I was adamant I wasn't going to apologise even though I knew it was my fault we'd argued. You spent ages talking to me, made me see that if I didn't get off my high horse then I could spend the rest of my life regretting it.'

'Well, I knew that you and Allen were meant for each other.'

'Like I strongly suspected you and Jeremy weren't.' Marion took a sup of her tea, then, cradling her mug in her hands, looked at Harrie keenly. 'So what do you feel for this Chas?'

'I told you, I just like him. He's a nice man.'

'Oh, you can tell me you just like him 'til yer blue in the face, Harrie. There's something about him that's attracting you, I can tell.'

'You're making too much of this.'

Marion cocked an eyebrow at her. 'Am I? We'll see.'

CHAPTER SIXTEEN

At just before eight that evening Nadine swanned through the door of the Rajah's Palace.

Rich dark red and cream flocked paper lined the walls and vibrant ethnic paintings adorned them. Gilded statuettes of four- and six-armed goddesses, ornate alabaster elephants and brasses, were positioned around the room in strategic places along with potted plants. All the waiters were smartly dressed in colourful traditional dress.

Nadine, in her ignorance of Gujarati custom, thought their chooridars were pyjama bottoms and wasn't impressed.

Without waiting for the majestic owner of the establishment to seat her, she barged her way over to a table in a secluded corner and, dumping her coat on the chair next to her, sat herself down.

A waiter who had rushed after her to pull out her chair instead picked up her coat. In her lack of knowledge about restaurant behaviour, she called sharply to him, 'Oi, you, where yer going with that?'

But he appeared not to hear her. With narrowed eyes she watched him weave his way through the occupied tables to the back of the large room and into a corridor behind where he hung her coat on a rack along with other customers' outerwear. Her astute eyes scanned the rack. Several coats looked to be in far better condition than her own and, if luck was on her side, by the time she and Chas left then one of them would be hers.

Another waiter appeared and without a please or thank you she took the proffered menu. After saying she was expecting her boyfriend to join her, she ordered herself a double vodka and black. At home she'd already drained a large bottle of Woodpecker cider while readying herself in the bedroom she shared with her children, ordering them all to shut up and go to sleep else the bogeyman would come and get them and lock them in a dark cellar and never let them out. Or worse still she'd let their grandmother loose on them. While she preened herself she never heard a murmur from her four terrified offspring. She hadn't bothered rowing with her mother over going out, just slipped out of the front door unobserved while Clarice was glued to the television. There would be hell to pay when she got back but Nadine couldn't give a damn.

She was feeling very pleased with herself. Chas would not know what had hit him tonight, and by the time she had finished with him she was in no doubt they would be planning on moving in together as a prelude to marriage as soon as she was free. No more living a hand-to-mouth existence, worried where the next penny was coming from, and once having entrapped him completely by marriage she would have a permanent babysitter on hand, allowing her to come and go in the evenings doing whatever she liked. And if Chas didn't like that she wouldn't make it at all easy for him to escape her clutches. She meant him to be her meal ticket for life.

She looked down at herself and a warm glow filled her. She was of the opinion that she did not look at all like a mother of four in the tight low-cut mini dress she had acquired via her gifted light fingers this afternoon on a 'shopping trip' in the town, and the new purple platform shoes and yellow handbag courtesy of Freeman, Hardy and Willis looked a treat against the fashionable fluorescent green of the dress.

The only thing that marred her good humour was the fact that her visit to Phil hadn't quite gone the way she had expected it to. She had thought he'd show some sort of reluctance to release her from their marriage, been ready for a fight with him about it, in fact, but instead he'd looked delighted, very eager to agree to her terms for as quick a divorce as they could get. Without even enquiring after the welfare of his children who she'd left with a friend while she did her errand, and before she could tap him for any money which she'd been about to do, he had wished her all the best and disappeared inside the flat, but not before making sure he'd got her key back from her.

Phil was in the past, though, and good riddance to him. Her future was just about to walk through the restaurant door.

She knocked back her drink and ordered another, occupying her time by studying the menu. As she did so she pulled a disgusted face. It all sounded like muck to her and nothing appealed. What on earth was curry? There seemed to be several varieties of it all with peculiar-sounding names that she could not pronounce.

Then she spotted a section offering English dishes. Chicken and chips would suit her nicely.

Nadine knocked back her second drink and glanced at the clock. It was approaching eight-thirty. Where was Chas? The likes of her current husband she would expect to keep her waiting but not the pushover who was her potential second. The waiter appeared and in his broken English asked her if she was ready to order.

She scowled at him. 'I told yer when I came in I was waiting for me boyfriend to come. Does it look like he's arrived, yer thick sod?' she snapped. 'Oi, and don't you dare look down yer nose at me like that,' she retorted angrily after seeing the look the poor man gave her because he could not understand her thick Leicester accent. Nadine was oblivious to the stares that other customers gave her. 'If yer that desperate for summat to do, gerrus another drink,' she demanded, thrusting out her empty glass at him which he took and scurried away. 'Oi!' she called after him. 'And put some proper music on outta the Hit Parade instead of that tinny-sounding stuff.'

'It's Indian sitar,' a man sitting opposite politely informed her.

She sniffed disdainfully. 'I couldn't give a toss whether they stand or sit to listen to it, it still sounds like wailing cats to me and I can't be expected to eat me dinner with that noise blasting in me ears.' She gave a disparaging glance at the dishes of food on his table. 'Christ almighty, looks ter me like dog food! If that's what they eat in foreign parts then they can bloody keep it.'

Her heart then leaped as she heard the outer door

opening. About time, she thought. She turned her head only to be disappointed to see a young couple coming in, looking very happy and very much together. That will be me and Chas shortly, she thought smugly.

The waiter arrived back with her drink which Nadine snatched from him. 'Took yer time, didn't yer?' she berated him. Then a thought struck her. 'Has me boyfriend left me a message saying he's going to be late?'

He looked at her non-plussed then gave a shrug. It was obvious he didn't understand her.

'Message? Note? Yer know, letter,' she snapped at him, miming the actions of pen on paper.

He gave another helpless shrug. 'You ready order, please, yes?' he eagerly asked, pad and pencil poised ready to take it.

A look of utter derision on her face, she exhaled loudly. 'I've already bleddy told yer that I'm waiting for me boyfriend. I'll let yer know when I'm ready to order. Now piss off and pester someone else.'

As he hurried away Nadine knocked back her drink and looked over at the clock. The numbers were blurred after her consumption of alcohol but she could just make out that it was after nine. A terrible foreboding began to swirl in her stomach as realisation dawned. Chas wasn't coming. Rage started to boil inside her. How dare he stand her up? Who did he think he was? Chas Tyme was nothing special. Far from it, in fact. It wasn't like he received an invitation to have dinner with a beautiful woman every day, if ever; the least he could do now was turn up. Her first instinct was to rush round to his house, bang down the door and demand an explanation for his non-appearance – and it had better be good.

Then she thought better of it. She knew without a doubt that Chas would have been over the moon that a woman like herself was showing interest in him. This was a man who helped old ladies and never took payment for his good deeds; had taken without retaliation all the abuse she and her brothers had heaped on him when young. Chas Tyme was not a man who would leave a woman sitting in a restaurant waiting for him. Something must have happened to stop him coming. Maybe he had left a message for her but that stupid waiter couldn't comprehend English well enough to pass it on. Maybe the note was back at home. Then another possible reason for his absence occurred to her. Had that snotty cow at Black's actually passed her message on to him at all? There was no way Nadine could find out one way or the other until tomorrow. But that had to be the reason Chas hadn't shown. Her face screwed up with rage. Well, that woman at Black's was certainly going to regret her lapse when Nadine got hold of her.

Then she gave a heavy sigh. It meant she had to go through this all over again. As it was, the thought of flirting with Chas, pretending to him she thought him the best thing since sliced bread, having sex with him when in fact he repulsed her, had been weighing heavily on her. Okay, she could pretend, pull it off to Oscar standards, but it was such bloody hard work.

She looked great tonight and Chas would have been bowled over by her, honoured to be in her company, and she knew without a doubt so grateful for what she was offering him. But because of that woman at Black's not doing what she'd been asked, he had no idea yet what Nadine had in store for him. Oh, why couldn't it just be as simple as telling him she had decided he was the man for her? Was bestowing on him the honour of being husband to her and father to her kids, affording him the family she knew an oaf like him would never have, and that was that. Life could be very difficult sometimes when it didn't run according to plan.

She was not going to let this set her back. Like hell it would. There was no going back for Nadine. She'd burned her boats as far as Phil was concerned, and the way things were going at home it was only a matter of time before her mother chucked her and her kids out and they were left with no roof over their heads. Chas was the perfect candidate for her particular needs, ripe for the taking. She'd just have to make another booking for dinner tomorrow night, but this time make sure he got the invitation. She'd give it to him personally, waiting for him at Black's premises tomorrow night when he finished his shift.

She made to summon the waiter to tell him she wouldn't be eating tonight but tomorrow instead and book them a table then, when a terrible thought struck her. She might not have had a meal but she'd had plenty to drink and those would need paying for. She hadn't any money on her as Chas would have been settling their bill.

Just then another waiter approached her. He was a big man and by the way he was dressed and held himself she knew without a doubt he was the man in charge. 'Memsahib, you ready order now, yes?'

Memsahib? What the hell was that when it was at home? Time to make my escape, she thought. 'Er . . . yeah, in a minute. I need the lavvy first.' She scraped back her chair, grabbed her handbag off the floor and stood up. 'Where are the lavvies?' she asked him.

He looked at her blankly.

Nadine gave a haughty snort. 'God's sake, do none of you speak English? Lavvies. Bog. Yer know, *the toilet.*'

'Ah, yes, Memsahib. Please, over there.' He pointed in the direction of the corridor at the back of the restaurant.

'I'll be back in a minute so keep me chair warm for me,' she said, giving him a wink and smiling sweetly.

The door leading into the toilet stood next to the coat rack. With a quick glance behind her to make sure no one was watching, which thankfully no one seemed to be, in a flash Nadine had unhooked two coats from the peg nearest to her and disappeared inside the toilet, bolting the door behind her.

The first coat she tried on was far too big and old-fashioned for her liking but the second of the two she'd have bought herself, money permitting, and she was more than pleased with her acquisition. She doubted the woman whose coat she had taken would be as pleased with what she'd been left in exchange.

Nadine's eyes settled on the window at the back of the toilet cubicle. She gave a disdainful click of her tongue. It was on the small side. Getting through it would be a tight squeeze but she'd manage it because the alternative was to race at high speed through the restaurant and possibly be chased down the street by the staff which she didn't fancy in the get up she was wearing, despite the fact she knew she'd escape their clutches because no way would they know all the back alleys and hiding places in these parts like she did, having used them all in the past for similar reasons.

Taking off her shoes, she shut the toilet lid and clambered up on to it. She then pushed up the bottom sash of the window which wasn't easy as it was sticking in places on the fresh paint. Finally it was open as far as it would go. Throwing out her bag, shoes, then the newly acquired coat into the yard outside, she stuck one leg through the window then bent double to manoeuvre her body through after it. In the process she heard a loud rip. It wasn't until she had both feet safely on the yard slabs that she discovered her dress had caught on a jutting nail and a big hole had been ripped in it.

'Fuck,' Nadine muttered under her breath, realising that she couldn't wear this again tomorrow night at wherever she rebooked their meal which meant she'd have to go 'shopping' again tomorrow afternoon.

Picking up her shoulder bag, she donned her shoes, let herself out of the yard then drunkenly swayed her way home. Despite her disappointment that the evening had not gone anything like she'd planned, in her inebriated state she could not help but giggle to herself. She would have given anything to have seen the look on the restaurant staff's faces when they finally broke down the toilet door and found she had absconded.

CHAPTER SEVENTEEN

At four-forty-five the next evening, Chas drew the car to a halt outside a large detached gabled house in the Leicester Forest East area on the outskirts of the city and beeped his horn to let his customer know he'd arrived. He was hoping this was his last job of the night. It hadn't been a particularly busy day considering it was a Saturday. Chas found hanging around for jobs far more tiring than actually being out on them.

As he waited for his customer to arrive his stomach started to rumble. Over four hours had passed since he'd eaten his lunch of potted meat sandwiches and he was ready for his dinner. Saturday night was usually sausage, egg and chips with slices of bread and butter and a dollop of HP brown sauce. He was looking forward to it. After he had helped his mother clear away and had replenished the coal bucket and done any other jobs that needed doing, they would settle down together. While Iris watched the television he would catch up with the daily news via the *Leicester Mercury*. Maybe his mother might fancy a bottle of stout from the off-licence. He could certainly do justice to a bottle of beer himself. Then a thought struck him. Iris hadn't been out in the evening for a while. She might like him to accompany her to the local bingo hall. He wasn't particularly fond of the game himself but his mother was partial now and again. Maybe Freda would like to join them as her husband usually went to the Blackbird for a couple of pints on a Saturday night and meanwhile she was left home on her own. Chas smiled to himself. He could just imagine his driver colleagues' reactions should they hear how he intended to spend his Saturday evening. Well, they might find it hilarious he was accompanying two old ladies to a game of bingo but if it gave his mother and her friend a couple of hours' pleasure then that afforded him as much back.

He turned his head to look at his customer as he got into the back seat.

'Good evening, Mr Graham,' he said, smiling at the old gentleman welcomingly. 'Thurcaston Road is where you want to go, isn't it?' That being the information Ralph had radioed him.

'Yes, please,' he replied. 'Could you make it quick?'

'I'll get you there as fast as I can, sir,' Chas responded politely. Despite the dark night and the limited light from the car's interior lamp he noticed the other man's flushed appearance and the fact that he was rubbing his temple. 'You all right, sir?' he asked in concern.

'Just a headache. I need to get home to take something for it.' As Chas turned around and started the car the old gent continued, 'I'm not surprised I've got one after the tough negotiating I've just had to do. I wasn't expecting it, thought we'd agreed matters and it was just the formalities I'd gone to deal with, but I was proved wrong. I've just sold my business, you see.

Rather sad but the time had come. It's been going downhill for a while and was only just supporting me, my wife, my two sons and their familes. A competitor has been after it for a while and it had got to the stage where if I didn't accept his offer, then there soon wouldn't be anything worth offering for. My buyer thought he had me over a barrel and he could beat me down on price at the last minute, but I stuck firm. I'd my family to think of. Now the deal's done I can take care of them. Me and my wife are going to be moving to the coast and my sons are buying a new business between them.'

Chas was of the opinion that there were three types of customer. The first, regardless of their own station in life, nevertheless saw taxi drivers as subservient to them, only speaking to issue instructions. The second was the sort that liked to pass the time of day as they journeyed along and rattled on about nothing in particular. The third type was the sort who viewed a taxi driver as a confidant and spilled out all manner of personal secrets and problems to the back of the driver's head, things they normally would never tell a stranger. This passenger, Chas realised, was the third sort. He politely listened, making suitable comments when he felt he was expected to.

'I expect you can't wait to get home and break the good news to them,' Chas commented as he expertly negotiated the traffic.

'That I can't. My poor long-suffering wife has waited years for this day. I must say, I never thought I'd hear myself say this but I'm ready to take things a lot more easily. No more having to set the alarm. What bliss.'

'Most certainly,' agreed Chas. Getting up when he woke, not when working hours dictated, a luxury he'd years to wait for yet.

He heard the back window being wound down. 'Is it too warm in here for you, sir?' he asked although to him it wasn't unduly so.

'No, it's fine. I'm hoping a blast of cold air might help ease my headache. That's all right with you, driver, isn't it?'

'Yes, of course, sir. You do whatever makes you comfortable.'

The icy draught from the open back window was swirling uncomfortably around Chas's neck but out of courtesy to his passenger he didn't say anything.

His concentration taken up with negotiating the evening traffic as they approached the town centre, it wasn't until he was waiting for a set of traffic lights to change in his favour that he realised his passenger had grown quiet. Chas turned his head to address Mr Graham, meaning to inform him that another fifteen minutes at the most should see him home safely. Instead his jaw dropped open in shock when he saw his passenger slumped against the back seat. Chas didn't need to possess any medical qualifications to know this man was not asleep but unconscious and needed to go to hospital as quickly as possible.

Thankfully the traffic lights had now changed. Chas was able to head straight for Leicester Infirmary Emergency Department.

Forty minutes later a grave-faced doctor came out to speak to Chas who had been sitting patiently in the corridor since the staff had whisked Mr Graham away as soon as they'd arrived. 'I'm sorry but there was nothing we could do. He suffered a massive brain haemorrhage. The police are on their way to inform his family.'

The old man was dead? Chas couldn't believe it. He looked at the doctor, mystified. 'Mr Graham complained of a headache when I first picked him up. Maybe . . .'

'He would have had no idea he was suffering from anything other than a bad head. There's no reason why you should have realised how ill he was either,' the doctor interjected. He looked at Chas sympathetically. 'Mr Graham suffered from one of those medical conditions that shows no prior symptoms. This is bound to have been a shock to you. Would you like me to ask a nurse to get you a cup of tea, Mr Tyme?'

'Thank you, doctor, but I'm fine. I need to get back to my firm's office and report what's happened.' As it was Chas knew Ralph would be wondering why he couldn't reach him on the radio as the job he knew Chas was on would not have taken him through any blackout areas.

It was a very sad Chas who drove back to base. He felt it most unfair that the old man should pass on just at a time when he had been going to reap the rewards of all his years of hard work and spend time with his wife, doing things they both enjoyed. The incident brought home to Chas the precarious state of health of his boss, the outcome of which was still so finely balanced. It was unclear whether Jack was yet to reap the rewards of all his years of hard labour or whether his wife, like Mrs Graham, was going to find herself a widow. He vehemently prayed Jack Black pulled through.

Meanwhile, back in the office Harrie looked up at the clock and was shocked to see it was nearly six o'clock. She was meant to finish at one on a Saturday but had volunteered to carry on without expecting any overtime in order to settle the outstanding paperwork. There was another reason she had decided to spend her free Saturday afternoon working. She was still finding it difficult not to fill every spare waking moment with planning her wedding.

Since Jeremy's proposal all her free time had been taken up with preparations for their forthcoming nuptials. Now she needed an interval in which to accustom herself to being a free agent again, filling her spare time with the things a single woman did, not an engaged one. She still had no regrets about her decision to end her engagement, but a large part of her felt it wasn't right to resume the old carefree single life-style that she had enjoyed before Jeremy had come on the scene. Not immediately anyway. As a result she had felt that immersing herself in work was a better time-filler than moping around the house, causing her father fresh concern.

Ready for the off, she came out of her office and was surprised to find Ralph still sitting at the radio-operator's desk. She couldn't help but notice that the old man looked tired. 'Doing anything nice tonight with Mrs Widcombe?' she asked him as she arrived at his desk on her way to the staff entrance.

He gave a despondent sigh. 'Me wife and me usually like to go for a drink down the working men's club on a Sat'day night, they generally have a good turn on, but by the time Marlene decides to turn up and relieve me, I doubt there'll be much of the evening left. I don't think that gel can tell the time, if you want my opinion. In normal circumstances I'd feel obliged to tell Mrs Black about her lax behaviour, but then we ain't in normal circumstances, are we?

'Besides, I ain't too long in the tooth not to realise that Marlene is taking liberties because she knows we have too much regard for what Mrs Black's going through to bother her with work-related problems. If you want the truth, though, lovey, if I'd known how long Mr Black was going to be off ill, I would have thought twice about offering to come out of retirement to help out. Not that I blame him. It's not his fault, is it? It's just that I'm finding this all too much now at my age. The extra money has come in handy, there's no denying it ain't, but we were managing fine without it on me savings and the bit of pension I get from the government. Me wife grumbled like hell when I first retired about me getting under her feet. Now she's moaning like hell about the fact I ain't there for her to boss about, and all the jobs I did for her aren't getting done 'cos I'm too tired when I get home.'

Harrie smiled kindly at him. 'Well, hopefully Mr Black will be back soon, Ralph, and then your wife will get you back again. And Marlene will be in shortly then you can get off home.'

'And pigs might fly,' he grunted. 'Look, can you hold the fort for a minute while I make a visit to spend a penny?'

'Yes, of course I can.'

Since she had commenced her temporary employment with Black's, Harrie had been itching to have a go on the radio. She didn't need to ask how it was operated. She had picked it up purely by observation on her visits to Ralph with queries he could help with. As she sat herself down on his chair she willed the telephone to ring so she could take details to radio through to a driver. To prepare herself to contact the nearest car to the customer she hoped would ring in, she began to study the book logging their pick ups and eventual destinations, and the relevant timings, so she could quickly calculate which driver was best positioned to fulfil any job that came in.

So engrossed was Harrie that she didn't hear someone come in through the outer door.

'Oi, you!'

Harrie's head jerked up. She saw a woman leaning on the counter, her face murderous with rage. Recognition dawned. It was the same woman who had called in yesterday asking her to deliver a message to Chas, the one she had passed on to Marlene. Harrie rose to her feet. As she walked across to the counter she asked politely, 'Can I help you?'

Nadine grunted, 'Like yer did yesterday, yer mean? I asked yer to pass a message on ter Chas.'

'Yes, I . . .'

'I ain't got time to listen to yer lies, lady,' Nadine cut in, wagging a finger warningly. 'You just thank God there's a counter between us else yer'd have no hair left on yer head. And be warned. Next time I ask for a message to be passed on to me boyfriend and it ain't, you won't live to regret it.'

With that she turned and stalked out. The outer door banged loudly behind her.

Harrie stared after her. Whether Marlene had or hadn't passed the message on to Chas was something Harrie would have to bring up with her when she saw her. She still couldn't understand how such a nice man as Chas had come to land himself with the likes of that woman. Obviously he saw good points in her that Harrie herself just couldn't. What did get her thinking, though, was why exactly Chas Tyme's choice of girl-friend should bother her so much?

On arriving back at the firm's premises Chas drove his car straight into the compound for security overnight. The very sad demise of Mr Graham was still weighing on him. The last thing he felt like doing was cleaning out the inside of the car and washing it down ready for work first thing Monday morning. The death of that old man had brought home to him how precious life was. He felt an overwhelming need to get home and see his mother, tell her he loved her and sincerely hope she took up his offer of a trip to the bingo hall. If Terry wasn't too busy, maybe he would clean out Chas's car, same as he did for the other drivers. That would save some time.

As he got out of the car Chas took a quick look around the yard in search of the maintenance man but couldn't see him. There was no light shining from the wooden hut in the corner of the compound where Terry conducted his business so it didn't seem he'd arrived for work yet. He could be in the office for some reason, Chas thought. He was just about to lock up his car and go in search when he felt a tap on his shoulder and jumped in alarm, spinning around to come face to face with Nadine.

She was grinning at him. 'Surprise!' she cried.

She'd more than surprised him, creeping up on him like that. Shocked him even. 'Nadine, what . . . what are you doing here?' he asked her, wondering why she looked so excited.

'Come to give you a message yer should've got last night only that silly office cow forgot ter give it to yer. But I've sorted her out so don't you worry, she won't be forgetting to do it again. Anyway, I've better things to talk about than about *her*. I've booked us a table at the Berni Inn for tonight at eight. Don't be late, I'll be waiting for yer. Now I've got to dash, I want to make meself beautiful.'

His heart sank. This was just the situation he had been desperate to avoid. His mind raced for a way to tell her that he couldn't accept her invitation without insulting or hurting her. He caught her by the arm. 'Nadine, look . . . er . . . I don't mean to hurt your feelings but as I've told you already there's no need to repay me for any help I've given you.'

'But I want to repay you, yer daft ha'p'orth. See you at eight.'

She was trying to pull her arm free from his grasp but he clung on tight, fearing she would leave before he'd resolved this situation. 'Nadine, I appreciate your offer, I really do, but I can't come out with you tonight. I've got other arrangements.'

She stopped struggling to free her arm and looked at him, stunned. 'Other arrangements? But you can't have! Who'd wanna go out with you?' Realising what she'd said, she hurriedly added, 'Well, I mean, I do of course. But you ain't got a girlfriend, have yer, so who else can yer be going out with?'

'My mother.'

'*Your mother!*'

'I'm taking her to bingo.'

Nadine's face twisted in astonishment. 'You're giving up the chance of a night out with *me* to take your *mother* out?'

Releasing his hold on her arm, Chas nodded. 'I appreciate your offer, Nadine, but I'm sure you won't have any trouble finding someone else to go with.'

'But I don't want no one else to go with me, I want you. So you tell your mother you'll take her to bingo another night and I'll see you at eight.'

Chas couldn't believe that she wasn't prepared to take no for an answer. 'I won't be there, Nadine. I've told you, I'm taking my mother out. Besides, she'll already have cooked my dinner.'

The woman was staring at him, astounded. She couldn't believe he was refusing her. Before she could stop it her temper flared and she blurted, 'Are you fucking thick or what? Can't yer see what I'm offering you, you flaming idiot? This meal ain't to say thanks for helping me with the rat trap or for when me mother brained herself, it's a date.'

He looked taken aback. 'A date?'

'I expect this date with me is the first you've ever been on but yer do know what a date is, don't yer, Quas . . . Chas?' She gave him a long lingering look while running her tongue over her top lip. 'I'm going to make sure I give you a date you'll never, ever forget and it'll be the first of many for us.' She lowered her voice to a seductive whisper. 'I'm sure yer not so thick you don't know what I mean, Chas?' She kissed the ends of her fingers then placed them on his lips.

A look of utter disgust crossed his face. Hastily he wiped his lips with the back of his hand. His voice was resolute when he said, 'I don't want to go out on a date with you, Nadine. I apologise if there's anything I've ever said or done to make you think I did.'

She seemed stupefied. 'You're turning me down! And when the flaming hell do you think the likes of you is ever going to be offered again what I'm offering you now?'

Chas could take no more of this unwelcome conversation. He couldn't understand what Nadine was playing at. What had got into her to make her think he would ever want a romantic attachment to her? There was nothing about her that attracted him and he'd never given her any reason to think in such a way. She must be drunk, there was no other explanation. 'Please excuse me, Nadine. I have to go into the office and report an incident that happened this afternoon.'

She grabbed his arm and frenziedly cried, 'I know yer want me, I know yer do!'

He peeled her hand away. 'Nadine, stop this nonsense. You're making yourself look stupid. I don't know what's got into you, I'm sure. Now go home, please.'

'Me making meself look stupid? It's you that's stupid! You're just a . . . a . . . you're weird, that's what you are. You're one of them queers, ain't yer?' she spat at him furiously. 'Yeah, yer'd have to be, turning a woman like me down,' she cried.

He looked at her sadly, shaking his head, and without another word walked away.

Dumbstruck she watched him go, powerless to do anything to stop him. All her dreams of a secure future for herself and her children were going with him. What on earth was she going to do now? A great rush of anger and frustration swelled within her. Spinning round to face the car she stood next to, she started hammering her fists on it. Blast the man! Fuck him! I hope he dies a horrible death, her mind was screaming.

Terry, who was just arriving for work through the compound gates, couldn't believe his eyes, seeing a woman standing there beating hell out of one of the firm's cars. He ran over to her. 'You all right?' he demanded.

Nadine spun to face him, fists raised as though to beat him instead of the car. 'Do I look all right, yer blind clot?'

'Er . . . well, no. You shouldn't be doing what yer are, though. You could damage the car.'

'Do I look as though I give a shit?' she hurled back. Then the thought of the police being called and herself carted off to jail made her drop her arms and unclench her fists. 'Who the hell are you anyway?'

'I'm the firm's mechanic.' That's what Terry told everyone who enquired about his job as it sounded far more important than maintenance man. He quickly scanned the woman before him. She was a good-looking piece, no denying it. 'Who are you?' he asked her back.

Nadine's temper was subsiding to be replaced by a

sense of real fear of what the future held for her now her dream of a golden life with Chas, free from monetary worries, was lost. She gave a miserable sniff. 'I'm a woman who's just been dumped by me boyfriend.'

He was pleased to hear that, but then she wasn't the type who'd look in his direction so there was no point in getting his hopes up. 'And yer've come in here to take it out on one of Black's cars? You do know yer trespassing, don't yer?'

'I'm not. Me boyfriend works here.'

Curiosity got the better of him. 'Who would that be then?'

'That great big oaf Chas Tyme. Well, I thought he was me boyfriend but it seems he ain't now. I can't believe he's turned me down.'

Terry couldn't either. The man must be mad. 'Well, he's got to be blind, that's all I can say.'

Nadine looked at him hard. He wasn't what she'd deem a good-looking sort, but he wasn't exactly ugly either. With the lights down low he could pass for Brian Jones from the Rolling Stones – well, just. He'd got a job which was a big plus as far as she was concerned. The possibilities of this man were certainly worth further investigation. She flicked her hand through her blonde tresses and flashed her eyelashes at him. 'Do yer reckon?'

He nodded. 'I don't think much of Chas Tyme meself, if that's any consolation.'

'Oh, why?'

Terry did not have the grace to bat an eyelid when he lied. 'He did me out of a job. That cabby's job he's got should have been mine by rights.'

'Oh, well, that gives us summat in common then, don't it? Chas Tyme's done the dirty on both of us. We should get our heads together, see what we can come up with by way of payback. You married?'

He shook his head.

'Attached at all?'

He shook it again.

Maybe her future wasn't as black as she had thought a few moments ago. 'Then it's your lucky night.' Nadine was just about to ask his name when the heavens suddenly opened. 'Shit,' she spat, 'that's all I need tonight.'

Instinctively Terry tried the car door next to him. It was locked. He stepped across and tried the one Nadine was standing by. The back door opened. Without needing to be told she scrambled inside and he followed.

Close together on the back seat, the sound of heavy rain beating on the roof, she turned to face him. 'Now ain't this cosy? So how d'yer fancy taking me out for a meal tonight then we can discuss ways to get back at that bastard for what he's done to us both?'

He couldn't believe his luck that such a good-looking woman wanted to go out with him. Chas might not want her but Terry certainly did. 'I'd love to, yer don't know how much, but I can't tonight. I'm working. It's me night off tomorrow, though. They do chicken in the basket at the Crow's Nest on Hinckley Road. Or yer could have scampi, if yer fancy?'

'I'm a girl who's used to rather more upmarket places but chicken in the basket at the Crow's Nest will do for a first date, I suppose.' Nadine moved up to snuggle against him and give him a kiss, something to remember her by until tomorrow evening. Her foot struck something on the floor by her feet. 'What's this?' she said, leaning over to retrieve it. She picked the object up to rest on her lap and opened it.

They both stared at the contents incredulously.

Chas arrived in the office just as Ralph was returning to relieve Harrie.

'Oh, there you are, Chas,' Ralph said to him, retaking his seat. 'I tried to get you on the radio a couple of times a while back but got no response from you. Car radio's working all right, ain't it?'

Chas looked apologetic. 'Yes, it's working fine. I switched it off. I should have told you before I did but, you see . . .' He proceeded to explain the details of what had transpired.

'Oh, dear,' said a grave-faced Harrie after he had finished. 'That must have been a terrible shock for you, a customer dying in the back of your cab. Are you all right yourself, Chas?' she asked with deep concern.

'It's Mr Graham's family I feel for. They've probably a meal ready waiting to celebrate their new future on his return. Instead they're going to get a knock on the door and find a policeman on the other side with bad news. I can't imagine what that's going to be like for them.'

Harrie's already favourable opinion of Chas rose even higher. After what he had just gone through most men would be wallowing in self-pity, encouraging everyone else to sympathise. This man's only concern was for others. She suddenly felt an urge to throw her arms around him and give him a comforting hug. She might have done if others hadn't been present. Instead she asked, 'Would you like me to make you a cup of tea?'

Chas smiled at her. 'I appreciate your offer but . . . well, this might sound pathetic . . . I just want to get home and see my mam.'

She returned his smile. 'I can appreciate your need to do that. It's made me want to rush home and check my dad's all right too. I feel this great urge to tell him how much I love him. Things like this happening make you realise how precious life is, don't they?'

'They certainly do,' agreed Ralph, looking pensive, privately wondering how much longer he and his wife had together. She might get on his nerves sometimes but he'd be lost without her.

Just then Marlene breezed in. As she began taking off her coat, revealing a ridiculously short skirt that hardly covered her underwear and a tight top accentuating her well-rounded bosom, she cast a glance at them all. 'Oh, a welcome committee. How nice. Darren's not signed out yet, has he?'

'He's on his way back from a run to Market Harborough,' Ralph told her.

She looked highly delighted by that news. 'Oh, good, then me tarting meself up ain't bin wasted.'

'Aren't you supposed to relieve Ralph at six, Marlene?' Harrie said to her.

'Me watch says it is six,' she snapped back defensively.

'Well, your watch is either slow or it's broken and you need a new one. It's getting on for twenty-past.'

Marlene scowled at her. 'Ronald Tyler is never on time to relieve me for the night shift and no one says anything about that, do they?'

Ralph and Harrie knew this was not true as Ronald was a meticulous timekeeper, known for arriving early to start his shift. There'd been a more than adequate excuse for the handful of times he'd been even a few minutes late over the years he'd been employed by Black's as their night-shift radio operator, starting at ten and working through the night until Ralph returned in the morning.

'And you've suddenly appointed yerself in charge, have yer, to be telling me I'm late?' Marlene continued. 'As far as I'm aware you're just the temporary office help with no authority here. If Mrs Black's gorra problem with me timekeeping then she can tell me herself. Shift, then,' she addressed Ralph.

He got up and she plonked herself down on the chair he'd vacated. The telephone started ringing but Marlene ignored it as she was busy taking a magazine and some cigarettes out of her handbag.

'Are you going to answer that, Marlene?' Ralph asked her.

'God's sake, give me a minute,' she retorted sharply. She lit a cigarette before she picked up the telephone receiver. 'Yeah?'

Harrie and Chas looked at one other with raised eyebrows.

'That girl really does take the biscuit,' said Ralph, joining them. 'All I can think is that she lied through her back teeth about having radio-operating experience when Mrs Black interviewed her. Soon as she gives us the nod that Jack's starting to rally I'm gonna say something, else I feel Marlene could single-handedly ruin his business and then he'll have nothing to return to.' Then it struck him that despite Marlene's receiving a call from a customer, he still had not heard her relay anything over the radio to a night-shift driver. 'Marlene, do you intend to alert a driver to pick up that fare or do you want me to call them back and tell them they might be quicker catching a bus?'

She was flicking through her copy of *Jackie* which was actually aimed at the thirteen-to-sixteen-year-old age group. Without lifting her head she said, 'What fare?'

Ralph signed. 'The one that's just rung in?'

'That weren't a fare.'

'Then who was it?'

'Mrs Black.'

'What did she want, Marlene?' Harrie asked her.

'She didn't want anything.'

'Why did she telephone then?' Chas asked.

'Eh? Oh, just to say that Mr Black died this afternoon.'

They all gasped in shock.

'Weren't you even going to tell us?' Ralph snapped at her.

She dragged her eyes away from her magazine reluctantly. 'Mrs Black never asked me to. She just said she was letting me know Mr Black passed away this afternoon.'

Despite reeling from this shocking news they were all looking at her incredulously.

'Did you offer her our condolences?' Harrie demanded.

The girl gave her a blank look. 'Our what?'

Harrie responded with an irritated sigh. 'Did you tell Mrs Black how sorry we all are to hear her bad news?'

'Well, how could I? I didn't know that you was all sorry.' And she added matter-of-factly, 'I never even met Mr Black so I don't feel nothing one way or the other meself.'

'What must Mrs Black be thinking of us all?' a worried Ralph asked Harrie and Chas. 'Do you think we should go round and see her? Ask her if there's anything we can do for her?' His face was drawn with grief. 'I can't believe Jack's gone. He is . . . was the sort of bloke you think will go on for ever. He was no pushover, wasn't Jack, a bit unconventional in his ways, but if you treated him fair, he treated you fair back.'

Chas laid a hand on his arm. 'The best way we can serve Mr Black's memory and help his wife, Ralph, is by making sure we do our best to keep this place going. Not go giving Mrs Black any reason to worry, so she can concentrate on what she has to do next.'

'Chas is right, Ralph,' Harrie agreed with him. 'We could have a collection on Monday, have some flowers delivered to her, and that way she'll know all our thoughts are with her.'

'That's a nice idea,' Chas agreed, smiling warmly at her. Harrie was very thoughtful, he thought, unlike Marlene who seemed to have no thought for anyone other than herself and Darren.

'I'll radio through and tell the night-shift drivers what's happened. We can't tell the others 'til Monday now,' said Ralph.

He left them to go over to the radio-operator's desk.

Something occurred to Harrie then. 'Oh, Chas, I believe I owe you an apology.'

He looked at her askance. 'You do?'

'Your girlfriend gave me a message to give you yesterday evening. I understand you never got it?'

'Oh, I see, yes. Well . . . Nadine had her wires crossed, she is *not* my girlfriend. It's all right, we've sorted it out.'

So that woman and Chas weren't an item? Harrie was surprised to realise how pleased she was to hear this. 'Well, I suppose there's nothing else for us to do here so we might as well go home.' She looked at him expectantly, hoping he'd suggest he should walk with her as they went the same way, although she lived several streets further along the Blackbird Road than he did. She would welcome his company, though. Maybe as they walked along she could get to know him better which was what she really wanted to do.

Chas knew they went in the same direction and was conscious it was now very dark outside. His natural instinct to offer to see her home was swiftly quashed when it struck him she might think he was acting too familiarly. He wouldn't want her to think badly of him. It was Saturday night and she was probably in a rush to get home and ready herself to go out with friends – despite his knowing from his mother that she had just broken off an engagement, he presumed an attractive woman like Harrie would have many more admirers waiting in the wings ready to show their hand when she let it be known she was available again. He'd seen for himself that Darren was most certainly interested in her. Was Harrie interested in return? Chas felt a stab of jealousy at the thought that she might be.

'Have a nice weekend, Harrie,' he said breezily.

He thought it was just his imagination that a look of disappointment crossed her face before she said, 'Oh, you too. See you Monday then, Chas. Goodnight, Ralph. Marlene,' she added as an afterthought, and wasn't surprised that the girl did not respond.

Ralph came across to Chas.

'Well, that's the night drivers told the news. They're all very shocked and said they'd happily give something towards some flowers for Mrs Black and a wreath for Jack. The others will be in agreement when we tell them on Monday, I know they will.' He gave a deep sigh. 'It's the end of an era. I've retired so it's not really of any consequence to me but I wonder what the future holds for Black's Taxis now?'

What indeed? thought Chas.

CHAPTER EIGHTEEN

Chas was surprised to find no sign of dinner on the go when he arrived home, but instead his mother dozing in the armchair by a low-burning fire. This was the second time in a few days he'd caught her asleep when he got home from work. He tiptoed across and knelt down before her, looking at her tenderly, worry building within him. Surely this was a sign that age was beginning to take its toll on her? Looking after this house and himself was obviously getting to be too much.

He felt positive the answer was a modern house with more labour-saving devices. In his savings account was just over two thousand pounds, an amount it had taken him the last ten years to accumulate. Would that be enough to cover the costs of buying a house, the legal fees, and whatever they needed to move into it? Trouble was, though, that with Jack Black's demise, Chas's employment was up in the air. Whether his job was safe or he'd be looking for another depended entirely on what Muriel Black decided to do next. He made up his mind, though, that once matters were settled on the job front, he'd speak to Iris and not give up until he'd made her see that a move was the best thing for her.

Iris suddenly roused herself. Sleep-fuddled, she stared at him blindly for a moment before recognition struck. 'Oh, my God, son, is that the time?' she exclaimed, struggling to right herself in her chair. 'I only sat down for a minute and I must have dozed off. You must be famished. It won't take me long . . .'

He put a hand on her shoulder. 'Forget cooking tonight, Mam. I'll pop out and get us some fish and chips.'

'Oh, would yer, lovey? I had planned to do us sausage and chips but the sausages will keep for another night. I quite fancy a bit of cod. I'll get the plates warmed through and some bread and butter cut and a pot of tea mashed while yer away.'

'I'll just stoke up the fire then I'll be off.'

After replenishing the fire he made to depart for the chip shop then stopped, to look back at her. 'I wondered if you'd like me to take you to bingo tonight? You could ask Freda to come as well, if you fancied?'

'Oh, that's a nice suggestion, son, but I've had quite enough excitement for one day as it is. Maybe next Saturday, eh? *The Rag Trade* is on later with that funny Sheila Hancock and Reg Varney, I'm really looking forward to watching it. Are you going to nip for a pint later? Look, why don't you, Chas? You'll never find a nice woman sitting by the telly with yer old mother, now will you?'

His mother was desperate for him to settle down and he daren't tell her she'd nearly got her wish today, if Nadine had got her way. He doubted she would ever approve of Nadine as a daughter-in-law, though. He still couldn't understand what had got into Nadine to made her act as she had, and doubted he ever would. The woman who did interest him he had no doubt Iris would most definitely approve of, but unfortunately the woman in question wasn't the kind to be interested in Chas.

A couple of pints and a chat with the locals he was acquainted with sounded just the ticket after the day he had had, but overriding that was his need to be with his mother tonight. Maybe not so much by his words but certainly by his actions he'd let her know how much he loved her. He'd surprise her by bringing her back a bottle of stout to accompany her fish and chips; he knew she'd enjoy that.

'The only woman I'm interested in spending time with is you, Mam. A night by the telly with you is all I need tonight.' Chas suddenly looked at her quizzically as something she'd said earlier came back to him. 'What did you mean by saying you've had enough excitement for one day? What excitement?'

She looked at him for a moment and he got the distinct impression she was about to tell him something then she gave a nonchalant shrug. 'You must have misheard me,' she said dismissively.

He knew fine well he had not misheard her and made to probe further when she stopped him by saying, 'I haven't asked you yet what kind of day you've had?'

He sighed. 'I'll tell you about my day when I get back with the fish and chips.'

When Harrie arrived home that night she was most surprised to be greeted by the record player blaring 'The Blue Danube' by Johann Strauss, but even more surprised to find her seventy-year-old father had pushed the furniture back in the living room and was dancing around the space he'd created, using a sweeping brush for a partner.

The unexpected sight was such a comical one that she couldn't stop herself from laughing.

As Percy spun around he jumped on spotting her and immediately dropped the brush. He rushed over and lifted the needle arm off the record, plunging the room into silence. Hands on hips, a twinkle in his eyes, he said, 'You find the sight of yer old dad having a dance funny then, do yer?'

'Not at all but I do your choice of partner.'

He bent down to pick up the brush and patted its head. 'Oh, she's not a bad sort is Gertie. She doesn't complain when I tread on her toes. I suppose she could do with a visit to a decent hairdresser, though.'

Harrie giggled then asked, 'What's this all about, Dad?'

He looked at her for a moment and it seemed to Harrie he was about to tell her something. Instead he gave a shrug and said, 'If you remember, me and yer mam used to love old-time dancing when she was alive and . . . well . . . the mood just took me. I thought, why not see if I still had what it took?'

'And from what I saw you have, Dad. So why not ask me to partner you?'

He beamed at her. 'You mean it?'

'I can't promise to be as uncomplaining as Gertie when you tread on my toes but I'd like nothing better than a spin around with you.'

Ten minutes later, Percy bowed to his daughter and

she curtsied to him. 'Well, I really enjoyed that, thank you,' he said. 'I never knew you could do the waltz.'

'I learned at school. I'm surprised I remembered all the steps because I haven't done one since.'

'You youngsters do all that jiggy stuff these days, don't you? That's not proper dancing. Anyway, waltzing is like riding a bike, lovey. Once yer learn, yer never forget.'

'Tell you what, Dad, when we've had our dinner, we could dance a bit more, if you like?'

'Oh, but aren't you going out? It's Saturday night, a night for you young things to be enjoying yourselves. It'll do you good to get out and have some fun with your friends, Harrie, after what you've been through recently. It'll help you get over it.'

'I appreciate what you're saying, Dad, but I fancy staying in tonight and enjoying myself with you.'

He looked at her in delight. 'D'yer mean that, ducky? Oh, I'd love that. I'm glad I never got rid of me old collection of records after yer mother died now. You stopped me, didn't you? I remember you telling me that I might be saying I'd never play them again now yer mother was no longer here to share them with me, but one day I might regret parting with them, once I'd got over her death. You was right and I'm glad I listened to you now.' A thought suddenly struck him and he exclaimed, 'Oh, yer dinner. By God, yer must be famished, our Harrie. I'd planned to have sausage and chips on the go for you. I must admit I was worried when I got home this afternoon and found you'd not eaten the sandwich I'd made you. Thought you finished at one on Saturday?'

'I didn't know you were planning to go out today, Dad. Where did you go?'

'Oh . . . just down the allotment, lovey, like I normally do. Anyway, I assumed you'd gone into town, but then when yer wasn't home on the four-thirty bus like you normally are when you go into town on a Saturday afternoon with Marion, well, I thought to meself, I bet she's stayed at work.'

'You were right, Dad. I wanted to get some more entering done in the account books to get them properly up to date for when . . .'

As her voice trailed off he saw the look on her face and asked, 'What's wrong, lovey?'

'Mr Black has died, Dad,' she said sadly. 'We got news just before I left tonight.'

'Oh, dear. Oh, I am sorry to hear that. What does that mean for you, Harrie?'

'I don't know yet. I don't suppose Mrs Black knows herself what she intends to do with the business with everything else she'll have on her mind. I've only been at Black's a week, Dad, but I really like it. I suppose I'll be kept on at least another week until after Mr Black's funeral. What happens to me then depends on what Mrs Black decides to do.'

'Well, by that time you might be ready to resume your secretarial work in a solicitor's office. That's what you're trained for, isn't it?'

'Yes, but now I've had a taste of something different, I'm not sure whether I want to go back into that. Secretarial work was interesting, Dad, but I didn't have the variety of work I have to do at Black's in running the office single-handed.'

'Ah, well, let's see what the future brings, eh, lovey? For what it's worth, yer mam always used to say there's no point in worrying about things that ain't happened yet. In the meantime, that dancing has made me famished. Tell yer what, how d'yer fancy fish and chips? The sausages will keep for another night.'

'Sounds good to me. I'll fetch them while you warm the plates and mash the tea.'

Harrie had expected the fish and chip shop to be packed, it being early on a Saturday evening, and that she'd have a long wait ahead. Instead she was surprised to find only a couple of customers in front of her.

'You've timed it just right, Harrie lovey,' Jim Waddall the owner greeted her when her turn came around. 'Half-hour ago you'd have been joining the queue outside.'

She looked relieved. 'Glad I didn't come half an hour ago then. But you had the queue because you sell the best fish and chips for miles around.'

'Kind of you to say so, ducky, and I happen to agree with you. Oh, did yer dad have a good time today?'

'Sorry?'

'At wherever he was off to when I seen him this morning. He was all spruced up in his best suit so I assumed he was off to a wedding or summat? I called across to him but he didn't hear me.'

'It couldn't have been my dad. He was down the allotment this morning and he certainly wouldn't be wearing his best suit to go down there.'

'Oh, well, it couldn't have bin him I saw then. Funny,

I could have sworn it was, though. So what can I do you for today?' Jim asked her.

Several minutes later, with her order ready, she prepared to hurry home. She felt something squelch beneath her shoe and before she could stop herself was losing her balance and heading rapidly towards the floor. Clinging protectively to her parcel, which she had no intention of losing, she automatically tensed herself for a heavy landing, but got the shock of her life instead to have her fall broken by a pair of strong arms that encircled her and held her tight.

'Oh, thank you,' Harrie exclaimed, looking up gratefully into the face of her saviour and getting the shock of her life when recognition struck.

She was no more surprised than Chas was to see just who he'd rescued.

Encircled in his protective arms, eyes fixed on his kindly gaze, Harrie suddenly felt a surge of emotion swamp her. It was like nothing she had ever experienced before. She knew instinctively that she belonged inside these arms, belonged with the man whose arms were holding her so protectively. She had never been so sure of anything in her life before. The shock of it shook her rigid. But what also struck her was the way he was looking back at her. He was feeling the same as she was, it was so plain to see.

Chas had never held a woman in such an intimate way. On the occasions he had wondered what such closeness felt like, he had never envisaged for a moment that it would feel like this. This woman felt so good in his arms, like she belonged there, and he felt a desperate need to scoop her up and run away with her.

Then the shock in her eyes registered. She was clearly embarrassed by the way he was holding her, worried anyone should see them and get the wrong idea. He dropped his arms and sprang away from her.

'You're all right now?' he blustered matter-of-factly. Then gave a nervous laugh. 'I couldn't believe my eyes when I entered the shop to see someone careering towards me. Glad I was on hand to save you from causing yourself damage. It was a chip you slipped on. Right, I'd . . . better get my order in as my mother's waiting. Goodnight then.'

With that Chas made his way to the counter and placed his order.

Harrie stared after him, stunned by his brusqueness. She hadn't mistaken that look in his eyes when he had been holding her, so why was he acting all distant with her now? Her mind a jumble of thoughts, she left the shop and made her way home.

As she arrived at the entrance that split the Harrises' house from the one next-door, Marion charged up to her.

'Oh, I was just coming to see you,' she breathlessly announced.

A distracted Harrie looked at her blankly for a moment before saying, 'Oh, why?'

'Well, yer could look more pleased to see me, Harrie,' her friend said, hurt.

'I am glad to see you, Marion, of course I am. I thought you were going out for a drink with Allen tonight so I'm surprised, that's all.'

'We are going for a drink but I've come to ask if you'd like to come with us? It'll do you good, Harrie, please say you will? You need to start getting yourself out and about, that's the best way to put the past behind you. Oh, and I found out today that Gillian Innes has split up with her boyfriend same as you have with Jeremy, only for different reasons. She found out he was seeing someone else behind her back and she's devastated, poor gel, but she'll get over it. But this means you won't be stuck for another single woman to pal around with, doesn't it? I quite envy you both in a way, being free and single, having fun going dancing and wondering who you might end up with if yer lucky at the end of the night. Eh, but don't tell Allen I told you that.'

'Thanks for the offer, Marion, but I'm having a night in with my dad tonight and I'm looking forward to it. We're going to be old-time dancing.'

Marion didn't look impressed. 'Oh, well, each to their own, I suppose. Next Saturday though, eh?' She suddenly stared at Harrie quizzically and grabbed her, dragging her over to stand under the street lamp and staring at her hard. 'What's happened?' she demanded.

'Sorry?'

'Summat's happened. You've got a sort of shocked look on your face and you're most certainly acting like you've summat important on your mind.'

Harrie sighed long and loudly. 'You're right, I have just had a shock. A bloody big one, let me tell you.' She eyed her friend earnestly. 'Marion, would it be so bad of me, considering I've only just broken off things with Jeremy and I thought I loved him, didn't I? Only I know now I didn't. I most certainly know now I didn't after . . . well, after what's just happened.'

'Harrie, you're babbling. Why would I consider you

bad? For what reason? What did just happen?' Marion demanded. She looked at the parcel in Harrie's arms. 'What *could* have happened on a visit to the chip shop?'

'Well, I knew I liked him but this ... well ... Oh, Marion, I think I've fallen in love. In fact, I know I have. Real love this time. He's the man for me, I know he is. He's such a kind man, the sort you feel safe with, and I know he'll be good company to be with, I just know it.' A look of pure rapture flooded Harrie's face. 'Oh, and when he held me in his arms ... well, I've never felt so ... so ... Oh, Marion, I knew when I met him he was going to mean a lot to me, and you suspected he could be the great love of my life though I didn't believe you, but he is, Marion, *he is*!'

Marion was staring at her. 'I take it you're talking about your cuddly bear man at work? Crikey, this is a turn up for the books. That clairvoyant was right, wasn't she? So when are you seeing him? Oh, I can't wait to meet him myself. We could arrange a foursome.'

'Slow down, Marion, he hasn't asked me out yet. That's if he ever does. You see, I'm not sure how he feels about me.'

'Oh, you must have some idea. We women just know when a man has the hots for us, don't we?'

'Well, I did get the impression he was feeling the same as I was when he was holding me in his arms after saving me from slipping. But afterwards, Marion, he acted like touching me had given him a nasty disease or something. I don't understand it, it's really confusing.'

'I'm sure you're imagining things. He saved you

from slipping, did he? Oh, how romantic. Tell me what happened!' she enthused.

Harrie did.

After she had finished Marion pulled a knowing face. 'He was just shocked like you were. Poor chap was reeling from what had just hit him.'

'Do you think so, Marion?'

'I'm positive. I bet he asks you out the first opportunity he gets. Oh, I wonder where he'll take you?'

'I don't care. I don't mind if we sit on the park swings, swigging pop from bottles, I just want to be with him. I've never wanted to be with someone so much in all my life. I can't believe this has happened to me.' She paused and looked worriedly at her friend. 'It isn't wrong of me, is it, to be feeling like this for another man so soon after breaking up with Jeremy?'

'Hey, gel, this is Mother Nature you're dealing with. You can't fight her. At least you and Jeremy had broken up before you fell for someone else. I know women who are still with their blokes while hankering after someone else or actually seeing them behind their blokes' backs. For all you know Jeremy has someone else already taking your place. Oh, I can't wait to hear the next instalment! You must promise to come and see me as soon as you leave work on Monday night. You do promise, don't you?'

'You're always the first to know when anything happens to me, aren't you?'

'Look, I'd better be off as Allen is waiting for me. I hope your dad likes cold chips.'

'Pardon? Oh, goodness, I'd forgotten about these,' she exclaimed. 'I'd better hurry too.'

CHAPTER NINETEEN

Despite enjoying the rest of the weekend in her father's company, Monday could not come quick enough for Harrie. She couldn't wait to see Chas again. Couldn't understand how she could be feeling as if every minute she spent away from him was a minute wasted. All she prayed was that Marion's interpretation of his reaction after he'd saved her was right and it had been caused solely by shock upon realising his feelings for her.

The atmosphere in Black's office on Monday morning was sombre. Each employee in turn learned the sad news of their employer's death, and most had private concerns about what the future held for them job-wise. They had no choice but to carry on with business as usual in the meantime and wait until Mrs Black made her decision after the funeral.

Chas was not around at all when Harrie arrived for work but out on a job. It was well after nine-thirty and she was busy in the office checking recorded mileage against petrol receipts when she heard Ralph say, 'Oh, hello, Chas. Glad you got your last job finished sharpish. Glenfield General has just called. They want a package picking up from the Haematology department at ten-thirty and delivered to the Pathology Lab at the Royal Infirmary. You've time for a coffee before you go.' And he added tongue-in-cheek, 'You might as well make one for me while yer at it.'

Grabbing a handful of petrol receipts, her prearranged excuse to go and see Ralph, Harrie shot out of her office and over to his desk just in time to catch Chas making his way to the drivers' rest room.

'Good morning, Chas,' she called brightly across to him.

He still assumed he had embarrassed her by his actions on Saturday night, and had been meaning to apologise to her for doing so. But this was not the right moment for him to pick as Ralph was within earshot. Instead he turned and looked back at her awkwardly, flashed her a brief smile and said a brusque, 'Morning.' Then he hurried into the rest room.

Harrie was stunned by his shortness with her. Then she reasoned with herself that he was unlikely to ask her out with others around. Chas was not the brash, full of himself sort like Darren whose conquests he liked to make common knowledge. She knew she wasn't wrong in her assumption that Chas would wish anything that transpired between them to be their business.

'Did yer want me for summat, Harrie?' Ralph asked her.

'Pardon? Oh, yes, I just wanted to know if you've any petrol receipts out here you haven't given me? I seem to have a couple missing, that's all.'

'Since you've started, the drivers put them on your desk themselves. Any excuse to come in and see you, Harrie.'

She smiled at him. 'The ones I'm missing have probably got hidden under the other paperwork on my desk. Sorry to have disturbed you, Ralph.'

'You can disturb me anytime,' he said, winking at her cheekily.

Just then the outer door opened and a man came in. 'I'll deal with him for you,' Harrie offered. 'Can I help you, sir?' she asked the new arrival, going across to the counter.

'I'd like to speak to one of your drivers if he's available. Mr Tyme?'

'Yes, you're lucky, he's just arrived back in. May I ask your name so I can tell him?'

'Geoffrey Graham. It's about my father.'

'Oh, yes, I was here on Saturday when Chas came back and told us what had happened. We're all so sorry about your loss. I'll get Mr Tyme for you.'

She made her way to the drivers' rest room and poked her head round the door. The room was empty except for Chas who was busy making two cups of coffee.

Harrie went across to him. 'Chas, there's a man at the counter asking to see you. It's Mr Graham's son. He's obviously come to thank you for what you did for his father.'

'Considerate of him to put himself out with all he's having to face at the moment. Thank you for coming to tell me.' He looked at her awkwardly for a moment before fixing his eyes on his hands. 'Er . . . Harrie?'

Excitement raced within her. He was going to ask her out. 'Yes, Chas?'

'I . . . er . . . apologise if I embarrassed you in any

way on Saturday night. It wasn't my intention. Right, better not keep Mr Graham's son waiting.'

She stared after him as he hurried out of the room. What on earth made him think he had embarrassed her on Saturday night when in truth it was just the opposite? She racked her brain for any reason she might have given him for thinking such a thing. She couldn't think of anything. In her urgent need to put him straight she rushed after him but he was already addressing the man at the counter so Harrie returned to her office, meaning to do the deed as soon as she got an opportunity.

Chas held his hand out in greeting to Geoffrey Graham. He looked like a pleasant man, in his mid-thirties and clean-cut, but it was very obvious he was suffering from deep distress. 'I'm sorry we meet in such circumstances,' Chas said sincerely.

Geoffrey gave a drawn smile. 'I represent the family. We'd like to express our gratitude for what you did for my father.'

Chas sighed deeply. 'I only wish I could have done more. If it's any consolation, as we drove along before . . . well, before he took ill . . . your father talked very highly of you and your brother, and said he was looking forward to spending more time with your mother on his retirement.'

Geoffrey gulped back a lump in his throat. 'We were very close. He'll be greatly missed. I'm glad I got to see you personally and thank you, I was concerned you might be out on a job. Anyway, I must get off. I've to see the funeral director at Ginns and Gutteridge at ten-thirty. So if I could just collect Dad's belongings?'

Chas looked at him, puzzled. 'His belongings?'

'The briefcase that was left in the back of your cab.'

Chas frowned thoughtfully. 'I don't remember any briefcase. I was sitting in the cab when your father got in so I never saw if he was actually carrying anything. I don't remember seeing any of the hospital staff taking a briefcase off with them when they took your father out of the back of my cab, but then at the time it was all quite frantic as I suppose you can appreciate.'

'My father definitely had it with him when you picked him up. It wasn't at the hospital when we went to identify him and collect his things so it must have been left in the back of your cab.' The man's face clouded over worriedly. 'Could your next passenger have picked it up, do you think?'

Chas paused momentarily to think back over events after he'd left the hospital before saying, 'Your father was my last job that night, the firm doesn't operate on a Sunday, and I've only had one job so far this morning and that was an old lady I took into town. She sat in the front with me. If I'd found it when I cleaned out the cab on Saturday night I would have put it in the lost property box which is here in the office. We get all sorts left in cabs as you can imagine. Most people remember eventually and come in to collect them. We keep stuff for six months.' A memory struck him. 'Ah, wait a minute. What happened to your father . . . well, it did knock me for six and I signed out on Saturday night without cleaning out my cab. I just wanted to get home, you see. The case will still be in the back.' He lifted the counter flap and joined Geoffrey Graham on the other side. 'Come with me and I'll take you to get it. My car's parked on the road outside.'

Minutes later Chas looked helplessly at Geoffrey Graham. 'As you can see for yourself, the case isn't here. Your father couldn't have had it on him when he got into my cab or else it's in the hospital somewhere.'

Geoffrey's face was paling rapidly. 'But they've checked everywhere it could be and it's definitely not at the hospital. My father left Mr Timminson's house in Leicester Forest East where you picked him up with his case in his hand. Mr Timminson's solicitor was there at the time and is a reliable witness. Mr Tyme, there was six thousand pounds in that case.'

Chas's eyes widened in shock. 'What?'

'It was the proceeds of the sale of his business. It's all we have in the world to secure our future.'

'Yes, your father told me he'd just completed the sale.'

A look of accusation filled Geoffrey Graham's eyes then. 'So you knew he had money on him?'

Chas flinched. 'Mr Graham, no, I most certainly did not know your father was carrying the proceeds of the sale on him. He just told me he had completed negotiations.'

A look of remorse crossed the other man's face. 'Look, Mr Tyme, you can understand . . .'

'Yes, I can,' Chas cut in. 'I am the obvious suspect, aren't I? Well, I can only give you my word that I knew nothing about the briefcase and say again that if your father got in my cab with it, it would still be here. You need to get the police involved. I'll willingly be interviewed by them and tell them all I know.'

As the implications of the case's absence sank in, Geoffrey Graham stared at Chas blindly for several long moments before his shoulders sagged despairingly and he uttered, 'I'll go and see them as soon as I've dealt with the funeral arrangements. I have to find that case.' He held out his hand towards Chas. 'Thank you, Mr Tyme.'

He accepted the gesture and they shook hands. 'I'm sure the police will turn it up,' Chas said, sincerely hoping they would but deep down wondering if there was a dishonest member of the hospital staff who was now revelling in their good fortune.

'You don't know how much I hope they do! It's bad enough coping with losing Dad. Without the money . . .' The man took a deep breath. 'Good day, Mr Tyme.'

A solemn Chas watched as he walked away towards the bus stop.

Harrie was coming out of her office to ask Ralph's help in deciphering Marlene's scrawl on a job she had logged into the book the previous Saturday evening and could not help noticing the gravity of Chas's expression when he returned inside the office. It was obvious to her that something had transpired between him and Mr Graham's son that had upset Chas badly.

She walked across to waylay him, the intended offer of support not just made towards the man who had won her affections but something she would have offered any work colleague in similar circumstances. 'Chas, could you spare me a moment in my office, please?' Without waiting for a response from him she made her way there.

As he joined her, thinking she needed to see him regarding the paperwork, he asked, 'What can I do for you, Harrie?'

'It's what I can do for you, Chas. Please sit down,' she said, indicating a chair to the front of her desk.

She was aware that he seemed very ill at ease but hoped it was because he realised he had strong feelings for her and didn't know how to proceed while they were both officially working. Wasn't she herself feeling all jangly inside in anticipation of what was to come? All it needed was for him to make a move so they could embark on the wonderful relationship she knew without a doubt they were going to share together. But at the moment it was clear Chas had other things on his mind.

She smiled warmly at him. 'It's obvious to me you're upset about something. I wondered if I could be of any help?'

He looked startled at that. He was confused as to why she had apparently been embarrassed by his actions on Saturday night, but now was offering him help as if she cared about him? Then he realised the intimate moment on Saturday had taken place in public where people could easily misconstrue the relationship between them, whereas now they were in a work environment and her concern was strictly that of one colleague for another. In that light he appreciated her offer and proceeded to tell her what had just transpired.

Harrie had no doubt at all that Chas was telling the absolute truth when he said he had no idea where the briefcase was. When he had finished, she said, 'I'm positive Mr Graham does not believe you've anything to do with the missing case, Chas, please put your mind at rest on that. People only have to talk to you to see how honest you are. I hate to think it, but if Mr Graham Senior definitely had the case on him when he got into your car then it has to have been taken by a member of staff at the hospital. The police will find out the truth.'

'I just hope someone comes across it slipped inside a cupboard somewhere. That money is crucial to the Grahams' future survival. I dread to think what's going to happen to them if they don't find it. If the police come to interview me when I'm out on a job, will you please make sure I'm radioed to come straight in so I can tell them all I know as soon as possible and they can get on with their investigations?'

'Yes, of course I will.' Here was the ideal opportunity to put him straight about thinking he'd embarrassed her by his actions on Saturday night. 'Er . . . Chas, about . . .'

Her words were interrupted by Darren breezing in to perch on the edge of her desk. A suggestive look on his face, he leaned over towards her and said, 'Hello, gorgeous. I've a couple of petrol receipts for you.' He fished them out of his pocket and held them out to her. 'Cream are doing a gig at the Ilrondo night club tonight and I've two tickets. How about you and me tripping the light fantastic together?'

Convinced he was in the way of Harrie and Darren making arrangements to go out for the evening, Chas got up. 'I've the hospital job and I'll be late if I don't get a move on. Thanks for your help, I appreciate it, Harrie. Darren,' he said, nodding at the other man.

Without giving Harrie a chance to stop him, he left.

She glared at Darren, annoyed at his intrusion on her private conversation. She had been denied her chance to put Chas right and had also hoped that with that out of the way he might have taken the opportunity to ask her out. Darren's untimely arrival had put paid to that.

'Thank you for the receipts,' she said to him shortly. 'You will excuse me, I've a mountain of things to do.'

'Yeah, 'course I'll let you get on.' He got up off the desk. 'That's a yes for tonight then, is it?' he said confidently. 'I'll meet you at eight, shall I, in the Stag and Pheasant and we can have a drink first?'

'No, that isn't a yes for tonight, and no, I will not meet you at eight. But whoever you take, I hope you have a good time.'

He gave a nonchalant shrug. 'Okay, maybe not tonight then, but you won't be able to resist my charms for long,' he said, giving her a confident smile. 'No woman can.'

With that he breezed out of the office.

Harrie couldn't believe his conceitedness but was more concerned that Chas would think there was something going on between herself and Darren. She planned to get Chas on one side as soon as she could but for the rest of the day he was busy on jobs.

Harrie had barely finished washing the dinner dishes that evening when Marion arrived.

'I couldn't wait to find out what happened today,' she said excitedly. 'I'm not stopping as I've Allen's dinner to get. So come on then, spill the beans. When yer seeing him? Where's he taking you? What yer wearing?'

As she dried her hands, Harrie realised her father was looking at her quizzically from the back room doorway. 'Women's talk, Dad,' she said to him.

'Oh, I see,' Percy said knowingly. 'I'll leave yer to it then.' He departed into the back room shutting the kitchen door behind him, affording his daughter and her friend privacy.

Harrie sighed heavily. 'Today went nothing like I was hoping it would, Marion. In fact, it turned into a complete nightmare.'

'Oh!'

She sighed again. 'Not only is Chas under the impression he embarrassed me on Saturday night, though I can't understand at all why he should think so, he's also under the impression there's something going on between me and Darren.'

Harrie told her friend exactly what had transpired that day.

'He seems to think he's God's gift, does that Darren,' Marion said when Harrie had finished. 'I wish I was working at Black's so I could bring him down a peg or two. You've got to let Chas know he didn't upset you on Saturday night, just the opposite in fact, and that there's nothing going on between you and Darren.'

'That's easier said than done, Marion. Chas and I might work at the same place but we don't come into contact that often. He's mostly out on jobs, and then actually catching him when he does come in with no one else around is another matter.'

'Well, he ain't going to ask you out until you do

put him right on both counts, so it's up to you to keep yer beady eyes peeled and grab him at your first opportunity.'

Harrie just hoped that such an opportunity didn't take too long presenting itself. But then she reminded herself of the saying: If something is worth having, it's worth waiting for. She had no doubt whatsoever that Chas Tyme was.

CHAPTER TWENTY

Jack Black's funeral took place that Thursday morning. It was a well-attended affair, the small church packed to bursting with family, friends, acquaintances and employees. A spread had been laid on in the church hall afterwards. Out of respect for Jack and for those employees who wanted to attend, the firm was closed during the morning but open again that afternoon to serve the clientele Jack had built up over his twenty years in business.

Harrie hadn't come into contact with Chas on a one-to-one basis since their chat in the office which had been abruptly cut short by Darren, a situation that was frustrating the hell out of her.

She was in close proximity to him during the funeral but had to quash her overwhelming desire to seize the opportunity. This was not the time or place to be thinking of her own personal problems. They were all gathered to pay their respects to Jack Black and be a support to his grieving widow.

During the service Chas had been very aware of Harrie and feared she was finding the sad occasion a strain. He had desperately wanted to offer her comfort but did not want a repetition of the incident in the chip shop. Besides, any offer of support should surely come from Darren as he presumed they were an item, though he couldn't understand why Harrie seemed to be shunning Darren's attentions recently.

Two noticeable absences from the gathering of employees at their boss's funeral had been Marlene and Terry. No one seemed surprised that Marlene hadn't shown herself. Terry hadn't shown up for his shifts at all this week and no word had been received from him as to the reason. It was presumed he was ill enough to be bedridden. Everyone hoped that his recovery would be swift as there was no one to cover his job. Thankfully no car had suffered serious mechanical problems while he'd been off, and any minor repairs the drivers had attended to themselves.

When they all returned to the office the telephone was ringing. Like the other drivers, Chas had immediately been despatched on a job while Harrie got stuck into her office work. They were all conscious, though, that it was only a matter of time now before Mrs Black informed them of her intentions regarding the business, and they were all secretly worried as to what the future could hold for them.

Harrie was leaving the office that night and just saying her goodbyes to Ralph when Marlene sauntered in.

She glanced Ralph over and cocked an eyebrow sardonically. 'What's with the suit?' Then she looked Harrie over. 'Posh coat for work, in't it?' Then, stripping off her own, she said, laughing, 'Ain't both bin to a funeral, have yer?'

'Well, actually, yes, we have,' said Ralph, and added stonily, 'As it happens, your boss's.'

'Oh, yeah, I forgot that that was today,' she said casually. 'Oh, did anyone bring any goodies back from the funeral lunch?' She was casting her eyes down the signing-in book to see if Darren had already left.

Ralph was just about to respond suitably to her flippant remark when Darren came in to sign out and, seeming oblivious to the way Marlene's face lit up at his entrance, immediately accosted Harrie.

No one spotted Chas enter seconds after Darren along with several other drivers who had also come in to sign out for the night.

'Hello, gorgeous,' Darren said to Harrie, his tone very suggestive. 'I saw yer looking at me at the funeral. Mind you, I can't blame yer, I was the best-looking bloke there.'

Before Harrie knew what was happening to her, someone had her pinned up against the wall and was screaming at her, 'You bitch, I fucking knew you were after my man!'

It was Marlene.

'I can assure you, I have no interest in Darren whatsoever,' Harrie retorted, desperately trying to push her away.

'Liar!' Marlene spat ferociously. 'You were eyeing him up at the funeral, I just heard Darren say so. You know he's mine, everyone does.'

She started beating Harrie hard with her fists. Harrie, eyes closed, had her arms over her face to try and protect herself while crying out, 'Marlene, stop it! Stop it, will you? You've got it wrong, I've no interest in Darren.' The blows suddenly ceased and she heard Marlene screaming, 'Get off me, will yer? Get off me!'

Harrie lowered her arms and opened her eyes to see that Chas had Marlene in a bear-like grip around her waist and was holding her away from him while she was kicking out her legs and screaming abuse at him. 'Put me down, you bastard. Let me get back at her to give her the pasting she deserves. Bleddy tart she is! Put me down, I said.'

Darren was looking on at proceedings with great amusement. He gave Ralph, standing next to him, a nudge in his ribs. 'Yer've gotta be summat, ain't yer, when yer've got two women fighting over yer?'

From the doorway a stern voice boomed, 'Marlene, I'd like to speak to you in the office *now*.'

Chas dropped Marlene and all the occupants of the room turned to see Mrs Black standing in the doorway. She did not look happy. A distinguished-looking man carrying a briefcase stood by her side. He looked appalled.

'It was her what started it, Mrs Black,' Marlene cried accusingly, pointing at Harrie. 'She attacked me 'cos I found out she was trying to get my man off me.'

'I'm not *your* man and never will be,' Darren spoke up, looking at her with a sneer. 'I wouldn't be seen dead with the likes of you, yer dozy cow!'

'That's enough,' the man with Mrs Black snapped. 'Show some respect, can't you? Mrs Black has buried her husband today who, may I remind you, was your boss.' He fixed his eyes on Marlene. 'Mrs Black asked you, young lady, for a private word in the office. And don't bother with any more lies as we were both witness to exactly what transpired. The rest of you, please wait here. Mrs Black would like to address you.'

Marlene, her face thunderous, slunk off into the office and Muriel Black followed, shutting the door behind her. The rest of them all milled round waiting for their employer to come back out. No one needed to wonder what she was going to speak to them about.

Chas was standing on his own by the drivers' rest room door when Harrie took the opportunity to go across and speak to him.

Her voice low so that no one else would hear, she said, 'I can't imagine what Mrs Black must be thinking of us.'

'Neither can I. I don't like to speak ill of anyone but I fear Marlene is about to get what she deserves. I couldn't believe it when I saw her launch herself like that at you, and unprovoked.' He looked at her closely. 'Are you all right? She didn't hurt you, did she?'

His concern was so genuine that Harrie smiled warmly at him. 'I've a feeling I've a couple of nice bruises on my arm but nothing that a dab of witch hazel won't sort out. My injuries could have been much worse if you hadn't stepped in so quickly. Thank you for coming to my rescue again, Chas.'

'Oh, if it hadn't been me who got in first, one of the other men would have,' he said matter-of-factly.

'But you did, Chas, and I'm glad it was you.' Harrie was feeling a prickling sensation all over to be standing so close to this man she desperately wanted the chance to get to know better. She was positive that once she did she had a wonderful future with him. She took a deep breath. 'Chas, it's important to me you know there is nothing between me and Darren and never will be. Also, I don't know how you got the idea I was embarrassed when you saved me from falling in the chip shop. I wasn't, far from it.'

He felt a sudden rush of joy that nothing was going on between Harrie and Darren, then it evaporated as it struck him that it didn't matter whether there was or wasn't as far as her looking in his direction was concerned. He couldn't understand why Harrie should feel it was important he should hear these things. He really wished she wouldn't look at him in that way. If he didn't know better he would be under the impression she fancied him. But he *did* know better. If good-looking, outgoing Darren was getting nowhere with her, then Chas stood absolutely no chance. He'd been such a fool in the chip shop, believing for those few seconds that she'd not scream in protest if he'd followed his mindless desire and scooped her up in his arms and run off with her.

'Well, I . . . er . . . appreciate you telling me, Harrie.'

She waited with bated breath, hoping that now he'd been put straight he'd suggest their going out together. To her disappointment he didn't. Then she remembered that despite not quite being in earshot of anyone they weren't exactly on their own at present. Chas had a sense of decorum, unlike Darren who seemed to possess none whatsoever. That thought only made her respect Chas more. She fought for something to say to keep conversation flowing between them and remembered she did have something to ask him about. 'How did your interview with the police go, Chas?'

'Oh, thanks for asking, yes, they seemed to be happy with everything I told them. I said I was available any time if they needed to question me further. I really do hope for the Grahams' sake that they find that case. I think the police suspect as I do that it's in the hospital somewhere.'

Just then the office door was thrust open and Marlene came storming out, shouting at the top of her voice, 'Who d'yer think you are, telling me it doesn't make any difference whether I felt provoked by that temporary office bitch or not? It's a poxy job anyway and you can stick it up yer arse!' She stuck two fingers up at Mrs Black who was coming out of the office herself, before grabbing her coat and shoulder bag from where she had left them on the radio-operator's desk when she had first come in.

As she reached the staff entrance she turned to look back at Darren, sneering at him. 'You say you wouldn't be seen dead with me, eh? Well, that's not what yer said when you was giving me one across the desk the other night when yer passed by on yer way home from the pub. I was good enough for yer then, wasn't I, yer bastard?' She stared across at Harrie. 'You're welcome to my cast-off 'cos I wouldn't have him now if he was the last man on earth. Oh, and in case yer don't know yet he's got a little dick and no idea what to do with it. Like me, you'll have to pretend yer enjoying it to feed his ego.' She cast an amused eye over them all. 'I shan't hold me breath for a leaving present and I can't tell a lie and say I'll miss you all. Ta-ra.'

With that she slung her coat over her shoulder and stalked off the premises.

They all stared after her for a moment speechless before Darren broke the silence by blurting, 'It's not true what Marlene said about me having a little d—'

'I'm sure none of us believed her,' cut in the distin-guished-looking man who'd accompanied Mrs Black. He turned to look at her. 'Would you like me to speak to the staff on your behalf?'

Muriel shook her head. 'Thank you but it's only right I do this.' She faced the gathering. They all knew the smile on her face was forced. Jack Black's widow was grieving deeply for the man she had loved for the last forty years. The situation she'd just had to deal with couldn't have helped either.

She took a deep breath. Clasping her hands in front of her, she began: 'As you can appreciate this has been a very sad day for me. Mr Grogin, Jack's . . . my . . . solicitor who's come with me today wanted me to leave what I have to tell you for another occasion, but I felt it only fair that you should know my decision about the firm as soon as I'd made it. First, though, I want to thank all those of you who came to the funeral today. Jack would have appreciated it. As you know, he lived and breathed his business and I always said that one day it would be the death of him. Hard work never killed anyone, it's said, but that's a lie 'cos it certainly did him no favours.'

She paused momentarily before continuing. 'I've decided to sell up. I've no head myself for business and under my charge it would more than likely end up bankrupt. And to be honest I've no heart for it now even if I had the necessary skills to run it.' They could all clearly see she was fighting to keep control of her emotions as she spoke. 'I've no idea how long it will take to find a buyer but I hope whoever does take this place will keep you all on. Be assured I'll tell whoever it is what a loyal and trustworthy bunch you are. Until then I know I can trust you to see that it's business as usual.

'Ralph, you were kind enough to come out of retirement when Jack first took ill and help out. I hope you'll stay on in the meantime? You too, Harrie. I'm more than happy with the grand job you're doing. I have no doubt many firms would like to snap you up, offering better pay and conditions than you're getting here, and it's probably a cheek of me to hope you'll consider staying like Ralph until ... until ...'

It all became too much for her then. She fumbled in her handbag for a handkerchief to wipe away the tears.

Mr Grogin took her arm. 'Let's get you home.' He flashed a brief smile at the gathering before he led her out.

'Well,' said Ralph, sighing sadly, 'that's that then. We can only wait and see what happens next. Like Mrs Black said, though, until the business is sold we carry on as usual.'

'Why does something like this always happen so near Christmas?' one of the drivers grumbled.

'Yer can't blame Jack for that,' responded another.

Chas could tell that discord was beginning to manifest itself and in order to defuse the situation said, 'At least we know we do have a job over Christmas and maybe for some time after that. It'll take a while surely for a buyer to be found and the deal to go through.'

'Yeah, I grant yer that, Chas, but I'm keeping me eyes and ears open in case summat more permanent comes along,' said Brian Kirk, one of the night-shift drivers.

Several other drivers mumbled their agreement.

'Well, that's everyone's right,' said Chas. 'But while we're employed by Black's it's only fair we're as loyal as we've ever been.'

'Chas is right,' piped up Harrie. 'And think about it this way. If a buyer sees how well this place is operating then he won't feel the need to make changes, will he, and your jobs will be safe.'

They saw the wisdom in what she was saying and nodded approvingly.

'We do have another more pressing problem,' Harrie continued. 'Now that Marlene has gone there's no evening-shift radio operator.'

Caught up with the announcement of the selling of Black's they'd forgotten about that problem.

'Well, I can't say I'm sorry to see the back of that little madam but Mrs Black obviously hasn't realised we need someone tonight. Then, it ain't surprising with all she's had on her mind,' said Ralph. 'It's going to take a few days to advertise and interview and then get someone started. I could stay on and cover for tonight, I suppose, although me wife ain't gonna like it.'

Chas smiled at the old man. 'No disrespect, Ralph, but you've been on your feet ten hours as it is and that's enough for anyone of your age. I'll cover for tonight. Jim, could you pop into my house on your way home and tell my mother what's happening or she'll worry?' he asked one of the other drivers.

'Yeah, 'course, mate,' agreed Jim.

'And I'll do tomorrow night,' said Harrie. 'I've

watched you, Ralph, and know how the radio operates.'

Chas looked at her in surprise that she should offer. But then the better he was getting to know Harrie, the more he realised she wasn't the type to stand back when someone needed help. She really was a woman in a million. He so envied the man she'd choose to share her life with.

'I don't mind doing my bit 'til yer get someone in permanent as I could do with the extra towards Christmas,' said a driver.

'Count me in too,' said another. And another after that.

Harrie smiled. 'I'll sort out a roster tomorrow.'

As she made her way home she felt terrible in the circumstances for the sense of disappointment she was experiencing. If Chas hadn't volunteered to cover this evening's shift he might possibly have suggested they walk partway home together and maybe by now, should things have gone the way she so vehemently hoped, they would have been planning an evening out together, the first of many.

She found her father bustling around the kitchen. It struck her that just lately Percy seemed to have found an extra zest for living, though she couldn't for the life of her think what could be the cause of it. Maybe it was because he'd had a reprieve, she wasn't leaving him to cope on his own now she was not getting married to Jeremy.

'You're a bit later than usual tonight, lovey,' he said, planting a kiss on her cheek. 'I hope the funeral went well.'

She told him about it and the reason for her lateness.

'Oh, dear, Mrs Black's selling up then, is she? Well, I suppose it's the only thing she can do, her having no head for business. Good thing you'll have a job there until the sale goes through at least. Yer never know, whoever takes it on might offer you the office job permanently. You've enjoyed it from the start, but the longer yer there the more yer getting to like it, lovey, I can tell.'

Harrie privately wondered if the fact Chas worked there was what really made her enjoy the job as much as she did.

'I've made us a cheese and potato pie for our dinner,' Percy announced proudly.

'Oh, is that what I could smell when I came in? I have to say, it smells good, Dad.' Despite her immense feeling of pride in him for what he was undertaking, nevertheless she said, 'You're taking this cooking lark seriously, aren't you? But you don't need to really, it's not like I'm leaving you to fend for yourself now.'

'Oh, yes, well, er . . . you will one day and I need to be prepared.' Percy's face lit up and he began, 'And I am so enjoying meself with . . .' before suddenly he stopped.

She frowned at him quizzically. 'Enjoying yourself with what, Dad?'

'Eh? Oh, with what I'm doing learning to cook and having a meal ready for you when you come home, instead of you having to do it.'

A warm glow filled Harrie. She had a wonderful father. Most men of his age and in his position would be sitting back, letting their offspring run after them, but not her father.

As he tucked into his pie Percy said to Harrie, 'All right, is it?'

It was rather bland for her liking, felt like it needed more seasoning, and she would never have dreamed of adding diced carrots, peas and chopped Savoy cabbage to it. She wondered what had made her father think of doing so. Nevertheless Harrie enthused, 'It's very good, Dad.'

CHAPTER TWENTY-ONE

After covering the radio-operator's position until ten, and considering he'd already done a ten-hour shift, Chas was almost falling asleep on his feet by the time he got home. He glanced down blankly at the plate of food his mother had just set before him. It looked very dried up but he couldn't blame her for that. When she had prepared it she would have had no idea it was going to be four hours after his normal home-time before he would be eating it. He guessed the white-looking stuff on his plate to be mashed potato with cheese mixed through it, and recognised the exposed peas and florets of broccoli, but he did not know what the white-ish chunks were. He had thought at first they were potato lumps as his mother wasn't the best at mashing potatoes but then he realised they weren't. Now it struck him these chunks were in fact diced parsnips.

'What yer staring at yer dinner like that for? It ain't gonna bite yer. Now tuck in, son, before it gets cold,' Iris told him, sitting down opposite cradling a cup of tea. Before he put his fork in his mouth, she said, 'I hope Mr Black's funeral went all right?'

'Yes, it did, Mam. Well, as well as funerals go, I

suppose. There was a really good turn out. Mrs Black came into the office tonight to tell us all she's decided to sell up.'

The response he received to this news wasn't quite what he was expecting. 'Oh, really!' Iris enthused, putting down her cup and looking at him excitedly.

'You seem pleased, Mam. You do realise that I could end up looking for another job if whoever buys it decides not to keep some of us on. They could bring in their own staff instead.' And, he thought, one not so near to home so he wouldn't be conveniently on hand should his mother have need of him.

'Yes, I realise that and that's how I come to have the answer to make sure you do keep yer job. I thought of this a while ago and wanted to tell you my idea but I never got around to it.'

'So what is this answer you've come up with?' he asked her.

'Well, it's really quite simple, son. You should buy Black's.'

He looked astounded. 'Me!'

'Yes, why not?'

'Why not? Well, for a start, what do I know about running a business?'

'What did Jack Black know before he started up, and he did all right for himself. And anyway, it won't be like starting from scratch for you. Everything's already in place for you to take over. You might even come up with some ways to make the business better and more profitable.'

His mother was showing a faith in his abilities he wasn't sure he possessed himself. 'But aren't you forgetting one big obstacle, Mam? Where am I supposed to get the money from to buy Black's with?'

'Oh, that's easy. You've yer savings and the rest you borrow from a bank.'

'You've thought this through, haven't you, Mam?'

Iris scowled at him. 'Don't look so surprised. I might only be a housewife but that doesn't mean to say I ain't a brain in me head.'

'I'm sorry, Mam, I didn't mean to imply that you haven't. But my savings are intended to buy you a new house that'll be nicer for you to live in and much easier to keep.'

'I keep telling yer, son, and I wish you'd listen to me: I'm happy where I am. If you buy that house and all these labour-saving machines you keep on about, you'll be moving into it and using the machines on your own. Now please, let that be the last of it. About buying Black's . . .'

'Mam, please, there's no point in discussing this because . . . because . . .'

'Because what? Oh, you don't need to tell me. I know. It's because you don't think you're capable of running a business.' Her face screwed up angrily. 'Those Dewhurst kids have so much to answer for, knocking your confidence right out of the window with their nasty antics when you was a kid. You *do* have it in you to do whatever you want to, Chas, and make a great success of it. What will it take for you to realise that? You're a good man, one who'd make a great boss people would be happy to work for and be loyal to. There wasn't much I could do when you was young to stop those Dewhursts plaguing the life out of yer.

They were such sneaky little so-and-so's that catching 'em at it was nigh on impossible, but what I can do now is stop you from passing up such a good opportunity. One which might never come your way again.'

She eyed him tenderly. 'For what it's worth, son, I love you too much ever to suggest you do anything you ain't capable of tackling. I know you ain't the type to want to seek revenge on anyone, but wouldn't it just be a kick in the teeth to those Dewhursts, eh, to show them that the boy they constantly taunted as being useless had grown up to be a businessman while they ... well, we all know how *they've* turned out.' She could tell he still wasn't convinced of his ability to aim higher. 'All right, I'll make you a deal. When yer make yer first clear profit that's enough to buy me one of them posh houses with all those labour-saving gadgets you keep threatening me with, *then* I'll move into it.'

His mother was blackmailing him. He knew she was well aware that his greatest desire was to make her life as easy as he could and that he was willing to do anything to achieve that. Chas wasn't the type, though, to go headlong into doing something without checking it out thoroughly first. 'All right, Mam,' he sighed. 'I suppose it wouldn't hurt to make some enquiries.'

A grin of delight split her face. 'That's the ticket, son. Now the first thing you should do is approach young Harrie to give you an idea what sort of profit the firm makes. As she's updating the books, she will be in the know. Then before you approach the bank you need to find out how much Mrs Black is expecting for the firm.'

Chas shook his head at her. 'You make it sound so easy, Mam.' He eyed her quizzically. 'How did you know Harrie was updating the books?'

'Eh? You told me she was.'

'I don't remember telling you anything of the kind. In fact, I don't remember discussing Harrie with you at all.'

'Well, you must have or how else would I know? So you'll get on to it first thing in the morning? No sense in wasting time or yer risk someone else beating you to it. Now eat yer dinner before it gets cold,' Iris ordered him. 'You're going to need all your energy in future when you're a boss.'

As he tucked in Chas's thoughts were whirling. It was madness his considering taking over Black's Taxis even if the bank would lend him the money. But then, what if he did? If the business did make a reasonable profit under his ownership, not only would he fulfil his ambition to make his mother's life better, he could also do his best to keep the other drivers and staff in work, maybe even pay them a little more in their wage packets to give them a better standard of living. He only had his mother and himself to keep on his wage. They might not live frugally but neither were they spendthrifts by any stretch of the imagination. How the other drivers coped with the costs involved in supporting themselves plus wives and children he'd no idea, even though he knew some of the men upped their wage by illegal means. He was also well aware what long hours taxi drivers had to work to earn their money, leaving them little time to be with their families. Maybe he could find a way to improve their lot.

As all these thoughts and ideas were going around in his head, not once did Chas think of the rewards that would come his way as the owner of a business. He thought only of what it would bring to others.

CHAPTER TWENTY-TWO

Chas didn't get the chance to approach Harrie until after eleven the next day. He'd slept badly the previous night, tossing and turning, going over in his mind the enormous undertaking his mother seemed to be absolutely certain he had every chance of making a success of, and battling all the time with his own terrible lack of self-confidence which was telling him the opposite. When he got up that morning, Iris had made him promise he wouldn't come home that night until he had at least approached Harrie and obtained some facts and figures, ascertained whether it was worth proceeding further.

Sincerely hoping that Harrie wouldn't mind his taking up her time on what he felt was more than likely a fool's errand, Chas tapped on her office door. On hearing her response, he popped his head round. 'Would it be convenient to have a private word, Harrie?'

Her heart pounded. At last. It looked like he was nervous and she didn't need to ask why. 'Yes, of course, Chas. Please come in,' she said enthusiastically. As he sat down on the chair in front of her desk she saw a look of discomfiture momentarily cross his face. 'Are you all right? she asked.

He rubbed his chest. 'I've indigestion. My mother made cheese and potato pie for my dinner last night and it's sitting heavy on me.'

'Oh, what a coincidence! My father made the same for my dinner last night. Mind you, I don't know where he got the recipe from as I've never had cheese and potato pie with an assortment of other vegetables in it before.'

'Isn't cheese and potato pie supposed to have an assortment of vegetables in it then?'

'No. Just cheese and potatoes, that's why it's called cheese and potato pie, Chas. Why did you ask that?'

'Oh, well, it's just my mother always puts vegetables in hers so I wouldn't be any the wiser.'

Harrie was desperate for him to get to the point. 'You wanted a private word with me?' she gently prompted him.

'Oh, yes, I did.' He scraped his hand through his hair. 'I don't know where to start really. I don't want you to think I'm mad even to be considering it . . .'

'I would never think such a thing of you, Chas,' she cut him short to reassure him. 'Now just ask me what you want to ask me?' she urged.

He took a breath. 'All right. Look, this isn't my idea but my mother's.'

His mother's! She would have preferred it to have been his idea but supposed she was pleased to hear that Chas's mother approved enough of her to suggest he ask her out. She had taken a liking to Iris when the woman had come to her and her father's rescue at the bus stop and had spent a pleasant hour afterwards in the café listening to her chatter. It was mostly about the son she was obviously proud of, and Harrie herself now knew that pride in him to be more than justified.

'Well, I would never have thought of it myself, you see.'

She looked taken aback. 'You wouldn't?'

'Oh, no. I can see her point, I suppose, about not letting this opportunity pass me by when I might not get another like it but . . . well, I don't know whether I'm up to it, you see, as I've no experience really.'

She liked the thought he hadn't been with many girls, it made her feel special, but she did wonder why he was telling her as usually men liked to brag about their experience not the lack of it. But then Chas wasn't most men and that was why she had fallen in love with him. 'Experience doesn't matter, Chas,' she reassured him.

'Do you think? That's a relief to hear. I thought it would be very important, you see, so as to make a success of it. If I do go ahead with this I want to do my best to make a success of it.'

She was so pleased to hear that. Her mind started to wander to what she would wear for their first date. Depending, of course, on where he took her. She didn't mind really but a meal would be nice then they could chat and get to know each other. There was so much she wanted to know about him and obviously he'd want the same. She wished though he'd stop going around the houses and just ask her for a date. 'Just ask me what you want to ask me, Chas?' she prompted.

'Oh, yes, I apologise for taking up your time. I do appreciate you're very busy. Is it making a profit?'

Harrie looked at him stupefied. 'Sorry?'

'Well, there's no point in me going any further with this if it's not in profit. I presume it is or else Jack would have thrown in the towel long ago but I need to know how much for when I approach the bank. Then I can be sure I can repay the loan comfortably as well as everything else. Provided, of course, they will lend me what money I need and Mrs Black isn't asking more than I can afford for the business.'

She gawped at him, stunned. 'Oh, so you want my opinion as to whether the firm is viable as I do the books and you're considering buying it?'

Now Chas looked confused. 'Yes, that's right.' His face clouded over. 'Do you think this is a hare-brained idea for me even to be considering?'

Harrie fought to hide the acute disappointment she was experiencing. 'No, not at all. It's just this isn't what I was expecting you to ask . . . er . . . Look, I'm sure Mrs Black won't have any objection to me divulging this information in the circumstances. I've just about got the books up-to-date and a regular profit is showing. This sort of business can have its ups and downs, but overall takings average out at five hundred pounds a week, give or take. Not huge by some firms' standards, and you need to work out how much the weekly repayment on the loan would be plus wages, rent on the premises, etcetera. But what you'd be left with, I feel, would be more than you're earning as an employee. I do know how much it is as I do the wages. It's certainly better to be your own boss than work for someone else, if you get the chance.' Harrie looked at him searchingly. 'I think your mother's right to tell you to consider buying the firm if you can. It's a wonderful idea. You'd make a great boss, Chas.'

'You think so?'

She nodded. 'I'd work for you.' I'd more than work for you if you'd give me the chance, she thought.

'Would you?'

She was surprised that he seemed so shocked to hear it. 'If anything goes ahead, would you consider keeping me on as your office staff?'

He couldn't envisage this office without her in it. 'If I'm successful in getting the business then consider the job yours, Harrie. I hope the other staff feel they'd like to work for me too. If this does come off, I was thinking that maybe I could shorten their hours or rearrange them somehow so they can spend more time with their families. I also hope it might be possible to pay them a bit more on the hourly rate so they can have a better standard of living.'

Oh, Chas, she thought, what a lovely, lovely man you are. How could you possibly doubt anyone would want to work for you? Yet he did, and she couldn't understand why he should have such a lack of confidence in himself.

'I have to say, I'm worried I'm about to bite off more than I can chew,' he said, looking undecided.

'I bet Mr Ford thought just that when he started planning his first production line to make cars.'

'Mmm, yes, I suppose. But are you sure it's not important to have experience?'

When she had said that she'd thought he was talking about something else! 'Well, maybe you haven't the office experience but that's what you'd pay me to handle for you, and it's not like you don't know how a taxi firm operates, is it? You're a cabby yourself so you must have a good idea.'

'Maybe not all the ins and outs but I have a good knowledge of the basics.'

'More than some people have when they start up a business. I bet you know more than you think you do, and what you don't know you can soon learn. Anyway, it's not like you're starting this business up from scratch, is it? Everything is already in place so really you'd just be taking it over.'

'That's what my mother said.'

'Well, we can't both be wrong, can we?' Harrie paused thoughtfully for a moment before saying, 'Tyme's Taxis. It's got a good ring to it. Oh, a good slogan would be: *On Tyme Taxis*.' She grabbed a piece of paper and wrote it down then showed it to him. 'I can just picture that on the side of the cabs.'

Chas looked impressed. 'That's very clever, you thinking of that. You really think I should seriously consider taking this further then?'

Harrie was pleased he liked her slogan and valued her opinion. 'I most certainly do, Chas. I think you should approach Mrs Black immediately to find out how much she wants for the place. In the meantime I'll see if one of the drivers will swap the radio-operator's shift with me tonight and then work late to get the books bang up to date so you'll be able to show the bank the figures should the price Mrs Black is expecting not prove too extortionate.'

How thoughtful of her to offer to do that for him, he thought. But then he guessed she would offer to do it for anyone. And, after all, she had shown a deep interest in working here permanently so all she was really doing was her bit towards securing a position for herself.

'You could go in your lunch hour to see Mrs Black,' Harrie suggested to him. 'No point in wasting time, Chas. You can be damn' sure if you dilly-dally on something like this, someone will jump in and beat you to it.'

And if I do dilly-dally it will give me time to think more deeply about what I'm going to do and there is a danger I will lose my nerve, he thought. He wondered if Harrie realised how much encouragement she had given him. Once again he was finding how easy he found her to talk to. She hadn't made him feel inadequate for considering doing something most people of his ilk wouldn't even contemplate. Once again he deeply envied the man who won her affections as Harrie seemed to him a rarity amongst women, certainly the women of around her age he had come across anyway.

He stood up. 'Thank you, Harrie.'

'My pleasure to help a friend, Chas.'

She considered him a friend? He felt a blush of embarrassment creeping up his neck, wondering what he'd done to deserve such an accolade. But he could do with a friend to help him through this if he was to proceed, especially one like Harrie. He felt privileged to have her.

Mixed emotions raced through Harrie as she watched Chas leave her office. She was pleased he had turned to her for help and advice regarding the enormous undertaking he was embarking on. But she was also greatly disappointed that he hadn't taken the opportunity to ask her out. Then she told herself that she was being unreasonable, expecting him to start a relationship with her while his mind was consumed by such important matters. Men were not like women who could easily handle several things at once. She needed to have patience, allow him to deal with buying the business, then once that was settled one way or the other, hopefully he would turn his attention to her.

CHAPTER TWENTY-THREE

Anyone witnessing the tall, well-made, smartly suited man walking purposefully up the Humberstone Gate the following Tuesday morning would have been very surprised to know of his inner turmoil. Armed with the facts and figures on Black's which Harrie had neatly typed out for him, Chas was on his way to attend an appointment with the bank manager.

Muriel Black had been astonished to find Chas on her doorstep a few days before. After apologising for disturbing her at such an emotional time, he'd awkwardly informed her of his interest in buying her late husband's business. To Chas's surprise she took his enquiry seriously and ushered him inside to discuss details over tea and Garibaldi biscuits. She was delighted, she told him, that someone like him would be considering taking over the business her dear late husband had given his life to. She'd much sooner that than it be swallowed up by a larger town-run firm who would possibly close it down because in truth they were just after the licence plates to expand their own fleet.

The sum of fifteen thousand pounds which she told him she was expecting from the sale sounded an absolute fortune to Chas. Fifteen thousand pounds would buy his mother three, or possibly four, four-bedroomed detached houses, complete with labour-saving devices, and have change left over to pay the wages of live-in help for at least five years at today's rates of ten shillings an hour including board and keep. Regardless of his savings of two thousand pounds, a sum it had taken him years to accumulate bit by bit, the bank would never advance him the rest, he was positive they wouldn't. He could picture the bank manager laughing at him for even considering such a thing. Beside that, how would he sleep at night with such a huge debt hanging over him?

Thanking Muriel Black for her time, and sorry that he had wasted it, Chas had returned to the office and given Harrie the disappointing news, also hoping his mother wouldn't be too distressed when he told her later that evening.

To his surprise Harrie had told him she didn't think the price Mrs Black wanted extortionate at all taking into consideration the fact that the sum asked was for the purchase of fifteen cars, not new admittedly but in good condition and none showing signs of major mechanical faults; plus the much-coveted fifteen licence plates authorising the carrying of passengers as well as the goodwill Jack Black had built up over twenty years. She was surprised herself that Muriel Black wasn't asking for more.

'You think I should still pursue this and approach the bank?' Chas had asked her.

'Well, of course that is your decision. You mustn't assume they'll turn you down, they could do the opposite. They'll look at you favourably because you told me you'd banked with them for years and they'll see from their records that you consistently saved each week. It might only have been small amounts but still regular savings, and that will stand you in good stead, show you're a reliable person. If they do agree to advance you the money, you still have the choice as to whether to go ahead or not.'

He knew his mother would be saying the same as Harrie, and was reminded of the reasons he'd bowed to Iris's blackmail attempt in the first place. He meant not only to improve her lot but also that of his colleagues who'd become his employees if this went through. 'All right, I'll make an appointment to see the bank manager and let Mrs Black know that I am interested after all.'

'Right, Chas, that's you sorted. Now I need to ask your advice.'

'Oh?'

'I don't know what to do about the fact that Terry Briggs seems to have disappeared off the face of the earth. Several of the drivers have complained there's no one to do their minor repairs for them and also no security guard watching over the compound at night in case vandals or thieves show an interest. It's over a week now that he's been off and he's not notified us of any reason for his absence. What do you think I should do about it?'

He scratched his chin. 'Well, I don't think we should worry Mrs Black unnecessarily with this, considering what she's going through, do you?'

'No, I agree we shouldn't.'

'Well then, we should give Terry the benefit of the doubt a little longer. I'm sure his excuse for being off is a good one. The men are capable of doing the minor repairs themselves in the meantime, and anything they can't they'll just have to get the garage to do. I know a little about engines as I had to make temporary repairs when I was on the road as a lorry driver, I can always see what I can do to help. Maybe we should ask Ronald Tyler, the night-shift operator, to keep an eye on the compound regularly during the night too. Hopefully we can manage this way until Terry does return to work.'

And you doubt your abilities to make a good boss, she thought. She wondered if Chas realised that he had just shown all the qualities a good leader should possess: compassion towards his fellow human beings, and well thought out solutions to counteract possible problems.

'You're spending a lot of time in Harrie's office just lately,' Ralph commented as Chas came out.

'Oh, er . . . just a query over mileage I'd logged against petrol receipts that needed clearing up.' He did not like lying to Ralph but what he was considering had better not become common knowledge yet.

Ralph quite rightly looked unconvinced by Chas's explanation. 'Huh, you sure there's n'ote going on between you two romantically?'

Chas stared at him stolidly. 'I can assure you there isn't, Ralph, and please don't let Harrie hear you talk like that. She could be insulted by the idea people would think such a thing.'

Ralph might be getting on in years but his eyesight

had not diminished that much. He had witnessed the way Harrie looked at Chas when she wasn't aware anyone was observing her and he knew she would definitely not be upset should anyone think they were an item. He'd seen the way Chas looked at Harrie when no one was observing him and knew the man had more than a passing fancy for her, whether he knew it himself or not. If the purpose of Chas's response had been to throw off the scent, then Chas was badly mistaken because Ralph was even more convinced now that something was going on between them.

On the morning of his appointment with the bank Iris had driven Chas mad with her continual offers of motherly advice as to how to conduct himself with the bank official, as well as fussing over his attire to make sure he was as well turned out for his interview as she could make him. His best suit had been sponged and hung up to air so no smell of mothballs lingered; his best shirt pressed several times to make sure not one minute crease remained; his shoes polished to a glass-like finish so Chas could see his face in them. After telling him he was as good as any other person asking the bank to advance them money, Iris waved her son off and sat down to drink endless cups of tea before he returned.

He had just alighted from the bus in town and was weaving his way through the throng of Christmas shoppers, passing by Lewis's department store towards the Midland Bank on the corner of Gallowtree Gate, when an expensively dressed woman, laden down with heavy shopping bags, caught his eye. It was Nadine.

He watched her flounce off to become enveloped

by the crowds of shoppers. He found himself wondering where she'd suddenly found the money from to buy her expensive clothes and whatever else was in her shopping bags. Maybe she had found herself a well-off man and he was funding her? Nadine might be coarse of mouth and spiteful of nature but she was a good-looking woman for a mother of four, he couldn't deny that. Then it struck him that it was a well-known fact how the Dewhursts had financed themselves in the past. There was a good possibility that was how she was doing it now, and if so she obviously hadn't lost her touch.

His own reason for being in the town then occurred to him and he continued on to his appointment.

Two hours later a very distracted Chas walked into Black's office.

Ralph looked at him, perplexed. 'Harrie told me you sent word in you were ill in bed. Yer don't look ill to me. So where yer bin, all dressed up like a dog's dinner?'

Harrie, who had been keeping her eyes peeled, ears alert for the first sign of Chas's appearance, came charging out of her office then to grab hold of his arm and pull him back inside, shutting the door behind them. Ralph sat staring at the door open-mouthed. It was obvious to him something was going on.

'How did it go?' she demanded. The stupefied expression on his face registered then and her own fell in dismay. 'Oh, they turned you down? Oh, Chas, I'm so sorry.'

'Eh? Oh, Harrie, no, they didn't. I'm still having trouble believing it. I'm in shock, if you want the truth, because I was fully convinced I'd be sent packing without a by your leave but the bank manager was very interested in what I put to him. You were right, the fact I'd banked with them for years went very much in my favour. He studied the figures you gave me and asked me to tell him as much as I could about the business and how I intended to run it. Well, I have to say I was a bit flummoxed by that as I hadn't really thought how I am going to run it yet. The same as it is now, I told him. It's doing all right and hopefully I can come up with some improvements to up the profits. I was honest with him, though, told him I was keener to improve the drivers' lot before the profits. I said you were managing all the office side, and how experienced you were and good at what you did and that you'd asked to be made permanent if I was successful in taking over. He seemed impressed I had a sizeable deposit. Told me he would put all this to the board when they next met and let me know their decision then.'

'Oh, Chas, that's great, just great,' she enthused excitedly. 'If the bank manager didn't think it was a good proposal he wouldn't be passing it to the board for approval. Were you given any indication how long we'd have to wait until we hear the outcome?'

He noticed she'd said *we* as if she was part of this, and didn't quite know what to make of that. Maybe it had been a slip of the tongue on her part. 'I didn't like to ask, Harrie.'

'Oh, it could be days or weeks, depends how often the board sits. Oh, Lord, the waiting is going to be terrible.'

'Well, there's nothing we can do but carry on as normal until then. I'd better get home and tell my mam what's what. She'll have my guts for garters if she finds out I called in here first. Thanks again for all your help, Harrie, I couldn't have come this far without it.' He felt a sudden overwhelming urge to grab her in his arms and kiss her by way of thanking her for all she'd done for him but hurriedly quashed it, knowing such an intimate display could well ruin the friendship that was growing between them, which was the last thing he wanted. 'I'll get changed and be back to work this afternoon. See you later, Harrie.'

A warm glow filled her at the knowledge that he had called in to tell her first what had transpired at the bank before he had gone home to tell his mother. But again she couldn't help but feel disappointed that no mention of their going out together had been made. But then, she couldn't expect him to be thinking of social matters when he had so much more important things to occupy his mind.

CHAPTER TWENTY-FOUR

Two weeks later Chas arrived home to find his mother dozing in her armchair. He stood looking down at her worriedly. Several times now he had found her like this. She had never been one for napping before so what had changed in her life to make her feel the need to do it now? Then he frowned as a thought struck him. The first time he had caught her was the Saturday evening of the incident in the chip shop with Harrie, but he felt sure each time since had been a Wednesday, the same as today. He wasn't sure whether there was any significance to that fact. Then he noticed his mother's best dress hanging on the door that led into the narrow passage where the front door and stairs were.

He realised she had woken and smiled down at her. 'All right, Mam, are you?'

She yawned. 'Yes, ducky, I'm fine, ta. Couldn't be better.'

'You sure, Mam?'

Giving a stretch, Iris looked up at him quizzically. 'What d'yer mean?'

'Well, it's just I've caught you asleep several times now and I'm getting concerned about it.'

'Caught me? You make it sound like I've done summat wrong.'

'No, I'm not saying that, Mam, you know I'm not.'

'I'm glad to hear it. There's no law against having a cat nap now and again, is there, son?'

'No, not at all. I just wondered, though, why it's always a Wednesday that I find you doing it?'

'Maybe I just get tired on a Wednesday. You keeping tabs on me?'

'Don't be daft, Mam, 'course I'm not. I just wondered if there's something you do on a Wednesday that tires you out then maybe I could do it for you, that's all.'

She wagged a finger at him. 'I know yer heart's in the right place, son, but you've got more important things to worry about than me having a snooze in the afternoon now and again. Heard 'ote yet?'

Chas shook his head. 'No.'

Iris gave a loud sigh. 'I can't stand this,' she grumbled. 'The suspense is killing me. How long does that bank need to make its decision whether to loan you the money or not?'

'They'll inform me as soon as they've made it, Mam, and not before. I'm not the only person applying for help from them and they have other business to deal with too.' A worried expression filled Chas's face then and he started to rub his chin distractedly.

Iris knew he was still having doubts he was capable of running a business and making a success of it, fearing not for himself but about letting others down. That was typical of her son and what she loved most about him, that he genuinely cared for others above himself.

Iris nursed a deep grudge against the Dewhurst children for the damage they had done him through their nasty remarks and mindless pranks in the past, but if it had in turn brought out the tender caring traits in his nature, to make him the man he was now, then for that and only that she was glad.

'Eh, don't you dare be thinking you ain't got what it takes to pull this off,' she scolded him. 'You can do this, son. If I wasn't sure of that I wouldn't have encouraged you to go ahead with it.'

Chas sighed, hoping she was right. He daren't tell her he'd not slept properly since he'd approached the bank, knowing that should they approve the loan he could not disappoint her by not going ahead when she was showing such faith in him. His eyes fell on her dress hanging on the door. 'Have you been out somewhere nice today?' he asked her.

Iris looked at him sharply. 'What made you ask that?' It was more of a demand than a question.

'I just noticed your best dress hanging up on the door. You only bring that particular one out for high days and holidays and as far as I know there are none of those in the offing.'

She looked across at it and Chas couldn't understand why a fleeting look of horror crossed her face before she said, 'Oh ... er ... I meant to take that upstairs. I must have forgot.' She looked blankly at him for a minute before explaining, 'I took it down to give it an airing. I was hoping we might have something to celebrate and then I'd need summat posh to put on.'

'Don't build your hopes up, Mam. I'd hate you to

307

be disa—' He stopped mid-flow as the sound of screaming children erupted outside. 'What on earth is that noise?'

'It's them bleddy Dewhurst grandkids causing mayhem. The older ones have been causing havoc since Nadine moved back, especially these past few weeks. They're giving us neighbours a hell of a time, just like when their mam was little and running amok with her brothers. Sounds to me like they're running riot out front,' Ivy said, getting out of her chair. 'I can't think what she's thinking of letting 'em out this time of night in this cold.'

They both went to the front door to have a look at what was going on and were stunned to see most of the other neighbours standing on their doorsteps, everyone's attention fixed keenly on what was going on outside the Dewhursts' house.

An authoritative man and woman were struggling to get Nadine's four hysterical children inside a parked car. Leaning on her walking stick in her own doorway, Clarice was shouting at the poor mites to do as they were told.

Freda came up to them. 'Clarice Dewhurst is handing her grandkids over to the authorities to take care of. It seems Nadine's done a bunk. Been weeks now since Clarice has seen her apparently.'

Chas was just about to inform his mother and Freda that he'd actually seen Nadine a couple of weeks ago on the day of his bank appointment when he was interrupted by Clarice shouting at the gathering.

'What you lot gawping at? Expect me to look after four brats, do yer, with my ailments? I'd like to see

308

you fucking lot try! And none of you offered to help me, did yer? Like hell yer did. All yer did was keep knocking on me door complaining about the racket the kids were making and blaming the older ones for causing mischief yer own kids had done. Call yerselves neighbourly? Huh!' she sneered.

The children were in the car now and the doors were locked so they couldn't escape. The woman and man got in and the car roared off.

Simultaneously an expensively dressed Nadine, struggling to carry a heavy-looking suitcase, arrived on the scene. She looked around at the gathering of neighbours and then at her mother. 'What's going on, Mam? Who was that going off in that car just now?'

'Yer bleddy kids, that's who,' her mother loudly informed her. 'I've handed 'em over to the authorities,' she said proudly.

Nadine stared at her before screaming, 'YOU'VE WHAT?'

Clarice reared back her head. 'Well, what did you expect me to do?' she spat. 'I ain't heard a word from you for weeks.'

'Two weeks, Mam,' Nadine thundered back.

'Four. Can't yer count, where you've bin? You've told me more times than I care to remember what a lousy mother I've bin to yer but one thing I never did was abandon me own kids.'

'I never abandoned my kids. I left them with you.'

Leaning on the door-frame for support, Clarice lifted her walking stick and waved it menacingly at her errant daughter. 'Listen here, lady, I didn't know whether you was alive or dead or ever coming back. So why have you suddenly turned up? Chucked yer out, did he, whoever you've been with? Seen what yer was really like, I bet, and got out while the going was good. It always amazed me yer kept yer husband in yer bed for as long as yer did, but then you pair was the same kind. Lazy good-for-nothings, neither of yer giving a shit about anyone else but yerselves.'

Clarice glared at her murderously. 'If you think yer stepping over this doorstep again, then yer've another think coming. You're no daughter of mine. I never liked yer anyway. I hate yer now. I can't stand them bawling brats of yours but they didn't deserve what you did to them. That Saturday night you disappeared, you said you was popping out to the corner shop for a packet of fags. Not a peep have I heard from yer since.

'Then you swan back here with yer fancy clothes and whatever is in that case, like yer've done nothing wrong. Sugar Daddy buy you all that stuff, has he, or did yer get it by yer usual methods? Don't bother telling me, I ain't interested. I bet there ain't nothing in that case for me or your kids, just stuff for you. While yer've been off enjoying yerself wherever it is yer've bin, did yer give a thought to how I was managing or for yer kids crying for their mammy? They're better off where they're going and I hope the authorities have the sense never to let you set eyes on 'em again.'

'You bitch, our Mam,' Nadine screamed out. 'You can't do this. They're my kids. You'd no right.'

'Oh, I see. *I* had no right to do what I felt was best for them kids, but *you* had a right to bugger off and leave 'em 'cos the fancy took yer? You want your kids back, you'll have to fight the authorities for 'em. First you'll have to prove to 'em yer've a roof to put over them kiddies' heads but don't bother giving this address 'cos I'll deny all knowledge of yer. Now get out me sight and don't dare bother darkening my door again.'

Clarice looked around the silent gathering. 'Give yer a good show, have we? I missed a good opportunity, didn't I? I should have sold tickets.'

With that she stepped back inside her house and slammed shut the door.

Nadine was shaking violently with rage. She launched herself at the door and hammered on it repeatedly. 'Let me in, Mother, you hear me? LET ME IN.' Getting no response she kicked the door hard, chipping the already flaking paintwork. Then she swung around and glared daggers at Chas standing several feet away from her. 'This is your fault, you bastard,' she screamed at him accusingly. 'If you hadn't turned me down this wouldn't have happened. I've lost me kids through you and now I've nowhere to live.'

Snatching up her case, she threw back her head and struggled off down the street to disappear around the corner.

Chas was staring after her dumbstruck. What she had said to him was preying on his mind. How on earth could she blame him for what had happened to her? Then the truth hit him. The date she had made for them in the restaurant had been meant as a prelude to their getting together. She had seriously believed he would jump at the chance of taking on her and her children, and providing for them. Did she think he was that desperate for a woman that he'd settle for one who had until very recently not wasted any opportunity to show revulsion for him? Now he saw why she had started to act kindly towards him. It had been purely to provide herself with a meal ticket, replacing the one she had lost with the break up of her marriage and, from what he had heard of her husband and how they had been living, securing a far better one for herself. Were there no depths that woman wouldn't stoop to to get what she wanted? Nevertheless he felt a twinge of pity for Nadine. She might not have proved to be the best of mothers and her children were probably better off being adopted by parents who would care for them properly, but it was obvious by her reaction to what her mother had done that Nadine did care for them.

Iris was yanking at his arm. 'What was she going on about, blaming you for what's happened?'

'Yeah,' said Freda, looking at him inquisitively. 'What did she mean?'

Chas thought it better Iris did not know what Nadine had planned for him. 'I've no idea,' he lied. 'I can only guess she had to blame someone for what happened and she picked me.'

Iris's face contorted angrily. 'You'd have thought that trollop would've had her belly full of picking on you and target someone else for a change. I can't believe she left her kids all that time with no word. I can't imagine what those poor mites have gone through. Nadine knows fine well her mother ain't fit to care for four lively youngsters. She weren't fit to look after her own before the illness struck her. Nadine's kids are better off where they're going if that's how she treats 'em. And good riddance to her! I for one won't lose any sleep if we never hear from her again.

'I didn't like the way she started calling on you, son, to help her out. Knowing her ways as I do from past experience, I couldn't help but worry she'd a hidden agenda. Thank God it seems she hadn't.' Iris gave a shiver. 'It's parky out here, I'm off back inside to get yer dinner. It's tripe and onions tonight only I ran out of onions so I'll do yer a fried egg to go with it. Ta-ra, Freda,' she called after her friend as she hurried back inside.

Chas cringed. He had never had the heart to tell his mother that he detested tripe. The way she cooked it made it reminiscent of rubber. And a fried egg wasn't really the best accompaniment. But as usual he would eat it and tell her it'd been grand. He realised Freda was speaking to him and looked down at her, smiling. 'Sorry, Mrs Lumley?'

'I was just asking, lovey, if yer'd take a look at Nell Hill's tap for her when yer've got a minute? It's drip, drip, drip, and driving her mad.'

'Of course I will, Mrs Lumley.'

'I said yer would. Yer a good lad, yer really are, Chas. I don't know what us old ducks would do without you helping us out, I don't. Now after all that excitement, I need a drop of whisky in me tea. Clarice was right, she should have sold tickets for that performance. It was better than some plays you see on the telly. Good night then, Chas.'

'Good night, Mrs Lumley.' Then he remembered he'd something to ask her. 'Oh, Mrs Lumley?'

She stopped and turned back to face him. 'You want me, lovey?'

He stepped across to her. 'I'm thinking of getting me mam one of those soap sets for Christmas. I know her favourite scent is Lily of the Valley but I can't remember her favourite brand and I thought you would, being's you're her best friend.'

'Yardley, ducky, same as mine is. My preference is Lavender, in case yer wondering.'

He hid a smile. 'I'll remember that. Thank you. Oh, Mrs Lumley, is me mam all right?'

She looked at him suspiciously. 'Why d'yer ask?'

'Well, I don't want to make too much of it but it's just I've caught her asleep for the last three or four Wednesday nights when I've come home from work and wondered if she does anything on a Wednesday that tires her out. Something I could help her with. You know what a stubborn so-and-so she is. She won't admit she's getting on and can't do as much as she used to.'

Freda clicked her tongue at him. 'Good Lord, Chas, when yer get to me and yer mam's age it's a poor shame if yer can't have a snooze now and again in the afternoon. Now listen to me, lad, stop worrying about yer mam. She's fine, never been better, believe me. Why, it's so excit—' She suddenly stopped talking and seemed to check herself before blurting, 'Oh, is that my Henry calling me? Best go. Goodnight, Chas.'

He responded accordingly. Watching her hurry off down the entry, he frowned. He hadn't heard Freda's husband calling out for her and there was nothing wrong with Chas's hearing. It fleetingly crossed his mind that Freda had used that ruse to get away from him, to stop him from questioning her further over his concerns for his mother. Was there something they didn't want him to know? Then he gave himself a mental shake. He was making far too much of the fact he'd caught his mother several times cat napping. Its being a Wednesday each time was just coincidence. Freda was right, there was nothing wrong with anyone of their advancing years having a snooze in the afternoon. Didn't he himself do it after his dinner on a Sunday, and he was less than half his mother's age.

The very next night Terry turned up to resume his post, offering no explanation for his four-week absence. It was Harrie who noticed the lights on in the hut where he carried out his duties when she was leaving for the night via the back staff entrance. Wondering if Terry had indeed returned or an intruder was inside, she crept across to investigate. Terry was donning his overalls and stared at her in shock when he saw her standing in the entrance.

'Oh, it's you, Terry,' she said, relieved. 'Thank goodness, I thought we could have burglars on the premises. You're fully recovered, I hope? Well, I assume you've been off sick. We were wondering what was going on as we hadn't heard a word from you for four weeks.'

He looked awkwardly at her. 'Yeah, well, it's me gran. It's her that's been really sick. I've had to nurse her day and night 'cos we ain't got no one else, see.'

'I'm so sorry to hear that. I hope she's fully recovered,' Harrie said solicitously.

'Yeah, she is, thanks.'

'You should have let us know what was going on. We didn't know whether you were sick, had left, if you were coming back or if we'd need to find someone else for your job.'

He looked alarmed. 'You ain't gave someone else me job, have yer?'

'No, but you're lucky as I was about to ask Mrs Black what she wanted to do about the situation. So next time you need time off, even a day, you will call in to let us know?'

'Yeah, 'course. Look, I'd better get on. I see there's a pile of jobs marked down in the maintenance book for me to do on the cars.'

'I'll leave you to it then. I'll let everyone know you're back.'

Despite Terry's explanation for his absence seeming perfectly plausible, something about his manner towards Harrie gave her the impression his whole tale had been a complete fabrication. She couldn't pinpoint exactly why. Well, the main thing was he was back, Mrs Black was saved the bother of looking for someone else during her mourning period and the men had a mechanic on hand again to deal with the niggling jobs. Terry could count himself lucky that everyone was too affected by the boss's death to enquire further as to what exactly he'd been doing.

CHAPTER TWENTY-FIVE

Chas blinked rapidly as the bright flash from a camera bulb temporarily blinded him.

'See, that wasn't painful, was it?' Harrie said to him. 'It's fantastic getting the *Leicester Mercury* here to do a piece on the changeover. Hopefully it's going to go into tonight's edition. Great publicity, and free.'

Harrie was right but Chas didn't like it one bit being in the spotlight, and would have much preferred to let the rest of the staff be in the photograph and leave him out of it. The reporter had insisted, though. Tyme's Taxis was the name over the door now and on the side of the vehicles, so it was only right Mr Tyme himself should take pride of place in the photograph accompanying the write up. Not many people found themselves in a position to take over the firm they were previously working for and *Mercury* readers would be inspired to learn of a local lad made good and be rooting for his success.

Chas was still reeling from how quickly all this had come about. Only just over two weeks had passed since the bank had approved the loan and deposited the money into his new business account, contracts between Muriel Black and himself been exchanged, and the organising and carrying out of the repainting of the sign over the premises and the alteration of the vehicles' logos had been carried out, all in time for them to take advantage of the busy Christmas period which was on them in three days. It had been Muriel herself who had pushed it through so quickly, wanting the burden of the business off her shoulders so she could concentrate on rebuilding a future without her husband in it.

The reactions of his colleagues had absolutely shocked Chas. He hadn't known quite what to expect when they had all been gathered and informed of the change in ownership. They had looked momentarily shocked before expressions of approval started to be heard. It was obvious they were more than delighted to find out who their new boss was, and the slaps of congratulation on Chas's back had resulted in a few minor bruises.

When he had broken the news that the bank would back him to his mother, she had not said a word, for the first time ever struck speechless, but the look on her face told him all he needed to know. 'Proud' was not a strong enough word to describe the glow that emanated from Iris.

It was one thing, though, having his mother's faith in him but Chas could not have done all this without Harrie's encouragement too. She had willingly tackled for him things he would never have had a clue how to go about. He had a lot to thank her for. He was feeling the pressure of the financial commitment he had taken on in order to buy the business, but somehow, with Harrie on board, his burden didn't quite feel so great.

It felt like everything would be all right as long as she was around.

One morning a couple of weeks ago he had come in from a job to see her desk was empty and no sign of her. For Chas it felt as if the heart had gone out of the office. Then she had come back, having been out to fetch fresh supplies of tea, coffee and sugar to replenish the empty containers in the newly cleaned rest room. Harriet had undertaken to clean this herself. After hours of hard labour it was now a much more inviting environment for the men to take refuge in than the dirty, smelly room it had previously been. As she walked back in, the office had instantly come alive again for Chas. It felt as if the sun had come out from behind a cloud and bathed his world in its warm enveloping rays.

He knew he was setting himself up for disappointment but Harrie had a warmth and allure that drew him to her.

'Hopefully this article will alert local people to Tyme's Taxis,' she was saying to him now.

Chas smiled gratefully at her. 'I have you to thank for getting that reporter and photographer here.'

Harrie wanted to say that she would do anything for him but it was not the time or the place. Now the business was in Chas's hands, though, she fervently hoped he would turn his attention to doing something about establishing a relationship between them, at least ask her out on a first date. What she did say was, 'Well, it's in my own interest to do all I can towards making your business prosper, now I work here permanently.'

Yes, of course it was, he realised with a twinge of disappointment.

The *Mercury* having finished, the staff all trooped back into the office. The interior looked very festive as Harrie had put up paper decorations and sprigs of plastic holly.

Ralph had stayed behind to man the telephone while everyone else had been outside for the photo shoot. As they all arrived back he called Chas over. 'As soon as I've seen the lads out on some jobs that have come in, could I have a word, please, boss?'

Chas still found it strange being called 'boss' but knew he had to get used to it. 'Yes, of course.' He had a feeling he knew what Ralph wanted to speak to him about and had been dreading this moment. He couldn't blame Ralph for wanting to resume his retirement, though. He'd stayed on far longer than the couple of weeks he'd initially thought he'd be doing when Jack Black was first taken ill. Chas was grateful to the old man for staying at his post until the new boss was safely on board, and planned to reward his loyalty by paying for a weekend trip to the seaside for him and his wife. Ralph's departure, though, presented Chas with the problem of finding a replacement radio operator which wasn't going to be easy at this time of year. Then he was reminded that in actual fact it was two operators he needed as the evening-shift post had not been filled while the change of ownership was going through.

'You don't want to consider doing the job yourself? The day shift at any rate,' Harrie suggested to Chas a while later when he had gone into her office to inform her of Ralph's desire to leave as soon as possible.

He looked horrified at the thought. 'I don't have to, do I?'

Harrie laughed. 'Chas, you're the boss. You can do whatever you like.'

He looked relieved. 'I like being out on the road. I wouldn't be any good at radio operating.'

'Well, you seem to do all right when you take your share of the evening cover,' she said encouragingly. She wasn't overdoing her praise. All the drivers who had volunteered their services had done their best to log everything down clearly and concisely, but her expert eye could tell that Chas had been extra-meticulous. She knew it wasn't just because he was aware that very shortly this would be his business; it reflected the sort of person he was, one who wanted to do the best job he could whatever he tackled.

Chas, not one to heap praise on himself, felt he had muddled through all right, but then the evenings weren't quite as hectic as during the day with so many drivers to organise. 'I think it's best I stick to what I know and let someone more experienced take care of that.' He paused thoughtfully for a moment. 'I found out about the vacancy for a driver through overhearing talk in the pub. I wasn't eavesdropping,' he added hurriedly, 'I wouldn't want you to think that. But maybe if we tell the lads to spread word we're looking for staff when they are out and about, someone might come forward.'

'I think that's a great idea,' Harrie agreed. 'It'll save money on advertising in the *Mercury*, but that's something we'll have to consider eventually if nothing comes up by word of mouth. Thankfully Ralph has said he will stay on until we do get someone and I'm sure everyone who volunteered to cover the evening shift will continue to do so until we get someone else. They're grateful for the extra money they're earning, especially at this time of year.'

'I'm lucky I've inherited a good bunch of people,' Chas said.

But Harrie had her suspicions about that. Because of little snippets of conversation she had overheard in the drivers' rest room when she had been making drinks, and also the way a couple of drivers clammed up whenever she was within earshot of them, she believed not all the drivers were as conscientious as Chas trusted them to be. It hurt her to think that because of his kindly, trusting nature they were able to pull the wool over his eyes. But then, Chas was far from stupid and she knew he would wise up eventually and deal with the situation in the best way he could. From what she had deduced Jack had been a fair boss but not quite as thoughtful towards his staff as she knew Chas was going to prove. In truth, she felt it was they who were the lucky ones in having him as their boss now. None of them had any notion yet that he was planning to review their working hours and see if he could up their hourly rate a little, as soon as he had a clearer idea how the business was doing under his ownership.

She knew he was worried about making a success of this venture and that this worry wasn't for himself but the prospect of letting his workers down, maybe even having to lay some of them off should business slacken for any reason. She was very aware from doing the books that the couple of months after Christmas was the firm's leanest time as people watched their money after the festive season. She wasn't sure if Chas was aware of that fact due to his lack of experience and didn't want to bring it to his attention now for fear of spoiling Christmas for him.

He was badly in need of at least one day's rest. He looked tired, a man who obviously had much on his mind. She was desperate to put her arms around him and help allay his fears that he hadn't taken on more than he could handle. As matters stood, though, that gesture would be far too intimate between employer and member of staff. Hopefully, though, her desire for a closer relationship between them would come to fruition sooner rather than later and then she wouldn't have to hold back from showing affection towards him. She did wish he would hurry up now as her yearning to be close to him was causing her sleepless nights.

She suddenly thought it extremely unfair that the accepted code of conduct meant that a woman had to wait for a man to ask her out unless she wanted to be branded forward. Why was it that most things in life were undertaken on men's terms? It really was an anachronism. It was about time that code of conduct was changed and favoured women a little more. This was the Swinging Sixties after all. Not that Harrie was free and easy herself but women nowadays had the contraceptive pill available to them so they could indulge in sexual encounters without fear of pregnancy. Institutions that had been closed to them previously were now welcoming women through their doors.

They were even being considered for the police force, an institution that had until recently been completely dominated by men. Other trades too, albeit slowly, were starting to include women in their ranks.

Her mind started to drift. Christmas was such a good time for making headway with someone you cared for. All that goodwill towards your fellow man, kissing under the mistletoe . . . She couldn't wait to feel Chas's lips on hers. She knew instinctively that his kisses would be gentle but passionate. In her mind's eye she pictured herself enveloped in his manly arms, crushed to his chest. Before she could stop herself she had let out a loud sigh.

'Are you all right, Harrie?'

She mentally shook herself, seeing Chas looking at her with obvious concern. Harrie was horrified to realise what she had done without realising it. How could she explain herself without embarrassing them both?

'I'm . . . er . . . er . . .' she said the first thing that entered her head '. . . suffering from indigestion. It's Dad's cooking. I don't know where he's getting his ideas for meals from but they leave much to be desired. I don't like to say anything, he's trying so hard and I wouldn't want to put a dampener on what he's trying to do.' What she had said was absolutely true if not strictly an account of the reason for her sighing.

Chas could appreciate what she was saying as his mother's cooking was similarly erratic. He found it a strange coincidence they each had a parent whose cooking skills left much to be desired.

Suddenly Harrie thought of a way she could prod

Chas into asking her out and get the ball rolling between them without appearing unduly forward. She could have kicked herself for not having thought of it before.

'Chas, you haven't toasted the success of the business yet. Be a shame not to.'

He looked at her aghast. 'Oh, no, I haven't, have I? With everything else on my mind I never gave it a thought. I can't imagine what the lads must be thinking of me. I expect they've been waiting for some sort of knees up. I'll see about taking them for a drink after work tonight. Christmas Eve they'll be wanting to get home to their families, won't they, so tonight's the best bet. I could get some bottles of beer for the lads on the night shift to take home with them. That should please everyone, shouldn't it?' He would have liked nothing better than to ask Harrie to join them, then worried she might feel insulted about being asked to join a bunch of men for a pint in the local. But might she not be equally insulted if he didn't ask her? What a dilemma. He decided to let her say for herself whether she wanted to join them or not.

It was me on my own I wanted you to take out, not the rest of them, Harrie wanted to shout at him. She didn't, though, begrudge the rest of the staff having a celebration drink with their new boss. She waited breathlessly for Chas to ask her to join them. When he didn't a terrible disappointment struck her. But she supposed he was thinking that everyone but her would be male, and when a gang of males had a drink in them they got rowdy and weren't exactly careful what came out of their mouths. Chas was being protective of her, that was all. She wanted to hug him for his thoughtfulness. Once he'd treated the men she was sure it would be her turn.

The next morning at just after ten Chas was about to leave on a job when a man came in. He looked clean-shaven and well-presented. Ralph was busy on the telephone so Chas went over to take his booking.

'Can I help you?' he asked politely. He thought this man looked vaguely familiar but couldn't remember ever meeting him before.

'Could I see the boss?' the man asked.

'I'll see if he's...' Chas stopped himself, feeling stupid. He was the boss now, wasn't he? 'That's me. What can I do for you?'

'My name's Stanley Slater and I'm after a job. Anything will do. I've plenty of experience as a taxi driver. Was one for years with a firm in Coalville. I can give you their number so you can check me out, if you like. I had to move to Leicester so my wife could be near her family as her mother's not well. I've been round all the other firms and they have nothing. I've tried getting work in a factory but the pay's terrible unless you've certain skills which I've not. I've put my name down for the Corporation buses and the Midland Red but they've stopped taking on until well after the Christmas period. I'm really desperate, Mr Tyme. So desperate I'd take anything you had to offer. I'm really hoping you've got something?'

The man's plight touched Chas deeply. He rubbed his hand across the back of his neck thoughtfully. 'Well, my licences are all covered, I'm afraid, and I can't see anything coming up in the near future for a driver as

I've no reason to believe any of my men are thinking of moving on.' Then a picture of this man's family swam before him. Chas could just see Stanley Slater returning home and his wife's disappointed expression when he informed her he hadn't found work. He saw them sitting around an empty grate on Christmas Day, table bare, no presents in the children's stockings. Chas could not send this desperate man away, not when he was able to help. He just hoped that as a driver the man wouldn't be insulted by what he was about to offer. 'If it's of any interest to you, I do happen to have a radio-operator's job going.'

Stanley Slater's face was a delight to behold. 'Oh, Mr Tyme, you have and you'll consider me? Oh, you don't know what this means to me. Radio operating is what I'd really like, absolutely it is. I'm experienced at it too. I covered the radio on loads of occasions when the firm I worked for were desperate. I was good at it. In fact, I'd sooner have that job, Mr Tyme.'

'You would? Well, that suits me just fine.' This man turning up out of the blue was really the answer to Chas's problem of finding a suitable replacement for Ralph. He seemed genuine enough. Articulate. Well-presented. Chas couldn't believe his luck. 'All right, you can start tomorrow, eight o'clock sharp. We'll sort out pay and conditions then, but don't worry, I pay a fair rate for a job well done. And . . . er . . . I suspect you're strapped for cash so I'll advance you some of your wages to tide you over Christmas.'

At his offer a look crossed Stanley Slater's face that Chas couldn't quite fathom. It was as if an offer to help this man provide Christmas for his family was the last thing he'd expected of Chas. Then he thought he must have been mistaken and it was just the shock of landing himself work that was written on Slater's face.

By now Stanley was holding out his hand to Chas. He accepted it and they shook to seal their deal.

Chas watched the other man leave. It felt so rewarding to be able to help someone out at this time of year. Slater could return home with good news. His family's Christmas was going to be far happier than it had promised to be earlier today.

Just as Harrie was leaving that night, Darren popped his head round her office door, waving a sprig of mistletoe at her. 'Me and you under this tonight, georgeous. Good of the boss, isn't it, taking us all out for a drink?'

Continuing her task of tidying her desk Harrie said, 'I'm sure you won't have any trouble finding someone to share your mistletoe with, Darren, but it won't be me. I'm not going. Mr Tyme is taking you men out to celebrate his acquisition of the business.'

His face fell in disappointment. 'I see. Oh, well, shame to waste this,' he said, a lustful expression on his face as he advanced on her. Before she could stop him he had grabbed her in his arms and puckered up his lips.

She struggled to evade them. 'Darren, control yourself!' she commanded, turning her face away so his lips missed hers.

Just then Chas walked in dressed for the off. Witnessing Harrie in the arms of Darren froze him rigid. Seeing another man embracing her in such an intimate way tore the very soul out of him. The man holding Harrie should be him. Darren had no right even to lay a finger on her. He fought a strong desire to grab the driver by the scruff of his neck and throw him out bodily, warning him severely that should he ever touch Harrie again Chas wouldn't be responsible for his actions. He knew then that he loved this woman, loved her with all his being, so much so he would lie down and die for her. Before he could check himself he'd thundered, 'Darren, shouldn't you be off home to get ready for tonight?'

Not having realised his boss had entered the office, Darren sprang away from Harrie. 'Just getting a Christmas kiss from our luscious Harrie, boss. No harm in that, is there?' It was then he noticed the murderous expression on Chas's face. The driver flashed a glance at Harrie, noticing the look of mortification on hers that Chas had caught her in such a compromising situation, and the truth dawned on him. Something was going on between Harrie and Chas. In fact, he'd go so far as to say they were in love with each other. But Darren knew better than to voice his discovery. He reminded himself that Chas was no longer just another of his colleagues to rib but his boss, in a position to fire him should he speak or act out of turn. But no wonder Harrie had spurned him! Chas was hardly the better-looking man by any stretch of the imagination but he certainly had far more than Darren could offer her. He would never have put her in the gold-digger category, had nursed high hopes of himself and the very fanciable Harrie getting together, but it was crystal clear to Darren he was wasting his time.

'I'll be off then. Good night, Harrie. See yer later, boss.'

With that Darren walked out.

Chas was staring awkwardly at Harrie. Realising the depth of his feelings for her had shocked him to the core, but those feelings were one-sided, hers for him no more than the friendship of an employee for her employer. He had no right whatsoever to interfere in her private life, should never have displayed such anger towards Darren. He vehemently hoped that Harrie had been too preoccupied at the time to have noticed his rage, Darren too. In future, unless he wanted to lose her friendship and risk her leaving his employment, he must never display his emotions in such a way again.

'I'm off then, Harrie,' Chas said briskly. 'Don't want to be late for meeting the lads tonight. See you tomorrow. Good night.'

In fact, Harrie had missed nothing. Chas's jealousy upon catching her in a compromising position with Darren had been very obvious to her. He had displayed all the emotion of a man in love, she had no doubt of it. So why didn't he ask her out? What on earth was he waiting for?

CHAPTER TWENTY-SIX

Harrie stole a glance at her father, her brow furrowed. Percy's newfound zest for life seemed to have dissipated today for some reason. There was a distracted air about him. She couldn't pinpoint why. He had seemed overjoyed with the presents she had bought him: cardigan and slippers, socks, and a box of his favourite chocolate-covered Brazil nuts. He'd devoured his dinner with relish, enthusiastically complimenting her on her efforts, and he'd enjoyed himself carrying out his usual Christmas Day ritual of popping in to see several neighbours, wishing them good cheer and readily accepting the tot of whisky they pressed on him in return.

Now he was relaxing comfortably in his armchair, eyes fixed on the television screen, seemingly engrossed in the Queen's speech. But, knowing him as well as she did, Harrie knew his mind wasn't fully on it. Why was he so preoccupied? Her father had no work problems to worry him. The allotment was resting over winter so he hadn't any concerns for failed crops. He was on friendly terms with all the neighbours he associated with so no disputes there that she was aware of could be concerning him. Then it struck her. Of course.

For some reason this year he must be missing her mother more than usual. It was six years since her death and Harrie was missing her too, but it had to be worse for her father as they had been partners, and very happy ones at that. Her heart went out to him. He must be so lonely. How she wished he could meet someone special to be a companion to him during his last remaining years. That wasn't likely, though, as he hardly went out socialising, saying he was too old for all that sort of thing now and happy as he was. But Harrie had a feeling that today he wasn't entirely happy though she didn't quite know what to do about it apart from making sure he was comfortable and well cared for.

'Can I get you anything else, Dad?'

He blew out his cheeks and loudly exhaled. 'Me darling, if I have anything else just now I'll burst,' he said, patting his stomach. 'You made a grand job of the dinner.'

'You helped too so I can't take all the praise. Er . . . Dad, just where did you come across that recipe for the stuffing for the chicken?'

'Well . . . er . . . a friend gave it to me. They said they were good at cooking, you see, and when I said I was teaching meself they offered to give me some of their recipes. Only I'm realising now, after following some of them, that they're not as good a cook as they think they are. I'd never hurt them by telling them, though. I might suggest instead they could try some of yours.'

She was honoured her father thought some of her recipes worth passing on, but then they had been her mother's originally. 'Who is this friend, Dad?' Harrie asked, interested.

'Oh, just someone I know,' Percy said dismissively. 'You usually pop round to see Marion after dinner on Christmas Day, don't you?'

Yes, she did, so the best friends could exchange presents and give their best wishes to each other. But this year because of Percy's show of melancholy she wasn't comfortable about leaving her father on his own, even for an hour. 'Well, I might give it a miss this year. See Marion tomorrow instead.'

'Why?'

'Because I prefer to stop here with you, Dad.'

He peered closely at his daughter. Harrie seemed like her usual cheery self, had done her utmost to make this day as special as she could for them both, but he knew her very well and there was something on her mind that was bothering her, although she was doing her best to hide it from him. He wondered what it was. She couldn't possibly be regretting her decision to break things off with Jeremy, could she? Percy set that notion aside. She had been emphatic that he was not the right man for her and had given him no reason since the break up to think she had changed her mind. So what then? Couldn't be her new job as she was really enthusiastic about how much she loved working there, really felt she was contributing to the firm. She had loved her job at the solicitor's but didn't derive from it quite the same satisfaction she did from running the office for Tyme's taxi firm. Had she met a new man and didn't know how to tell him? No, that couldn't be it. Harrie would have told him if she'd started seeing someone new, she always had done in the past.

Then he realised what the matter was. Not that she

didn't usually miss her mother, but today of all days she was missing her more than she normally did and wasn't voicing her emotions for fear of upsetting him. That had to be it. What a dear thoughtful daughter he had.

He eyed her tenderly. 'Don't you think you've spent enough time with this old fuddy-duddy today, me darlin'? You get yerself off out and be in company of yer own age for a while, it'll do you good. Marion will be looking forward to seeing you. I can have a snooze while you're gone and look forward to our supper later on.'

Marion was delighted to see her and welcomed her in with a big hug.

'Merry Christmas, Harrie. Where's me present then?' she demanded impatiently.

Marion was thrilled with the latest Walker Brothers LP, delighted that Harrie had remembered her strong hint that that was what she wanted, Harrie equally as delighted with the latest Jimi Hendrix LP Marion had bought for her.

They sat down at the kitchen table with a pot of tea and plate of mince pies, though neither could face eating again after just having dinner.

'Allen's snoring his head off in the armchair so we won't be disturbed for a bit and we can have a good catch up,' Marion said. 'Being married does have its drawbacks, yer know, Harrie. We've just had a massive dinner at his mam's, and we've a massive tea at my mam's to look forward to in . . .' she lifted her eyes and glanced at the kitchen wall clock '. . . a couple of hours. Oh, bloody hell, I hope I've managed to make room by then. I shall be glad when tomorrow comes so I can give me stomach a rest.' She paused long enough to pour out cups of tea and pass Harrie's to her. Sipping on her own, she looked keenly over the rim at Harrie. 'Right, let's cut the chat and get to the nitty-gritty. What's the latest on you and Chas?'

Harrie gave a despondent sigh. 'There is no latest, Marion. He's still not asked me out and I can't understand it. Nothing's changed, in fact, since the last time I saw you. Oh, except for something that happened in the office a couple of nights ago.' She told Marion about Chas catching Darren trying to kiss her under the mistletoe and the look on his face when he'd reprimanded the driver.

'Yes, he certainly didn't like catching you in another man's arms, did he?' said Marion, pulling a knowing face. 'Definitely jealous. The man's in love with you, isn't he?'

'I have no doubt he is,' Harrie replied with conviction. 'I've never been so sure of anything in all my life. So why hasn't he asked me out yet, Marion?'

She stared at Harrie thoughtfully for a moment before she said, 'It's just a thought, but I wonder if he's afraid you're going to reject him if he does and that's what's holding him back? Yes, that could be the reason, yer know. He might not be quite sure you like him enough to go out with him, and you did say you'd got a good friendship developing between you. Well, he could be worried that by asking you out and being turned down he could ruin that friendship. Then things would be very awkward between you, especially as you work together.'

Harrie gave a despondent sigh. 'Well, I feel I've made very plain to him how I feel about him.'

'Not plain enough obviously.'

'Well, apart from telling him outright of my feelings, what do I do to let him know?'

Marion gave a disdainful tut. 'Men drive you mad, don't they? We women drop all the hints we can to them but nine times out of ten we end up having to spell it out to them letter by letter before they finally cotton on. Let me think . . .' She sipped tea for a moment as she did so. Then, after putting her cup down in its saucer, she folded her arms, leaned on the table and fixed Harrie with her eyes. 'Well, it seems to me you've two choices. Either you just have patience and wait for him to pluck up the courage, however long that takes, or else it's got to be you who asks him out.'

Harrie sighed loudly. 'I've already tried that, Marion. I suggested a drink to celebrate his taking over the business but Chas took it as meaning he should take all the staff out. He didn't even ask me to go along, though I do understand why. He was being thoughtful, not wanting me to be in a bunch of drunken men's company all night.'

'Yes, that was nice of him. Wish my Allen was as considerate. He actually thinks I do enjoy being in rowdy male company and encourages me to come along when he's meeting his mates down the pub.'

'Well, Allen's right, you do. When you've had a drink you're more raucous than the men are.'

'Yeah, well, maybe I am,' Marion grudgingly admitted, knowing she did make her presence known when she had a few drinks inside her, though she was never coarse or vulgar like some women were. Marion's eyes suddenly lit up as an idea struck her. 'I've got it! Get Chas to take you to the pictures. America put a man on the moon in July this year, surely you can do a simple thing like get him to take you to the flicks! There's loads of good films on just now. *Midnight Cowboy, Easy Rider, The Love Bug* . . . No, maybe not that film, it's funny but more for kids. Oh, I know! *Butch Cassidy and the Sundance Kid*.' Her eyes glazed over dreamily. 'Paul Newman makes my toes curl with them blue eyes of his, but then Robert Redford . . . boy, is he sexy! I know you'd like the film and I'm sure Chas would too, it's got plenty of action in it. Use all your womanly wiles to get him to take you, Harrie.'

She pursed her lips thoughtfully. 'Mmm, it's worth a try. Actually, I really do fancy seeing that film. I suggested it to Jeremy when I was with him but somehow we never did go.'

'Yes, well, we both know now that he wasn't the sort to sit in the back row sharing a bag of sweets and having a good giggle over a *Carry On* film. You're well out of that, Harrie, as you well know. Anyway, you could sort of bring up the subject casually with Chas, let him know you really want to see the film but have no one to go with. He can't not take a hint like that, surely. And he can't suggest taking the whole firm to the pictures either. If he does then you're flogging a dead horse, Harrie.'

She knew she wasn't. Marion's suggestion was a good one. She'd give it a try at the first opportunity.

She hadn't been able to get Chas out of her mind all day. Whatever she'd been doing, a picture of him kept popping up in her mind's eye and she hadn't been able to stop her thoughts from dwelling on him, wondering what he was doing. Was he having a good Christmas Day? What presents had he been given? The fact was she'd have liked to have given one to him herself, something personal that he would treasure. If Chas had taken the plunge and asked her out before Christmas Day she could have had that pleasure. She wondered gloomily if this time next year she'd still desperately be waiting for him to do the deed. Now Marion had opened her eyes – and her friend was good at doing that – to one possibility why he was procrastinating. If Marion was right and he was not sure of Harrie's feelings for him, stalling because he feared she'd reject his advances, then he wasn't going to be left in any doubt for much longer. Chas and she were meant for each other, Harrie had absolutely no doubt about that, and all her instincts told her he felt the same. She just prayed she wasn't wrong or else she was about to make one hell of a fool of herself.

Meanwhile in the Tyme household Chas was feeling stuffed to bursting after his huge Christmas dinner. Having helped his mother clear away, he was relaxing in the armchair, feet stretched out on the hearth being warmed by a blazing fire, watching *The Perry Como Christmas Show* on the television. It wasn't his preferred viewing but his mother liked these variety shows, and if she was happy so was he.

Trouble was, he wasn't sure if his mother *was* entirely happy. Oh, not that she hadn't shown great delight with the presents he had given her: a new pink candlewick dressing gown with a pair of matching slippers, a Yardley Lily of the Valley soap and bath-cube gift set, and a pound box of Terry's All Gold chocolates. She had bustled cheerily around the kitchen preparing the dinner and enthusiastically welcomed in Freda for their ritual glass of sherry mid-morning, toasting each other's good health and exchanging token gifts. Freda was delighted with the soap set Chas had bought her, remembering her favourite fragrance was Lavender. It was just that, knowing his mother as well as he did, she seemed a little distracted today, as if part of her mind was elsewhere. He wondered if she was suffering from some ailment she wasn't telling him about because she didn't want to worry him. But then she didn't appear to be ill at all. The picture of health, in fact. She and Freda were on the best of terms as he'd witnessed this morning so no disputes there for her to be worrying over. Although, he did wonder what they had been whispering about when Iris had first greeted Freda at the door. He had witnessed Freda wagging a stern finger at his mother before they had both started giggling like naughty schoolgirls sharing a secret. When he had asked to be let in on the joke, they had stared at him like they had been caught doing something they shouldn't, before Iris had accused him of being nosey, and of being a bad host and not offering her a festive drink. After Freda had left, his mother's mood had returned and it wasn't until during the Queen's speech, when Her Majesty had told her subjects she hoped this day was uniting families across her domain, that he realised the truth behind his mother's preoccupation. For some reason this year she had been thinking of past Christmases when his father had been alive and of the happy times she had shared with him before his untimely death. Chas's heart went out to her. She obviously still missed him terribly, even after all these years. Iris had many friends as she was well liked and respected but she must be lonely for companionship of the male variety. It was such a pity she couldn't meet someone she got on well with, someone who liked her back and would share her remaining years. She wasn't exactly a regular participant at social events, much preferring her own fireside these days, but neither was she a hermit. Chas was hopeful that one day she'd meet someone who took her fancy while she was out and about.

But then his mother wasn't the only one whose mind wasn't entirely focused on what was going on around her. Try as he might Chas himself could not stop a vision of Harrie from continually coming to mind. It was only yesterday evening that he had wished her goodnight and a Happy Christmas but those intervening few hours seemed an age to him. He couldn't wait to witness her smile when he saw her again at work the day after Boxing Day. The rest of the workforce was in tomorrow as Christmas Day and New Year's Day were the only days of the year taxi firms did not provide their services to the public. Despite knowing he'd miss her Chas had generously given Harrie the extra day off as she had worked so hard since she'd joined the firm, been invaluable to him while the takeover was going through. She more than deserved a good break and any office matters could wait to be dealt with until she returned.

He was very aware that he was heading for a painful time if he continued to allow himself to harbour secret desires for a woman who would never be his, but try as he might to stem his feelings, he just couldn't. Stupid, he knew, but he felt Harrie was part of him, as if he'd only been half-functioning for all the years before they met, and her arrival in his life had made him whole. All he could do was try and prepare himself for the devastating hurt he knew was coming his way when she met the man she would marry, which was going to happen sooner or later considering the sort of woman she was. He just hoped that by that time he had managed to get his feelings for her into perspective, so he could wish her well and truly mean it.

He gave himself a mental shake as he realised his mother was speaking to him and looked up to see her holding out a plate of mince pies. 'Oh, no, thanks, Mam. After that wonderful dinner I doubt I'll eat for another week,' he said, patting his stomach. His mother really had excelled herself for once. The chicken hadn't been dry at all but maybe that was because he hadn't put it in the oven when she had asked him, hiding it in the pantry instead and waiting until an hour later which thankfully she hadn't noticed. But whatever had possessed her to substitute salted peanuts for walnuts in the new recipe for stuffing that she said she had taken down from a cookery programme on the television? Either she had misunderstood the ingredients when the television chef had been relaying them or she had decided that nuts were nuts and any would do, which seemed quite likely, knowing Iris. He'd had to force down the peculiar-tasting stuffing and pretend he was enjoying it, which in fact was far from true.

'Well, I'm glad you enjoyed it all,' Iris said proudly. 'I'll put these pies on the table and you can help yerself if yer change yer mind.' She settled herself down in the armchair opposite and looked at Chas. Her son didn't seem quite with it today, his mind was elsewhere and she worried that something was troubling him. 'What's on yer mind, son?' she asked.

'What made you ask that, Mam?'

'Oh, it was just that you seem a bit distant today and I wondered why?'

He would like nothing better than to discuss the truth, reveal to her that he'd been stupid enough to allow himself to fall in love with a woman he knew would never return his feelings, ask her advice on how to handle what he was going through. But he knew that to learn the truth would be so worrying for her, he couldn't bear to put her through that. This was something he had to deal with on his own.

'I'm fine, Mam, really,' Chas said lightly. 'Nothing is bothering me.'

He wasn't being truthful with her and Iris wondered why. She knew instinctively he was fighting some inner turmoil and wished he'd open up to her so she could help him deal with it. While he was growing up he had kept from her many painful incidents so as not to upset her. Those incidents had eventually come to light through neighbours' gossip but too late for Iris to do anything about them. Chas was an adult now, and though still gentle by nature would hardly stand by and do nothing when someone was causing him grief.

She knew he must still be grappling with his change in status from employee to owner of a business. That must be what was on his mind. She had no regrets about spurring him on to do what he had. Iris just wished he'd have a little more faith in himself, and hoped that would come in time when the facts and figures proved to him the business was thriving even more under his ownership than it had under Jack Black's.

'You told me you'd set a new bloke on as radio operator to replace Ralph Widcombe. You don't have any worries over him, do you?' Iris probed. 'He was rather a Godsend, turning up like that just when yer needed someone.'

Chas's mind flew back to two days ago when he had spoken privately to Ralph, asking his opinion of his replacement. The two men had sat side by side for an introductory day before Ralph left to resume his retirement.

'Well, if yer want me honest opinion then I have to say the man's claim to be experienced in this business is highly exaggerated,' Ralph had said candidly. 'Most taxi firms operate in more or less the same way, so after what you told me about him I was surprised I needed to go through everything with him from start to finish. I can't see how he can say he's experienced, meself. Having said that, he's keen, I'll say that for him, and he picked things up quick and asked me lots of questions about all the ins and outs which I did me best to answer. I'm sure he'll do fine, boss. He's competent enough now to manage by himself. Give him a few days at it and he'll be handling the radio as well as I do, with all my years of experience.'

Chas was appreciative of Ralph's honest opinion, if a bit concerned that he'd set a man on who maybe hadn't been entirely truthful with him about his knowhow. But then, it had been very apparent how desperate Stanley Slater was for work. If Chas had found himself in such circumstances, Christmas upon him, no money coming in and a wife and family to keep, then wouldn't he have done anything to secure himself a job, just like Stanley had?

Chas had been expecting Ralph to be quite emotional when it came time for them to part company but the old man seemed very relieved that his stint back at work was now at an end. He was, though, deeply touched by Chas's generous gift of twenty pounds extra in his final pay packet to pay for his wife and him taking a weekend together at the seaside.

Chas was aware that along with the extra he'd given Ralph as well as the ten-pound bonus he'd paid all the drivers, with the same for Harrie as he felt it was only fair to treat her equally, he was leaving himself just about able to pay the firm's bills, rent and incidentals, and cover his first loan instalment to the bank as well as seeing his mother right for housekeeping. He just prayed that takings kept up to the level they had been under Jack and did not dip for any reason or he'd find himself in financial trouble. Regardless he did not regret at all what he'd done to help make his staff's Christmas a better one.

'Yes, he was a real Godsend, Mam, and he's doing fine as far as I can tell. What's really surprised me is that he's offered to work evenings as well. I pointed out to him that it would mean doing a sixteen-hour shift, six days a week, but he said he needed the money and was more than happy to do it. I have to say it saves me finding someone else so I've agreed as long as he tells me straightaway if he's finding it too much.'

'Well, yer can't blame a man for taking on extra work to provide for his family. Then everything so far at work is fine, I'm glad to hear. So what is bothering yer, son? Summat is, I know. Don't forget yer can talk to me about anything and I'll do me best to help you in whatever way I can.'

His mother cared so much for him and wouldn't give up until she had wheedled it out of him, but he had no intention of telling her what was really on his mind. He needed to change the subject. 'Actually, I was trying to think of ways to drum up new business, Mam.' Despite his lack of business acumen, he was aware that to sit on his laurels and assume that Jack's clients would remain for the duration of his ownership was an attitude that courted disaster. He'd need to start thinking of the future now the firm was in his hands.

She eyed him, impressed. 'You'll come up with ways of bringing in new business, I've no doubt, and damned good ones, too. Ready for a piece of Christmas cake?'

He groaned. The cake did look good. She had peaked the icing, creating a snow scene with little plastic Christmas figures dotted here and there, and a thick red ribbon was tied around the side. Whether the mixture was made up of the usual Christmas cake ingredients or his mother had added extras remained to be seen.

CHAPTER TWENTY-SEVEN

Harrie's first opportunity to manoeuvre Chas into asking her out came after a frustrating morning back at work once Christmas was over. Her ears were pricked for the sound of his arrival on the premises, and she was having terrible difficulty concentrating on the pile of work she had to do. The constant stream of jobs coming in meant that Chas and the other drivers were kept busy out on the road, and while she knew she shouldn't be annoyed, she wished today could have been one of their slacker days instead of one of their busier, so that she could do what she had to do and, hopefully, have an evening with Chas to look forward to.

It was Wally Bender's voice that she heard first filtering through her open office door and her heart leaped as she realised who he was speaking to.

'Some morning that was, Boss. Non-stop for me, at any rate. I ain't had time to stop for a bite of lunch yet and it's after two.'

She heard Chas's reply. 'Take the opportunity now, Wally, and if anything comes in I'll take it on.'

'Yer a decent boss, Chas, I'll give yer that. I don't mean to speak ill of the dead, but Jack Black wouldn't have been so considerate. I'll just take long enough to eat me sandwiches then I'll report back for duty.'

The telephone started ringing and Harrie heard Stanley answer it. She pretended to be immersed in her work but secretly willed Chas to come into her office. Her wish was cruelly dashed when she heard Stanley say, 'Boss, that was Fred Owens calling from a telephone box. He's had a slight accident that has knocked his radio out and he needs someone to go and give him a push to get the car started.'

A while later, Chas surveyed the scene before him in dismay. Fred's slight accident had been an under-statement. The front of his car was embedded in a low, front-garden wall and, apart from the obvious dents, Chas would only know the full extent of the damage once the car had been towed into the garage. It seemed that no other vehicle had been involved and he wondered how this could have happened on such a quiet road. Chas's first concern, though, was for Fred's well-being. 'Any harm to you, Fred?' he asked the middle-aged, wiry man, whose sparse head of greying hair and lived-in face, that other drivers likened to a pickled walnut, had earned him the nickname Nutty.

'No, Boss, well, just a bruise to me head where I hit the windscreen when I came to a halt. Oh, and me neck hurts a bit,' he said rubbing it.

'Well, maybe I ought to take you down to the hospital and get you checked out.'

'No, I'm fine, Boss, honest. A couple of Aspro will sort me out.'

'If you're sure. How did this happen, Fred?'

The man looked awkwardly at him. 'Well, er . . . it

were like this, Boss. I'd picked up a woman at a house up the top end of Narborough Road as Stan had radioed through to me. Posh house 'un all, and I was thinking to meself that anyone living there was bound to tip well. But when she came out she was . . . well, she weren't as well dressed as I thought she'd be. I realise now just what she was and why she was in a house like that. Anyway, she asked me to take her to a street up the Clarendon Park area. She insisted on sitting up front next to me, as she liked to chat, she said. Well, she rattled on about n'ote in particular and, to be honest, I wasn't really listening. Then suddenly she asks if I'd like a special sort of payment for the fare instead of the usual kind. Before I knew it she had her hand on me . . . me . . . well, me credentials and . . . well, yer know . . . I was so shocked I lost control of the car and you can see for yourself what happened, Boss. The woman scarpered before I could stop her so she can't have been hurt.' His face then puckered into a frown. 'Eh, listen, Boss, this mustn't get back to me wife. She's a jealous woman is my Edna and there's no telling what she'd do if she found out just who that woman was. Murder, believe me.'

If the situation hadn't been so serious and poten- tially life threatening to Fred, Chas would have laughed out loud at the comical vision in his mind. He wondered what the insurance company would make of this tale when Chas put in the claim. 'We'll keep this to ourselves, Fred, you have my word. As far as I'm concerned you swerved to avoid a dog.'

'Ah, thanks, Boss,' he said gratefully. His face then screwed up worriedly. 'This means I'm gonna be off the road while the car is repaired. I ain't gonna have no wage coming in. Oh, bloody hell and just after all the expense of Christmas.'

Fred wasn't the only one who would lose out because the car was off the road. Chas's own predicament, though, was overridden by Fred's worry about not being able to pay his bills. 'Well, let's hope the garage can do the repairs as quickly as possible once the insurance company give us the go ahead and, in the meantime, you can use my car so you won't lose out money-wise.'

Fred looked at him gob-smacked. 'You really are a gent, Boss. God, we're lucky it was you who took over and not some money-grabbing so-and-so who doesn't care a jot for the staff.'

Satisfied that Fred was fit enough to drive, Chas sent him back to the firm's premises in his own car for a much-needed cup of tea. He stayed with the damaged vehicle to see it safely stowed on the back of the garage tow truck, knowing they'd accommodate a lift for him. Fred was to ask Harrie to organise it all as soon as he arrived back. He also had the foresight to put a note through the door of the house whose wall had been crushed, apologising for what had happened and promising to repair it. As he had sat waiting for the tow truck to arrive a policeman had approached him wanting to know what had gone on. Thankfully, he had accepted Chas's version of events, particularly as no one had been injured, and he went on his way.

As a result, Chas did not return to the office until well after Harrie had left for the night. She had stayed much later than normal, but had become fearful of arousing suspicions amongst the remaining workers as to why she was hanging around for the boss to come back.

Her wish to talk to him privately, though, was granted just after she arrived for work the next morning. She had just begun to update the account books when Chas tapped on the door and walked in.

'Sorry to disturb you, Harrie, but I wanted to thank you for organising the tow truck yesterday. Fred's car's in the garage and they'll telephone you with an estimate of the repair costs as soon as they can, so you can fill in the insurance claim forms and we can get their go ahead so it's not off the road longer than necessary.'

Harrie had already overheard two drivers discussing Chas's generosity in handing over the use of his car to Fred while his was off the road. From what was said it was obvious that they hadn't noticed her arrival.

'Nutty was lucky not to write himself off let alone the car,' said Dan Peters, a thick-set man in his forties, who'd been a taxi driver for several other firms before landing a job at Black's five years ago. 'I'd have run the bleddy dog over instead of smashing into a wall.'

'Oh, come on. Things like that happen so quickly yer can't predict what yer'd do in the circumstances,' replied Sonny James. 'I nearly had a cyclist off his bike the other day when he careered at break-neck speed around a corner and it was only his good fortune that I happened to be looking his way and saw him in time.'

Dan Peters rubbed his hands, a look of glee in his

eyes. 'Yeah, well, one thing this has proved to me is that our new boss is a soft touch. He's gotta be ain't he to give over his own car to a driver who's caused damage to his own. Jack Black weren't a bad boss in the big scheme of things, but I doubt he'd have done that. I've learned a few ways to make extra money during my time, but Jack knew all the scams better than we did, and we knew better than to risk doing 'em for fear of the sack. Well, our Mr Tyme ain't bin in this game long enough to know what ter look for, has he?'

As Harrie listened to the two men, an anger burned inside her. Before she could stop herself, she spun round to face the two men and called over, 'It would be a mistake to interpret Mr Tyme's generosity as him being soft. Mr Tyme might not have had years in this business but his eye is on the ball, let me tell you, and if he got a whiff that any of you drivers was up to anything you'd be out. I count myself extremely lucky that I have a kind and considerate boss like Mr Tyme who puts his employees' welfare before his own. You should count yourself fortunate too instead of planning ways to fleece him to line your own pockets.'

Dan Peters' face fell. 'Now, look here, Harrie, lovey, I didn't know you was there and I was only having a bit of fun with Sonny. Wasn't I, Sonny? I didn't mean none of what I said, honest, Harrie. I don't really know any scams, I was just trying to impress Sonny. That right, Sonny?'

She knew Dan was lying but hoped her words had put a stop to anything untoward. Chas was so trusting she doubted it'd crossed his mind that any of his staff would do anything to harm him. He had enough on his plate worrying about keeping the business afloat without her heaping this on him. She decided to keep her eyes peeled, on his behalf. She would try and work out herself what scams could be worked and do her best to prevent them.

She fixed her eyes on Dan. ''Course I know you were having a joke. I know you're not a stupid man, Dan, who'd risk his job for a few extra shillings.'

Now, as she looked at Chas, her stomach was turning somersaults. Should anyone or anything interrupt them this time she would personally lock and bolt her office door until she had fulfilled her quest. She smiled warmly at him. 'I'll do my best to chivvy the insurance company along once I get the repair figures from the garage. I understand you've handed over your own car to Fred while his is in for repair, so what will you do in the meantime?'

'Oh, I'll find something to keep me busy. You did a grand job of cleaning up the drivers' rest room, so I thought I'd give it a fresh coat of paint to make it look better. Plus the sink in the toilet is hanging off the wall . . . Oh, well, I could keep myself occupied for at least a month with the repair jobs that the landlord should take care of but never seems to get around to doing. I thought I could also give Terry a hand with some of the minor repairs that have piled up while he's been off looking after his sick gran. Also, I need to give a lot of thought to ways of bringing in new trade. If I do come up with any ideas, do you mind if I run them past you?'

'Oh, I'd be delighted to give you my opinion, Chas.

Now I've the books up to date and am managing to keep them that way, I've more or less got the office work under control, so I'll put my thinking cap on too and see if I can come up with anything.'

Harrie knew he was about to make his excuses and leave. Now was the time to put her plan into operation. She suddenly felt very nervous that she'd mistaken his feelings for her and was about to make the biggest fool of herself. But then she told herself there was no way she had mistaken the look in his eyes when he had held her in his arms in the chip shop and neither was she mistaken over his jealousy when he had caught Darren trying to kiss her under the mistletoe.

Pulling a copy of the previous Friday's *Leicester Mercury* towards her, she said, 'Oh, there's an article in last night's paper that I thought would be of interest to you and, not knowing if you read the *Mercury*, I brought it in for you to have a look at.' Not giving him time to respond, she opened the newspaper out at a page she had already marked as the one she wanted to open it at and then swung the paper around so he could look down at it.

He scanned the page quizzically. 'I can't see any articles on this page, it's the cinema page you've shown me.'

She planted a puzzled look on her face and spun the newspaper back around to face her. 'Oh, so it is. Oh, damn, I've picked up the wrong newspaper as this is last Friday's and the article was in last night's.' She then exclaimed, 'Oh, just look what's showing at the Fosse Picture House: *Butch Cassidy and the Sundance*

Kid. I so badly want to see that film. It's supposed to be really good.' She looked forlorn. 'But I've no one to go with me. All my friends are either courting or married.' She then looked as though a thought had just struck her. 'Have you seen the film yourself yet, Chas?'

He wondered why she wanted to know. 'Er . . . no, no, I haven't.'

Oh, she was so relieved to hear that. 'Oh, then you wouldn't take me, would you?' She then added meaningfully, 'I really would like to go with you, Chas.' There. She couldn't have been plainer, could she? Even the dimmest of men would know from what she had said and how she had said it she was asking for a date with him because she liked him, liked him very much.

Chas was thinking that Harrie really must be desperate to see the film if she was asking him to accompany her. She had no idea what she was asking of him though. Apart from the fact he'd never been to the pictures with a woman before and this would be a whole new experience for him, knowing how he felt about her, it was going to be so difficult for him to act the perfect escort, when all the time he would be fighting to stop himself from scooping her up in his arms, to proclaim his love for her, then to kiss her so passionately she would need to beg him to stop. He wished she wouldn't look at him the way she was doing. If he didn't know better, he would swear she liked him far more than just the work friends that they were.

'Well, I could take you, I suppose.'

'Tonight?' she said eagerly.

Goodness she was keen to see the film. He'd nothing else planned to do that evening 'Well, yes, I could.'

'I'll meet you then at seven thirty, outside the Fosse Picture House.' She noticed the anxiety on his face. 'Have I said something wrong, Chas?'

'Oh, no, no, it's just that it's very dark now at that time of night and . . . well, if you're entrusting me to make sure you get there and back safely wouldn't it be better if I called for you at your house?' As soon as he suggested it, he realised Harrie maybe didn't want to be seen walking along with him. 'But, if you prefer we meet outside the pictures, then that's fine with me.'

Not many men these days would put themselves out to offer what he had. More and more she was being convinced that this man was the man for her. 'I'd like very much if you'd call for me. Shall we say seven?'

Her request for him to call for her shocked him as he hadn't expected her to want that. 'Oh, right, seven it is then? Er . . . just what was the article about that you thought I'd be interested in?

'Oh, er . . . do you know, I can't remember now. I'll rack my brains and, if I remember, I'll tell you later.'

As Chas walked out of Harrie's office he kept reminding himself that this definitely wasn't a date. He was just accompanying her to the pictures because she had no one else to go with.

As he left the office, Harrie wanted to clap her hands and jump up and down with glee. She had done it. She'd finally got Chas to take her out. Their relationship had begun and she had never felt so excited at the prospect of a date with a man in all her life.

As Chas left the office he noticed a smartly dressed man waiting at the counter. He looked irritated.

'Can I help you, sir?' Chas asked him as he arrived at the counter.

'Finally, I get service?' the man snapped. 'I've been waiting at least two minutes. I want to speak to Harriet Harris. Hurry up, man, I haven't got all day.'

Chas did not like this man's attitude and wondered what he wanted with Harrie. He was a very good-looking man and appeared well set up to Chas. 'Who shall I say wants her?' he asked politely.

'Just fetch her, man, I've already told you I haven't got all day.'

Chas popped his head round the office door. 'There's a man at the counter wanting to see you, Harrie.'

She looked askance. 'Who, Chas?'

'He wouldn't say.'

As soon as Harrie saw who had summoned her, her heart plummeted. She had thought she had seen the last of Jeremy. Before she could ask him what he wanted with her, he requested she accompany him outside.

In front of the premises of Black's now he looked at her mystified. 'I couldn't believe it when I saw the article in the newspaper about this place and saw you in the picture amongst the staff. Harriet, what on earth are you playing at, reducing yourself to working in a place like this? Anyway, that's by the by. I've given you ample time to come to your senses and enough is enough. I realise that you must be feeling rather stupid for acting so childishly, therefore, against my better nature, I've come to see you so we can get this over with and get on with our wedding preparations. Mother has persuaded the Belmont to rearrange our wedding date . . .'

Harrie was staring at him dumbstruck. She couldn't believe that he had not taken on board at all what she had said to him but had continued to believe that during their separation she was still suffering from pre-wedding nerves. 'Jeremy,' she interjected. 'I meant what I said to you. Our relationship is over. I know I'm not right for you and you're not right for me. I don't like hurting you more than I have already but I can't marry you just to make you happy. There is someone else for you, Jeremy, who will make you the sort of wife you want, but that woman is not me. Now, please, leave me alone, Jeremy, and I mean that.'

Before he could stop her, she had spun on her heels and disappeared back inside the firm's premises.

During her absence, Chas had been hovering inside the office, wondering who this man was and why he'd taken Harrie outside to speak to her. As soon as she came back in he went across to her and asked, 'Everything all right, Harrie?' He could tell by her face all was not well.

She looked upset and Chas wasn't fooled by the smile she planted on her face when she responded, 'Oh, yes, thanks, Chas, everything is fine. That was just a friend who I'd lost touch with who'd seen the article in the paper about Black's and saw me in the photograph and came to ask how I was. I'd better get on with my work.'

He stared after her as she returned to her office. He had a feeling that the man was more than just a friend. Several possibilities sprang to mind as to who he was, some of them evoking jealousy within Chas. Regardless, though, one thing did strike Chas: Harrie was acquainted with men like him and possibly others of his ilk and, in that respect, the likes of himself stood no chance whatsoever with her in a romantic way and he was stupid to even dream otherwise.

CHAPTER TWENTY-EIGHT

'You're home sharpish tonight, son,' Iris said to Chas as he walked through the back door just after six that evening. 'Good job yer dinner's all ready. It's shepherd's pie. Go and sit yerself down and I'll bring it through. Work's not slack, is it? Hope that's not why yer home earlier than normal.'

'No, Mam, I'm glad to say it's not. That article in the *Mercury* that was printed the day before Christmas Eve has brought more customers in. Harrie said it would do and she was right. I'm just hoping they're all pleased with our services and will continue to use us when they need a taxi.'

'You're pleased with what Harrie's doing in the office, ain't yer, son?'

'If you want the truth, Mam, I couldn't manage without her.' He happened to catch the look on her face as he lifted his fork to his mouth and said, 'We just work well together so don't get any ideas, Mam. And don't say you weren't because I know you were.'

'Well, I really took to her when we met. She's such a nice girl and you're such a nice man and . . .'

He eyed her sharply. 'Mam, I know you really want

nothing more than to see me happily settled but stop getting your hopes up that it could be with Harrie because I'm not her sort and I'm certainly not stupid enough to think I am,' he said, remembering the calibre of the man who had visited Harrie in the office earlier. He frowned quizzically then. 'Er . . . just what have you done to this shepherd's pie?'

Iris looked worried. 'Why, what's wrong with it?'

'Nothing, it's delicious.'

'So yer saying my other ones weren't, even though you said at the time they were?'

'Er . . . well, they weren't as tasty as this, Mam,' he said diplomatically. 'Have you done something different to it?'

'I've used a new recipe I was given by a friend.'

'Oh, Freda?'

'Er . . . yes, that's right. Well, if it's so delicious I'd better stick to using that one in future instead of me own. And here was me thinking mine was best.'

'Oh, but Mam, I didn't mean . . .'

'It's all right, son,' Iris cut in. 'Sometimes even I have to admit that someone else's recipe is better. I've some more pie left in the dish, if you want it?'

'Well, I'll pass if you don't mind, Mam. I'm going out tonight and I'm in a bit of a rush to get ready.'

Her eyes lit up. 'You're going out? Good, I'm glad to hear it. Who with?' she asked keenly.

She was clearly hoping he was going to tell her he'd a date with a woman. Well, he was going out with a woman but it was definitely not a date and in order not to get his mother's hopes up he felt it would be better to tell her he was going by himself.

'I'm going to the pictures on my own, Mam, because there's a film I want to see.'

'Oh? Well, you might meet someone nice there that's gone on their own too, mightn't you? Eh, and if you do and she shows interest in you, don't you dare think you're not good enough and miss an opportunity.'

Chas pushed away his empty plate. 'You don't mind if I don't give you a hand with the dishes tonight?'

'No, 'course I don't, son. It's not often you decide to go out for some enjoyment even if it is on yer own. About time you did. I know there's a nice woman out there waiting for you to come along, son, but you won't meet her unless you go out and find her, will yer?'

Percy was pleased to hear his daughter was going out for an evening's entertainment with a friend who he assumed to be female. She had hardly been out socially since her break up with Jeremy and he felt it was about time she did. She wouldn't find the man of her dreams sitting in a chair by the fireside.

Harrie had decided to let him assume that it was a female friend she was going out with as she had already made one mistake in going out with a boss and didn't want her father worrying she might be making another with Chas until their relationship was on a firm footing. Then she could bring Chas round to meet him and Percy could see for himself that this time she definitely was not making a mistake.

Before she left, though, Percy made her promise to be very careful when she walked home that night as he'd read a report in the *Mercury* that evening about two women on separate occasions having their handbag snatched from their hand by an assailant who then jumped into a car which sped away. Harrie promised him she would be very diligent and felt a little guilty for not putting his mind at rest by saying her escort was a man who definitely would not let any harm come to her while she was with him.

Immediately Chas knocked on the door of the address Harrie had given him it was pulled open and Harrie stood beaming at him.

The sight of her dressed very becomingly in an ankle-length peasant-style dress in soft pastel colours, over which she was wearing a long black maxi coat with fake fur around its collar, almost knocked him for six. She'd looped her hair up at the back and tendrils framed her lovely face. He couldn't believe that this beautiful woman had requested his company when she could have any man she wanted. Even more surprising, she was looking very pleased to see him.

Harrie was thinking how handsome Chas looked in his black polo-necked jumper, over which he wore a smart navy blue blazer. He wore blue casual trousers which she was pleased to note were not the flared type that were all the rage just now as they were more for stick-thin dandy-type men which Chas certainly wasn't and would not suit his more well-proportioned manly shape. How proud she was going to feel, walking down the road with him by her side.

'Right on time just like I knew you'd be,' Harrie said to him. She turned her head and called back down the passageway, 'I'm off now, Dad, won't be too late.

Then, joining Chas on the pavement, she closed the door and again surprised him by hooking her arm through his. Smiling up at him, she said, 'Shall we go then?'

At just after eleven o'clock that night they stood facing each other once more on the doorstep. Harrie had had a wonderful evening, just as she'd known she would. She had learned much more about Chas as they chatted easily on the way to and from the picture house. She had heard about his great love of music, the huge collection of records he regularly played, and was thrilled to find out that some of his preferred artists were hers as well. She hadn't met a man before who admitted he enjoyed reading, and after his enthusiastic accounts of several of his favourite novels she wanted to read them too.

He had insisted on paying for the tickets so she had offered to treat them both to an assortment of sweets. Despite the film's being riveting, usually the type she would have lost herself in, Harrie had remained very conscious of the man sitting next to her. Throughout the performance she willed him to hold her hand or put his arm around her and was disappointed that he never attempted any intimate gesture towards her whatsoever. But maybe he didn't want to push his attentions on her too quickly. After all it was their first date. Maybe on their next one he would be bolder and show more affection towards her.

Chas had had a wonderful evening too. Harrie was very good company, very easy to talk to, and seemed so interested in his likes and dislikes. It surprised him to learn they had quite a lot in common in their musical tastes and both liked reading, and although she'd never been to speedway before she said she certainly would after Chas had made it sound so exciting. It had been difficult for him as they sat side by side to keep his hands clasped firmly in his lap except to accept a sweet from the bag when she regularly offered it to him. He was desperate to hold her hand, or even better put his arm around her and pull her close to him. But once again he was reminded of the man who'd visited Harrie and that he wasn't of her calibre.

'I've had a wonderful evening, Chas, and thank you so much for taking me,' Harrie said, back on her own doorstep.

'I've enjoyed it too. It was a pleasure.'

Harrie fully expected him at least to kiss her cheek or preferably her lips before suggesting another date soon. What he did next stunned her speechless.

He held out his hand to her, which she automatically shook. 'Well you're home safely so good night then, Harrie. I'll see you at work tomorrow.'

She watched in astonishment as he marched off down the road.

She felt sick with disappointment. How could she have been so badly mistaken about Chas's feelings for her? Obviously after his actions of tonight she most definitely had been. She hadn't held back over allowing him to see how she felt about him and had given him more than ample opportunity to take their relationship further should he want to. Whatever type of woman Chas preferred, Harrie was without doubt not his sort. A great sense of loss filled her. She felt bereft. She had no choice but to accept Chas's rejection of her, see that she was no more to him than an employee he got on well with. But whoever she met in the future and settled for, she would always know deep down that Chas Tyme was the man she should really be with.

Marion was stunned when next evening Harrie told her what had transpired.

'I can't believe it, Harrie, I really can't. He showed no signs of fancying you at all?'

Miserably she shook her head. 'Treated me like a friend, that's it.'

Marion affectionately patted her hand. 'Well, yer can't win 'em all, gel. Plenty more fish in the sea. You won't be on yer own for long,' she said by way of cheering Harrie up. It was obvious she was heartbroken that she hadn't after all got the man she'd been sure she was meant to spend the rest of her life with. 'How did you manage today at work, Harrie? It must have been awful for you?'

'Oh, Marion, it was, I can't tell you how awful. As Chas is not out on the road at the moment until a damaged car gets fixed, but on the premises all the time. As soon as I arrived I saw him looking over the log book to see what jobs had been done the previous night. I wanted to leap into his arms and demand to know what was so wrong with me that he didn't feel attracted to me. How I managed it I'll never know but I just acted towards him like any employee would to her boss and he was the same to me as he always is. But what I can't understand, Marion, is why his eyes looked the way they did those times if he hasn't got strong feelings for me?'

She shrugged. 'Search me, Harrie. Maybe you wanted to see what you thought you did.'

'Imagined it, you mean? Yes, seems I did, doesn't it?'

'Look, Harrie, wouldn't it be best if you got yourself another job? That way you'd get over the man quicker.'

That thought had crossed her mind as she lay tossing and turning the night before, so devastated by her disappointment she couldn't sleep. 'It would be the sensible thing to do but I love my job, Marion. I feel as if I'm more than earning my money, and Chas does pay me a decent wage for what I do. And I want to do what I can to help him make a success of his business. He really needs someone with my office experience to run that side for him, he's not up to doing it himself yet. It'd be childish of me to give up a job I really enjoy just because the boss doesn't like me the way I like him, don't you think? Best thing I can do is throw myself into my work and accept that you're right, Marion, you can't win them all. As much as I would so love to have won this one.'

But when it came to Chas, Harrie knew this would be a lot easier said than done.

CHAPTER TWENTY-NINE

True to her word Harrie threw herself into her work, doing her best to submerge her feelings for Chas and hide them away. It was far from easy. She would be glad when Fred's car was ready to be picked up from the garage and Chas got his own back, then he wouldn't be physically on the premises so often and she not constantly coming into contact with him.

If her father had noticed she was not quite her usual self then he had elected not to say anything to her, for which she was grateful. She had noticed, though, that the extra spark Percy had had about him recently, and which he seemed to have lost on Christmas Day, was back again. What was causing this newfound energy and joy within him she had no idea.

On New Year's Eve Marion had begged Harrie to join her and Allen, his mates and the rest of the revellers, at the Blackbird pub which had laid on entertainment: a group who specialised in playing chart-topping music and a comedian renowned for having his audience rolling in the aisles. Harrie knew it wasn't going to do her any good sitting at home moping and wondering how Chas was celebrating the start of the seventies so she agreed she'd join them.

To Harrie's surprise she did manage to enjoy herself, though she constantly found herself scouring the crowds, hoping for a glimpse of Chas. She knew this pub to be the one he used when he did venture out for a drink and was disappointed when he didn't appear. She told herself off for that. It wasn't as if she could rush up to him, throw her arms around him and kiss him for New Year. Now she knew he didn't care for her in the way she wanted him to care, she was best off putting all romantic thoughts of him from her mind. She was glad when the evening's frivolities were over and she could make her way home with the rest of the crowd, most of them extremely inebriated.

On the first Friday morning in January Harrie was tackling the wages when she realised she hadn't got the details of Stanley Slater's tax code or National Insurance number so she could add him to the payroll. Unable to proceed further without them, she went out to see him.

Stanley was on the telephone taking details of a job from a customer. As she stood waiting to speak to him slightly behind him, she noted he was jotting the details down on a piece of paper which struck her as odd. All jobs were usually first logged in the book lying on the desk in front of him. Having concluded the call, he put the telephone back into the receiver and the piece of paper in his jacket pocket.

He must have sensed her presence then as he jumped and turned his head to look at her. 'Oh, blimey, you gave me a scare, Harrie. I didn't know you were there.'

'I'm sorry, Stanley, I didn't mean to but you were taking down details of a job and I didn't want to disturb you. I need to speak to you but I don't mind waiting until you've radioed that job through to a driver.'

'Eh? Oh, it's not for today but tomorrow. I can do it later. What did you want to speak to me about?'

'Just to ask if you'd brought your P45 in yet like I asked you to do when you first started. I need your details to make up your wages.'

'Ah, well, I haven't got a P45. You see, my last firm insisted on all their staff being self-employed. It saved them the bother of paying tax and National Insurance for their employees as we were responsible for paying our own. It'd be easier for you if I continued as self-employed. Save me a lot of bother, too, getting my status changed at the tax office and having to wait weeks for my code to come through while paying full-rate tax on every penny I earn. I know you get the over-paid tax back eventually but in the meantime I'd have to pay out and I can't afford to, what with my wife not being able to work while she looks after her sick mother. So it's all right with you then, is it, Harrie, if I stay self-employed?'

It would make her life easier, not having to calculate and deduct his dues each week, plus Chas would be saving his employer's contribution. 'If it's all right with you then it's fine with me,' she confirmed.

Stanley seemed very relieved by this.

'Are you still happy to be working all hours, Stanley, now you've been doing them for a week?' she asked. 'A sixteen-hour shift, six days a week, is a tall order for anyone.'

'Oh, I'm more than happy,' he insisted. 'I need the money.'

'Well, remember what the boss said to you when you first asked to be allowed to do it. If you do find it getting too much for you, then don't hesitate to say so and we'll get another operator in to cover the evening shift.'

As Harrie made her way back to her office to resume her own work she thought this man must be desperate indeed for money, to be prepared to work such long hours to earn it. Still, she did admire Stanley for what he was prepared to do in order to provide for his family.

A little later that morning she was making herself a drink in the rest room. While the kettle was boiling she took a look at a copy of last night's *Mercury* which someone had left on the table. The front-page article immediately caught her eye and she was reminded of something her father had warned her about on the night of her ill-fated outing with Chas. BAG-SNATCHING EPIDEMIC, screamed the headline. It seemed from the article that six women now had had their handbag stolen as they walked home alone late at night, all it seemed by a person dressed from head to toe in black, head covered by a balaclava, who immediately after snatching the handbags from the surprised victims ran off down the road to where a parked car was waiting. As soon as the thief was safely inside it sped off. As yet all the victims had been far too stunned by the speed of events to have had time to take down the vehicle's number for the police to trace.

She realised someone had entered the rest room and lifted her head to see who it was. It was Chas. Despite fighting hard to play down her feelings for him, the sight of Chas still managed to set her heart racing and her thoughts pondering miserably what might have been.

Harrie planted a smile on her face. 'Hello,' she said brightly. 'Get the sink in the toilets fixed?'

'Finally,' Chas replied. 'It's now firmly back against the wall and I hope it stays that way.' He took a glance around. 'I can make a start on freshening the walls in here now I've done all the smaller jobs.'

'You're enjoying yourself doing all the odd jobs around here, aren't you?'

'I have to say I am, though I'd prefer to be out on the road earning the firm some money. Any news yet from the garage?'

'Oh, yes, they called a few minutes ago. As soon as I'd made my drink I was coming to tell you about it. Fred's car will be ready on Monday. The insurance company has pushed through the claim and will settle the bill as soon as the garage sends it to them.'

'Oh, that is good news,' said Chas, relieved. 'Thanks, Harrie. I know it's through your hard work this has all gone through so quickly. Well, seems my stint of odd jobbing is at an end. I'll have to come in on Sundays to paint this room up. One Sunday might even do it if I start early and don't finish until it's done.'

'Maybe one of the drivers will offer to help you?'

'Oh, I wouldn't expect them to give up their day off after working hard all week.'

No thought for himself after all the hard work he'd put in all week, she noticed. 'Coffee?' she asked, moving across to the table as the kettle started singing to announce it had boiled.

'Tea if you don't mind, please, Harrie.'

She didn't mind. Despite her devastation on learning he didn't return her feelings she'd still do anything for Chas, would make him a hundred cups if that's what he wanted.

Chas's eyes fell on the article Harrie had been reading. 'Oh, dear, those poor women must have been terrified, having their handbags stolen from them as they walked home. A couple of them were carrying as much as twenty pounds on them at the time. God, that's a lot of money to have stolen! I hope they find the culprits soon before many more women are attacked like that. Oh, thank you, Harrie,' he said as he accepted his mug of tea gratefully from her. He couldn't bear the thought of anything like this happening to her and, before he could check himself, asked, 'You do take care when you're out late at night, don't you, Harrie? Especially with people like this on the loose at the moment.'

She had learned to her cost not to misconstrue his show of concern for anything more than it was, a boss worried for the welfare of a female member of staff. 'I'm not often out in the evening on my own these days so don't worry about me, Chas. But all the same, thank you for doing so.' She hardly went out in the evenings nowadays, except to call on Marion, not feeling in the mood for socialising at the moment while still struggling to accept the fact that the man she knew to be perfect for her would never be hers.

From what she said Chas interpreted this as meaning that when Harrie did go out she had the protection of a male companion. A boyfriend most likely. He had warned himself not to expect that a woman like her would be unattached for long. Nevertheless, he hadn't envisaged the news hurting as much as it actually did. He felt like his guts had been ripped open. 'Well, that's good to hear,' he said matter-of-factly. 'I'll leave you to it then.'

Harrie watched him go, feeling utterly dejected.

As the weeks passed, try as she might, Harrie's feelings for Chas did not diminish in the slightest. Well, she would just have to learn to live with them. She was in love with him and true love did not die. She dreaded the day she would learn that he had found a woman who suited him, vehemently hoping she could sound convincing when she wished them both well for the future.

CHAPTER THIRTY

One morning at the start of April found Harrie staring into space, her brow creased into a worried frown. She had just finished updating the end-of-month figures in the accounts book. Since the beginning of January Tyme's had taken approximately fifty pounds a week less than Jack Black had done. Harrie could not understand this state of affairs. It seemed to her they should have been making more profit than Jack had due to several changes in the way the firm operated that had been made over the last three months, as well as the article in the *Mercury* that had been published the night before Christmas Eve and had brought many new customers walking through the door.

Besides all that, Harrie had also put her brain into overdrive and come up with several new ideas to improve profits. Chas had been delighted to hear them and she in turn delighted he'd put them into operation.

On Chas's behalf she had negotiated with the local garage a penny a gallon discount, which over a year added up to quite a saving on their fuel costs.

The customer waiting area had also been made a much more pleasant environment than it had been in

Jack's day in the hope that people would choose to spend extra on a taxi rather than catch a bus. The walls in the waiting section at the front of the premises were now painted an inviting bright yellow and potted plants stood on the window ledge. More comfortable chairs had been provided to sit on, along with an assortment of magazines to read. Facilities to make a cup of tea or coffee while people waited had also been made available and were proving very popular.

To improve the overall image of the firm to the customer, all drivers had been issued with smart new navy blue jackets and matching trousers so none had any excuse for presenting a scruffy appearance as they had previously tended to do.

Harrie had also worked out a possible way the drivers could be lining their own pockets. Fares were calculated by drivers on arrival at the destination. They would log the actual mileage then double it to include the return to base. The total mileage was then multiplied by the mileage rate which at the moment was a shilling a mile. Unless a very astute customer logged the vehicle's mileage when they first got into the taxi and again when they arrived at journey's end, which she doubted many would consider doing, Harrie could see that drivers could very easily charge customers for an extra half-mile or mile on that trip, the passenger being none the wiser. The driver could pocket the extra shilling or so charged, along with his tip, and over a week, even only carrying out this scam on half the allotted jobs, a substantial sum could be made by defrauding the customer and Chas who bore the cost of the vehicle and petrol.

Fair-minded Chas hated the thought that any of his drivers could be up to no good, preferring to give them the benefit of the doubt, but Harrie had finally convinced him that this was a business he was running. If a way to undermine that business presented itself then he had no choice but to take action to protect his own livelihood.

The solution to this particular situation was simple, Harrie explained. Each driver would be issued with two separate, carbon-copy, numbered receipt books. At the end of each job a receipt must be written out for the cost of the journey, the top copy being given to the customer in exchange for their fare, the carbon to remain in the receipt book. Each night that day's receipt book would be handed in to Harrie by the driver along with their takings. The next day they would take the other receipt book out with them. Harrie would keep a separate account book for each driver. In that book she would log the details on each receipt, checking the numbers ran consecutively and none were missing or she'd want to know why, and also make sure the takings handed in tallied with the total mileage recorded. Due consideration was given to wrong change being given due to human error but a rule was put in place that for any shortages over ten shillings a week, the driver would have to be responsible. In order to ensure drivers furnished every customer with a receipt, they were informed that regular random checks with customers would be done by the management, not only to verify that they had been given a receipt but also to clarify that the service they had received from Tyme's Taxis had been first class.

Harrie pointed out to Chas that implementing this system would prove one way or another if any of their drivers were up to something. If they were, and were not happy that their way of making extra for themselves had been ended, they were quite at liberty to terminate their employment with Tyme's Taxis and take up a position elsewhere.

After the system was introduced in the middle of February, Chas was delighted that none of his drivers resigned their post. After pondering this, Harrie herself could only conclude that the firm must have lost more customers than it had gained through the article in the *Mercury* and the changes they had since implemented. The reason why customers had possibly chosen to leave them and use other cab firms remained a mystery to her. Surely Tyme's offered the best service in the area?

Harrie knew Chas was desperately worried about the fall in profits, feeling that under his ownership the company was failing despite Harrie's own assurances to him that he was proving to be a more than exemplary boss, well respected by his staff. She knew it also grieved him that if this trend continued it could reach a stage where he'd have to start laying off men instead of upping their hourly rate to compensate for the shorter shifts he had planned to introduce: three shifts of eight hours each instead of the two at twelve they worked now, affording the drivers more leisure time to spend with their families. Chas also had the added burden of repaying the bank loan. If he failed to do that each week the bank would have no choice but to foreclose on him.

Harrie strongly felt that it would be a crying shame if the business did go under. Chas had done everything in his power during the short time he'd owned it to make it a success. Tyme's Taxis was a slicker operation by far than ever Jack had run. Whatever lay behind their loss of custom, Harrie knew it was nothing to do with Chas's management of the business. All she could hope, like him, was that those lost customers would come back and the profits rise again.

Harrie rubbed her hands wearily over her face and gave a deep sigh. Having now updated the accounts book to show the figures for March, she knew she was going to be adding to Chas's worries. She closed the books and placed them on the shelf above her desk, ready to show Chas when he came in as he knew she was closing the balance on the month of March figures that morning. She felt a great need for a cup of coffee before she began her next task. She was just coming out of her room when her attention was drawn to the outer office. She saw two rain-coated men entering. Glancing across the room to see that Stanley was busy on the telephone, she went over to deal with them herself.

She was stunned when the older of the two men introduced them.

'We're police officers,' he said. 'I'm Detective Wright and this is Detective Newman. We'd like to speak privately to the owner.'

'He's not in,' she told them. 'We've a contract with Marconi to supply taxis as and when required. Mr Tyme personally has taken one of the staff down to Marconi's office in Basildon. I don't know when he'll get back.

My name is Harriet Harris and I'm in charge of the office. Can I help you or would you like me to ask Mr Tyme to contact you when he comes back?'

'Well, perhaps you can give us the information we're after. Could we go somewhere private?'

Inside her office with the door closed, Harriet looked at them expectantly.

'I don't know if you're aware of the spate of bag-snatching that's been going on recently?' Detective Wright began.

'Yes, I am. I read an update about it in the paper last week. It said twelve women had now had their handbags stolen from them while walking home late at night.'

'Yes, that's right, only now it's fourteen. Two more were attacked last night.'

Harrie gasped. 'Oh, that's terrible!' Then she looked at the detectives quizzically. 'But what has this to do with us?'

'Well, that's what we're here to clarify – whether it is or it isn't anything to do with Tyme's Taxis. The last victim has been able to give us more details than any of the others up to now. She gathered her wits about her quicker than the rest and gave chase to her attacker. She witnessed him getting into a car which then sped away but she noticed that the car in question had writing on the side of it, like private-hire taxis have, although she couldn't make out the name, unfortun-ately.

'If this information is correct then it appears for that particular incident at any rate, a taxi driver and his accomplice are the likely culprits. We're visiting all the

382

taxi firms in Leicester to find out what vehicles they had operating that night, and what areas they were in at the time of the crime so we can rule that firm out. The incident we're checking out took place last night at around ten-forty-five on Latimer Street soon after the victim had left the Crow's Nest public house. You can give us information about your drivers' whereabouts at that time, I trust?'

'Yes. We have three drivers covering the night shift which runs from six in the evening until six in the morning. The jobs they do are all logged in the night-shift job book. But, officer, none of our three drivers would be involved in anything like this, I know they wouldn't,' she said with conviction. 'They're all decent family men. In fact, Sam Little is a grandfather.'

'Could we have a look at the book, Miss Harris?'

'Oh, yes, of course. I'll fetch it.'

Back in her office Harrie opened the book at the relevant page and scanned down it. The drivers had been kept busy that night but at the time in question it seemed all three men were in the office, waiting for work to come in, so they could vouch for each other. She relayed this information to the policemen then clarified her statement by showing them the log book.

Satisfied no driver from Tyme's Taxis could be involved in the incident the previous night, they thanked her and she politely accompanied them to the counter to see them off the premises.

No sooner had they walked out than a smartly dressed, matronly woman walked in. Harrie flashed a glance across at Stanley to see him once again busy on the telephone. Turning back to face the woman, she smiled welcomingly and asked if she could help her.

'Yes, you can, dear,' the woman said in a baritone voice. 'I tried to telephone earlier but the line was continually busy. As I had to come this way, I decided to call in personally. I've arranged for a taxi for Thursday at nine o'clock to take me to see my daughter in Coventry. Unfortunately my arrangements have been changed and I won't now be going tomorrow but on Friday instead. My name is Mrs Jackson, 33 Anstey Lane. If you could make new arrangements for me at the same pick-up time, I'd be grateful.'

When Harrie arrived at Stanley's desk he was busy radioing through a job to a driver and it seemed he was having difficulty as the driver's radio kept cutting out. Sooner than wait for Stanley to finish, which could take a while she guessed from what she was over-hearing, Harrie thought she'd help him out by doing it herself.

Sliding the book from in front of him, she turned the page to show the next day's jobs. Details of several pre-booked fares had been written down and she quickly scanned them, searching for Mrs Jackson's booking. It wasn't there. Thinking she had missed it, she scanned the page again. No, she hadn't been wrong, there was no booking for a Mrs Jackson, nor even a name that could be mistaken for Jackson or an address anywhere near the one she had given to Harrie.

Stanley had by now managed to get the information he needed to the driver and had snapped off the radio-mic.

'A radio-operator's job isn't an easy one, is it, when

you get situations like that, Stanley?' Harrie said to him. 'I enjoyed my stint before you started with us but I don't think I'd like to do it all the hours you do, six days a week.'

'Well, when you need the money you can't turn down the chance to earn it, can you?'

'No, you can't,' she agreed, knowing that if she was in Stanley's situation she would be doing just what he was to look after her family. 'Anyway, can you help me? A Mrs Jackson has just called in to the office. You were busy at the time so I dealt with her for you. She says she pre-booked a taxi for tomorrow to go to Coventry but her arrangements have changed and now she wants to rearrange her booking for Friday. I can't find an entry for her at all in the book tomorrow, though.'

He stared blankly at her. 'Oh, I see. Yes, well . . . she couldn't have booked it with us then.'

'She seemed so positive she had a taxi booked with us for Thursday.'

'Well, maybe she came in here thinking we were another taxi firm? The one she had in fact booked with. It's an easy mistake to make.'

'But we're the only firm in this area. Oh, we could be trying to work out what's happened for the rest of the day but as far as Mrs Jackson is concerned she's cancelled her taxi for tomorrow and rearranged it for Friday so we have no alternative but to send her one. I suppose it's only fair I should call all the other taxi firms to find out which one she booked it through and then cancel it . . . this is naughty, I know, but I won't tell them we're now providing her taxi and hopefully

Mrs Jackson will be so pleased with our services she'll use us for all her future business.'

'Well, as I know you're busy, Harrie, give me Mrs Jackson's details and I'll log down the job and call round the other firms for you.'

'But you're busy too, Stanley. Have you had a break at all today? You know I've told you I'll cover the telephone and radio for you whenever you need relieving, if no one else is around to take over. You've only called on me a couple of times since you started here, Stanley, and that was just while you nipped out to spend a penny. Anyone would think you and the desk were part of each other.'

'Well, I may as well sit here and work than idle my time away reading a newspaper in the rest room.'

Harrie smiled at him. 'We were lucky to get you, Stanley. Not many men are as willing and conscientious in their job as you are.' She handed him the piece of paper on which she had taken down Mrs Jackson's details. 'I'll leave you to it then.'

Harrie was right, Chas was visibly distressed on learning that the profits were down for the third month in a row. This big, wonderful man she loved so much it physically hurt had looked so tired when he arrived in the office after his long journey to Basildon and back. Receiving this news on top of it seemed to drain the life from him. Harrie desperately wanted to give him a comforting hug but he had made his lack of feelings for her very plain on the night of their outing to the cinema and she felt he wouldn't welcome the gesture.

Rubbing one big hand wearily over his face, Chas gave a deep sigh and said, 'I'm going to end up bankrupt at this rate. I've tossed and turned for nights over this and decided that if the profits were down again at the end of March then I'd no alternative but to throw in the towel. I'm obviously not cut out to be the owner of a business.'

'Oh, but you are,' she insisted. 'You have got what it takes. You have.'

He forced a smile. 'I know you're trying to make me feel better, Harrie, and I appreciate your efforts but it's obvious by the fall in profits that I've not. I haven't got what the likes of Jack had to make my own business a success, it's as simple as that. If I put the firm up for sale now, hopefully someone will buy it who has the know-how to make a go of it. That way the men's jobs and yours will be saved and hopefully I'll get enough to pay off the bank loan. I might even be lucky enough to get a job from whoever buys it.'

'Oh, Chas, please can't I change your mind?' she begged. 'At least give it a little longer. I'm sure next month will see a rise in the profits. Look, I could be wrong about the reason for the fall being down to customers using another firm. It could be we're going through a longer post-Christmas lull than usual. Maybe other taxi firms too are going through it. I could try and find out.'

'Harrie, please, there's no point. Look, I might not have a business brain but I have enough sense to realise that if I give it another month and the profits take another fall then the firm will be worth even less. I'm not worried for myself, Harrie, it's the staff that concern me. I have to do my best for all. And there's also my mother to consider. If I'm back on a wage and still repaying what I owe the bank, I might not be able to give her all she needs for her housekeeping. It's not right that she be reduced to living on the breadline at her age, not if I can help it.'

Chas stood up. 'Thank you for staying behind to tell me the end-of-March figures. I know I don't need to ask you to keep my decision to sell to yourself, Harrie. I don't want the men worrying over possibly losing their jobs for as long as I can keep this from them. Well, I'd better get off home and find the right moment to break this news to my mother.'

Then a thought struck him. It was Wednesday so his mother would be having her usual snooze. In all these months he'd never got to the bottom of why exactly Wednesdays affected her in this way. He felt sure it was because on that day she went to town and tired herself out looking around the shops, and didn't want to come clean to him because she knew he wasn't happy about her going far on her own.

When he reached home and saw his mother, peacefully asleep in her chair, Chas couldn't bring himself to tell her the distressing news. He didn't want to worry her any sooner than necessary, and he also knew she was going to be very disappointed. He felt he had let down her faith in him and that was the hardest thing to bear.

The next day he informed Harrie that he'd an appointment the following Tuesday afternoon with a firm that handled the sale of businesses. He'd need the account books to take with him so they could give him an idea what they felt the company was worth. They would then find a buyer for him, and the quicker the better, so he could get this over and done with.

CHAPTER THIRTY-ONE

It was a very subdued Harrie who next Monday morning sat logging the details of the previous Friday's individual drivers' receipts in their separate log books and checking that their takings balanced with the total amounts written on the receipts. When she had finished, only three of the drivers had shortages in their money for that day and then only by a matter of pennies. Harrie got out her purse and made the balance up herself.

As she made to start on Saturday's receipt-logging, she remembered that tomorrow afternoon Chas had an appointment to begin proceedings to sell the firm and it reminded her of the day he went to the bank all smart in his suit to ask them for a loan to buy the business. He would be smart in his suit again tomorrow but how far removed the appointments were. How ironic it would be, she thought, if things should start picking up suddenly, those lost customers start using them again, and people like Mrs Jackson be so pleased with their services that they used Tyme's in future instead of whoever they had before.

Then a memory stirred. Mrs Jackson had been going to Coventry on Friday but Harrie couldn't remember a receipt made out for that fare in any of the drivers' receipt books when she had logged them all earlier. Had the driver who had done the job for Mrs Jackson forgotten for some reason to give her a receipt? Yet the takings had tallied with the amounts on the receipts apart from by a few coppers. Harrie gnawed her bottom lip anxiously, not at all liking what seemed to be glaringly obvious. Did this mean that one of the drivers was on the fiddle? Had Mrs Jackson not been given a receipt for her fare because the driver had pocketed the money and taken a chance that Mrs Jackson would not be one of the customers randomly checked by management? Harrie just couldn't believe that any of the drivers would do this to Chas, after he'd more than proved himself to them to be such a considerate boss, always putting his staff's welfare above his own.

Anger rose within her. Chas of all people didn't deserve this. She wouldn't let whoever this driver was get away with what he'd done. She would find out who it was then confront him and make him pay back the fare he'd pocketed. She'd speak to Chas about it as soon as she could and see what he wanted to do with the culprit. She felt, though, that he would have no choice but to sack whoever it was, as how could he continue working for them when they knew he was dishonest? What a foolish man to risk his job for the sake of a few pounds!

She'd find out who Stanley had allocated the job to via the job-logging book. He had just finished relaying details of a new job to a driver over the radio when Harrie went over.

'Can I just check with you which driver you allo

cated to Mrs Jackson's job on Friday, please, Stanley? If you remember, she's the lady who mistook us for another firm and you were left with all the rigmarole of calling round all the others to find out which one she'd really booked her taxi with.'

He looked blankly at her for a moment then said, 'Oh, yes, Mrs Jackson. Oh, er . . . but she telephoned in a while later to apologise as she realised she'd mixed us up with another firm, like we thought she had. Thankfully it was before I'd wasted my time calling round the others.'

'She did? Oh!' So Harrie was wrong and a driver hadn't fiddled the fare after all. Mrs Jackson's job had never taken place. She felt terrible for mentally accusing one of their men of doing something she now realised he hadn't.

'There isn't a problem, is there?' Stanley asked.

'Oh, no, no,' she said hurriedly. 'After logging the drivers' receipts for last Friday, I remembered Mrs Jackson and wondered why I hadn't come across a receipt in her name. Now I know why.'

Neither of them had noticed that a woman had come in and was standing at the counter until they heard her call, ''Scuse me, I'm sorry to interrupt, but can I get some service? I'm in a hurry.'

Stanley shot up out of his chair and hurried across to deal with her.

Harrie was halfway back to her office when the telephone started to ring. With Stanley already busy at the counter, she turned back to deal with the caller before they gave up and rang off.

'Good morning, Tyme's Taxis. How can I help you?'

A deep baritone voice boomed back at her. 'Mrs Jackson here. I left a scarf in the back of the taxi on Friday. I can manage without it so no point me making a special trip down to fetch it but if you have a driver passing my way sometime soon, I'd be obliged if you could drop it off to me.'

'Oh, er . . . Mrs Jackson, this is Tyme's Taxis you've called.'

'Yes, I'm well aware of that.'

'But you cancelled your taxi with us for Friday.'

'I most certainly did *not* cancel my taxi for Friday. If I did, why did one with your name on the side come and pick me up? It's you that's muddled, dear. Please have my scarf sent round for me as soon as you can, it was a gift from my late husband. Thank you.'

With that she rang off.

Harrie stared blankly at the receiver in her hand. So Stanley had lied to her about Mrs Jackson's cancellation. But why would he?

As he approached the desk to resume his seat after dealing with the woman at the counter's requirements, he noticed the confused expression on Harrie's face and asked her, 'Anything wrong?'

Something obviously was but she wasn't quite sure what. She needed to get back to her office and think about all this. One thing she mustn't do was alert him to the fact that she suspected he was up to something until she was sure one way or the other. 'Pardon? Oh, no, nothing at all, Stanley.'

Once seated back behind her desk, her head in her hands, Harrie's mind was racing. What reason could Stanley have for lying to her about Mrs Jackson's booking? Mrs Jackson was adamant that a Tyme's taxi had arrived to pick her up and take her to her destination and that she had left her scarf in the back of it. Why then hadn't Harrie come across a receipt for Friday with Mrs Jackson's name on it? She sat for a moment puzzling over this problem. Then a terrible thought struck her. Was it possible that Stanley and a driver were in league together and had split Mrs Jackson's fare between them? All the facts seemed to be pointing that way.

If she was right this was terrible. She couldn't believe it of him. Stanley seemed such a pleasant, trustworthy man. Chas had given him a job when he was desperate for work. Had advanced him money on his wages to tide him over Christmas. Allowed him to earn himself extra by agreeing to let him cover the evening shift as well as the days. Now she realised why he was so keen to do that, it was not just for the extra income. That way he could pick and choose all the plum fares to share with his accomplice, during the evening as well as during the day.

Then another memory stirred. A vision rose before her of witnessing Stanley writing details of a job he was taking over the telephone on a piece of paper instead of straight into the book. He'd put that piece of paper into his pocket and told her he was going to deal with it later. Oh, he was going to be dealing with it later all right – by handing those details to his partner-in-crime, whoever that was. But she had witnessed the incident weeks ago. Stanley and his accomplice had probably been operating this scam for a while. It could well be the reason for the fall in profits over the months since Christmas. There was still one question that bothered Harrie, though. How was the mileage on the firm's cars being falsified to cover these jobs? Maybe the culprits when brought to book would answer this question, Harrie couldn't fathom it.

She still couldn't work out which driver could possibly be in league with Stanley. They all appeared to be such decent men. But then, so did Stanley himself.

Her first instinct was to tackle him with her suspicions right now and see what he had to say in his own defence. But she knew that as owner of the business it was up to Chas to tackle him. This was going to devastate him, she just knew it was. But would her findings be enough to change his mind about selling the business? She supposed that depended on how much Stanley and his accomplice had been getting away with.

It was a nerve-racking time for Harrie, trying to carry on as normal in front of Stanley until Chas arrived back and she could divulge her grave suspicions.

Time ticked past and there was still no sign of him. She was desperate to get this matter resolved, very conscious that while Stanley was left at liberty behind the radio-operator's desk, under the impression he was getting away with things, he could be plotting another scam. But she had no alternative but to sit it out until Chas came in.

Harrie's leaving time came and went and still he hadn't returned. Tonight of all nights a job had kept him out late. The day-shift drivers had all signed out, the three night ones had taken over. It was after eight o'clock by now and she knew her father would be wondering where she was. Stanley too must be wondering why she was working so late.

She jumped as the man himself popped his head round her door. 'Oh, er . . . hello, Stanley. What can I do for you?'

'I just wondered if you'd like a cup of coffee as I'm about to make myself one? You don't usually work this late, Harrie. Well, you haven't since I've been working here.'

She hoped she sounded convincing when she told him, 'Oh, I'm just finishing off a job and thought I might as well stay until I'd done it. Give me a clear desk in the morning so to speak. I'd love a cup of coffee, thanks. Er . . . I noticed the boss's been out all day and hasn't come back yet?'

'Oh, yeah. I radioed him this morning to pick a man up and take him to the station to catch the train to London. Chas radioed me back a while later to say the chap had changed his mind about catching the train and wanted Chas to drive him instead. By my reckoning he should be back anytime now.' The telephone started ringing. 'Oh, better go. I'll bring that coffee through as soon as I get chance to make it.'

CHAPTER THIRTY-TWO

Chas finally arrived back at nine-thirty that night.
He was surprised to see the light still on in Harrie's
office and made his way straight in to ask what she
was still doing at work at that time of night.

As soon as he came into the room, she leaped up
from her desk, went over to the door and shut it behind
him, conscious that he was staring at her in bewilderment.

'Harrie, what's going on?'

'I need to talk to you, Chas, without Stanley over-
hearing us. I think you'd better sit down,' she advised
him.

Several minutes later he was staring at her, looking
astounded. 'I can't believe this ... You've got to be
wrong, Harrie.'

'I'm not, Chas. Mrs Jackson is adamant a Tyme's
taxi took her to Coventry on Friday. She said she left
her scarf in the back and wants us to have it taken
round to her. She was quite put out when I asked her
if she'd called the wrong firm, mistaken us for another.
She didn't come across to me as the type of woman
who'd easily make a mistake. Don't forget she called
into the office when she rearranged her taxi. That would

mean she'd mistaken us for another firm twice, and I find that hard to believe.'

'I'd better get Stanley in and find out what he's got to say about all this.'

The radio operator entered, smiling at them both. With his eyes on Chas, he said, 'Yes, Boss, what can I do for you?'

Chas invited him to sit down and began, 'Well, it's just that we have a mystery on our hands, Stanley, one we hope you can clear up for us. You see, a customer called Mrs Jackson is adamant that she left her scarf in the back of one of our taxis after it took her to Coventry on Friday, only there's no record of her having ordered a car in the book and neither is there a driver's receipt for such a trip. I'm not accusing you of anything, Stanley, I'd just like to clear the matter up, that's all.'

He gave a shrug. 'Well, it's as I told Harrie, Boss. Mrs Jackson cancelled her taxi so she couldn't have left her scarf behind in it because she never had one from us. She's got our firm muddled with another, that's what she's done.'

Chas flashed a look at Harrie as though to say, I have no alternative but to accept this man's version of events. It's Mrs Jackson's word against his that she actually had a taxi from Tyme's.

Stanley got up. 'Well, if that's all you wanted to see me about, I'd better get back to my post.'

Harrie watched him closely as he turned and made to walk out. She knew Mrs Jackson had been telling the truth and that she had had a taxi on Friday from Tyme's. Stanley was lying. But how could she prove it? Then an idea suddenly struck her.

'Stanley?' she called after him.

He stopped and turned back to face her. 'Yes, Harrie?'

'Would you mind turning out your pockets, please?'

Chas glared at her. 'Harrie! What on earth is possessing you to ask Stanley to do that? What's in his pockets is personal to him, surely?'

'I'm not so sure about that, Chas, and I need my suspicions confirmed. If Stanley has nothing to hide he will do as I ask.'

The man stared at them both frozen for what seemed like an age. Then his shoulders sagged and he blurted out, 'You know what's in my pockets, don't you, Harrie? It's details of jobs. You've sussed me, haven't you? But me and my brother were only getting back what was *ours*. As soon as we had all the money back that would have been it. We're not thieves.' He glared at Chas accusingly. 'It's *you* that's the thief, Mr Tyme, isn't it? It was you who took my dead father's case and then used what was inside it to start up your own business. Did you give a thought to the state you left my mother in, and me and my brother and our families? That money was to provide for us all. You go around pretending to everyone you're such a nice man and they have no idea what you're really like, have they? No idea at all.'

Chas was staring at him, astounded. 'You're Mr Graham's son? You think *I* took his briefcase? You're wrong, Stan— Mr Graham, you're so wrong. I didn't use your father's money to start this business. It was my own savings I used, along with a large loan from the bank. I've hocked myself up to the eyeballs, can easily prove everything I say. I have no idea who took your father's money, Mr Graham, but it wasn't me. I told the truth when the police interviewed me.'

Harrie, who couldn't believe what she was hearing, nevertheless shot to Chas's defence. 'I can confirm all he is telling you. You're badly mistaken, branding him a thief as you have.'

Graham stared at Chas, horrified. 'You didn't steal it then? Didn't use our money to buy this place?' He sank down on the chair in front of Harrie's desk, cradling his head in his hands. 'Oh, no, no. We were positive it had to be you after seeing the article about you buying this place in the *Mercury*. Oh, God, I . . . I don't know what to say. I'm so afraid we've made a terrible mistake. It's not you who's the thief, it's me and my brother, isn't it? Oh, dear God, dear God.'

Chas was looking confused. 'Would you care to tell me just what exactly has been going on here, Mr Graham?'

The other man raised his head and looked at him guiltily. 'Yes, you deserve to know what my brother and I have been doing and then I'll leave it to you to decide what to do next. But you have to believe me we thought we were justified in what we were doing. Thought we were taking back what was rightfully ours. Clasping his hands, he took a deep breath. 'My name is Gordon Graham – you've met my brother Geoffrey. You know how Dad died, and Geoffrey told you about the money in his briefcase. When the police had exhausted their investigations and couldn't find any trace of the case, they concluded that it must have been taken out of the back of your taxi by an opportunist thief at the hospital while you and the staff were concentrating on getting my father inside.

'As if it wasn't bad enough for all of us losing him, our future depended on what was in that case. The shop hadn't been doing well for a long time and so my brother and I persuaded Dad that he had no choice but to accept a cash offer for the business from a competitor.

'Mum and Dad were going to be selling the house they'd lived in all their married life and using that money to buy a bungalow on the coast, something they'd always wanted to do. With two thousand of the money from the sale of the business to help eke out their government pensions, Dad was giving me and my brother the other four thousand between us to put down as a deposit on a newsagency and work there to support both families.

'When the police told us three weeks after Dad's death that they'd drawn a blank on what had happened to the case, my brother and I had no choice but to give up our plan to buy a business and get ourselves whatever jobs we could, trying to help Mother out between us as well as looking after our own families. I found myself a job as an electrician in a factory and my brother worked as a machine operator. We just hoped that whoever had taken our money was proud of themselves for ruining the futures of those they'd stolen from. We felt it best to try and forget it and get on with making the best future we could for ourselves.

'Then the night before Christmas Eve I read the article in the paper about you buying this business. I went straight round to see my brother and showed it to him. It just seemed such a coincidence to us that one day you were a taxi driver and the next you'd bought this business. Well, we could only draw one conclusion – you must have done it with our money. We felt there was no point in going to the police as they'd already interviewed you and were happy with your statement. We also thought that if you were clever enough to convince the police it wasn't you who had taken our money, then you'd be clever enough to have a story ready as to how you got hold of the capital for the business.

'We were faced with two choices. Either we let you get away with what we thought you had done or else we tried to get what was ours back from you.

'We hadn't a clue how but felt if one of us could get a job with you and be on the inside, so to speak, that would be a good place to start. Neither of us is what you'd call criminally minded but we both felt that to achieve what we wanted, we had to start thinking that way. It was decided it would be me who tried to get work with you as you'd already met my brother when he came here to ask after the case. Our first hurdle, though, was for me to get a job with your firm

'I couldn't believe my luck when you believed my sob story and took me on starting immediately. I wa prepared to take anything just to get set on, and wher you offered me the radio-operator's job I just hope I could make a stab at it. I'd arranged with my brothe what to do if you wanted references. The number I' given was actually my brother's telephone number an he was all geared up to pretend he was my pas employer and give me a glowing reference. You di shock me, I have to say, when you offered to advance me some money on my wages to tide me over Christmas. I couldn't understand how a man who had done what you had could show such compassion . . . Then I thought it was just an act you were putting on, wanting to make everyone believe you were a kind man when in truth you were the opposite.

'When I told my brother what job I'd been given he was over the moon because he said that, unbeknown to you, you'd given me the best job you could have for us to stand a chance of getting back what was ours. Radio operators had control over what jobs were given to the drivers. If he became a Tyme's driver then as radio operator I could make sure all the good jobs went his way.'

Chas was looking puzzled. 'But I haven't taken on any new drivers since I bought the business, how could he have become one of Tyme's men?'

'It was unofficial. You didn't know my brother was working for you. We used our own car, had two magnetic signs made up that we stuck to the side-front doors each time the car was being used as a taxi. We took them off when it wasn't being used illicitly. When you issued the men with their new trousers and jackets for work, my brother bought himself a set too. The signs and working outfit were the only outlay involved for us. All we had to hope was that you didn't cotton on that some of the jobs coming in weren't being done by your official drivers. We did realise you could become concerned about any fall in your profits, but if so much as a whiff about that was heard in the office then I would made a quick exit.

'I was very relieved when you, Harrie, accepted my request to work as self-employed because it meant I didn't need to keep finding an excuse to fob you off for not giving you my P45. Well, I couldn't because you would have known then I wasn't Stanley Slater. The home address I gave you when I first started obviously isn't my real one.

'I was terrified that you'd suspected I was up to something when you saw me writing those job details down, Harrie. I was so relieved that you seemed to believe the excuse I gave you. I was managing on average to pass over to my brother jobs that brought us in about two hundred pounds a week. Out of that money, of course, he had to fund the petrol for all the jobs he did and pay maintenance for the car but we put the rest of it aside to accumulate. We wanted to keep things going until we'd made all of Dad's six thousand back, or as much as we could of it. We'd all moved in with my mother and tried as best we could to survive on my wages from here. It's been tight for us but it was worth it. It seemed the only chance we were going to get of regaining Dad's money and buying our own business. As time passed and no one here seemed to have any idea what was going on, I really thought we'd pull it off. Until today, that is. When I passed that original booking of Mrs Jackson's over to my brother I had no idea it would end up . . . well, proving to be the thing that would be our downfall.'

He gave a deep sigh. 'Well, now you have it, Chas You have to believe me that since we thought you'v stolen from us, we felt justified in our actions. It didn' seem like a crime to us. My brother will be besid himself when he learns all this. We will give you the money we've made back, every penny of it. You have my word on that, for what it's worth. Obviously what you decide to do with us is your decision.'

Harrie spoke up first. 'I don't know what to say about all this, I really don't. I feel I ought to ring the police and have you and your brother arrested, but then I also feel you were right to try and get back what was yours when you thought Chas had stolen it from you. Oh, what a mess.'

Chas slowly slid to his feet from where he'd been sitting on the edge of Harrie's desk. He walked across to the door and stood facing it for several long moments before turning back to look at Gordon. 'The money you and your brother made from me . . . I don't want it back.'

Gordon stared at him in utter shock. 'You don't? But I don't understand . . .'

Chas sighed. 'The case was stolen from my car and I have to take some responsibility for that fact. I want you to put what you've made towards doing what your father intended.'

The other man couldn't believe what he was hearing. 'You mean that?'

'Yes, I do.'

'Well, I . . . don't know what to say.'

'There's nothing to say.' Chas held out his hand to Gordon who slowly shook it. 'Goodbye, Mr Graham.' He held the door open for Gordon to leave.

Only Chas would have done what he just had, Harrie thought to herself. Chas Tyme was the most generous man she had ever come across or was ever likely to.

He was looking at her gratefully. 'Once again I have a lot to thank you for, Harrie. I don't know how I can ever express my feelings.'

In fact, he could think of one way last doubted she'd welcome it.

I know how I'd like you to thank me, Harrie thought. By grabbing me in your arms, kissing me passionately and telling me you love me. But you won't, Chas, will you, because you don't love me. She planted a smile on her face. 'There's no need for thanks, you pay me for what I do, Chas. I'm just glad we got to the bottom of this. I wonder who did take that case?' she mused.

'Well, like Gordon Graham said, I hope whoever did it is proud of themselves.'

'They probably are,' she said dryly. 'Proud they got away with it, I mean. And I hope that money brings them nothing but misery. But, Chas, you know what this means, don't you? Gordon said that he and his brother were making themselves about two hundred pounds a week. Your profits haven't been declining after all but going up – and by a lot. This changes everything, doesn't it?'

He smiled at her. 'Yes, it seems it does. I'm not quite the failure I thought I was, am I?'

'I always knew you weren't. So you'll be cancelling your appointment tomorrow?'

'Well, I won't have time to go, I'll be too busy trying to find replacements for Gordon, won't I? But one thing I have learned from all this is that before I take on anyone else for such a responsible position, we must check them out thoroughly first. Until we find replacements, I'll have to do my best to cover the job.'

'I'll help where I can, and I'm sure the other drivers will pitch in when they can until the vacancies are filled. Best we tell all the staff that Gordon, or Stanley as he's known to them, just decided he'd had enough and left, don't you think, Chas?'

'Oh, yes, I certainly agree with that.'

Harrie was suddenly very conscious of the time. 'I really ought to be getting off home,' she said, moving around her desk to unhook her coat from the nail on the wall that she used as a makeshift coat hook. 'It's getting on for eleven and my dad is probably frantic, wondering where I am.'

'Oh, goodness, yes, me too,' Chas exclaimed. 'My mother will probably have called the police out by now and half the Leicester force will be searching for me. I'll drive you home, Harrie, it's too late for you to be walking alone at this time of night.'

'Oh, I couldn't put you to all the trouble of getting your car out of the compound.'

Nothing was too much trouble when it came to Harrie. Didn't she have any idea he would do anything for her? 'It's not in the compound, it's parked around the corner. When I arrived back tonight I found some kind soul had blocked our entrance by parking a van across it. Hopefully they've gone by now. I've got to move the car anyway. To be honest, Harrie, I don't fancy the walk home myself so after dropping you off I intend driving home and for once leaving the car parked outside my house. Come on then.'

CHAPTER THIRTY-THREE

Moments later Chas turned to face Harrie who was seated beside him. 'Comfortable?' he asked.

She smiled at him. 'Yes, thank you.'

'Good. I'll have you home in a jiffy then.'

Starting the car, he drove it the short distance to the junction with the main Blackbird Road where he needed to turn right. A car was approaching, travelling in the same direction that Chas needed to go in, and he waited for it pass. As it did he had a clear view of what was painted boldly on the side of it.

Harrie had seen it too and commented, 'One of the night drivers off to do a pick up?'

Chas frowned. 'All the drivers were out when we left just now. Anyway, I caught a glimpse of the first couple of letters of the number plate and that's the car allocated during the day to Harry Gibbons. That car isn't being used by any of the night drivers this week.'

She looked at him quizzically. 'Well, if the night drivers are all spoken for, and that car isn't one of theirs, then it shouldn't be out at all but parked securely in the compound.' She gasped as a thought struck her. 'Oh, Chas, do you think it's being stolen?'

'Oh, hell, that's the only explanation, Harrie. God,

that's all we need after what we've just been through. What a day this is turning out to be! And I pay Terry to keep that compound secure as part of his job . . . Oh, no time to think about what I'll be saying to that young man. Harrie, I'm sorry . . .'

'Shut up, Chas, and just get after it.'

'Hold tight then,' he warned her.

They were so consumed by their need to chase after the car that neither of them gave a thought to radioing through to Ronald Tyler and telling him to alert the police to what was going on, enlisting their help in the chase to reclaim the stolen car.

Flashing a quick glance up and down the road to see that his way was clear, Chas pressed his foot hard down on the accelerator and swung the car expertly out into the main Blackbird Road, setting the tyres screeching.

Harrie was eagerly scanning the road ahead, looking for the car. She couldn't see it. Then she spotted its back end disappearing around a corner ahead of them.

'I see it,' said Chas, pre-empting her.

'What are you going to do when we catch up with it?'

'I don't know. Stop them somehow before they caus any damage to it.'

'Drunks, do you think, having fun?'

'More than likely. Obviously a drunk who know how to hot wire, though.'

'Sorry?'

'Now's not the time to explain what it means, Harri not while I'm trying to concentrate. Where has the c: gone now?'

Harrie's eyes darted. 'There it is, look! It's just turned down the Loughborough Road. I wonder where they're headed?'

'I just hope it's not a patch of waste ground to be abandoned after they've set it alight. We've just had an insurance claim for Fred's car after his accident and with another coming so soon afterwards . . . well, the insurance company could start getting suspicious about us.'

Harrie clung on tight to the edge of her seat as Chas spun the car expertly into the Loughborough Road and then along its curving length, eventually leading on to the Belgrave Road. Chas slowed right down to manoeuvre a tight bend just after they had passed by the busy Checkett's public house. The road ahead straightened out. There was no sign of the car they'd been following.

Chas drew his car to the side of the road, taking his hands off the wheel and holding them up in bewilderment. 'Well, where did they go, Harrie?' he exclaimed.

She looked mystified. 'Not ahead, we'd see them as we weren't that far behind. They must have turned off on one of these side streets. But which one? We'll lose them for sure if we don't try and look. Go down that one,' she suggested, pointing in the direction of a tree-lined street just slightly ahead and to the right of them.

Knowing the area well through his job as a cabby, Chas said, 'But that only leads to another maze of streets. There's no waste ground down there to my knowledge. Oh, we'll lose them by sitting here! Okay, let's try the street you suggested.'

Moving off again, he turned right into the street and set off down it.

It was Harrie who spotted the woman half-lying on the pavement. 'That woman, Chas, she looks like she's had an accident!'

He looked across and spotted her. Being the man he was, he automatically slammed his foot on the brakes, pulling the car to a halt at the kerbside by the prostrate woman. Leaping out of the car, he dashed over to her and squatted down beside her. He could smell drink on her. One of her stockings was ripped and blood was pouring from a deep graze on her knee.

Before he could ask what help he could give her, she cried, 'He got me handbag! It all happened so quick. I'd just left the pub and was on my way home when I was attacked. All in black the man was, one of them balaclavas pulled down over his head. He ran off before I could stop him. But I saw him getting into a car parked just down there,' she said, pointing ahead of her. 'It was a dark car and as it turned the corner at the end of the street I saw it had white writing on the side. Don't mind about me, I need me handbag back. It's got all me stuff and money in it. Get after them and get it back. Go on,' she urgently cried. 'Go on!'

Chas jumped up and dashed back to the car. He hurriedly clambered inside, slamming the door shut behind him, just in time to stop Harrie from getting out to come and offer her help to the woman. 'Shut the door, Harrie,' he ordered her, revving the engine.

Doing as he said, she spun to face him, looking stunned. 'What about that woman . . .'

'Harrie, whoever's stolen our taxi has just snatche

her bag. We've got to try and catch those bastards who did this to her and get her bag back. Now we know why they wanted a vehicle . . . it certainly wasn't to ride around in for a bit of fun. Is this a coincidence, do you think, or are these the same people who've been doing this to women for the last few months? Hold on tight, Harrie.'

She just had time to cling on to the edge of her seat before he sped off in the direction the woman had indicated.

Harrie had never seen Chas angry or heard him swear before in her company but she felt it to be well justified in the circumstances. A memory struck her then. 'Oh, Chas, I forgot to tell you after everything else that's happened today . . . two policemen turned up this morning to see you. Two more women were attacked last night and it seems one of them saw the getaway car. She said it had writing on the side, like a taxi. The gang are obviously stealing taxis to do their dirty work from, Chas.'

'And tonight it was our turn,' he hissed. 'Well, let's hope their choice of our car was a bad one for them, eh, Harrie?'

They caught sight of the stolen taxi a little way ahead of them as they turned the next corner.

'There it is!' she cried. 'Put your foot down, Chas, and catch up with it.' She was surprised, though, when he actually did just the opposite. 'You're slowing down, Chas. Why?'

'Well, if they get an inkling they're being followed they could try and lose us. If they succeed we've achieved nothing and they're at liberty to keep on doing this. I've a suspicion they'll abandon the car soon and then we can follow them on foot. Hopefully they'll lead us to an address. We can give that to the police and let them take it from there.'

Harrie looked impressed. 'Oh, good thinking. Look, they've turned right to head back down the Loughborough Road.'

Following a safe distance behind, it soon became apparent to them both that the car was heading back towards the Blackbird Road.

'This doesn't make sense,' said Harrie, confused. 'They seem to be going back towards our premises. You don't think : . . no, they can't be . . . but they do seem to be taking the car back to our compound.'

'I have a feeling you're right but we'll soon see,' he responded gravely.

Moments later Chas drew his car to a stop a short distance from the office. They sat in bewildered silence as they watched the car entering through the open gates to the compound. It drew to a halt in a space next to several other vehicles parked for the night. Immediately the driver's door opened and a man's figure got out and hurried across towards the hut at the back of the compound where Terry did his jobs. It disappeared inside. Seconds later they saw the driver's-side back door inch open just wide enough for another figure to emerge. It was dressed from head to toe in black, head completely encased in a balaclava-type hood. It slipped out and ran across to the hut, carrying something over its arm. The shed door closed behind it.

The onlookers stared at each other mystified, neither having a clue what was going on.

Chas opened his door and prepared to get out. 'Harrie, go and telephone for the police,' he ordered her. 'Tell them to hurry.'

'Where are you going?' she demanded.

'There are two robbers on my premises, Harrie. What they're doing in there I have no idea but there's no time to try and work it out as they could make a getaway. There's also Terry to consider. I'm worried they could have harmed him so they could get away with stealing that car.'

Her face paled. 'But those men could attack you. It's two against one, Chas. I'm coming with you!' She made to open her door and leap out to accompany him, but he grabbed her arm to stop her. 'Harrie, do as I say,' he ordered her. 'Go and telephone the police. I can look after myself.'

'But, Chas . . .'

He had already got out of the car and was making his way across the road towards the compound whose gates were still open.

Harrie's heart started thudding painfully. Fear for Chas's safety flooded through her. She was torn. To go and telephone the police was the sensible thing to do, but the man she loved with all her being could be heading towards danger. Those men in the shed were capable of attacking a defenceless woman and robbing her of her handbag, might also have hurt Terry so they could steal the car, so there was no telling what they would do to Chas when he confronted them. She could not abandon him to face two criminals alone. As soon as she was certain he was in no danger she would summon the police.

As stealthily as his large frame would allow him, Chas arrived outside the shed. Stopping just long enough to steel himself, he pushed open the door and stepped over the threshold.

He hadn't known quite what to expect but certainly hadn't expected to see Terry perched on a stool in front of his work bench, rifling through a woman's handbag.

To the side of him the person dressed all in black was in the process of pulling their balaclava off while saying, 'Another success, eh, Terry? God, we're getting good at this. Well, me really, as I do all the hard work while you have the easy bit. Yer should have seen that woman's face tonight when I surprised her. God, was she scared!'

Chas didn't need the balaclava to be fully removed to know whose face was concealed under it. He'd know that voice anywhere, having been at the receiving end of its nasty comments often enough in the past.

The balaclava fully off now, Nadine shook her head and ran her fingers through her hair. As she did so her eyes caught sight of the figure filling the doorway and her face froze in shock for a moment only to relax into a broad beaming smile as recognition struck.

'Well, look what's crawled in out the woodwork. If it isn't Quasimodo. Whoops, sorry, I shouldn't be so disrespectful to yer boss, should I, Terry? Yer don't mind, do yer, Terry's boss, that I've popped in to see me boyfriend for a minute while he's working?'

One hand still inside the woman's handbag, Terry was staring at Chas, wild-eyed. 'Oh, er . . . Boss. Yeah, Nadine's just popped in to see me. Yer don't mind, do yer? Er . . . what brings you here at this time of night? Summat I can help yer with?' His hand was out of th bag now and he was desperately trying to hide it under a piece of oily rag.

Outside the shed Harrie stood behind the open door, riveted by what was going on inside. She was stunned rigid that Terry appeared to be one of the robbers but who his woman accomplice was she didn't know, although her voice and manner did seem familiar. The woman obviously knew Chas, though. Harrie did not like the way she was addressing him. She was still torn as to whether to obey Chas's orders for her to fetch the police or wait and see if he was in danger. She decided to wait just a little longer, to make sure he had the situation under control.

Inside the shed Chas's face was a blank mask. 'I wouldn't normally have any objection to a friend or relative dropping in on my staff while they're at work, but I do object to your presence here, Nadine. I know what you've both been up to.'

Nadine gave a mocking sneer. 'So yer caught us taking one of the cars out for a spin. Well, so what? Terry don't get any other perks in this poxy job of his. Anyway I'm glad you're here, Quassie, 'cos it gives me chance to thank you. We've got a lot to thank your boss for, ain't we, Terry?'

'Nadine,' he hissed at her warningly.

'Oh, shut up, you,' she shot back at him. 'Chas has a right to know what he did for us. It certainly helped to make up for the way he turned me down. You've got a fucking nerve turning me down,' she spat at him. 'Who d'yer think yer are, eh? I told yer what he done to me, didn't I, Terry? Led me on to believe he'd give me the world, only to toss me aside when he changed his mind. And you ain't exactly his best friend neither, are yer, Terry, him taking that cabby's job off yer like he did.' She narrowed her eyes and glared at Chas murderously. 'And after me lowering meself even to consider giving an ugly git like you a chance.' Then her face lightened. 'But I forgive you, see, because if you hadn't done what yer did that night, we would never've found it, would we, Terry?'

'Nadine!' he stormed at her. 'Will yer shut yer trap before yer say summat yer shouldn't?'

She shot a glance at him. 'No, I won't shut up. He can't do anything, no one can, 'cos they can't prove we ever had it. Have yer forgotten, we spent all the evidence and got rid of what we found it in, in the canal? Now will you stop yer whittling, I want Quassie to know that through him we had so much fun. Best holiday I've ever had. First holiday I've ever had. And money no object. Boy, did I enjoy spending it.

'When we found it, we couldn't believe our eyes, could we, Terry? More money than either of us had ever seen in our lives.' She gave a wicked grin. 'Surprising what yer can find in the back of a taxi when yer sheltering from the rain.'

Chas gasped as realisation struck. 'It was you who stole the case?'

She looked mortally wounded. 'Stole? We never stole nothing,' she erupted. 'We found that case, and as far as I'm concerned, finders is keepers.'

'But you had no right to that money, Nadine, and you knew you hadn't,' Chas accused her. 'The man who owned that case had just died and what was in it belonged . . .'

'Oh, well, he had no use for it then where he was going. Someone else might as well put it to good use,' she interjected before Chas could finish. 'Oh, and we certainly did put it to good use, didn't we, Terry? We booked ourselves into the Grand Hotel that night in the best room they'd got and spent a great week blasting the shops. Then I thought to meself, I've never been out of this hole of a city, now's me chance. So we caught a train to London and booked ourselves into one of them posh hotels, The Dorchester, I think it was called, and we shopped 'til we dropped. We ate in lots of fancy restaurants too where waiters dress like penguins. Got chucked out of a couple an' all, didn't we, Terry?' she guffawed. 'Anyway, I got quite a taste for the high life. Took to it like a duck to water, I did. Shame, though, when yer living like that, money don't go far, does it? So we had to come back until we'd decided on our next money-making scheme.'

'You blew the whole lot?' Chas exclaimed, horrified.

Terry was by now cradling his head in his hands, deeply regretting the day he'd happened across Nadine out in the compound and got involved with her. Little did he know then what this woman had been about to lead him into.

'Too bloody right we did!' Nadine shot at Chas as though he was stupid. 'So Terry had no choice but to come back to work for you. At least that way we had some money coming in until something better turned up. He moved back in with his grandmother and I went back to my mother's meantime. Only I found out that the bitch had turned me kids over to the authorities and wouldn't let me back in her house.'

Terry's head jerked up. 'Kids! You never told me you had kids, Nadine!'

'Well, yer know now, don't yer? And you'll make 'em a lovely dad when I get them back. We're working hard at being able to afford our own place, ain't we Terry? After me mam chucked me out I had nowhere to go, see, so I had no choice but to move in with Terry and his gran. Well, I thought *I* had it bad with the mother I'd been cursed with but, as God's my witness, I ain't never heard anyone nag like his grandmother does. That's why I been popping down here at night to see him now and again, so I can get away from her. She flashed Terry a sweet smile. 'Anyway, best be off darling, and leave you to it. I'll keep the bed warm for yer for when yer get home in the morning. Don't work too hard now, keep some strength for me.'

Chas held up his hand in a warning gesture. 'You're not going anywhere, Nadine, except down to the police station.'

'And why would I want to go down there?' she snapped.

'Taking the car out for a spin wasn't really what you were doing tonight. We found the woman you attacked and whose handbag Terry is trying to hide in front of him. It's my guess she's not the first you've done this to. How many is it, Nadine?'

She sneered at him. 'You ain't got n'ote on me. You ain't found me with no handbag on me tonight, and the police can come around to his gran's and search the place from top to bottom but they won't find n'ote in my belongings 'cos I'm too clever to hang on to incriminating evidence.' She wagged a finger at Terry. 'It's him you saw with his hand inside that woman's bag when yer came in, not me. I'm just an innocent bystander and as far as I'm concerned the police can lock him up and throw away the key, 'cos I'm fed up with him anyway. Plenty more where he came from and I'm off to find meself one.'

She made to get past Chas but he blocked her route. 'I told you, Nadine, you're going nowhere. Neither of you. I might not be able to prove that you stole that briefcase or that you'd any involvement in those other bag snatches, but I can prove this one tonight as you've still got the evidence. The police will be here any minute.'

'And I told you, yer thick cretin, I ain't going to no police station tonight or any other night.' Glancing around her, Nadine grabbed up a monkey wrench and waved it menacingly at him. 'I'll brain you if you don't get out of my way, you big ugly bastard!'

Before she could take a swing at Chas, he had lunged forward to grab her arm and shake the wrench from it. With her arms pinned to her sides, he grabbed her round the waist in a bear hug.

They were all surprised by the figure that then burst through the door, crying, 'You lay a finger on him and I'll swing for you!'

Chas was alarmed to see Harrie. 'What are you doing here? I told you to call the police and wait for me in the office. I don't want you involved in this.'

'I was worried you were in danger, Chas.'

He was desperately trying not to mind the painful

kicks his shins were receiving from Nadine's heels as she thrashed wildly against him. 'You can see I'm not. Now please fetch the police. In fact, when you leave the shed, lock us all in,' he commanded.

'But, Chas . . .'

'Do it, Harrie.'

A long time later Chas came back into the office. He'd just seen a policeman off the premises after he'd taken Chas's and Harrie's statements. Terry and Nadine were already down at the police station, being charged by the police. Apparently they'd found a safety deposit key in Nadine's handbag and it looked to be hopeful that at least some of Mr Graham's missing money would be recovered, though Terry seemed stunned to hear it.

Harrie rushed over to him and took hold of his hand to examine the painful-looking bite he'd received from Nadine as she'd tried to free herself from his clutches in a vain attempt to make a getaway before Harrie locked them all in the shed.

'That needs medical attention, Chas.'

'It's fine, Harrie. I'll bathe it with TCP when I get home.'

'But I noticed you limping too. What else did that woman do to you after you made me lock you inside the shed and fetch the police? You shouldn't have made me do that, Chas. I was frantic while we waited for them to arrive, knowing you were in the shed with those two, hearing that woman screaming abuse at you. Such nasty things she was saying, evil woman that she is.'

It was after two in the morning and Chas was desperately tired, still reeling from the shock of all that had happened that day. His usually placid nature was stretched to breaking. Before he could check himself, he snapped, 'Harrie, please stop fussing.'

After all that had happened to her that day, Harrie too was feeling the strain. 'Fussing!' she exclaimed. 'How dare you accuse me of fussing? You have no idea how I felt when you were in that shed. I was imagining all sorts. Waiting for the police to arrive to rescue you and march those two off to jail was the worst wait of my life.'

'I don't know why you're getting yourself so het up, Harrie. I . . .'

'You don't know why I'm getting so het up?' she interjected. And before she could stop herself blurted, 'Because I was terrified you'd be seriously hurt and I couldn't bear the thought of you getting hurt because . . . because . . . I care. I care because I bloody well love you, that's why.' It then struck her just what she had divulged and horror flooded though her. 'Now, on top of everything else today, you've made me go and make an idiot of myself. But don't you dare feel sorry for me. I realised a long time ago that you didn't have the same feelings for me as I do for you and I've accepted it. Right, I'm going home now. And, no, I don't want lift. I'll walk, thank you.'

She made to storm past him but he grabbed her arm and pulled her to a halt in front of him, looking deep into her eyes, his face mystified. 'Did I hear you right, Harrie? You love me? But how can someone like you be in love with me?'

She looked up at him wide-eyed. 'What do you mean, how can I love you?'

'Well, I'm not handsome, I know that, and I'm big and . . .'

'Just the most wonderful, kind, considerate, compassionate man I've ever met in my life! I'd marry you tomorrow if you asked me to.'

He couldn't believe what he was hearing. 'What?'

'You heard me. Now I really *have* made a fool of myself and I want to go home. In fact, right this minute I wish the ground would open and swallow me up. If I've embarrassed you . . .'

'Embarrassed me? Oh, Harrie, you could never embarrass me. I've worshipped the ground you walk on almost from the moment I set eyes on you. I just never thought for a minute you would ever feel that way about me. I never dared dream you would. That man who came in to see you in the office, well, I might be mistaken, but I got the impression he was more than a friend looking you up as he happened to be passing. That's the sort of man you attract, Harrie. My sort . . . well . . .'

'Oh, Chas,' she interjected sharply. 'You are my sort. Fine clothes don't make a man, Chas, it's what's inside that counts. You're right, that man wasn't just a friend. He was my ex-fiancé who wouldn't accept that our relationship was over. But he wasn't for me, nor was I for him. Jeremy will find another woman who will suit him far better than I ever would, I've no doubt of that. And he will be much happier with her than he would ever have been with me. We weren't suited. Not like you and I are suited. Oh, Chas, all this time we've been wasting.' She looked at him expectantly. 'Would you please do something for me?'

'Oh, anything, Harrie. Name it?'

'Just kiss me.'

It was everything they had dared hoped it would be and more. Neither of them wanted that kiss to end.

It was a breathless Harrie who pulled away first but only because she had a crick in her neck as Chas was so much taller than she was.

Eyes beaming with love, she looked up at him and said, 'Saturday then?'

He looked disappointed. 'Oh, have I to wait that long? But if it's the soonest you can manage, that's fine by me. Where would you like to go? To the pictures again?'

'No, maybe another time. On Saturday I want you to take me to the church to get married.'

Laughing loudly, he scooped her up in his arms and crushed her to him.

CHAPTER THIRTY-FOUR

An exhilarated Chas drew his car to a halt outside the neat-looking semi-detached house. He was having great trouble behaving with his usual calmness when in reality all he wanted to do was stand on a soap box in a crowded area and proclaim to anyone who'd listen that he was loved by the most beautiful woman in the world, and as soon as they could arrange it they were going to get married.

Before he and Harrie had reluctantly parted the previous night they had made firm arrangements to take the afternoon off work the next day, first paying a visit to a jeweller so Chas could buy her an engagement ring, then seeing Iris to break their wonderful news to her, and then Percy. Hopefully both parents would join their respective son and daughter for a celebration meal that night. Parents dealt with, next stop was the vicar.

Before an excited Chas could go and collect an equally excited Harrie back at the office, though, he still had to finish dealing with the customer in the back of his car.

'Well, here we are safe and sound. I hope you've had a comfortable journey with Tyme's Taxis. That will be seven and six, please.'

A ten-shilling note was pressed into his hand. 'Thank you. Please keep the change. Yes, I have had a very comfortable journey, Chas. It is Chas, isn't it?'

He manoeuvred his body around so he could take a proper look at the smartly dressed woman seated in the back. He didn't recognise her. 'Yes, it is,' he said quizzically.

She smiled at him. 'I can see you don't remember me. My name is Sylvia Vines. Well, Sylvia Blaydon now as I'm married, you see. I used to live with my parents in the shop on the corner near where you lived. I often think of you, Chas. I wish you knew the number of times I've prayed to have a chance to say how sorry I am for how badly I treated you that night.

'I did love you, Chas. You were my first love. I'd loved you for a long time before you even noticed me. But I never dreamed for a moment a handsome boy like you would look at a thin ugly thing like me. When I realised you liked me back, well, I couldn't believe it. I was so excited when you plucked up the courage to ask me to meet you in the entry that evening because I knew you were going to ask me out.'

Her face fell then. 'Trouble was, somehow Nadine Dewhurst found out about our arrangement. I don't know how she did but then Nadine always had a knack for finding out things that could be of use to her. Before I met you that evening, she collared me and threatened that if I didn't do exactly what she said, she and her brothers would set fire to my parents' shop. Well, you can imagine what a situation I was in. I so much wanted to go out with you, Chas, but I was worried for my parents. The shop was their livelihood and I had n doubt Nadine and her brothers would do what they said if I didn't do what she told me. I had no choice. But I can't tell you how much it grieved me to say what I did to you. I assure you they were Nadine's words, not mine. For weeks afterwards I cried myself to sleep, knowing that what I'd done must have hurt you terribly. But I couldn't risk putting you right because if Nadine and her brothers found out they would have carried out their threat.

'The Dewhursts never treated any of us kids well, terrorised us all in truth, but I could never understand why they hated you so much more, Chas, what it was they had against you. I know you'd never have done anything bad to them. Then one day I found out what the reason was. My mother had sent me round to deliver a loaf of bread to Mrs Dewhurst and when I arrived at the back door I could hear this almighty row going on inside. Nadine was screaming at her, "*Why couldn't we have a mother like Chas's got? Why did we have to get you?*" Well, then I realised exactly why Nadine and her brothers hated you so much. You had something they hadn't and would never have. They were jealous of you, Chas. You had the one thing they couldn't steal or extort through their threatening ways, like they got everything else they wanted. You had a good mother.'

Sylvia took a deep breath and flashed him a bright smile. 'You don't know how good it feels to get that off my chest. Well, it's been lovely to meet you again. I don't need to ask you how well you're doing as the company's in your name, I see. I have no doubt there's a lovely woman waiting at home for you. Now I'm going to go and cook my lovely husband his dinner. Goodbye, Chas.'

With that she slipped out of the car and hurried inside her house.

A stunned Chas sat for a while going over all Sylvia Vines had said to him. He had never understood why Nadine and her brothers had picked on him in particular to be the brunt of their endless tormenting. Now he knew. He didn't need this final piece of information, though, to lift the great burden of self-doubt the Dewhurst offspring had left him with over their years of abuse because Harrie had already done so the previous night.

CHAPTER THIRTY-FIVE

Later that afternoon Chas opened the back door of his house and politely stood aside to allow Harrie to go before him. Closing the back door behind them, as pre-arranged Chas went ahead to warn his mother he had someone with him so she could prepare herself to greet their visitor.

As he walked into the back room his mouth dropped open in shock to see his mother sitting side by side on the settee with an elderly man. They were holding hands and chatting and laughing very intimately together. On the table before them was a tray of tea things and a plate of biscuits.

Sensing another presence in the room, Iris turned her head to see who had come in. When she saw who it was her face drained and she dropped the man's hands, jumping up from her seat like a scalded cat.

The man too jumped out of his seat and stood next to her, putting one arm around her protectively.

Thinking that by now Chas would have prepared his mother for her visitor, Harrie walked in to join them.

On seeing her, Iris's face turned even paler and she exclaimed, 'Oh, my God, Percy, we've been sprung!'

Her eyes darted backwards and forwards between Harrie and Chas, panic-stricken. 'We were going to tell you both about us. We were, honest,' she blurted.

'Yes, we were,' insisted Percy, pulling Iris closer to him. 'We just didn't know how to, that's all. We didn't know how yer'd both take it. We were bothered you'd think us too old to be wanting to get married again. And the last thing we wanted either of you to think was that just because we'd found each other we cared less for the dear departed. And we worried that you two worked together. I mean, we knew you got on well from what yer both said, but we didn't know how yer'd feel about us two being together. But we couldn't help falling in love, could we, me darlin'?' he said, looking tenderly at Iris.

'No, we couldn't,' she agreed, looking tenderly back.

'Look, it's all my fault,' explained Percy. 'It was me who asked Iris to meet me again in the café after the day we first met. I couldn't help meself, you see. There was just something about this lovely lady that struck a chord with me. I felt comfortable with her. I was so chuffed when she agreed to see me again.'

'And I was just as chuffed that you'd asked me,' said Iris to him. 'If you hadn't, I would have asked you meself 'cos I knew yer liked me.'

'Did you?'

'Oh, yes. We women know these things. And we've had such fun together since, ain't we, ducky?'

'Oh, yes, we most certainly have. We've been for walks in the park, and up the town together, and after you finding out I loved dancing, I've been teaching you to dance ever since at the old-time dancing on a Wednesday afternoon.'

'Yes, and I'm getting really good at it now. And I've been teaching you to cook, ain't I, when you told me you wanted to learn to help yer daughter out.'

'Er . . . yes, you certainly have, my dear.'

'What d'yer mean by that?'

'Nothing, me darlin'. But let's just say I know what I'm buying you as a wedding present and I'm going to make sure you stick to the recipes written in it to the letter because your days of slinging whatever you think fit together are over.' Percy glanced at Harrie and Chas who both seemed staggered. 'Now, look here, I don't know how you found out about us but I'm glad it's all out in the open and we don't have to sneak around any more.'

'I'm so glad too,' agreed Iris. 'Freda's the only one who knew about us. Well, I had to tell her as she's me best friend and I needed someone to talk to. But I was getting sick to death of you asking me why I was having a snooze on a Wednesday evening, son. Now you know. It's 'cos I was bushed after dancing me feet off all afternoon.' She looked warily at Chas. 'Are you angry with me?'

'Are you with me?' Percy asked Harrie.

'Oh, no, most definitely not,' they both answered in unison.

A delighted beam lighting her face, Harrie held her arms wide and rushed over to her father, hugging him tightly. 'Oh, I'm so pleased for you, Dad, really I am.' She let go of him then to envelop Iris in her arms. 'I couldn't wish for anyone better for Dad than you,' she said sincerely, kissing her cheek. 'Would you mind if I call you Mum when you're married?'

'Oh, ducky,' Iris said, tears of happiness filling her eyes. Then she looked at Chas. 'What about you, son? Are you happy for us too?'

He had been desperately trying to swallow down the lump in his throat. He came towards her and hugged her fiercely. 'I'm more than happy for you, Mam.' Releasing her, he held out his hand to Percy and they shook. 'If Harrie is being allowed to say Mum, have I your permission to call you Dad?'

'With pleasure, son,' said Percy, beaming proudly.

'So how did you suss us?' Iris asked.

'We didn't,' Harrie answered.

Ivy and Percy looked puzzled.

'Well, what did bring you both here then?' Percy asked, bewildered.

Harrie grinned at them both. 'Well, it's a long story but in a nutshell, how do you fancy a double wedding?' she asked, flashing her solitaire engagement ring at them both.

Iris's eyes darted from Chas to Harrie. Percy's darted from Harrie to Chas.

As the truth dawned on them both the loud eruption of delight had Freda running in to see what had caused such a commotion in the house next-door.

No Going Back

Lynda Page

Looking back over the past forty years, Judith Chambers realises she has led a sad and lonely life. Her parents never loved their only daughter, and by forcing Judith to stay at home they stopped her from making friends or finding happiness.

Then her father's death gives her the chance to spread her wings. At first, she struggles to survive in the outside world, and just as she is making headway, an unexpected visitor forces her to deal with difficulties she is ill equipped to cope with. But for Judith Chambers there's no going back.

Don't miss Lynda Page's other sagas, also available from Headline.

'A welcome read for fans of Cookson and Cox' *Daily Express*

'Full of lively characters' *Best*

'It's a story to grip you from the first page to the last' *Coventry Evening Telegraph*

'A terrific author' *Bookseller*

0 7553 0879 4

headline

Whatever It Takes

Lynda Page

Kay Clifton has waited five, lonely years for her husband Bob to come home from the war. But, despite her excitement, she can't help feeling anxious as she goes to meet him at the station.

Hopes of a romantic reunion are ruined by the presence of Bob's fellow soldier Tony. Bob is indebted to Tony for saving his life and he invites Tony home with them. Tony is not the sort Kay would wish for as a friend to her husband and when he shows no sign of moving on and Bob himself starts acting strangely, Kay knows she must do whatever it takes to bring out the Bob with whom she first fell in love. Only then can they forge the future that they had envisaged before the war wreaked its havoc.

Praise for Lynda Page's previous sagas:

'A welcome read for fans of Cookson and Cox' *Daily Express*

'Full of lively characters' *Best*

'It's a story to grip you from the first page to the last' *Coventry Evening Telegraph*

0 7553 0881 6

headline

You can by any of these other bestselling
books by **Lynda Page** from your bookshop
or *direct from the publisher.*

FREE P&P AND UK DELIVERY
(Overseas and Ireland £3.50 per book)

Evie	£6.99
Annie	£6.99
Josie	£6.99
Peggie	£6.99
And One For Luck	£6.99
Just By Chance	£6.99
At The Toss Of A Sixpence	£6.99
Any Old Iron	£6.99
Now Or Never	£6.99
In For A Penny	£6.99
All or Nothing	£6.99
A Cut Above	£5.99
Out With The Old	£6.99
Against the Odds	£6.99
No Going Back	£5.99
Whatever It Takes	£5.99
A Lucky Break	£5.99

TO ORDER SIMPLY CALL THIS NUMBER

01235 400 414

or visit our website: www.madaboutbooks.com

Prices and availability subject to change without notice.

WORLDS APART...
SHAKING EV...
BROUGHT THEM TOGETHER. . . .

DORIS: She had spent her life alone. She never married. Aging, ill, she thought she was dying. Instead, she gave birth.

SHOCKLEY: As a young composer, he had astonished the music world. As an aging professor, his talent spent, he had just one hope.

JACOBSEN: Impresario extraordinaire, the hustler's hustler, he would manage the child's "career."

IRINA: Blond, beautiful, she moved with a gentle, seductive grace. Who would take her for a kidnapper?

FATHER FITZGIBBONS: A man of God, he had championed many causes, been jailed for his beliefs. Now he believed in a miracle.

BABY

"ASTOUNDING . . . AN UNCONVENTIONAL NOVEL BY A SPELLBINDING STORYTELLER." —*ALA Booklist*

"COMPELLING . . . LUCID . . . SATISFYING . . . BUILDS INEXORABLY TO AN ABSORBING CLIMAX."
—*The Hartford Courant*

BABY

Robert Lieberman

A DELL BOOK

Published by
DELL PUBLISHING CO., INC.
1 Dag Hammarskjold Plaza
New York, New York 10017

For my sons, Zorba and Boris,
who always wanted
a book dedicated to them

Thanks to
Jim Salk, attorney
David Berman, musician
Two FBI agents who wish to remain unnamed
One other lawyer, who will also remain anonymous
Don Smith, for help in Los Angeles, Ithaca, and Caracas
And, of course, Gunilla, who sparked this idea

Page 408:
ROCK-A-BYE YOUR BABY WITH A DIXIE MELODY
words: Sam M. Lewis & Joe Young music: Jean Schwartz

© 1918 WATERSON, BERLIN & SNYDER CO.
© Renewed 1946 WARLOCK CORPORATION &
MPL COMMUNICATIONS, INC.
International Copyright Secured. All Rights Reserved.
Used by Permission.

Dell ® TM 681510, Dell Publishing Co., Inc.

ISBN: 0-440-10432-7

Reprinted by arrangement with Crown Publishers, Inc.
Printed in the United States of America
First Dell printing—September 1982

Music to me is a power that justifies things.
—IGOR STRAVINSKY

There was something distinctly remarkable about the child. It was not just the extraordinary fact that she was born to a woman nearly sixty years of age. Nor that her mother was to insist vehemently that there was never a father. Nor the fact that, in this age of modern medicine, she was born in a field outside Ithaca, New York, without the benefit of obstetrician or blessing of a birth certificate. Nor that the child would never carry a name other than Baby. All this was definitely strange. These oddities would be whispered about, openly discussed, ultimately examined in minute detail in the nation's media. But all this was peripheral. At the center of the maelstrom was Baby herself, born to Doris Rumsey, a child allegedly endowed with an incredible talent, a little girl who many said was nothing less than a miracle, a sacred gift to the world. Others, less generously inclined, called her and her performance a fraud, a carefully orchestrated hoax.

ONE

1

By any measure, Doris Rumsey was an odd woman. She was a spinster in the classical sense, an anachronism, a woman with a prominently curved spine and a sense of dress that was fashionable in the early years of World War II. She could often be seen lunchtimes, when free of her duties at the Boynton Junior High Library, walking up Cayuga Street toward the Ithaca Commons. Hunched over as she had been since her teenage years, Doris would, if the weather were mild, be clad in a vintage crepe dress with padded shoulders, her hair perched on top of her head in a stiff roll. When it was bitingly cold, as it was now, those dresses would be hidden by an old wool coat, her hairdo covered by a matching hat decorated with a feather or a little bundle of berries.

Invariably during the school year, Doris Rumsey followed the same lunchtime route. It took her south along Cayuga Street, across Court, Buffalo, and then Seneca streets, and finally she would end up at the Home Dairy, a cafeteria where she would get on line with the other older folks, pick up the plat du jour and a cup of tea, and sit with her tray at the same corner table she had occupied for nearly thirty years.

Despite her contorted spine and her out-of-style fashions that set her apart from the rest of humanity, Doris

Rumsey was a pleasant woman who tried in small ways to be sociable. Reticent and shy, she would nevertheless always make a point of stopping and exchanging greetings with the people she knew in town, offering a smile and some small talk about the weather or the flowers if they were in bloom, or the colors of the leaves if they were flaming and then, with her head thrust forward like a turtle, she would trudge the length of Cayuga Street back to school.

Originally, Doris Rumsey had worked as the sole librarian in the St. John's Elementary School on Buffalo Street, a few blocks from her home on Willow Avenue. It was a formidable brick structure with wire mesh protecting the windows and a high, cyclone fence encircling the yard. Doris had liked working in the elementary school, especially with the younger children. Once a week each class would line up and march down in a double line to Doris's domain on the first floor for their "library hour." An old classroom fitted with shelves and racks, Doris's library in the west wing was bursting with books and periodicals and encyclopedias. It was so crammed that with a class of twenty-five or thirty children, there was barely enough room for them to turn around. The little ones always arrived boisterous and fidgety, poking one another and laughing at silly jokes, but Miss Rumsey knew just how to handle them. Without waiting for the shoving and giggling to subside, she would reach for one of the storybooks on the shelf above her desk and in a slow, steady voice start to read. Without fail, within a few lines the children—especially the first- and second-graders—quickly fell into a mesmerized silence. For half an hour she would read them stories of adventure, of explorations in the wilderness, of children who played detectives, of heroic dogs, and of pioneering families. For the remaining minutes, while she had their attention, Doris Rumsey would tell them of the library, how this small, musty room packed with books was a "warehouse of knowledge" where they could find anything in the world they wanted to know, how it was all arranged in a simple order, and how there was no such thing as an "old" book. All books, she would earnestly tell them, are new books if we haven't read them.

Though Doris Rumsey was never married, would never have a child of her own, it was apparent to the students that she loved them—apparent in the even, gentle-voiced manner in which she dealt with them, in the comforting way she might put her arm about a distressed child, apparent in her soft eyes. Miss Rumsey's barrenness was a source of sore disappointment that she had come to accept ever since her fifteenth year, when her spine began to inexplicably sag and bend under the weight of her upper body. Despite the use of all types of braces, consultations with specialists in Rochester and New York, her back continued to curve, becoming more deformed each year until, at the age of eighteen, she was for all purposes considered a hunchback. No man would ever look at her, she knew, nor, as the doctors told her mother, would she ever have a child. Her older sister married, left town, and was killed in a tragic accident on her honeymoon. Her parents died within a year of each other. Alone in the world, Doris Rumsey stayed on in her modest family home on Willow Avenue, took a job with the school system, and tried to come to terms with her life. She adopted two stray cats that ultimately became four, sponsored a half-dozen children through the Christian Children's Fund, which gobbled up a large chunk of her monthly paycheck, began sporadically attending the Methodist church of her parents, and told herself there were surely worse afflictions in life than a U-shaped spine. Childless she was not, she would remind herself in moments of weakness. She had more than two hundred children of her own, not to mention those poor little ones overseas. Doris Rumsey was not one to complain. Not even when life dealt her one more cruel blow.

"Maybe it's time for a change," she had said with a fatalistic shrug when told that she was to be transferred to the new junior high.

"We're going to miss you, Doris," said Olive Eldridge, the principal, who was a friend as much as a colleague. Olive was a large, big-boned black woman with a world-wise smile and deep circles under her worried eyes. When she broke the news she couldn't look at Doris.

"You make it sound as though I'm moving to the end of the world," Doris had said with a smile.

That had been in 1969. Her words later struck her as prophetic. The junior high school was a sprawling, noisy complex in a state perpetually bordering on anarchy. There, a library was no longer a library; it was now called a resource center, and the children who came to her classes were not to be pacified with a fairy tale or a book of adventure. They were big, clumsy ruffians, silly as teenagers can be, and often as rude. Unlike the cramped but cozy little library at the elementary school, the junior high library was situated in the middle of the first floor, wall-less like the rest of the classrooms in this "open" school. There was a central hall, encircling the library from above, through which the students passed on their way between classes. From this balcony the students were afforded a tantalizing bird's-eye view of the resource center and their aging, hunchbacked librarian. The temptation seemed too much to withstand, and without fail there rained down from above paper planes, butter patties from the lunchroom, pieces of chalk, books grabbed from an innocent student, eggs. Once a Coke bottle crashed by her desk and Miss Rumsey finally broke her silence. Her desk was moved to a more protected area, and two teachers were posted on either side of the balcony during class changes to prevent further incidents. Nonetheless, they continued and so, too, did the thefts and the needless destruction of books.

Doris Rumsey tried to make sense out of what was happening around her. She tried to come to grips with the ways of these students just as she had learned to live with her deformity, the childlessness of her life, and the long, empty weekends.

"I suppose I'm just getting on in years," she confided to Olive Eldridge when she ran into her one lunch at the Home Dairy. It was an unusual confession for Doris, who was becoming progressively more indrawn—and more tired. She just didn't seem to have the spunk that she used to have.

"Things aren't like they used to be," said Olive with a nod, but she didn't bother elaborating. She, too, was getting on in years and felt equally baffled and overwhelmed by all that was going on in the world.

"Another—how many years is it?" Doris asked herself as though trying to measure out her energies and beginning to wonder if, maybe, she was feeling so low because she was coming down with some bug. "Six."

"And then?" Olive questioned with a full mouth, polishing off her eggplant parmigiana.

"Then I'll retire. I've always wanted to travel. That's it." Doris brightened. "I'll go on a trip!"

That meeting had occurred in early January. Making

her way down the slush-filled streets just a week after
that lunch, a biting north wind howling down Cayuga
Lake and chilling her to the bone, Doris finally realized
that there was indeed something strange going on in her
body. Not only was she perpetually tired, but she
couldn't seem to tolerate the cold anymore. The winter, supposedly the mildest in years, seemed unbearable. Every time she went out, the cold ate right through
her, causing her body to tremble and her teeth to chatter. To add to that, the very act of walking was becoming a chore. Her steps felt leaden and waterlogged. Just
lifting a leg required an inordinate effort so that what
ordinarily might have been a casual stroll, even in this
weather, was making her huff and pant. Now that she
thought about it, whatever it was that was happening
had been going on for weeks already, maybe a month.
Her wrists and knuckles were now swollen, she recognized, flexing them under her gloves. Her breasts
ached, and her gut felt inexplicably bloated. As she
headed into the icy wind that viciously cut through her
old fur-collared coat, it suddenly occurred to Doris that
she might be seriously ill, that she might not even make
it to retirement, that her dream of travel would be nothing more than that, a dream.

The Oltzes were the first to sense something amiss
with Miss Rumsey. A retired couple who lived in the
large stucco house on the corner of Willow Avenue,
they were the self-appointed guardians of the neighborhood. In the warm weather they would pull out chairs
and post themselves on their porch, scrutinizing each
passerby. They scolded dog owners who let their pets
pee on their bushes, ordered children who dropped gum
wrappers on the sidewalk to pick up their litter, reminded their neighbors when it was time to cut the

grass or rake the leaves that were in imminent danger of blowing over onto their own immaculate lawn.

Aside from spending their days tending to their grounds, clipping their grass in a blade-by-blade fashion, stooping down to pick up individual leaves, shoveling their walk at the first hint of flurries, Charlie and Edna Oltz made it their first order of business to watch the comings and goings of their neighbors. They knew, for instance, when Muzzy, the alcoholic realtor who lived around the corner on Yates, was picked up by the ambulance after one of his severe bouts with the bottle; knew when that no-good daughter of the Hickeys had another fight with her parents; knew each and every time that black woman, Olive Eldridge, came over from her neighborhood across the creek to say hello to Doris Rumsey. It was therefore not unexpected for them to spot the change in Doris.

"Whatsa matter, Doris?" Charlie Oltz asked, leaning on the handle of his ice chopper and adjusting the red-checked hat on his head. His cheeks were flushed from the cold, and his walk was the only one on Willow Avenue that was perfectly ice free.

"Matter?" echoed Doris as he moved aside for her to pass on the walk. "Must be the winter," she smiled, forcing herself to pass briskly along.

"Can't complain about this one. Not yet, anyway," Oltz said and, taking off his wool cap, scratched his bald head as he watched Doris move down the street. Just as she had done an infinite number of times during the school year after lunch, she climbed the steps to her porch, picked up her mail, quickly checked her cats, and then hurried back to school. Oltz was still studying her as she walked in her hunched-over gait up the far end of the block and disappeared around the corner.

"Told you so, didn't I?" said Edna, slipping up unexpectedly next to her husband. She had been watching Doris from the window and, as soon as Doris was out of sight, she had rushed out to confer with Charlie.

Charlie Oltz took a long breath and exhaled a stream of white vapor. His eyes remained fixed on the vacant corner and then shifted down into the frozen creek bed that ran the length of the street. "Yeah"—he nodded thoughtfully—"she does look a mess. All sickly and pale and—"

"If you ask me, it's cancer. Or maybe something worse."

"Like what?" asked Oltz, turning to his wife and getting distinctly uncomfortable.

"God knows."

"Hope to hell it's not contagious."

Irwin Shockley lived on the Hill, as they say, meaning of course East Hill. He lived there with his wife, Ruth, and their four children in a rather sumptuous old stone house in Cayuga Heights that the family had painstakingly restored. His home sat on a little promontory, affording him vistas of the lake, West Hill, and the Fall Creek environs occupied by Doris Rumsey and her neighbors.

Professor Shockley was a tall, wiry man with dark, hungry eyes and a goatee lined with early threads of gray. He was a composer of music, a musician, though he now earned his livelihood teaching at the university. He taught a series of large lecture courses in music appreciation, gave instruction in theory and composition as well as occasional lessons in violin and cello. His teaching had been a compromise made several years ago when it seemed the only way he could earn a living and still be free to compose.

"Sometimes," he confessed to Ruth one afternoon when they were alone in the kitchen, "I feel that life is like a hunk of salami."

"Oh?" said Ruth, puzzled. She was a bubbly, quick-witted woman who taught math at the college on South Hill. Large-boned, with dark, curly hair and an ever-present white smile, Ruth was the sort of person who rarely if ever was plagued by dark thoughts.

"A hunk of salami. And every day a slice is shaved off. If you try to object they say, 'What are you belly-aching about? It's only a thin slice.' But one day, I'm afraid, you wake up and find that the whole salami is gone."

"Sounds more like baloney to me," quipped Ruth, trying to buoy him.

Shockley smiled weakly, but his eyes, which were focused off into the distance, betrayed him. In his mind's eye, spread out before him like so many slices, he saw his history—saw himself again as a young man, barely twenty, envisioning a career as a full-time composer, a creator of music. A top grad of the Eastman School, Shockley had been invited to become a protégé of the famous Gunther Schuller. Studying composition at Tanglewood under the venerable composer's tutelage, Shockley had written a number of progressively more promising pieces. Then 1965. At the age of twenty-four Shockley completed work on a tone poem, *The Last Star*. It was a deceptively simple piece born without terrible pain or labor, but it was a brilliant work, carrying all the earmarks of genius, and it burst upon the musical scene like a comet. It yanked him from the anonymity of struggling student to the heady heights of feted composer. He was wined, dined, and treated like visiting royalty. Every notable group in the country scrambled to perform the new work. *The Last Star* was played by the Baltimore Symphony, the Houston and San Francisco symphonies—to mention but a few. It was a powerful orchestral work that a notoriously vitriolic critic for *The New York Times* hailed as a singular modern masterpiece. Shockley could still quote the review: "Chromatically tonal with unique orchestration,

Shockley's *Last Star* is a superb example of music that is harmonically rich and imaginative with a melody line that goes in unimagined directions."

Showered with lucrative invitations to conduct his own work, give lectures, just show his face, Shockley finally got the ultimate in recognition. Until the day he died he would never forget the thrill of receiving that telegram announcing his Pulitzer Prize.

Praise came in torrents. He was showered with offers of grants. The Koussevitsky Foundation. The Fromm Foundation. You name it—they were there trying to push money on him. With that kind of support and fired with optimism, Shockley went back to work. Employing the same basic and simple approach he had used to create *The Last Star,* he began to turn out new works.

But something was wrong. Looking at a new piece, he could see something was amiss but just couldn't put his finger on it. He would begin to rework it, making nervous changes, throwing out whole sections only to pick them up again and then discard them in a fit of rage. What had been a straightforward labor of love became convoluted agony.

The more he fiddled and rearranged, the more muddied the waters. People in the business began to talk. His scores that once had been so eagerly snapped up by major orchestras could now find only second-rate groups. Slowly the grants dried up.

Finally, in the midseventies, near broke, Shockley accepted a position at the university and came to Ithaca. He knew then, as he knew today, that he was cashing in on his Pulitzer Prize. It was going to be a thick slice, but what else could he do? He had a family to feed, at that point three growing children who ate like horses. Teaching music appreciation to freshmen didn't have to

be the end of the line, did it? He would still compose—
compose no matter where he was or what he was. He
was born a composer and he would die one.

At the university he did, in fact, continue to compose. Determinedly he worked weekends, early mornings before class, sometimes nights. He whipped himself
into generating prolific streams of composition, but the
old joy and excitement of creating seemed to have
evaporated, leaving in their place a dull and tasteless
residue. Lofty sentiments aside, Irwin Shockley began
secretly to fear that he had nothing more to say.

"You missed the punch line," said Ruth, poking him
lovingly in the ribs and trying to rouse his spirits.

"Huh?" said Shockley, shaken from his reverie and
looking up absently.

"Oh, Irwin, you're hopeless," she said and kissed
him. Instinctively he wrapped his arms around her, held
onto her tightly as though he could get a grip on the
world through her.

"I understand," she said quietly a moment later when
he moved away from her. He wondered if she really
and truly did—if deep down inside, she, whose life had
been so ordered and easy and linear, could really grasp
his anguish.

"Sometimes I wake up at night—" he said, walking
over to his favorite window that overlooked the valley,
his sentence trailing off. His eyes traced Cascadilla
Creek as it sliced across town, the ice-choked stream
moving from the mouth of the gorge and out into the
foot of the lake. For an instant his eyes settled on the
point where Willow Avenue ran parallel to the creek
bed, then moved on, and he picked up his thoughts.
"Wake up in a cold sweat and think that I'm finished.
That I'll never write another note. That this is just the
tail end. The death throes."

"There are worse things," said Ruth worriedly.

"Oh. Of course." Shockley snapped out of his gloom. He was thinking of her and his children, and shuddered at unspeakable thoughts. "Then, other times—" he trailed off.

"Yes," Ruth prompted.

"I have this odd feeling that—"

He turned to look at her and, as he had guessed, she was wearing a nervous smile, her teeth big and gleaming.

"Go on."

"Oh, it's nothing." He laughed at himself.

"Tell me," she insisted.

"Well, that I'm at the turning point of my life. That this is just a phase. A hiatus. That I will do something, discover something, create something, that will forever transform me and those around me. Just like before. That *The Last Star* will turn out to have been the first star."

"That sounds optimistic to me," said Ruth.

"Yes. It is—I think."

Doris tried to ignore her growing list of complaints. She tried to forget the insidious nausea that came in the early morning and usually slackened by school time. Her fainting spells were few and far between, and things like that, she consoled herself, did happen as women got older. No matter how much she slept, Doris awoke in the morning feeling exhausted, and that, too, she tried to dismiss. What troubled her, however, were the nagging pains in her back. No matter what position she slept in or sat in, no matter how she held her frame, her back was killing her. Too, she was gaining weight despite the controls she tried to exert on her ravenous hunger. It was her growing weight, she reasoned, that was exerting more pressure on her spine and precipitating the pain. Buried deep in the back of her mind was the fear that her spine was softening again, that her hunch would worsen until she was bent over like a pretzel and reduced to a helpless cripple. If there was one thing Doris Rumsey didn't want to be, it was dependent on others. She would, she once told Olive, rather be dead than helpless.

Doris rarely saw a doctor. What she feared most about a visit with a physician was that she might have to undress and expose her disfigured body. She had all but ruled out going to a doctor when, coming home one gloomy February afternoon, the choice was made for her.

It happened on one of those typically leaden Ithaca days with the sky hanging dark and heavy, a low, sluggish veil dragged across the university that stood on the hill towering over her Fall Creek house. On that February afternoon, a Thursday to be exact, Doris had been shopping in the P&C Supermarket on Hancock Street. Her arms loaded with two unwieldy bags of groceries, she was trudging up Willow Avenue, sidestepping the treacherous patches of ice in front of the Poyers', who were off wintering in Florida, when suddenly and inexplicably her heart started to pound and she burst out into a rush of sweat that drenched her in a matter of seconds. Frightened, she picked up her pace and made a mad rush for her house. As she pushed forward on legs of jelly, Doris tried to still her terror by concentrating on her house. If she could just make it to the front door, she told herself, she'd be safe. Nearing her walk, she was concentrating on the peeling porch trim when suddenly the entire house began to lurch. The sidewalk heaved under her, the trees on the street rolled over to one side, and then everything went black. When she opened her eyes a few seconds later, Charlie Oltz was already there, dressed in shirt-sleeves and bending over her.

"Oh, I must have slipped," Doris said, struggling to find her feet that were somewhere under her. She was lying amidst a clutter of broken glass, cracked eggs, and cat-food tins. A head of lettuce had rolled away and come to a stop at the porch steps.

"You didn't slip. You conked out!"

"Call an ambulance, Charlie!" ordered Edna, who was standing there breathlessly.

"No. It was ice," objected Doris, still on her back.

"Ice, my foot!" argued Edna stridently. "We were standing in the window and saw you. You conked out. Are you going to call an ambulance, Charlie, or do I have to?"

"No. Please," said Doris, as she pulled herself up, hanging on to Oltz's arm.

"You shouldn't let her move," Edna reprimanded her husband. "I'm calling the ambulance myself," said Edna, beginning to storm away. Edna believed in positive action.

"Mrs. Oltz. Please," Doris called out weakly. She tried to go after her, but her knees began to cave in, and forlornly she settled down on the front stoop with the help of Mr. Oltz. Edna stopped and turned around.

"Look at you," Edna said. "You can't even stand on your feet."

"I'm just a little shook up."

"I think you'd better see a doctor." Edna softened her stance now that the color was coming back into Doris's face.

"OK," Doris conceded.

"Charlie'll get the car; you just sit there."

"Now?" Doris asked, distressed.

Edna had called ahead to Dr. Melcher's office, and when Charlie drove up, the doctor whisked Doris past all the other patients in his waiting room, taking her directly into his examination room. Making her lie down on his table despite her objections, Dr. Melcher felt her pulse, listened to her heart, and took her blood pressure. He looked under her eyelids, peered into her throat and ears, and asked her about her general health. Reluctantly Doris told him about her back pains.

"Did you have them before you fainted?"

"I don't remember," she answered.

"Look," said Melcher, absently twisting the tubes of his stethoscope, "I don't see anything immediately wrong, and I can't give you a full physical right now. I'd like you to go up to the hospital and take some tests."

"What kind of tests?"

"Oh, all kinds," he answered evasively.

"When?"

"We could send you up right now. How are you feeling?"

"Perfect," said Doris with a shrug and a purposeful smile.

"Do you think you can go home and come tomorrow for the tests?"

"Sure," said Doris, who was actually feeling well, as well as usual—which made her feel foolish taking up the doctor's time.

"Tomorrow, then," Dr. Melcher said and watched as she walked out of his office.

"What'd the Doc say?" asked Oltz, jumping to his feet when she emerged into the waiting room. He followed her out of the building on Buffalo Street and led her to his parked car.

"Nothing. He says I'm fine. Perfectly healthy."

"When's he going to see you again?" asked Oltz, who needed some worthwhile tidbit to report to Edna.

"He isn't," answered Doris and, lifting up the end of her long wool coat, she carefully lowered herself into the car.

Doris's condition began to steadily deteriorate in March. Her back pains became progressively more severe, with the moments of relief few and far between. Continuing to gain weight at a frightening pace, her thighs and midsection and breasts were now swollen to proportions that seemed to her almost double what they had once been. The dresses that had served her so well through the years no longer fit, and Doris was forced to go out and replace them. Even her trusty gray wool winter coat that had once been so floppingly comfortable could hardly be buttoned around her. To add to her distress, she was plagued by unmentionable afflictions—her bowels were forever churning and producing vile gas, she suffered from extreme constipation and, as a result, developed painful hemorrhoids. To top it all off, Doris's teeth were rapidly deteriorating—old fillings began falling out, new cavities were developing, her gums were bleeding, and she was plagued by a sour breath that even she could smell and that no amount of mouthwash could disguise.

Doris's condition distressed her and made concentrating on her work nearly impossible. She dropped books. She lost vital loan records. On a number of embarrassing occasions, she tripped over her own feet in front of a library class. Sensing her decline, some of the crueler students at the junior high took the opportunity to goad Doris from the balcony with taunts of "Clumsy Rumsey!" She tried to ignore it, but the fun caught on and inevitably the slogan appeared as graffiti on the walls, scribbled under caricatures depicting one grossly bloated and hunchbacked school librarian.

Though Doris was able to ignore her morning nausea, learned to anticipate her fainting spells, managed to somehow muddle through the day, the aches in her teeth became unbearable, and she finally went to see Dr. Markowitz, the kind, old dentist who had his office on the third floor of the Bank Building.

Markowitz peered into her mouth, poked around with a tool for a few moments and then, pushing his glasses up over his forehead said, "Mrs. Rumsey, your teeth are in terrible shape. And your gums too. Are you eating right?"

"The usual," answered Doris, trying to hide her anguish.

"Maybe you should try to leave off the starchy foods and eat more healthy things," he gently suggested, purposely avoiding looking at her recently developed double chin. "Milk. Skim milk, preferably. Eggs. Cheese."

"I do."

"You need more calcium. Also vitamin C."

"I understand."

"You know they have to go."

"Who?"

"Your teeth. I can't save them."

"Oh," she said, fighting her tears.

"Not all. We can try to save the bottom row. But the top—There's nothing left there to be filled," he said sympathetically. "I can fit you with a plate and it'll look even better than before. No one will know."

Though he considered himself above superstition, Irwin Shockley believed that fate always dealt its cards in clusters. That is, bad news—or good—had a way of being bunched up and delivered to the recipient in rapid-fire order.

Stepping out of his house on a windy January morning, only the vaguest hint of a thaw in the air, the sky overcast as it had been most of the winter, Shockley sensed from the outset that this was going to be a dismal Monday.

On the way to work, whether by self-fulfilling prophecy or just plain luck, Shockley's car skidded on a solitary patch of ice, and he ended up slamming his wheels into the curb and knocking the front end out of alignment.

Then, at school, Shockley ran into his colleague, Ernst Rosenzweig, who was standing at the foot of the stairs leading up to his office.

"Did you hear?" said Rosenzweig, making small talk.

"About Tuesday's meeting?" asked Shockley, reading Rosenzweig's mind. The hallway was crowded with students moving off to their first morning classes, and the two men were momentarily jostled together against the banister.

"Doesn't look good," said Rosenzweig, tugging at the

long strands of white hair at the nape of his neck.
"Doesn't look good at all. There's going to be some big
changes. Austerity, they say."

"No sense anticipating. The best thing is—" Shockley had begun when, suddenly, he caught his name
mentioned above the general din. He strained to listen.
A familiar voice at the top of the staircase was talking.

"Shockley?" The voice from above laughed. "Are
you kidding? Shockley's a fucking has-been!"

Feeling his pulse race, Shockley tried to speak but
his voice deserted him. Anxiously he looked at Rosenzweig, who was busily pretending not to hear.

"It was good. I'll grant you that," continued the
voice belonging to Martin Gross, a grad student who
was taking a composition course with Shockley. "But it
was a fluke. A stroke of luck. Call it what you want.
But one piece doesn't make a career."

Shockley stood rooted to the ground, looking at Rosenzweig, who kept staring at his shoes.

"Look, Irwin," said Rosenzweig, gathering his wits,
"I've got to run off to class." And before Shockley
could say anything, he quickly disappeared into the
milling crowd.

Shockley stood abandoned at the bottom of the staircase. From above he could still hear Gross dissecting
his career.

"Tell me, what's he done that's worthwhile in the
last—?"

Taking hold of the railing, Shockley turned and
slowly marched up the stairs to his office. Step by step
he climbed toward the second floor.

"Like I said, one piece doesn't make—"

When Shockley got to the landing, sure enough, there
was Gross talking to a new grad student, a young
woman. When he saw Shockley, Gross's jaw fell open.

The girl blanched and almost dropped her books. Without breaking stride, Shockley walked past them, his eyes meeting Gross's for an instant. Holding himself erect, he walked down the wooden planking of the hallway, his footsteps echoing loudly in his own ears. He reached his office, unlocked it, stepped in, and closed the door sharply. Gross, he thought to himself tossing his briefcase on his desk, who was he but an arrogant, two-faced little twerp! He had yet to write a single original piece himself. What did he know about music, much less life. And with that, Shockley dismissed the man from his mind.

But the words returned to him all through the morning as he labored to prepare his classes. *A fucking has-been!* Shockley struggled to shrug it off, but Gross's words had already burrowed themselves deep into his mind and sat there like a parasite, draining his energies. He knew he should give it no credence. That, even if it were true and he was washed up, Gross—who had a tin ear—was in no position to hand out death warrants. But—But—The words stung.

Maybe, Shockley mulled as he sat alone over a cup of coffee in the Temple of Zeus in Goldwin-Smith Hall, maybe Gross was right. Shockley looked up from his tepid coffee and noticed the heavy plaster replicas of Greek statues lining one side of the basement coffeehouse. They seemed to be staring down at him, admonishing him. Perhaps, as he had said to Ruth, this was just a bleak period. When you most need the muse to strike, it deserts you. A work of art must gestate like a fetus. Patience, he reminded himself, patience.

When Shockley got back to his office, there was a note stuck in the door. It was from Krieger, his department chairman, asking him to drop by his office.

"Times are getting harder," said Krieger, deciding not to mince words. Krieger was a diminutive fat man, who seemed lost in the immensity of his overstuffed chair. He was a reputed expert in fourteenth-century lute notation and really didn't give a damn about Shockley's music.

"Which means?" Shockley asked, though he sensed what was coming.

"Which means we have to cut back. A decision's been reached. The university's curtailing our funds." Krieger reached over and lifted a piece of paper as though it lent more authority to what he was saying. "I'm letting three of our faculty go. We're all going to have to pitch in and take up the slack. That means no more released time for composition."

"But—"

"It's not just you," Krieger interrupted him, and then Shockley knew that he was being singled out. "You're going to have to take some more of the freshman courses this term."

"The big ones."

"Yes. And they're going to be even larger." Shockley nodded, showing no emotion.

"Look, Irwin," Krieger said after a moment's silence. "It's not the end of the world. You'll still find time to compose."

"I will," answered Shockley, and he said it as much for his own benefit as Krieger's.

Oblivious of his surroundings, Shockley walked the short stretch of corridor back to his office. His mind was in a turmoil. First there was Gross pronouncing the death sentence on his career, he thought bitterly. Now Krieger had come along and precipitously stolen his last remnants of free time. If bad news really came in clusters of three, he thought, slumping down at his desk, what would the third thing be? What else could they possibly do to him?

The phone on his desk rang.

He reached for it.

On the other end was Burt Marra, director of the university orchestra. When Marra started to hint what was on his mind, Shockley almost burst out laughing.

"You're kidding!" Shockley exclaimed.

"No. I wish I were. I know what it means to you, Irwin. But we're making some changes. The students need a more balanced repertoire. They're complaining that they want to play some of the standards."

Shockley listened but remained silent.

"And your works are expensive." Marra fidgeted uncomfortably. "I have to bring in extra harpists. You need eight horns, I have only four. Try to understand. We have to pay these people. And now with the new belt-tightening, well, something had to give."

Silence.

"It was a consensus agreement," Marra said, trying to squirm off the hook. "But it's just for the summer concert and next fall," said Marra, meaning that they would not be performing Shockley's new works. "By the winter season things will probably improve." He tried to dangle out a little hope. "Look, if we get some additional funding, your works will be the first to—"

"If," repeated Shockley, breaking his silence.

"Irwin, it's not the end of the world," said Marra, oddly enough invoking the same words that Krieger had used but an hour earlier.

That day Shockley went through the motions of teaching. He gave his lectures, met with his grad students, and managed to muddle through his private lessons. When the day was over, he bundled up and went to his car. Driving numbly through the darkened streets, he tried not to dwell on the misfortunes of the day. There was nothing to be gained pursuing them. Tomorrow, he thought, slowing down as he neared his home, tomorrow he would salvage what he could, re-think his life. He was damned if he was going to give up composing just because things weren't exactly going his way. Shockley pulled into the garage, grabbed his brief-case, and headed for his warm house.

"We've got a problem with Randy," said Ruth before he was hardly in the door. She was referring to their thirteen-year-old, whose primary interests, as of late, were girls, coins, electronic games, and expensive clothes—in that order.

"Again?" he asked.

"He was thrown out of violin class. Mr. Hoover just called with the good news. If Randy's not going to prac-tice, he doesn't want anything more to do with him."

"The world of music will never be the same," said Shockley, a little distantly.

"Is that all you have to say?" asked Ruth.

Shockley shrugged. He had come to the point where he had all but abandoned the hope of seeing any of his children turning into musicians. Randy, his only son, was a lost case. Annette at fifteen was a different matter. Though she practiced her violin unstintingly and was technically sound, she lacked the indefinable little something separating accomplishment from art. Just at that moment, as though for his benefit, he heard the discordant sound of a cello groaning in the den. Stepping into the room, he took a peek at Julie, his ten-year-old daughter, who sat half hidden behind her in-strument. The raspy sounds ceased, and she looked up.

"Hi, Daddy." She smiled tentatively, her smile remi-niscent of Ruth's.

"Don't try to con me." He tried to look menacing but then broke into a grin.

"Oh, I wasn't," Julie said in her usual open way, her eyes searching his. "I meant to start earlier, but—"

"So start," he urged and stood listening for a minute, feigning interest as she laboriously weeded her way through an exercise.

"That's my little girl." He stood over Julie, urging her on gently, watching her little fingers bridge the strings. "Don't rush. You're not trying to catch a train. Keep the notes clean. Yes, yes, that's it. And put a little feeling into it," he said, trying to sound a note of encouragement. But at that moment he still felt removed from his home and feared that his tone undercut his words. He headed to the kitchen, where he could hear Ruth preparing dinner.

"What are we going to do about Randy?" asked Ruth, hunting in the cupboard for a pot.

"Huh?" Shockley asked. He was staring out the doorway at Cindy, his youngest. She was stooped over a miniature table she had set up in the far end of the living room. Seated around the table was a slew of dolls, a family Shockley surmised, doing a quick count. Mother, father, three daughters, and one son. Knees to her chest, with her pink undies peeking out, Cindy was carrying on an animated discussion with her family, and Shockley longed to eavesdrop. For a moment he stood watching her play, drinking her in. With big, brown eyes and long, silky tresses, she was still slightly chubby, still a baby. Seeing her, Shockley never failed to be overcome with the urge to protect her. Of all his children, she seemed to be the most sensitive, the most vulnerable. He was scrupulous to avoid favorites, but he knew that there was one. In her, right or wrong, he saw himself as a child.

"I was asking you about Randy, but you seem off in some other world."

Shockley drew a long breath.

"What can you do? Obviously he wants out. We could break his arm, but it's only going to make it tougher for him to practice."

"He's going to regret it," Ruth said, sounding an ominous note.

"Tell him, not me."

"I have."

"I give up," he said, sounding more resigned than bitter. "From now on it's every man and woman for themselves. If Randy or the girls don't want to learn an instrument, that's fine with me," said Shockley, who came from a long line of musicians. Four generations to be exact. Four generations of performers and composers and conductors. Try as he might, he knew that the tradition was now at an end and there was really little he could do about it.

"You can't take that attitude. If you do, Julie will give up before she's even started. And Cindy. She's flighty like Randy. If you don't give her encouragement—"

"I suppose you're right," Shockley agreed halfheartedly.

"What's the matter with you these days? You agree with everything I say. Which means you don't care."

"And I agree with that too." Shockley grinned, pouring himself a drink, and for the first time, Ruth noticed that his hand was shaking.

By the time late April rolled around and all the daffodils and crocuses around the Rumsey house were out in full bloom, Doris's request to the school system for a leave of absence was all but a formality. She had already repeatedly lost days on end to illness, and on those days that she did drag herself to work, she could barely function at her job.

Mr. Lisk, the acting principal, finally called her on the phone during one of her stretches of absence and suggested that she take the leave.

"I was thinking of that," admitted Doris.

"If you could get us a doctor's note, you could have a medical leave."

"Yes," Doris agreed, but she knew that she would no more seek out a physician for a note than she would return to Dr. Melcher for those tests or go back to Markowitz, to be fitted with the false teeth that would replace the upper row he had already removed. For Doris had ceased being distressed about the future. Standing naked in front of the mirror one evening—an act she had scrupulously avoided all her life—she saw the grotesque swelling in her midsection, observed the way her insides all but seemed to explode, extending her belly and pressing out her navel, saw that and knew that the malignancy that had grown to the size of a football was taking over her body. Looking down at the enormousness of the hard, protruding mass, she realized that there could be little time left and, furthermore, she didn't seem to want much more. Nothing could have been further from her mind than to subject herself to operation after operation. To chemotherapy. Or radiation. Or heaven knows what. She had witnessed what they had done to her good friend, Theresa Thames, and, thank you, wanted no part of it. When she left this earth she wanted to leave it in one whole unmutilated piece.

Resigned that she had reached her last days, Doris took to walking. Though her feet ached, her back pained, she felt compelled to wander. Each morning she would get up, eat breakfast when the nausea was tolerable, and pulling on her old winter coat, would begin one of her long, agonizing treks. Some days she would walk south along the floor of the valley, beginning in Ithaca and heading toward mountainous Newfield. Despite her cumbersome weight, she would waddle up the steep hills leading out of the city, climbing until she reached a height where, looking back, she could see Ithaca spread before her like a child's play village.

Drawn to the outdoors, Doris became something of a movable fixture in the county. An odd sight, Doris Rumsey could be seen walking sometimes across the university quads, shuffling along in her now-crumpled shoes, her feather-bedecked hat perched awkwardly on her head, her top teeth missing, her stockings loose and wrinkled and worn with holes. As she passed through the university, students who had not seen her before would stare and she, unfazed, might acknowledge their looks with a nod or even a gentle smile before moving on.

At peace with herself and her fate, Doris Rumsey

walked and walked and walked. Along the dangerous
trails that wound along the lips of the deep gorges. Beside the highways that skirted the east and west shores
of the lake. Through the residential neighborhoods of
the downtown and once right past the front door of the
Shockley home in the Heights.

Though Doris would not be likely to confess why she
walked, in her soul she knew the reason: She was going
to die, and in her last days she wanted to experience
everything that there was to see, to hear, to taste, and to
feel—all that might have escaped her in life. And the
only way to see it was on foot. Out in the open air she
could smell the fecund soil stirring with spring, touch
the soft, new buds on the trees bulging and ready to
burst, witness the geese as they flew overhead in forma-
tion back home to the north, laugh and pity the inevitable straggler honking its way back into line. An aging
vagabond, guiltless and cut loose from the world of responsibilities and job, Doris would plant herself on a
hilltop and sit there listening, entranced by the mellifluous sound of wind whistling through the bare
branches of a tree. By a slow running stream she would
pause and listen for the familiar notes caused by the
silky, cold water caressing the rocks. The birds sang to
her a new song. The trees creaked in harmony. The
leaves rustled in a gust that miraculously melted her last
vestiges of anguish.

On the days that she felt poorly and couldn't face a
long hike into the countryside, Doris would usually
manage to walk the five short blocks leading to the
Commons. It was a small but pleasant pedestrian mall
that had been formed by cutting off a section of State
Street and installing trees where there had once been
parking meters. On the Commons Doris would find
herself a warm, sunny spot and, like many of the stu-

dents from the college or university, would buy herself a bagel and sit in her sheltered nook contentedly chewing, pressing the tough meat of the bread against her now-healed upper gums, chewing and chewing like a teething infant until the bread was soft enough to finally swallow. And there she would pass her time reminiscing about the old days when she was a young girl in this town, the days before her spine had weakened. She would remember going to the State Theater when it still was a music hall. Joining her father fishing on the banks of the lake. A winter sleigh ride in the countryside.

In her mind's eye, as she sat dozing in the sun, Doris saw her life pass before her, and she told herself that it had, after all, not been so bad. Admittedly she had not had a man to love her. (She could still remember the envious way she used to watch couples strolling arm in arm, stopping to steal a kiss. And even now, she could not help but watch a pair of lovers through the corner of her eye.) Nor had she been able to experience having a child of her own. But all things considered, she had had almost sixty years of health. What more could anyone ask for? Nothing, perhaps, except to pass quietly and painlessly from this earth. And for that she prayed. Prayed fervently.

Surrounded by long tortuous hills, the roads around Ithaca were something of a cyclist's nightmare. A notable exception was the stretch from Shockley's house in the Heights to the university, which was a near-level run broken only by a few mild grades. In May, when the rains stopped and it turned dry and hot and the grass was growing dense, Shockley dusted off his bike and began cycling to and from work. The trips were an invigorating pleasure for him that kept him in shape,

saved gas, and made him feel mildly virtuous. Perhaps
most importantly, they gave him a chance to clear his
head and make the transition between work and home.

Riding home early one evening, the sun low, yet
agreeably warm, Shockley let his mind run while absently making his way along University Avenue. As he
pedaled over the steel-mesh bridge spanning Six Mile
Gorge, water gushing through the yawning chasm
hundreds of feet below, Shockley was thinking back to
the dreary January day when he had been assaulted by
that barrage of bad news. Though that bleak day stood
in stark contrast to this glorious spring evening, its effects, he mulled, pedaling on, continued to ripple
through his life. The extra courses overflowing with
bodies, the endless papers that had to be graded, the
small hassles that ordinarily were manageable, all had
conspired to take a chunk out of his life. The remnants
of time that he still managed to carve out for himself
were unproductive. Though he had resolutely promised
himself that he would continue to compose in the face
of all adversity, when he did sit down to work, his mind
was scattered in a hundred directions and, try as he
might to focus on a new piece, there was always some
little item popping up in the corner of his mind to dis-
tract him. Though he rarely complained, Shockley wondered how much longer he could go on.

Coming off the end of the bridge onto the macadam,
Shockley gave a quick backward glance to the cascading waterfall at Beebe Dam and then turned onto Wait
Avenue. He was moving along at a steady clip, still lost
in his thoughts and the rhythms of his stride, when suddenly, looking up, he saw smack in his path the
rounded back of an old woman moving directly ahead
of him in the road. With but inches to spare, Shockley

frantically jammed on his brakes and, yanking his wheel to the left, managed to just brush past her before finally coming to a jerking halt and nearly tumbling off his bike.

Collecting himself and beginning a profuse apology, Shockley watched in bafflement as the woman, apparently oblivious of the near collision, continued unfazed along the side of the road, mumbling to herself as she moved along. His heart still pounding, Shockley got back on his bike and, tramping on the pedals, began to move on. A few hundred yards farther down the road he found himself slowing down and turning around to catch a glimpse of this strange woman. Everything about her struck him as odd. Though it was a balmy evening and Shockley was comfortable in only shirtsleeves, the old lady, he noticed, was dressed in a clumsy winter coat with matching feathered hat. Her gait also seemed strange. It was a slow, shuffling walk in which, hunched over, under her coat, she propelled herself forward by dragging her feet ahead and stepping down on the backs of her crushed shoes. There was a sidewalk that followed Wait Avenue, but here was this queer lady walking in the street alongside the gutter. Well, he thought to himself with a perplexed shrug as he turned onto Cayuga Heights Road, Ithaca sure has some peculiar people. And then, before he could give her much more thought, he was turning into his familiar driveway, pedaling up the slow incline toward his garage, and a familiar child's voice was calling out to him.

"Daddy!" cried Cindy, spotting him from the backyard. Deserting her toys in the grass, she rushed forward to greet him and, as he stood straddling his bike, she leaped up into his arms, nearly bowling him over.

"Whoa there!" He laughed, catching his balance as

she wrapped her arms around him and hugged him tight. "Take it easy on the old man." He grinned, tickled by her effusiveness.

"Take me for a ride," she said, turning her face up to him. "One of those speedy rides."

"What about dinner?"

"It can wait. Please," she pleaded.

"OK, hop on." And putting her on the crossbar, he turned back down the drive. "Now hold on tight and keep your feet away from the spokes," he said as they careened down the inclined drive.

"Faster. Come on. Lots faster," she urged him, laughing excitedly as he shifted gears and began to force the pedals harder and harder, the bike picking up speed until they were whizzing down the street of stately homes, Cindy's mouth open to catch the wind as she hung on for dear life.

"More, more," she coaxed, and Shockley continued to pour on power, putting his might into his feet until his muscles began to ache and he could barely catch his breath. Then he coasted, slowed down, and, wheeling in a wide circle, headed back to the house.

"Wow," uttered Cindy, catching her own breath.

With sweat dripping into his eyes and a momentary sense of well-being invading his entire body, Shockley shifted down to his lowest gear and turned into his drive. As he closed the last few feet to the top of the knoll, he suddenly realized he was thinking about that crazy old lady. He had seen her somewhere before in Ithaca, he thought, coming to a stop and letting Cindy slide off, but just couldn't place her.

By the time Doris finally figured out just what it was that was happening to her, it was too late to do anything about it. There was no single symptom that finally made it dawn on her that rainy Tuesday in mid-June. Rather, the revelation was brought about by a mounting backlog of evidence—edema, sore and grossly swollen breasts, morning sickness, protruding belly, lethargy, and those strange internal movements—singular events coalescing in her mind like fine particles of mist merging spontaneously to form a single, perfect droplet. As she wandered through the streets of town, the dribbling trees soaking the feathers on her hat, the truth finally assailed her. Those sharp spasms she had first attributed to gas could be only one thing—the undeniable kicks of a growing fetus.

She was pregnant. Gravid. With child. As absurd and ludicrous and shameful as it was, there was no denying it. Parthenogenesis. She remembered once reading about it, and that day Doris pulled herself over to the library and looked it up again. High in the stacks of the county library, she read of how, instead of the normal situation in which the male gamete enters and activates an egg in the female of a given species, it was possible for an egg to develop spontaneously because it had inexplicably acquired the full diploid number of chromosomes and become self-activated. Parthenogenesis. It was common among plant lice and aphids, bees, crustaceans, and lizards. Thumbing through the cumulative sets of *Index Medicus*, Doris discovered how parthenogenesis had been experimentally induced, how unfertilized frog eggs pricked with a needle amazingly developed into living young, how rabbit ova subjected to temperature change or saline solution had ultimately produced living rabbits, how local anesthetic and tranquilizers had induced parthenogenic activation of mouse oocytes. When it came to humans, mythology was filled with stories of virgin births. But so, too, Doris found, was history, alleged cases occurring around the globe—none ever satisfactorily confirmed, but then, none ever scientifically disproved. Among Doris's research, one sentence discovered in an encyclopedia lodged in her mind, and long after she had left the library that day, it kept repeating in her thoughts: "In origin, parthenogenesis is not primitive but has arisen by mutation in many species." In this infinite universe all things were apparently possible. Though the odds were one in ten billion, it had nonetheless actually happened. And it was to her, she realized. Miss Rumsey. Doris Rumsey. A singularity. An aberration. A mutation. A freak!

But why? Why me? She shuddered. Better to have died a slow, agonizing death, consumed by a malignancy, than to be a freak, she railed against the stormy heavens. Why, of all the human beings on this planet, why had she been singled out for this curse?

Later that night, when the rains lifted and the skies cleared, Doris looked up at the stars that glowed beyond the halo of light surrounding the city and wondered if this thing, this infant that was surely in her, weren't a punishment brought on by her secret longing for a child, brought on, perhaps, by unvoiced envy?

A few days later, Olive Eldridge came by to see her.

"It's been ages, Doris," she said, trying not to be too obtrusive as she glanced around the house. It was not by chance that she dropped in. Olive had heard all the rumors around school about Doris's disintegration and she had come by to take a look for herself—and see what she could do for her old friend.

Once in the house, Olive couldn't help but notice how Doris's ordinarily tidy house seemed neglected. The furniture was covered with dust. There were piles of forgotten refuse spilling over the garbage bags in the kitchen. Dirty dishes lay piled in the sink. The kitty-litter box looked as if it had gone unattended for weeks, and the stench of rotted food caused Olive to gag.

"Is there something I can do for you?" asked Olive, trying to disguise her disgust. "Are you ill? Are you—"

"I'm fine," said Doris, shamefully averting her eyes.

"Let me give you a hand cleaning up. You can't live like *this*."

"I was going to straighten everything up tomorrow. I just haven't gotten around to it."

"Doris, let me help you. Let me take you to a doctor."

"No!" objected Doris adamantly. She knew that if the truth ever got out, whatever peace she had left in her life would be taken from her. It was her shame, her punishment, and what she needed most was privacy.

"Just let me—"

"Please. I just want to be left alone," said Doris, shaking her head. "I think you'd better go now," she uttered, and, shuffling through the dark hallway, showed Olive the door.

After Olive left, Doris sank down on the couch and

wept bitterly, crying until she fell into a deep, dreamless sleep. The next morning she got up and, without so much as breakfast, pulled on her coat and headed out the door. That day she walked and wandered until dark, praying to God for forgiveness and understanding. Once she even considered stepping into a church, but she didn't want to be seen like this, seen in her sin.

The days passed. The weather turned hot and sticky for a spell, then rained, cooled off under a north wind, then started the cycle all over again. As Ithaca finds itself caught on the break point between the sultry heat of the southern states and the crisp arctic air of Canada, a mere wind determining a violent shift in temperature, so too was Doris's life balanced on a fine line. One minute she might find within herself the steely determination to meet whatever future waited for her, the next she might be staring down from the lip of a gorge into a rocky abyss contemplating the ultimate sin.

Doris wept, prayed, debated, despaired, gained courage, lost it again. But through it all, the days marched on, and the thing within her womb continued to develop and expand and slowly descend. It kicked her, poked her, jabbed her with sharp bones from within, and turned around in her stomach as though it were doing somersaults. Mercilessly it grew and expanded until the skin that stretched over Doris's belly felt paper thin and ready to burst. Then in the early morning hours of June 21, the day on which the sun reached its zenith, the inevitable and unmistakable warning pangs aroused her from her sleep. Pulling herself from bed, Doris Rumsey dressed, washed herself, combed her hair for the first time in weeks, and, putting on her coat, headed out into the countryside to meet her long-dreaded appointment.

Hurrying along the road that led north out of the city, Doris began to sense within a few miles the telltale drip that ran down her legs. Anxiously she pushed on, halting only when her contractions came in cruel clusters, forcing her to double over at the side of the road. In even shorter stretches between pains she determinedly plodded on and on, panting and puffing and murmuring, driving herself to the very limit of her endurance until, just outside of Lansing, her waters broke with a sudden gush, and looking worriedly down at the inert puddle that lay on the macadam, she knew she could go no farther. She turned off the road into a field planted with young oats and, stepping as cautiously as she could over the tender plants, trekked across the seeming vastness of the clearing. Finding a secluded spot in a hedgerow at the far end of the field, Doris Rumsey accepted the commandments of her pain and, sinking to her knees, she slowly lowered herself to the earth.

The pains came and went, returning each time with greater frequency and more violence. They lasted all that morning, through the afternoon, and into dusk. As the sun exploded on the horizon, burning a fiery red in the streams of high clouds above her, Doris cried out, beat her fists into the ground, bit down on her sleeves until they tasted of blood. The racking pain came without abatement, twisting, tearing, contracting her aged body until it was a single knot of torment, and Doris was now certain that this was what hell must be like. And then, in her instance of greatest anguish, she let out a piercing howl that echoed across the still countryside.

"Oh, Lord!" she wailed. "What have I ever done to deserve this?"

And at that moment, Baby was born.

Even before she returned home the next day with Baby swaddled in her old, gray coat, Doris knew there was something distinctly unusual about her newborn infant.

After a long, arduous delivery, mother and child had slept out that first night in the hedgerow, the two of them falling into a deep, exhausted sleep. When Doris awoke the next morning at dawn, she opened her eyes with a start. Around her birds sang, insects buzzed, a bee alighted noisily from a wild flower just behind her head. A breeze blew across the field, ruffling up her hair. She had been sleeping outside in the country, she realized and then, feeling the dull residue of pain inside her, recalled what had happened. Looking down she saw the baby that lay against her body. The infant's eyes were already miraculously open, and she was looking up at her mother as though patiently waiting for her to rise.

Lifting herself on an elbow, Doris took a closer look. In the early morning light that reached just over the hill, she saw for the first time what a beautiful child she had gotten. Born with golden wisps of hair, fine, even features, and a cherubic countenance, the child looked to Doris like nothing short of an angel. As she continued to examine her, marveling at her perfectly formed little hands and feet, Doris realized that the baby was actually watching her, staring back up at her with a knowing, expectant look in her powder blue eyes.

Clutching her baby tightly, Doris slowly got up and sat on a large shale rock that jutted out of the ground. She squinted out at the sun rising behind the trees in the distance. Overhead and in the fields on either side, the birds were busily beginning their day, their calls and chirps filling the air and getting louder as the sun rose. It was their activity that finally made Doris aware, by contrast, how oddly silent her baby was. Since birth, her baby had not issued so much as a single sound. Frightened that the infant had been born mute, she began to shake her baby, hoping to elicit a cry. She shook her repeatedly, jolting the child almost violently, yet the baby gave not a whimper or cry, but just continued to look up at her mother, a puzzled expression coming into her eyes that made Doris stop.

Instinctively Doris opened her blouse and offered the child her milk-heavy breast. Finding Doris's nipple between her lips, the baby began to fumble unsurely with it and then, with a little coaxing, she finally began to drink, sucking away hungrily. In a few minutes the child emptied both breasts, and Doris found that she had barely enough milk to satisfy her. When the child was finished and pulled away, Doris waited hopefully for some sound, but other than a small burp there was nothing. Finally she gathered the baby up in her coat and began the trek home.

In her attic Doris found an old wicker basket. She put a pillow in it, covered it with a fresh sheet, and put the child in the makeshift crib. Still, as the day wore on, the child neither cried, nor called, nor complained. Later, holding her tight to her breast, she fed the child, and then, finding a comfortable spot near a window that looked out on her garden, she put the baby to sleep in the basket. From a distance she continued to observe her. She saw how the baby's eyes looked out the window to follow a passing bird, how she seemingly studied the roses that were beginning to bloom, watched intently as a fly bounced against the windowpane. This was surely no ordinary child, she said to herself and, going back to her, couldn't help but pick her up. Clutching the child in her arms, Doris felt shivers running up and down her spine.

"Baby, Baby, Baby," she murmured, rocking the child, bestowing on her the name that would never be erased.

"I told you," Charlie Oltz whispered conspiratorially to his wife. "There was a baby wrapped in that coat when she came back."

"I wouldn't have believed it if I hadn't seen it with my own eyes!" said Edna, who had sneaked around the Rumsey house and spotted the infant through the garden window. "She's got the thing stuck in a basket."

"What are we supposed to do?" Charlie scratched his bald dome, as he did whenever he was troubled.

"Well, we gotta do something."

"Maybe she's baby-sitting?"

"That baby's not even a couple of days old. I know a newborn when I see one."

"What are you thinking?" he asked, turning to look at her.

"You know what I'm thinking," she said, and together they quickly resolved to take action.

" 'Scuse me," said the young man standing in Doris's doorway. He was wearing a plaid sports jacket and maroon slacks and had a dark moustache.

"Yes?" asked Doris, pulling her robe tight around her neck. The young man looked clean-cut and reminded her of one of those Mormons or Jehovah's Witnesses who came around, except he didn't have a book in his hand.

"I'm Detective Iacovelli, Ithaca City Police," he said, flashing a set of papers.

"Oh," said Doris nervously.

"We have a report that you have a baby here," he said, looking at the woman who appeared disheveled, old, and rundown.

"And?" asked Doris suspiciously.

"Well," began Iacovelli uneasily, looking down at his shiny shoes, "*do* you have a baby in the house?"

Doris paused and looked straight at the young man.

"Do you?" he persisted.

"Yes," answered Doris.

"How old is the child?"

"It's new," she said tersely. She would have liked to lie, but all her life she had always stuck to the truth.

"Whose is it?" asked Iacovelli.

"Mine," answered Doris, and before the man could ask another question she had closed the door.

"I checked the wire and there's no report of any missing baby anywhere." Iacovelli told Chief Lean when he made his report back at the police station behind Woolworth's.

"I don't see what you're bothering me with this crap for," said the chief, letting out a disgusted grunt. "Last night we had five break-ins, a gas station on Elmira Road was knocked over in an armed robbery, and a co-ed got raped just off the campus, and you're asking me about a simple case of a misplaced baby?"

"I just never ran into anything like this before," explained Iacovelli, stymied. "I don't want to go out and get a warrant."

"So don't! Why don't you talk to her?" Lean clamped his teeth down on the stub of an unlit cigar.

"I tried. I just didn't get anywhere."

"Try again. Make her produce a birth certificate." The phone on Chief Lean's desk rang. "How old did you say the lady was?" he asked, picking up the phone. "Lean here," he said into the receiver.

"Late fifties"—Iacovelli raised his voice to keep the chief's attention—"maybe sixty."

"Are you kidding?" Lean rolled his eyes to the ceiling. "No, not you," he said into the phone. "Look"—he covered the receiver and turned to Iacovelli—"I've got my hands full. Do the best you can, huh?" Then he turned back to the phone. "You got him?" Lean barked into the phone while Iacovelli continued to stand there, his hands at his sides. "Well hold the son of a bitch! That's right. Sit tight. I'll be right down!" Lean said, shoving his chair away from his desk and scrambling to his feet. "Come on, tiger"—Lean grinned and gave Iacovelli a playful punch on the shoulder—"go get her."

"I'm sorry to bother you again, Mrs. Rumsey," said the detective uncomfortably. "Can I come in?"

"No," said Doris flatly but politely.

"I can get a warrant if I have to," he said, and over the man's shoulder Doris could see her neighbors, the Oltzs, watching from down the block as they pretended to work on their lawn.

"OK, come in." She motioned and Iacovelli followed her into the house.

Iacovelli looked around. It was an old house, he noticed, one of those that had probably been built in the early 1920s. There was a large, wooden staircase that came down into the entranceway, hardwood floors in the hall and living room, faded linoleum in the kitchen. The oak trim and wainscoting that had originally been built into the house had not been painted over and the wood was still evident through layers of old varnish. The house seemed dark and smelled musty and sour. The inside seemed dirty, Iacovelli thought, but he had seen worse.

"I'd like to see the baby, please," he said, lifting up his dark eyebrows, and Doris took him to the wicker basket that stood by the garden window.

Baby was awake in her makeshift crib and, looking down, Iacovelli, a father himself, noted that she seemed alert and healthy. Instinctively he reached down and tickled her tummy. Baby smiled and Iacovelli smiled back.

"You say this is your child?" he said, still looking down into the basket.

"Yes," answered Doris, watching the detective.

The walkie-talkie on his belt burst out with a garbled message.

"May I ask if the father is around?"

"There is none," Doris answered evenly.

"Oh," said Iacovelli discreetly, opening his pad and beginning to write.

"Your age?"

"Do I have to answer that?"

"I need it for the records, ma'am."

"Uh-huh," she said and muttered something.

"Huh?"

"Fifty-something."

"Fifty what?"

"Fifty-eight," she said and knew it was just a small fib.

"And this is your child?"

"Yes, that's what I said," she answered firmly.

"Er . . . do you have a birth certificate you could show me?"

"No."

"No?"

"No."

"Where was the child born?"

"In Lansing."

"In a home out there?" he asked, realizing that there was no hospital out that way.

"No."

"Then where?"

"Out there. In the country."

"You mean *outside*?"

Doris nodded.

Iacovelli took a long breath and slowly exhaled. For an instant he felt like going out and throttling those neighbors down the block for dragging him into this stupid mess.

"Look, Mrs. Rumsey. Let's try to make this easier for both of us, OK?" The walkie-talkie barked again and he turned it down.

"I'll try."

"This all sounds a little unreasonable."

"I understand."

"If you could just in some way prove to me that this is your child or that—let's say—you're taking care of it for a granddaughter who maybe got into a little trouble. Or—"

"But it *is* mine."

"Then I could be on my way. I've got a lot of pressing cases."

"But it *is*."

Iacovelli nervously played with his walkie-talkie.

"OK. Fine. Could you take me to the place where you gave birth to the child?" he asked, deciding to call her bluff.

Doris paused for a moment. She weighed her situation, realized that this man had the power to take Baby from her if she didn't cooperate, and then finally relented.

"Yes," she told the surprised detective. "I'll take you."

Doris gathered up Baby in her blanket, and as the Oltzs watched, she got into the detective's car. Iacovelli called into headquarters, waited for a response, and then pulled away from the curb.

"This way," she said, directing him out Route 13, and by the time he reached the top of the hill he realized he was already out of his jurisdiction. What he was doing was definitely not by the rules, but neither was this case.

"Turn left here," she said, holding Baby protectively so that if he stopped short the child would not be hurt against the dash. The radio in the front seat crackled, and a series of calls went back and forth between a cruiser and the dispatcher as Doris pointed out the way.

"Stop there." Doris finally motioned as they came over a rise.

"Now where?" Iacovelli asked when he had parked the car. They seemed to be somewhere out in the sticks.

Doris got out, cradling Baby, and began walking into the field, stepping over the young stalks of oats as Iacovelli followed, a foolish look on his face.

"She doesn't cry much, does she?" he said, trying to make conversation. The sun was hot and he was beginning to sweat under his polyester sports jacket.

"Baby's an angel," said Doris, and Iacovelli could see from the gentle way she held the child that she loved it.

"Here," she said when they arrived at the shale rock that jutted out of the ground by the hedgerow.

Iacovelli looked around. The grass around the trees was, indeed, matted. Someone had been here recently. His eyes began to scan the area and almost immediately fell on a foul, bloody mess that was covered with flies. It was an afterbirth. He wrinkled his nose and looked away.

"That it?" he asked her.

Doris nodded with lowered eyes. Iacovelli quickly scribbled something in his pad and then they left.

"Jesus!" said Iacovelli through his teeth when they reached the car.

"What?" asked Doris.

"Nothing."

That evening when Detective Iacovelli came home from work he was still thinking about his encounter with the old lady on Willow Avenue. Later when his children were fast asleep and he lay in bed with his wife, Sandy, he told her about Doris Rumsey, the fifty-nine-year-old lady who had actually given birth to a child—and out in the middle of a field of all places. Sandy Iacovelli worked as a secretary in the engineering department at the university and, during the morning coffee break the following day, she told some of the other women in the office about it. Naturally each of the women couldn't help but relay the unusual tale to at least one of her friends. One of the women present that morning at the coffee break was Helen Scaglione, who was a good friend of Carol Place, who just happened to be an old school chum of Mary Sullivan. Mary Sullivan, it turned out, was a reporter for the Ithaca paper and it was precisely through these kinds of contacts that she got some of her best stories. It was therefore not at all odd that Mrs. Sullivan appeared at Doris's house the very next evening.

"Are you Mrs. Rumsey?" asked the woman standing on Doris's porch. It was dark outside, but Doris could see that there was a man standing behind her.

Doris said nothing.

"I'm Mary Sullivan from the *Ithaca Journal*," chirped the woman. "And this is—" She began to introduce the man, but as soon as Doris spotted his camera, she reached for the door. In one quick instant the camera suddenly came up, a blinding flash went off, and Doris slammed the door shut. Locking it tight, she stood leaning against the door, waiting for her sight to return. As soon as the white ball burning in front of her eyes began to fade, Doris hurried around the first floor pulling all the blinds. She carried Baby in her basket up to the second floor and there went around drawing all the curtains and blinds, resting only when she was sure she had sealed herself off from the outside world.

"Hey, will you look at this?" said Shockley the next evening. He and Ruth were sitting around the table after dinner while Julie and Annette took their turn washing the dishes. From Randy's room upstairs came the irritating grate of hard rock, which Shockley tried to block out.

"At what?" asked Ruth, looking from her section of the *Ithaca Journal*. She always took first crack at the section that held real estate ads, while her husband began with the world and local news.

"I know that old lady. I almost ran her down with my bike a couple of weeks ago," he said, holding up the fuzzy front-page picture. On top of the photo was the caption:

60-Year-Old Woman Gives Birth to Child

"That's really incredible," exclaimed Shockley. "Sixty years old!"

"Ah"—Ruth waved away the article—"the *Journal* always gets its facts screwed up."

When Doris picked up a copy of the *Journal* with her groceries and recognized the picture of the startled woman on the front page she suspected that her troubles had only just begun.

As she opened the front door, the phone was already ringing. Instinctively she grabbed for it.

"Hello?"

"Mrs. Rumsey?"

"Yes," she answered against her better judgment.

"This is Andrew Scott, Associated Press in Syracuse. I'm calling to verify a story that—"

Doris hung up. She went over and checked Baby, who was lying in her basket on her stomach, her eyes open, the child silent as ever. Doris turned her over onto her back, checked to make sure she was still dry, and smiled at her. Baby looked quizzically up at her with her wide, pale eyes, her fine wisps of golden hair pressed against the pillow.

Taking her groceries into the kitchen, Doris went about unpacking them, trying not to dwell on the call, on her photo in the paper, nor the way the checkout girl at the P&C had kept staring at her as she rang up her meager order, Pampers and all.

The phone summoned her again.

Doris let it ring. She lifted a container of skim milk

out of the paper bag and put it into the refrigerator. Then cottage cheese. A couple of oranges. A small bunch of bananas. All as Markowitz had recommended. For Baby's sake she was determined to eat right, take care of her health, try to lose a few pounds.

The phone continued to sound. Finally she went and answered it. It was a woman from United Press International.

"Please, I need to be left alone," Doris pleaded.

"I won't take more than a minute of your time," began the woman, trying to wheedle her way in. "I'd just like to ask you—"

Doris broke the connection.

Later, while she was trying to breast-feed Baby, the phone rang again. It rang and rang. Finally, after ten rings, it stopped and Doris heaved a sigh. A few minutes later the phone started in again, but this time Doris no longer heard it. Her attention was completely absorbed. She was riveted to another sound. Baby, lying on her tummy in Doris's lap, seemed to be issuing a faint noise. Doris was almost sure of it. Anxiously she put her ear close to Baby, straining to ignore the shrill echoing of the phone. Nothing. But there had been something coming from Baby's lips. She had heard a muffled, cooing type of sound. She could have sworn to it.

Quickly she turned Baby over. The infant was smiling, a little bit of cheesy milk dribbling out of the corner of her mouth. Sliding her hands under Baby's armpits, Doris raised her up and, holding the tiny infant in front of her face, waited tensely. Baby looked around the room distractedly. The phone finally ceased, and the house became almost silent. All Doris could now hear was a large truck rumbling in the far distance along Cayuga Street. The noise faded and there was total silence. A moment passed as mother and child looked at each other. Then Baby took a short breath, opened her mouth, and a faint sound emerged, filling the void. Doris's own mouth fell open. It was not a cooing sound, she realized, listening in astonishment to the continuous utterance. No. Rather, it was a kind of—yes—music. Baby was singing. Actually singing. Coming out in the high voice of an infant was a faint though coherent series of notes, a melody of sorts. Holding her breath Doris sat spellbound, listening to the unearthly strain emerging from the lips of this child, who for days since her birth had shunned all sounds, listened as Baby sang for her mother, her notes pure and crystal and perfect. Never had she heard such strains. It was the bell-like music of a flute, the high resonant notes of a plucked harp, the perfect strain of a violin. It was all of these and yet none of them. But whatever it was it caused the tears that welled in Doris's eyes to break loose as her soul became buoyant, taking flight as though the unspeakably heavy burden she had carried for so long was suddenly being lifted. And as Doris clutched her infant, holding Baby with great tenderness as if fearing she might crush the faint song, a radiant smile spread across her tear-stained face, a face that no longer looked quite as creased and haggard.

The phone rang again, but Doris could no longer hear it. Baby's song had already transported her far from the confines of her dreary house. In that moment, as the phone continued to urgently peal, a startling revelation was dawning upon her. Suddenly, in that span of an instant as wide as time itself and as short as the gap between those rings, the purpose behind all the trials and travails of the last months made sense. Baby had never been meant as a punishment or a curse. Baby had been intended as a present, a very special gift, she realized, weeping in open thanks, as Baby sang for her her unworldly, childish melody.

Each passing day Baby's voice grew gradually stronger, the notes of her mellifluous song surer, her crystalline sounds yet clearer. As the Oltzs could hardly fail to notice, other significant changes were also taking place in the Rumsey house. The blinds that had been kept drawn day and night were now open again, leaving the sunlight free to splash into the house. Doris even began to venture out for more than a quick dash to the supermarket down the street. On a number of occasions she was seen working in her garden, humming happily to herself as she tended her yard, pruning the forgotten roses planted by her father or weeding the unruly flowerbeds at the edge of the house. And the Oltzs, when by chance they met Doris on their walk, were mystified to be greeted by their neighbor with a sweet, benevolent smile.

After a stretch of balmy July weather, a week was marked by one of those bleak rainy spells endemic to Ithaca. The cold, damp air sent people scurrying back into their houses, where they lit wood fires to drive out the persistent chill. For that dismal week Doris was hardly seen by her neighbors. Then late one night the heavens secretly cleared and, the next morning when people arose to go off to work, they were greeted by the beginnings of a glorious day. Above the town the sky blazed a perfect dome of blue, extending cloudless so far as the eye could see; a rippleless lake sparkled in the azure of the sky; the green of the summer foliage sprang forth lusher than memory could recall, and a splurge of flowers filled the air with a heady, fragrant perfume.

It was on that day, that inordinately paradisiacal day, that Doris decided to take Baby on her first outing. Wrapping her child in a thin blanket, she wandered up Yates Street to Cayuga Street, and when she passed the public library she crossed the street and walked into Dewitt Park. There, finding an empty bench among the sunworshipers, she sat down and, opening the blanket, let the morning sun fall on Baby's delicate skin. Although it was still early, the park was already moderately busy. Two young boys on skateboards were zigzagging down the pavement practicing turns and nearly colliding. In the grass a group of young people lounged around a trio strumming guitars. An old wino sat backward on another bench, his feet pushed through the slats as he sipped from a paper bag. Two sulky-looking youths with long hair and army jackets sat propped up against a marble monument, rolling some suspicious-looking cigarettes.

Turning her face up to the sun, Doris closed her eyes and dozed for a few moments. She awoke, checked Baby to make sure she wasn't too hot, saw that her child was content, and then closed her eyes again. For a few minutes Baby lay still, soaking in the warmth of the morning sun. Then she let out a yawn, stretched her arms and, taking a long breath, began to sing. The two youths sitting on the monument across from Doris stopped rolling their joints and, looking up in sudden puzzlement, nearly dropped them. Couched in her blanket, Baby continued to sing, her melody now getting louder as it climbed and fell like water tumbling through a stream, her little voice sure and velvety. The drunk on the nearby bench sat up erect and gaped as a rivulet of red wine ran down his chin. The youths at the monument exchanged bewildered glances as Baby sang on. For a moment they continued to sit frozen and then, certain of the source of the music, they stuffed their paraphernalia into their pockets and went over to where Doris was sitting.

"Wicked!" mumbled the first one, spellbound, as the pair stood looking down on the old lady with her singing child.

"That's so fine it's pitiful!" gasped the other, shaking his dirty curls.

Doris opened her eyes and, looking up at the pair, gave them a knowing smile. Quietly they sank down and sat cross-legged on the walk by the bench.

The kids on the skateboards whizzed past and, catching a few of Baby's notes, nearly fell off their boards. Executing a sharp turn, they came back for a second pass. When they reached the bench and again heard Baby's song, they jumped free of their boards, letting them run off down the walk until they flipped over and lay forgotten in the distant grass.

The drunk on the neighboring bench disentangled his feet and stumbled over.

"Did you ever—?" he began, and the two youths sitting on the walk silenced him with their hands, their earlier glower now replaced with smiles of peace and contentment.

The crowd around Doris's feet grew rapidly as new people came past, stopped at the sound of Baby's song, and ended up sitting down to listen. What had started with a few people had now grown into a few dozen sitting in an awestruck circle around Doris's bench. Yet more people arrived until, suddenly and without explanation, Baby stopped singing. For a moment there was dead silence. Then a long, unanimous sigh went up in the crowd. The people who had sat in rapt silence began to slowly stir and fidget as though awakening from a trance. Patiently they remained seated waiting for more,

but clearly the child had finished singing and the spell
was broken. A few people moved away embarrassedly.
Others lingered on, puzzled and uncertain just what it
was they had heard. Doris tickled Baby under her chin;
the little girl smiled, emitted a burp, and then, closing
her eyes, fell asleep in her mother's arms. Doris closed
the blanket, got up from the bench, and, weaving her
way through the stunned throng, headed back home to
give Baby her feeding.

Word of Baby's song traveled fast, especially among
the younger people of Ithaca—the students and hangers-
on, ex-students and teenagers—who frequented the
park and Commons. Within a few days something
of a ritual was established, Doris returning each morning to Dewitt Park to find a sizable crowd waiting expectantly. Not one to disappoint Baby's admirers, Doris
would sit down, open Baby's blanket, rock her in the
sun until, sure enough, Baby would draw that telltale
long breath, open her little mouth, and begin to trill for
her enraptured audience.

Ithaca now buzzed with tales of Baby. She soon became the number-one topic at school, surpassing sex,
sports, and rock. The kids talked about her in the halls,
passed notes during class, and discussed her animatedly
after school in the game room at the Pyramid Mall,
their voices raised above the whines and beeps and
crashes of the electronic games.

"Did you hear her sing?"

"Who?"

"Why, Baby, you dink!"

"Where've you been living all this time? Under a
rock?"

"A baby?"

"No, not *a* baby. Baby."

And it *was* hard to believe. Who had ever heard of a month-old child who could sing, actually *sing*? But she did, and what came from her lips was nothing short of incredible.

"Her music's sort of like a bird's chirping," some would say, trying to grapple with a description.

"No," others who were more poetically inclined might differ. "It's more like a brook babbling, or—"

"Or the wind whistling through the trees."

"Or glass chimes tinkling in the breeze," sighed a young girl still under the spell of Baby's song.

In Doris's mind, they were all correct. Baby's music seemed to be a distillation of all the mellifluous sounds of nature, of wind and songbirds, flapping geese, and rushing water. It was as if Baby, while still in Doris's womb, had absorbed all these colors of sound, for the lyrical melody that she sang could only be that of a wanderer.

As the news of Baby's music continued to spread, Baby's audience continued to swell, subtly changing in composition. Where once there had been mostly young people, there could now be discerned, sitting in the grass by the bench, older people—a smattering of retired folks, a few laborers, secretaries, even a well-manicured banker in a three-piece suit, who came by whenever he could pull himself away from business.

Once heard, Baby's sweet-noted song could hardly be resisted. It buoyed the spirits, enticed the soul, planted hope where before there had been fallow despair. That, and apparently more.

"You know those gruesome headaches I had," said a woman to her husband. "Well, they're gone. Vanished. That baby did it."

"I'd been depressed for months," confessed a widower with dark circles under his eyes. "I couldn't sleep.

Nights were hell. Days were even worse. I considered ending it all by jumping in the gorge. Then I heard her. That little baby. And suddenly my perception of everything changed. Oh, sure I still hurt, but I can live with it. You ought to give it a try."

"There's this little, teeny-weeny baby," said Randy Shockley to his parents over dinner. Randy spent a good deal of his time hanging around the downtown area looking for girls and by chance had wandered past the park a few days earlier. "And she sings."

"Sings?" asked Ruth Shockley, tilting her head in puzzlement. As of late, Randy had been acting queerly. He seemed to have gotten unusually subdued, and Ruth secretly feared he was dabbling in drugs.

"What kind of baby?" asked Shockley, his curiosity pricked.

"A little one. A newborn."

"And she sings?" he asked, a smile stretching his lips.

"I heard her with my own ears. She's got this weird kind of song," said Randy, and he tried to imitate it, but it came out sounding wrong to his own ears and he shrugged it off.

"You're telling me that there's a baby that sings?" Shockley laughed aloud.

"No, it's true, Dad"—Annette came to her brother's rescue—"I heard it from Laura Epstein. She was down in the park. This old lady has this baby—"

"This *newborn* baby?" Ruth questioned. She prided herself on being a logical person and wanted to pass on to her children a smattering of that precision.

"Well, I don't know if she's newborn, but she's very little. Like this," she said, approximating Baby's size with her hands.

"And she holds a tune," said Shockley sarcastically.

"No, sings!" Randy flushed.

"I heard it too," Julie chimed in.

"With your own ears?" Ruth asked.

"Well, not exactly. Stevie DeFilipis told me."

"Oh, *him*"—Shockley rolled his eyes—"that kid's mother is a Bible-toting, certified looney."

"But *I* heard it!" Randy insisted, and then, giving up in disgust, went back to picking at his potatoes.

"And I suppose you heard it too, kitten?" Shockley gave his youngest a tickle under her arm.

"I didn't hear nothing," said Cindy with an innocent shrug.

"Anything," corrected Ruth.

"Huh?" said Cindy.

People soon found out where Doris lived, and what had begun as a morning affair now occured twice daily—once in the morning as usual at the park, then again later in the early evening on Willow Avenue.

Emerging onto her porch with Baby in her arms, the gentle light of dusk casting long shadows, Doris was always sure to find each evening a crowd of local people waiting in front of her house. There, clustered in respectful silence, would be men, women, and children, mothers holding their own babies, others pushing strollers or carriages, laborers with coarse, grease-lined hands, bowlegged old folks leaning on canes. Lining the sidewalk they would patiently wait, their numbers often growing so large that they spilled into the street, blocking the road almost up to the edge of the creek. With the street filled, passing cars would be forced to slow down and wait for the crowd to part. And, if by chance Baby happened to be singing, the drivers would inevitably leave their cars and end up joining the audience, causing traffic to hopelessly jam up.

"This is getting to be a goddamn circus!" Charlie Oltz had fumed when once the crowd had swelled to such proportions that they had trampled some of his shrubs.

Angrily he and Edna had charged over to complain.

"Hey, just one second here!" He had elbowed his way through the crowd toward Doris, who sat with Baby on the front stoop, Edna following in his wake.

"Hush!" said Muzzy, the realtor, who lived around the corner. "A person can't hear with you shouting like that."

Oltz had stopped long enough to catch it. The baby. That little baby that Doris Rumsey had stolen was singing. Acutally singing.

"Edna. You hear it?" he said, his anger melting.

"I got ears," said Edna, a dreamy, youthful look coming into her eyes.

"Hush," said Mrs. Muzzy softly.

"Holy shit," muttered Oltz to himself later as he walked away after Baby had finished. He was so touched he could hardly swallow. "If I hadn't of heard it with my own ears I wouldn't have never believed," he said, his skin still tingling. "Not in a million years."

"That woman's got a gold mine there," said Edna as they watched the late show on television, the effects of Baby's song having slowly worn off.

"And she doesn't even know it," echoed Charlie wistfully.

"See, I told you," Randy admonished his father. "You just *never* believe me, do you?" he asked, but Shockley was too absorbed in the *Journal* article to answer.

"Infant Sings to Ithaca Crowds" read the caption.

There on page one was a picture of that toothless old

lady Shockley had almost run down on Wait Avenue. She was grinning and proudly displaying a tiny infant in her arms.

"Oh, this is getting screwier by the day." Shockley shook his head. "Here, listen to this, Ruth," he called out. Ruth was sitting curled up in a chair trying to grade some math prelims. " 'The child,' " Shockley read aloud, " 'who, the mother claims, is only five weeks old, is able to sing a continuous melody, which some Ithaca residents claim possesses curative properties.' My God, what a crock!"

Ruth looked up from her papers.

"Maybe it's true," she said, with a pencil still in her teeth.

"Come on, Ruth, do you really think a baby who's barely a month old can hold a tune?"

"Anything is possible, I suppose."

"Oh, yeah. Then listen to this: 'Ithaca-born Doris Rumsey, fifty-nine, purported mother of the child, alleges that there was no father involved in the conception of her child.' "

Ruth grinned.

"Not only do we have a month-old child that can sing. We also have a virgin birth on our hands! Now this is just absolutely ridiculous!" he said, slamming the paper down on the rug. "I really don't see why we keep subscribing to this rag!"

"And I don't see why you're so upset."

"She usually comes out around this time of night," said a man with gray stubble on his cheeks. The man talking to Shockley was at the far edge of the crowd by the banks of the creek and was standing on tiptoes, straining to see over the heads of the others. Though the throng was probably close to a hundred people,

Shockley found it surprisingly subdued, people hardly speaking and then only in muted voices. Feeling awkward and a bit foolish, Shockley had selected a place far from the street lamp in the hopes of not being recognized. It was an unusually hot, sultry night with barely a breeze, the sourish odor of perspiration hanging in the air. Shockley was sweating profusely himself and could feel his shirt sticking to his body. The air in the valley basin was so humid that, sighting down the row of street lamps lining Willow Avenue, he noticed that each globe stood surrounded by an eerie halo of white.

"Hey, there she is now," said the stubbled man, and a sudden murmur went up in the crowd. Raising himself up on tiptoes, Shockley watched through a jumble of heads as a familiar hunchbacked lady emerged from the front door of the house. A tiny infant in her arms, the aged woman acknowledged the people with a soft smile and nod and, moving over to a rocking chair that stood on the porch, carefully took a seat. The buzzing in the crowd subsided. Feet that had been shuffling froze. Whispers died half spoken. The street fell absolutely still as the crowd held its breath as one. Shockley drummed his fingers on his thigh and waited, feeling sillier than ever.

"When does she—?" he whispered to the man.

"*Sh-sh*!" said the man, putting a finger on his lips.

Shockley grumbled silently to himself and felt like an idiot. He checked his watch.

A half hour passed and still there was no action from Baby.

"How long does it take?" he whispered to a pretty, well-dressed woman who stood with her arm around her young daughter.

"Be patient," said the lady, touching him softly with her hand, and, embarrassed, he shrank away.

Shockley was peering at his watch for the third time when, suddenly, he felt the people around him tense expectantly. He tilted his head to one side and listened. From the far distance at the head of the crowd came a faint sound. A voice of sorts, he thought. Getting up on his toes he craned his neck and strained his ears. A car roared by a few blocks away, blanking out all sound. When the noise finally faded, his hearing returned and with it that same curious, high sound. He stretched his neck upward trying to peer over the crowd. From what he could see the infant was moving its lips and, yes, yes, she seemed to be, sort of, sort of singing, he thought, dumbfounded, picking up bits and pieces of Baby's song. Inexplicable little shivers coursed up and down his spine. Shockley labored to hear, but was too far removed to catch more than just snatches. Carefully he began inching his way through the crowd, an ear cocked forward as he maneuvered between the tightly packed people, a look of intensity growing on his face as he neared the porch. Managing to wedge himself deep into the crowd before the bodies became too dense to budge, he came to a halt midway in the steamy press of people. Standing motionless, his hands at his sides, Shockley held his breath and listened. Listened and gaped.

"My Lord!" he muttered in astonishment, hearing the unearthly song issuing from the porch. "Is that actually coming from that little—?"

"*Sh-sh,*" said someone behind him, putting a quieting hand gently on his shoulder.

Shockley pressed ahead a few more feet, his head craned intently forward. Closer to the porch, he was now in a position to see, unobstructed, both mother and

child. Yet what he saw and heard defied the very foun-
dations of all he knew and believed he knew. It was
some trick. It had to be. Some electronic gimmickry, he
thought, trying to shake off the music. Reaching into
his shirt pocket he took out his glasses and put them on.
For the longest moment he stood fixating on the child's
mouth, carefully observing her lips. They were moving.
Moving in perfect synchronization to the voice. And
what a voice, he thought, barely able to contain his
emotion. Whatever in the world it was, it was incredibly
beautiful. Absolute perfection. In his entire life he had
never heard the likes of this heavenly sound. Dumbfounded, Shockley listened as Baby swung through the
sphere of her music, her voice cool and velvety in the
low range, smooth in the middle, bright and birdlike in
the upper.

He closed his eyes and let himself go with the music,
feeling, as it tugged at the very root of his soul, the
golden currents of Baby's song rushing in, cutting him
loose and sweeping him aloft. Bathed in the melody of
Baby's sweet song, Shockley could feel himself being
lifted until he seemed to float on the undulating waves
of her music, his absorption so complete that he was
now oblivious of the hot, clammy skins pressed against
his, unaware of the sour, stagnant breath of the
crowd—Shockley engrossed to the point where he felt
himself a solitary figure standing before this miraculous
child, placed there as Baby sang for him and him alone,
elevating him above all the adversities of life, moving
him far beyond worldly cares and daily drudgery.

Lost in the midst of Baby's music, Shockley was
caught unawares when the child reached the end of a
passage and, without warning, stopped.

A single, audible sigh went up among the people and,

opening his eyes, Shockley realized that his sigh had merged with theirs.

He looked back up at the porch and watched as Doris, smiling benignly, tucked Baby back into her blanket. The crowd stood mesmerized as Doris slowly rose from her chair. Gathering his wits, Shockley quickly nudged through the tight throng, fighting to near the porch as Doris headed for the door.

"Excuse me. Excuse me." He weaved his way forward through the unyielding bodies. "Wait," he called out as Doris reached for her door.

Doris turned. Shockley reached the steps to the porch.

"Mrs. Rumsey. I'm Irwin—" He began breathlessly to introduce himself.

"I'm sorry," said Doris, who thought Shockley was another reporter, "but I have to go." And she opened the door and went back into the house.

When Shockley got home that night, he was still under the influence of Baby's music. His nerves hummed. His skin tingled. The child's song was still ringing in his ears. Losing track of time, he paced the downstairs, stopping only when Ruth called to him.

"Are you coming up?" she asked from the top of the stairs.

"A little while," he answered absently and then, looking at his watch, saw that it was already past midnight. Baby's song, he thought. He should get her melody down while it was still fresh in his head, before it escaped him.

Taking a notepad from his study, he sat down in the living room and began to quickly jot down as much as he could recall. Although his memory was haphazard in everyday matters, when it came to music it was phenomenal. In a short while he managed to get down a good deal of what he had heard, making the direct transition from sound perceived in his brain to notes on paper. When he was finished, he went to the piano and, with one hand, began to play from his hasty scribbles. Over and over again he listened to the refrain he had transcribed, but as he concentrated on the melody, he felt none of the enthralling emotion he had experienced back in that Fall Creek neighborhood.

He stopped playing and got up from the piano. Something was bothering him and it wasn't Baby's music. Somewhere in the recesses of his consciousness, there was another song battling to come forth.

"Irwin?" Ruth called again.

From upstairs he could hear Julie's distinctive snoring.

"In a minute," he replied and went to get his pad. In his head Baby's music was suddenly vanishing and, as though a curtain were parting, in its place he was now listening to another song, his own song, melodic motives echoing in his brain, rhythmic patterns coalescing out of thin air. For the first time in ages he could feel fresh ideas beginning to flow.

Fumbling with his pad, he tore off the top sheets and, slumping down in his chair, began to set down a few tentative notes. He hummed them to himself, chewed on the pencil eraser, added a few more notes. Pleased, he went back to the opening, followed the line and then, without even humming, began to write feverishly, the music pouring from brain to paper, spilling out faster than he could record it.

By 2:00 A.M. Shockley was drenched in sweat, spent but exhilarated. He had finally broken the long, dry spell.

He was composing again. He had started a tone poem, gone back to his point of departure and, in the heady rush of creativity, he was certain it was going to be better than *The Last Star* had ever been. Somehow, by some miracle, he had recaptured his youth, his exuberance, his lost optimism. His brain finally winding down, Shockley leaned back for a second and immediately fell into a deep, exhausted sleep, his pad in his lap, his pencil lost on the floor.

In the morning Ruth found her husband slumped in his favorite chair. He looked so peaceful that she let him sleep an extra half hour, awakening him just before she went off to work.

"Care for some coffee?" she asked, holding out a steaming cup.

"Yes, definitely." He sat up, stretching and yawning. "Such service," he said, as he pulled her close and gave her a kiss. "Ugh," he grunted a few minutes later, staggering to his feet. His head throbbed and his face felt as though it had been run through a wringer.

"Why didn't you come to bed?" asked Ruth, gathering up her books.

"I meant to." He smiled sheepishly and, taking a few sips of his coffee, told Ruth about his experiences last night, about the crowd around the Willow Avenue house, about Baby, about his new work that had miraculously materialized out of thin air.

"So, the child sings?" she said, a grin forming on her face.

"You don't believe me, do you?"

"I didn't say that." Ruth laughed, sidestepping the question. What was uppermost in her thoughts was that her husband, for whatever reasons, was finally composing again. It meant that he would be happy and such contentment usually had a way of reflecting itself through the entire family.

After Ruth left, Shockley called up the departmental secretary and had her cancel his summer-school classes for the day. Now that he was composing again, he had no qualms about playing sick.

After a second cup of coffee Shockley went into his study. He opened his pad and began by reviewing his previous night's scoring. He changed a few bars, nervously fiddling with some notes and rests and then, approaching the point where he had left off, tried to pick up the pieces. He tried to concentrate, but the kids were in the kitchen making a racket. When he got there he found Annette and Julie squabbling with each other about who would get to pour milk first on their cereal—Annette with her round, saturnine features and pubescent body squaring off with spirited, sticklike Julie.

"Hey, what's going on here?" he asked.

"Annette's hogging the milk," said Julie, still holding on to the container.

"I am not. I had it first," Annette objected righteously, refusing to relinquish her own hold. "It's not fair."

"Girls. Please. I've got important work to do," said Shockley, who had gone through this same scene countless times before, always losing his temper and usually ending up by taking the milk away from both children. "I want a single, honest answer. Who had the milk first?"

"I did!"

"I did!"

The girls looked nervously at their father.

"This is silly." He smiled benignly and the girls exchanged a fleeting look. "In the time that you've spent arguing you could already have poured out enough milk for an army," he said sweetly.

"But it's the principle of the matter," insisted Annette.

"Yeah, and I had it and she tried to grab it away."

"Well, we can either cut the container in half"—Shockley smiled—"or, better"—he went to the refrigerator and took out a fresh container and placed it before Julie—"let you each have your very own container."

"But—" sputtered Julie.

"But what?"

"But you've *always* told us we're not allowed to open a new one until we've used up the old one."

"When did I say that?"

"Yesterday, as a matter of fact," said Annette, mystified.

"Well, that was yesterday. And today is a different day," he said pleasantly and, giving each girl a pat on the head, went back to his study.

Awaiting him at his desk was his open pad, exactly as he had left it. He sat down and, hunching over it, tugged at his hair. He went back to the beginning and tried to recapture last night's inspiration. What, he asked himself, had he intended to do after that last bar? He should have left himself some scribbled reminder before dozing off.

Shockley pulled himself away from his desk and walked to the window. He looked out. It was going to be another beautiful, sunny day. A few faint wisps of clouds hung over the north end of the lake. He could tell by the number of sailing boats tacking across the blue waters that there was a stiff breeze up. For a moment he wished he were out on a boat knifing across the water instead of sitting in this room staring blankly at some squiggled pencil marks. He tried to clear his mind but, looking back at his desk, felt a sinking sensation overtake him.

Breakfast. That's what he needed. A good breakfast. He went into the kitchen. Randy was making his favorite: pancakes. The kitchen was a mess, full of spilled batter, the air heavy with oily smoke.

"Want some, Dad?" asked Randy cheerfully over his shoulder.

"Yeah. Looks good."

"How many?"

"Load up a stack."

"Sure thing. One stack coming up," chirped Randy, who, like his mother, was blessed with a naturally sunny disposition.

"When does she come to the park?" Shockley asked his son after the boy proudly served him a mound of partially burned flapjacks.

"Who?" asked Randy, who knew what he meant but just wanted the satisfaction of hearing it from his father's lips.

"You know, the old lady with the baby," he said with a full mouth.

"Oh, *her*," he said, biting his tongue to keep his freckled face from splitting into a grin. "I'd say around ten-thirty or eleven. If the weather is good. Hey, where are you going?" he called as Shockley headed out the door to his car, his pancakes half-eaten.

"They were excellent." Shockley stuck his head in the kitchen window an instant later, surprising his son. "I'll finish them when I get back," he said, trying to sound sincere. "I promise."

Randy laughed and watched as his father made a dash for his car.

By the time Shockley found an empty parking spot on the Buffalo Street edge of the park, he discovered he was already late. Through the windshield he could see people positioned on the grass around a bench on which sat a stooped figure holding an infant in her arms. Leaving his car without locking the door or putting a coin in the meter, he sprinted across the park. When he reached the crowd, Baby was already singing. Quickly, he scanned through the mass and, noticing an empty patch of grass not far from the bench, he cautiously clambered over the people, careful not to step on any outstretched hands or legs.

Sliding down into the vacant spot, his chest still heaving from his sprint, Shockley tried to still his panting. From where he sat, he could clearly hear Baby's voice. What she was singing, he noticed, was a variation on the melody she had sung the previous night. Slowly Shockley's breathing quieted down and, wiping the sweat that ran into his eyes, he began to concentrate. Her music, he thought, sounded even better than last night. Her voice seemed to have gained a measure of fullness, her notes struck him as even purer. Shockley closed his eyes and listened, listened with sheer pleasure as his body began to sway to her music, a fresh glow spreading from his stomach, extending outward until it caressed his thought and lightened his head.

Then Baby stopped.

Shockley opened his eyes abruptly. Baby let out a long yawn and stretched her little arms. She was finished, he realized, feeling vaguely cheated that he had been able to catch only the end of her song.

As the crowd began to stir and slowly straggle away, Shockley got to his feet. Looking over the array of bobbing heads, he watched as Doris rose and began to

make her way through the parting crowd. As she shuffled away Shockley stood debating with himself.

"Mrs. Rumsey," he called, pursuing her long after
she had left the park. "Please. I'd like to talk to you,"
he said catching up.

Doris turned to look at him and stopped. She was
standing by the curb on Court Street waiting for the
light to change.

"My name is Irwin Shockley. I'm a musician," he
said hurriedly.

"Oh, that's nice." Doris smiled innocently, and when
the light changed, she simply turned and walked off
with Baby, leaving Shockley standing there baffled.

Shockley remained on the corner, watching as the
old lady trudged up Cayuga Street, her back hunched
protectively over Baby. Finally, shrugging to himself, he
turned and strolled back to his car. Halfway across the
park, his nostrils were assaulted by an increasingly foul
but familiar odor. He stopped and sniffed, trying to locate the smell that seemed to pursue him. He checked
the soles of his shoes and then, turning at the waist and
pulling around the seat of his pants, suddenly discovered why that prime patch of grass by the bench had
been vacant.

"Ugh," he moaned disgustedly, looking at the
crushed fresh leavings of a dog. Finding a stick, he
cleaned off the mess as best he could and continued
across the park.

When he got back to his car, Shockley found a
piece of paper awaiting him on the windshield. It was a
violation for overtime on the meter.

Normally, either one of the two distasteful events
that had transpired might easily have sent Shockley into
a fit. This morning, however, he accepted his fate with

equanimity. Calmly pocketing the ticket and covering the driver's seat with a rag, he slipped into his car and drove home.

The next day it rained on and off. When Baby failed to appear in the park for her morning sing or on Doris's porch that evening, Shockley found himself unable to work on his new tone poem. The day proved a complete loss. It was on the second day, however, when he got up in the morning and saw it pouring again that Shockley began to panic. He knew from experience that once the wet weather set in, it could take interminable days for it to lift, sometimes weeks. Why, the previous July it had rained the entire month. And what was he supposed to do in the meantime? On the second day he realized that it was Baby's music he needed, if only a few notes, to keep him moving. Damn! he muttered in disgust, pounding his fist into his palm and pacing the house. Unable to work, Shockley knew he should return to school, but he was afraid that the demands of teaching might further snuff his spark of inspiration. He took off yet another day and passed the morning looking blankly at his earlier work, trying to push further the development. Whatever he did manage to write, however, came out tinny and contrived. Without Baby's euphonious song lingering in his ears, his own music refused to budge.

By ten the rain was coming down in sheets, and Shockley knew that Baby surely would not be out. He walked the confines of his study mumbling to himself and finally, against his better judgment, jumped into the car and drove down to the park. There, sitting in his car, his windshield wipers sweeping away the cascading torrents, he looked out forlornly on the soaked and deserted bench.

* * *

"You've got to hear this child," Shockley explained to his wife in the early evening as he alternately checked his watch and the weather. "Then you'll understand."

"After all this talk," said Ruth emphatically, "I *would* like to hear her."

"Come with me."

"In this beastly weather? But you said she hasn't been there in the rain."

"Tomorrow then."

"Sure," she said, and Shockley thought he detected a patronizing tone.

"Where are you going?" Ruth asked worriedly when he grabbed his trenchcoat and headed for the door.

"Out," he said, turning up his collar.

"I ran into Krieger today," she called after him. "He was very concerned about your health."

"Ruth, you didn't—"

"No, I didn't tell him you were playing hooky. But Irwin, this is a small town. Sooner or later you're going to bump into him. And what then?"

"So I bump into him."

"You can't do this. You can't take on a responsibility and then just chuck it."

"I have to. This is more important."

"You don't even have tenure. They can fire you on the slightest whim."

"All the more reason to take that chance. Do you think I want to spend the rest of my life at the mercy of their whims?"

Doris had been up in the attic rummaging through the family trunks when the doorbell chimed. Searching in hope of finding some old baby clothes, she had inadvertently come across some forgotten photos. In the dim light of the attic she had curiously shuffled through the pile—pictures of grandparents and aunts and cousins now long dead or moved away—when, by chance, she had come upon a dog-eared snapshot of herself as an infant. Staring at the picture, she found she couldn't put it down. The resemblance was so striking she had to shake her head and laugh. The photo could have been that of Baby. As an infant, apparently, Doris, too, had had those blond wisps of hair, those big, pale eyes, those angelic features. Why, they could have been twins, she mumbled. Then the doorbell chimed, shaking Doris from her reverie. She sat motionless holding the picture and waiting. Sure enough, it rang again.

Gathering together the odds and ends she had managed to dig up for Baby, Doris closed the trunk and carefully descended the rickety wooden stairs leading back to the second floor. When she got to the landing and snapped off the attic light, the person at the front door stopped ringing and began rapping loudly. Doris checked Baby as she slept in her basket and then, as the knocking persisted, she resignedly went down the stairs.

It was not easy getting accustomed to the endless
stream of visitors, people who, at any hour of the day
or night, would come by to sneak a peek at her child, to
question Doris, to have their picture taken with Baby—
there was always some request. Though Doris tried to
be civil, it was very trying. Tonight, maybe because of
the gloomy weather, she felt particularly tired and
would have liked to pass a quiet evening reading or
watching a TV program.

The knocking stopped.

Snapping on the porch light, Doris stared through a
chink in the lace curtain on the front door. It was that
man, she recognized, the tall one with a goatee who had
tried to approach her twice before. She switched off the
porch light and turned to leave, but the knocking began
again, this time more frantically.

"Oh, dear," she sighed, realizing that he was not
going to give up.

Doris went back, turned on the porch light and, leaving the chain on, opened the door slightly.

"Mrs. Rumsey, I beg you," began Shockley, who was
soaked to the bone. His hair was plastered to his head,
and water was dripping off his long nose. "I've got to
speak to you."

Doris looked at him blankly.

"It's *really* important." He shivered, and Doris,
seeing his desperation, finally took pity on him.

"OK, come in." She closed the door, took off the
chain, and then opened it barely enough for him to
squeeze through.

"Whew," he said, standing apologetically in a puddle
and shedding his coat. "It's pouring outside."

"Let me take that," she said and hung his coat in the
bathroom behind the kitchen.

"I won't take up much of your time," he began when she returned.

"I've got lots to do," she fibbed.

"I'll try to be brief."

"You're not a reporter, are you?"

"No. I swear to you. I'm a musician. A composer. And I've been listening to Baby."

"Yes, I've seen you," Doris said, and Shockley noted she seemed pleased when he indicated his interest in Baby. "Would you care to come and sit inside?" She said, leading the way.

Shockley followed her into her living room. It was a rather grim room with dark, flowery wallpaper that had been in fashion forty years ago. Her somber furniture, worn and old, seemed to match the period. Doris motioned for Shockley to take a seat. He sat down on the sofa beside a sleeping cat, who languidly opened her eyes, looked at him, and then went back to sleep.

"Mrs. Rumsey," he began cautiously, wetting his lips and swallowing, "Baby's had a very profound effect upon me."

"Upon many people." Doris smiled knowingly, her gums showing briefly.

"No doubt," he said a little brusquely and caught himself. For an instant his eyes fell on six photos taped to the living room mirror. They were pictures of young, dark-skinned children, four boys and two girls, all stiffly posed with their hair neatly combed and their scant clothes pulled straight. They were obviously foreign, and the pictures puzzled him.

"I'm working on a piece of music," he struggled to explain, looking back to Doris, who had been watching him.

"Yes, you mentioned you were a composer," she

said, detecting the lofty tone in his voice and just wanting to let him know that, though she might be old and tired, she certainly wasn't senile.

"Mrs. Rumsey—" Shockley struggled with himself trying to find the best approach. Every time words came to mind, they seemed lame. Finally he threw up his hands, deciding on the truth. "Look, before I heard Baby sing I had come to the point in my life where—where—well, I just couldn't write. Sometimes I'd start to compose a new work, get maybe to the halfway point, but then run out of steam and not be able to finish it. Or, if I did, it would turn out to be garbage," Shockley confessed, and noticed that Doris was observing him intently with her pale, rheumy eyes.

"I don't know if you'll understand this," he said and then, despite himself, began the story of his life, the words springing from his mouth. He told her how as a young boy he used to wander by the shore of the bay near his parents' Long Island home singing to himself, composing in his mind, nurturing dreams of bringing to the world music more moving, more beautiful than had ever before been created. "It was a childish fantasy, I admit, but it was what drove me and sustained me." Doris listened and nodded. Shockley continued to talk about his early years as a violinist, about his harsh father, the conductor, who was convinced his children were prodigies, his cowed mother, his sister, who ultimately hanged herself in her room. He disclosed to Doris the pains of his life, the rewards, and confided in her things he realized he had never told even Ruth. He spoke of his first success, of his prize, of the seemingly endless grants that came to an end. With the old lady nodding sympathetically, Shockley opened his heart and told Doris of his deepest dread, that he was finished as an artist, about his growing sense of uselessness, of the gulf developing between him and his family that he loved.

Shockley stopped and looked straight at Doris. In the old woman's eyes he recognized a tender look of compassion that absolved him from feeling foolish for having made this confession to a total stranger.

"But," he said finally, brightening, "since hearing Baby it's all changed. I'm now working on the piece that I'm sure will give people everywhere as much pleasure as Baby has given us here in Ithaca. Mrs. Rumsey, I need Baby."

"Need her?" Doris suddenly went rigid.

"I mean, to hear her," he corrected himself. "Regularly. I can't lose precious days because it rains or you won't take Baby outside or—"

"Well—" she said thoughtfully.

"The piece I'm working on," he said, the words pouring out of their own volition, "I'm going to dedicate it to Baby."

Doris sat motionless, continuing to stare at him, but he could already see that he had struck a responsive chord.

"It'll be *her* piece as much as mine."

Silence. Shockley sat perfectly still, his eyes moving about as though searching for something. Doris sat staring down at her hands. A long minute later she looked up.

"I'll go get her," she said suddenly, surprising him. "I can't promise you that she'll sing, though."

"Your teeth have been sitting here waiting for you," said Markowitz amiably when Doris appeared at the dentist's for her long-overdue appointment. She was neatly dressed, he noticed, and her hair had been braided and rolled into a bun. "They had almost given up hope," he joked as the nurse took Baby and Doris sat down in the chair. Markowitz had read the stories in the paper about Doris and her "wunderkind" but decided not to mention anything about Baby unless she brought it up.

"Let's see now," he said, adjusting his light and peering in. "H'm. Looks like it's healed nicely," he remarked, and went to get Doris's upper plate from his little lab in the back room while his nurse cooed to Baby.

Checking the fit, Markowitz began to hum to himself as he put the finishing touches to Doris's new teeth. He ran his grinder over the pink plastic that would sit against her gums, checked for conformity, took out the plate, and filed down a high spot. He was still humming above the whine of his tool, when he realized that there was someone else singing in the background. Markowitz let his machine wind down to a stop and tilted his head. Lying in the nurse's arms and staring at the ceiling, Baby was singing to herself in a high but gentle voice, her dulcet song meandering slowly between notes. A smile appeared on the dentist's round face, growing wide until it stretched from ear to ear.

"Oh," said Markowitz with a sigh, "that's beautiful. Perfectly gorgeous." He was a music lover who traveled all the way to New York City once a month just to hear an opera at the Met. In his time he had heard some of the greatest singers. But this! This!

"My teeth," said Doris, reminding Markowitz, who was off in a reverie.

"Oh, yes," he said with an embarrassed grin and reluctantly went back to work, forsaking his machine for hand tools as long as he could.

Baby stopped singing, and in short order Markowitz completed the job.

"There," he said proudly, holding the mirror for Doris. "Now you look like a teenager," he laughed.

Doris grinned and her new teeth gleamed.

"That child has the loveliest voice I have ever heard," said Markowitz, taking the bib off Doris. "Funny, you know it reminded me of my mother, bless her soul. When I was a little boy, she used to sing these Yiddish melodies to me. I had almost forgotten them." He nodded to himself and then began to hum, his eyes turning misty.

When Doris opened her pocketbook to pay the nurse at the desk, Markowitz went to intervene, leaving another patient waiting in the chair with open mouth.

"Listen, there's really no rush," he said, holding up his hand. "Whenever you have it—"

"I have it," she said, fumbling with some bills.

"How much are you charging this fine lady?" he said, looking over his nurse's shoulder. "No. That's wrong," and with a stroke of his pencil he cut the amount in half.

"Dr. Markowitz?" Doris ventured before she left. Markowitz struck her as a worldly person—certainly more than she was—and her instincts told her she could trust him.

"Yes, dear!" He smiled.

"Do you know a man by the name of Shockley?"

Shockley? Shockley? he thought, scanning his brain.

"He's a professor," she said, motioning with a finger toward East Hill.

"Yeah. A musician. A composer. Writes crazy kind of music. Not that it's so bad. I mean, who am I to be a judge? He has all these kinds of electronic noises and banging." Markowitz shrugged indulgently. "My wife and I used to go to concerts a lot up on the Hill. Why are you asking me about Shockley?" he inquired, his curiosity piqued.

Doris hesitated for an instant and then opened up. She told him about Shockley, about their first encounters, his need for private visits in addition to the public singings, the daily visits that had now gone on for almost two weeks, how he brought Baby gifts, listened to her music, making copious notes, about his altogether consuming interest in every facet of Baby's life.

"And you don't want him to come?" Markowitz probed.

"No, it's not that."

"What exactly is it he wants?"

"That's what troubles me. I'm not quite sure."

"Well, I'd be very careful. Whatever you do, don't sign anything and don't make any commitments. You really ought to get some good legal advice," warned Markowitz. "You've got a very valuable little baby there."

Somewhat reluctantly, almost a full three weeks after Shockley had first seen Baby, Ruth finally let her husband drag her down to the park one morning and there, for the first time, she, too, heard Baby sing. Astonished by what she witnessed, Ruth then often joined her husband when he went for his private hearings at Doris's. Although Ruth found herself touched by Baby's music, the child's song had none of the all-encompassing hold that it had on her husband. She went along on these visits, she suspected, because she couldn't resist the chance to hold a little baby. Whenever she came, Ruth always made a point of bringing along some useful gift for the child, and on this particular Saturday, when she and Irwin went down to the flats to visit Doris Rumsey, she brought along the little knit suit with matching booties that her mother had made for Cindy. In addition to his usual notepad, Shockley decided to lug along his tape deck.

"What's that for?" asked Doris when she saw the unwieldy machine.

"It's a recorder," he said, plugging in the device and putting on a large reel. "I want to record Baby's singing. It won't hurt her in any way. It's just a simple tape machine," he repeated.

"It looks very complicated," Doris said.

"It's like a run-of-the-mill recorder, except a bit more sophisticated. With it I can get reproduction with almost perfect fidelity," he said, and, noting her adverse reaction, realized he had been wise in delaying it these weeks. But the recordings were vital. With them, he reasoned, he would have Baby's song always close at hand, easily summoned forth by the push of a button. Too, Shockley felt it incumbent upon himself to amass as much material on Baby as possible—notes, transcriptions of her music, recordings, even a daily diary—though to what ends he was still not quite sure.

"Ah, here we are!" said Shockley, holding out his hands when Doris brought Baby into the living room. She was dressed in Cindy's pink suit and seemed actually pleased. Even Doris looked delighted. "And how's my favorite little singer?" he said, taking the child in his arms and holding her for a moment until she smiled. Shockley had a great fondness for small children, and holding Baby reminded him of the days when his own kids had been infants. As he held Baby against his body, feeling her respond to his little strokes and tickles, Shockley noticed through the corner of his eye the leery way Doris was watching him. Quickly he returned Baby. "Here we go, back to mommy," he said with a flourish, but felt a small twinge of regret.

Putting the microphone close to where Doris sat in her rocker with Baby, Shockley turned on the recorder and then joined Ruth on the sofa. Ruth took out some mending she had brought along, as as Doris rocked Baby, the three sat waiting patiently.

"I wonder what it is that precipitates her singing," said Shockley, breaking the silence.

"There doesn't seem to be any pattern," said Ruth, looking up, tearing a thread with her teeth.

"She knows," said Doris obscurely.

"Knows what?" asked Shockley, and as Doris opened her mouth to answer, Baby suddenly began to sing.

Ruth put down her sewing in midstitch. Shockley checked the microphone, pushed it closer, and then leaned back on the sofa to listen. Doris continued to rock Baby, looking down pleased as Baby opened her little bird's mouth and sang out to her, mother and child exchanging knowing glances.

Baby sang for a good ten minutes, her voice with its infant's coloring sweeping through her full range, her sweet tune folding back on itself like waves hitting the shore. When she stopped and Shockley was certain that she was finished, he snapped off the tape machine.

As Doris readied herself and Baby to go out for her morning stroll, the Shockleys continued to hang around, Irwin busying himself by rewinding his tape, taking more time than obviously necessary.

When Doris went out to the back porch to put Baby into Cindy's former carriage, which the Shockleys had brought the previous week, Ruth approached her cautiously.

"Baby's seven weeks old now," said Ruth gently, trying to approach her on a mother-to-mother level.

"Six and a half," corrected Doris. Somehow being with them, she always felt the compulsion to let them know that she was on top of matters.

"I don't know if you noticed, but, well, she seems a little thin."

"She's OK," Doris mumbled, lowering Baby into the carriage.

"A baby that age ought to be a little, a little plumper. Just a little."

"What are you trying to say?" Doris looked up at Ruth.

"She may not be getting enough food," answered

Ruth, treading carefully. She and her husband had discussed the matter for almost a week now before daring to bring it up. They didn't want to do anything that would jeopardize his access to Baby, but on the other hand, they genuinely felt that the child was not getting enough nourishment.

"What is it you want me to do?" asked Doris.

"I think it would be a good idea to see a pediatrician." Doris remained silent.

"Baby has never seen a doctor. She should probably be getting some vitamin drops. Maybe—"

"No," said Doris obstinately.

"Look," said Shockley bluntly, joining the discussion when it was at an impasse. "You've got a responsibility to Baby. To make sure she is in the best of possible health. Now if you're concerned—"

"I am."

"Well, then you should take her for regular checkups."

Doris looked from husband to wife. Though she knew they were right, her instincts warned her.

"She's supposed to be growing now. It's critical that her progress be monitored," Ruth urged.

"If she's not getting the proper nourishment, she could get sick," Shockley warned, Baby's eyes on him.

"She's going to need vaccinations, too. She's—"

"Mrs. Rumsey," said Shockley, peeved by her thickheadedness. "You've got the life of a baby in your hands," he said with emphasis. "Do you *want* her to get sick?"

The Shockleys had already made an appointment with the pediatrician on Albany Street before they brought up the subject, and to their minds, it was only a matter of getting Doris to go along.

"But what about the people waiting in the park?"

Doris asked, concerned, as they bundled her and Baby into their car.

"Let them wait," said Shockley. "This is more important."

"It'll take only a half hour," Ruth tried to soothe her as they pulled away from the curb.

"And don't worry about the bill. We'll take care of it," said Shockley, waiting at a red light.

"I can pay," she said, wondering if going to the doctor constituted a commitment, as Markowitz had warned.

"I'm sure you can, but please let me," said Shockley.

"You've already done too much," said Doris, only the faintest edge in her voice.

"For Baby, nothing's too much." Shockley smiled, pretending not to detect the double meaning. "Here we are," he said, a moment later pulling up in front of the old Victorian off Clinton Street that housed the pediatrician's office.

Ruth and Doris went in with Baby while Shockley waited in the car.

Inside, the place was busy, the waiting room packed with kids—lying on the floor playing with toys, thumbing through storybooks, or sitting listlessly in a parent's lap. There were children coughing, children sneezing, children waiting fearfully for shots. As soon as Ruth presented herself at the desk, one of the nurses ushered Doris and Baby directly into an examination room. Ruth followed behind into the small room, but when she saw the doctor approaching said, "I'll be out in the waiting room," and slipped away.

Doris watched nervously through the open door as Ruth moved down the corridor.

"Well, what do you know?" Dr. Waterhouse smiled after introducing himself. "Here we have our little celebrity." He was a short, middle-aged man with bifocals and a soft-spoken manner. From the loving way he took Baby's diminutive hand in his, Doris could tell he cared for children. She let him take Baby to the examination table and watched as he carefully unbuttoned her new pink suit. Observing Dr. Waterhouse as he systematically examined Baby, cooing comfortingly to her as he listened to her heart and chest, palpated her intestines, weighed her, peered into her ears and mouth, Doris began to feel foolish about all her misgivings. It had been downright silly of her to have delayed bringing Baby in for a checkup.

When the doctor finally completed his examination and had elicited from Doris some basic facts about Baby's habits, he was brief and to the point.

"She looks basically healthy, I'd say. But she's definitely underweight. She's also a bit short for her age," said Waterhouse, looking at Doris over the tops of his glasses. "I think we'd better take her off the breast and put her on a fortified formula immediately."

Doris looked questioningly at the doctor.

"Yes"—he nodded, responding to her unasked question—"it's important."

Obediently Doris went with Ruth Shockley to the drugstore on the Commons and bought the formula. She let Ruth, who was obviously experienced, help her prepare the first batch, show her how to sterilize the bottles and nipples. She even permitted Ruth to give Baby her first bottle-feeding, which Baby readily accepted.

Late at night, however, when Doris was lying in her bed listening to Baby sleeping in the basket at her side, she felt possessed by a queasy sensation. She sat upright and turned on the light and looked at Baby. For a few minutes she sat perfectly still, watching as her child's small, bony chest heaved and sank. Looking at Baby's tiny fists that lay on top of the covers, Doris reached over and worriedly caressed those perfect little hands. She tried to allay her qualms, telling herself that her fears were groundless, but her distress continued to grow, her worries feeding on themselves until she became frightened and her heart began to race. Deep down inside, Doris realized, what she really feared was that this formula business was just the first step, that they were conspiring to wean Baby away from more than just her breast. At that instant Baby suddenly awoke and, blinking her eyes, glanced up at her mother.

That night Shockley, too, was plagued by insomnia. He tossed and turned. He got up and closed the windows. When the room turned hot and stuffy he got up again and opened them. He threw off his covers, got cold, and pulled them back on. Something was nagging at the back of his mind and wouldn't let go.

In the afternoon he had finished the initial sketch to his tone poem. It was now basically all down on paper, the fragments, the rhythmic runs, the melodic motives, the piece tentatively welded into a large first-draft conception. In the rush of inspiration that had come over the weeks, he had even assigned some of the notes to particular instruments, perhaps scribbling at the head of a passage, when the insight came, *WW* for woodwinds; or, backtracking on his previous notes he might think, This would be perfect for oboes and clarinet together with strings, and he would quickly jot it down lest he forget. That afternoon, thanks to Baby's help, he had come to a point where he had finally tagged and committed to paper all the ideas that had flown through his mind. In essence, he had come to grips with the toughest part—to nail down the abstractions of the composition into a concrete form. All that remained now was that day-to-day task of craft, of hammering those whimsical notations into a unified and orchestrated form. Though it would take tedious months, Shockley was over the hump. He could return to his neglected grad students and private lessons at school while tending daily to the laborious but straightforward grammar of his tone poem.

When he had finished the sketch that afternoon, adding those final bars, rather than experiencing elation at the end of a good job, Shockley had felt let down. It was odd and it troubled him. Perhaps, he had mulled, it was the postpartum blues. Spurred on by Baby, he had driven himself relentlessly. He was thoroughly drained and exhausted—that was it. Maybe he should put the music aside? Go away with Ruth and the kids for a weekend. Have a good time.

Wearily Shockley had gone into the living room and, taking the tape he had made that morning, had threaded it through his deck. At that faltering moment Shockley desperately craved Baby's music to revive his spirits. Turning on the tape, he had hunted through the endless feet of silence until coming to the squeal marking Baby's song. Backtracking, he had put the machine into its normal mode and, lying on the floor, had positioned himself close to one of the speakers. With his head cradled in his arms, he had closed his eyes and waited as the beginning of the song snaked its way toward the heads. Soon the hiss of the tape had given way to Baby's familiar sound, her light-voiced trilling echoing as it had in Doris's living room. Shockley had listened to the familiar melody, its simplistic line, those childish combinations of vowels and consonants that

constituted Baby's otherwordly language. He had let
the music play over him, concentrating diligently as the
tape ran on but—but could feel nothing—the effect
from the tape giving little more than the flat, emotion-
less response he had gotten when he had tried her melody on the piano. Whatever it was in Baby's music, one
couldn't capture it and hope to keep its effect. It was
neither the notes, nor the melody, nor the language, nor
all of these together that created that thrilling aura. It
was Baby herself, he had realized, who held the magic.

"Are you sick?" Ruth had inquired when he refused
dinner and just moped around the house.

"Me?" he had asked absently. "I'm fine. Perfect. I
just finished the sketch today."

"How is it?"

"Good. As a matter of fact, great." He had tried to
drum up his enthusiasm.

But at night he couldn't sleep—he who had always
been such a sound sleeper. Shockley stared upward and
watched the light from an occasional car play across the
ceiling. Outside in the sticky August night the summer
crickets chirped. Downstairs, he could hear the refrigerator humming. I need a rest, he told himself. And he
resolved to stay far away from his music and Baby for a
while.

Shockley knew of a quaint inn right in the heart of
Pennsylvania Dutch country. It was a rather exclusive
place set amidst miles of rolling, manicured lawns. The
advertisements for the stately old mansion-turned-guest
house boasted of golf courses, tennis courts, horseback
riding, saunas, pools, and fine cuisine. It was a rich
man's retreat, without a doubt, something they could ill
afford—which was why he decided to splurge.

Shockley liked to spring surprises on the family and, without telling Ruth or the children where they were going, loaded the whole gang into the station wagon.

"But where are we going?" Cindy repeatedly whined. She didn't like surprises.

"Are we going to like it?" asked Annette eagerly.

"You'll hate it." Shockley laughed.

"Are there girls there?" Randy asked, combing his hair for the umpteenth time.

"Millions."

"Yeah, but are they good-looking?"

"Each one guaranteed to be a dream."

"I know," said Ruth when they got near Allentown and she guessed it. "But how are we going to afford it? We're still far behind because of the house and—"

"Plastic money," said Shockley with a wink.

"You have to pay that in the end, you know," said Ruth with a grin.

"You do? Gee, if I had known that—" Shockley feigned worry and announced to everyone that he was immediately turning around.

"Why didn't you tell me?" asked Olive Eldridge, leaning over Baby, who was taking her midday nap. Looking at this startlingly perfect baby it was hard for her to grasp that it had come from poor Doris. "Even though I was out of town, you could've reached me by phone."

"I was ashamed," said Doris.

"What's there to be ashamed about, woman?" she said, turning around and planting her feet squarely apart. "I'm a friend of yours. Don't you know what that means?"

"Yes—I do now," Doris admitted, embarrassed by Olive's effusiveness, yet touched.

"That is just one gorgeous baby." Olive shook her head in honest admiration. "What do you call her?"

"Baby," said Doris matter-of-factly.

"Yes. Sure. But she's got a real name, doesn't she? Like Olive. Or Doris. Or—"

The phone began to ring. It rang repeatedly, and when Doris made no move to answer it, Olive looked at her with puzzlement. "Aren't you going to pick it up?"

"It rings all the time."

"Who's calling?"

"Everybody under the sun," answered Doris. "I was thinking of having it disconnected."

"But who?" persisted Olive.

"Oh, folks from the newspapers. From television programs. Like these," she said, going into the kitchen and grabbing a handful from the stack of mail that lay on the table. To one side there were three opened envelopes with foreign stamps, letters from her foster children overseas.

"So, she really does sing?" said Olive, thumbing through the pile.

"You stay around until she wakes up and you'll hear it too," Doris couldn't help but boast.

"Most certainly will." Olive laughed uncomfortably. "Mind if I look at these?"

"That's just today's," Doris said as Olive went through some of the letters, her eyes nearly popping out.

"Do you know what's in here?"

"I've read some of them from before. They keep sending these letters. Calling. I even get telegrams. What I need is a secretary," Doris laughed good-naturedly.

"Look at this! They want you to appear on the 'Donahue' show. And here's one from 'Good Morning America.' And another one from—"

"It's not me they want. It's Baby."

"And here's one from Warner Brothers. In Hollywood." Olive moved her lips as she read. "They want to discuss a film contract," said Olive, flabbergasted. "They want to put Baby in the movies!"

"I know," answered Doris.

"Look at this, will you? They're offering you here five thousand dollars for a one-time appearance on the 'Tonight' show. Doris, do you know what this means?"

"Yes. It means that Baby's staying here. She's not

going on any television shows, and certainly not into any movies."

"But why? You could do it in such a way that it wouldn't hurt the child. And you could make a fortune. She'd be set for the rest of her life. And so would you."

"That isn't the point."

"What is?" asked Olive, who came from a poor family, and all her life, until finally being appointed principal, had had to scratch for a living.

"Baby was not meant to be used like that. She was not meant to be exploited for money. Don't you see?"

"No, I don't see."

"She was a gift from God."

"Phooey!" said Olive, who was a pragmatist.

"If I would do that—put her in the movies, put her on TV shows, sell her music—he'd take her away from me."

"You don't *really* believe that?"

"Oh, I most certainly do." Doris nodded her head. "And I don't think I could bear to lose her."

Shockley knew that he should be having fun. The resort more than lived up to the promise of its brochures. Nestled below the branches of high, ancient oaks, the inn sat encircled by sweeping lawns that undulated far off into the rolling hills. The interior of the old Victorian mansion proved as ornate as the scrollworked exterior. The rooms were lavishly appointed with Oriental rugs and fine period antiques. The cuisine was authentically French, the chef having been lured over from a renowned Paris restaurant. What they served for breakfast alone would have sufficed Shockley for an entire day. There were servants to attend to every whim—bellboys and waiters and maids, personnel to serve drinks by the pool, cabana boys to give out deep, fluffy towels that smelled of sun. Because it was costing him far more than he could afford, Shockley felt that he should be enjoying himself. He went through all the motions. He was visibly enthusiastic at dinner when the escargots, smelling of drawn garlic butter, were brought out on silver platters. He swam and played tennis with apparent gusto. He bantered with the other guests over cocktails. But, as much as he forced himself to indulge in his surroundings, he wasn't really enjoying himself.

For the first day of that three-day weekend Shockley had managed to keep up the pose for his family. By Saturday, however, after walking the same corridors of the inn, exploring the dining rooms, the gym, and the lounges, he realized that there was really only one thought in his mind—Baby. During lunch he spoke not a word.

"Daddy," said Cindy, sidling up to her father as he got up from the table. She took his hand and held it to her cheek. "Tell me a story."

"Not now, kitten," he said, slipping his hand free.

"Please," she pleaded. "You haven't—"

"I said, not now. Later, maybe," he answered and walked off.

"I thought we'd play a game of doubles with the Purcells," said Ruth, catching up with him. She was wearing a bathing suit, and her healthy suntanned skin was in marked contrast to her husband's pallor. "They seem like such a nice couple."

"Why don't you go ahead and play with them? I had something else in mind."

"Play doubles with them? But—" she began to object, but Shockley was already on his way.

Shockley wandered up over the hills behind the inn,

crossing the golf course that sat on a plateau high above
the mansion. Moving obliviously across the field of
players, bright distant swatches of color standing out
against the uniform green, he entered the woods that
rustled and hummed with unseen life. Continuing to
walk aimlessly mile upon mile, Shockley struggled to
clear his head, but all he could think about was Baby,
her and his own damn music and how they seemed
connected. Here he was, living at the veritable pinnacle
of luxury, the sketch for a promising new score on his
desk, the prospects for the future getting brighter, yet—
if he were to be reasonably honest with himself—he
was utterly miserable. All he could do was dwell on
Baby, long to hold her, and have her wondrous song fill
his ears. If only, he thought, if only I could see her for
just a few minutes.

Shockley pushed the image of the infant out of his
mind. This craving was a form of lunacy. A passage
from his new piece sang through his head, and loudly
he whistled another tune to drown it out. He marched
on, picking up his pace, but in a few minutes the woods
came to an end and he arrived at a highway lined with
fast-food joints, gas stations, and a muffler shop. It was
a rather hideous strip and Shockley laughed to himself. Here he thought he had succeeded in leaving behind the realities of life, when, in actuality, just beyond
a ring of woods it was all still there.

For a few moments he stood watching the traffic as
it moved along the strip, cars snaking busily in and out
of the parking lots. Then he turned and went back into
the woods. Retracing his steps through the bog, the
noises of the highway quickly lost, he was suddenly
thinking about his childhood. To mind came the image
of him sitting with his father on a stump in the woods
by a hotel, oddly enough something like this place, and

the old man was saying, "Remember, whatever it is that
you do in life, just be sure that you're the best at it.
Always the best." Shockley recalled the way his father,
for emphasis, had raised one of his bushy eyebrows, fixing him with his hard, unyielding stare—the memory of
which still to this day made him shudder. Too, he could
still feel that same old frustration, that familiar anguish
that he knew was making him so desperate about his
own music.

Shockley crossed the golf green and saw the inn coming into sight. He felt himself sinking deeper into melancholy. Removed from Ithaca, he felt aimlessly adrift
and, though it was only Saturday afternoon, he was already counting the hours.

Though he felt bone weary, Shockley managed to appear cheerful at dinner. That night he went to bed early
and quickly fell into a deep, exhausted sleep. Within
minutes he was dreaming. It was a strange dream in
which he saw himself riding a long traveling belt of the
kind used in airport terminals. He was being transported along the band in the direction of what should
have been the departure gates, but instead of moving to
the ramps where the planes took off, he was being carried toward a bright, blinding light. In his ears there
echoed the singing of children, a chorus of a hundred
infants, their mouths opening in unison as though appearing in trick mirrors, their voices fusing in an over-
powering and peculiar harmony. The music grew louder
and louder until it became deafening. The light brightened in intensity until he became totally blinded. Suddenly Shockley felt something placed in his arms. His chest
was bare and the object felt pleasantly warm against his
skin. The belt reversed itself. The light began to recede,
and when his sight returned, Shockley looked down and
saw that he was holding Baby against his chest. The

music from the chorus slowly subsided, and he clung protectively to the infant, who glowed in his arms. That music, he was thinking, still clutching the warmth to himself, such odd harmony. Then he awoke with a start, awoke to find that he had Ruth's arm clasped against his bare skin.

Shockley opened his eyes and checked his watch. It was only two. He had slept at most a couple of hours. He got up and went to the bathroom to urinate. Groggily watching the tail end of his stream, he tried to recall the harmony of that dream chorus, but though it had been very real then, it now eluded him. He went back to bed and lay down beside Ruth, convinced that he wouldn't be able to sleep anymore that night, that ahead of him lay a long, weary six hours. He closed his eyes for a second. When he opened them again, Ruth was already long since up and it was nearly ten.

Shockley got up, dressed, shaved, and had breakfast. All through the morning he continued to think about the dream. After lunch he paid the bill while Ruth packed. They loaded the car and began the trek home, Shockley still plagued by that lucid dream and hardly speaking.

When they began to approach Ithaca in the late afternoon Shockley felt noticeably better. The depression that had engulfed him at the inn began to dissipate. His senses started to tingle.

"Slow down, please," Ruth warned, and he glanced down at the dash to discover that he was speeding wildly.

He drove in toward Ithaca on the Slaterville Road, and then, instead of turning north toward the Heights, Shockley continued down State Street right into town. Ruth looked at him questioningly as he cut down Aurora Street, took a left on Yates, and pulled up on Willow Avenue. Leaving the engine running, he slid out of the car and closed the door.

"Why don't you drive yourself and the kids up to the house?" he said through the open window to his flabbergasted wife. "I'll get a lift up later myself." And then he was gone, eagerly racing up the steps of Baby's house.

Shockley took a cab up the hill to his house. With Baby's music fresh in his ears, he felt he couldn't afford to waste a precious second.

"Irwin"—Ruth tried to stop him when he charged in the door—"what in the world is going on?"

Shockley raised his hand, begging indulgence, and wordlessly scooted past her into his study.

Going to the drawer where he had left his new piece, he took out the thick sheaf of papers and brought them over to the spinet. Hunched over and squinting at his notes cluttered with insertions and erasures, Shockley began to play his way through the work, filling small gaps with improvisations as he went, all the while disciplining himself to listen to his own music as though with a foreign ear. He played through the entire composition without pause and when he finished he sat looking at the keyboard.

"Well?" said Ruth, who was standing at the door.

He looked up to see her, a curious smile playing over his lips. "You heard."

"I heard." She nodded. "It's good. It needs work, but it's good."

"Yes," he agreed, that strange smile still present. "It's innovative, graceful, melodic. A bit romantic," he said as though he were a critic. "I'd say some of the passages are pleasingly infectious, wouldn't you?"

Ruth nodded again. She didn't like the look on his face. It worried her.

"Polished and orchestrated, it would probably be the best thing I've ever done."

"Would be?" she echoed, picking up the subjunctive.

"Come," he said, patting the vacant spot on the bench beside him, motioning for her to sit. Ruth came over and sat down.

"If," he said, lifting a finger, "if I had never heard Baby's music, at this point I'd probably be dizzy with joy."

"But," she prompted nervously.

"But— Here, listen to this," he said and played through a short passage.

"Sounds wonderful to me."

"No, listen," he said, annoyed, his smile fading as he played the bars over again.

Ruth remained silent.

"Don't you hear? It's not my music. It's Baby's. It has her nuances. Her color. Her little twists and turns," he said. "Yet," he continued sharply, closing the cover to the keys, "yet it's got none of her depth. None of that soul-shaking power. I knew back at the inn there was something bugging me."

"I think you're being very harsh on yourself." Ruth tried to calm him, but saw that it only goaded him, and she stopped.

"Harsh? No." He shook his head. "Ruth"—he turned to her, and when she looked at him, his eyes seemed wild and frenetic—"it's *her* music, Baby's, not mine, and a lousy imitation at that. Don't you understand?"

"I understand that you're tired. You've just had a long drive. Your nerves are still frazzled from all the work."

"That may well be true, but it's also true that hearing Baby has drastically changed my perceptions. Ruth, darling," he almost pleaded, "this piece, or any piece that I do in the future, will at best be a second-rate copy. Trivial."

"That's a rather depressing view."

"No. No, it's not. In fact, it clears up a lot, a hell of a lot. I finally understand," he said, taking the sheaf of notes and rolling it mercilessly into a tight roll, "after all these agonizing years of trying to compose, what it is that I *really* should be doing."

"Which is?" Ruth asked, her eyes on the roll as he continued to twist it, the skin on his knuckles turning white.

"Everything has been preparatory. I was being shaped—or shaping myself—being honed to the point where I would be able to recognize the profundity of Baby's music when I finally heard it. Somehow I feel—" He hesitated, perceiving how silly his thoughts might sound. The recollection of his dream suddenly sprang to mind and he decided to mouth his sentiments. "I feel as though—Well, I've been singled out to protect Baby, selected as the one to bring Baby to the world. Now, I know it sounds ridiculous." He laughed a little sheepishly.

"No," said Ruth uncomfortably. "It sounds fanatical."

"I'm no fanatic." He laughed and, putting an arm around Ruth, gave her a hug.

Disarmed, Ruth smiled.

"I just know what I have to do."

"And what's that?" she questioned, following as he got up from the piano with his twisted sheaf of notes and moved into the living room.

"First I'm going to put an end to this nonsense," he said, hesitating for a moment in front of the fireplace and then impulsively tossing the entire roll onto the grate. The papers landed with a thud and began to unwind.

"Irwin. No!" she said as he hunted on the mantel for a match.

"Where the hell are the—?" he said and went into the kitchen. When he came back with a book of matches, he found Ruth on her knees hurriedly gathering up his composition.

"Please. Don't." She looked up at him beseechingly.

"May I?" he asked, trying to take the papers from her grasp. She held to them firmly. "They're mine, you know," he said, tilting his head.

"Don't burn them," she said, reluctantly releasing her grip. "You'll regret it."

Wordlessly he spread the papers on the layer of cold coals that lay on the grate.

"Oh, Irwin," she gasped, watching as the fire licked the edge of the pile, layer after layer curling up and burning with a bright, almost blinding flame.

Shockley lost little time in approaching Doris with the plans he was formulating for Baby. Early the next morning, under the guise of bringing Baby some freshly pureed fruits, he paid her a visit. Doris was still in her kitchen preparing Baby's morning bottle.

"Baby's no ordinary child," he said when Doris was sitting quietly, Baby drinking in her lap.

"That's obvious," Doris replied guardedly.

"She's got an absolutely phenomenal gift."

"What is it that you want?" she asked, cutting to the heart of the matter, Baby pulling away from the nipple to take a rest.

"I want you to share her with the world."

"That's what I've been doing," said Doris. "I take her out to the park when the weather's—"

"Ithaca's not the world. It's only one little town in one little state. I'm talking about the *world*."

Doris looked a little overwhelmed and Shockley backed off.

"Let me help Baby," he urged softly.

"You've helped her already," she said as she held Baby against her shoulder and burped her.

"I meant in terms of her future. She has one, whether you want to face it or not."

Doris fell silent, her pale eyes troubled, and Shockley knew he had hit a tender spot.

"You won't be here forever." He followed his advantage.

"No, I won't," admitted Doris, putting Baby into her lap and looking squarely at her child.

"When Baby's thirteen, still a young girl, you'll be almost—almost seventy-three."

"If I'm still around," she said without looking up.

"Yes. That's exactly the point. She won't always be an infant. She's got a life ahead of her. She'll have needs—"

"I still don't understand what you're leading up to."

"What I'm saying is that the right moves now could guarantee her a secure future. She could have money, all the money she'd ever need. There could be emergencies, or maybe she'll want to go to college, or travel, or—"

"I'm not going to put her on TV shows or in movies," she said adamantly.

"I'm not talking about that."

"Then what?"

"I'm talking about letting her go on tour, letting her sing for others, letting her give concerts."

"It's the same thing."

"No, it's not. She wouldn't be displayed as an oddity. She would be a singer, singing for people who love music. There's a world of difference."

Doris opened her mouth to speak, but Shockley held up his hand.

"Hear me out, at least. Please."

Doris heaved a sigh.

"First I want to take her to meet some key musicians around the country. I'd like them to hear her sing. Get their endorsements. Then she could go on tour. It would be no big deal. She could sing for small groups just exactly as she does here. And you'd be with her. Traveling with her. We could have a nurse along to help. She'd be given the best of everything. For the rest of her life she would never want for anything."

"And what do you get out of all this?" said Doris with unusual acerbity.

"Nothing. Absolutely nothing but the pleasure of knowing that others have had a chance to hear her."

"No," said Doris tersely, getting up.

"What do you mean, 'no'?"

"Just that. No. She's not leaving Ithaca."

"You can't bury her here. Keep her under house arrest. It's criminal," Shockley flushed.

"She stays put. Right *here*," said Doris, plunking Baby into her basket by the garden window. "And that's that!"

By the time September rolled around and the university was in full swing, it was vexingly apparent to Shockley that there was an ever-widening gap between his plans for Baby and Doris's uncompromising and shortsighted view of her child's future. Each small concession had to be painstakingly wrung out of this old woman, who seemed to be getting more obstinate by the day.

Shockley wanted to take Baby to the Eastman School in Rochester just for the morning to present her to some colleagues there.

"No. She stays in town," said Doris obdurately. "I told you that before."

"Then let me at least take her up to a departmental meeting here at the university. There's one next week."

"I don't know—"

"You can even come along."

"We'll see." Doris put off the decision, and of course, when the date rolled around, she nixed the idea without so much as an excuse.

In the month that followed, Shockley exhausted every conceivable approach. He tried pleading with Doris, threatening her, cajoling her. Sometimes he backed off and ignored her completely. In early October he again tried reasoning.

"Doris, please," he appealed to her. "Don't put me in the position where I have to badger you and coddle you and play all these games."

"You put yourself in that position. Why don't you just enjoy Baby's music and let it go at that?" she asked.

"Because I honestly feel that it's selfish. Doris, tell me, how long will she be able to keep singing like this? Will it be another year? Another five?"

"It might be forever."

"Or she might stop next month. Then it'll be all gone."

"I suppose it's in God's hands, isn't it?" replied Doris fatalistically.

"Perhaps. But what she does with her gift is in ours. Yours. Baby was meant to be heard. Can't you grasp that?" he pleaded.

"I can," she said evenly. "But it doesn't mean that I agree."

"Oh, you're like a stone wall," he muttered and, walking over to Baby's basket, peered in. Baby, who was lying on her stomach, lifted her head and, recognizing Shockley, gave him a big, toothless smile. Turning her over and holding out his hand, he felt her firmly grasp his finger in her fist. Well over three months, she was now rapidly developing. With Doris agreeing to feed her solid foods—the fresh apples, bananas, and cooked vegetables that Ruth pureed daily in her blender—Baby was finally putting on weight and growing. Her cheeks were round and chubby, her limbs plump, and she had a thick head of curly, blond hair. Baby released her grip on his finger, and Shockley stood by the makeshift crib watching in fascination as she reached out for the toys that hung above her head. Knocking a stuffed monkey on a spring, Baby laughed and cooed delightedly when the bells on its neck jangled. One of Doris's cats jumped up on the basket, following the bobbing toy with a paw. Looking in horror at the outstretched claws, Shockley shooed away the cat.

"If you could only give me one good reason," he said to Doris, containing the impulse to warn her about keeping those damn cats away from the child, "why, for instance, we can't take her to just a couple of schools."

"I know why," she said, looking over at the basket. "Why?"

Baby lifted her head above the edge of her basket and looked at her mother. Doris smiled back at her child. "I have my reasons."

* * *

"I hate Baby," said Cindy bitterly during a Sunday morning brunch that the family had in a downtown restaurant.

"But how can you hate her?" asked Shockley, cracking off the top of a soft-boiled egg in a single stroke. "You've never ever seen her."

"I don't have to." Cindy pouted, playing with a spoon in her cereal.

"She's a cute little baby and she—"

"I know. I know. 'She sings like an angel,' " Cindy mimicked.

Shockley and his wife exchanged glances.

"Why don't you come along with me this morning when Mommy drops me off, and we'll visit her together?"

Cindy shrugged her shoulders indifferently.

"Cindy's such a spoiled brat," muttered Julie in disgust.

"That's not nice," Ruth interceded quickly.

"But it's true," Julie answered and, shoving her chair back, got up from the table.

"Women," muttered Randy, trying for a laugh. Ruth fixed him with a stare and he became silent.

After breakfast Ruth drove her husband and youngest daughter to Willow Avenue. Holding the shopping bag containing the usual jars of freshly prepared food and other odds and ends for Baby, Shockley took his daughter's hand and led her up the walk to Doris's house.

"You're really going to like her," he said, extolling Baby's virtues as they climbed the stairs. "If you're very careful, maybe you can hold her."

"Can I feed her?" Cindy tested.

"I suppose so," said Shockley, smiling down at her. As her father rang the bell, Cindy stood on the porch waiting, tapping her feet, and turning around to watch the creek that gurgled past the house. The door opened and Doris appeared. Greeting Shockley, she looked down with mild surprise to see his daughter.

"And how are you, young lady?" asked Doris, who always made it a point of paying attention to children.

"My father says I can feed Baby," Cindy blurted out as she marched in. Doris looked noticeably taken aback by the girl's brusqueness and tried to smile.

"No, I said—" Shockley began to explain as they entered the hallway, but stopped abruptly when he spotted a well-dressed man sitting on the living room sofa. The stranger was holding Baby, and Shockley felt his heart begin to race.

"Who's that?" he asked curtly.

"Oh, let me introduce you," said Doris as they entered the room. "This is Dr. Nolan. He's from the Rochester—"

"Eastman School," said Nolan, returning Baby to Doris and rising to greet Shockley. "Mrs. Rumsey has been telling me about you." He smiled.

"What's he doing here?" Shockley challenged openly. Though he didn't recognize Nolan by face, he knew the musicologist by reputation.

Nolan stood with his hand still outstretched.

"He just came by to hear Baby. And I thought—" Doris stammered confusedly. Nolan took back his hand.

"You should have called me." Shockley turned a deep crimson.

"Hey, hold on one second," said Nolan, facing Shockley squarely. "You don't *own* the child."

Cindy's eyes darted from one tense adult to the next.

"Let's go," said Shockley, angrily slamming down his shopping bag, the jars inside clanking together dangerously. Grabbing Cindy's hand, he yanked her out of the room, passing Doris without a glance.

"But I didn't even get to hold Baby," Cindy protested, dragging her feet as they left the house.

The front door slammed shut, and Doris watched through the window as Shockley marched furiously down the block, his little girl repeatedly turning around. Perplexed and shaken, Doris remained at the window for a moment staring out at the maple leaves that tumbled from the trees onto her walk. She felt tangled in contradictions. Shockley had been badgering her to expose Baby. And here she was, finally complying with his wishes only to have him fly off in a rage.

"Maybe you'd better go, Dr. Nolan," said Doris a few minutes later, feeling weak and spent.

"But I haven't had a chance to—" Nolan started to object.

"Some other time," said Doris, her head starting to spin. She had been feeling poorly for days and was worried about it. "I just don't feel up to any more people today." She apologized, showing him the door.

"Well, you have to understand, Irwin's moody," explained Ruth the following day. Monday afternoons she had a three-hour gap between classes and decided to take advantage of the time to bring Doris some fresh jars of food and look in on Baby.

"I'd say that he was jealous," said Doris, who sat in her favorite chair rocking Baby.

"That's probably also true." Ruth smiled, noticing how wan Doris looked. "He feels that he discovered Baby and—"

"But he didn't discover her. He wasn't the first."

"No. But he was the first musician," said Ruth, trying to smooth over the situation. "And I think he's very concerned about her future and her welfare. In a very unselfish way, as a matter of fact."

Doris shook her head languidly and, rising with difficulty, made a move toward the kitchen, where her kettle was whistling loudly.

"Coffee?" she asked.

"Oh!" gasped Ruth and then quickly regained her composure. She was looking at the cushion on which Doris had been sitting. It was soaked with blood. Doris slowly turned, staring back at the chair, and out of politeness Ruth hastily averted her eyes. Doris paused for a long moment, her eyes going from the cushion to Ruth and then back to the cushion.

"I've been bleeding a little lately," she finally admitted with embarrassment.

"A little?" asked Ruth, looking back at the large, sticky stain.

"It wasn't this bad before. It seems to be getting worse," she said, holding Baby in one arm as she fumbled to untie the cushion with the other.

"Here. Let me," said Ruth, going over and unfastening the stained cushion. She noticed that the whole lower back of Doris's dress was drenched with blood. It became obvious to her that the woman was very ill. The flesh on Doris's face hung lifeless and limp. Her eyes had a distant glazed-over look. Every breath seemed to require a great effort.

"Why don't you see a doctor? I have a good gynecologist—"

"I've thought of it," Doris said, and she looked so weak that Ruth quickly took Baby from her arms.

"Here, sit down again." Ruth helped her over to the sofa. "Maybe you want to stretch out for a minute," she said, slipping a pile of newspapers under Doris to protect the couch.

Doris surrendered to Ruth's suggestion, and she lay back gratefully as Ruth fitted a pillow behind her head. Ruth looked down at the old woman and then, instinctively, lowered Baby into her arms.

"I was going to see a doctor," said Doris haltingly. "But I was afraid. Maybe I'd need an operation or something—"

"If you need it, you need it," said Ruth, who tended to be practical.

"But then what would happen to Baby while I was in the hospital?"

"We'd take care of her for you; you know that," said Ruth as though it were a foregone conclusion.

Doris opened her eyes and stared at Ruth. Ruth read her mind.

"We'd take care of her while you were sick and then, just as soon as you'd be well and strong enough—" she began to explain and then interrupted herself. "But this is silly! You don't even know what's wrong with you. Maybe it's nothing serious at all. Perhaps all you need is a simple D and C. And that's no big deal. It takes only a day."

"Yes," said Doris, brightening, the color slowly returning to her face. "You're probably right." She smiled and then laughed at herself. "I do have a way of making mountains out of molehills."

"Please, ma'am," begged the man standing in Doris's doorway, his hat deferentially held in his hand. "We won't take much of your time. And we ain't gonna be much of a bother." The man's ears stuck out from the sides of his head, and from his clothes Doris could see that he was of poor countryfolk.

"I'm sorry. It's just not a good day for me," she said, gripping the doorframe.

"We came all the way from Ohio," he said, turning back to his junker, which stood parked in front of the house. It was an old, pockmarked Ford with its rusty fenders held on with straps. Doris looked out and could see the girl with glasses sitting in the car, watching expectantly, a wheelchair folded in the rear seat. "I know that if she could just visit up close with Baby, maybe let the little one touch her."

"Baby can't help you that way. She doesn't heal. She just sings. Please, I have to—"

"It can't hurt none to try," said the man desperately. "The doctors, why they've done just about everythin' and—"

"Please. I'm sorry," said Doris, closing the door. Immediately afterward she was stricken by guilt pangs. Leaning against the wall, she stood in the hallway debating with herself. She peeked through a chink in the curtain and watched as the man went back to the car and stood talking to the girl through the open window, motioning with his hands and looking back at Doris's house. The girl looked young, maybe fourteen or a frail fifteen. Doris nervously chewed her lip in indecision, then reached for the doorknob. By the time she opened the door, however, the car was moving down the street, a loose tailpipe dangling below the bumper.

Doris went back into the house, closed all the blinds, disconnected a wire leading to the doorbell, and took the phone off the hook. In a little while, she surmised, people would be gathering in front of her house for the customary listening. She had not been up to facing the morning crowd in the park, and she doubted she had the strength to face them this evening. She needed to conserve her energy for what lay ahead.

"I'd recommend a hysterectomy," Dr. Gaskins had told her. "The bleeding is profuse and it seems to be coming not only from the uterus but—"

"Is there a choice?"

"Not really," the physician had said in a businesslike manner. "Matter of fact, it should be done immediately."

"Can I be out in a day?" she had asked, knowing full well that it was a fatuous question.

The doctor had smiled indulgently. "You'll need some time to recover."

"Oh," she had said, fighting the tears forming in her eyes.

"It's not an unusual operation." He had put his hand on hers. "We do them all the time," he had reassured her, deciding to play down the possible complications.

"Can I think about it?"

"I'd like to reserve a bed at the hospital today," he had pressed.

"I need time."

"There isn't much," he had persisted. "You've lost an awful lot of blood. You shouldn't even be on your feet."

Sitting at the Formica table in her kitchen and looking blankly into a cup of tea gone cold, Doris tried for the umpteenth time to reason her way through her dilemma. She was afraid to leave Baby. Once out of her hands, there was no telling what might happen to her.

"I'd be very careful." Markowitz's words rang in her ears. "You've got a very valuable child there."

"We'd take care of her while you were sick," said Ruth. "And then, just as soon as you'd be well—"

Doris wrung her hands together. For an instant she saw before her Shockley's youngest daughter, and the image of that child impudently saying "My father says I can feed her" worried her.

Doris moved through the downstairs of her house toward the rear window where Baby's basket sat. The sun was getting low and the garden was couched in dark shadows. In her bones Doris could feel the first rawness of winter that was but weeks away. She peered into the basket. Baby was up, patiently waiting for her feeding, quiet and uncomplaining as always.

"You are such a perfect little angel," said Doris, tears welling up in her eyes. Baby looked up at her expectantly. "Mommy's a bit of a coward," she said, and a solitary drop rolled off her cheek and splashed on Baby's face. Doris took a finger and wiped it off her infant's smooth skin.

Reaching down, she carefully lifted Baby from her basket, holding the child's head in the palm of her hand. As she shuffled back to the kitchen, Doris could feel the warm dampness of blood moving threateningly toward the edges of her napkin, and she wished it would all just stop and go away. Outside her house she could hear the first murmurs of people.

"I have no choice, do I?" she asked, and Baby looked back at her, her delicate brow furrowing as though she grasped every word and desperately wanted to help. "If I don't go for the operation we'll lose each other forever. If I go, it'll be a long time. And who knows what will happen," she murmured, realizing how helpless she now was, and how utterly dependent she would be on the Shockleys. "Will you remember your mommy, huh?" She stroked the curls on Baby's head with two fingers as the child peered back searchingly. "Oh, how I wish you could talk," she said as Baby's eyes darted worriedly from side to side and then suddenly stopped as she stared fixedly at her mother.

Baby drew a long breath, her small chest swelling until it could grow no more. Her delicate lips parted and then, as she slowly exhaled, there emerged a song, a new song, a plaintive melody that Doris had never heard before, the child remarkably capturing and distilling the melancholy mood of the moment. It was as though Baby comprehended the impending trials that they would both face and through her song was urgently trying to convey that understanding to her mother.

Doris closed her eyes and listened to Baby's new song with its long-held elegiac notes and sorrowfully meandering melody, Baby's voice low and barely audible as if she had taken the measure of her audience of one.

"Baby, Baby, Baby." Doris sang along in her own creaky voice, weeping openly as her child's compassionate melody granted her comfort, giving her the fortitude to face the harsh realities that waited in the days ahead. "Baby, Baby, my angel Baby." Doris sang out from the depths of her heart, lost in the moment of the song.

Within the span of a single day Baby's presence rapidly transformed the tone of the Shockley household as all activity began to revolve around the new arrival. Shockley, who had never particularly troubled himself with the mundane needs of his own children when they were little, was now changing Baby's diapers, powdering her bottom, making formula, feeding her, and worrying about the ravages of diaper rash. Annette, who from the start fell under the spell of Baby and her music, eagerly took on the role of surrogate mother whenever she could.

"She's not a pet or a plaything," Shockley had joked when Annette started dressing her up like a doll for the third time that day.

"Oh, Daddy. She's so gorgeous," Annette gushed, holding up Baby in a frilly little nightgown and matching booties.

Julie appointed herself official walker and that afternoon, when she returned from school, she proudly pushed Baby's carriage up and down the sidewalk under the watchful gaze of her eldest sister.

Even Randy, loath to partake in any domestic activity that might endanger his *reputation*, volunteered in the privacy of his home to hold Baby while she drank, taking secret pleasure in watching the little girl as she eagerly tugged at the nipple. When Baby rewarded him with a song, he was tickled with pride.

Of all the children, Cindy showed the least interest in the new visitor, and Shockley correctly assumed that it was her closeness in age to Baby that made her so standoffish, though from the start he had scrupulously tried to head off any rivalry.

Bringing Baby home that morning after helping Doris to the hospital, Shockley had made it a point of letting Cindy be the first of the children to officially greet her.

"Wouldn't you like to hold her?" he had said, extending Baby to her.

"Well——" Cindy had pouted, swaying her hips from side to side with studied indifference. "Well, I suppose so," she finally conceded.

Shockley had put Baby into her arms. "Now, hold her carefully. And use your arm like this to support her head."

"I know!" Cindy had responded, piqued. "I'm no dummy," she'd said, peering down at Baby, a mixture of curiosity and suspicion crossing her face. Lying in Cindy's arms, Baby had suddenly become agitated, her eyes taking on a desperate look. And then, for the first time in Shockley's experience, Baby had begun to cry and struggle.

"I'd better take her," he had said, shaken, unable to disguise his own distress. "You may be holding her too tight," he'd added as an afterthought. "It takes a little experience."

"Who cares, anyway?" she had muttered, sauntering off to her room. "She's just a stupid little baby who poops in her pants."

"Maybe you'd like to feed her," Shockley had worriedly called after her.

"Not now. Maybe later," Cindy had said, tossing her head back and slamming the door to the room.

Unsettling as it was, the incident with Cindy did serve to substantiate a suspicion that had been with Shockley for some time.

"Not everyone is affected by Baby's music," he said, sitting bolt upright in bed in the wee hours of the morning. "Ruth," he said, shaking his naked wife who had been snugly curled up against him. "You awake?"

"No." She smiled sleepily at the ludicrous question.

"Until now we've only seen the people who're attuned to Baby's music. They're the ones who've made themselves evident. But not everyone is touched by it."

"Nor," said Ruth, yawning and then completing the thought, "to the same degree."

"Precisely! You can see it among our own kids," he said, but Ruth was already deep asleep.

The following morning after the kids went off to school, he excitedly continued the discussion.

"There seems to be a hierarchy of effect," he said, as he gulped his coffee and burned his tongue.

"There was no reason to think otherwise," said Ruth matter-of-factly. "In nature, in biological phenomena, there's usually a continuous, often Gaussian type of distribution. You know, a bell-shaped curve." And she drew it in the air with her hands.

"But this is not biology."

"Most certainly not," Ruth agreed, with a smile. "It's religion."

"Aw, come on," Shockley said with a mouthful of toast.

"And even in religion, there's probably some sort of distribution with a small collection of atheists, skeptics, and assorted disbelievers on one end, then a growing number of moderate people somewhere in the middle and then, finally, a diminishing number of zealots at the other extreme."

"Sounds like a good Ph.D. thesis," Shockley joked.

"It's all yours," said Ruth as she drained her cup and gathered up her dishes.

"Seriously though," said Shockley, stuck on the subject, "if you look at our kids, the effect of Baby's music seems to go by age. Annette is the most profoundly affected, then come Randy, Julie, and finally Cindy, who's totally deaf to it."

"Now that's not fair!" Ruth objected defensively.

"I didn't mean it disparagingly. I love her as much as you do."

"She's not deaf to it. She hears it. It amuses her. She just isn't quite as moved."

"Because of her age?"

"Who knows?"

"What about us?" he probed thoughtfully, wiping his lips with a napkin and putting his dishes in the sink.

"I'd say that although I'm very touched by her music, you're far more profoundly influenced. I'd put you in with the zealots," she grinned.

"Hmmm," said Shockley, standing in the middle of the kitchen, rubbing his chin thoughtfully. He was still working on his theory, trying to plug others he knew into a slot.

"Now don't try to point out that I'm a year younger," she said, heading for the hallway, "and attempt to draw an inference from that."

"Now you're joking with me," he said, pursuing her.

"Oh, Irwin." She lovingly stroked his cheek and then, turning, hunted through the hall closet for her coat. "You'd make a hell of a scientist," she laughed.

"But what's wrong with—?"

"There's nothing wrong with your theory except that you're trying to draw conclusions from isolated observations. You don't even have a decent statistical sample."

"I'm grasping at straws, I'll admit it, but I'm trying to make sense out of it all."

"Isn't it possible that there is no 'sense'? That there is

no physical correlation? That age or sex or height or even musical ability doesn't necessarily matter?"

"In some way people are predisposed to her music. In some way they are more or less open, more or less receptive."

"I'll grant you that," said Ruth, pulling on her coat. "And it could just be that that receptivity is not quantifiable, at least not in any earthly way. Do you find that so hard to accept?"

"From you, absolutely! I thought you were the pragmatic, scientific brain in this house and I the sensitive, emotional, whimsical artist."

"Turns things around, doesn't it?" Ruth gave him a wet kiss and, with an enigmatic wink, hurried off.

That very afternoon Shockley had another revelation about Baby's music.

It was almost five when Shockley was finally able to break away from his last class at the university, and by the time he came home Annette had already relieved Mrs. Holger, the helpful neighbor who had agreed to look after Baby during the day. Ruth was in the kitchen making dinner with Julie and Randy—Randy objecting loudly about getting stuck with the dull job of peeling potatoes. Annette sat in the living room doing her homework, one eye on Baby, while Cindy lay on the floor working on a jigsaw puzzle.

After spending a few minutes with Baby, Shockley began to wander aimlessly around the house. His offer to help fix dinner rebuffed, he took out his violin. He was scheduled to get together with his chamber group later that evening and he thought it a good idea to run through some of the pieces they would play.

"How much longer?" he called out to Ruth, tightening his bow. The house now smelled enticingly of frying

meat and freshly baked bread, and he could feel the
juices in his mouth beginning to flow impatiently.

"A bit," she answered vaguely. "Can't you entertain
yourself for a while?"

"What's a while? I'm starved," he said, thumbing
through his notes.

"Me too," said Cindy, hunched intently over her
puzzle, her knees pulled up to her stomach.

"Me three," joked Annette.

Shockley picked up his violin and played a passage
from a Haydn string quartet that had previously given
him some trouble. He played through part of a Mozart
piece and just started a Bartók work when Ruth called
them to dinner.

Annette and Cindy dashed off to wash their hands as
Shockley hurriedly put away his violin. He was just
closing the case when Baby began to sing.

"Ruth," he called out urgently after an instant.
"Come quickly!"

She appeared, wearing her apron, the children coming from all directions.

"What's the—"

"Listen!" he said, pointing to Baby as she lay in her
basket.

"Baby's singing," said Julie matter-of-factly. "She always—"

"No. Listen again," Shockley said, closing his eyes
and tracing her notes with a finger in the air.

When Baby had finished he turned to Ruth, who
stood with tears in her eyes.

"You heard," he said, beaming, and she nodded.

Annette had gooseflesh on her arms.

"It was a different kind of song," she said, filling the
silence.

Baby turned to look at the collection of faces encircling her basket and smiled.

"A new song."

"It sounded a little like the Mozart you were playing," said Randy, who had a good ear.

"And maybe a touch of the Haydn," added Ruth thoughtfully.

"Are we ever going to eat?" asked Cindy, but she was ignored.

"Ruth, my God," said Shockley delightedly, "she's learning. She's picking up new ideas—a little of the whimsy of Haydn, a touch of Bartók's lyricism—and synthesizing them in her own way. She's taking from the masters and going beyond."

"Far beyond," admitted Ruth.

"What does it mean?" asked Julie, baffled.

"I'm not sure, but from now on we're going to give her a chance to hear other kinds of music. The best. There's not going to be a music-free moment in this house anymore." He reached over and pulled Baby's shirt down over her bare tummy. "Our little singer here is going to have a blitz course in music appreciation."

"That's great"—Cindy pouted—"but what about dinner?"

"Don't you see?" Shockley said to Ruth late that night when he got back from his chamber group. "Baby's trying new modes of expression. She's moving beyond that same basic theme we've heard for weeks. She's actually developing a repertoire."

"Two songs don't compromise a repertoire."

"You're a cynic."

"A realist," Ruth shot back. "Why must you always jump the gun?"

Shockley tried to sleep but couldn't. His mind was in a jumble. He was thinking about Doris, who was scheduled for surgery the next morning; he was thinking about Baby, about the two of them together. He tried not to dwell on the future.

"The reason she didn't evolve any new forms," he said later to Ruth, who was trying her utmost to doze off, "is that in Doris's home she was never exposed to any music."

"Maybe she's just maturing, and tonight the time just happened to be ripe." Ruth stifled a yawn.

"In Doris's home she was deprived," he said, a little dogmatically.

"If that's what you want to believe—But I'm sure that Doris probably had the radio or television on some time. There's always some—"

"I mean *music,* not junk."

A few minutes later Shockley was talking again.

"I was thinking—" he began.

"I really wish you'd stop thinking. It's late. I'm tired. I don't know about you, but I have to work tomorrow." Ruth got testy. "And I want to get some sleep."

"Oh. Sorry," he apologized innocently. "I was just thinking—"

"So what is it already?"

"We can't let Baby go back to her, to that bleak house."

"There's no choice."

"There is," he said, chewing his lip. "I had an idea. We could let Doris move in here after she gets out of the hospital."

"Forget it," said Ruth and rolled over, turning to the wall.

Doris came out of the anesthesia in agony. The wound, which ran from hip to hip, was one white-hot, searing pain. Her insides felt torn and stretched, cut and twisted around. There were tubes in her arms and her nose, a catheter in her urethra. When she vomited, it felt as though she would burst her stitches, and all she could do was try to lie perfectly still on her back, which also ached. If she dared to make the slightest movement, perhaps turn to her side, her pain became torture. Doris found herself trapped in a living nightmare in which she moved between sleep and wakefulness, unable to differentiate between them, time marked by the short-lived relief of injections—the faces of the silver-haired surgeon, the Shockleys, the nurses and orderlies merging with the apparitions of her wild dreams until she was unsure whether those people had actually been there at her bedside or in her dreams. When the suffering became unbearable and the next injection seemed an eternity away, when she no longer believed that she was alive and was convinced she had landed in hell, Doris would cry out in a low, desperate moan for Baby. She would call for her child until her strength failed and then fall into an exhausted sutpor, wondering if there really ever was a Baby or if that little, golden-haired infant had also been no more than a figment of her dreams.

On the second day things didn't seem much better. Doris was still in torment. She seemed even weaker and hardly conscious of her surroundings. The ordinarily persistent nurses, who were instructed to get their patients moving the day after surgery, didn't have the heart to force her up. When they tried to merely roll her on her side to halt the developing bedsores on her back, Doris wailed in pain.

"How are you feeling?" asked Ruth on the third day when Doris opened her eyes.

"Bad," groaned Doris through cracked lips, and then closed her eyes again.

"Well, it's not healing quite as it should," Dr. Gaskins explained to Shockley a day later. "And she's running a fever."

"Which means?"

"She may have an infection. But don't worry. I've already put her on antibiotics. These things happen, but they usually resolve themselves quickly. Though—"

"Though what?"

"She's not exactly young. And she was not in the best of shape when she finally came to me. She was torn apart inside. She had lost an enormous amount of blood. There was internal bleeding. She was anemic. She—"

"It sounds to me like you're hedging your bets," said Shockley bluntly.

"No. I'm just trying to give you a realistic assessment."

"Do you think she's going to die?" he asked straight out.

The doctor looked only mildly surprised. He paused

thoughtfully and then finally said, "There is that possibility, though that kind of pessimism isn't warranted. Not yet."

"What is?"

"Caution," said the doctor. "We're going to have to watch her very carefully. I'm considering opening her up again to put in a drainage tube."

"Is there anything else we can do?"

"Hope for the best."

It didn't take long for Shockley to get an inkling of how Baby's presence was to disrupt his family's ordinarily quiet life. With Baby absent from her downtown home and word spreading of her whereabouts, Baby's followers now began to appear at the Shockley house in ever-growing numbers. They came on foot, by bike, car, taxi. They arrived individually or in large groups spilling out of vans. They hung around the Shockley house, clogging the street and angering the neighbors, who lived in the Heights precisely because it was supposed to be private and excluded what they considered "town riffraff."

"What the hell's going on there?" Dr. Dusenburg, the Nobel laureate physicist, who was Shockley's neighbor on the north, called to complain.

"I don't care if Jesus Christ himself is living in your house!" fumed Mrs. Rifkin from across the street when a couple accidentally trampled one of the sprigs in a new hedge she had planted just last spring. "Get rid of them or get rid of the baby."

"There must be some law against it," said Dr. Garfinkle, the historian, conferring with Simpson, the famous economist and presidential adviser next door.

"Maybe there's a zoning ordinance against babies," quipped Simpson, who always found humor in everything, but later lost his temper when someone's car inadvertently blocked his driveway.

"I'm sorry." Shockley nervously confronted the crowd standing on his lawn. The last leaves of the season were drifting down from the ancient oak overhead as he spoke, and in the background he could hear the phone ringing in his house. He couldn't be sure if it were another neighbor, or the press, or God-knows-who. "Mrs. Rumsey is seriously ill and until she gets better there won't be any listenings. Please. I must ask you to leave. The neighbors are complaining."

Some of the people left with grumbles and resigned shrugs. Others were more insistent. They took to hanging around at all hours, leaning against their cars and smoking or sitting cross-legged on his lawn. One couple, who had come from Buffalo, even had the audacity to demand their rights.

"Look, you're just going to have to go," Shockley had insisted a bit more firmly.

"But when can we hear her?" asked a petulant girl, who was dressed in an army fatigue jacket and looked like a former student of his.

"If you don't leave, I'm going to call the police," Shockley warned.

"I don't want Julie taking Baby out for walks on the road anymore," Shockley later told his wife.

"Baby's safe. They just want to hear her, that's all."

"That was Doris's mistake. We're not running a circus here. Baby will be heard. At the right time and in the right place."

"When and where is that?"

"I haven't decided," Shockley answered perfunctorily. The demands on Shockley were growing, and he seemed to be getting progressively more short-tempered.

In addition to the people who hung around the

Shockley house in the hope of catching Baby's song, the calls and requests that had previously besieged Doris were now being redirected to the Shockleys. In a single day a deacon from some fundamentalist church in Binghamton appeared, demanding to see Baby; two fanatical women describing themselves as born-again Christians tried to force their way in, claiming that they had been divinely appointed to exorcise the devil that had possessed the infant; a blind woman plunked herself down on their front step and refused to budge until her sight was returned. And at the university, Shockley's colleagues were hanging on his heels as if he were a dog in heat, begging for an invitation to his house; and, of course, the same television people who had been working on Doris were still trying to get their foot in the door.

"I'm simply not going to discuss any proposals on the phone," Shockley tried to put off a particularly insistent ABC news producer who was trying to finagle an immediate booking for Baby on "20/20." "All inquiries should be made by letter, setting forth the terms."

"But we've done that already," the man objected in frustration. "In fact, we've sent about six letters and I don't know how many goddamn telegrams to Mrs. Rumsey."

"Well, I'm not Mrs. Rumsey. Why don't you do it again, but this time address it to me? You may have better luck."

As the days passed and Doris's condition appeared to worsen, Shockley soon found it impossible to fuse in his mind the disparate worlds of Doris's misery, the meaningless drudgery of school, and his buoyant life at home with Baby. Encased in the sterile sphere of the hospital, there was the old lady, tubes running into her body, dark yellowish urine haltingly dripping into the bottle under her bed, life measured in sluggish drops. Awaiting him each day at the university were his new music-appreciation classes, so crowded that students had to sit on the floor of the lecture room, students and teacher locked in by requirement not choice. And at home was Baby, lying in her crib, the glorious sounds of Beethoven or Brahms or Britten filling the air, the little girl listening and looking expectantly as if she were waiting just for him. Moving from school to hospital to home, Shockley felt he was being torn into three distinct pieces.

Returning home from the county hospital one evening, a little more than a week after Doris's surgery, Shockley suddenly blurted out what had been in the works for days.

"I'm taking Baby for a trip," he announced.

"A trip? But where?" Ruth asked, puzzled.

"She's going on a tour with me to see some people around the country."

"But why? I don't understand."

"Why?" he echoed as if it were self-evident. "To give her a little exposure. To let people hear her. Other people. People outside this town. People who know music. Baby was meant to be heard, not hidden. Too much time has already been wasted. I—"

"You can't do that!"

"It's all arranged. I made the reservations this afternoon. We're already expected. I'm going to USC, to Peabody, to Juilliard—"

"But what about Doris? You know how she feels about Baby being—"

"Doris? She doesn't even know what's happening."

"She's the mother."

"She's sick and dying, a crazy old lady who in the last fifteen years hasn't ventured out of a five-mile radius, who—even in her best years—probably has always been out of touch. Look, Ruth, I feel sorry for her. Honestly I do. She's a sad shell of a human being. A tragic case."

"And you have a responsibility to her."

"Yes, I do. But I have a larger one too. I feel a moral obligation to make sure that Baby is heard, an obligation that goes far beyond the one to Doris."

"She entrusted us with her child."

"God Almighty! We're not boiling the kid in oil. All I want to do is take her to see some people. I'll be back in less than two weeks."

"Two weeks!" Ruth all but gasped. "But what am I going to tell Doris?"

"You don't have to tell her anything. If she asks, just say that Baby's happy and fine. And it'll be the truth."

"And what about your job? You can't just take off. If you lose it, then what?"

"God'll provide," he said with a confident smile.

"Sure," said Ruth sourly.

The phone rang.

"That must be for me," Shockley said, rushing off. "I'm expecting a call from Lenny Bernstein. I'm trying to set up a meeting. Keep your fingers crossed."

Almost from birth, Irwin Shockley was drawn into the world of music. Even before he was old enough to lift his own miniature violin and scratch out a tune, Shockley was being exposed to an impressive sampling of the most eminent composers, conductors, and performing artists in the business. Though Maestro Henry Shockley was never to attain the heights of fame he had always assumed were his due, he did nonetheless possess a savvy instinct for rubbing shoulders with the musical luminaries of his day. A list of the people whom young Irwin had come into contact with almost from the start of his life might read like a *Who's Who*. Aaron Copland, who used to stay weekends at the Shockleys' Long Island home had—according to Shockley's mother—changed baby Irwin's diapers during an emergency. Eugene Ormandy had gotten down on the floor on all fours to play horsey with Irwin. Arthur Rodzinski had once held a serious conversation with the promising five-year-old that Shockley could still recall today. Dimitri Mitropoulos had shown the fledgling violinist a nifty new way to finger strings. And on and on. Walter Piston. Samuel Barber. Fritz Reiner. Leopold Stokowski. Shockley had been exposed to his father's contemporaries almost without knowing who they were. They had all dropped by at one time to have a drink or chat with Henry Shockley—an outwardly warm, considerate, and affable man.

From the age of six and onward, Irwin Shockley's contact with the august world of music became more formalized. Observing the agility with which his son taught himself the violin, Henry Shockley had come to the conclusion that young Irwin had all the earmarks of a prodigy. Above the weak objection of his wife, he sent the headstrong six-year-old off to study with Ivan Galamian. Galamian, whose later students included Itzhak Perlman and Pinchas Zuckerman, was quick to spot not only the boy's inherent talent, but also his rambunctiousness, which could prove a problem. As a favor to Maestro Shockley he accepted the boy, assuming he could channel Irwin's energies into the violin. He was wrong. The young Shockley was no easy student. He cut classes, stubbornly refused to spend the required five hours a day in uninterrupted practice, and was more interested in play than playing.

After a frustrating year, Galamian, sapped by the demands, threw up his hands.

"Listen, Henry," said Galamian, breaking the news, "he's a sweet kid. I like him. A competent violinist he can be, that's obvious. But a genius he's not. Take my advice. Don't push the boy. Let him develop. He's a wild kid who needs to have fun, to mature. He's got a good ear and a nice touch." Galamian had tried to soften the blow. "Who knows what direction he'll take? Maybe he'll become a great conductor like his father. Or another Mozart," he laughed.

Irwin's failure, however, was no laughing matter. Nor was it to be accepted. Galamian didn't know what the hell he was talking about. Off went Irwin to the next violin master. And then the next. Never one to learn from experience, Henry Shockley also discovered in his daughter the makings of a prodigy. A pianist, this time. Karen proved more malleable than her older brother. With her father's coercion, she practiced endless hours without a whimper or complaint, forsaking the carefreeness of childhood for the rigors of the keyboard. By the age of twelve, this high-strung, frail girl had been formed into an accomplished soloist. By fourteen, she was on the road giving recitals around the country. By sixteen, she had ended her life. With Karen's death the light went out of Henry's life. The house became cold and barren, devoid of visitors and music. Irwin Shockley fled to school and never returned. Henry's wife left him without warning. A couple of years later Maestro Henry Shockley died a lonely, disappointed, and impoverished man.

Aside from the debts against his estate, Maestro Shockley did, however, leave his son a legacy of sorts—

the Shockley name. It was a key that, if not guaranteeing success, did at least open doors a crack. Just as Galamian had so astutely predicted, Irwin Shockley had moved in other directions. He put away his violin and became a composer. All those early contacts paid off handsomely in admittance to the best schools, scholarships, fellowships, grants, recognition. And today, thanks to the lasting image of his father, Shockley still had entré. All he had to do was pick up a phone. Which was what he had done for Baby.

"Zubin," said Shockley when Maestro Mehta finally returned his call. "How good to hear from you. The reason I called—"

On the morning of his departure, Shockley was the first one up. It was a crisp November morning with a layer of frost covering the grass and, after turning up the heat in the house, Shockley hurriedly packed. For Baby he filled up a large suitcase with diapers and extra bottles and blankets, her vitamin drops, a tube of ointment, and a sampling of her best clothes. For himself he packed a much smaller bag. After shaving and eating a hasty breakfast, he dressed in a new suit and went up to the guest room that had been converted into a nursery. Still deeply asleep, Baby was lying on her stomach, her hands placed by her head, her knees tucked under her, elevating her tiny bottom into the air. Reluctantly Shockley awoke Baby, rolled her over and changed her diapers as she stretched her mouth in a long yawn, her face still creased from sleep.

"We're going for a big trip," he told her after her breakfast, when the airport limousine pulled up in front of the house and honked.

Baby looked back at him confusedly, and laughing, he touched her nose and gave her a quick loving peck.

At the Ithaca airport Shockley checked the bags and boarded the waiting jet. The engines roared, shaking the cabin. Fastening his seatbelt, he held on tightly to Baby, muttering soothing words to the child, who seemed alarmed by the noise. As the massive machine plunged headlong down the runway, its shell quivering violently, Baby's apparent fear suddenly became infectious and a terrifying thought raced through Shockley's mind. What if the plane couldn't lift off and crashed at the end of the runway, trapping them in a fiery heap? Pressing his forehead against the cold plastic of the window, Shockley forced the vivid image from his mind as though that unmentionable thought had the power to shape events.

The plane lifted its nose with a groan, banked steeply, and started to climb. Shockley let out his breath. Distorted through the scratchy plastic of the window, he could see the roads and houses turn to doll-like proportions. A stretch of forest with bare-limbed trees merged to an even blanket of dark, cold brown. The choppy waters of the lake passed below, yielding to the neat squares of outlying farms.

Shockley pulled himself away from the window and, looking down at Baby, saw to his surprise that she was sucking her thumb. It was the first time in her life that she had done it, he thought, gripping her tightly as the plane continued to climb, bouncing through the thick, ominous clouds. The jet lurched and jolted. Finally it broke through the gloom, and they were now moving in an unobstructed field of brilliant, blue light, riding smoothly above a frothy, white layer cushioning them from the ground. The plane reached altitude and, as the noise in the cabin began to abate, Shockley noticed that Baby was singing, or trying to sing, her thumb still lodged in her mouth. Curious, he bent forward, bringing his head close to hers, his nostrils picking up her scent of powder and milk. She was not exactly singing, he observed above the drone of the engines. Rather, she was humming to herself, humming around that thumb. He pressed his ear tightly against her curled fist and strained to pick up the bits and pieces of her slow, melancholy song. How I wish Ruth were here to witness this, he thought, touched by the pathos of this new melody. He had been right. Baby had it in her. Another new song, he muttered jubilantly to himself. And though it was a new song to him, it was, in fact, the same elegiac melody that Baby had sung for her mother on parting, one that she had, unnoticed, come to sing to herself in her moments of distress or longing.

By the time they reached Los Angeles, Baby was clearly exhausted. She had not slept a wink on either the first flight to Chicago or the connecting one to the coast. She was tired and irritable and refused to eat. Afraid that Baby might balk at singing, Shockley debated delaying the scheduled appearance before the USC music department. If he did, however, it would foul up the entire itinerary and, worse, might start raising suspicions.

"Are you going to sing tonight?" he asked nervously, and when Baby finally took her bottle he decided to push ahead with the appearance.

"You may have to be patient," he explained to the gathering of academics and musicians.

"Is this a joke?" asked one of the men peering into Baby's portable crib that sat on a table at the front of the rather large and austere lecture room.

"She doesn't sing on cue," continued Shockley uneasily, ignoring the comment. "You're going to have to sit very quietly and just wait."

They all sat and waited. Overhead the fluorescent lights hummed noisily. Outside on the street a siren wailed. A dog barked. After half an hour some of the people in the room started fidgeting in the hard, wood-backed chairs. Forty minutes later people started drifting out of the stuffy room.

"Please," said Shockley, almost angrily, to those who were getting up. "Give her a chance."

Looking over at Baby, who was lying there inertly staring at the cold ceiling lights, Shockley felt a wave of resentment sweep over him.

After an hour and a quarter, with the audience dwindling down to less than half, Shockley was beginning to feel like a fool. His nerves were ragged, and he knew that if Baby didn't sing, he would never live this down.

"Maybe she's tired," he suggested, preparing for his downfall. "She's been traveling all day. Let's give her another quarter of an hour," he pleaded, and the remaining audience grumbled but stayed.

Then, moments before the time was up and Shockley was at his breaking point, Baby suddenly relented. Opening her mouth she drew a long breath and began to sing. It was a variation of her earliest melody, and though she sang barely loudly enough for the assemblage to hear, Shockley fell back in his chair in exhausted relief. A murmur of surprise went up, then quickly subsided as people strained to hear, Shockley delightedly observing their faces, which registered the full range from rapt attention to startlement to blissful tears. When Baby finished, there was dead silence.

A man at the rear started to clap tentatively. Someone else joined him. An instant later the assemblage burst out in loud, unanimous applause.

"Hurrah!" someone shouted.

"More!" cried a woman, as though she were at a concert.

The people rose to their feet as one and for three long minutes gave Baby a standing ovation.

With a grin Shockley took a bow for Baby's benefit.

"Thank you. Thank you," he said when the applause finally began to subside. "Please inform your colleagues about what they missed."

Zubin Mehta was still in town and Shockley took a cab over to his house to catch him before he left for a concert in Tel Aviv.

"So you're the little singer." Maestro Mehta laughed, spreading apart the blanket and peering curiously down at her face.

"I have to warn you," said Shockley, hedging his bets, "it's not always easy getting her to sing. It took almost two hours at USC today."

"For me she'll sing," said the swarthy man, holding out his arms and accepting the infant. "Come, darling, sing for Uncle Zubin," he coaxed gently, and without a moment's hesitation, Baby began to open up. She sang basically what she had sung earlier that evening.

"Divine," said Mehta, shaking his head. "Can you do more?" he asked, puckering his lips in the form of a kiss.

"She's got another song," Shockley started to explain, and Baby interrupted him by singing her plaintive song, singing out loud, and finished by sticking her thumb into her mouth.

"What a sad song!" said Mehta, obviously stirred. "What's she trying to say?" he asked.

Shockley shrugged.

"What are you going to do with her?" questioned Mehta when Shockley was getting ready to leave.

"I want to share her with the world. I want everyone to hear her."

"Yes, of course. But you must be careful," said Mehta sagaciously.

"Don't worry, I am," said Shockley, meeting his dark eyes.

"I've never seen anything like this. But I do know that with children you have to be exceedingly careful. Talent can be burnt out," he said with a raised eyebrow. Mehta had heard the tale of Shockley's sister and knew he didn't have to say more.

The next morning Shockley flew with his protégé to the State University of Arizona at Tempe where Baby—in noticeably better spirits after a good night's sleep—performed without a hitch. From Tempe they went east to the University of Indiana. The grapevine was working at high speed and, when they landed in Bloomington, they were greeted at the airport by a contingent of eager musicians.

A day later the pair arrived at West Texas State. Baby's reputation had apparently preceded her here, too, because, though she stalled for a good two hours, not a single person in the packed auditorium wiggled so much as a toe. While at the Peabody Institute in Baltimore a week later, Shockley received a long telegram from Pierre Boulez, the former conductor of the New York Philharmonic, requesting a private audience. Boulez was known for his interest in avant-garde music, and Shockley was exceedingly pleased by his request. It just added further credibility to an already accepted Baby.

"Shockley's Find Is the World's Find!" raved a critic

for the *Los Angeles Times* who had waited out Baby's performance at USC, knowing that, no matter the outcome, he would have a good story.

"Composer and Infant Hitch Teams," read a large headline in *Music World* over an article replete with pictures of Shockley and Baby—eight pages of the normally staid journal devoted to the infant prodigy and her impresario. Scattered throughout the article were shots of Shockley standing over the makeshift crib taking notes, Shockley holding Baby aloft before an overflow audience at West Texas State, even a photo of Shockley feeding Baby her afternoon bottle.

At the New England Conservatory, Shockley was mobbed outside the building where Baby was to perform, and mounted police had to be called in to clear a path through the crowds for Baby's limousine.

"You wouldn't believe what's going on," Shockley breathlessly told Ruth in a short phone conversation they had one night. He was trembling with excitement and had to grip the phone with both hands.

"I believe it," she said dully, having just read about Baby in *Newsweek*.

They talked for a few brief minutes and then, as Shockley was saying good-bye and was about to hang up, she said to him, "You know, Irwin, you haven't even asked me about Doris."

"Oh. Doris. Yes. How is she?" he asked, still flushed with success.

"Feeling better?" inquired Dr. Gaskins, leaning over his patient.

Doris opened her hooded eyes a little more and tried to swallow. Her throat was parched. Sensing her thirst the physician lifted her head and held to her lips a pa-

per cup filled with ice chips. Doris took a mouthful of
the cold chips and, pressing them against the gums
where her upper teeth had once resided, felt the soothing, melting water ease down her throat.

"You had us all a little worried," he said, taking out
a blood-pressure sleeve. Pumping it tight, he rolled his
eyes upward, concentrating on the stethoscope plugged
in his ears. "H'm." He smiled a little too cheerfully. "It
looks good."

Doris swallowed the remaining ice that had turned
to slush, her eyes searching the doctor's face.

"The worst is over," he said, meeting her gaze.
"Your fever's down. Your red count's improving. By
tomorrow I want you up. OK?"

Doris gave a weak nod. She tried to smile, but the
muscles in her face refused to obey.

"I know what hell is like," she said when the doctor
was leaving.

He turned and laughed. "Well then, you can warn all
us sinners." He grinned and turned on his heels.

"Up to the bathroom," said the nurse the next morning, a few hours after Doris's catheter had been removed. "Doctor's orders."

"Oh, please." Doris protested feebly as a team of
nurses disconnected the tubes and hoisted her up despite her moans.

"Now that wasn't as bad as you thought it would be,
was it?" said the young nurse when they led her back to
bed and covered her.

"Worse," said Doris, and they were sure she was joking.

She wasn't. What did they know with their young
bodies that had never been sliced in two?

In the afternoon Doris ate her first meal: Jell-O, a half slice of toast, and a cup of tepid tea. It all tasted faintly like plastic, but she knew that if she were ever to get out of this place—and not in a pine box—it was vital to eat. For Baby's sake. When they took her tray away, Doris lifted the covers and for the first time peered down at the drainage tube that emerged through the gauze and tape of her bandage-covered wound. Quickly she covered it up again and tried not to dwell on the fact that it ran deep into her body.

In the evening Ruth came by with a smile and some flowers.

"You're looking much better," she said, and Doris had the feeling she was hiding something. Maybe she was dying and they didn't want to tell her the truth?

"How's Baby?" was the first question she asked.

"Oh. Baby," Ruth blustered. "She's fine. Happy. Well."

"Why do you seem so surprised that I asked?"

"It's the first time you've asked anything." Ruth shrugged nervously.

"Where is she?"

"With Irwin."

"I'd like to see her."

"They don't allow children to visit the surgical wards," Ruth said and realized that her answer had come out a little too quickly.

"Maybe you could bring her tomorrow. Outside the window," Doris said, motioning behind her head to the long window that looked down three stories into a grassy courtyard.

"Maybe." Ruth smiled. She suspected that Doris had been thinking about it all day.

* * *

"She wants to see Baby," Ruth explained to her husband when she finally located him. He was on the way to New York. "Tomorrow!"

"Stall her."

"I can't. I tried."

"You have to. Tomorrow I see Boulez and Bernstein."

"Why am I stuck with the disgusting and utterly onerous job of lying?"

"I didn't say lie. I said stall."

"Why should *I* be the one?"

"Because I need you to. Look, a few more days. What the hell difference will a few lousy days make?"

"Plenty."

"Can't explain now. Listen, darling, I've got to be at a meeting tonight. Tomorrow it's Juilliard."

"Now *you* listen."

"A few days. What's a—Wait! I've got it. They don't allow children to visit in the surgical ward," he said frantically rushing his words. "Tell her that."

"I did already. She wants me to bring Baby to the window."

"What floor's she on?"

"Why?"

"What floor?"

"Third."

"Great! Wrap up a blanket and parade it down in front of her window. It'll work out perfectly. Doris'll be tickled. You'll be off the hook. And everybody'll be happy."

"I will not!"

"You will."

"Why carry on this charade? Sooner or later she'll find out."

"Maybe. But let it be later."

* * *

When Doris saw somebody standing below in the courtyard holding a pink bundle, she fumbled for her glasses. Seeing that it was Ruth holding Baby, she burst into tears.

Forcing herself up in her bed on an elbow, she moved closer to the window and waved, dabbing at her eyes with a tissue.

"Baby, Baby," she called from behind the sealed panes, pressing her hands against the icy glass.

Ruth tipped up "Baby" and pointed her toward her mother. Doris laughed through her tears.

"Just seeing her," Doris confessed when Ruth came upstairs later, "makes me feel well already. I feel like hopping out of this old bed and charging home," she laughed exuberantly. Ruth swallowed uncomfortably. "But if you're up here"—Doris suddenly stopped, her smile fading, lines of worry registered on her face— "then who's with Baby?"

"Cindy's sitting with her in the lobby. She's OK," Ruth said reassuringly and felt like strangling Irwin for putting her through this.

"It's not that I don't trust you," Doris quickly apologized.

"I understand," answered Ruth, wanting to leave.

"I'm always worried about her."

"That's normal."

"I suppose when you have a child this late in life and with so much trouble you get to be silly and overprotective," she said, looking down at her white hands that were splotched with freckles and lined with blue veins. "I've always been afraid that if I let go of Baby even for a minute I'd lose her forever. It's ridiculous, I know, but that's why I acted the way I did when I left her with you. But you've taken good care of her. I can see that,"

Doris said, becoming uncharacteristically loquacious, her hand coming to rest on Ruth's. "How can I ever thank you people?"

"You don't have to," Ruth said and with a mumbled excuse finally rushed from the room. She took the elevator down to the main floor and met Cindy, who was sitting in the lobby, one of her lifelike dolls held in her lap, the pink blanket trailing to the ground.

"I don't get it," said Cindy, probing her mother's face with her dark, deep-set eyes.

"There's nothing to get. Come on. Let's go," she said, taking her by the hand. "We're late for your lesson."

"Was Mrs. Rumsey supposed to—?"

"Will you mind your own business!"

"I was just asking."

"Well, don't!"

When they moved Mrs. Skibinski into the empty bed in Doris's room, Doris knew it was a sign that she was recovering—though she wished that they would have found anyone but Mrs. Skibinski. The thirtyish woman with owllike features had undergone removal of a tumor in her right breast and from the moment she awoke from the anesthesia and learned that the lump had been benign, there had been little peace for Doris. Mrs. Skibinski chewed gum, talked incessantly, and was visited by an endless string of friends, relations, and co-workers who crowded the tiny room and stayed for hours. Worst of all, Mrs. Skibinski's husband had rented a television for her, which blared unabated from early morning to late night. In vain, Doris had once requested Mrs. Skibinski to turn down the set, please.

"It's down as far as it'll go. If I turn it down any

more," said the woman testily, "I won't even be able to hear it."

Doris resigned herself to the television, trying to concentrate on the books that the hospital volunteers brought her, aware that her irritation was a healthy sign. Before, they could have dropped a bomb in her room and she wouldn't have noticed it. On and on the television ran as Mrs. Skibinski whimsically changed the channels, giving the tube no more than a cursory glance. Sometimes Doris would look at the oblique screen, catch snippets of a dull soap opera or gameshow or the shrill commercials that vied for her attention. Mostly the programming filtered into the background of her consciousness, returning to haunt her in her sleep in the form of jingles that looped over endlessly in her head.

The second night of TV, as Doris was finishing her dinner, a news report coming over the cable from New York abruptly broke through the wall of her consciousness.

"And, coming up," the newscaster was saying, "Mayor Koch calls for yet another cut in city workers. A tragic fire in Brooklyn. And a baby who can sing takes the city by storm. All after these brief messages."

Doris dropped a spoon into her rice pudding.

"What's that!" she gasped, her heart standing still.

"It's the news," said Mrs. Skibinski, lighting up a forbidden cigarette.

"What did they *say*?" Doris asked, feeling the blood drain away from her head, her chest tightening as she fought for breath.

"The usual." Mrs. Skibinski shrugged.

Doris's mind began to race. A baby that can sing.

Takes New York by storm. That's what he said. She was almost positive. And how many babies in this world can sing? she wondered, throwing off her covers and shuffling barefoot across the icy floor.

"What's the big deal?" asked Mrs. Skibinski, who thought Mrs. Rumsey a pain but was curious to see her suddenly interested in something on television.

Doris moved up to the set.

"You're blocking it," said Mrs. Skibinski, who didn't want to miss whatever it was that excited her roommate.

Standing hunched in front of the screen, her eyes riveted to a bleach commercial, Doris didn't budge. After the first ad there was one for toothpaste, followed by an interminable dramatization about floor wax in which two women were arguing about who had shinier floors. Doris was still worrying about what she thought the man had said. Feeling woozy and weak, she took a step backward and leaned against Mrs. Skibinski's bed for support.

"Make yourself at home while you're at it," said Mrs. Skibinski caustically.

The newscaster came on again. There was a story about Mayor Koch. Some sanitation workers were interviewed. Angry faces threatened with mayhem in the form of uncollected garbage. Then there was a scene of flames shooting out of a brick tenement, and Doris tried not to let her imagination fly as she saw bodies wheeled away on stretchers.

The newscaster came back on and introduced the next story. The picture switched to a black reporter standing on a city street holding a microphone.

"Well, John, we weren't allowed in, nor for that matter were our cameras, but we have it on reliable advice that there's a most unusual three-month-old baby in town. And she arrived quietly in New York about two days ago."

The picture cut to a shot of a man emerging from the rear of a limousine. The car was flanked on either side by police holding back an eager crowd of reporters and onlookers. Doris, who berated herself for not bringing her glasses, moved back to the set, bringing her face close to the tube until the picture became distorted. She turned up the sound.

"The baby, who goes by the name of 'Baby' "—the newsman let a chuckle slip into his voice—"has been on a tour of . . ."

The camera was being jostled, and Doris held her breath as it searched through the confusion of people, found an opening, and slowly started zooming in.

"According to our sources, this three-month-old little girl can actually *sing.*"

The camera was now closing in on the man and child.

"Oh!" cried Doris in anguish.

" . . . discovered by music Professor Irwin Shockley of Cornell University, this little girl is causing quite a stir around the country. Purportedly . . ."

The newscaster came on screen again and the report was over before it had hardly begun.

"Well, a baby that croons," said the announcer with a laugh and a wink, wrapping up the program on a light note. "That's a new wrinkle. And that's it for this evening. Chuck Bates will be back at eleven with the final roundup. From all of us here at TV 10."

Doris slumped down on the corner of Mary Skibinski's bed.

"Hey, Mrs. Rumsey. Are you *the* Mrs. Rumsey who—Oh, wow!" she exclaimed, realizing her roommate was a star.

"Wait till I tell Hank about this!"

Doris sat in bed the entire day waiting in turmoil for Ruth to appear, rehearsing in her mind what she would finally say to her. In her lap sat a copy of *The New York Times* opened to a second-page article headlined "Infant Prodigy Stirs Juilliard." Under the headline was a picture of Shockley holding her Baby. Doris had read the article over eight times and there were phrases she could quote verbatim:

"After a hectic cross-country swing . . ."

"Experts at the University of Southern California . . ."

"At Baltimore's Peabody a group of eminent . . ."

"Shockley was purposely vague about his plans to. . . ."

Doris tried to reason through her predicament, her thoughts torn by anger and despair and bitter fury. Ruth had lied to her. Straight to her face. Had tricked her. How in this world could one human being do such a heartless, deceitful thing to another? How could one mother, who had given birth to children of her own and knew the feelings it engendered, be so callous to another mother? Shockley she could understand. He was pushy, arrogant, self-centered. But his wife. How could she have taken part in this heinous deception?

Ruth never appeared that day, and the speech Doris had so carefully prepared went unused. That night, feeling wretched and helpless, Doris cried herself to sleep. She awoke early the next day before the morning shift of nurses had arrived, feeling as though she hadn't slept a wink. At lunchtime she looked up over her tray to see Ruth standing in the doorway. The television was squawking loudly, but all Doris could hear was the thunder of blood in her own ears. Ruth remained framed in the doorway, giving a tentative smile, the corners of her mouth twitching nervously. The instant her eyes met Doris's she realized that the old woman knew.

"I'm terribly sorry," she said, aware that it was a lame apology.

Doris stared at her with narrowed eyes, her fists bunching up the sheets, her nostrils flaring with each breath. She tried to speak, but the words she had prepared failed her.

"I can't tell you how bad I feel. You're angry. I understand. I would be furious too."

Doris continued to stare fixedly at her, her features frozen and hard, her expression going beyond anger or pain. She swallowed with difficulty and then, finally, the words she could muster issued from her lips.

"You betrayed us," she said succinctly and turned her back to Ruth.

"Don't be rash," said Dr. Gaskins, who had learned of Shockley's deceit. "Stay at least until you're strong enough to cope with the situation."

"You can't keep me here against my will," said Doris firmly.

"No, I can't," he admitted. "But if you go, I won't be responsible for what might happen."

"I didn't ask for that."

"Give yourself a few more days. You've made a splendid recovery. Why ruin it?"

"I want to go now."

"Wait at least until the morning."

"Now."

"There are forms to be filled out," he stalled. "The business office needs time to—"

"Now," she said obstinately.

"You'll have to sign a release waiver."

"Whatever."

* * *

"It was a stupid thing to do," said Ruth, breaking the silence as she drove her husband home from the airport, Baby dozing in his lap.

"It was and it wasn't, Ruth." He turned to her in the darkness, the headlights from a passing car harshly chiseling the lines of his face. "I had to grab the chance. If I hadn't done it now, I might never have had the opportunity. Now they all know. The child exists."

"And to do it you duped Doris and you used me."

"I don't deny it. I admit it."

"And you're not contrite."

"No, not especially."

Ruth stopped at the intersection to Route 13 and waited for the long lights to change. The motor idled noisily and Shockley thought about getting the car tuned.

"How are the kids?"

"You should ask first how Doris is."

"I'm afraid to."

The light flashed green and Ruth turned on to the highway. She drove down the long incline, passing the malls flanking both sides of the road, their parking lots busy with cars. The sign of a Holiday Inn glared to one side. An electronic sign alternated numerals, 35°, 8:45, 35°, 8:45.

"OK, OK. It was wrong. Morally despicable. What else do you want me to say?"

"Nothing," she said, but her words belied her meaning.

"Look, I couldn't help myself," he burst out after a moment. "Whenever she sings, I have no choice. I feel impelled to do something. I can't just sit on my hands and let this magnificent child get buried alive. Do you understand?" he asked, looking down on Baby's placid features and noticing that her thumb was again in her mouth.

"No,"—Ruth glanced away from the road for an instant—"not really. I don't understand."

"Boy, I'm glad you're the one who has to confront her now, not me," Ruth said as they pulled up the driveway to the house. "I don't think I could ever look her in the eye again. Or for that matter myself in the mirror."

Ruth got out of the car, but Shockley remained in the front seat, holding Baby.

"Would you mind driving us to the hospital?" he ventured meekly.

"Right now?"

"I'd rather face her now and get it over with. I don't like things hanging over me."

Ruth got back into the car.

"Maybe," he said as they passed through the octopus exchange at the far end of town and began to climb up West Hill to the hospital, "maybe I can reason with her."

"Fat chance," said Ruth.

"Checked out this afternoon," said Mrs. Skibinski, with a smile on her face and a fresh wad of gum between her teeth.

"Left?"

"The doctor told her she was nuts." Mrs. Skibinski shrugged. "I'm getting out myself tomorrow morning. None too soon for me. I work up at the—Hey, you're the professor we saw on television, aren't you?" she called out as Shockley left.

"We called a cab for her," said the head nurse when Shockley found her. "I assume she went home, because the doctor arranged for a nurse to visit her daily but—"

Shockley hurried to the elevator and pressed the button. The elevator was in the basement and seemed to stop at every floor. He grew impatient and hurried down the stairs two steps at a time.

"She's left," he said, getting back into the car and taking Baby, who had dozed off.

Ruth looked stunned.

"But where to?"

"Home," he said tersely.

Ruth started the car and drove back toward town. She cut through the west end of the city, drove over the small bridge on Cascadilla Creek, and turned on to Willow Avenue. The lights were on in Doris's house, and Ruth and her husband exchanged worried looks.

"You can wait here," he said, getting out with Baby, who was waking up.

"I'll go with you."

"You're not responsible for what happened."

"I know what my responsibilities are. I don't need you to define them," she said going along.

Shockley rang the bell. No one answered.

He rang again. Still no sign.

He peered in through a parting in the curtains of the front door. Looking into the hallway, he could see no one. He rang again, holding the button. Suddenly Doris's face appeared framed in the curtain opening and for a moment the two stood fixed eye to eye, Shockley feeling himself wilt under her slitlike gaze. The door slowly opened. Doris stood planted in the doorway, her body blocking the way.

"Give me Baby," she said, holding out her hands.

Shockley hesitated.

"Doris, I want to explain—" he began.

"Give her the child," said Ruth emphatically.

Obediently Shockley handed over Baby.

Doris took her child and looked down at her as though examining Baby for damage. When she was finally satisfied, she lifted her face and directed her words to Shockley.

"You're never to come around here again, or see Baby again," uttered Doris in a low, quaking voice. "No one is. Forget about Baby," she said and with that slammed the door.

"Come on," mumbled Ruth, going back to the car.

Shockley remained on the porch, stunned. He stood there staring blankly at the door, watching as the downstairs light went off, shivering from the chill of the evening, from trip fatigue, from the incisive awareness that Doris Rumsey truly meant what she said. The door was to be closed. Forever.

TWO

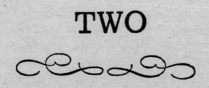

Shockley busied himself raking leaves in the yard. Ordinarily it was a task that he enjoyed, relishing the smell of crisp leaves and deriving a certain satisfaction from the orderly swaths of lawn that followed in his wake. Today, however, it gave him little pleasure, and he did it only to kill time.

Leaning his rake against his shoulder Shockley anxiously checked his watch for the third time. By the time he glanced up, a stiff gust had done a good job of scattering his neat pile. He tried to round up the tumbling leaves, but the wind tricked him, picking up speed and repeatedly switching direction. A frigid blast swooped up from the valley, cutting him to the bone and turning his fingers numb. Helplessly he watched as the last leaves on his pile scattered over the expanse of dormant grass.

The sky turned dark and for a moment there was a rush of wind-driven snow. The heavens lightened, the sun peeked through a blue chink above the rim of West Hill, then disappeared. A few vagrant snowflakes fluttered to the ground, as low, boiling clouds charged recklessly overhead. Turning up his collar, Shockley thought about the desolation of the incipient winter, a winter without the consolation of Baby. In his mind's eye he could already picture the snow dunes blowing blindly across the roads, see the deep, rutted piles of salted slush clogging the city street. Shockley shivered at the prospect. In Ithaca it was always the weather, the damn weather. It governed conversations, moods, needs, the condition of the pocketbook, the outlook on life, even sex. Looking into the skies one could almost forecast the state of the day's events. A cluster of snow stuck to his eyelashes and, wiping it away, he tossed aside his rake and went inside to the phone.

Picking up the receiver, Shockley waited for a dial tone, but none came. He jiggled the button, but still there was no signal. It was then, hearing the static in the receiver, that he realized that someone was on the line.

"Hello?" he questioned the hiss.

"Hello," echoed a distant female voice, sounding surprised. Apparently he had picked up the phone an instant before it was going to ring.

"Professor Shockley?"

"Yes?"

"One moment, please," said the woman and, before he could even inquire who was calling, the line was switched and a man with a familiar foreign accent was on the line.

"This is Jacobsen. Ivar Jacobsen," said the man with the guttural pronunciation.

"Oh, Mr. Jacobsen," said Shockley, taken off-guard. "I'm terribly sorry. I meant to get back to you."

"I was waiting for your call," replied Jacobsen rather brusquely.

Ivar Jacobsen was a powerful booking agent with offices in New York, London, and Rome. Representing some of the most distinguished opera singers, performing musicians, and conductors, he flew around the country in his private jet replete with communications equipment and staff, and Shockley had no idea where he might be calling from. While in Texas, Shockley had been contacted by an associate in Jacobsen's New York office. The famous Mr. Jacobsen, he was informed at the time, wanted very much to speak with him. Shockley was flattered, and an appointment of sorts had been arranged. At the appropriate time, he was told by the caller, Mr. Jacobsen would find him. Ultimately Jacobsen had caught up with him in New York.

Emerging with Baby from the auditorium at Juilliard after her performance, Shockley had been getting ready to run the gauntlet of reporters awaiting them outside the hall when he spotted a tall man with regal bearing standing discreetly off to one side of the crowd. His head towering over all the others, he was a strikingly ugly man with long, exaggerated features, a heavy brow, thick jaw, and long strands of whitish blond hair encircling his bald dome. The man's eyebrows were nearly transparent and his skin so light he looked almost albino. Though Shockley had never met him in person, had only seen pictures of him, he immediately recognized Jacobsen. Before Shockley realized what was happening, three of Jacobsen's assistants had encircled him and Baby and were deftly whisking them past the reporters and into Jacobsen's waiting limousine—a small contingent of cooperative police holding back the onlookers who pressed close. It was, in fact, that very limousine that Doris would later see on Mrs. Skibinski's television.

Holding Baby, Shockley had silently ridden with Jacobsen and his crew to Central Park South, the limo pulling up in front of the Pierre Hotel. Until they reached Jacobsen's top-floor suite not a word was exchanged, Jacobsen's aloofness and stern bearing cowing the normally irrepressible Shockley.

Jacobsen's suite was lavish. A pair of large crystal chandeliers hung from the vaulted ceiling of the main room, the gleaming furniture was solid mahogany, and on the floors were rugs that appeared to be authentically Persian. Shockley was staying with Baby in a rather ordinary motel on the West Side and, gazing around in awe at the splendor of Jacobsen's rooms, he promised himself—and Baby—that the next time they visited New York they would also live in style like this.

"I don't have much time, so let's get right down to business," said Jacobsen bluntly after they were seated in armchairs facing each other. Lighting up his fifth cigarette since they had met, the Dane exhaled a flood of smoke. Baby coughed and wrinkled her face, but Shockley didn't dare object.

"What sort of business did you have in mind?" asked Shockley, his attention caught by a Teletype chattering away in the next room.

"I'm talking about Baby, of course. I had a chance to hear her today."

"She is remarkable, isn't she?" Shockley beamed.

"Yes," replied Jacobsen without emotion, "but what you're doing with her is certainly less than remarkable. In fact, if you'll pardon me, I think it's a disaster."

Shockley's smile fell.

"I think you ought to realize that if you're trying to set up a career for her, you've gone about it in the worst possible way," he continued, snuffing out a half-smoked cigarette.

"I'm not sure that I do want to set up a career for her," said Shockley defensively.

"Well then, what is it that you're trying to accomplish?"

"Frankly, at this point, all I'm trying to do is to give her an opportunity to be heard."

"By the greatest number of people?"

"Yes. Of course."

"Well," said Jacobsen, his mood suddenly shifting and turning cordial, "in that case it looks like you need some help, doesn't it?"

"Perhaps," Shockley hedged.

"Come on, Dr. Shockley, let's not beat around the bush. I want to put Baby on tour." Jacobsen absently fumbled for another cigarette. "But I'm talking about a *real* tour, not this half-hearted farting around with music schools. I'm talking about a tour that can draw big box office, big money," he raised a hand. One of his gold cuff links caught a gleam of light and Baby strained forward to get a better look.

"I'm not interested in money. That's not my motivation."

"Fine. But what about her?" said Jacobsen, motioning to Baby, who sat in Shockley's lap attentively watching the agent's every move. "Did you ask her?"

Shockley laughed.

"Sure," said Jacobsen, "she's only a little baby now. But one day she'll be big and her gift could be gone. This might be her only chance in life and it could end up being squandered. Have you given her future *any* thought?"

"Well," Shockley stumbled. "Not really. I'm taking this one step at a time."

"Yes, that's obvious. But maybe you should be looking ahead. Five, ten steps. Not one. With an extraordinary child like this you have to think big, really big," he said, the near-transparent flesh on his face flushing. "If for no one else then for *her* sake."

"I suppose you may be right," Shockley conceded, suddenly feeling his own inadequacy in the face of this man who had shaped the lives of countless performers.

"I *am* right," he said, not mincing words. "Look, let me make a proposal." Jacobsen wet his lips. "I want to put Baby on tour. I want to put her in the biggest, most prestigious concert halls in this country and overseas. You want her to be heard? She will be heard. That I can guarantee you. And she'll make money. Bundles of it, which we'll put away in a trust fund for her. Then, when she's old enough, she can decide whether or not she wants it. If not, let her give it away to charity!" He laughed. "Dr. Shockley"—he suddenly turned serious—"you know as well as I do that I can get her bookings anywhere I want."

Shockley swallowed and nodded.

"Well? Do we have a deal?"

"I have to think about it."

"Well, think."

"Right now? You want an answer this instant?"

"No." Jacobsen chuckled. "Take a few minutes."

"You're joking."

"I'm serious. I want an answer before you leave. If you don't want to do business, that's fine with me. We'll shake hands and part friends. It was a pleasure to have met you. If you want to do business, then we'll get right down to brass tacks."

"Only one go-around."

"You've got it," Jacobsen looked at him squarely, his face taut and etched with deep furrows.

"I see," said Shockley, looking down at Baby. Nervously he stroked her hand with his finger. Baby turned abruptly and looked up at him.

Silence.

"There are other booking agents in the business," said Jacobsen helpfully, but implicit in that suggestion Shockley knew was the affirmation of Jacobsen's supremacy.

Silence.

"OK," said Shockley hoarsely a long minute later. "OK. You'll take care of her bookings. But that's all."

"Good," said Jacobsen affably, his face turning magically smooth and bright. "Good man. You've done the right thing," he said and, motioning for his secretary, he began dictating a letter of agreement.

"She is yours, isn't she?" Jacobsen suddenly interrupted his letter and turned to Shockley.

"Yes. It looks that way."

Jacobsen arched an eyebrow, paused, and turned back to his dictation.

After Jacobsen finished the agreement and his secretary had gone to type it, he turned back to Shockley.

"You heard my terms, didn't you?"

Shockley nodded.

"There's one more thing we have to understand, and that's reliability."

"Pardon?"

"Is she reliable? Will she perform on schedule?" he asked, irritated by Shockley's apparent thickheadedness.

"So far she has. Sometimes it takes a little while."

"I noticed."

"Generally, I'd say yes."

"Are you reliable?"

Shockley laughed, then looked offended. "Yes. Of course."

"Good," said the Dane, rising to his feet, "Hans," he called out to his associate, who had been awaiting his cue.

"Mr. Jacobsen," said the man deferentially.

"We're ready to roll." He nodded, and clasping his hands behind his back and looking up at the ceiling, Jacobsen began his litany, reeling off names that made

Shockley's head spin. "Try Symphony Hall for the fifteenth, Severance for the twenty-sixth," he said, pacing
the floor and scanning a mental list. "I think we have a
hole there, but you'd better double-check." The man
looked up from his pad and then went back to scribbling. "Try—"

"So soon?" interrupted Shockley nervously.

"You said you wanted a tour. So I'm setting up a
tour," Jacobsen said, fixing him with a hard stare that
made Shockley wilt.

"Yes, of course. It's just that I didn't think it would
all go so—so—"

"So?"

"So fast!" He forced a smile.

"Is she ready or isn't she?"

"She is," Shockley said, trying to sound determined.
"I just have to clear up a few matters back home."

"I was waiting for your call," repeated Jacobsen.
"You said you'd call to confirm as soon as you returned. It's now—"

"I'm sorry," he apologized lamely. "We've had some
minor problems on this end."

"I've already set up the dates."

"There's been a hitch."

"What kind of hitch? You gave me the go-ahead,"
snorted Jacobsen.

"That was subject to my clearing up certain matters.
Besides, Baby's got a cold."

"A cold? I asked you if she's a reliable performer."

"My God, how can we control a—?"

"Hang on a second," mumbled Jacobsen distractedly, and Shockley could hear another voice in the

background. "I've got an urgent call from London. Could you hold on for a couple of minutes?"

"Why don't you call me back when you're finished?" suggested Shockley, trying to put off the man. At the moment, uppermost in his mind was another call.

"OK," said Jacobsen, abruptly breaking the connection.

Shockley hung up for an instant and, checking a number he had carried around all day, hurriedly picked up again and dialed.

It rang on the other end.

"Come on. Come on," mumbled Shockley as it repeatedly rang. Finally the ringing stopped and a woman answered. "Mrs. Rudd? Shockley here."

"Oh, yes, Mr. Shockley," said the visiting nurse, sounding cheery, her false gaiety rubbing him wrong. "I just got in the door this second," she said breathlessly. "Some weather, isn't it?"

"Did you see her?" he inquired, hardly able to go through any pleasantries.

"Yes. I changed her dressings and—"

"The baby? How's the baby?"

"I couldn't spend much time staring at the child. Mrs. Rumsey was watching me like a hawk. Wouldn't let me hardly near her. The best I could do was sort of casually take a peek—like you suggested."

"And?"

"She looked OK, I suppose," she said circumspectly.

"What do you mean?"

"Mrs. Rumsey's awfully weak. Matter of fact she can hardly move. She's barely strong enough to care for herself, much less her child. And the place—well, it's not what I'd call exactly neat," said Mrs. Rudd.

"And the child?"

"She seemed healthy."

"You sound hesitant," he tried to draw her out.

"Well, I am. I took a look in the fridge when Mrs. Rumsey wasn't looking. Heaven knows what they're eating. It was just about bare. And she's certainly in no condition to go shopping. Why, she can barely make it to the bathroom."

Shockley remained silent for a moment, assailed by visions of Baby hungry.

"You still there, Mr. Shockley?"

"Yes. Look, do you think you could go shopping for her?"

"It's not exactly my job, but—Yes. Sure I could."

"I'll bring some money right over. I want you to get whatever you think they might need. Especially for the baby. I'll pay you for your time and trouble."

"That won't be necessary."

"I insist."

"Well, if you—"

"It's important they have anything they need. Spare nothing. I don't want them suffering in any way."

"You're a very kind man," said Mrs. Rudd warmly.

"Just don't tell her where it's coming from."

"If that's the way you want it."

"It is," he said and, as an afterthought, added, "please."

Shockley put down the receiver. The phone rang almost immediately.

"Mr. Jacobsen calling for Dr. Shockley," said a young male voice.

"He just stepped out."

"When is he expected back?"

"Not till late tonight. I'll have him return the call."

* * *

"What does she see?" asked Cindy when the screen filled up with the terrified face of the actress.

"Huh?" asked Shockley, turning to his daughter in the darkened theater. He had been sitting there for almost an hour, staring blankly at the movie, without anything registering. He had been thinking about Baby.

"I said, 'What does she see?' " Cindy repeated.

"I don't know." Shockley shrugged distractedly. "Why don't you wait and see?"

An instant later Cindy's question was answered. It was a decapitated body covered with blood, and Shockley was wondering why he'd let her talk him into taking her on a sunny Saturday afternoon to such a morbid film. He suspected he had gone along in the hopes of occupying his own thoughts but, here he was, dwelling on Baby, vexed at how Doris was undoing all he tried to accomplish, and at how damn helpless he was to do anything about it. He tried to push Doris out of his mind. Tried, but she was like a festering sore.

"What's she going to do now?" asked Cindy a minute later, again breaking into Shockley's thoughts.

"Don't ask me," he snapped irritably.

"OK," mumbled Cindy, hurt, turning back to the screen and reaching deep into a near-empty bag of popcorn to dig out a few stray kernels.

A minute later, however, Cindy was again bugging him with questions.

"What's going to happen now?" she asked, gripping his hand.

"How should I know? I didn't make the damn movie!"

"Quiet!" hissed someone behind them.

"I was just asking," Cindy whispered. She was glad to have her father back again, doing things with her,

like going to a movie in the middle of the day. It felt
good, even if he was grumpy.

"I think she's gonna be murdered," she explained a
few minutes later.

"Maybe," said Shockley, guilt-stricken for snapping
at the child and wanting to apologize.

"See!" Cindy crowed delightedly when the woman
fell over dead, a knife in her back. "Gross, isn't it?" She
grinned, wide-eyed.

When the movie was over they filed out of the theater. The brightness of the afternoon was blinding, and
Shockley felt a dull headache throbbing at the back of
his skull.

"Where are we going?" she asked when they didn't
go directly back to the car.

"I've got to take care of something," he said, a dime
already in hand as he stepped into a phone booth on
State Street.

"Not Baby *again*," she muttered to herself as her father dialed a number.

"This is Shockley," he said into the mouthpiece, covering his free ear to block out the sounds of passing
traffic.

"Oh, I'm glad you called," said Mrs. Rudd.

"How is she?"

"Getting stronger."

"The baby. The baby."

"The diaper rash is worse. Mrs. Rumsey's hardly
ever changing her diapers. And now it's getting ulcerated. I tried to tell her not to use the rubber pants, but
she keeps doing it anyway. I gave her some salve, but
the baby looks very uncomfortable. I told her it's almost better to leave everything off, but she doesn't trust
me. She's a strange woman, very strange."

"Is she taking the baby out?"

"No. Not at all. I told her that a child needs fresh air, but it's like talking to a wall."

Silence.

Shockley stood by the phone thinking. For an instant his eyes shifted to Cindy, who stood waiting, her hands on her hips in an expression of impatience.

"You know, Mr. Shockley, somebody ought to do something," said Mrs. Rudd. "That's just not a good situation. That woman should be back in the hospital, and that baby should be getting proper care. I know it's not really any of my business, but, well—"

It all happened so fast that Doris hardly knew what hit her.

"Mrs. Rumsey?" questioned the woman standing on the porch and rudely trying to peer past Doris into her house. Actually, she was more a girl than a woman, Doris judged. She looked almost like one of those college students with her longish, straight hair and stern, wire-rimmed glasses. "I'm Miss Cassaniti"—she introduced herself as Doris held a ready hand on the door—"I'm from social services."

Doris felt her heart stop.

"What do you want?" she asked, swallowing dryly.

"I'm here to investigate a complaint."

Doris's eyes widened. The veins at the side of her neck bulged.

"About a possible child neglect—"

Before the woman could complete her sentence, Doris shoved the door closed, locking it with the dead bolt.

Neglect. Neglect. Neglect.

The words exploded in her ears, keeping beat with the deafening thud of her pulse.

The woman knocked on the door. She knocked again. Gave the bell a few perfunctory jabs. Surrendered.

A scant few minutes after the investigator left, Doris began to worry that she had made a serious mistake. Watching through the upstairs window as the woman questioned her neighbors on either side, Miss Cassaniti motioning with her pencil toward Doris's house, Doris was plagued by second thoughts. Her instincts told her to summon back the woman, explain her first, frenzied reaction, show her Baby, how happy she was, perhaps even let Baby sing for her. Logic was one thing, her panic another. It was real, palpable, and left her paralyzed. The next hours were fraught with fear as she tried to guess just what was in store for her and Baby. If only she had had the presence of mind to handle the situation, she cursed herself. Twice in the span of those hours she started to call Olive Eldridge, but never completed the call. She even went so far as to look up the number for social services and sat for a half hour staring worriedly at the listing in the telephone directory.

By late afternoon Doris's forebodings materialized in the form of a lumbering deputy sheriff mounting her porch. The man was so enormous and looked so fiercely determined that Doris feared that if she didn't instantly open up, he was likely to come crashing right through the door, dead bolt and all.

"Doris Laura Rumsey?" he asked, filling the doorway.

"Yes," she responded meekly, looking up at the square-jawed, humorless face.

"Sign here," he said, handing her an official-looking document and pen.

"What is it?" she asked, holding the pen in abeyance.

"Subpoena," he answered tersely.

"What for?"

"I'm not a lawyer, lady," he said, motioning impa-

tiently with his chin toward the pen. Obediently Doris
signed.

Long after the patrol car left, she remained riveted in
the doorway. Finally she opened the document, bringing it close to her eyes to read, the wind shaking the
paper between her fingers as if trying to tug it free.

Halfway through, a cry escaped her lips.

"Oh, my!" she moaned, rereading the words. The
paper was not just a subpoena. From what she could
gather she had been served with something called a
show-cause order from the family court. She was to
show cause within five days why the court shouldn't
terminate her custody of Baby.

The next days were an unsettling mixture of despair
and anxious waiting punctuated by brief glimmers of
hope. Somewhere in that period Doris managed to
gather her strength, enough at least to consider looking
for a lawyer—though she really didn't quite know
where to begin. She had never been in need of an attorney, nor for that matter had her parents. All their lives
the Rumseys had lived a notably quiet existence, never
getting into any squabbles with anyone, much less any
legal entanglements.

Doris knew she had to seek help from a lawyer. Olive Eldridge had once mentioned Frank Kiely. Doris
had seen his picture in the local paper more than once.
No doubt he was as good as any of them, and probably
just as expensive.

Counselor Kiely turned out to look just like his picture. He was a robust, portly man with jowls, double
chin, and a wide, outgoing smile. Dressed in a pin-
striped suit with a bright red tie and diamond stickpin,
he struck Doris as an intelligent and sophisticated man.

"Mrs. Rumsey. How are you?" said the lawyer, stepping out of his office and greeting her with his rich baritone. "This way, please," he said cordially. He motioned her into his office and followed behind as she shuffled painfully toward his desk, which was piled high with papers. It was a sturdy early American model, and the rest of his furniture also seemed to be antique. The walls were lined with leather-bound volumes, there were hanging plants in front of the window, and some paintings of local country scenes hung on the wall. Entering the room Doris felt as though she were taking a comforting journey back into the past.

Kiely pulled up a chair for Doris, and when she was seated he sat down behind his desk.

"Now, how can I help you?" he said, and Doris handed him the subpoena.

"Oh, my," he said, glancing at the order and invoking the same words Doris had. "This is not good. Not good at all," he muttered, and then his phone rang. His phone, in fact, kept interrupting every few minutes until, sensing Doris's exasperation, he had his secretary hold all calls.

"Now I want the whole story," he said, fixing her with his stern eyes and exuding such a strong sense of confidence that Doris's misgivings started to vanish.

"Where do I begin?" she asked.

"Start at the beginning," he said coaxingly, his features softening, and taking up a legal pad began to makes notes.

Doris told him about Miss Cassaniti, who had come from social services. She tried to explain how, in a moment of terror, she had foolishly locked the woman out. Kiely muttered something about impeding an investiga-

tion, shook his head sternly, and told her to continue.
Doris explained about the deputy serving the paper.

"Where is the baby now?"

"At home."

"With whom?"

"She's alone," she conceded, but explained that Baby
was sleeping safely and that, because of her recent operation, she didn't quite yet have the strength to push
her carriage or carry her.

Kiely pressed for details. What operation? Who was
the attending physician? Why had she left the hospital
early? What was the name of the visiting nurse? Did she
feel her child was getting proper care? Could she in any
way document it? Were there friends? Family? Priming
her with questions and continuing to take copious
notes, he let Doris talk, her pent-up frustrations pouring
out. In the matter of a scant half hour Doris had managed to span the entire story of Baby, of her birth, her
talent, Doris's experiences with the Shockleys, her own
physical condition. When she had finished, Kiely sat for
the longest time chewing thoughtfully on the rubber
eraser on the tip of his pencil, his eyes fixed on the pad.
Then he slowly looked up at her, a smile spreading
across his face.

"I think we can take care of this," he said, tapping
his pencil on his pad, and Doris heaved a long, relieved
sigh. Here was someone who apparently knew just what
to do, who could take this mess off her hands.

Kiely sat silently looking at Doris, drumming his fingers on the desk, his head tilted back expectantly as
though waiting for Doris to say something. Doris
looked at him blankly. Kiely cleared his throat.

"I'll need a retainer to take on this case."

"Oh, yes, of course," she said, embarrassed.

"It may get expensive," he warned her.

"Whatever it costs," she said ingenuously. "I certainly don't want to risk losing Baby."

"A thousand dollars," Kiely said. "That's my minimum fee," he added as an afterthought.

Doris already had her checkbook out and was filling in a check.

"Do you think you could call me a taxi?" she asked, handing over the check. She would have to go to the savings bank to cover that big a sum and doubted she could make it on foot.

"Why, certainly." He smiled.

"Now remember," said Kiely as he left her in his outer office to wait for her cab. "Be sure to be on time at the family court on Friday."

"You don't have to worry about that," she said absently, thinking about her dwindling savings.

"You know where it is?"

"In the courthouse?" She checked.

"Right. Second floor. Ten sharp. And please bring the child."

Doris arrived an hour early all keyed up for the hearing. She came to the courthouse dressed in a freshly pressed suit. Her hair had been washed and set, she had put on lipstick and a touch of rouge, and hanging from the lobes of her ears were small earrings studded with imitation diamonds. For the hearing Baby had been bathed and powdered and dressed in one of those new frocks with matching hat she had once gotten from the Shockleys. Even her blanket had been scrubbed the night before in the tub.

Leaving nothing to chance, Doris had arrived at nine sharp, and in the intervening hour she sat expectantly on the hard wooden bench with Baby on her knee, watching people file in and out of the courtroom. Each time someone passed, Doris would look up searchingly, hoping to see Mr. Kiely's familiar face.

Ten o'clock arrived, yet there was no sign of counselor Kiely. By ten-thirty Doris started getting nervous. The frightening thought suddenly occurred to her that she might have missed her lawyer—that the hearing might at this very minute be going on without her. Raising herself with effort, she cautiously moved over the marble floors to the swinging doors marked Family Court.

"I'm Doris Rumsey," she said softly when a uniformed man appeared on the other side of the doors, blocking the closed hearings. "I'm supposed to appear this morning." Through an opening in the door she could see into the courtroom. A woman was sitting on the stand holding a handkerchief to her face, and the sight gave her a sinking feeling.

"One second," whispered the court assistant, and he let the doors close. A moment later he returned.

"You're not on the docket today. It was changed to Tuesday," he said, reading from a clipboard.

The doors swung shut and Doris stood in front of them, baffled. Turning, she descended the long arch of stairs leading to the lobby and went to the pay phone. Propping Baby against the shelf next to the phone, she searched through her change purse for a dime and then called Kiely's office.

"Oh," said Kiely, his voice booming on the other end. "Didn't the court call you? They were supposed to. Your case was delayed. It was moved to Tuesday. Eleven-thirty. Be sure to be there on time. We don't want to keep the judge waiting."

* * *

When the brick exploded through the picture window, showering the room with glass shards, Ruth felt as though it had crashed through the brittle shell of her life. For a moment, too stunned to move, she just stared at the missile that lay in front of her on the glass-strewn rug, then at her husband. By the time she had gathered her wits, Shockley was already on his feet racing out the front door. Ruth stood and shook the glass out of her lap and then, closing her eyes, carefully brushed her face for splinters. She opened her eyes and looked down at the brick. It was wrapped in a piece of paper. Bending down she untied the paper, her hands trembling.

"Free Baby," read the note scrawled in childish block lettering.

"There are some people out there as usual," said Shockley, returning, looking flushed. "But they insist they didn't hear or see anything. I'm calling the police," he said and then, turning to go, stopped abruptly. "Are you OK?"

Ruth nodded and he hurried to the phone.

In a couple of minutes the police were there, questioning everyone and clearing the street. The neighbors stood watching from the safety of their houses.

Picking off the stray shards of glass that lay on the far side of the sofa, Ruth cleared a place for herself and sat down. Staring in disbelief at the gaping hole, at the mess of glass at her feet, she felt a wave of nausea rise from her gut.

"Don't worry about it," said Shockley when he came back. He looked harried and frightened. "The insurance'll pay for the damages," he explained, trying to cheer her up, and immediately realized he had said the wrong thing.

"I don't give a damn about the money," she said hoarsely.

"It's the fucking principle of the thing," he agreed readily and knew that he had again put his foot in his mouth. It seemed that no matter what he said to Ruth it came out wrong.

"Here. A little message for you," said Ruth in disgust, handing him the note.

"Free who? Are they nuts? She's not even here!"

"If Baby had been here, would it have made more sense?"

"Don't be ridiculous," he said irritably, watching as Ruth got up.

"Baby's brought us nothing but trouble," she said, stooping down and carefully gathering in her hands the bigger fragments of glass.

"How can you say such a thing?" he uttered, looking down at her, troubled.

"It's the truth," she said, controlling her rage, her face turning a deep crimson.

"You mean because a rock comes sailing—?"

"I don't mean just this," she said, standing up to face him. "Since this whole damn thing started, it's been hell living with you."

Shockley stood with his hands at his sides, facing her.

"I've been difficult, I know," he admitted.

"You've always been difficult. I knew that when I married you. That was part of the package. It also came with the redeeming fact that you cared for me, for us, all of us."

"But I *do*."

"It's not like it used to be," she said, dumping the pieces with a crash into the wastepaper basket. She went to the hall closet to get a vacuum.

"I love you and the children," he said, following on her heels. "Nothing has—"

"Everything's changed. The most important thing in your life is Baby. It's the only thing!" She spun around accusingly.

Shockley tried to reach for the vacuum, but Ruth blocked him.

"Since the day you saw her she's ruled your life, our lives. Admit it."

"She's important. Yes."

"The most important."

"I wouldn't say—" he hedged.

"At least be honest!"

"OK, OK. Right now she's the most important. She's on my mind. I'm not going to deny that."

"You're deserting your own children for someone else's."

"Why must you always speak the absolutes?" he shot back, and knew that they were at each other because there was no other culprit to blame for the brick—knew it but was still helpless to control his own anger.

"Because absolutes are all you understand."

"I'd better put some plastic over the window," he mumbled, turning to leave.

"Coward!" she called after him, and though Shockley pretended not to hear, the word stung.

When Doris returned on Tuesday for her rescheduled hearing, the edge was off her fear and she was now more resolute than timid, convinced that with forceful Mr. Kiely on her side the truth would be out and once and for all she would be free of all these meddling people. The last days had taken their toll in anguish and sleepless nights, she thought, taking a seat on the now-familiar wood bench. Even Baby was tense and restless these days, prone to upset stomachs and fitful sleep. How she wished that people would just let them alone and let them live in peace.

Doris awoke from her thoughts to find a man standing in front of her. He had a large shock of light hair that covered part of his forehead, and with his wide, chubby cheeks and big grin he looked like a young boy. He introduced himself as Robert Bennett.

"Mr. Kiely's associate," he added by way of explanation.

"Where's Mr. Kiely?" asked Doris, puzzled. Baby's eyes moved from her mother to the young man and back again.

"He's asked me to take over your case while he's out of town."

"Out of town?" she echoed.

"Mr. Kiely's on another case," explained Bennett a bit sheepishly.

"Another case? I paid him a thousand dollars to represent me!"

"I'm a lawyer too," said Bennett sympathetically. He was dressed in a three-piece suit that seemed to accent his round, boyish face, and when he spoke there were deep dimples in his cheeks. If this kid is a lawyer, thought Doris, giving him a second look, then he must barely be out of law school.

"I'm sure you're a lawyer," said Doris, trying to control her frustration. "But how can you help me? You don't know the case." In the back of her mind she was wondering how in the world, in just a few minutes, she could possibly go through all those explanations again.

"I've consulted with Mr. Kiely and tried to familiarize myself with your case."

Though he fixed her with his clear eyes that looked honest, the word *tried* stuck in her mind.

Bennett nervously checked his watch. "Shall we go?" he asked tentatively.

"I don't have much of a choice, do I?"

"You do. You could try to request a delay and retain another lawyer."

Doris debated. She saw herself forking over another thousand dollars.

"One way or the other, you have to decide fast," he said, as Doris's thoughts raced around in her head.

Doris nodded reluctantly.

"How old are you?" she asked as they went together through the doors.

"Twenty-eight." He grinned.

"You look a lot younger," she said, but seemed mildly relieved.

* * *

"That's Tony Tribble. He's the assistant county attorney," Bennett whispered to Doris as the lanky man with wavy hair approached the judge sitting behind the raised oak bench. Doris and her young lawyer were seated together at a table toward the front of the small courtroom, Baby quietly taking her late-morning bottle, the sounds of Baby's drinking punctuating the momentary silence of the high-ceilinged room. "Tribble is going to act in the capacity of what you might call a prosecutor—though he's not really a prosecutor. This is supposed to be something of an informal hearing."

Doris was listening to her lawyer with one ear as she watched the presiding judge. His name was J. S. Warren, she could see by the nameplate in front of him. He was a man with gray hair, deeply set eyes, and hollow cheeks that gave his face a sepulchral look. Beneath his robes, Doris could see that he was bony and small, but it was his eyes that gripped her attention. They struck her as cold and distant, as though they had seen too much misery and anger, as though a wall had been constructed blocking out all emotion. His manner, too, seemed abrupt and impatient, rushed.

When Doris turned her attentions back to the proceedings, county attorney Tribble had already made a short statement and was requesting permission to bring in a first witness. When the social services caseworker marched through the door and took the stand, it came as no surprise to Doris. After being sworn in and asked a few preliminary questions, the woman was requested by Tribble to summarize her report.

"After receiving the complaint, I attempted to question Mrs. Rumsey," said Miss Cassaniti, glancing up from her notes to look at the defendant's table, her eyes falling on Baby for an inordinately long moment. Tribble cleared his throat to catch her attention. "I attempted to question the mother," she said, quickly returning to her file, "but she refused to cooperate with the investigation. I was also denied access to the premises. I interviewed a number of the neighbors in an attempt to corroborate—"

"Your Honor!" Bennett was up on his feet to object. "If we're going to introduce hearsay—"

"Counselor"—the judge rapped his gavel—"let me remind you, this is just a hearing, not a trial."

"But an adverse decision from this court has the power to remove Mrs. Rumsey's child—"

"Continue, please," said the judge, turning back to Miss Cassaniti. Bennett sank down deflated. He mumbled something apologetic to Doris, noticing how the baby in her arms had been fixedly watching him. He tried to shift his attention back to the stand but could hardly wrench his eyes away. There was something uncannily adult about the child, he thought, and it made him uneasy.

Miss Cassaniti continued to read from her report. From what she had been able to see through the doorway of Mrs. Rumsey's house, she explained, the place appeared to be in a state of disarray and neglect. The outside of the dwelling seemed in general disrepair. There were weeks' worth of garbage on the back porch, uncovered or improperly bagged—an invitation to roaches and rodents. She went on to testify that she interviewed four different neighbors, all of whom expressed serious questions about the infant's welfare. Citing the names of three additional city residents, people whom Doris had never even known existed, Miss Cassaniti indicated that they, on their own initiative, had approached her to state their concern that the baby seemed grossly neglected.

"That's a lie! A horrible lie!" Doris objected loudly to her lawyer.

"Quiet! I want you to warn your client to refrain from any further interruptions," the judge snapped.

Bennett muttered something inaudible.

After a brief and fruitless cross-examination by Bennett, Miss Cassaniti was dismissed from the stand and, at the behest of the county attorney and despite the strenuous objections of Doris's young lawyer, Judge Warren accepted into evidence Miss Cassaniti's entire file.

Following the testimony by the caseworker, Tribble began what seemed an endless parade of witnesses.

He brought in Detective Iacovelli.

"On the twenty-third of June I was called to investigate what was an alleged kidnapping," explained Iacovelli in response to the county attorney's query, the detective looking down at his hands as they wrestled each other.

"And would you tell us what you found?" pressed Tribble.

"What do you mean?" asked Iacovelli, flushing when his eyes met Doris's.

"Would you tell us about the conditions in which this child was living?"

"Well, like I told Mr. Tribble, the place wasn't exactly neat."

"Would you call it unhygienic? Adverse to the health of a newborn infant?"

"I'd seen worse," Iacovelli tried to soften his remarks.

"Please answer the question," ordered the judge.

"I'd call it messy."

"Would you say that it was the proper environment for a newborn—"

"Your Honor!" Bennett was on his feet again, Baby's eyes still on him. "Counsel's leading the witness!"

"Overruled!" Judge Warren brought down his gavel with a bang.

Doris looked over at Bennett and tried to smile encouragingly. He wasn't so bad after all. He was really trying his best, she thought, but Doris couldn't help but wonder how Kiely would have done.

Iacovelli went on to describe the alleged site of the birth.

"It appeared that she had given birth in the hedgerow," he explained.

"In the hedgerow?"

"Yes, sir."

Attorney Tribble looked meaningfully at Judge Warren, who gave a noticeable shudder.

"Thank you," said Tribble, turning away from the stand. "Counselor?" he addressed Doris's lawyer.

"Mr. Iacovelli," said Bennett, rubbing his chin intently as he approached the witness. "You said that you had seen messier homes. Could you elaborate on that?"

"Your Honor!" Tribble was now on his feet. "This is completely irrelevant. The question in point here is whether Miss Rumsey's house was a suitable place for an infant."

"Sustained."

"Isn't it true, Mr. Iacovelli," continued Bennett, "that there are homes in this county, in your experience, housing infants, that are in far worse—?"

"Objection! Counsel is rephrasing the same question."

"Sustained."

Bennett took a long breath and wet his lips. Beads of perspiration were forming on his forehead.

"From what you could see, Mr. Iacovelli, of the interior of Mrs. Rumsey's home, didn't it strike you as one adequate for bringing up a child?"

"Well—" Iacovelli shuffled his feet nervously. "Well —it wasn't *that* bad," he admitted.

"And didn't the mother seem loving?"

"Yes. Very definitely so."

"Thank you. No more questions," said Bennett, stopping while still ahead.

Tribble called in his next witness.

"Well," said Mrs. Oltz, drawing a long breath as Doris sat in stunned shock. "After I knew that there was a baby living there, I just took a walk over to have myself a look. I took a peek into the house and, let me tell you, she had that poor little baby stuck into a basket. A dirty, old laundry basket. She didn't have any clothes on. The baby, that is. And it was cold then, damp. Her place was a mess too. For the last months," volunteered Mrs. Oltz, "before she got hold of that baby, Miss Rumsey was sick. You could see it. She could hardly walk. Her clothes were in rags. Why, she didn't even have hardly a pair of shoes on her feet, they were all broken down. And then she got that baby— don't ask me how. I still think she stole it. I mean, did you ever hear of a fifty-nine-year-old woman—"

"Mrs. Oltz, would you please limit yourself to your observations?" said Tribble, bringing her back on track.

Baby, sitting up in Doris's lap, let out a loud yawn. The judge looked over, annoyed.

Mrs. Oltz then went on to explain how the baby looked malnourished, how the mother was exploiting her singing ability, keeping her up to all hours of the night and forcing her to sing for folks, how people would crowd around the house and make nuisances of themselves in the neighborhood, how—

"Mrs. Oltz," said Bennett when his turn came to

cross-examine the witness with the birdlike countenance. "You've never had a child, have you?"

"Well, no, but—"

"Please just answer the questions," said Bennett,
trying to impeach her testimony.

"Have you ever cared for a child?"

"I did baby-sit for the Muzzys when their mother
went to the hospital."

"When was that?"

"Oh, 'bout a year or two ago."

"Isn't it true that you don't have any recent and real
experience regarding the care of an infant, that you are
in no position to judge whether Mrs. Rumsey is an adequate mother?"

"Objection!"

"Overruled."

"Well—I mean, I am a woman." Mrs. Oltz flushed.

"Isn't it also true," he probed, hoping to show pre-
conceived prejudice, "that you think there's something
disgusting about a fifty-nine-year-old woman having a
baby?"

"Sure is strange, isn't it?" She chuckled.

"Mrs. Oltz, do you drink?"

"Objection! Counsel is—"

"Overruled."

"Do you drink, Mrs. Oltz?" he pressed.

"I have taken an occasional little nip. You know,
when we have company or—"

"Had you taken an alcoholic drink before you went
over to spy on Mrs. Rumsey through her window?"

"Objection!"

"No! Absolutely not! I was as sober—why, as sober
as the judge here sitting on the bench!" she snorted indignantly.

"No more questions," uttered Bennett, turning his back.

After Mrs. Oltz had left the courtroom, Bennett approached the bench.

"Your Honor," he said in a subdued voice, "this is ridiculous. So far, counselor Tribble has not brought in one valid, expert witness."

The judge looked at Tribble.

"Be patient," replied the county attorney, pushing his glasses back up on his nose and, with a confident nod, motioned to the court assistant. The doors opened and Dr. Waterhouse, the pediatrician, appeared.

"Why are they doing this to me?" asked Doris forlornly when Bennett returned to her side.

"Well, the child was underweight," admitted Dr. Waterhouse under questioning. "Yes, I'd say so," said the doctor, taking his glasses and cleaning them on his handkerchief. Without his spectacles, his eyes looked small and tired.

"Why was she underweight?" pressed Tribble.

"From what I was able to gather, the mother was trying to feed the child solely from her breast."

"On whose advice?"

"On her own."

"Had she ever consulted you before?"

"No."

"Had she ever consulted another pediatrician?"

"Objection!" Bennett jumped to his feet. Doris, afraid that he was going to blunder into dangerous water, grabbed his sleeve.

"I never did," she warned him in a low whisper, and withdrawing his objection, Bennett slowly returned to his seat.

"Let me amend that," said Tribble magnanimously, looking at his colleague with undisguised sympathy.

"Had she ever consulted another pediatrician so far as *you* know?"

"No."

"Did you specifically question her on this point?"

"I did."

When the county attorney was finished, Bennett strode to the witness stand.

"Would you say, doctor, that the child was malnourished?"

"As I said, she was underweight for her age."

"Does that constitute malnourishment?"

"Not necessarily."

"Is being underweight an unusual occurrence among children?"

"It happens."

"Is it always caused by neglect?"

"It can be."

"But you can't specifically say—"

"We've gone through this line of questioning already," said Judge Warren, who wanted to move the case along. He had a long, jammed schedule of hearings, other cases of neglect, child abuse, custody battles, orders of protection for wives whose husbands beat them, women seeking another twenty dollars in child support, men fighting for denied visiting privileges.

"I'm being railroaded," said Doris to her lawyer when the next witness was called. It was Mrs. Rudd, the visiting nurse. "Can't we stop this?"

"You'll have your chance to tell your side of the story," said Bennett, putting a comforting hand on hers. "After their last witness. I promise."

Doris looked at Baby and felt like crying.

Mrs. Rudd began her testimony by substantiating Mrs. Oltz's contention.

"It's certainly no place to raise an infant. Nor is Mrs.

Rumsey up to the job. And I base that on my years as a registered nurse. Let me give you an example," said Nurse Rudd all too eagerly. "The child had been suffering from a severe rash, which, because of inattention, had turned into ulcerated sores. I tried to advise Mrs. Rumsey about the child's condition, suggest treatment, but she refused to listen," she continued without prompting. "To top it all off, there was no food in the refrigerator and, until I took the initiative, no way for her to get it. Mrs. Rumsey was in no condition after surgery to administer to her own needs, much less those of a small child."

"And you'd say, without reservation, that this was a case of child neglect?"

"Without reservation," said Mrs. Rudd emphatically.

"Any more witnesses?" asked Judge Warren, who couldn't help but wonder why the county attorney was going in for overkill.

"The people have no further witnesses, Your Honor."

"Do you have any witnesses?" the judge addressed Bennett.

"The defendant, Your Honor, will offer testimony on her own behalf," said Bennett. Trembling, Doris made her way toward the stand, her child clutched possessively in her arms.

"This is all unfair," she said, her lips quivering. "You've all made up your minds. This trial is a sham." Then tears welled in her eyes, and despite her best efforts, she broke down and wept.

"This is a hearing, Miss Rumsey, not a trial," the judge corrected her, apparently unmoved by her tears. "If there's something you wish to say on your behalf you're free to say it," he explained, fixing her with his steely eyes. "Please take a seat."

Doris's lawyer approached the stand and began to question his client gently. He asked her if she knew how to care for a baby, eliciting from Doris the fact that she fed her child regularly, kept her clean and dry and warm. He questioned her about her experience with children, with Doris indicating how she had spent her entire adult life working with children.

The judge sat listening to Doris's testimony and after a few more queries finally interrupted.

"Would counsel have any objection"—he addressed Bennett—"if asked a few questions?"

Bennett nodded his consent.

"Miss Rumsey," said Judge Warren, shifting in his chair and leaning toward Doris as she dabbed at her eyes, "there are a couple of matters this court would like clarified."

Doris blew her nose, snuffled, and looked at him.

"Miss Rumsey, did you have any prenatal care at all?" Doris shook her head.

"You have to answer with words," he said referring to the stenographer.

"No," she replied, her voice cracking.

"Other than your single visit with Dr. Waterhouse, did you have any postnatal care for the baby?"

"No," she answered again.

"Where is the father?"

Doris mumbled something.

"I'm sorry, what did you say?"

"There is none," said Doris, stroking Baby's cheek. The judge cocked his head to one side.

"You mean you don't want to identify him, is that it?"

Bennett was hurriedly approaching the bench. The judge held up a warning finger and Bennett obediently froze. Holding his breath Tribble stared at the witness, his eyes narrowing as though sensing a kill.

"No," said Doris hoarsely.

"Let me understand this," said Warren, confused. "You're saying that there *is* no father."

"That's right. That's why I didn't go to any doctors. I didn't even know I was pregnant. And when I realized it I was too ashamed. How could anybody ever have believed me?"

"You maintain," interrupted the judge leaning farther over the bench toward her until she could almost feel his breath flowing past her, "that this is a *virgin* birth?"

Doris hesitated. She looked at Bennett, who was frantically trying to warn her off with his eyes. She glanced at Tribble, who stood to one side of the room, poised. She looked down at Baby. The room became utterly silent.

"Yes," she answered, raising her head and breaking the silence. "Yes. I do."

The judge's face blanched. He fell ominously silent, and only a telltale twitch tugged at the corner of his lips. What this woman was saying was absurd, insane, and it made all the reports and testimony offered this morning suddenly superfluous.

"Counselor"—the judge addressed Bennett—"do you wish to continue?"

Dutifully Doris's lawyer approached the stand and tried to pick up the threads of his previous line of questioning. He asked Doris about where the child slept, if the house had adequate plumbing and heat. He tried to raise the matter of why people might, in view of the child's unusual talent, want to have her removed from Doris's custody. Though he went through all the motions, Doris knew they were already beaten.

When Bennett finished, Doris sat on the stand, drained and empty.

"Thank you, Miss Rumsey," said the judge, dismissing her, but Doris remained rooted in the chair, her eyes dry, her jaw set.

The judge sat at his bench, uneasily fingering his gavel, avoiding the sight of the old woman and her child. Bennett stood waiting at the defendant's table. The stenographer sat at her machine, her hands in her lap, her gaze lowered. The court assistant stood slouching against the outside door. Tribble busied himself closing the notes on his desk. The air seemed to crackle with tension. Baby's eyes began to dart around the room, moving from adult to adult. Deep furrows formed on her forehead. Restlessly she squirmed in her mother's lap. Judge Warren started to speak again, but before he could utter a complete word Baby drew a quick breath and, opening her mouth, began to sing. Mustering her strength she sang out into the courtroom, her notes emerging in an urgent rush, her desperate and compelling plea filling the air.

Tribble looked up from his papers. The court assistant straightened himself. Bennett stared at the child with undisguised bewilderment.

"Quiet that child!" snapped the judge, banging his gavel. "She'll have to be quiet or be removed from the court!" he shouted irritably, loudly rapping his gavel as though trying to drown out her music.

Doris pressed her finger onto Baby's lips and instantly she stopped.

"Later," whispered Doris, giving her child a kiss, "later."

"We'll have a recess," said the judge, rising abruptly from his chair. "Ten minutes," he said, stalking out through the oak doors that led to his chambers.

* * *

After the short recess Judge Warren appeared again from his chambers. Everyone rose and waited for him to take the bench.

"I'm issuing a temporary order of removeal pending a dispositional hearing," he said in a noticeably calm voice. "In that period Miss Rumsey will be required to meet the following conditions." He paused and, putting on his glasses, lifted a paper from his desk. Doris's grip tightened on Baby.

"That she undergo a thorough psychiatric examination," read the judge, clearing his throat. "That, following that examination and in the event she receives an evaluation confirming her competency, she radically alter the living conditions in her home so that they are conducive to the raising of a child and meet the standards to be set by the Department of Social Services. That, further, Miss Rumsey obtain assistance with child-care as well as clearly demonstrate her own competency in that area."

"How long is temporary?" Doris asked her lawyer when the judge had finished.

"That depends," said Bennett, poker-faced, determined to leave before they wrenched Baby from her arms.

Andrea Cassaniti turned out to be a blessing of sorts. That such a cooperative young lady came to the position where her judgment would be instrumental in determining Baby's fate was, oddly enough, a direct consequence of Baby's musical gift.

A recent graduate of the university, Miss Cassaniti had been hanging around Ithaca trying to figure out what to do with her life and new degree when, one morning in late August, she stumbled across a crowd assembled around Doris's bench in the park. Edging up to the outside of the mass, Andrea Cassaniti picked up the strains of Baby's music and before the child's song was completed knew that her fate was foreordained: it was here it Ithaca, close to this miraculous child, she was meant to stay.

Hunting around for work, Andrea Cassaniti accepted one of the rare but poorly paying jobs available and in early October became a caseworker for the Department of Social Services. Shortly thereafter Doris was taken to the hospital for surgery, the Shockleys took over the care of Baby, and the child that had kept Andrea Cassaniti in Ithaca became inaccessible. When Miss Cassaniti was assigned to investigate a complaint alleging Baby's neglect, there could not have been a more fortuitous turn of events, and Andrea Cassaniti was determined not to let the opportunity slip by. In return for placing Baby in the legally sanctioned foster care of Professor Shockley and his wife, Miss Cassaniti extracted a number of small concessions for herself. For her efforts in securing Baby's fostership for the Shockleys as well as appearing before the court, which was to appoint Dr. Shockley guardian *ad litem*—a cozy arrangement empowering him to execute contracts on Baby's behalf—Miss Cassaniti was to be granted the privilege of private audiences with Baby. Further, according to another agreement privately reached between Miss Cassaniti and Professor Shockley, in return for a guarantee of only *pro forma* interference in the matter of Baby's custody (leaving Baby free to travel outside the state), Miss Cassaniti would receive a modest monthly "consultant's fee" intended to supplement her present low wages—said payment to be derived from Baby's future earnings, skimmed before insertion into her court-directed trust fund and to be kept off the books. What had initially seemed like a dull and unrewarding job dealing with the dregs of Ithaca society turned out to be a golden opportunity for Andrea Cassaniti.

"It stinks," mumbled Shockley to himself when Miss Cassaniti finally delivered Baby. "But it's got to be done."

"As soon as things settle down," he later told Ruth, "I want to let Doris move in. We can put her in the guest room."

"To soothe your conscience?"

"Yes. As a matter of fact, I don't enjoy being a bastard. There's no reason to punish her more than necessary."

"Necessary?"

"She's a crazy old lady who backed herself into a corner. Now that the rules are established and she knows she can't bury Baby, as far as I'm concerned she can spend every minute of the day with Baby. It was never my intention to deprive her of her child. Never!"

"Tell it to Doris," said Ruth.

"I will. As soon as the time is ripe."

"Hello. Jacobsen?" he said later on the phone. "Shockley here."

"Professor Shockley," said Jacobsen. "What a pleasure finally to hear your voice."

"We're on," said Shockley, ignoring the snide tone. "We've had some difficulties on this end, but we're all set now."

"Are you sure?"

"Positive."

"Well, that's fine, because I'm not!"

"Look, I'm sorry about all—well, all the back and forth."

"I'm not interested in your sorrys, Shockley. What

the hell do you think you're doing? Do you think you can dangle me on a string? Jerk me around any time you want? I don't play games like that!" he shouted.

"We've had problems on this end."

"*You've* had problems!" he whined. "Do you have any idea of the chaos you've created? What you've cost us already? The liabilities we've incurred?"

"Listen, I'm sorry, but it was unavoidable. If you're trying to tell me that you don't want to represent Baby, then just say it."

"I want to represent her all right," said Jacobsen, slowing down. Shockley could hear him puffing furiously on his cigarette on the other end. "It's *you* I don't want to represent."

"What are you talking about?"

"Shockley, if I'm going to take on the child it's going to be under *my* terms."

"Which means?"

"I want a binding agreement with you."

"That's certainly reasonable. I don't—"

"A booking *and* management contract."

"But I'm Baby's manager."

"Not if I'm going to represent her. If you want me, then we tear up our previous agreement, which you've already violated, and start anew. From now on I make the sole decisions as to when and where Baby appears and in what format. I call all the shots."

"That's not acceptable."

"It's got to be."

Shockley sat in stony silence.

"Shockley"—Jacobsen took a long pause—"I understand you're a good musician. Quite a composer, I hear. You probably are. But let me tell you one thing, you're a hell of a lousy businessman."

"That's never been one of my goals in life."

"Precisely! And at the rate you're going, you're going to end up burning yourself out and getting nowhere. You didn't know what you were doing when you first tried to start a tour, and you don't know what the hell you're doing now when it comes to managing."

Shockley didn't respond.

"Come on, let someone who knows the business take care of the child's affairs," said Jacobsen soothingly.

"You?"

"Exactly," said Jacobsen. His other phone buzzed and for an instant he covered the mouthpiece, then returned. "Look, the pie is big enough for everyone to have a nice, fat slice."

"I'm not after money. I've told you that before."

"Who's talking about money? Here's my suggestion. It's very simple. I'll be her manager; you'll be her impresario. I'll take care of her tours; you'll attend to her artistic needs. As a businessman, I'll direct the course of her business life. As an artist, you will attend to her artistic life," explained Jacobsen, his voice all sweetness.

Shockley swallowed uneasily, his mind racing. Although there were other booking agents, none even approached Jacobsen. His major concern, he reminded himself, was to ensure that Baby had an audience. What difference did it really make who her manager was? When it came to Baby's music, he could not allow his own feelings to interfere.

"She'll always be your find," said Jacobsen, breaking into Shockley's thoughts. "No one can ever take that away from you. And through me she will have access to places you could only hope for in your wildest dreams."

Shockley sat at the phone, playing with a pencil.

"Well, what's it going to be? In or out? I don't have all day."

"OK," said Shockley tensely. "I'll go along with it."

"In writing."

"I'm a man of my word."

"One thing I've learned in this business is, always get it in writing from an artist," he said, his lips caressing the word *artist*. It flattered Shockley. "You'll get a contract in the mail tomorrow. I want it all in writing."

"In writing."

"It'll protect you also."

"What do you mean?"

"Nothing. Just that," he said offhandedly. "Someone could grab Baby from you too," he said and laughed loudly.

"Too?" asked Shockley, but the connection was already broken.

Olive Eldridge sat on the edge of her seat, her purse in her lap, both hands planted squarely on it. Uneasily she looked around the sterile fourth-floor visiting room of the Willard Psychiatric Center. Green cinderblock walls. Barred windows looking out on a gray, snowy day. Near her sat a woman with thinning hair and drooping features, absently fingering the seam of her gown, oblivious of her husband's imploring voice. A teenage boy with wild eyes swimming in their sockets stood in front of his mother, giggling hysterically into his hands. An old man on the other side of the room was rocking his body back and forth, peering over his shoulder at Olive as he whispered conspiratorially to a visitor.

When Olive saw Doris coming down the corridor with the attendant she immediately rose to her feet, watching anxiously as her friend approached. Olive couldn't help but see that there was something decidedly truculent and determined in the way she proceeded. Though hunched over as Olive had always known her, Doris seemed to move like an aging, wounded cat, threatened, poised, and ready to spring.

"I came as soon as I heard," she said, hugging Doris. "Oh, dear, I'm so sorry."

"I'm glad you came," Doris said, and characterisically there was no self-pity in her voice. "I didn't want to call you, but I really didn't know who else to contact at this point."

"Hush!" said Olive lovingly. "Now why don't you just tell me what's going on?"

"There is nothing much to tell." Doris pulled her hospital robe tight around her. "Somebody complained that I was neglecting Baby. Before I knew what happened I was in court, they were taking her away from me, and they stuck me here because I'm supposed to be nuts," she said angrily.

"Why didn't you get yourself a lawyer right away?"

"I did," explained Doris, and she went on to tell Olive the story of Kiely, how he had seemed so competent and optimistic and how, in the last minute, Mr. Bennett had appeared in his place.

"Did you say Kiely?" asked Olive, as though disbelieving her ears.

"Frank Kiely. On Tioga Street. I had heard you mention his name once and I figured that—"

"Oh, dear Jesus!" said Olive, putting her hands to her graying temples and shaking her head.

"No?"

"No. Absolutely no. The reason I had mentioned Kiely was because my sister-in-law, you know Frieda, had gone to him because of a lawsuit. He ended up botching up the whole case and sticking in one of his 'associates.' If anything, I was warning you away from the creep. Not recommending him. Kiely? Why, he's absolutely worthless. A bum. A slumlord in Collegetown."

"Oh, my," said Doris, now suddenly remembering the connection in which she had seen his picture in the paper.

"He's the one who's been accused of all those building violations. It was in one of his hovels that those four students burned to death last year. Doris, honey, he wasn't on another case. He just took your money and sent in one of his flunkies, that's all."

"I've got to get out of here," said Doris, searching her friend's face.

"We'll get you out. We'll start by getting you a lawyer. A good one, this time."

"Then I want Baby back," said Doris, getting up her pluck.

"I'm with you."

"Olive, I'm so tired of being such a soft touch, of being pushed around."

"Good girl!" Olive beamed.

"I'm going to fight this thing to the end. If it takes every last penny and every last ounce of strength I have, I'm going to get Baby back. I'll get justice even if I have to go all the way to the Supreme Court," said Doris, getting carried away.

"Heavens!" said Olive. "Maybe you *are* crazy." She slapped Doris affectionately on the knee and laughed. She had been afraid to come here and find Doris a vegetable. "There's a young lawyer I know," said Olive, drawing close to Doris.

"Not another young one," said Doris apprehensively.

"Oh, but he's a fine young man. His name is Harry Terkel. From what I hear he's one of the best in town. A real fighter. Brash and hard driving—and that's what you need."

"Is he expensive?"

"Probably. But you get what you pay for. That's what my Al always used to say. Don't worry about the money. It'll come from somewhere. It always does," said Olive, taking Doris's hand. "Now, let's just concentrate on getting you out of here and getting Baby back to her mother, right?"

Doris nodded but looked at her askance.

"Are they giving you any pills here?" asked Olive suspiciously.

Doris lifted a flap in her gown and with a guilty grin showed her a pocket full.

"They try," she said.

"Lord!" Olive exclaimed. "How did you do that?"

"It wasn't easy," said Doris proudly. "But they're not going to mess me up. I know what I want."

"Good for you," said Olive, standing up and retrieving her coat. Olive had always been a quiet rebel herself, and Doris's gumption was certainly impressive.

"You know, Olive," said Doris, her courage waning and her mood turning melancholy as she watched her friend buttoning her overcoat, "I've spent a lot of time here thinking about all that's happened. And it's funny," she laughed sadly to herself.

"What's that?"

"The more I think about it, the less I understand. I bring something beautiful into the world and—what happens to me?—I'm crucified for it. I don't understand it. Just don't understand. Why, Olive?" Doris shook her head.

"Doesn't make any more sense to me, honey. But for that matter, most everything these days doesn't make sense," she said, tying a scarf around her neck and putting on her fur hat. Outside it was still snowing, and Olive didn't relish the slippery trip back to Ithaca. "These are wicked times," said Olive, as much for her own sake as Doris's. "And it seems as if all the junk's floating to the top instead of sinking. Well, got to take care of some business for a friend." Olive winked and, giving Doris a peck on the cheek, hurried down the corridor to the locked steel door.

* * *

"What do you mean 'strange'?" Shockley questioned his eldest daughter when he came home from work on Tuesday. "Either Baby sings or she doesn't."

"Well, she sings," Annette explained uneasily. "I mean, she starts to sing," she corrected herself. "But then just stops after a couple of notes. She just sort of runs out of steam."

"Baby's been acting funny ever since she came back," said Julie, taking Baby's hand in hers as Baby sat propped up, listless, in her seat on the kitchen table, her dish of food getting cold.

"I think she's sad," said Annette, stroking Baby's face. Baby looked up at her, her appearance decidedly dejected. Her cheeks were slack, her mouth slightly open, her forehead wrinkled like an old person's.

"Maybe she misses her mother," said Randy, joining the group.

"She's been with us before," said Shockley, trying to stem the panic that was edging closer. In four days Baby was scheduled to make her first gala public appearance in Cleveland's Severance Hall. Everything was set. Jacobsen had taken care of all the publicity, pouring a small fortune into advertisements. The media had been primed, the papers full of stories. Tickets were being sold. Another couple of days and it would be impossible to halt the juggernaut without lawsuits and losses and irreparable damage to Baby's image. The word *reliable* rang through Shockley's brain and he trembled.

"Maybe she was starved and didn't get enough food," said Julie, looking compassionately at Baby with her own serious eyes. "And now she doesn't have enough energy."

"Put some music on," ordered Shockley. "Here, heat up her food again," he said to Annette. "Come on, sweetie." He tickled Baby under the chin, trying to elicit a smile. "Gee, she seems cold," he said, touching her cheek, then forehead.

"Maybe she's sick and dying," said Cindy, sauntering by casually and driving a stake into Shockley's heart.

"Don't talk like that!"

"It was just an idea. Ideas don't hurt. You've always said—"

"Not now!" Shockley snapped. "Please. Come on, Baby. Sing a little song for us. La la la," he tried to induce her with his own voice, but Baby just turned away and stared out the window off into the snowy distance. "Shit!" he muttered. "Hell, don't put on Wagner!" Shockley called out when the music came blasting over the speakers in the kitchen. "Put on something light. Try Vivaldi. Or even some pop music. That's it. Put some junk on. Maybe that'll bring her out of it."

But it didn't.

"I knew I shouldn't have gone to classes today!" said Shockley to his wife, passing back and forth in the kitchen while dinner cooked. "The first day she's back and look what happens."

"I doubt if your being here would have made any difference. I don't think she's sick. She doesn't have a fever. She looks well to me. She's just a little confused, probably. It's not good to shuffle a little baby back and forth," said Ruth in her usual levelheaded way.

"Do you think her singing's winding down?" he asked later, fear creeping into his voice.

"Who knows?" said Ruth. "If it is, I doubt if there's anything you could do about it, anyway."

"She's got a concert on Sunday. That's only four days away," he said, visions of Jacobsen's skull-like head appearing before him.

"She *may* have a concert on Sunday."

"I'm quitting the university. This is the end. The last straw. I'm not leaving Baby's side. Not for a minute."

"I was waiting for that," said Ruth fatalistically.

"It was inevitable. I warned you."

"You didn't have to warn me. You just have to figure out how to pay the mortgage and the orthodontist and the car payments. The peanuts they call my salary won't keep this production on the road."

Shockley went upstairs to check on Baby. She was lying fast asleep in her crib, her thumb in her mouth, her little rear raised. He turned on a small light and brought his face close to hers, the milky smell of Baby reaching his nose as he listened to her breathe. As she slept, he noticed, her eyebrows were busily knitting, her lips tensely moving about her thumb, her cheeks working away.

"Please, Baby," he whispered forlornly, stroking her tiny back, "don't stop singing. We love you so much. We need your music. Don't let us down," he murmured, and suddenly realized that he was weeping, large tears careening down his cheeks and falling onto her curled-up little form.

Doris turned sixty on the Friday she was released from Willard. She had spent a scant four days undergoing "observation," but it might easily have gone on to be four weeks or even four months had not Harry Terkel deftly pulled a few strings. Considering her ordeal, the indignity of being held with all the other crazies, real and suspected, Doris looked remarkably fit. For the first time since her operation she had a chance to eat regular meals, get nursing help as well as some direly needed rest, and it showed. Her incarceration also produced a report for Judge Warren and the family court, a copy of which was already in Terkel's possession. He was, in fact, reading it when Doris arrived at his office. Basically, what the evaluation—a consensus report by three resident psychiatrists—stated was that "Though Miss Rumsey was capable of holding rational and logical discussions, was cognizant of her surroundings, aware of her actions and how they affected others, she still suffered from religious delusions; Miss Rumsey persisted in the belief that she had given birth to a child through a virgin birth brought about by divine intervention. Exhibiting certain paranoid tendencies, she nonetheless impressed the observers as being, for the present at least, lucid, responsible, and capable of caring for herself in a noninstitutional setting."

"That's damning you with faint praise," said Terkel, putting down the report. "What they're saying is that you're as sane as the other nuts that they've been turning loose lately because of state cutbacks."

Doris looked back at him in surprise.

"*I'm* not saying that," he said, pointing to himself. "I'm just reading between the lines," he laughed loudly. Terkel was a little man, probably in his early thirties, who had dark, curly hair, a pug nose, and seemed to bristle with energy. Whenever he spoke, his hands were in motion, pointing, gesticulating, waving in the air, and Doris wondered if he were doing it for her benefit. "A noninstitutional setting," he repeated and laughed, shaking his head. "That's big of them. Listen, Doris— can I call you Doris?—don't feel bad. If they put me in there, I wouldn't get half as good grades." He laughed again, and Doris nodded her head in agreement. "Sending you for psychiatric evaluation—what nonsense!" Terkel snorted. "Jack Warren should have been thrown off the bench years ago. He's totally incompetent. And" —he took a breath—"if you had had decent counsel, you would have known from the beginning that you didn't have to identify the father."

"But there was none."

Terkel's smile faded.

"Oh," he said and stood up and walked over to the window. From his office on Court Street he could see the brick building that was the sheriff's office and jail. On the third floor a prisoner, one of his clients, stood with his face pressed against the barred, snow-encrusted window. The man was awaiting trial for the rape-murder of his mother. Terkel knew all about sanity—sanity and insanity. It was getting to be his specialty in Tompkins County. That and criminal law. From the vantage point of the cases that staggered through his office, the county seemed to be crawling with crazies, crooks, druggies, or a combination thereof. Eccentric old ladies didn't throw him.

"First of all, let's lay down some ground rules, OK?"

"Depends," said Doris cautiously as he turned back. She was struck by how small Terkel actually was when he stood. He was about the height of a large midget or a small teenager.

"If you want me to represent you, you have to agree to them."

"Well?" she said, wanting to hear him out before making any commitments.

"First of all, if any question arises in any further hearings, 'examinations' "—he lifted the psychiatric report and dropped it back on his desk—"court proceedings, depositions—whatever—you will neither mention nor make any allusions to a virgin birth."

"But—"

"I don't care if it's true or untrue. For all we know the good Lord himself came down out of the skies and—and—well, whatever." He cleared his throat. "If you're ever asked again in court, just say that you refuse to identify the father. Period."

"I don't want to lie."

"It's not a lie!" Terkel tore at his hair as Doris watched imperturbably. "It's an evasion. If you had done it to begin with, you wouldn't be in such a mess today. Please."

"OK," sighed Doris, who was not used to lying *or* evading.

"Next thing. Make sure that your person and living premises are immaculate." Terkel stopped short, recognizing his unfortunate pun. "You know, buy a couple of new dresses. Get in a cleaning lady. Scrub the place down from A to Z. Hang up some bright curtains. Go to the beauty parlor. Get your hair and nails done. And let everybody know it."

"What about Baby?" questioned Doris, trying to bring the lawyer back on base.

"That's exactly what I'm talking about. I'm getting to the gist of the matter. What I'm trying to do is establish that, first"—he raised one finger—"you are not only a fit mother but also a loving, competent, and totally sane one. For that we're going to send you to two psychiatrists of *my* choosing for evaluation." Terkel paused to let it sink in. When Doris didn't object, he continued. "Second," he said, adding another finger forming a victory sign, "we are going to attempt to substantiate collusion."

"All that time I had to myself back at Willard," said Doris, catching the spark of Terkel's enthusiasm, "all that time I kept wondering, of all those witnesses they brought in—"

"Noticeably absent was Mr. Shockley. Yes. Funny,

isn't it?" Terkel grinned, pleased with his client. "Equally odd is the fact that Mr. and Mrs. Shockley were given custody of your child. I did a little snooping around yesterday and I learned that it was Miss Cassaniti, the young lady who testified against you at the hearing, who conveniently arranged for the Shockleys to have foster care. Which brings me back to my second point. We're going to try to show collusion between this Shockley character and our Miss Cassaniti—whoever the hell she is. Also, if possible, I'm going to try to establish some connection between Shockley and the other witnesses."

"I wouldn't want him to go to jail," said Doris worriedly.

"Oh!" Terkel slapped his head dramatically. "He can steal your child, stick you in Willard for an indeterminate sentence, and you don't want him to go to jail? Miss Rumsey, Doris," he brought himself close to her, his hands outstretched, his head thrown back.

"I just believe that two wrongs don't make a right."

"I wish I had you for an adversary," he said, rolling his eyes heavenward.

"I don't think Professor Shockley really meant evil. I think he just couldn't help himself. And, in his way, he felt he was doing it for Baby's sake."

"You're a true Christian," said Terkel, who wasn't. Doris just shrugged.

"Now. Where were we? Yes. Our attack," said Terkel, checking his watch and beginning to speak quickly. "Point three"—he resumed with his fingers—"I'm going to file a notice of appeal today with the family court. Four, I'm also immediately filing a brief with the appellate division in Albany."

Doris smiled. She liked Terkel's forthrightness. Particularly, she liked the word *immediately*.

"How long will it take?" she asked. "Until I get Baby back, I mean."

"That depends."

"On what?"

"It can take some time for the appellate court to get to our brief."

"How long?"

"Well"—he hedged—"they're swamped. I suspect, it could take a few months. Four, maybe five," he said, almost timidly.

"Ooooh," said Doris, letting out a pained sigh.

"I'll try to petition the appellate court that your case be given preference. We'll get it moved up if I can convince them it's a critical case."

"But it *is*," insisted Doris.

"Yes. To you and me. But we have to convince an appellate judge," explained Terkel, watching Doris's initial enthusiasm start to wilt. "Look, I'm going to attempt something else," he said, hoping to buck up her spirits. "But I don't want you to hold your breath."

Doris nodded.

"Before I do anything else, I'm going to petition the appellate court for a stay of the lower court's order pending review. To get the stay, I'd have to show that we'll prevail in the ultimate decision. If we got it, Baby would be returned to you prior to any rehearing."

Doris smiled at the prospect.

"I said *if*," cautioned Terkel uneasily. "It's a long shot. You've got to understand that. I don't want you getting your hopes up and then have them dashed. With the child already removed from your custody it's going to be an uphill fight. It's going to take some time, though we *will* prevail. I just want you to try and be patient. Please," he said, touching her gently with his hand. "I know what you've been through and what you're going through."

"Do you?"

"I'm a father. I can understand." He glanced again out the window at the brick prison. "But look at it this way. You *do* have visiting privileges. You're *out* of Willard. And we've got a heck of a good chance to win this case. Try to look on the bright side of things."

"I am, but it's not very bright without Baby."

"Go see her."

"I don't know if I could bear to see her and then have to leave."

"Take each day at a time."

"I do. I will. The days are OK. It's the nights, Mr. Terkel, the nights."

"I'll be in your corner fighting for you."

"I'm counting on it."

There was a silence. It filled Doris with a sense of déjà vu, except that this had actually occurred before. In Kiely's office. And at about the same time in the course of the conversation.

"And your fees?" asked Doris, saving Mr. Terkel the trouble.

"It's going to run into money."

"I thought you'd say that."

"I understand your circumstances. But you must also understand that there are going to be out-of-pocket expenses to meet. For an appeal there have to be twenty printed copies of a bound brief. I'm going to have to go to the appellate court in Albany. Maybe a few times. You're going to have to pay for the private psychiatrists' evaluations. There'll probably be a few visits to each one. These men are highly respected, the best in the profession. Their word carries weight in this state.

I'll see to it that they give you a break, but they're not cheap."

"How much?"

"You'll have to travel to Rochester and New York to see them. There'll be overnight lodgings. Bus or plane fare," he continued his litany. "There's—"

"Altogether. What do you think?"

"Then there are my fees," he continued obliviously. "I'm very expensive. In your case I'll make an adjustment. I'm interested in your case," he said, sounding sincere.

"Well?" she pressed. "I have to know."

"I'd figure if I were you probably—in the neighborhood of a few thousand, minimum."

"That much?"

"If you want to protect your rights, you're going to have to pay for it."

"I don't think I have that much."

"You mean to say that after all these years of working you don't have any savings?" he asked puzzled.

"Well, I was never much of a saver," Doris admitted reluctantly. "Being alone, whatever extra I had I, well, I usually sent away."

"To whom?"

"Till now I was sending money to my children."

"Your children?" he asked, flabbergasted, his eyes nearly popping. "You didn't tell me anything about—"

"They're not really my children." She smiled. "They're foster children, overseas. You know. Here," she said and, opening her purse, took out pictures of the same children whose photos sat taped to her living room mirror.

Terkel rummaged through the stack.

"This is wonderful!" he exclaimed. "How long have you been doing this?"

"Well, these six for the last four, no five, years, but before them there were others."

"Doris Rumsey! This, this," he said, holding aloft the pictures, "is what, in the end, is going to save you. When the court finds out that you've been supporting six other children, that—" Terkel drew a breath. "We're going to win back Baby. That I can assure you—I think."

"If I can solve the money problem."

"Yes," he said, rubbing his chin thoughtfully. "But there must be a way. Your salary?"

"I'm on leave without salary. The earliest I could go back is next fall. I'm still too young for early retirement."

"You could"—Terkel thought to himself—"go on disability. You were ill, you had a—"

"No!" said Doris firmly. "If I applied for disability that would be just one more reason not to let me have Baby back."

"Good. Good thinking."

"I do have a house."

"Yes." Terkel nodded and waited.

"I suppose I could sell it."

"You could."

"And rent somewhere," she said, blinking madly to hide the tears that threatened to come.

"It'd only be temporary," said Terkel firmly. "After, when you get Baby back and you're feeling better, you could return to your old job."

"Yes," said Doris. "I was hoping to."

"Look, Doris. I'm not worried about my fees," he said, sensing her distress. "If you can just cover the real, out-of-pocket expenses, I'll help you with the rest. If things weren't quite so tight on my end, why, I'd cover the whole—"

Doris cut him off. "I wouldn't think of it. I'll get the money. I'll manage," she said stoically.

"Now, there's only one thing more," said Terkel.

"Yes?"

"I want you to promise that you're not going to worry, that you'll let me do the worrying for both of us."

"I promise." Doris smiled confidently, knowing that she had finally found one terrific lawyer.

"It's not going to be easy. It'll be a hard, protracted fight."

"I understand."

"But we'll take it step by step. Cross one bridge at a time." He smiled, and a minute after she left, he rushed off, late, to the criminal court, where a jury selection awaited his ministrations.

"She's singing! She's singing!" rejoiced Shockley, waltzing through the house with Baby.

"Ruth! Baby's singing again!" he exploded over the phone after having a secretary summon his wife out in the middle of class.

"Thank goodness," said Ruth, relieved. She, too, had been worried that something was wrong with Baby, but for different reasons from her husband's worries.

"She sang two complete songs already. Two songs," he bubbled. "And—listen!" He held Baby close to the receiver. "You hear that? It's another one. A new one! Do you hear it?"

"Yes, I do," she said, and through the line Ruth could hear the makings of a joyous song that seemed to echo Shockley's sense of deliverance.

"She's happy! She's chirping like a happy little bird! You can pack your bags; we're off to Cleveland."

"Count me out," said Ruth quietly.

"You still mad at me for making you trick Doris?"

"That and all the lies I had to tell."

"I'm sorry. How many times do I have to say it? It's past. Let's forget it. I just want you to come along to Cleveland, to be with me for the gala opening. Please. You'll have a swell time; you'll see."

"I doubt it."

"Oh, come on, darling, give it a chance. Give me a chance. And Baby needs you too."

"Well—"

"I swear to you, Ruth, I'll never again in this lifetime ask you to do anything that goes against your own scruples."

"Is it *really* so important that I come along?"

"Yes. For me it is."

"It's just going to cost more money."

"I don't care. I can't worry about money at a time like this."

"Money is exceedingly tight right now," explained Mrs. Cornish, the real estate lady from Futterman's Showcase of Homes, surveying the downstairs of Doris's home. "Interest rates are skyrocketing. Mortgage pools are drying up. The banks have even stopped giving conventional mortgages," she said, stepping into the first floor half-bath.

Mrs. Cornish peeked into the hall closet and jotted a note on her clipboard.

"I'm telling you all this, Mrs. Rumsey, so you don't get your hopes up for a quick sale. We're by far the best in the business," she said, moving briskly over to the staircase, "but even for us it's not going to be easy. If we put it on multiple listing maybe we can sell it by spring. I say maybe. Mind if I go upstairs?"

Doris nodded and was about to speak, but Mrs. Cornish was already heading up to the second floor.

"I really can't wait until spring," said Doris, tagging behind the skinny woman with horn-rimmed glasses as she tramped up the stairs.

"Being a college town, this is a seasonal market," said Mrs. Cornish, checking out the bathroom. "Oh, you've got one of those old tubs with feet. I just love those," she remarked, noting on her form the absence of tile. "Now, with winter here, there just isn't much movement in the housing market. Is that another bedroom there?"

"I need the money now," explained Doris as Mrs. Cornish breezed through the second bedroom.

"Well," said the real estate woman, standing in the middle of the small room and turning full circle. "If you'd be willing to sell on land contract or hold a mortgage, that might expedite matters. You know, a small down payment to cover the commission and closing costs. Amortized, it would give you a tidy little something for retirement."

"I don't need a retirement, Mrs. Cornish. I need cash. Immediately."

"Oh, I see," said the saleslady. "Is that the attic up there?" she pointed with her pencil.

"Yes," said Doris, exasperated, as Mrs. Cornish went up by herself into the icy attic to check for roof leaks.

"That could be finished off into a nice study," she said, coming down the stairs and writing it down. "With a little spiffing up, a little modernization, this would make a very nice starter home for a young couple."

Doris followed her back down the stairs as she went back into the kitchen.

"Those cabinets and the sink would have to be

changed. The floors redone. The walls stripped," recited Mrs. Cornish, letting her imagination run.

In her mind's eye, Doris could see the young couple moving in, ripping out the cabinets and sink and walls. Too, she could see the reproving looks of her dead parents. She tried not to dwell on the agonizing task that lay ahead, of moving, of going through two generations of belongings and deciding what was to be eliminated forever.

"It's all a function of price," Mrs. Cornish explained later, when they were seated in Doris's living room. She took a small, cautious sip of her coffee and finally looked Doris in the eye. "If you're willing to lower the price so that it becomes sufficiently attractive, there are always people with cash watching the market and ready to step in."

"How low and how fast?"

"Tomorrow," said Mrs. Cornish, offering a strained laugh. "For instance, I know a gentleman with just oodles of ready cash. He's a lawyer here in town. All I have to do is give him a call."

"His name isn't Kiely, is it?" asked Doris.

"Why—Why, yes!" Mrs. Cornish admitted, taken aback. "But how did you know?"

"What's going on?" asked Shockley.

"Let me explain. There isn't much time," said Jacobsen, anxiously checking his watch.

Dressed in a new tuxedo Shockley was standing in the stage manager's office in Severance Hall clutching Baby and looking bewildered. On stage, behind the curtain, the Cleveland Symphony was tuning up as the last of the audience were taking their seats in the cavernous hall.

"I don't get it. What's the orchestra for?" asked Shockley. "This isn't the way I planned it."

"That's what I'm trying to explain. If you'd just listen for a second." Jacobsen gritted his teeth. "Look, there are two ways of doing things. You can either throw Baby out on that stage cold with the audience unprimed and hope for the best. Or"—he paused, wetting his heavy lips—"or, you can—Oh." Jacobsen spun around as a man in powder-blue tux and garishly frilled shirt peeked his head into the office. "Jud!" he exclaimed, waving him in. "Just the man I was looking for. I want you to meet Dr. Shockley and, of course, our little star here." Jacobsen smiled at Baby, who was all spiffed up for the occasion in a red dress.

"Well, well," said Osgood in the deep, resonant voice that was his trademark. He chuckled. "This is certainly a great pleasure for me," he said, pumping Shockley's limp hand and chucking Baby under her chin. Shockley looked at the man with unveiled surprise. He didn't need any introduction. Anyone who had ever watched television in America could spot that high-cheeked countenance a mile away. With his toothy smile and self-assured manner, Judson Osgood was a household name, a living piece of broadcasting history who over the last decades had hosted innumerable variety shows, celebrity awards, and television specials. Trying not to stare, Shockley took a second look at the man. Though Osgood was getting on in years, he looked remarkably trim and vigorous. Standing next to him, Shockley was struck by how much shorter he seemed in real life and, despite the layers of makeup, Shockley could see that the taut, masklike skin on Osgood's face was pockmarked like the surface of a meteor-impaled planet. Nonetheless, Osgood impressed Shockley as a strikingly handsome man, as good as or better looking than he appeared on the tube—the performer filling the room with his notable presence.

"Well, shall we get on with the show?" said Jacobsen, sounding deliberately cheery.

"Fine. I'll take Baby now," said Osgood, stretching out his arms and flashing his famous smile.

"Take Baby?"

"Yes."

"No!"

"I'm not going to keep her." Osgood laughed good-naturedly. "I'm just going to introduce her, that's all." He smiled at Baby, who was watching him curiously.

"She stays with me." Shockley hung on to Baby.

"Shockley, let's be sensible. You're not a performer," said Jacobsen, trying to ease Baby from his arms. "What do you know about showmanship, huh? This thing calls for a professional. Now give me the kid and let's get this show on the road."

"I understood that *I* was going to take Baby out on stage."

"There was never any such understanding. I would hardly have agreed to such a thing."

"Come on, Professor Shockley." Osgood smiled patronizingly. "Be reasonable. What's the difference who takes her out, huh?"

"Shockley, we've got to hurry," insisted Jacobsen tensely. "You're being very difficult and I can't stand here arguing with you. It's too late. It's all been carefully rehearsed."

"For two days we've been busting our asses preparing for this show," said Osgood, looking hurt.

"The program's printed and the audience is out there now, reading it."

"Do you want to screw up everything in the last minute?"

"I've got to think about this," said Shockley, perplexed and outgunned.

"Don't worry. You'll get to take more bows than your back can stand," said Osgood, trying to sound comforting. He was beginning to sweat, large drops running through his makeup.

"Three minutes to curtain!" A stagehand popped his head into the office. "We've got a packed house out there, Mr. Jacobsen. S.R.O.!"

"Look. If this thing is to come off without a hitch, everyone has to do the job he's best at," said Jacobsen, speaking in a rapid-fire manner. "I'm the manager. You're the impresario. And Jud here is the showman," he said, pointing in turn to each of them, his finger trembling. "And, of course, Baby is the star. We should never forget that." He touched her cheek with his bony hand. Baby opened her mouth wide and burped.

"One minute!" called the stagehand.

"Shockley. For God's sake, let him have the baby!" said Jacobsen, turning a deep crimson, his voice low and controlled and tense.

Shockley's gaze swung from one to the other.

"Let him have her. Trust him. He's not going to *eat* the child."

"Relax," said Osgood, massaging Shockley's shoulder with his hand. When he smiled, his makeup began to crack at the crow's-feet around the eyes.

"Shockley, if you go out you'll fuck it up permanently. Let Osgood do it; he's the best in the world. Stop bucking everything."

"Go with the flow," urged Osgood soothingly.

"Do what's best for Baby, not what's best for yourself."

"Forget your own ego, man."

"It isn't ego," Shockley objected.

"Then what is it?" asked Osgood, fixing him with his hard eyes.

"I don't want Baby out of my sight."

"She'll be in your sight." Jacobsen held out his hands. "You'll see her. It's as simple as that."

"You can't use microphones. Remember, no microphones. It won't work with them."

"No microphones," Jacobsen echoed indulgently. "I promised you and I'm a man of my word."

Slowly Shockley released his hold on Baby.

"Good," said Jacobsen, sighing in relief. "Good," he mumbled, taking out a handkerchief and wiping the beads of perspiration from his upper lip as Osgood dashed from the room with Baby.

* * *

By the time Shockley reached his seat, the curtain was up and Isaac Popov, the famous Russian exile conductor/composer was mounting the podium to the loud applause of the audience. On stage the orchestra had risen to its feet, the violinists vigorously tapping their bows.

"You're here?" asked Ruth, surprised as her husband pulled an extra chair in the box next to her and sat down.

"Change of plans," he said in a clipped, lowered voice barely audible over the dying applause.

"So I see," she said, looking at her program.

Putting on his glasses, Shockley took the program. Quickly he scanned it, his eyes picking up on the first sweep the names of Popov and Osgood. In bold letters at the top of the bill stood:

BABY IN CONCERT

At the bottom in small caps was:

A JACOBSEN/SHOCKLEY PRODUCTION

Shockley went back over the program and began to read. For the occasion, explained a short paragraph, Isaac Popov had been commissioned to write and conduct an original work called *Ode to Baby*. After the orchestral piece there would be an introduction by Osgood and then, finally, Baby was to sing.

"How's Baby," whispered Ruth.

"Calm," he said, looking out from their box over the vast hall. Searching among the sea of elegantly dressed humanity, Shockley couldn't locate a single empty seat. "Jud Osgood's going to present her," he said, trying to sound upbeat.

"Yes. I saw his name on the program," she answered woodenly.

"I'll introduce you later." He gave an uneasy smile.

Without reply Ruth turned back to the stage.

After a few stray whispers the audience fell silent.

Popov stood frozen at the podium, waiting, baton poised, his eyes ranging over his players.

The orchestra tensed. The violinists raised their bows. The horns glistened in the overhead lights. A drummer behind the kettles took a last-minute squint at his notes.

Popov brought down his baton in a swift stroke, and the orchestra broke into a deafening thunderclap rocking the hall—the explosion quickly followed by the violins bowing furiously. The opening reminded Ruth of the brick bursting through her window. To Shockley it brought to mind the explosive birth of a planet.

The violence of the opening soon gave way to a melodic strain as the music moved into a cloying passage that to Shockley sounded like the worst of Mozart, Brahms, and Strauss rolled into one sticky ball.

Ruth watched as the Russian went through his theatrics—Popov leaning into the music, gyrating his torso, jumping up and down on his stubby, little legs, his long mane of graying hair flying behind him.

The music became more ethereal, taking on a cosmic, eerie tone—the violins following a tremulous line, the horns growing in the distance, promising revelation. The music set Shockley's hair on end, giving him chills. It was having the same effect on the audience. Maybe Jacobsen really did know what he was doing, it occurred to him as the theme began to fade and the lights on the orchestra slowly dimmed.

"Ladies and Gentlemen," announced a disembodied voice. "Mr. Judson Osgood!"

There was a brief flurry of applause, but the clapping failed to break the spell of the music that continued to issue from the darkened stage. A lone light reached out from above the rear balcony and caught Osgood as he marched solemnly out onto the stage approaching a microphone that rose out of the floor, his powder-blue tuxedo blazing brightly in the spotlight.

"Once in a small eternity," he intoned, his deep voice filling the hall and reverberating off the walls, "the earth is blessed with a miracle." The violins began to pick up. "A miracle of such profundity that humanity, people everywhere, must stop." The drums were now picking up, thudding ominously in the background. "Stop!"

The music stopped short, and the audience, as though dangled on a thin filament, seemed to hold its breath lest the string snap. A lone flute began to play, penetrating the stillness with haunting refrain.

"Stop and behold."

The oboes and violins began to join in behind the high flute. Shockley felt himself sweating. His shirt was damp, and perspiration seemed to ooze from every pore.

" 'And I saw an angel standing in the sun,' " quoted Osgood from the Book of Revelation, " 'who cried in a loud voice to all the birds. . . .' "

Shockley's throat felt parched, and he swallowed tensely. For an instant he glanced over at Ruth, who sat stiffly in her seat, then quickly shifted his eyes back to the stage as Osgood's voice began to rise compellingly.

"The miracle is *now* and it is *here*," cried Osgood, as the kettledrums thundered deafeningly and a pair of beams suddenly shot across from opposite ends of the hall, training their lights on the pit at the forefront of the stage.

An audible sigh traveled up over the audience, moving from front to rear like a surging wave.

"For us to *behold!*" exclaimed Osgood, as Shockley glimpsed something bright rising up from the blackened pit.

Shockley leaned forward against the railing of the box and stared. There, sitting in a nest of white satin ruffles, was Baby, slowly rising out of the dark. The child's face was rouged, her lips painted, and in that satin-ruffled seat she looked as though she were entombed in a sarcophagus. Looking on in stunned silence Shockley noticed that instead of her red dress, she was clad in a pink gown trimmed with lace and dotted with sequins. On her head was an outlandishly large, pink bonnet. Continuing to rise up as the music swelled and pounded, Baby was squinting out into the glaring lights, the sequins on her dress and bonnet shooting out a myriad of tiny, dazzling beams.

The music came to an abrupt halt.

"Ladies and Gentlemen. We must now ask for your undivided attention," said Osgood with chilling firmness. "For your complete and utter silence."

The light on Osgood flashed off and, in the darkened hall, there remained only Baby, sitting alone in her nest of satin, her eyes peering out curiously at the flood of ghostlike humanity that sat there holding obediently still, stifling their coughs and sneezes and restless feet, two thousand people holding their breaths for a single infant.

"Quiet. Please. Perfect quiet!" reiterated Osgood from the darkness, and the hall became yet stiller.

Shockley sat pressed forward against the railing, chewing tensely on his knuckles. The ventilation that had been running in the hall was abruptly shut off, leaving an emptiness filled by the blood pounding in his ears. Inhaling in slow, controlled breaths, he could feel himself breathing in unison with the multitude around him. As he watched as Baby sat there in her nest, now elevated above the stage, her eyes trying to penetrate the blackness, a single worry raged through Shockley's mind: Would she sing?

The air in the hall became heavy, damp with breath and the smell of humanity. Someone in the balcony stifled a cough. A spring in a seat squeaked deafeningly. An infinity of eyes focused on the little head encased in the oversized bonnet.

"Baby," said Osgood's voice returning from the depths of the darkness, "sing for the people!"

A careless hand rubbed across the string of a violin and gave off a brief cry and the audience stiffened, thinking it was the child.

"Sing for us, Baby. Sing!" Osgood commanded.

Baby sat there lost in the converging spotlights. She tentatively lifted her thumb to her mouth, and Shockley was ready to burst out of his seat, run onto the stage, and pick up Baby in his arms. With him, he was sure she would perform.

"Sing! Sing!" urged Osgood, his voice echoing.

Baby let her hand fall back into her lap. She fidgeted with the lace on her dress, shook her head with the big bonnet, trying to free it.

"Sing!" cried Osgood, as Baby wrinkled her forehead in obvious suffering. "Sing! Sing! Sing!"

From the box Shockley could see her eyebrows knitting in conflict.

Slowly he rose from his seat. Ruth turned to look at him and just as she did Baby also turned and looked up as though spotting him. Gripping the back of his seat, Shockley froze and watched as Baby, cocking her head to one side, suddenly took a large breath. Noting it, the

audience also caught its breath. And then it came. The
voice. A small point source of music, a high rapturous
sound emerging from that little mouth on stage, faint
yet clear, note after note diffusing through the crowd,
her uncanny melody drifting out and enfolding the
waiting multitude, her crystalline, flutelike song distilling the essence of humanity's love and aspirations and
longings—a solitary voice calling out in an unearthly
language that all could grasp.

His heart thumping, Shockley gaped and listened as
Baby's tentative music began to grow in confidence, her
voice now a chorus of fine small voices, harmonies
within harmonies. She was taking long deep breaths of
the dank air and proudly singing out her music, her
songs merging into one another as she weaved in and
out of themes, her medley going from passages of hope
to elegy to passion. In the audience people were weeping, men and women alike, swollen tears coursing un-
checked down their cheeks, their faces set in rhapsodic
expressions of devotion, their hands clasped tightly as
though in prayer. Baby continued to sing, going long
beyond Shockley's wildest expectations as though she
were drawing strength from the packed crowd, sensing
their needs and giving all she could muster. Lungful
after lungful, she exhaled in a loud determined voice,
her face damp with sweat, the fringes of hair peeking
out from under her hat, plastered against her skin.

Enough. Enough, thought Shockley, wanting to spare
Baby, but she seemed unable to stop, and he began to
fear that she would exhaust herself and sing herself out.
Enough, enough, he called out to her in his mind, but
she continued to trill, her music rising to unattained
heights, her voice promising to rid her listeners of despair and anguish, her optimism rising to a fever pitch.
Higher and higher she climbed until, reaching a cres-

cendo, her voice began to fade, her music wound down, her strength began to ebb. Finishing with a short bird-like strain, she came to a stop and her thumb went into her mouth.

The audience remained suspended.

Suddenly the lights flashed onto the orchestra. As though caught in a dream, the musicians fumbled for their instruments. Popov, looking obviously shaken, brought up his baton and, robotlike, led the orchestra through the closing section of his piece—Baby's music still ringing in his ears.

A moment later the cymbals crashed, the trumpets blared, and the audience broke into wild cheers and applause as Osgood, beaming his smile and proudly holding Baby, took bow after bow.

The audience rose to its feet.

Extending a hand to Maestro Popov, Osgood signaled the Russian to take a bow amidst a deafening ovation. Popov motioned for the musicians applauding him to take a bow themselves.

A spotlight swung over to Shockley's box catching him unawares and confusedly he, too, took a bow to the thunderous applause. The light swung back to Osgood. The curtain went up and down and up and down, the applause continuing unabated. Shockley left the box and joined Popov and Jacobsen on stage, joining hands, and took a rousing new round of cheers, Osgood holding Baby aloft to the crowd.

"Well," said Jacobsen out of the corner of his mouth, as he took a long, last bow, "do I know my business, or do I?"

Squinting in the bright light, Shockley looked up at the box where he and Ruth had been sitting. It was empty. Ruth had left.

* * *

That evening, for the first time since his college days, Shockley got drunk. It happened in the grand ballroom of the Shockleys' hotel at the celebration honoring Baby. Thrown by the Friends of the Symphony, the party was an extravagant affair mobbed by jet-setters and the cream of local society, and overflowing with catered delicacies. Long tables stood brimming with imported caviars and exquisite cheeses, smoked salmon and oysters, and endless mounds of jumbo shrimp piled high on ice. Uniformed waiters edged their way through the tangled crowds, serving champagne and canapés. Two bands took turns entertaining, vying with the din of hundreds of excited voices that filled the hall. There was barely enough room to move as people pressed up against one another, the men dressed in dinner jackets, the women in long evening dresses, their faces flushed, all animatedly discussing Baby. And, it seemed, everyone wanted to meet Professor Shockley.

"Oh, so you're Dr. Shockley," said an elderly man with flapping jowls, elbowing his way into a group encircling Shockley. "My wife's just been dying to meet you," he said, a lithe, blond girl in tow.

"How *ever* did you discover Baby?" asked a woman with bluish gray hair, her ears and wrists heavy with diamonds.

"I understand you won a Pulitzer Prize," said a famous film actor trying to squeeze a word in edgeways.

The drinks came in endless rounds. They appeared on the passing trays, at the four strategically placed bars, and they were slipped into Shockley's hands by considerate guests eager to hear anything about Baby.

"Well, it hasn't exactly been easy," said Shockley to a rather attractive steel heiress as he searched the crowded room in the hopes of spotting Ruth. Since the performance she was nowhere to be found, not in their suite or apparently anywhere in the hotel. "We've had our ups and downs with her. Why, tonight," he said, downing something that tasted like a martini, "Baby had me really frightened."

"When did she first start singing?" asked a man who introduced himself as a local music critic.

"What a gold mine you've got," said Isaac Popov, giving Shockley a playful poke in the ribs before he was whisked away to meet someone important.

"I'd like to have a serious discussion with you," said a toy manufacturer. "Not tonight, of course." He forced a loud laugh. He was hoping to get Baby's endorsement for his new line of educational toddler toys.

"When are we going to see Baby?" asked a double-chinned matron weighed down in gold.

"Yes," agreed her escort. "Where is that enchanting child?"

"Well, we thought we'd bring her in for a few minutes later," Shockley slurred.

"She's sleeping and we don't want to disturb her," injected Jacobsen, appearing suddenly from out of the depths of the crowd. "I just checked with the baby-sitter," he added for authenticity.

"Well, if she's seeping we slertainly don't want to—" said Shockley, leaning up against Jacobsen for support.

"What a pity," sighed another woman in a tantalizingly low-cut dress.

"Shockley." Jacobsen pulled him aside. "A hard and fast rule: Nobody sees her without paying. Get it?" he said, and then disappeared into the crowd.

Shockley continued to drink, occasionally popping into his mouth a cracker heaped high with caviar or a lone slice of rare roast beef that tasted like fur, his perceptions of the party becoming progressively more obscured by a strange fog. Despite his inebriation sometime during the night, something caught Shockley's eye. He was standing with Osgood at the time, struggling to appear sober when he spotted it. It was a pendant that one of the more chic women guests was wearing around her neck, a minuscule gold charm cast in the shape of a pair of oval lips. Shockley tried to point it out to Osgood, but before he could speak, it was gone. Later on he thought he saw the same pendant on another woman, but by that point he neither trusted his powers of observation nor cared.

There was something else, too, that Shockley noticed that night at the party. It was a woman. He had spotted her early in the evening talking quietly with a man. She was tall and svelte. Young. Early twenties, he had guessed, unable to take his eyes off her. Her cheeks were high and broad, almost Slavic-looking, and her skin was smooth and flawless. Her beauty was so extraordinary that she had caught his eye almost from the moment he had entered the crowded ballroom. Once, later that night, while he was engaged in small talk with a television newsman, their eyes met for a fleeting second. She was watching him. He was sure of it. And then she was gone. As he drifted through the party that night, yanked from one group to the next, he had kept searching for her, hoping for the chance to speak to her. At one point, when he discovered her close to where he stood, he had been tempted to pull away from a conversation and go over to her, but finally hadn't dared. She was so breathtakingly gorgeous that Shockley found himself intimidated by her beauty. Yet, as he drank his way through the party, his eyes continued to scan the crowd, still hoping to find her.

Around midnight, when the celebration began to wane, Shockley queasily took the elevator up to his rooms.

The woman who had been installed to watch over Baby rose quickly to her feet when he entered the suite.

"She's just been a perfect little angel," she gushed, as Shockley groped in his wallet to pay her. "I brought along some sewing, but I just couldn't take my eyes— Oh, heavens, what's this?" she asked, looking at the wad of bills. "I couldn't take that," she said, and Shockley noted as she put on her coat to leave that she, too, was wearing a pair of those golden lips around her neck.

After the woman had left, Shockley went into the bedroom and checked Baby, who was fast asleep in her crib. Looking over at the double bed, he could see that it was still freshly made, untouched. Shedding his clothes, he wearily pulled aside the covers and slid into the large, cold bed. He closed his eyes and immediately dozed off. A short while later he was briefly awakened by movements next to him. It was Ruth coming to bed.

"The lips," he uttered groggily.

"What?" she asked distantly.

"The lips," he mumbled, trying to concentrate, but his brain refused to pursue the thought and he fell back into unconsciousness. After that he slept only fitfully, waking up repeatedly, dreaming in short, vivid bursts, dreaming about Baby in a sarcophagus, about that dark, svelte woman who had looked at him, about those golden lips. In the early morning he awoke, sick to his stomach, nausea churning in his guts. He tried to stem it by pushing all thoughts out of his head, but the nausea just grew. He tried sleeping on his back, on his stomach, on one arm. Finally he surrendered and, dashing from the bed, hung over the toilet, vomiting repeatedly and swearing to himself that he was not going to get drunk again for at least another decade or two.

* * *

The following morning Ruth flew back to Ithaca, and for the next five days Baby continued to play Cleveland. Almost from the outset it became clear to Shockley that things were changing. To begin with, the character of the audience was altering drastically, shifting for each performance from that chic, opening-night crowd to more ordinary folks. Tux and evening dresses gave way to suits, which, in turn, were being infiltrated by jeans and sweat shirts. The audience, which had started out with the wealthy and powerful, now consisted of laborers and school teachers, drop-outs, aging hippies, and street people.

"I don't like the way the audience is changing," said Shockley after one of Baby's performances.

"Christ, Shockley, stop being such an elitist," said Jacobsen. "As long as they pay, why give a damn who they are?"

"You wanted exposure, didn't you?" said Osgood, handing Baby over to Shockley. "Well, that's what you're getting."

"You don't understand. That's not what I'm talking about."

What Shockley objected to was the program itself. It had taken yet another turn that made him uneasy. The change had occurred after the second performance when Osgood, according to plan, had commanded Baby to sing.

"Sing! Sing for us, Baby!" Osgood had called out from the darkness. Looking a bit overwhelmed, Baby had sat in her nest, silent. "Sing for us, Baby!" Osgood had tried again and again.

Then in the growing tension someone in the first balcony, losing control, had suddenly cried out, "Sing!"

Heads had abruptly turned to locate that lone cry,

but a second later another voice coming from the mezzanine had punctuated the darkness.

"Sing!" called a high voice.

"Sing!" called a baritone.

Soon the entire audience was chanting in unison, stopping only when Baby opened her mouth to finally sing.

"Keep it in the show," said Jacobsen after the incident as Osgood, looking shaken, waited in the wings for Baby to end her performance.

"What?"

"It's perfect, don't you see? It puts the responsibility for the performance squarely on the audience instead of you. When Baby sings, it leaves them the feeling that they've elicited the song."

And from that point on, Osgood made a practice of encouraging the audience.

"It's hokey. It's rowdy. It's even worse *schlock* than that first night," said Shockley the next night in Baby's dressing room, taking off her bonnet and drying her sweat-soaked hair. "And I want it stopped."

"Do me a favor," said Jacobsen, watching as Shockley undressed Baby. "Please limit yourself to your own area of expertise. I have control over the format of the programs. You read your contract before you signed it, didn't you?"

"Contracts can be broken," said Shockley, turning and coming eye to eye with the Dane.

"Try to break it," said Jacobsen, a cigarette locked between his teeth.

"And?"

"You'll find out," he said, stalking from the room.

There were other points that also irked Shockley. Those tiny golden lips, for instance. They were becoming more and more prevalent, appearing on fine chains around people's necks, on lapels, in earrings. They made Shockley uneasy.

Then there was the matter of the media. What had started out as an exclusively positive press was now turning mixed and often vicious. In particular, Felix Lyons in his nationally syndicated column was coming out with almost daily attacks on Baby.

"If there ever were a good old-fashioned hoax," he wrote in one of his assaults, "it's being perpetrated on the masses by a team of sharpies and hipsters using an innocent infant as a front." Lyons went on in that article to accuse Jacobsen and Shockley of employing "electronic chicanery" to make it appear that Baby was singing; that Baby by some gimmick had been taught to move her lips to some decidedly weird-sounding music. It was the old back-tent circus con, and anybody shelling out twenty-five dollars for a ticket would fare better spending it on a psychiatrist.

"Why's Lyons doing this?" asked Shockley, handing the newspaper over to Jacobsen as they flew in the agent's private jet to Boston for Baby's Symphony Hall show.

"Maybe he's got some share in a psychiatric clinic," quipped Osgood, giving Baby her late-morning bottle.

"Let him say what he wants. What's the difference?" said Jacobsen, tossing the paper to one of his assistants. "Besides"—he took a tentative sip from his snifter of brandy and rolled the liquor around his tongue—"he's giving Baby enormous publicity. People are going to buy tickets just to see for themselves if Baby is a fake. They're not going to take Lyons's word. Would you?"

"Does everything boil down to money?" asked Shockley, as the plane banked and began to make its approach to Logan.

"Ultimately," said Jacobsen unabashedly. "Look, this is a stupid discussion. The trouble with you," he said, zeroing in on target, "is that you're on this morality kick that says that making money is evil. Well, I don't think it's necessarily so. I make money. Lots of it. But I also give most of it away to very worthy causes and people who need it. I've supported many a starving performer until they made it. And some who never did."

The engines on the plane cut back and the flaps came down.

"Stop trying to be all things to all people. You want to be loved by the whole world. Forget it. It's impossible. And forget this asshole Lyons," continued Jacobsen, as Shockley took Baby back into his lap. "He's not worth a second thought. He's doing it because he's one of those born-again Christians."

"What's that got to do with it?" asked Shockley, as the landing gear locked into place with a loud clunk. Jacobsen gave an enigmatic shrug.

"We're late as usual," he said, glancing at his watch and changing the subject.

Holding Baby tightly, Shockley looked out the window and saw the ground rising up to greet them. As the beginning of the landing strip came into sight the thought of Doris suddenly popped into Shockley's head. Then the tires hit the runway with a squeal, the plane lurched, and the thought was jarred from his mind.

After two days in Boston, Baby looked exhausted.

"She needs a rest," warned Shockley.

"She'll get a rest," said Jacobsen, trying to concentrate on the itinerary. There had been a last-minute cancellation for their Seattle date and he was trying to plug in a substitute in nearby Vancouver.

"When?"

"When the first part of the tour is over. We stick to the schedule. No deviations."

"Jacobsen, you're pushing your luck."

"And you're pushing me! Now be a nice guy and take care of Baby and see that she's ready."

Later, Jacobsen apologized.

"Hey, I'm sorry. I didn't mean to be rude. I've been a real son of a bitch lately, I know it," he said, putting his arm around Shockley. "It's the pressure."

"Yeah. It's getting us all," said Shockley, taken off balance by his candor. Just when he was convinced that Jacobsen was a cold-hearted, hard-driving businessman, he would surprise Shockley in some small way.

During the shows in Boston, Shockley took to nervously pacing around the theater to kill time. Secretly he was glad that Osgood was up there on stage taking the strain. It was no easy job and Osgood, too, was beginning to show the signs of fatigue.

On the night of the third performance, as Baby's ruffle-enclosed nest was rising up out of the pit and the audience was chanting for Baby to sing, Shockley was wandering around the theater when, by chance, he walked out into the lobby. There, where they were setting up for a last-minute sale of refreshments after the show, amidst the cold orange drink and wine and plastic-wrapped sandwiches, Shockley spotted a case holding a display of golden lips. There were lips that could be fastened to chains or bracelets. Discrete miniature lips that might almost disappear on the lapel of a suit, big obtrusive lips that could be worn on a ponderous chain. Together they formed a chorus of a thousand infant mouths opened in song.

"If you don't see what you want," said the old woman behind the counter, "just ask."

"What are they?" he asked.

"They're lips," said the lady matter-of-factly.

"I can see that."

"Baby lips."

"Oh."

"We've got them in all price ranges. We've got them, like these here, in pure gold," she said, unlocking a glass case and holding them out to Shockley. "Aren't they darling? And then we have them in gold plate, like these."

"Are you selling many of them?"

"They're selling like crazy. Why, I must have sold eight dozen tonight alone. Boy, I wish I owned this concession."

"You don't?"

"Oh, heavens no!" said the lady, waving him away and smiling, the lines on her face folding into deep gorges. "If I did, I'd be in there listening to that wonderful child, not out here working." She shook her head. "Heavens no"—she laughed—"I work for the Jacobsen outfit."

Following the Boston concerts, Jacobsen ferried Baby's entourage across the country for a West Coast swing, kicking off the tour with a three-day appearance before packed crowds in the Los Angeles Civic Center.

After L.A., Baby and Osgood did a one-night stand in San Diego, where Jacobsen experimented with yet another twist to the program. He had asked his old friend and pop lyricist Jay Kramer to see if he could come up with some lyrics to Popov's *Ode*. Excerpting one of the melodic refrains from the Popov piece, Kramer managed to hone a very catchy, moving tune, and Jacobsen decided to give it a whirl in San Diego. Before the orchestra began the Popov number, Jacobsen had a local choir troop onto the stage and sing Kramer's song.

> Baby, Baby,
> Our voice from heaven,
> Easing our pains
> Our hope you do leaven.
> Lifting our burdens with your sweet song,
> When you sing, the world can't be wrong.
> Baby, Baby,
> Baby, Baby.

By the time the choir was into its encore, the audience was on its feet. Joining hands and swaying to the infectious rhythm, the audience sang along in perfect harmony, and Jacobsen knew he had a hit. The song, recorded then and there in San Diego, was pressed and hurriedly put into production. In less than a week it was in retail stores and being played on radio stations around the country. On the flip side was the orchestral overture of Popov's *Ode* recorded live at the Cleveland opening. Hopes were high that the record would do a brisk business as a single. If initial sales were any indication, it looked as if the song would be up on the charts in a matter of days.

After San Diego the company flew to Vancouver, Kramer's song already an integral part of the program. Vancouver gave way to Dallas, Dallas to Chicago, Chicago to Detroit. Through all the travels, Felix Lyons continued to take potshots at Baby, his vitriolic attacks joined by a number of other journalists. Picking up a stateside paper in Vancouver shortly before the second show, Shockley read one of Lyons's more recent columns and finally understood the source of the man's virulence.

"There are those," Lyons wrote, concluding his column, "Babyists among them, who would have us believe that a messiah has arrived, who would have us cast off two thousand years of religious belief for a passing gimmick, who . . ."

It was the first time that Shockley had actually heard the word *Babyist,* and it confirmed his suspicions and made the connection between the fervor of the audience and those golden-lipped pendants. They were obviously more than just souvenirs.

"Looks like we've got an honest-to-goodness religion on our hands," said Osgood breezily, studying the article from the wings as the orchestra moved toward his cue.

"Here, let me see that," said Jacobsen, taking the paper and scanning the column. "What the hell's Lyons crusading about now?"

"You know very well and you've known all along!" said Shockley, his temper suddenly flaring.

"Lower your voice," Jacobsen whispered back. "They can hear you all the way out in the audience."

"I don't give a good goddamn if they do hear! I know what you've been up to all along. You're the one who's been feeding the fires. You're the one behind those damn lips. You're the one who's been selling them."

"Now hold on just one second!" Jacobsen's face burned a deep crimson. "I've been marketing them. I don't deny that. But I think you're confusing cause and effect. I just responded to a need, that's all. I certainly did not start these people going. My people sell the lips. Nothing more. Period!" he said, turning on his heels and marching away. A few feet later he stopped. "And by the way," he added, raising a finger, "the profits from those trinkets are not just going into my pockets.

They're going into Baby's earnings as well!" And with that he spun around and stormed off.

"Christ Almighty, how many times do I have to tell you I don't care about—" Shockley shouted after him, but Jacobsen was already out of earshot.

"Jud, she's a singer, not a messiah," Shockley insisted in a firm whisper as he watched Baby being taken to the pit below.

"I think you're being a little unfair to Ivar," said Osgood, his hand poised on the curtain. "He was telling you the truth. He's not behind it. I know that for a fact. You've got to understand, the man's a businessman. His mind doesn't work like yours and mine. If he sees an opportunity to make some money and it's not illegal or immoral, he'll take it. Try not to be too judgmental. I learned that a long time ago in this business. It makes life a lot easier. And don't worry about these Babyists. They're OK. Relax," he said, touching Shockley's arm and smiling reassuringly. "Relax. Oops," he said, missing his cue from the conductor and, leaving in a hurry, he solemnly marched onto the spotlighted stage.

After Vancouver, Shockley heard the name Babyists again. He saw them mentioned in Dallas and Chicago papers. At the end of the week, *Time* magazine carried a brief article on the Babyists in its section on religion, including a photo of Baby in her costume, the picture credited to the Jacobsen outfit. In the lobby of one theater Shockley was handed a pamphlet by a matronly woman who had tried to hit him up for a donation. Around her neck she wore an enormous pair of golden lips dangling on the end of a thick chain. She introduced herself as Sister White, a member of the lay clergy. Fortunately, she didn't recognize him, and he was able to escape before she got too far into her sermon on the goodness of Baby and the pressing need for a temple. Later in Baby's dressing room, as the wardrobe lady was putting the finishing touches on Baby's makeup, Shockley took a moment to study the pamphlet. It was published by something called the Assembly of Babyists. He began to read:

For the fleeting moments in eternity that we hear Baby we become one with our great Master, who created her song. Through her we receive his message, fathom his intentions.

He tried to read further, but the booklet contained a lot of gobbledygook and biblical references to the new messiah. He soon got bored and crumpling the pamphlet, tossed it into the trash.

"What absolute drivel!" he said to Baby.

Baby smiled back at him, then scrunched up her face as the woman carefully dabbed it with a puff of powder.

When Baby was ready, Shockley lifted her into his arms and headed out the dressing-room door. In the hallway he hesitated, turned around and going back, extricated the pamphlet from the trash. Smoothing it out, he folded it into his pocket.

"I tell you, this Babyist business spells trouble," warned Shockley during a quick huddle before the Atlanta performance.

"Take it easy. You've nothing to worry about," said Jacobsen, trying to calm him. "They're absolutely harmless."

"I've been talking to some Babyists and they're really *good* people," Osgood added, noting Shockley's agitation. "Sometimes they come backstage to speak with me and—"

"They do?" This was all news to Shockley.

"All they really want is to listen to Baby and, if they can, serve her in some way," explained Osgood compassionately. "Where is the harm in that?"

"I don't like any of it," Shockley eyed him suspiciously.

"You can't tell people what to believe," said Osgood logically. "It's a free country, man."

"Don't cut them off," said Jacobsen sagaciously. "You never can tell."

"They might come in handy some day," echoed Osgood.

"How?" snorted Shockley. "By selling more tickets?" The Dane smiled indulgently, and Shockley could see the wheels spinning in his head. He was looking for dollar signs in Jacobsen's eyes, but saw them only in Osgood's.

"I don't care what you two think," said Shockley, taking Baby after the show and heading directly to his hotel. "But I'm not taking any chances!"

"Nobody's saying you should," said Jacobsen, accompanying him to the door of his hotel room. "Take good care of her. That's fine with us. Just don't get paranoid about the whole thing."

From that moment on, Shockley made a strict point of always keeping Baby within sight. He had all his and Baby's meals sent up to his room. He no longer ventured out onto any of the city streets either with Baby or by himself, which would have meant entrusting her to another person. At night when he slept, he kept her crib close to his bedside, guarding his little singer jealously, often waking in the night to check her.

The strain of the shows, the endless travel, the new cities, the strange hotel rooms, the crazy hours and odd meals, his growing worry about the Babyists, all were slowly beginning to take their toll on Shockley. In everything he began to see the portents of imminent danger. The plane, while parked on the ground, could be sabotaged and they would crash. The food could be poisoned and Baby would be lost. The audiences, packing the poorly ventilated theaters, were infusing the air with potentially lethal bacteria. Before every performance he always checked the exits, outlining in his mind an escape route for Baby. The lips, which began to appear in profusion, greeting them as they arrived in each new city, chilled Shockley to the marrow. The Babyists who repeatedly tried to make appointments to speak with him regarding Baby were denied access. The less he had to do with them the better. The country was crawling with nuts and assassins, and he was not taking a chance with any maniacs who might want to martyr the child.

The mounting pressure became so intolerable that Shockley felt he was starting to see things. Driving in from the Atlanta airport, he thought he caught a glimpse near his hotel of that dark, svelte woman he had fleetingly seen the night of the Cleveland party. Now that he thought about it, he suspected he had spotted her once in Los Angeles and another time early in the tour on Boyleston Avenue near Symphony Hall. He knew his mind was playing tricks on him, but he felt helpless to stop it.

I don't know how much more of this any of us could take, he thought to himself on the night of the last performance. They were scheduled to return to Ithaca for a short break preceding the big New York City opening, and it was none too soon. Baby was tired, sometimes cranky and, as of late, she often had an upset stomach.

Spontaneous songs had now become a rarity as though, calculatedly, she were saving her singing for the rigors of the show. When she did sing for him in private, Baby's songs struck him as morose and lonely. She was now sucking her thumb almost constantly, refusing a pacifier, her eyebrows knitting frequently. Shockley tried to cheer her up, with new toys, by talking to her, singing her lullabies, even telling her fairy tales. Nothing seemed to help. Baby seemed distant and preoccupied.

The tour had been too long. Osgood was showing the signs too. Without makeup his face looked old and haggard, and his hands were developing a small but perceptible tremor. Jacobsen was smoking up to four packs a day. He had gone through three assistants; two had been summarily fired, and one had collapsed in exhaustion. Every time Shockley boarded the plane, he seemed to be greeted by a new face on the staff. They all needed a rest. Badly. Ithaca came as a welcome relief.

It felt great to be back in Ithaca. The minute Shockley's feet touched the macadam at the airport, all of his fears and forebodings seemed to vanish. Even Baby looked suddenly happier.

"Have you heard anything from Doris?" he asked, hardly in the door.

"Not a word," said Ruth, accepting the child from his arms. "Boy, Baby really looks pooped."

"Nothing that a good few days' rest won't cure," he said, slumping down into a couch, putting up his feet, and swearing that nothing could make him budge.

A few minutes later, however, he was on the phone, calling Andrea Cassaniti.

"Oh, Dr. Shockley, you're back in town. I'll be right up," she said and hung up before he could object.

"Baby's sleeping now," Shockley apologized, letting Cassaniti in. "She's awfully bushed."

"Oh, I was really hoping—"

"Tomorrow. I promise you. She'll sing."

Cassaniti brightened, her eyes sparkling behind her glasses.

"One reason I called you was to inquire about Doris Rumsey. Ruth hasn't heard anything from her, and I was wondering, well—if you had?"

"Nothing." Cassaniti shrugged, slouching in her seat. "She's got visiting privileges," she said, twirling a strand of hair around her finger.

"I know," he said, watching her. "That's why I find it odd that she hasn't contacted us."

"I don't find it so odd. We deal with a lot of strange cases, a lot of strange clients. You wouldn't believe some of the weird parents we encounter. When we try to remove their children, they fight like crazy. They lie. They try to steal the kids. Try to smuggle them out of town. Then, once they're removed from their custody, the parents are actually glad. This job is better training in human psychology than any course I ever took up there," she said, motioning with her chin toward the campus.

Shockley nodded and smiled indulgently.

"Well," said Cassaniti, moving to get up. "Gotta be going."

"Yes," said Shockley, his eyes caught by a sudden gleam that appeared low in the front opening of her blouse. Subtly maneuvering his head, Shockley peered down into the fissure between her breasts and saw what it was. It was a small set of lips hanging on the end of a chain.

* * *

"As long as Baby's in town for the week, I was thinking of asking Doris to come and stay here," said Shockley that night while brushing his teeth.

"Is that a request or a statement of fact?" asked Ruth, appearing behind him in the bathroom doorway.

"It's both," he replied, a ring of white foam encircling his mouth. "I'm asking if you'd object," he said, looking up into the mirror to see her reflection.

"We're getting very considerate these days, aren't we?" she said quietly.

"Ruth. Please," he rinsed his mouth and turned to her. "Do we have to fight?"

"We're not fighting," she said, skirting around him to get at the sink.

"Can't we talk?" he asked, coming up behind her and wrapping his arms around her waist. Through the sheer nightgown he could feel her stiffening under his grasp.

"That's all we do, talk," she said, slipping away from him. "I'm tired of all the words."

"I feel very bad about Doris," he added a little later when they were together in bed. "The thought of her being deprived of Baby keeps haunting me."

"Obviously you feel guilty."

"Of course I do."

"Well then, instead of having her come here to be with Baby, why don't you let Baby stay with her?" she asked, sitting up on an elbow and facing him.

"Because we can't. According to the custody decision she's supposed to stay in our house, under our supervision."

"Irwin," she said, looking deep into his eyes, "how did we really get Baby?"

"I've told you. When I heard about the action, I

quickly volunteered our names. I certainly didn't want her going to God-knows-what other family. Did you?" he asked, avoiding her penetrating look.

"Is that the whole truth?"

"Basically."

Ruth heaved a long sigh and lay down.

"OK," she said a few minutes later, staring up a the ceiling. "Ask her if you want. It's fine with me if Doris wants to stay here."

"I was sort of hoping that you'd ask her," he ventured tentatively.

"No," said Ruth flatly, snapping off the light on her side. "If you want her to stay, *you* ask her. Don't ever use me or put me in a position between you and Doris again. Ever!"

Shockley's first full day in Ithaca turned out to be a busy one. There were loose ends to be tied up at the university as well as a multitude of legal and financial matters that required immediate attention. Baby's first check from the Jacobsen organization had just arrived, and a trust fund and corporate shelter had to be established. Shockley didn't quite know where to turn. Fortunately, while picking up his last paycheck from Krieger's secretary, he ran into Burt Marra.

"Oh, I saw you and Baby in the Sunday *Times*," said Marra, greeting him like a long-lost friend. "How's everything going? Are you in town for a while? Why don't you and Ruth come over to the house for drinks tonight?"

Although he made a polite inquiry about Shockley's composing, professing a newfound eagerness to perform some of his latest works, it was obvious that all Marra really wanted to talk about was Baby.

Shockley took out a few minutes to talk to the rotund, little conductor. Marra, he knew, had inherited a small fortune from his wife's family and, when he wasn't rehearsing the university symphony, he was actively orchestrating his portfolio of stocks, bonds, options, and commodity contracts. He was obviously the right man to ask about Baby's financial needs. At the appropriate moment, Shockley slipped in a question about business.

"Sounds to me, what you need is a good lawyer," said Marra. "A man who knows tax laws, contracts, annuities, setting up trusts—the whole *schmeer*."

"Got any suggestions?"

"Matter of fact, I've got just the man for you." Marra's tiny eyes lit up. "Does all my work. He's absolutely the best. Knows the angles."

"What's his name?"

"Kiely. Frank Kiely. He's a real bullet, if you know what I mean." Marra gave a knowing wink.

"Thanks," said Shockley with a grateful nod.

"Always glad to help a friend. By the way," Marra called after him, "you can mention my name."

"I will," said Shockley, who was already thinking of his next stop.

When he wheeled around the corner on Willow Avenue, Shockley was immediately struck by the appearance of the Rumsey home. Devoid of curtains and blinds, the house looked hollow from a distance. Climbing onto the porch, he peeked in and discovered that not only were the windows bare but the front rooms were totally empty. The place looked as if a bomb had hit it. The wallpaper had been peeled off the walls, and the floors were littered with debris. Hurrying around to the side of the house, he anxiously checked a rear window. Then another. The dining room was bare. The kitchen had been stripped of its cupboards, and all the plumbing had been ripped out. Someone had started to spackle the deep cracks in the ceiling, and the only thing in the room was an old kitty-litter box abandoned in one corner of the desolate room.

"Where's Mrs. Rumsey?" he finally asked one of the neighbors, who had been scrutinizing him as he looked into the vacant house.

"Moved," said Mrs. Oltz tersely. "An' none too soon."

"Where to?"

"Been pulling down the whole neighborhood," grumbled Charlie Oltz, coming up to her side.

"Good riddance to bad rubbish," added Mrs. Oltz.

"Where'd she go?" Shockley persisted.

"Moved out to the trailer park," explained Charlie, blowing on his bare hands to keep them warm. "Leeming's Trailer Park. Up by Etna. You know," he added, noting Shockley's confused expression. "Hang a left by Gas and Electric."

Shockley jumped into his car and drove out onto the highway that angled up over the east lip of the lake. Climbing to the plateau above the city, he passed the shopping malls and then the airport. He took a turn off the highway and, checking his map, began a zigzag shortcut through the countryside. He had never ventured out this way in all his years in Ithaca and what he saw surprised him. After a short span of squat ranch houses built in the middle of what had once been hay fields, he began coming upon stretches of road lined with dilapidated houses and ramshackle trailers with tacked-on additions. They looked as if someone had slapped them together and missed. Between them were pockets filled with squatters' shacks that had been built of scrap lumber and corrugated steel. They were so small and shabby that Shockley was sure that no one could be living in them, except that there were TV antennas on the roofs and wood smoke curling out of chimney pipes. Everywhere there seemed to be piles of junk: old car carcasses that had been turned over and scavenged for parts, abandoned washers and mowers, trash galore.

After three wrong turns Shockley finally found Leeming's Trailer Park. Driving in on the rutted, muddy road he found the place worse than anything he could have imagined. "Park" was a euphemism carried to the nth degree. The place was crowded with old, crumbling trailers that looked as if they had been stolen from junkyards. They were wedged together so tightly that a person could almost step out of one and into the next without setting a foot on the ground. As he rounded a turn, Shockley saw a child dressed in ragged clothes playing desultorily in the frozen dirt in front of a peeling green trailer. The boy's face was pale and smeared with grime, his expression vacant. A dog chained to the trailer barked relentlessly as he danced about at the end of his chain, his paws ankle-deep in piles of frozen turds.

Cutting a wide circle around the snarling dog, Shockley went to the trailer and knocked on the door.

An obese woman holding a child against her billowing hip answered the door. Her face was bloated and round as a ball, and her breasts were so large that they lay against the top of her protruding belly. Both she and her baby had the same pale look of abject vacancy as the child playing outside in the dirt, and both were lacking teeth, though for different reasons.

Shockley asked her if she knew Doris, as the dog continued to yap.

"Shadup!" she snapped at the unrelenting mutt. "Ya mean tha' ol' hunchback lady?" She turned back to Shockley, her eyes lost in the flesh of her face.

Shockley nodded uncomfortably, watching through the corner of his eye as two mangy dogs rummaged through the garbage oozing out of a pile of plastic bags.

"Just 'round there. Third one in," instructed the woman, and Shockley left his car where it was parked and walked on. As he cut across through the cluster of trailers, he came upon more of the same. Small children dressed in rags, without gloves or hats despite the biting cold, their faces hollow. Strewn trash. Lone dogs snapping viciously on their lines. He could hardly believe that this was just a short spin outside allegedly civilized Ithaca, home of an Ivy League university.

Shockley saw Doris about the same moment that she spotted him approaching. She was seated by the window inside a small pink-and-aqua trailer, staring out at the leaden day. When their eyes met, the muscles in her face went taut, the bones in her jaw jutting out through her transparent skin.

"Well?" she asked, coming to the door. There was an edge in her voice that Shockley had never heard. A blue vein at the side of her head pulsed with each beat of her heart.

"Baby's back in town—" he began falteringly.

"I know," she answered tersely. Her cat jumped up on the window ledge and looked curiously at Shockley.

"I thought—maybe—you'd like to see her."

Doris stood impassively. The dogs that had been scouring the garbage near the fat woman's home had trailed Shockley and stood eyeing him at a respectful distance.

"Ruth and I thought you might care to move in for the week," he continued uneasily, filling the silence.

"That way," he went on, "well, that way you could be with Baby."

Doris fixed him with her pale eyes. Her cat continued to stare at him. Shockley swallowed.

"You want to see her, don't you?" he asked.

Doris stood tensed, her body rigid, as straight as she could hold it. A telltale finger at her side twitched nervously.

"Actually, it's not just for the week. I was hoping that, ultimately, you could move in and live with us," he ventured unsurely.

"Move into *your* house?" she asked, her upper lip quivering.

"Yes," Shockley nodded, trying to sound enthusiastic. "That was the general idea."

"Move in with you to condone your theft? Is that the idea?"

"No, that's not it at all," said Shockley defensively.

"Move in until you felt like throwing me out? Is that your plan?" Doris asked, her gnarled fists clenching at her sides.

"I was—"

"Mr. Shockley," she said, holding up her head. "*Professor* Shockley, I would rather be dead and roast in hell than set a foot in your house!"

Shockley swallowed, his heart thudding in his ears.

"I want to see Baby. I want to hold her more than anything in the world," she said, tears flooding her eyes. "But the next time I see Baby she'll be mine," she uttered, biting her lips.

"Doris, come on. Be reasonable," Shockley pleaded. "You're only hurting yourself."

"I have been reasonable," she said, a lone tear coursing down her cheek. "That was my big mistake. I should never, never have opened my door to you!"

"Look, I'll bring Baby to see you. Here, if you wish. I can—"

"No! Don't! How many times do you have to crush me?"

"Doris, please," he begged.

"Please nothing!" she uttered. "The next time I see her, it'll be for keeps. If it takes every last penny, every last drop of my blood, I'll get her back. She was given to me, not you. Now, for God's sake, go away and leave me in peace!" she said, slamming the door, her cat fixing Shockley with an unblinking stare.

Although the tour had stopped, the attacks on Baby continued to mount, and for each passing day there were fresh assaults, new slurs, and accusations disputing her gift and denouncing Shockley's motives. The mere existence of the Babyists was polarizing sentiment, and Shockley could sense the situation rapidly deteriorating to the point where one either worshiped Baby or viewed her as an insidious threat—which had absolutely nothing to do with Baby's music.

Picking up the lead from Felix Lyons and his cohorts, a reporter on the "Nightly News" did a scathing report on Baby. Using some unauthorized footage of Baby in concert, the correspondent broadcast the sound of the child's singing to prove his point that Baby's socalled music was nothing more than a case in point of mass hypnosis and hysteria. Included in the highly biased report was an interview with some academic type from the Harvard Medical School, who, even though he had never heard more than the recording of Baby's voice, felt free to pontificate at length on the hazardous powers of mind control manifested by this "child worship" and the progressive erosion of the country's moral fiber by the burgeoning number of cults.

Following the TV coverage, Shockley was deluged with bags full of hate mail, his phone service was flooded with calls, and the newspapers went into high gear, feeding the flames with even more pulp about Shockley's alleged scam. On the weekend, a group calling themselves Clergy United to Reject Babyism (CURB) took out a full-page ad in the Sunday *New York Times*. Warning of the perils inherent in worshiping a false messiah, the coalition called on the members of their congregations and faiths-at-large to reject the idolatry of this paganism and to boycott the upcoming Lincoln Center concerts. The list of endorsees on the CURB petition filled four columns, eight-inches long with fine type. Included among the signatories, Shockley noted, was the archbishop of the New York diocese, a number of prominent Lutheran, Episcopal, and Baptist clergy and lay-people, as well as one lone rabbi.

That petition was the final straw. Armed with copies of the accusatory articles and a videotape of the television report, Shockley went to see his new lawyer. This whole thing had gotten out of hand and the time had come to put an end to it.

"The accusations against Baby are insane," he said, plopping the pile on Kiely's desk. "It's not a case of gimmickry or hysteria or hypnosis. There's never been any attempt on my part to represent her as a messiah or any other kind of religious figure. I want to stop this thing right in its tracks. Now."

Kiely rummaged through the pile, glancing at a few of the articles.

"How about initiating a libel suit?" Shockley suggested.

"That's a possiblity," said Kiely, turning an unlit cigar in his mouth. "But it's slow and cumbersome. What you want is something fast and effective. A sharp, swift cut."

"Yes."

"Something that will pick up the challenge. Nip this damn thing in the bud."

"Exactly."

Kiely thoughtfully licked the end of his cigar.

"Why not fight fire with fire," he suggested, a self-pleased smile forming on his ruddy face.

"How?"

"Use the media. Turn it on the bastards," said Kiely, the springs squeaking in his chair as he leaned back, his head cradled in his arms. He was thinking about his own ongoing war with the housing authority and how he had deftly managed to muddy the waters in the press. "Find yourself someone in the media who you think will give you a fair shake. Then use him."

"It's not a bad idea."

"Think about it," said Kiely, who had yet to hear Baby sing. As far as he was concerned, Baby's music was essentially a matter of indifference. His job was to handle the vast sums flowing in, administer her trust, pay her expenses, file for incorporation, minimize taxes, buy off people like Cassaniti and others, grease the wheels. Between his tenements in Collegetown and the lucrative work brought about by this singing kid, he had his hands full. The last thing in the world that he wanted was a protracted libel suit. There was no real money in it, just hassle.

Later, when other news programs started carrying a series of less-than-flattering items on Baby and her entourage, Shockley finally became galvanized into action. He decided television was the answer. He needed network coverage. If he were going to get a good audience for a single shot, he knew his best attack. Picking up the phone, he called Jim Fowler. The "On Line" producer had been eagerly seeking an interview for the last four months, and in a few minutes an appointment was firmed up for the following day in Ithaca. After the arrangements were finalized, Shockley felt an immense sense of relief. He was convinced that he had made the right choice. Almost everybody in the country watched "On Line," and the program was bound to give him the fairest shake. Once and for all he would make it clear that his intentions were solely musical, not religious. He'd nip this damn thing in the bud, just as Kiely had suggested.

Early the next morning, preceding the arrival of the camera crew, the Shockley home was in a minor uproar. The house was a mess and needed to be cleaned from top to bottom if it were going to be shown on national television. The children had been allowed to stay home from school so that they might be included in the program and, though they had all vowed to help, in the end they did little but add to the general pandemonium. There was furniture to be polished; there were rugs to be vacuumed, piles of magazines and books and papers to be put away; the broken blinds in the nursery had to be temporarily tied up; Randy's coin collection that littered the den had to be removed; Cindy's doll carriage and dolls had to be taken out of the living room and lugged back up to her room; Julie's bike had been left right smack in the middle of the front drive and the first car in would probably crush it. Through all the last-minute tidying up the kids expended most of their efforts horsing around, Julie and Annette getting into a knock-down, drag-out fight over a record they had found, each vehemently insisting it was hers.

Shockley ran the vacuum and tried to straighten up in the living room while Ruth attended to the kitchen. She had initially objected to letting the network people into her house, but realizing that her husband was under attack, she had grudgingly relented.

"I want everything to look shipshape. This program has got to go off without a hitch," he had warned the troops at breakfast. "This is Baby's big moment and we don't want to do anything to spoil it. And please, Cindy, when you're on camera, no dirty words."

"Yeah, and don't pick your nose." Randy grinned.

"Oh, screw you," said Cindy, giving her brother the finger. Annette giggled. "And screw Baby too," said Cindy, sulking, when her father had grabbed the offending finger and given it a small but painful twist.

"I mean it, Cindy," said Shockley, still holding that finger. "Just answer the questions, if there are any. And try to say nice things about Baby—for a change."

Outside it was beginning to snow heavily as they made the final preparations.

"Gee, I hope they don't get snowed in at the airport," said Shockley, peering apprehensively out the window. "There's already a good three inches on the ground and it looks very slippery. Do you think they'll close down the runway?"

"I wouldn't worry," said Ruth, preparing a lunch for the visitors. "They'll be here. They want this interview as much as you do. Probably more."

"We've only got this one day." He continued to fret. "I should have taken their advice and waited until we had a couple of full days for the shooting. I knew it." He worriedly looked out again at the dank day. "If we could only make more time. If only we didn't have to leave for New York tomorrow. Damn!" he muttered to himself, a sense of foreboding nagging like an itchy rash.

Shockley checked his watch a little later.

"They should be landing in fifteen minutes," he announced.

"Take it easy. The planes are never on time," said Ruth, and in her voice Shockley detected a note of reconciliation. They were over the worst, he told himself. Time would heal all.

"I want to go out and shovel the walk. Do you think you could get Baby up and ready?" he asked, giving her an appreciative hug. "I'm all thumbs today."

"Sure," said Ruth and, drying her hands on a dish towel, went up the stairs to the nursery. When she got there, she discovered Baby sitting up in her crib, a proud smile on her face. It was the first time she had sat up by herself, and Ruth was tickled to discover it.

"Look," she said to Cindy, who had tagged along. "Our little television star is sitting up all by herself."

"You want to give her an Oscar for it?" asked Cindy cuttingly. Ruth let the comment pass.

"Well, how about you and I giving Baby a bath, huh?"

Cindy shrugged.

"We'll get her all spruced up and smelling like a rose." Ruth lifted Baby and nuzzled her bare tummy with her nose as Cindy looked on in unveiled disgust.

"Can you keep a hand on her?" asked Ruth after she had put Baby on the changing table and taken off her diapers. Keeping her eye on Baby as Cindy held her, Ruth went to the closet to get Baby's plastic bathtub. "She rolls around a lot by herself, and you have to be *very* careful she doesn't slip off the table."

"I know. I know," said Cindy, pressing her hands down on Baby's hips. Baby's skin felt soft and rubbery, almost like warm plastic. Cindy looked down at the cheese dribbling from the corner of her mouth.

Ruth went out and Cindy could hear the water running in the bathroom.

"Drooling little creep," she muttered to Baby. Baby looked up nervously at the little girl pinning her to the table.

"Keep your eyes on her at all times," Ruth called out over the sound of rushing water.

"What do you think I'm doing?" Cindy shouted back, but she was looking intently out the window at her father, who was hunched over a shovel in the driveway. Red-faced and puffing, he was intently cleaning line after line of asphalt. The snow was falling so rapidly that his hair and beard were already covered with white.

Ruth came quickly back into the room to find Cindy standing there obediently holding Baby, her eyes fixed on the infant.

"Good girl," said Ruth, patting her with a damp hand.

Double-checking the temperature of the bath, Ruth took Baby from her daughter.

Cindy watched as her mother cautiously lowered Baby into the tub, the water lapping her chubby legs and back and then stomach. Baby cooed and laughed and started flicking the water with her hands, making happy little splashes. Ruth let Baby sit against the rim of the tub as she lathered her with a soft cloth, starting at Baby's neck and working under her arms and down to her toes. Baby wrinkled her face as Ruth gently washed it. She stuck out her tongue and tried to lick the soapy water. Just as Ruth finished washing her, the phone rang.

"Why doesn't somebody downstairs pick it up?" Ruth turned distractedly as the phone beckoned loudly from the bedroom.

"Could you pick up the phone?" She started to dispatch Cindy, but then suddenly changed her mind. "No. Wait. I'd better get it. It could be important," she said. It occurred to her that it might be the television people trying to get through.

"Cindy, can you hold on to Baby again for a second?" she asked, and Cindy, dutifully putting her hands under Baby's arms, watched as her mother dashed from the room.

Holding Baby upright in her bath, Cindy glanced down at her for a moment, then looked out the window at her father, watching, absorbed, as he puffed behind his shovel. She noticed the snow was now coming down hard, as Baby slipped from between her hands and slid down under the surface of the water.

Outside, Shockley was now at the far end of the driveway, putting the finishing touches to the last neat patch of snow. Though his back and arm muscles ached, it felt invigorating to be working outdoors in the fresh air. The exertion was a welcome relief after all those tense weeks on the road, being cooped up without exercise in hotel rooms and conveyances.

Shockley shoveled clear a last, long line, touched up an area of newly fallen powder and then, with pleasure, straightening his back, let his eyes trace the cleared driveway and walk. A man needs a routine of hard physical work, he was ruminating philosophically when something at the nursery window caught his attention. He turned up to look. It was Cindy. Cindy with her face pressed against the sealed window.

Cindy smiled and waved at him, and instinctively Shockley realized that something was wrong, terribly wrong.

"Ruth," he cried out. "Ruth! Ruth!" he called into

the wind. "Cindy, where's Mommy?" he shouted up at her. Cindy shrugged.

Dropping the shovel, Shockley started toward the house, inexplicable fear suddenly gripping him. He broke into a trot, then began to race forward, his feet skidding on the slick pavement.

"Ruth!" he bellowed, bursting through the front door and starting up the stairs.

Halfway to the second floor landing he heard Ruth let out a shrill scream. As he dashed into the nursery, Ruth pulled Baby from the water.

"Oh, my God! Oh, my God!" she gasped.

"Baby!" uttered Shockley aghast.

"She's not breathing!" Ruth wailed, holding the limp infant in her arms, her sleeves soaked from the water that ran off Baby's inert body.

"Call an ambulance! Call a doctor! Call somebody!" sobbed Shockley, looking down at Baby in horror. Her eyes were open and she was staring blankly up at him, her pupils wide.

Frantically seizing Baby, he opened the child's mouth and, putting his lips to hers, began to blow.

"It's Baby!" wailed Annette, arriving at the room. "Cindy's killed her."

"The little brat drowned her!" cried Randy, afraid to look at his father and Baby.

"She's dead," Julie buried her face in her hands and wept. "Poor Baby's dead!"

"Wait," said Shockley, pulling his mouth away, his body trembling uncontrollably. "I think—I think she's breathing."

Baby's chest started to heave. She gasped for breath. She took a second frantic gulp, coughed, and emitted a short bleat. Then she took another breath and started coughing weakly.

"She's alive," uttered Shockley, almost afraid to hope.

"Quick!" said Ruth, grabbing her purse and keys, her face streaked with tears. "The hospital."

Taking Baby, she hurriedly wrapped her in two large towels and bolted with the child to the garage, Shockley right behind her.

Fumbling with the keys, Shockley got the car started on the second try and, throwing it into gear, lurched blindly backward down the driveway. At the end of the drive he wrenched the wheel, spun the car in a half circle and sped off, skidding and fishtailing down the street.

"Cindy's going to catch hell," said Randy, as the three Shockley children stood huddled at the front door watching the wheels kick up a tail of snow.

Doris realized she was breaking her vow but couldn't help herself. In the early morning she had been stricken by a sudden painful tightness in her chest that was forcing her to fight for each gasping breath. No matter how deeply or how often she inhaled, she felt as though she couldn't get enough air and was slowly but surely suffocating. At first Doris was sure it was her heart giving out. Then she realized that the pains were actually lower down, in her diaphragm, as if someone had hit her in the gut and knocked the wind out of her. It was anxiety, she belatedly recognized, panic, not a heart attack.

Doris had been thinking about Baby when the seizure struck and, as she quickly dressed in layers of clothes, wrapping two scarves around her head, her sense of alarm continued to mushroom. Something was amiss with Baby. She was lost. She was hurt. She was sick. She was dying. Doris was sure of it, as sure as of the pain in her chest. Baby needed her and there was no time to waste.

Once outside her trailer in the icy air, Doris found that she could breathe with less difficulty, though that looming dread continued to plague her. Taking her bearings, she headed out of Leeming's Trailer Park, the snow swirling around her in blinding squalls. She struggled through the deepening drifts on the unplowed country road and, in minutes, her coat and head scarf were thick with white. She reached the large plowed highway and, cutting onto it, began to trudge the long straight miles to town.

As Doris lumbered through the ankle-deep slush at the edge of the open highway, the relentless wind drove the snow into her face, filling her neck with dripping ice. Passing cars showered her with briny slosh. Her boots became waterlogged, her feet numb. Once she slipped on an icy spot, wrenching her arm and soaking the back of her coat. Determinedly she picked herself up and pushed on. As she made slow but steady progress into the vicious headwind, Doris tried to keep from thinking, tried to take hold of that insistent fear. She counted steps. Measured the miles by paces. Sang a childhood song to herself while flapping her arms to keep warm. Nevertheless, in her mind's eye Baby's face kept returning, the infant crying out, crying for her, her mother.

"Baby. Dearest little Baby," she mumbled, shuffling on now in an almost hypnotic gait, oblivious of the storm, her frozen feet clumping down in a monotonous rhythm that seemed to keep the worst of her horrors at bay.

"Baby, Baby, Baby," she continued to chant. "Baby, Baby."

Three frigid miles later Doris passed the airport road. Another mile and she reached the outlying shopping malls, their plethora of bright lights emerging suddenly out of the screen of snow. The traffic was now getting heavier as she neared town, and to avoid the dirty spray she was forced to squeeze farther onto the shoulder of the road, often having to climb up on the steep piles of compressed snow left by the early plows.

Doris crossed the highway on the overpass just beyond the Howard Johnson's and waded through the snow-choked peripheral roads leading into Cayuga Heights. Following her instincts, she negotiated the inner winding streets of the Heights. Here it was quieter, seemed warmer, the houses more protected from the storm, the snow less hostile, the tall pines beautiful under their crushing burden of snow. When she reached the street she had sought, her body began to quiver uncontrollably, her bottom row of teeth chattering against that lifeless upper plate. Her back ached, her hands throbbed, her feet felt like leaden stalks.

At the head of the street she came to an abrupt halt. A half block farther and across the street, through a veil of snow, she saw the imposing stone house that was the Shockleys' home. As she looked at it, her heart began to leap and her chest tightened. The large house stood shrouded in a halo of white. The driveway and walk had been recently cleared. The garage stood open and abandoned and, though there was no car, she could see the shadow of the fishtailed tracks gouged through the snow. Doris riveted her attention on the stone facade of the building, stared and stared as if with her rheumy eyes she might penetrate its formidable opacity. She moved closer until she was almost across the street. The snow began to pick up, falling in large, wet clumps, striking with an almost audible splat, covering the Shockleys' drive and filling in the fishtailed sores. Doris remained fixed and waiting, planted in her spot, her solitary vigil unrelenting. The storm waxed and waned. Shafts of wind gusted through the street, driving up clouds of white that whistled through the wires. A big tree dropped its load of snow and shuddered in relief. Doris remained at her post, a lone figure engulfed by the storm, white and as unseen as the heavy-laden pines in the Shockleys' front yard.

Annette picked up the phone.

"How is she, Daddy?" she asked tremulously.

"Perfect," exclaimed Shockley. "It's nothing short of a miracle. No water in her lungs. She didn't even swallow a drop. No injuries of *any* kind. She had nothing but a nasty scare. She's even smiling a little now," he explained, and listened as Annette relayed the message to the cheers of Randy and Julie. "As a matter of fact, your mother and I are in worse shape than she is." He forced a chuckle, his body still trembling. "Have the television people come yet?" he asked a moment later.

"No," answered Annette, her voice noticeably subdued. "Wait!"

Shockley could hear Randy in the background running to the door.

"They're here. They're just coming up the drive. A whole mess of cars. What should we do?"

"Annette. Listen." Shockley's mind began to race.

"I'm listening."

"Tell Randy to come back. Not to open the door." He waited as Annette repeated the message.

"OK," she said when Randy was back by the phone.

"I'm going to need the help of all you kids."

"Yes?"

The doorbell chimed.

"I don't want any of you to breathe a single word of what's happened. Do you understand?"

"Yes," she replied submissively.

"Now, tell that to Randy and Julie." He waited. "Where's Cindy?"

"Upstairs hiding. I think she's in the attic."

"I want you to go to her, stay with her and tell her Baby's not hurt. That's very important."

"I understand."

"And don't let her out of your sight. Try to comfort her. Tell her we're very upset but not angry."

"I don't particularly feel like talking to that little murderer," said Annette disgustedly.

"She's just a baby herself. She didn't know what she was doing."

"Oh, I wouldn't be so sure," she said bitterly. In the background Shockley could hear the doorbell chiming again.

"Let's get something straight. It's not for you or your sister or brother to judge her. I want you to make that clear to the others," he explained. "Now."

Annette repeated the message.

Shockley's throat felt tight and parched and he tried to swallow. His saliva felt like sand going down his gullet.

The doorbell chimed for the third time.

"All right," he continued tensely. "Let the television people in and let them set up. Just pretend that everything is perfectly normal. Tell them we got delayed somewhere. We're going to go through this as if absolutely nothing had happened. OK?"

"Sure, Daddy."

"The show must go on," he said, a trace of sadness in his voice.

"If you say so."

When Shockley and his wife returned home with Baby, the TV crew was already set up in the living room. The furniture that had been so carefully arranged earlier in the morning had been dragged away, and the lone couch shuffled to one side of the fireplace was being lit with kliegs. The rugs had been rolled back, and a sound man was taping down wires on the bare floor. A large camera perched on a tripod was having its magazines loaded with film while a man with a light meter circled the couch. The room was a jumble of boxes and wires and lights and people.

"Hi. I'm Jim Fowler," said the producer with the dark, droopy moustache approaching Shockley. "We spoke on the phone," he smiled cordially, holding out a hand.

"Sorry to be late. We had an unexpected problem," said Shockley, forcing a smile. Behind him stood Ruth holding Baby, who was resting flaccidly in her arms, the child still occasionally shuddering and emitting a residual sigh. "Baby's feeling a bit under the weather," he continued uncertainly. "I really don't know if she's up to going on for very long," he said, motioning to her. Annette stood in a far corner, fixedly watching her father as he spoke.

"In that case we'll try to make her part as quick as

possible. Mrs. Shockley." He greeted Ruth, taking her hand, which was cold and limp. There were dark circles around her reddened eyes, and to Fowler she looked weak and ill.

"Well, it looks like we're ready to go," said Fowler loudly, catching the attention of his people, and it was then that Shockley noticed Joel Webster sitting off in a corner of the dining room with a woman, the two of them going over some last-minute notes. "Joel?" Fowler called out to him.

The woman looked up. Webster turned and, taking off his reading glasses, smiled toward the group. Although Shockley had never met him, Webster's angular and intense face was so thoroughly familiar that it felt as though he had known him all his life. Webster gathered up his papers in a neat sheaf and ambled over, his walk heavy-footed. Fowler introduced him. Webster mumbled some pleasantries to each of the adults and grinned at the infant in Ruth's arms. His manner was polite and polished and definitely businesslike. Webster's aloofness made Shockley uneasy.

"Shall we?" asked Webster, motioning toward the sofa after some strained small talk.

"Don't you want to outline with me beforehand what we're going to discuss?" asked Shockley, puzzled.

"No. I don't think it's necessary. Actually, I think we'll just start rolling, if that's OK with you, Jim?" He checked with Fowler, who readily nodded, as though it had all been prearranged.

"Let's have all the kids in this opening shot," suggested the woman who had been sitting with Webster. She waved the three over, and Shockley excused himself as the family gathered by the couch. In a few minutes he returned with Cindy in tow. She looked pale and terrified and was unusually tight-lipped.

Shockley himself felt unsteady, and faint waves of nausea periodically rose and ebbed in his gut. He looked over at Baby, who lay passively in Ruth's arms, her eyelids heavy with exhaustion. Reaching out, he soothingly stroked her head, thinking to himself how lucky they were, how incredibly lucky. Furrowing her brow, Baby shifted her eyes and glanced over at him, a pained expression on her face.

The cameras started to roll.

They began with the kids, taking individual close-ups of each of the children for later cut-ins. Webster talked with them, asking them how they liked having a famous star like Baby living with them, what they thought of her music. Cindy answered with terse yeses and noes and nods of her head while the others tried to carry the ball. Watching them, Shockley felt pride at seeing how they behaved in the face of calamity.

Ruth went on camera. Haltingly she spoke about Baby's general routine in the home, how she fitted in, how the children had come to love and accept her—her eyes fleetingly meeting Shockley's.

The kids were then dismissed. The cameras were reloaded with fresh film and then Webster, moving a chair directly across from Shockley, started to question him.

WEBSTER: You're aware, Professor Shockley, of the skepticism, of the furor that's arisen since you've taken Baby on her latest tour around the country.

SHOCKLEY: Yes, Joel, I am. In fact, it's because of that skepticism, because of the attacks on Baby, her music, and even on me, that I've consented to this interview.

WEBSTER: You claim that Baby can sing.

SHOCKLEY: Yes.

WEBSTER: And she'll sing for us today?

SHOCKLEY: I hope so, though I can't guarantee it. She's her own master. [*Looking down at her.*]

WEBSTER: When did she start singing?

SHOCKLEY: Shortly after her birth.

WEBSTER: Which was?

SHOCKLEY: In June. [*Vaguely.*] Late June.

WEBSTER [*Sensing his reluctance.*]: I understand her mother was a fifty-seven-year-old woman.

SHOCKLEY [*Tersely.*]: Fifty-nine.

WEBSTER: Who claims the birth was a virgin birth.

SHOCKLEY: I really don't know anything about those claims. [*Trying to slough over the point and shift the line of questioning.*] That has never been my concern. The important point is that the child can and does sing.

WEBSTER: Do you attribute this to [*Struggles theatrically with his hand in the air as though probing for the word.*] to the hand of God? Is this child [*Looks down at Baby, who yawns loudly.*] the daughter of God?

SHOCKLEY [*Firmly.*]: Maybe this is a good time to set the record straight.

WEBSTER [*Giving a magnanimous smile, one eye directed toward the camera.*]: Be my guest.

SHOCKLEY: The fact that Baby can sing, could in fact sing almost from birth, is a marvel. To listen to her music is to be raised to lofty heights. With her songs she can stir the soul as I, as a composer—

WEBSTER: I understand you won a Pulitzer prize for one of your works.

SHOCKLEY [*Modestly.*]: Yes. That's right. As I was saying, she can move people's emotions in ways that my music, or the music of other mortals, could never, ever, aspire to.

WEBSTER: Baby's a miracle.

SHOCKLEY [*Correcting.*]: A prodigy. A wonder, if you like. But—But that's where it stops. She is not the daughter of God. Nor is she a messiah. Nor a messenger or what have you. Neither I nor Ivar Jacobsen, her manager, nor anyone else connected with her has ever maintained anything of that nature.

WEBSTER: Then how did this whole thing start?

SHOCKLEY: You mean the Babyists?

WEBSTER: Yes. Among others.

SHOCKLEY [*Surprised.*]: Others?

WEBSTER [*Firmly.*]: Others.

SHOCKLEY [*Heaving an audible sigh.*]: I don't know how it got started. I truly wish it hadn't. It can only make public access to Baby's music more difficult. As far as I'm concerned, these people, whoever they are, are misguided. [*Pauses.*] They're a bunch of fanatics and zealots. They're making it hard for Baby to function in the role that she was meant to function in.

WEBSTER: And that is?

SHOCKLEY: As a singer. As a performer.

WEBSTER: As a freak show?

SHOCKLEY: I resent that.

WEBSTER: Dr. Shockley, you launched Baby's career by first visiting a number of music schools around the country.

SHOCKLEY: Yes. That's correct. I anticipated a certain measure of skepticism and felt that she needed acceptance by some of the most prominent people in music today. That tour struck me as the best means to that end.

WEBSTER: Did you have permission from the mother to take her child on that tour?

SHOCKLEY [*Taken aback and unprepared.*]: Well, tacitly. Er, I suppose you could say so. There were many factors involved—including the mother's health.

[*Clears his throat.*] The woman was very sick and apparently dying. Yes. I would say that there was a tacit understanding.

WEBSTER: Let's go back to her birth.

SHOCKLEY: I really don't know much about it.

WEBSTER: How did you discover her?

SHOCKLEY [*Reluctantly.*]: The way others did in Ithaca.

WEBSTER: And how was that?

SHOCKLEY: She was taken out by her mother to a local park, and she would sing there. For small audiences. Er, there, or in front of her house. But this is really not germane to the—

WEBSTER [*Pointedly.*]: Why don't you let me decide that?

SHOCKLEY [*Looking at the cameras as they continue to whirl, unabated.*]: I'd really prefer limiting our discussion to Baby's present tour.

WEBSTER [*Oblivious of the objection.*]: Who is her mother?

SHOCKLEY [*Vaguely.*]: Er, Doris Rumsey.

WEBSTER: How did you get the child?

SHOCKLEY: She was placed in our foster care by the Department of Social Services.

WEBSTER: Why?

SHOCKLEY [*Swallows uneasily.*]: Why? [*Shrugs and tries to appear nonchalant.*] Apparently she was being neglected in her previous home.

WEBSTER: Was she?

SHOCKLEY: Well, according to the people at social services and according to the courts and whoever else was involved, it was determined that she was not getting proper care. I really don't know much more about it.

WEBSTER: Come now, Dr. Shockley. You don't

mean to say that you didn't know the mother well *before* the child was placed in your custody.

SHOCKLEY [*Reddening.*]: I saw her singing. I listened to it. I was taken by it. If you're implying in any way that I was instrumental in her removal from the mother's custody, the answer is emphatically no! When I learned of the court decision my wife and I offered our services. Period.

WEBSTER: And not before?

SHOCKLEY [*Irritably.*]: I said *no*. If you want to know more, why don't you talk to the authorities? This is not a line of questioning I'm interested in pursuing. I thought you came here—

WEBSTER: Just what was your relation to—

SHOCKLEY [*Continuing.*]:—because you wanted to learn more about Baby.

WEBSTER: Were you in any way involved in the court procedures that led to Baby's removal from her home?

SHOCKLEY [*Vehemently.*]: I don't wish to pursue this line of discussion any further. It serves no purpose. Now is there anything more you'd like to know about Baby herself?

Shockley moved uncomfortably in his seat. His eyes strayed from Webster, and looking beyond the glare of lights, he briefly caught sight of a snow-clad hunched figure moving past his window and up the street.

Shockley fervently hoped that the New York City performances would go off without a hitch. After New York, Baby's next appearance was to be a series of Christmas concerts in Miami, and Shockley was looking forward to having Ruth and the kids join him there for the holidays. He figured that if he could just squeak through the New York shows without incident they could all celebrate Christmas together in the Florida sunshine and try to mend some rifts that had come between them. Almost from the start, however, his hopes were quashed.

When Shockley checked into the Plaza with Baby, he was met by a slender young man with blond hair and effeminate ways who introduced himself as Rolf Pettersson, another of Mr. Jacobsen's ubiquitous assistants.

"We anticipate a *little* trouble tonight, sir," he said deferentially, after the bellboy had left and they were standing in Shockley's suite. Baby sat in the middle of the Oriental rug in the living room. Overhead a glittering chandelier caught her eye, and bending her head all the way back, she reached out her tiny hand as if she could grasp it.

"What kind of trouble?"

"Mr. Jacobsen wanted me to assure you that it's nothing."

"Well, what is it?"

"The CURB people are planning a demonstration outside of Avery Fisher. You know, the usual sort of thing."

Shockley shook his head. What was the usual?

"In order to avoid any kind of incident, we're going to use two cars as a diversion."

"Oh, Lord," said Shockley anxiously.

"This evening when you leave the hotel to go to the concert you'll, as usual, get into the limousine we'll have waiting in front. Instead of driving directly to Lincoln Center, it's going to head east to Third Avenue. There you'll change to a regular passenger sedan. The limousine will turn and take the regular approach to Lincoln Center. Inside will be someone who looks like you and he'll be carrying a bundle. Meanwhile, you and Baby will come in through a special back route."

"How do I know which sedan to get into?"

"That'll be easy. I'll be driving it. It's an old red Volvo. My car," he smiled sheepishly.

"And how the hell do I know that you really work for Ivar Jacobsen?"

Petterson lifted up his eyebrows in confounded surprise.

"Well—Because—I—" he stumbled. "Why don't you just call up Mr. Jacobsen?" he said, finally gathering his senses.

"I will," said Shockley.

After Pettersson left, Shockley locked the door and went to change Baby, who was soaked from the long trip.

He scooped her off the rug and laid her on the bed in the adjoining room. First taking off her snowsuit, he slipped off her dress and unfastened her wet diapers.

Baby lay quietly on the bed sucking her thumb, her knees brought up into a fetal position, her eyes peering expectantly up at him.

"Such a little troublemaker," he said, lovingly stroking her soft, pliant flesh. For a moment he stopped and studied her. Now almost six months old, she was beginning to look more like a little girl than an infant. Her eyes were still as large and luminescently blue as ever, but some of the early baby fat from her face had melted away, giving it a slightly more mature appearance and defining the bones that formed her high cheeks. In the intervening months, her wispy hair had grown thick and dense and ever curlier, forming a blond halo that encircled her head. With her features more clearly defined, her babyish pug yielding to a thin and rather elegant nose, her chin emerging with a well-cut curve, Baby promised to be one very beautiful little girl—far more striking than she had ever been as an infant. Shockley searched her face and tried to match her features with those of Doris, but try as he might he could discern no resemblance and was secretly glad. He gazed down over her body. It was sturdier and plumper now than at any time since he had first seen her. From the length of her legs, her chubby but elongated fingers and her arms, he could see that she would ultimately be tall. No doubt, one day she would grow into a beautiful woman. It was hard for him to fathom that one day she would be a woman, imagine that she would have a lover, a husband. The thought made him shudder with a kind of fatherly jealousy. Somehow, previously, he had never thought of her in those terms. In his mind her image had been frozen, unyielding, as if she would always be just as she was now, just Baby.

Shockley took her into the bathroom, held her red and wrinkled rear under a stream of lukewarm water that gushed from the sink spigot. Carefully he patted her dry and carried her back into the sleeping quarters of the large suite. As he went about dressing her, he was reminded of his own Cindy when she was little like this, a pretoddler. And then he was thinking about Cindy as she was today.

"I didn't mean to do it! Really! I swear!" Cindy had shattered into tears as soon as the television people had left.

"I know," Shockley had said, trying to comfort her, touched by how she had fought back her emotion until this moment, and battling back his own tears. "I haven't been paying much attention to you lately, have I?" he asked, cuddling his daughter on his lap as Baby lay in Annette's arms intently observing it all.

"I was just bathing her with mommy," she said, as emotionally spent as they all were. "And the next thing I knew she was under water."

"It's OK," he had said, and Cindy looked at him with puzzlement. Then she had buried her head in her father's chest and wept bitterly.

That evening they had given Cindy dinner in bed, and after telling her a story, Shockley had tucked her in and turned out the light.

When Ruth was sure Cindy was fast asleep, she had finally broken her own silence.

"We can't take a chance again. No matter what she says."

"I really think it's going to be fine," he had said in a lowered voice.

"It's never going to be *fine*," Ruth spat out his words. "We'll never know for sure. I don't ever want to go through that again. Never ever!"

"What am I supposed to do?" he had asked worriedly. "Move out with Baby?"

"I've thought of that."

"I'm certainly not going to break up this home for Baby," he had replied determinedly. But he was also not going to give up Baby. Though he hadn't said it, he knew Ruth tacitly understood.

"Are you putting me to a choice?" he had finally asked after a long silence.

"No," Ruth had replied cautiously. "Not yet."

By six o'clock there was already a mass of noisy pickets concentrated in front of Avery Fisher Hall. By seven, still a good hour before Baby's concert, the ranks of the pack had swollen to an ugly, shoving mob barely containable by riot-equipped police.

From the safety of a window in Baby's dressing room Shockley watched the milling horde, their strident cries mingling and echoing up garbled from below. With a pair of opera glasses he tensely began to scan the waving placards.

"DENOUNCE THE PAGAN PROPHET" read one.

"THE LORD PUNISHES HEATHENISM" said another, bearing a large red crucifix.

He caught a momentary glimpse of a third that made his heart skip a beat. It read

"DEATH TO BABY."

He tried to read it again, but it disappeared from sight. Anxiously he kept searching the maze of signs, and when it popped back into view, he read it for a second time and saw that it actually said "DEATH TO BABYISM." He checked again, and though he was now sure that it read "Babyism" instead of "Baby," it seemed a paltry consolation.

Everything leading up to this show seemed to foreshadow disaster. Although he and Baby had been quietly ushered through the service tunnel running below the complex, the decoy car arriving a few seconds earlier had not fared as well. From what Shockley had learned, the limousine supposedly carrying Baby had been attacked by the crowd, people throwing themselves at the car, kicking it, and viciously smashing at the windshield with the poles from their signs. When the limousine had finally escaped under a rain of bottles and bricks, the mob had given off a unanimous cheer, certain that they had succeeded in aborting Baby's concert.

Shockley pulled himself away from the window and turned back to Baby, who sat in a portable crib in the darkened room. He picked her up and was about to shut the window when suddenly a deafening hue went up from the crowd, the sound expanding contagiously and building like the rumble of thunder. Holding Baby, he quickly went back to look. Below him he could see a contractive wave spreading over the mass and focusing on a single point at the periphery. Shockley picked up his binoculars and, following the wave, trained them on the point. From what he could make out amidst the pandemonium there were people scuffling with the police. With horror he watched as a cop lifted his club and brought it down on the head of a man. Then again on another man. Then a young girl. Shockley gagged in horror. Then he saw what was going on. A short distance away someone was being engulfed by the crowd at a point where the barricade had been breached. A man carrying a sign bearing the oval-lipped emblem of the Babyists had haplessly ventured too close and was being lunged at by the mob. Shockley heard piercing screams, the cries for blood going up. From across the avenue there came the wail of sirens as the pack tore at the man. Incredulously Shockley watched as the Baby-

ist, covering his head, stumbled blindly under a rain of
blows, men and women viciously tearing at him from
all sides, kicking and stomping their crumbling victim.
A phalanx of police was trying to break its way in to
extricate the fallen man now consumed by the crowd,
the cops swinging their clubs and driving a wedge
through the unyielding cluster. Above the wail of sirens,
the screams and bellows, the sounds of multiple explo-
sions punctuated the air, echoing dully between the
buildings. Shockley saw the clouds of gas billowing.
The choking crowd pulled back as a team of gas-
masked cops swept into the gap and dragged away the
limp body of the Babyist, his face a bloody mass. From
a block away there came the loud wail of an ambulance, its flashing red turret cutting through the haze.

Sickened, Shockley turned away as Baby, clinging to
his shoulder, maneuvered her head trying to look out.
He pulled closed the window with his free hand and,
drawing the blinds, turned on the lights in the dressing
room. Baby blinked in the brightness, still straining toward the window. Shockley checked his watch. Another
half hour until showtime. He wished Jacobsen were
here. Osgood, who was doing a series of commercials in
a downtown studio, would be arriving at the last minute. Shockley felt isolated and vulnerable alone with
Baby. Three shows, he told himself, and we'll be out of
this insane city and in the warm Florida sunshine. Already he could feel the healing rays soaking into his
skin, see Baby tanned and content sitting with him in
the hot sand at the edge of a surf-licked beach.

Osgood arrived still wearing his television makeup,
and seemed hardly fazed by the crowds outside.

"Just a bunch of nuts," he said breezily. "It'll pass."
Once the orchestra started up and Osgood had the

audience in control, the people singing along to Kramer's song, Shockley began to relax for the first time since arriving in New York. He smoked a cigarette he had bummed from one of the stage crew and stood in the wings listening to the audience as the wardrobe lady went through her last-minute preparations, tying on Baby's head the oversized pink bonnet.

> Baby, Baby,
> Our voice from heaven,
> Easing our pains . . .

Shockley took a peek through the space in the curtain. Compared to the frenzy outside, the audience seemed safe and civilized as they stood holding hands, swaying as they sang.

> Lifting our burdens with your sweet song,
> When you sing, the world . . .

Almost everywhere Shockley looked he could see those golden lips.

> Baby, Baby,
> Baby, Baby.

"Dr. Shockley?" said an elderly man, catching Shockley unawares as he took a fresh puff on his cigarette.

Shockley spun around and coughed.

"I'm sorry to startle you," he apologized softly, a benign smile creasing his ruddy-complexioned face. "I'm Thomas Fitzgibbons," he explained and waited.

Shockley looked at him puzzled. The man had a striking head of snow-white hair combed straight back

from his high forehead, accentuating a big, broad smile.
Though he had heavy jowls that weighed down his features, there was a distinct youthful bounce to his manner, and when he spoke, he had a distinguished air that
reminded Shockley of an aging stage actor. Though he
couldn't immediately place the face, Shockley knew
that he had seen him somewhere before.

"Thomas Fitzgibbons," the man repeated, seeing his
confusion. "Father Tom."

"A Babyist?" Shockley inquired warily and then saw
the heavy gold lips that hung from a chain partially hidden by his tweed jacket.

"Yes, I'm one of them," he admitted openly. "I've
wanted to talk to you for some time, but, until now
you've been unreachable," he said candidly. "Matter of
fact, I had to sneak back here." Fitzgibbons smiled, his
eyes twinkling. "So if you wish, you could easily have
me thrown out."

"Why would I want to do that?" asked Shockley, disarmed by the man's frankness.

"Well, we've tried to contact you before—" He
shrugged, and it was then that Shockley suddenly recognized him.

"Weren't you?" said Shockley, trying to put his finger on Fitzgibbons's past. "Weren't you involved in the
antiwar movement?" he said, finally placing the face.
"Yes. Fitzgibbons." Thomas Fitzgibbons. The activist
Catholic priest. Very early on in the war he had heard
Father Tom—as he was called by the students—speak
on campus. It was ancient history now, but Shockley
could remember being in sympathy with the man from
the start, admiring his guts and determination and ultimate bravery. "So, from Jesuit to Babyist," said
Shockley without a trace of malice. "That's quite a
leap, isn't it?"

"Yes," agreed Fitzgibbons rather matter-of-factly.

The ineradicable image of the Babyist outside the hall being mauled by the crowd popped into his head. It now all made a bit more sense. With defections from people of Fitzgibbons's stature, it was little wonder the established churches felt threatened.

"A Babyist," Shockley repeated to himself, as though letting it sink in.

"Some of us have seen the light," Fitzgibbons said, and then, with a touch of humor, added, "or heard the song."

Shockley grinned. The man had a seductive way about him, and considering his record, the years he had sat in prison for what he believed in, he would be a hard man to simply discount.

"From what I understand, you think that we're a bunch of nuts."

"Well, I've"—Shockley searched for words—"I've never said quite that," he hedged.

"The reason I've been so eager to see you is that I'd like to dispel that image."

Shockley remained silent.

"I think it's important, now more than ever, that I tell you a little about us, about our beliefs, about how we feel."

"I think I know. You think she's the messiah, right?"

"Yes. In a sense. We feel that Baby is a gift from God."

"You could say that of all children, couldn't you?"

"Certainly."

"If you believe in God," Shockley added, quickly setting the record straight.

"For us—and we believe in a Supreme Being—he is speaking to us through the song of this child, his child, his daughter, just as he did through his son Jesus

Christ." Fitzgibbons paused. "Her music," he continued, closing his eyes and going off into a reverie, "her music is the distillation of life itself, each precious drop bringing us closer to heaven, bringing order to chaos around us." He opened his eyes and looked directly at Shockley, who seemed unaffected. "Her music taps the springs of earthly human experience, compelling the spirit to burst forth. When I listen to this child, I am listening to all that is pure and good and heavenly."

"Well, you've got no argument there," said Shockley, recognizing that Fitzgibbons's words were so close to what he had once read in a Babyist pamphlet that he suspected Fitzgibbons to be the author. "But what you're talking about is the role of art, of music, not the direct hand of God."

"Well, if you want to call it art, fine. It's the Creator's art. Ultimately all art goes back to God—if you believe in him," said Fitzgibbons, gently backing off.

"You're not going to convert me to Babyism, you know," said Shockley defensively.

"It never was my intention. There's no need. Baby makes her own converts," he said succinctly. "All I've wanted to accomplish is to let you know we're here to protect Baby, support her. Whatever it is that she needs, we're here to provide."

Shockley looked at him, a glimmer of suspicion growing in his eyes.

"We're here to serve her," he repeated emphatically, sensing Shockley's skepticism and wanting to leave no room for doubt. "To give. Not to take."

"But there is something you want. Otherwise, why would you be talking to me now?"

"Just to keep the lines of communication open. That's all."

"OK, they're open." Shockley nodded.

"We just wouldn't want anything—" said Fitzgibbons, almost as an afterthought, "anything to occur that might interfere with our being able to hear Baby," he said and, without elaborating, clasped his hands together and turned to the stage as Osgood finished his introduction and Baby came rising up from the depths of the pit.

"Sing, Baby. Sing!" cried the audience in eager anticipation. "Sing!"

Outside, the crowds were assembling again for a new confrontation.

Shockley had reservations on the midnight flight to Miami, and when Baby completed her last concert in New York, he made a dash with her through the back tunnel to Rolf Pettersson's waiting Volvo. Their bags were in the car and everything was set.

Shockley and Baby, however, never made it to Miami. It had been snowing all afternoon, and by nightfall the highways were so bogged down in deepening snow that Pettersson was forced to turn back when they reached the expressway in Queens, the Volvo narrowly making it back through the thickening maze of stranded vehicles clogging the roads.

"Consider yourself lucky," said Pettersson, heaving a sigh when they finally pulled up in front of the Plaza. He knew what the city roads were like, and had it not been for Shockley's insistence, he would never have ventured even as far as Queens. As it turned out, all flights in and out of the city were ultimately canceled as of midnight. Up and down the Atlantic Coast from Bangor to Norfolk airports were being shut down as a sprawling blizzard that had been brewing in the Ohio Valley began dumping a record three feet of snow along an eight-state-wide swath. Following on the heels of this storm, according to the ominous forecast, was another deep, low-pressure system, carrying with it the promise of yet more snow.

By the time Shockley checked back into the Plaza, the city was at a virtual standstill. Bus service had long since ceased, subways were stalled, phones malfunctioned, and there were many areas in the boroughs without power. Though thwarted in his quest for sun, Shockley realized that he was more than lucky to get back his familiar suite at the overflowing hotel.

As city crews began to tackle the overwhelming task of digging out amidst freshly accumulating mounds of snow, Jacobsen was on his Teletype attempting to reshuffle Baby's bookings, Osgood's agent was racking his brains seeing if he could fill in his client's downtime with some quick commercial spots, Shockley was trying to get through to Ithaca to let Ruth know the trip was temporarily off, and Mayor Koch, frantically manning his crisis center, was declaring a state of emergency and pleading with the governor to call out national guard troops.

It looked as if it were going to be one long siege.

Shockley tried to make the best of the coming days. Keeping to his suite of rooms, he had all his meals sent up. He read, watched television, and tried to entertain Baby. To break the monotony, he repeatedly called Ruth to get an update on an equally snowbound Ithaca. Inactivity never wore well with Shockley and by the end of the second day he finally understood the term *cabin fever*. From that point on he was constantly on the phone to the airlines, booking and rebooking space on phantom flights south. Concert or not, he and Baby were going to get out of this miserable cold for at least a few days, and he was damned if the family was not going to be reunited for Christmas. Dealing with the airlines was exasperating. The phone lines were forever busy. When he finally got ticket agents on the line, they usually gave contradictory information. Yes, there would be flights by the next morning. No, the airport was snowed in and, because of the blowing drifts and an approaching new storm, it was likely to stay that way until the end of the week.

Shockley felt himself in a state of suspension, which unnerved him. He felt the overwhelming need to utilize the time profitably, but that dangling sense of expectancy kept him from doing little more than reading the novels he had gleaned from the racks in the magazine stands in the lobby. Those and some of the Babyist literature that Fitzgibbons had insisted on leaving with him. Only once did it occur to him to try his hand at composing. He immediately dismissed the notion. It was, he told himself, a closed chapter.

But there it was, the nagging need to *do* something, to be active, to fight against the restraints of inertness. Secretly he envied those who knew how to let loose, to have a grand time, to have—fun.

After three days of confinement, Shockley knew he could not look at another paperback or television show or crossword puzzle or Babyist brochure without letting out a shriek. He had had it. He and Baby were going out that night. For dinner downstairs, and afterward —afterward a show, or something—anything! The hell with the Babyists and CURBists and all the other damn *ists*!

With Baby in one arm, Shockley passed the Palm Court, the strains of a violin fiddling some schmaltzy Viennese waltz drifting out between the palms. For an instant he considered going into the lobby restaurant with its plethora of rich desserts displayed on a cart by the entrance, but then he changed his mind and headed toward the Edwardian Room. There in the vaulted dining room with dark oak paneling and white pillars, red walls above the dark wood and ponderous chandeliers, he and Baby were shown to a small corner table. The maître d' lifted a finger and instantly a waiter appeared with a high chair. In a moment they were seated and Shockley was scanning the menu.

"Tonight you and I are going to have some fun for a change," he told Baby, handing her a piece of pumpernickel to nibble on. Baby bit down on the hard crust, kneading it against her bottom gums, where her first teeth were just starting to cut through. Desultorily she glanced around the sparsely populated dining room, then tilted her head back and stared up at the high ceiling. A small rivulet of drool mixed with crumbs cascaded down Baby's chin, and Shockley, putting down the menu, wiped it off with his napkin. As Shockley turned back to the bill of fare, his attention was suddenly caught by someone being shown to a distant table across the dimly lit room. Pretending to busy himself with his choice, Shockley peeked over the top of the card. His eyes nearly popped out. Being seated there by herself at a red-curtained window was, he could have sworn, the woman he had seen at the party the night of Baby's opening in Cleveland—that Slavic-looking beauty with the wide, high cheeks and svelte body. It had to be. After ordering, to make doubly certain, he put on his glasses and let his eyes drift over in her direction. Yes, it was. Not his imagination, as had happened before. He was positive. How could he ever forget a face like hers! What a coincidence! What luck!

Nervously he sipped his water, put down the glass, and watched as the waiter, who had been hovering attentively in the background, came forward and filled it again to the brim.

Baby dropped her piece of bread. The waiter picked it up and with a smile gave her a new piece. Another waiter appeared from the kitchen with a tureen of steaming soup. After he was served, Shockley poured off a little of the clam broth into a separate dish, careful to strain out the pieces. Blowing on each hot spoonful, he fed Baby, who noisily slurped up the liquid, half of it running down onto her chin and bib.

When Baby finished her portion, Shockley began to

work on the remaining soup, his eyes perpetually shifting back to the woman by the window. In fact, as the meal progressed through the filet mignon, the asparagus tips in sauce Béarnaise, the tossed salad, even through the strawberry soufflé, coffee, and Grand Marnier, Shockley found that he could hardly take his eyes off the woman. She was, as he had first realized that drunken night in Cleveland, one of the most gorgeous women in his memory.

With coffee he requested a pack of cigarettes and lit one up. He inhaled and watched the smoke drift upward from his lips. He toyed with his cigarette, knocked off some ash, took another puff, his thoughts obsessively returning to the woman.

Shockley glanced over again to her table. She, too, was finished with dinner, and he realized that if he didn't talk to her now, get up and introduce himself this instant, he might never again in his life have the chance. He looked over at Baby, who was playing with the remains of her meal, moving crumbs and strands of noodles around the tray of her high chair in busy patterns. It was now or never, he told himself. He tried to lift himself from his chair but was gripped by fright.

When the check came, Shockley signed it and finally rose. Sliding Baby out of her chair, he stood by his table and felt the veiled gaze of the waiters upon him. He could hear his heart pounding in his chest, and he cursed himself for being such a coward. Slowly he headed for the dining room exit. Nearing the door, he suddenly stopped and, as if just discovering her, turned and approached her table.

"Excuse me," he said, as she looked up at him for the first time, her green almond eyes meeting his and causing him to melt. "This may sound silly," he began tremulously, "but I think—I think we've met before."

She smiled, her eyes flashing.

"Aren't you—Aren't you?" She wiggled her long fingers in the air as if trying to extricate his name.

"Irwin Shockley," he coaxed.

"And this is Baby," she said, reaching out and taking Baby's small hand in hers.

Baby looked down at her with bored disapproval.

"We met—?"

"In Cleveland"—he jogged her memory—"you were at Baby's gala in Cleveland."

"What a memory you have," she said, her voice having the faint tinge of an accent.

"I always remember faces," he lied.

"We didn't even have a chance to speak."

"But we do now," he said, a glint in his eye.

Would she mind if he and Baby joined her?

Of course not. It would be a pleasure.

Would she care for an aperitif? Perhaps some more coffee?

Waiter, a little more coffee for the lady. We'll also have Cointreau. No, just for the two of us, he joked. The baby isn't drinking tonight.

What fantastic luck meeting her, he thought. These days in New York were not going to be a waste, after all.

Her name was Irina, she told him in nearly faultless English.

"When I first saw you, I was certain you were Russian," he bubbled.

"Well, that's almost right. My father was Russian. My mother's Italian. But my father's parents were partly Polish and Hungarian. I'm a real mutt." She laughed, biting down delectably with her sharp teeth on her tongue.

"Well, despite all the handicaps, you seem to have turned out remarkably well," Shockley joshed exuberantly.

She told him that she lived in Cleveland, that she was in New York on business. A pending divorce. Sorry, he commiserated. Oh no, she said, she was happy. Now she was finally free, and rich, she laughed naughtily.

Baby sat momentarily forgotten in the high chair that the waiter had carried over from Shockley's table, her head moving from one adult to the other, watching the ongoing ritual.

Would Irina care for another drink?

Would she, Shockley ventured unsurely, care to join them in their suite upstairs? These days, what with all the publicity and troubles, it was best not to be out in public too much. Perhaps she'd care for some champagne? Yes, a bottle of champagne. After all these days of being holed up in his suite, he was feeling in a festive mood, he explained to her.

In the elevator up, he hinted at how, after spotting her at that party in Cleveland, he had not been able to forget her.

When they toasted each other in the sitting room, toasted her divorce, Baby's future, Shockley confessed that he had noticed her as she came into the dining room but had been afraid to approach her.

"Silly man," she said, her eyes locking with his and then drifting down his face to his lips.

I can't believe this, he muttered to himself. When he put Baby into her crib in the bedroom, he noticed that his hands were shaking. For a fleeting moment he thought about Ruth, thought about her and pushed her from his mind.

He came back into the sitting room and found Irina waiting on the sofa with an empty glass. Eagerly, too eagerly, he poured it full. It foamed over and ran onto her dress. Nervously he apologized, patting her lap dry with a handy diaper, his face feeling as though it were on fire.

"I—I—" He started to speak, but his voice failed him.

"Yes?" she asked, looking up at him, her face alive and glowing from the champagne.

"I know this is going to sound ridiculous."

"We won't know until you say it, will we?" she said coaxingly.

"I want you," he finally blurted out, looking hungrily at her. "From the first moment I set eyes on you, I've wanted you." He swallowed and, taking quick, shallow breaths, waited.

"I know," she said matter-of-factly. "Is that so ridiculous?"

"Oh, God, no," he blustered, relieved to finally have it out. "That's not what I meant. It's just that I had to say it," he apologized. "I've never been very good at keeping things in." He rushed over his words.

"Don't explain," she said, sitting there expectantly.

The smile on Shockley's face froze. Cautiously he moved toward her. He sank down next to her on the sofa and paused as though waiting to be rebuffed. She remained motionless. He brought his face close to hers. They looked at each other for a short eternity. She was young, so very young, he thought. Her skin flawless. Her eyes luminescently green. There was an exotic appeal to her face that drew him ever closer. Awkwardly, he pressed his lips against hers. Her lips parted. He felt her arm caress his neck and gently pull him close. Her tongue touched his and he began to tremble, his entire body shaking in anticipation.

It's a dream, said one side of his mind over and over.

The other side was trying to remind him that she was just a woman, an exquisite one, certainly, but just a woman. No more, no less. The tug-of-war, however, was an uneven one, and knowing it, he surrendered and eagerly led her into the bedroom.

In her crib Baby was lying on her back, her thumb planted in her mouth. Her knees were flexed up to her stomach, and with her free hand she was idly playing with her toes. Her eyes shifted to the pair when they entered the room.

Shockley began to undress Irina, fumbling with the front buttons on her dress. She saw his trouble, smiled, kissed him, and helped. Overwhelmed, he watched as she slid out of her dress, out of her slip, out of her pantyhose.

"Did anyone ever tell you you're beautiful beyond words?" he said, beholding her long silky legs, her narrow waist, her firm breasts, which stood pertly by themselves. His eyes again traveled down the length of her, stopping at the light patch of pubic hair incongruous with her long black tresses.

"Never," she said disingenuously. "Now it's your turn." She laughed and began unbuttoning his shirt.

Shockley took off his shirt. Confronted by the youth of her body, he felt unequal. He undressed and pulled himself close, his throbbing groin pressed hard against her belly. He reached around her and stroked her body almost too carefully, as if afraid that if he touched too firmly she might evaporate.

He flung off the covers to the bed, and they melted into the cool, fresh linens, which smelled fragrantly of soap. Shockley tried to think, to make sense of what was occurring, but pressed as he was against the smooth warmth of her body, his mind refused to cooperate.

Then, almost without knowledge, he was sliding into the very soft core of her body, an audible cry emerging from deep within her throat. She was so beautiful that, as they made love, he felt compelled to keep his eyes open. Pulling back, his hips moving in an hypnotic rhythm of their own, he drank in her being, her lanky legs that were brought up around him, her arms that reached out to stroke him, her narrow pelvis that undulated under him, her face frozen in a distant, ecstatic smile, her teeth gleaming through her warm lips, the mounds of her breasts capped by bright, taut nipples. He soaked in her image, savoring it, burning it indelibly upon the memory of his brain so that he could never in a lifetime forget her. He tried to hold himself back, delay this flashing instant in the continuum of time, the days and months and years that made a man's life, preserve it, store it. His eyes caressed her body, and then, for an instant, he caught a glimpse of Baby in her crib. Holding on to the bars, she was standing and watching them. Blindly he groped out for the covers, trying to pull them over, but it was too late. The tension had mounted in his loins until he could bear it no more; his body quivered, his eyes slammed shut with an explosive force, his cries mingled with hers, and there was nothing in the world but the two of them.

When Shockley got up out of bed, Baby was still standing there, holding on to the edge of her crib, her eyes following him as he padded across the room and into the bathroom. Irina lay curled up in bed, asleep.

As he adjusted the water gushing out of the spigot, clumsily alternating between the extremes of burning hot and freezing cold, Shockley was wondering about her, the woman in his bed. He was wondering if she had been attracted to him or if she were no more than a

groupie of sorts. He hoped to hell she wasn't a Babyist.
Though it was unlikely. If she were, she would have
been wearing a pair of those fool lips, would have paid
more attention to Baby.

Shockley washed and then dried himself. He looked
at his face in the mirror. Under the harsh light above
the medicine cabinet it looked old to him, old by com-
parison to hers. There were lines on his forehead,
crow's-feet by his eyes, a deep furrow running between
his eyebrows. Where was all this going? he asked. What
was it leading to? He stood staring at his reflection. He
knew that by all rights he should feel ashamed and
guilty, yet he felt preponderantly guilt-free. Happy, in
fact. For the first time in ages he felt invigorated.
Young. Only those damn lines on his face contradicted
his feeling of rebirth.

Shockley wrapped a towel around his waist and
sauntered back to the bedroom. He found the covers
drawn back, the bed empty. Irina's clothes, which had
been lying on a chair, were gone. Instantly his eyes shot
over to the crib expecting to see Baby's curious little
head still peering over the bars. No head. No Baby. The
crib was empty.

He rushed into the sitting room. It was deserted. He
ran back into the bedroom, then back again into the
sitting room. He even looked into the bathroom.

Frantically he raced from window to window, checking each one. He went to the door of the suite. It was
unlocked. Clad still in only his towel, he sprinted out
into the corridor. He charged up and down the inter-
secting hallways, then raced over to the bank of eleva-
tors. The arrows were pointing up and down in a confusion of signals. Bolting for the fire exit, he raced down
ten flights of stairs, checking each level. He reached the
lobby and ran toward the main entrance.

Hitting the bronze front doors, he burst through, nearly bowling over the astonished doorman. He was flying barefooted down the snowy steps when he saw the car pull away—Irina sitting in the front seat holding a blanket-clad bundle against her as the car skidded off through the deep snow.

"Baby!" cried out the voice rising from the depths of his soul. "Baby! Baby!" he bellowed forlornly, the snow rising up over his ankles.

THREE

"Now let me get this straight," said Detective Feldman to Shockley, his Brooklynese tinged with suspicion. "You never met this woman before in your life, right? Yet she just waltzes in here and takes off with the kid?"

"Well—I—I saw her at a reception in Cleveland, and I think I may have spotted her after that a couple of times. I'm not sure, but I never talked to her before this evening," said Shockley, hunched in his chair. As he ran his hands nervously through his hair, his gaze fell on one of Baby's toys that lay abandoned on the sitting-room rug, and a sharp pain stabbed at him. He looked back up at the cop, who was hovering impatiently above him.

"Look, if we're going to get your child back you're going to have to cooperate a little—level with us," said Detective Hoover, standing with his hands in his pockets and looking out the window at the traffic that crept along the south rim of the park. He was a barrel-chested man, whose clothes seemed almost too small to contain him. Wearing a perpetually somnolent look, he had until this moment remained silent, seemingly content to listen. "With all due respect," he continued, "this sounds like a lot of bullshit to me."

"Was she a hooker?" asked Feldman.

"No, of course not!" said Shockley, pressing his hands together to keep them from shaking. "Listen, I've given you a complete description of the woman. The waiters downstairs can corroborate it. I've told you the car was an older Ford, maybe '70 or '71."

"But you have no license number."

"No. I didn't get it. I've told you that. Why the hell don't you check with the doorman? He must have seen more than I did. That car was probably waiting for her out there all the time. Look"—he gritted his teeth—"I've told you everything I know."

"Have you?" asked Hoover, and his apparent insouciance rattled Shockley.

"If she's a known hooker we could probably have her picked up in less than an hour," Feldman persisted.

"But she's *not* a hooker! Can't you get that straight?"

"How can you be so sure if you don't know her?" asked Hoover, zeroing in.

The phone rang. Both cops suddenly jumped to life. Feldman grabbed Shockley's hand as he reached for the phone and held it for a moment.

The muscles in Hoover's face tensed, tight strands of tendon protruding through his skin as he moved away from the window. On the third ring he motioned for Shockley to pick it up. Again reaching for the receiver, Shockley felt his heart race.

"Hello?" he said anxiously, and listened.

The cops looked at each other.

"It's for you," said Shockley a moment later, and he could see the detectives sinking back into their lethargy, punctured, Feldman gravitating down on the arm of the sofa as his partner took up the phone.

Hoover mumbled something, his lips barely moving, then hung up.

"That's Franken over at the Bureau," he said. "They're coming in on the case. Now"—he turned menacingly on Shockley—"you're sure it's a kidnapping?"

"No, I gave her Baby!" Shockley spat out angrily.

"There'll be hell to pay if it isn't," warned Feldman.

"Tell us about the woman again," said Hoover, forever circling the same point like a vulture sensing carrion. His gaze drifted around the room, taking in the ornate fixtures and furnishing, and in his eyes there was unveiled contempt. He never particularly liked rich people, folks who lived their lives sealed in their fancy hotel suites and penthouses, moving in air-conditioned limousines between safe points in a rarefied space, insulated from the everyday dirt and mayhem of the street.

"Again?"

"Again. And start at the beginning."

"There's nothing more to tell. I met her in the dining room. She came up for a drink. I went to the bathroom. When I returned she was gone and so was Baby. That's it. Period," he said. He recalled Baby's innocent little face, how she stood up in her crib for the first time in her life, and he felt a pang of emptiness as though a hole had been permanently punched out of his life.

"You been sleeping?" asked Feldman, looking into the bedroom.

"Huh?"

"The bed," he said, motioning with his chin. "It's all mussed up." He strolled into the room, walked first over to the crib and then the large double bed. "Hey, this your long, dark hair?" he called, lifting a strand from the pillow and, coming back into the room, dangled it in front of Shockley before slipping it into an envelope.

Shockley stared down at his hands.

"Come clean," said Hoover irritably. "Shit, man, we weren't born yesterday."

"You're insulting our fucking intelligence," muttered Feldman.

"Are you in on this in some way? Is this a con?"

"Was she a partner?"

"What?" Shockley asked, astounded.

"What's the scam, huh? Insurance money on the kid? A publicity stunt?"

"Scam? My child has been kidnapped and you're standing here accusing me of a scam?" he said, livid. "You should be out looking for her, not standing here hassling me."

"Yeah? Well, tell us where."

"You got any hot tips?"

"Maybe," said Shockley, looking up, a rim of red underlining his eyes. "I'm not sure."

"Who?"

"It's only a hunch."

"Who?"

"The Babyists."

"Huh?" asked Feldman.

"You know," explained Hoover, "the ones with the lips."

"Why them?"

"Why not?" said Shockley, warming to the idea. The more he thought about it, the surer he became. It was a setup right from the beginning in Cleveland when he had first spotted Irina and those lips. He struggled to remember if she had been one of those wearing a pair of lips that first evening. "They've been dying to get their hands on her."

"That doesn't mean they took her."

"This guy Fitzgibbons, Thomas Fitzgibbons, approached me during one of the shows here in the city—"

"And?"

"It's what he said."

"Yeah?"

"He said"—Shockley racked his brain to recall the words—"he said, 'We just wouldn't want anything to happen to Baby that might interfere with us being able to hear her.' "

"Doesn't sound very incriminating to me."

"It's not really what he said; it's how he said it."

The cops looked at each other for a moment.

"Why don't you question him? He must know something."

The buzzer to the suite sounded, and Feldman opened the door. Behind it stood two men dressed in squarely cut dark suits. Rushing up the corridor directly behind them were a television crew and a group of reporters. The detective let the two men slip in and held the others back with a raised hand.

The door closed on the newsmen, and the four conferred in a quick huddle.

Shockley sat and watched, helpless. He was thinking about Baby. He just hoped to God that Irina—or whatever her name really was—hadn't already sneaked Baby out of the city or, worse, out of the country. He hoped that she was taking good care of her. That Baby was being fed, kept warm, that she wasn't terrified by the strangers. If only he could just get his hands on that lousy woman, he'd strangle her pretty neck with his bare hands. Shockly stared morosely out the window. It had stopped snowing, and the dark night sky was beginning to clear. Above the illuminated haze of the city he could make out through chinks in the clouds the light of a few solitary stars. The storm had run its course. His had only begun.

"There's more to the story," Shockley muttered.

The cops all turned around.

"Good," said Detective Hoover, with a glint in his eye. "Now we're finally going to find out what you were doing running around outside with just a towel on."

"Let me start at the beginning," he said, and knew that he had fooled no one but himself.

Once the FBI took over the case, they decided that the most prudent approach would be to keep a low profile. Attempting to simulate the appearances of minimal police intervention, they immediately pulled back the city police as well as their own agents, keeping a tight but invisible surveillance on the hotel.

That night, Shockley sat by the phone in his suite hoping against hope for contact by the kidnappers. The line was coupled to the Manhattan field office of the FBI, where an agent also sat vigil, waiting for the ring that would give the investigation its first substantive clue. As the long night wore on and no attempt for ransom was initiated, Shockley became more convinced than ever that it was the Babyists. They had stolen Baby, so his reasoning ran, because they feared that he might end Baby's tour as a result of the continuing violence at the concerts. Fitzgibbons's concern about access to Baby, suddenly voiced after all these weeks, solidified Shockley's conviction.

Going on Shockley's lead, the FBI began rounding up for questioning prominent Babyists across the country. One of the first to be pulled in was Father Thomas Fitzgibbons.

"That's not the way we operate," Fitzgibbons told his interrogators, appearing genuinely distraught. "A kidnapping is contrary to everything we hold sacred. It's a vicious, deplorable act."

What was he doing backstage?

"I was hoping to initiate a dialogue from which we might develop a way for us to serve her."

Why suddenly then, just two scant days before her kidnapping, had he made his approach?

"Pure coincidence. The time was ripe. The opportunity presented itself."

They showed Fitzgibbons a sketch of the alleged woman kidnapper done by a police artist. Fitzgibbons studied it carefully for a long minute.

"To the best of my knowledge," he said, "I've never set eyes on her in my life."

"He's lying!" Shockley told the agent, who called at 4:00 A.M. to inform him of the questioning. "If Fitzgibbons is not behind it, then it's one of the other Babyists," he injected as an afterthought.

After the call Shockley tried to catch some sleep, but his conscience gave him no peace. Over and over he replayed the evening's sequence of events, hunting in vain for a clue. Repeatedly he berated himself for not having the presence of mind to take down the license number of the car, cursed himself for ever having left the suite, for ever having gotten involved with that damn woman.

As he lay tossing in bed, Fitzgibbons's reply to the police began to bother him, too. As he recalled the Babyist literature he had read, Fitzgibbons's response did have the ring of truth to it. The Babyists, from what he had been able to glean, were Christians—neo-Christians, as they called themselves. They accepted the Old and New Testaments as part of their faith, the appearance on earth of Jesus as the son of God. Although their prayers and liturgy now recognized a new trinity—the Father, the Son, and the Daughter—they did preach a return to fundamental Judeo-Christian morality, to purity, honesty, and goodness, all that they heard in Baby's song. Could they really steal a child without violating their own tenets? ˈ

Shockley gave up sleep and continued to wait by the phone, watching the sky turn bright as morning broke over the city, the sun filtering in shafts of red through the gaps between the buildings lining the East Side. The day promised to be clear, cloud free, and bitterly cold. A sanitation truck with plow moved noisily up and down the street, pushing back the high banks of still-clean snow.

Just after seven, Shockley notified the FBI man by means of the newly installed auxiliary phone that he was stepping out for a minute. He rode the elevator down to the lobby, went into a phone booth, and, granted that modicum of privacy, called home.

"Ruth, darling," he said hoarsely, feeling spongy and wrung out.

"Irwin?" she said, surprised to hear from him so early in the morning. "Is something wrong?"

"Matter of fact, yes," he said, and knew that she hadn't yet turned on the radio. "I wanted to talk to you before you hear the story from somewhere else."

"Oh, my God," she said. "Something's happened to Baby."

"Yes," he said tersely. "She's been kidnapped."

Ruth gasped.

"The police are on it. The FBI. The New York police. Don't panic. I'm sure we'll get her back," he tried to sound reassuring, but his voice belied the message.

"Oh, Irwin, can I help? Should I come in?"

"No, not right now," he stalled. "Listen, there's something else you should know."

"What?" she asked, short of breath. "How did it happen?"

"That's what I wanted to talk to you about"—he hesitated—"before you hear it from other sources." Shockley struggled to recall how he had planned to break the truth, but his rehearsed lines evaded him.

"Is it bad?" she asked, sobbing quietly.

"There was a woman," he said.

"I don't understand," she questioned, but he knew she did.

"I got—involved—with a woman. A stupid thing." Silence.

Shockley waited for her voice, but all he could hear was the faint, indistinguishable background of cross-talk riding the waves of static.

"She took Baby," he struggled to explain.

Still silence.

"I'm sorry," he said lamely, hearing her cry on the other end. "Terribly sorry," he lamented when her silence became unbearable. "I just had to tell you," he continued, but the connection had already been severed and he was speaking to a dead line.

"Oh, good. I'm glad you called," said Harry Terkel, standing by the desk. He had just stepped in his office and was still wearing his overcoat. "I've been trying to reach you."

"I haven't got my phone yet," said Doris, standing in her neighbors' trailer and trying to hear Terkel above the racket of their five small children.

"Well, I've got good news and I've got bad news," he quipped. "Which do you want first?"

"Whatever," answered Doris. She was in no mood this morning for jokes. All last night she had had trouble sleeping and had awakened with an excruciating headache and chills. She wondered if she were coming down with a flu.

"The good news first. The appellate court has granted your case preference. That means they're going to move it up on the calendar," he added when she gave no response.

"When are they going to hear it?" she asked. An infant was crying loudly in the background, and as she stuffed a finger into her free ear, Doris was thinking about her own Baby, that sweet angel who had never cried, never complained.

"I can't get a straight answer out of the clerk, but, I'm only guessing now, I think it'll be sometime after New Year's, probably in the latter part of February."

"But that's two months away!" Doris objected. "And that's the *good* news?" she asked testily.

"Very good news," Terkel responded defensively, surprised by her ingratitude.

"And the bad news?"

"The stay we requested for the family court order was denied."

"Oh," said Doris, trying to think through the haze of her throbbing head.

"But I told you that was a long shot. Remember?"

"Yes. I know you did," Doris answered wearily, heaving a long sigh.

"Don't worry." Terkel tried to cheer her up. "We'll get her back. It's just a matter of time. Hang in there."

"Hey, Fay, she's starting again!" called the man standing guard at the shattered window. Peering out over the line of plastic that had been hastily tacked up to cover the missing lower panes, he nervously scanned the empty street, trying to ignore the singing that issued from the far-rear room. Though his face was covered with a growth of thick stubble, he was a ruggedly handsome man. With chiseled features and a square jaw, clear, piercing brown eyes, and carefully cut dark-blond hair, he looked noticeably out of place in this condemned South Bronx tenement. A car moved down the snow-clogged street, and quickly he hid to one side, watching as it disappeared around the corner. "Come on," he called out as the singing continued. "Shut her up, for Chrisake!"

"I can't," answered the woman from the other room—a room that had once been a kitchen before repeated fires and scavengers had mercilessly gutted the building. "I've got my head in a bucket of water. You're closer, Sloan. Why don't you?"

Pulling tight the collar of his overcoat, Sloan moved through the cold, cavernous apartment littered with broken glass and plaster and went into the room where Baby lay shivering under her thin blanket on a stained and grubby mattress.

"Shut up, kid!" he growled just as she opened her mouth to emit another desperate stream of song. "And I mean it," he warned, standing menacingly over her. Baby closed her mouth, and muttering to himself, he stalked back to his post by the window. Hardly had he sunk down on his mat and begun to roll a joint than Baby started in again.

"Oh, shit!" he cursed, spilling the weed in his lap. Angrily he marched into the kitchen and confronted his girlfriend. "Look, I've got to watch the window, and you've got to watch the kid," he said to the woman, who stood leaning over a pot of water, giving her hair a final rinse. The stove and plumbing had been rudely ripped from the room, and all that remained of the fixtures was a section of jagged counter that dangled from the crumbling wall. Precariously balanced on it stood two lone bottles, peroxide and dye.

"I can only be in one place at a time, Sloan," she said, squeezing dry her newly shorn hair. Blindly she groped out for a towel as water dripped on the shoulders of her elegant coat.

"Screw the hair," he said, handing her the towel. "You can always play with that later. Listen to what's going on out there," he said, motioning with his head toward the other room, where Baby lay singing. "If she keeps up like this, we're going to have the whole goddamn world in here buying tickets."

"I thought you said that this place was safe," she asked, wrapping her head in the towel.

"It is. It is. But there's other people here, too. They may be junkies and winos, but they sure as hell aren't deaf. What do you want to do, advertise that we've got the kid?"

"Jeez," she mumbled, exasperated but, then, looking

at him, her eyes meeting his, she suddenly relented. "OK," she said and obediently went to the rear room.

Sloan headed back to his post by the window, stopping momentarily to warm his numb hands by the small portable kerosene heater near the window. When the feeling in his hands returned, he slumped back down on the mattress and picked up his cigarette paper. He rolled a fresh joint and lit it. Taking a deep drag, he held it in as long as he could before finally letting the smoke burst out between his lips. He closed his eyes and tried to relax, but the damn kid was still singing. Scrambling to his feet, he stormed back into Baby's room. There, sitting on the edge of Baby's mattress was Fay, stroking the child's white face as Baby trembled under her blanket, still trying to sing.

"I said shut her up, not play with her," he snapped.

The woman who had once called herself Irina but whose real name was Fay Dworkin and who was of midwestern heritage rather than Russian, looked up at her boyfriend.

"She's cold. Can't you see that? And I'm freezing, too."

"This is not supposed to be a picnic," he said as Baby kept struggling to sing out. "Quiet!" he snarled, and reaching down, he grabbed Baby's arm and shook her violently.

"Sloan!" the woman screamed, grabbing his hand and wrenching it free. "What's the matter with you? Have you gone crazy?" she asked, hanging on to his arm, her eyes wide. He threw her hand off his and charged out of the room.

Dumbfounded, Fay watched as he left. Then she looked down at Baby, who lay stunned on the mattress, her jaw trembling.

"He didn't mean anything, sweetie," she said, taking off her coat and covering the child. "You try to sleep a little," she said, tucking the coat tight around Baby's body. "You go to sleep, and before you know it you'll be right back home," she murmured softly and thought again about Sloan. In the two years that she had known him, had worked with him in that Off-Off-Broadway showcase, had gone to all those auditions with him, those cattle-calls, even these last three months they had lived together, she had never witnessed this side of him. Though he was an intense man, strong and determined and unswerving—which is what attracted her to him in the first place—she had never seen him mean like this. Realizing what it was that she had done, how by a single act she had irrevocably committed herself to Sloan, she became frightened. It had been one thing letting her imagination fly, splurging their last money on clothes, travel, and finally that extravagant dinner, becoming for a few hours Irina, the exotic divorcée with the foreign accent. The consequences, however, were another, and now they were painfully dawning on her. Rubbing her arms, she rose to her feet and went into the front room and stood by the smelly kerosene heater watching Sloan as he leaned up against the wall near the window nursing his ill-humor. Grudgingly he looked at her for an instant, then, taking a toke of his joint, turned back to the street below.

"I've never seen you act like this," she said, unwrapping the towel and shaking her head to fluff up her damp hair.

"It's the pressure," said Sloan, taking another drag and holding the joint out to her.

Shaking her head, she waved it away.

"Take it," he insisted through his teeth, holding his breath. "You need it."

Ignoring him, Fay took out a mirror and looked at herself. All traces of the black dye were now gone from her hair and in its place was a clipped version of her original chestnut red. For the first time since leaving school it was short and felt strange, as though she had cut away more than just a length of hair.

"You know," she said, slipping the mirror back into her purse, "you're not the only one under pressure. And even if you were, it wouldn't give you the right to bully me around like this and beat up on that little baby."

"Oh, please, spare me."

"The reason I went along with this," she continued, enunciating her words through her sharp, even teeth, "was that I felt we were building a future together."

"We are. We are," he said, watching through the milky plastic as a black man staggered past the front entrance of the building four stories below.

"That it was a way for us to get out of this rattrap of a city and start a new life."

"Brazil," he said. "Now tell me, doesn't that sound like a new life to you?"

"It doesn't matter really where we go, it's what's going on between us now that counts. And I don't like what's happening."

"Look, Fay, honey." He approached her and held her about the waist. "This just isn't the time to start discussing our future. In fact, it's the worst possible time," he said, as she looked searchingly into his face. He moved his head close and kissed her on the lips.

"I did something—a number of things—I don't really like myself for. I went to bed with—"

"Come on. Don't start playing the blushing virgin. I was not the first man in your life and—"

"But you are the only one—" She turned in his arms.

"I understand," he said soothingly.

"Do you? Do you really?"

"Sure. Of course. But it's the feeling that counts, not the act itself. I mean, do you think I feel so great about having my girl—well—Look, let's just forget the whole thing." He waved his hand and went back to the window.

She watched him as he maneuvered his head to get a better view of the cross street down the block.

"How long is this going to take?"

"Not long," he said. "Not long at all. Just don't start getting antsy and pressuring me. OK?"

"I just want to know, that's all."

"We've got to wait this thing out. Let them stew for a while. The longer we wait, the bigger the stakes, and the less likely this guy Shockley will be to cooperate with the police. We want him desperate, at his wit's end. So eager to deal that he'll even cross the cops."

"Sure, but how long do we wait?"

"Till the vibes are right," he said, evading her eyes.

"How many hours has it been?" asked Jacobsen, even though he had a watch and was perfectly capable of making the simple calculation.

"It's five-thirty now," said Pettersson, his eyes following Shockley as he again circled the room restlessly. "That makes it—almost twenty hours, Mr. Jacobsen."

"Twenty hours," Jacobsen repeated to himself, strumming his fingers on the arm of his chair.

"The longer it goes, the worse it is," worried Osgood.

"That's not necessarily true," said Jacobsen and then interrupted himself. "Damn it, Shockley! Will you stop marching in circles? You're making me dizzy. Try to come up with some ideas instead of wearing out the carpets."

Continuing to pace, Shockley looked over at Jacobsen and mumbled an obscenity.

"I've got an idea," said Osgood, who had been staring out the window at a Santa Claus who stood on the street ringing a bell. "Let's offer a reward."

"Yes," agreed Shockley, stopping in his track. "I've thought of that too. It's not a bad idea." He had spent half the day looking through mug shots of women, and to his sleep-deprived, addled brain, any suggestion of action seemed better than the endless waiting.

"It stinks," said Jacobsen.

"No, it doesn't," replied Shockley obstinately. "Offer a large reward, say ten thousand dollars, for information leading to the return of Baby."

"Dead or alive," added Jacobsen cuttingly, still rankled at Shockley for succumbing to the oldest trick in the world.

"That's vicious," said Shockley, whose guilt didn't need stoking. A moment earlier, before Osgood had come up with his suggestion, he had been thinking miserably about Ruth, his kids, about the Christmas that would be coming up in two days and their planned holiday together that would never be.

"Use your head," said Jacobsen, dismissing the notion of a reward. "If someone kidnapped her for money, you'll be hearing from them. Don't worry. If it wasn't for money, no reward is going to bring them out of the woodwork."

"But someone may have seen something," Osgood persisted. The more he thought about it, the more he liked the idea. "It might be just the impetus needed to bring someone forth."

"OK. You want to offer a reard, offer it. But out of your pocket," said Jacobsen, hoping to stop Osgood short.

"That's all right," said Osgood evenly. "It's the least I can do for Baby."

Shockley looked at him, surprised.

"I really appreciate that," he mumbled.

Osgood shrugged, embarrassed.

"I'll call the papers," Pettersson volunteered.

"It can wait another hour until this evening's press conference, can't it?" Jacobsen stopped him.

Shockley nodded and went back to pacing.

Osgood turned back to the window. With his hands clasped behind his back, he watched as the street lamps began to flicker on up and down the streets encircling the park. The snow that had inundated the city only a day earlier was now a filthy mess lying in oozing humps along the gutters. Under the harsh glare of the arc lamps, the piles took on the sepulchral appearance of funeral mounds.

"You know," began Osgood a moment later, his eyes searching the approaching night, "I have this feeling—"

"Oh?" said Shockley.

"This odd feeling that—well, not only Baby's life is in the balance," he continued earnestly, "but that we're being tested, as well. We, as people."

Shockley stopped and looked at him squarely.

"Please," said Jacobsen, who was staring at the phone. "Please spare us the religion. We've got enough headaches as it is."

"I don't believe this!" said Sloan, slamming his fist into the wall when Baby began to sing again. As he stumbled to his feet, Fay caught him, putting a hand on his shoulder.

"Let me," she said and hurried to Baby's room.

Sloan got up and followed her.

"She's blue with cold," she said, hunched over the

child and turning to see Sloan standing framed in the doorless jamb. "Can't we at least move her to the front room where she'll be closer to the heater?"

"So everyone can hear her better from the street? Is that the idea?"

"If she's warmer she'd probably be quiet," said Fay, holding Baby tightly against her as the child looked up at her beseechingly.

"This is utter bullshit! I've had enough. Put a gag on the kid already!"

"What?"

"I said, put a gag on the kid," he repeated. "You know, take a handkerchief or something and stuff it in her mouth."

"Are you absolutely crazy?"

"Then you can move her anywhere you want," he said logically.

"If you put a gag on her, she could spit up her bottle and end up choking."

"Nah." He waved her away.

"You could kill her!"

"Chrisake, stop getting hysterical," he grumbled, and in his eyes Fay saw a ruthless look that in a single glance obliterated all her hopes—of escape, of riches, of a new life with this man. Frantically her eyes searched his face, looking for familiar landmarks, something to connect with the man she had loved, or thought she had loved. There were none.

"It's Father Tom," said Shockley, covering the mouthpiece to the auxiliary phone. "He's downstairs with hotel security and wants to come up."

"Is he carrying a ransom note?" asked Jacobsen sarcastically, crushing a butt into his brimming ashtray.

"He just wants to talk."

Jacobsen shrugged his indifference.

"It can't hurt," said Osgood, who believed that there was strength in numbers.

A few minutes later Rolf Pettersson let Fitzgibbons in.

Osgood, who was slumped in a chair, looked up and gave Fitzgibbons a smile and a polite nod.

Jacobsen, following his usual tactic, remained silent and waited for Fitzgibbons to make the first move.

"Well?" said Shockley.

"I was horrified to hear what happened," he said, addressing the room, his eyes moving over to Shockley, who looked old and haggard. There were dark circles under the man's eyes, and deep lines ran across his face. To Fitzgibbons he looked as though he had aged ten years.

Silence.

"There's been an enormous outpouring of concern from our people all around the country."

Silence.

Jacobsen groped in his pocket for a fresh cigarette. Pettersson got up, yawned noisily, and stretched.

"Have there been any developments?"

"We were hoping that *you* might have some word," said Shockley, trying his best to sound mistrustful, but Fitzgibbons's demeanor undercut his suspicions. As he looked at Fitzgibbons, with his upright bearing, his open, honest eyes, it was hard for Shockley to continue nursing his suspicions about the former Jesuit. True, he had once doused a draft-board office with blood. True, he had once broken in with some of his followers and burned government records. But in those actions there had been a clear-cut, moral forthrightness. Kidnapping, Shockley had to admit, was just not up Fitzgibbons's alley. If he had been part of a conspiracy to take Baby, he would have owned up to it, just as he had done during the war.

"I know what you've been thinking," said Fitzgibbons, drifting over to Shockley.

"I've been thinking a lot of things lately," said Shockley wearily.

Father Tom smiled at him.

"No," he said finally. "I don't think you were involved. I'm sorry."

"You don't owe me an apology," said Father Tom. "You only did what was natural. I was a logical suspect." Father Tom looked at him. The two men were of nearly the same height and as their eyes locked, Fitzgibbons detected a sadness in Shockley's eyes that verged on tears. "We're only flesh," he said quietly reading Shockley's thoughts and giving him the first words of consolation since the kidnapping. "If they hadn't gotten Baby this way," he said, his hand touching Shockley's arm, "they would have gotten her another."

Shockley swallowed with difficulty.

"I appreciate that," he said, clearing his throat uncomfortably. "Even if it's not true." He smiled wistfully.

The phone rang.

Shockley looked up abruptly.

It rang again.

"It's the hot line," gasped Pettersson, pointing at the table holding the two phones.

The phone rang again.

"Hell, man, answer it!" said Jacobsen, on his feet and ready to leap at the instrument.

Shockley held up a hand, let it ring one more time, and then reached for the receiver. Tensely he put it to his ear. From the other end he could hear above the faint, crisp static the sound of distant traffic.

"Hello?" he said, his eyes darting nervously from side to side, his nerves humming.

"Dees da professor?" asked a high, nasal male voice with a distinctly Hispanic accent.

"Yes, it is," answered Shockley, his heart racing.

"You wan' dee baby bock, meester?"

Shockley's voice failed him and he nodded mutely.

"You wan'?" repeated the high voice.

Shockley felt the blood draining from his head. Dizzily he lowered himself until he was perched on the edge of the low table.

"Is she all right?" he asked hoarsely.

"Do like you tol', understan'?"

"Yes, but is she *OK*?" Shockley persisted. The police had warned him to keep any callers on the line as long as possible, but though their advice was lost in the terror of the moment, Shockley's own needs made him stall.

"She fine—for dee time being."

"What do you want? Please, we want her back—"

"We wan' dee money, meester."

"Yes. Yes. Whatever. Just—"

"Three million dollars. Cash. No marked beels. Meexed beels. Understan'?"

"Yes. Yes. I understand."

"No bait money. No serial numbers. Or she one dead baby."

"Yes. Of course," agreed Shockley, who would have agreed to anything.

"Tomorrow."

"But where? I mean, to whom do I give it? Who—?"

"You' find out," said the voice, and then the connection was broken.

Dazed, Shockley surrendered the phone to Fitzgibbons, who put it into its cradle. An instant later the auxiliary phone began to ring and Jacobsen grabbed for it.

"Did you get it?" he shouted to the Fed on the other end and then waited tensely. "Shit!" he muttered a minute later, slamming down the receiver. "It was a phone booth. They didn't have enough time to dispatch a car."

It was then that the enormity of what he had done began to dawn on Shockley. He had just blithely agreed to deliver an enormous ransom.

"Three million dollars," he muttered forlornly. "Where the hell are we going to get that kind of money?"

"Fay babe, we're in!" said Sloan, winded from racing up the flights of stairs.

With Baby slumped in her lap, Fay looked up.

"By tomorrow we'll be on our sweet way, three million smackeroos richer," he crowed. He grabbed her shoulder, but she pulled away abruptly. "I can't believe it's going this easy," he continued as she rocked the listless infant in her arms. "I could have said eight million and that professor would still have jumped," he beamed. "Hey, come on, honey. Cheer up. What's with you? I thought you'd be tickled."

"Did you really?" she asked sullenly and went to the heater, where a bottle was sluggishly warming in an old dented pot. "Where's the baby food?" she asked suspiciously.

"Oh shit!" He slapped his head dramatically. "In all the excitement I forgot."

"I'll bet you did."

"OK, OK, so I didn't. She's got milk, doesn't she?"

"She needs food, not just milk. She's a child, not a calf."

"Look, I can't walk into a grocery store and start buying up scads of baby food. Now how would that look, huh? Use your head," he said, glaring back at the infant, who followed him with her glazed eyes. "We'll give her some of our stuff."

"Oh sure, popcorn, pizza, beer—"

"Listen," he warned, raising his eyebrows, which joined in the middle, "I don't want you to get stuck on the kid." He had been watching the way Fay had taken to the baby, cuddling her and rocking her, holding her close and letting her quietly sing to her. And he didn't like it. Not one bit.

"Don't worry about me," she said determinedly. She thought about the money. Sloan could have said thirty thousand or three hundred thousand and it would still have sounded like a fortune to her.

"Look, honey," he cajoled, "we're almost over the hump. In no time we'll be rich and on our way to paradise. We'll start a new life, a good one," he said, sensing the direction of her thoughts. "I promise," he added, trying to fix her with his eyes.

"Don't bullshit me, Sloan," she said, busying herself with the bottle, shaking it up and testing it on her wrist.

"Would I—?"

"You lied to me. And you keep lying to me. Every second word out of your mouth is a lie. I should have known I could never trust you."

"Oh, come off it! Why must everything with you—you—" He stopped short. He was going to say women and managed to catch himself in the last minute. Fay knew what he was going to say even before it came out, knew what was going through his mind. For the first time in two years she knew she was seeing him for what he really was. A callous con man, a go-getter. Just as he had screwed friends out of bit parts with his shenanigans, he was trying to pull a fast one, run circles around her. He was the kind of unscrupulous creep who used people, and she was damned if he was going to steamroller her.

"As far as I'm concerned," she said, avoiding his eyes, "from now on this is strictly a business arrangement."

Sloan scratched the stubble on his chin.

"We"—he shrugged—"it's not what I had planned, but if that's the way you want it."

"Sloan, will you, for God's sake, cut the crap?"

"Crap?" he asked, innocently wide-eyed.

"You haven't heard a word I've said, have you?" asked Jacobsen.

"Huh?" Shockley looked up blankly at Jacobsen, as if rousing from a dream.

"Do you have any idea how much money that is?"

"Yes. But we've got to get Baby back," said Shockley, wetting his parched lips. "I don't care what it takes."

"Fine. I understand your sentiments. But try to be logical about this thing."

"You shouldn't have given in to everything right up front," said Osgood, with the clarity of hindsight. "You should've tried to hold out, bargain."

"I'm not bargaining with Baby's life."

"But where the hell are you going to get three million dollars? And by tomorrow?"

"I don't know. I was hoping—well, at least some of it might come from Baby's future earnings." He looked over at Jacobsen.

"In other words, you were counting on *me*," said Jacobsen.

"Well, partially, yes," he said, feeling himself plummeting into despair.

"Forget it," said Jacobsen, but seeing the wretched look on Shockley's face, he finally took pity on him. "Look, friend," he began in one of his unexpected turnabouts, "if I could help you, I would. Believe me. But if I had that kind of cash, do you think I'd be in this business?"

"Then what the hell are we going to do?" asked Shockley, rubbing his hands over his face, trying to clear his mind.

"Don't ask me," said Jacobsen. "My experience in the ransom business is very limited. Fortunately."

"By agreeing to their demands, Dr. Shockley may have locked himself in," said Pettersson, echoing the thoughts of most of those in the room.

"Maybe," said Father Tom. "But Irwin did the right thing. Any of us would have done the same in his shoes. He'd have been crazy to try and haggle at this point. I think we should look at it on the positive side. The important thing is we've made contact."

"If they really have her," injected Pettersson.

"They probably do," said Jacobsen. "If they have any brains in their heads—and these people have probably been planning this for some time—they know that we're going to demand proof before any payoff."

"I feel she's safe," said Father Tom. "For the time being, at least. And I think we should concentrate on raising the money."

"Father Fitzgibbons," said Jacobsen, his mind working, "how about your people? Your church? Is there any chance—?"

"Three million? Not a ghost of a chance." Father

Tom shook his head. "We're not the Catholic Church," he said with a smile. "We're a young church. A loose federation at this point. And without any money to speak of."

"Damn," muttered Shockley miserably. "There's no way we're going to raise that kind of money."

"There probably is a way," said Father Tom, who wasn't easily defeated. "It's just that we haven't come up with it, that's all. If we put our heads together," he said, fighting to dissipate the gloom that was settling down on the room, "we can lick this thing and get Baby back. The important thing is to have faith."

"Yes," snorted Jacobsen, who naturally fell into the role of iconoclast. "To get down on our knees and pray."

"Right," said Father Tom, but before he could seize the opportunity, the auxiliary phone rang. It was the FBI again. Just as Shockley had expected, they had no new ideas to offer, just consolation.

"Stall," said the agent. "Keep them dealing. We'll get them, don't you worry. It's just a matter of time. Let them think that you're really trying to raise the cash."

"We are," said Shockley, and the agent wasn't quite sure which way he meant it.

"Ruth, please. Don't hang up on me," pleaded Shockley from the phone booth in the hotel lobby. "We've got to talk."

"So talk," she said perfunctorily, and Shockley tried, but the words didn't quite come. He had planned to tell her about the kidnapper's call, about the depths of his despair, about his regrets at hurting her, how he felt himself being dragged helplessly along in a current that threatened to drown him. He wanted to tell her about Father Tom, who was now up in the suite with the others, all of them racking their brains, trying to come up with the ransom. He wanted to confess how he now longed for the old life, for those relatively simple days when he had taught at the university and composed, how he missed her, their children, the familiar surroundings of their home, which they had so lovingly restored with their own hands. He wanted to tell her that and much more, yet he felt overwhelmed as though sensing the futility of the task.

"I'm scared," he finally blurted out. He swallowed and waited.

"Yes," she said a long minute later. "I figured you would be."

"Of what's happening to us through all this."

"Has happened," she corrected, but there was no malice in her voice, only a profound sense of disappointment and weariness. The anger she had first felt when she had read the papers and seen the news reports that seemed to rub her nose in the lurid details of the kidnapping had now yielded to melancholy, to the point where she could almost empathize with her husband.

The phone line fell silent again, and Shockley knew that she was reviewing their lives together as he himself was doing, running through the tape of their existence at high speed, picking out discrete spots, images that seemed to distill their lives into its very essence: The birth of Annette, their first child—Shockley present as his little girl was born after fourteen hours of labor. His Pulitzer Prize—the heady excitement, the whirl of parties and congratulations, and the promise of seemingly unlimited happiness. Ruth getting her doctorate. Julie born. Annette's ruptured appendix—the ghastly fear of losing their child. Her recovery. Their tears. Through Shockley's mind in that short instant of time there flashed other quick shots, small but meaningful events that seemed at this moment filled with content. A dinner with Ruth's father days before he died. A long walk along Park Avenue with Ruth one warm summer evening. Another summer the two of them lying together in bed, exhausted from making love, outside the surf pounding on a beach—a vacation somewhere. Cape Cod? Spain?

"Too much has gone on between us for it to end just like this." He struggled to clear his thoughts.

"It's over," she said.

"It can't be. Not like this. Just because of—"

"Not just because of—of her," she said, meaning the woman in the Plaza.

"Then why? Why?"

"Because of everything. Because you've changed. Because you're not the man I married. Because you made a choice without ever thinking about us, about me."

"You mean Baby?"

"Exactly!" she said bluntly.

"I had to."

"Yes, I understand. You had to. I don't blame you. But you also have to live with the results."

"You mean to say we're breaking up because of a little baby girl?" he asked, trying to sound incredulous.

"You're trying to simplify it. It's not because of her per se. It's because of all the misery and trouble she's brought us. You called her a blessing."

"She was. I mean"—he corrected himself—"she is. *Is*," he reemphasized.

"She's been a curse," said Ruth harshly. "To our lives, at least."

"Ruth—"

"She's damaged Cindy. That poor child still goes

around crying all day. And now she's convinced she's somehow responsible for Baby's kidnapping."

"Ruth—"

"You've given up composing, quit your job. And for what? To become a promoter. A hipster. Irwin, you're the laughingstock of this town."

"So that's it!"

"No, that's not it. I don't give a damn what anybody else thinks, not really," she said, but he suspected that she did. "It's what *I* think. Irwin, you've changed. And I don't particularly like what you've become. Can you understand that?"

"No," he objected. "Not quite. Look, Ruth, I can change again. You think I like what I've become? I'm not any happier than you are."

"Because you're miserable, why should I be?" she went on, and suddenly Shockley understood that she was talking not only about the last six months since Baby; she was thinking about all the years she had passed with him, supporting him with her life tissue as he struggled to compose, bouncing through the highs and lows of his roller-coaster existence. Baby, he realized, was but a catalyst. Ruth was tired. Tired of him. The ups and downs.

"What a holiday this turned out to be," he said forlornly before hanging up.

"Merry Christmas," she said to herself long after he had gone.

Subdued, Shockley rode the elevator back up to his suite, keeping to the rear of the car. The elevator was crowded with guests, jovial people, their faces still red from the cold, Christmas gifts tucked under their arms. They joked, bantered, laughed, all of which seemed to drive home Shockley's sense of isolation. Without his family, without Baby and her song, he felt cut loose from the world. As the elevator stopped on the second floor to disgorge a noisy couple, he tried to imagine life without Ruth, but it eluded him. As far as he could see, the future was a blank, and he knew that he had reached the lowest point in his life.

Seventeen years together, he thought as the elevator slid open at the next stop and the remaining people spilled out, leaving him finally alone. Seventeen years in which they had shaped each other, fitting together like matched pieces of a puzzle, a single, fused, living unit that breathed in unison. Yet—yet now all that was out the window, and the prospect of facing life alone made him shudder.

What was odd, he thought, leaving the elevator and advancing over the soft carpets to the door of his suite, was that this was happening to *them*. In recent years he and Ruth had watched from the safety of their marriage as many of the couples they had known in Ithaca— friends and neighbors, colleagues and acquaintances— people like the Stearnes and the Pompilios, the Halperns and the Todds and the Millers, steady, solid couples, had dissolved their homes and marriages. They had watched it all from the sheltered distance of their union, safe and secure. Theirs was an island of stability in a turbulent sea of recriminations and custody battles and property squabbles. Yet here he was being sucked into the same morass, aware of what was transpiring, but utterly helpless to stop it. And the catalyst? he thought to himself, reaching for the doorknob. A baby of all things. An infant, sweet and innocent as the morning dew, a child blessed with song.

* * *

After calling Terkel in the early morning, Doris had gone directly back to her trailer. The chills she had awakened with had gotten worse, and no matter how much she turned up the heat or put on extra clothes her skin was still covered with goose bumps.

Piling all the blankets she could find onto her bed, Doris had crawled under the covers in an attempt to warm up. Hardly had her head hit the pillow than she fell into a deep sleep. For hours she lay beneath the layers of blankets, lost in a dark, dreamless pit, her body quivering with shivers. Toward nightfall her sleep was suddenly invaded by a ghastly vision. In her dream she saw Baby naked and wandering, lost in an icy blizzard. Her lips were blue with cold and she looked as though she were freezing to death. Above the merciless howling of the wind Baby was trying to sing, calling out to Doris in a tremulous and fading voice. Doris reached out her hand but couldn't quite grasp ahold of Baby. She lunged forward toward her child, but Baby kept retreating back into the storm, still frantically crying out for her mother.

Doris suddenly awoke and realized that she was sitting up in bed. Dazed, she looked around, her heart thumping, her body cold as ever. She glanced out the window. It was already dusk, and the people in the neighboring trailer had turned on the string of colored Christmas lights lining their doorway. Sliding her feet into her slippers, Doris wrapped herself in her coat and turned on a light.

What a horrible dream, she thought, shivering by the furnace duct as the warm air streamed past her. The headache she had had in the morning was still with her. Her bones ached and her back was acting up again. She was sick, Doris realized, probably one of those viruses that were going around the trailer park. She went to the medicine cabinet and swallowed two aspirin. She took her temperature and, to her surprise, found that it was normal. If only she could shake this darn headache, she thought, as she put on some water for tea. While waiting for the tea to steep, she sank down at the kitchen table. That dream, she thought, running her fingers over the Formica pattern on the table, her mind drifting back. She couldn't recall ever having had such a vivid or frightening dream. She knew it was silly. Baby couldn't walk. She was barely six months old. But Baby's plea in that dream had been startlingly real.

Doris poured herself a cup of tea, and taking a sip, she suddenly felt ravenously hungry. Busily she set about making herself a meal, her stomach churning in hunger. She boiled two eggs, dropped some bread into the toaster, poured herself some milk as Markowitz had recommended—even took out the orange juice she had been rationing for a week. What was odd, however, was that when her meal was all prepared and she sat down to eat, she could hardly stomach a morsel. Though her belly was knotted in hunger, she could only manage to swallow a bite of toast.

It was all crazy, she told herself, as she bent down with pain to feed her cats. Chills without fever. Hunger without being able to eat. And that terrifying nightmare.

She watered her plants and went about tidying up her trailer. She felt so sick, however, that after a few minutes she gave up and slumped down in her chair by the window, closing her eyes for what seemed a moment. When she opened them again, it was already late at night and someone was banging loudly on the door. It was Mrs. Schooley.

"They're asking ransom!" said the fat woman,

breathless from the short walk, a toddler tucked under one arm. When she spoke, her words issued out into the cold night in a stream of smoke lit by the light from Doris's trailer.

"Ransom?" asked Doris confused, trying to shake off her lethargy. She had just had that same dream over again, and she couldn't comprehend what her neighbor was talking about.

"It's supposed to be on the news again. Johnny thought you'd want to see her. Hurry," she urged.

The cold was pouring into the open door, and rather than questioning the woman, Doris grabbed her coat and followed Mrs. Schooley over the trampled path of snow.

"They're asking three million dollars!" said Johnny Schooley by way of greeting. He was a skinny man, as bony as his wife was fat. His ears stuck straight out from his head like wings, and the creases of his neck and hands were always lined with mechanic's grease. Getting up from his recliner in front of the color set, Mr. Schooley motioned toward Doris to sit in his place.

"What are you all talking about?" she asked, rubbing the sleep from her eyes.

"Why the kidnapping, 'course!" said Mrs. Schooley.

"Of Baby," echoed her husband.

Doris turned white as a ghost, and the couple suddenly became scared that she might pass out right then and there in their double-wide trailer.

"Oh, cripes!" said Mrs. Schooley, slapping her hand over her mouth. "And we thought you knew! Why we never would—"

"She doesn't know?" asked Mr. Schooley, baffled. How could she not know? The whole freaking world knew.

"I think I've got it," said Father Tom, looking up with a full mouth of lasagna and breaking the deadlock. By that time the four men had spent the entire day brainstorming. Trying to come up with a scheme for freeing Baby, they had gone through and dismissed everything from raising the ransom by levying a tithe on every Babyist on Father Tom's mailing lists (too slow and clumsy) or floating bank loans (Jacobsen: "On what collateral? On a star we might never get back in one piece. Bankers are businessmen not philanthropists.") to stuffing a suitcase with paper and letting the police nab the person who made the pickup (Osgood: "By the time he—or she—spills the beans, the others will be miles away and Baby might be dead.").

Up until the evening press conference, the four repeatedly consulted with the FBI man on the other end of the auxiliary phone. One after the other he effectively punctured all their schemes, suggesting instead that Shockley continue to stall, holding off the consummation of *any* deals until their officers had exhausted every possible lead. What kind of leads? The FBI wasn't telling.

"If you give in to their ransom demands," explained the gravel-voiced Fed on the other end, "and on a prominent case like this, then you can be sure as hell we're going to have a rash of these kidnappings around the country."

"Obviously you're more concerned with the fallout than freeing Baby."

"Oh no, we want to get her back, Dr. Shockley," the cop objected. "But we also have to deal with the wider implications. We have responsibilities. And so do you. You don't want this thing happening to other people, do you?"

"Does that mean you're going to interfere if we try to make a drop?"

"No. We gave you our word on that. But we're certainly not—at least at this time—going to encourage you to give in."

"I think I've got it," said Father Tom, looking up from his plate, his eyes brightening.

The men in the suite held their forks in abeyance, looking at him expectantly.

"A way," he continued, swallowing eagerly, "of raising a large quantity of money, relatively fast."

"Go on," said Shockley. With a warm meal in his belly, he was ready for a new surge of hope.

"Well?" pressed Jacobsen.

"A benefit."

"A what?" asked Shockley.

"A benefit performance. A Christmas benefit for Baby," said Father Tom.

"Yes. A concert. A show," said Osgood, immediately picking up on the notion. "Big names. A variety show of sorts. Singing. Dancing. Acting."

"Exactly!" Father Tom grinned.

"With the right people," said Pettersson, wetting his lips thoughtfully, "you could pack them in, run performances head to tail."

Jacobsen sat expressionless, his eyes following the speakers, absorbing what they were saying.

"There are lots of show people who really care about Baby," said Father Tom, turning his attentions to Jacobsen. "Why, off the top of my head I could name a half dozen," he said eagerly, hoping to ignite Jacobsen.

"Name them," said Jacobsen coolly.

"Well—Well—For instance, Joan Baez," said Father Tom, grabbing at a name. "And Barbra Streisand. And Redford. Robert Redford. I know they'd help."

"That's three."

"Wayne Newton," Osgood chimed in excitedly. "I'm positive we could count on him for a good cause."

"Lenny Bernstein," piped Shockley enthusiastically. "He's in town. And I'm almost sure he'd lend a hand."

"How about McCartney?" added Pettersson, looking at his boss. "We could fly him over from London. On the Concorde he could be here in a matter of hours."

Jacobsen still didn't react.

"Baryshnikov," Fitzgibbons tossed in as the room became electric. "Now he's absolutely crazy about Baby. And Dolly Parton. Pat Boone. How many more do you need?" He laughed happily.

Jacobsen sat silent, an unlit butt dangling from his lower lip.

"It's not a bad idea," Pettersson cautiously prodded.

"Bad idea? It's one hell of a good idea," exclaimed Osgood, congratulating Fitzgibbons. He could already envision the show, see himself as master of ceremonies.

"If you could take care of arranging a theater and ticketing"—Fitzgibbons faced Jacobsen—"we could probably in less than a day round up the stars."

"No," said Jacobsen, shaking his head.

"No?" asked Shockley his smile fading. "What do you mean 'no'?"

"No theater," answered Jacobsen.

"No?" echoed the other men.

"No," answered Jacobsen, rising to his feet, and there was the hint of a smile on his lips. "Television," he continued tersely, nodding his head to himself.

"Yes," uttered Osgood in a near whisper, catching the spark.

"A telethon for Baby," said Jacobsen, pointing a single finger skyward.

Shockley watched him, holding his breath, almost afraid to hope.

"Look at it logically," said Jacobsen, now himself, and busily pacing the floor. "A theater has a limited capacity. What can it hold? Five hundred seats? A thousand? Assuming you can get one quickly, by the time you've paid the rent and security and ads and God-knows-what-else, your net is down to nothing. Theaters, even bowls and stadiums, they're all finite, all regional. But, on the other hand, television"—he beamed—"blankets the country, the world. It's essentially infinite. It can reach every man, woman, and child. It's fast—almost instantaneous. It's clean, easy, and it's lucrative, very lucrative," said Jacobsen, who had always wanted to move into that area.

"We can have people calling in their pledges," Pettersson chirped excitedly.

"Pledges?" scoffed Jacobsen. "Forget it. Stick to plastic money. With Visa or Master Card or American Express, we can convert numbers to immediate cash."

"Not everybody has credit cards," said Fitzgibbons levelly.

"But anybody can wire in money," said Jacobsen. "And in urban areas we can set up collection centers. Why, think of it, within twenty-four hours we could have three million—or close to that—sitting in piles right in this very room."

"But they want the money *tomorrow*. Christmas Eve."

"Screw them!" roared Jacobsen, feeling his oats and taking control. "If they want that kind of money they're going to have to give us a couple of days," he said, extracting a little black book of phone numbers. Wetting his finger, he hastily thumbed through the leaf-thin pages. "Rolf," he ordered, pointing to the phone, "get me Silverman. If you can't raise him at the station, try him at home."

Pettersson was scribbling madly on a pad by the phone.

"Hurry, man," said Jacobsen feverishly. "We don't have all day."

"Yes, sir," said Pettersson, grabbing the wrong phone and flashing an alert in the FBI office.

"Some winter we're having," said the man sitting across the aisle from her on the night Greyhound.

Doris turned in the darkened bus and saw the elderly man with his cane resting between his legs, his pale, freckled face illuminated by the passing traffic. She nodded courteously and then turned back to stare out her window.

"Never seen it this cold," he added a little later as the bus droned on through the flatlands of New Jersey. "And I've been around seventy-five years. Seventy-five years!" he repeated.

Out of politeness Doris turned again toward him and tried to smile.

"Got all my own teeth still," he said, taking his upper teeth between his two fingers and yanking them theatrically. "And my own hair!" he said, taking off his hat and bending his neck so Doris could see the top of his head.

"That's very nice," said Doris dully, and was staring back out the window. Over the eastern, icy marshlands the sky was slowly reddening, and as the bus shook and swayed over the potholed road, Doris was trying to think ahead. She was hoping that it would be light by the time they pulled into New York City. It was more than fifteen years since she had visited the city, and her imagination took her no farther than her arrival. Beyond that stretched a blank.

"Some folks say that it's all these nuclear accidents," said the man across the aisle a few minutes later.

"Huh?" Doris awoke from her thoughts.

"The weather. The ice age. Why it's coming back," said the man, desperate for conversation. "But I know that's not the reason. It's because of our wickedness. We're being punished."

Doris looked at him blankly. Her head ached as ever, and she felt herself removed from the world.

"You ask me, the whole planet's going plumb crazy," he offered without being asked.

Doris looked away. She was in no mood for small talk. She was, in fact, interested in only one thing: finding Baby. Since the Schooleys had driven her out to route 79, where they had managed to flag down the night bus from Rochester, Doris had been able to think of little else. Even when the bus, just out of Binghamton, had skidded off the slick road into an abutment, lurching and coming to a crashing halt, Doris still had had her mind on Baby. New York. She had to get to New York, she had repeated to herself while the passengers sat stranded at the side of the road, waiting

those interminable hours for a replacement bus to come
and rescue them. New York. That's where Baby was.

"Now you take the kidnapping for instance," said the
old gent reaching into a paper bag. Tearing apart a
sandwich, he extended half to Doris. Without thought
she accepted it and as she bit into the dry bread, her
tongue made contact with something that tasted like
warm salami. "Now if that isn't wickedness, pure and
simple, I don't know what is," snorted the man.

Doris stopped chewing in midbite and turned to look
at him. There were large, luminous tears in her eyes,
and through them the man's face appeared misty and
distorted.

"Now how can somebody do a thing like that? Take
an innocent baby, a gift from God Almighty himself,
and steal her?"

Doris shook her head as the tears coursed down her
cheeks.

"What a pity!" said the man, wiping his own eyes.
"What a crime of crimes." He blew his nose loudly into
a stained handkerchief and, rolling it into a ball, stuffed
it back into his pocket. "I know just how you feel,
lady—" He shook his head in commiseration. "I'm a
Babyist myself," he said. "See?" He opened his shirt
and held up the golden lips that hung around his sinewy
neck.

Doris leaned across the aisle and stared at the lips
that dangled between his fingers.

"Baby," she muttered into her fist, seeing the lips
that were a perfect replica of Baby's little birdlike
mouth. "My sweet Baby." She broke down at the sight,
weeping openly, the remains of the half sandwich flopping to her lap.

"Gee whiz, lady," said the man, taken aback by her

copious tears. "There, there, now," he said, sliding into the empty seat next to her and patting her hand. "Everything's going to turn out all right. That's why I'm going to New York. Because of Baby. Sure," he said, when Doris quizzically turned her tear-splotched face up to him. "To see that telethon tomorrow. My nephew's a big shot, a cameraman for the network"—he grinned proudly—"does all the top shows. Said he could get me into the telethon. Knows how I feel about her music and all," said the man, still holding Doris's hand. "Why maybe he could get you in too," he said, noticing the way Doris's eyes were still fixed on the lips that now hung out of his shirt. "Here," he said, carefully removing the chain over his head. "You need this more than I do." He handed the lips to her. "Genuine fourteen carat gold-plated," he said wistfully. "But that's the message," he explained in his disconnected fashion. "Of her music. To share. To give a part of yourself to others who need it. I've heard her sing with my own ears. Yep. Really," he insisted when Doris looked at him through her continuing stream of tears. "Heard her in Cleveland. In Chicago once. Even heard her in Atlanta. I'm quite a bus rider"—he laughed at himself—"got myself one of them passes. They call them Discover America. I call them Discover Baby." He chuckled, trying to cheer up his silent companion.

"My heavens," he remarked later, still holding Doris's hand as they entered the Lincoln Tunnel. "You're cold as ice," he said, trying to warm her with his own bony hands.

Doris gave him a weak smile. She had been sitting for the last half hour with those golden lips pressed to her own lips. Watching her, the man knew now that he had done the right thing in giving them to her, that the act of parting with what he held most dear was the re-

ward in itself, just as he had heard Father Tom once
say.

"Well," he said, gathering up his meager belongings
as they pulled into the Port Authority Terminal, "it's
been nice riding with you. You don't talk an awful lot,"
he said candidly, struggling to his feet with his cane,
"but you're sure a good listener."

From the very moment of its conception, the Christmas Day Telethon began to take shape as if possessed of
a will and energy all its own. Everywhere doors magically opened. The network and its affiliates coast to coast
agreed to push aside their scheduled Christmas programming to make way for the telethon. Some of the
biggest names in show business—actors, singers, dancers, and comedians—were falling all over themselves
to offer their talent. Volunteers were coming out in
droves to man the phones and the collection units to be
stationed in major cities. By daybreak of Christmas
Eve, the telethon was already a reality, and even Father
Tom, a staunch believer in divine intervention, couldn't
help but be astounded by the speed and ease with which
everything fell into line.

With a star-studded cast, everyone was predicting an
unprecedented 95 percent Nielsen share of the Christmas Day audience. The network had already sold the
commercial time, sandwiching the telethon for a phenomenal three times the going prime-time rate—the
revenues, the network president explained, earmarked
to cover the costs for the show. "Otherwise," he told
Jacobsen, "consider the air-time and facilities *our* gift
to Baby."

As Father Tom and Pettersson and Osgood worked
with Jacobsen at his Madison Avenue office, feverishly
putting together the program, Shockley found himself

once again alone at the Plaza, waiting for the next contact from the kidnappers. He tried to fill the intervening time by listening to the news or reading the papers, but mostly he ended up sitting in the bedroom on the edge of his bed, staring at Baby's empty crib.

As the hours wore on, Shockley found himself alternating between the depths of despair and glimmering hope, his moods swinging wildly from minute to minute, giving him no respite. Yes, he would think in a flash of hope, he would get Baby back. Happy and healthy. No, he'd realize on second thought, as in the Lindbergh kidnapping, she was already dead. And all this activity was merely a futile death throe. Then he would remember the drowning, Baby's miraculous survival. Surely someone was looking over Baby, someone who would protect her now, he thought in a moment of near prayer. No! If she were protected, this would never, never have occurred.

When his patience was near the breaking point, Shockley picked up the auxiliary phone and made contact with the same gravel-voiced Fed who had been on the case almost from the beginning.

"How're you holding up?" asked the man, sounding weary himself.

"Badly."

"Try to be patient. These things can take time. Time is in our favor." The cop tried to soothe Shockley.

"Have you ever been involved in a kidnapping before?" asked Shockley pointedly.

"Well, no," the man answered honestly.

Shockley laughed.

The man laughed.

"But seriously"—the cop tried to allay Shockley's fears—"we're trained to handle things like this. We've got over ninety men out in the field on this case."

"By the way," asked Shockley, hungry for conversation. "What's your name? We've been talking to each other all this time and I still don't know it."

"Nisbet. Jeff Nisbet."

"Nisbet," repeated Shockley, trying to imagine the face. "Look, Nisbet, do me a favor. Level with me. Do you *really* have any leads?"

"We do," he answered succinctly.

"Well?"

The man became silent.

"Come on, tell me," Shockley coaxed.

The line remained silent.

"I'm not going to talk about it. Do you think I would screw myself? Who the hell am I going to talk to, anyway?"

"OK," said Nisbet, knowing that Shockley needed something tangible to keep him going. "We know that the woman who slept in your bed did not have dark hair."

"So?"

"She was a redhead. She had dyed her hair black."

"And?" Shockley waited for the rest.

"Well, that's a clue."

"You're joking!" said Shockley. "Tell me, how many redheaded women are there on the loose in the city at this moment, huh?"

"There's more."

"Go on," Shockley prompted.

"We think that the kidnappers are part of a Puerto Rican nationalist group. That they're the same people who set off bombs in the Bank of America offices in Chicago and New York last week."

"Based on what?"

"They're trying to raise money to finance a revolution to break Puerto Rico free from the United States.

They operate out of the South Bronx. The call you got from the kidnappers came from that part of the city."

"How does that connect with the red hair?"

"One of our informers identified the composite you made with our artist as looking like Mama Libre, one of the heavies in the organization."

"This woman was no Puerto Rican," said Shockley, thinking back again to Irina. When he visualized her in bed with him, chills ran up and down his spine.

"We've only got a description of her, no pictures, but from what we understand she's an American girl, one of these little college-type bleeding hearts—" The cop stopped himself.

Shockley sat silently holding the phone.

"You still there, Shockley?" asked the husky-voiced Fed.

"Still here, Nisbet." Shockley heaved a long sigh. "Not going anywhere."

"Listen, this was strictly between us."

"Don't worry. My lips are sealed. Your job is safe."

"Good," mumbled Nisbet, only vaguely relieved.

Shockley put down the phone. He sat trying to imagine Irina dressed in army fatigues, moving through the jungled hills of Puerto Rico carrying a machine gun. By no stretch of the imagination could he fit her into that image. There was something about her, however, that continued to nag at him. There was something indefinable he had spotted in her from the beginning, something that went deeper than her beauty, a certain sense of genuine kindness, of compassion, of warmth. Yet, yet that miserable bitch had stolen Baby. The contradiction made him dizzy.

*　*　*

Leaving the bus and emerging into the Port Authority Terminal, a shopping bag in hand, Doris was immediately overwhelmed. On this morning before Christmas
the bus station was sheer bedlam. The crowded hall was
swirling with holiday travelers, people scampering back
and forth with their bundles and bags, bawling children
dragged along behind their arm-yanking parents, all
kinds of people frantically rushing around. And there
were lines everywhere. Lines snaking through the hall
to the ticket counters. Lines to the information booths.
Lines for doughnuts and coffee. Lines for escalators. As
Doris stood on tiptoe searching for an exit to the street,
a huge woman lugging a suitcase charged smack into
her from the rear, nearly bowling Doris off her feet—
the woman pushing on without so much as a second
look. An instant later a teenager with festering pustules
covering his face tried to interest her in a digital watch
hot off the trucks. Overhead speakers blared out garbled messages. A vendor vaulted over the counter of his
stand and dashed past her, chasing a woman who had
stolen a pack of M&Ms. Swept up in the eddies and
swells of the crowds, Doris finally found what appeared
to be an exit and, before she knew it, was propelled out
the door by the surge of bodies.

Out on the street, Doris stood for a moment on the
corner near the terminal trying to get her bearings
amidst the morning rush of trucks and cars bouncing
through the slushy potholes, the noise of jackhammers
and horns and sirens blaring in her ears. Finally she
picked a direction and began to walk.

Blowing on her frozen hands and pushing them deep
into the pockets of her old wool coat, her shopping bag
dangling from above her wrist, Doris pushed on
through the thickening crowds streaming past her in all

directions. She was looking for Baby, she told herself, beginning to realize the enormousness of the task that lay before her. Somehow time and memory had shrunk New York to the manageable proportions of Ithaca. But this was no Ithaca. This was madness, sheer chaos. Yet, she thought, crossing the street in the sea of people, somewhere amidst all this pandemonium, somewhere in this city, was that woman who had stolen her Baby.

"I've just got to find her," she said to herself, reaching a wide avenue. Turning onto it and instinctively heading northward, Doris continued to trudge on, the icy headwind freezing her cheeks and causing her nose to run.

"Oh, dear God," she prayed ten blocks later, when her feet began to ache, her hands had gone beyond numbness, and her resolve had begun to falter. "Please give me the strength to find my Baby," she uttered, looking up into the gray sky lodged between the buildings. A lone snowflake fluttered down and hit her in the eye.

Shuddering in the icy, raw air, Doris pushed on. She managed another few slushy blocks and then, looking for a place to rest, noticed a small luncheonette. She went in, thawed out her hands while waiting for an empty stool, then sat down at the counter and ordered tea. While people stood behind her waiting for an opening, she sat nursing her cup of tea and trying to puzzle out a plan. She sat and sat and sat over that half-finished cup, stalling, waiting, hoping, praying as the waitress came past repeatedly, busily cleaning the counter in front of her and trying to shame her into leaving.

When the morning rush had finally thinned, Doris picked up her bag and continued her northward trek.

When she reached the edge of Central Park, Doris sensed she knew where she was—she had been here once during a school-librarians' convention in 1958. Recalling the horses and carriages she had seen that year, that very happy year, she turned east on the cross street and soon found herself standing in the small plaza near a rather ornate hotel. Reading the sign on the awning, she made the connection with the news report. Finding a telephone booth down the street, she slid in, closed the door, and hunted in her purse for a dime.

When the hot line sounded, Shockley could barely restrain himself from picking it up. With clenched fists he stood poised over it and finally, on the fourth ring, grabbed the receiver.

"Dees da professor?" asked the now-familiar voice.

"Speaking."

"You got dee money, meester?"

"How's Baby?"

"She happy as a bird. Now, dee money."

"We're getting it."

"What you mean? We tol' you, mahn, today ees dee day!"

"I know you did. But you're asking for an extraordinary amount of cash. If you'd consider a smaller—"

"Hey, you playin' games weet me?"

"If you want three million dollars you'll have to—"

"You know what we wan', meester. You don' fuck weet me or dat baby—"

"Look. Try to be sensible. There's no way in the world we could have scraped together that kind of money in a few hours. You must know that," said Shockley.

"Meester, I don' wanna hear 'bout your problems."

"It's your problem too," said Shockley bluntly.

"I wan' dee money an' no bullsheet, meester, get it?"

"If you're willing to take less, you can have it now. I could give you a hundred thousand in a matter of an hour."

"Three million, mahn. No less!" The man sounded enraged and Shockley backed off.

"OK, OK, but we need time."

"Today, meester, or your baby she is dead."

"Three days," said Shockley.

"Today!"

"We've got a telethon benefit coming on tomorrow to raise the money. Surely you must have heard—"

"Hey, mahn, you stallin'?" The man sounded worried.

"No, no. But we need time. Give us at least two days then."

"Mahn, what you talkin' about?"

"Two days. And that's the best we can do," Shockley pushed on stubbornly. "We'll give you three million dollars, any denominations, any way you want it."

"You agreed today."

"Impossible. It's *absolutely* impossible. What's an extra couple of days going to matter to you?"

"Stop hustlin' me, mahn!"

"Three million dollars. It's yours. All of it. But you've got to give us a chance."

"I gotta think, mahn—"

"Just two lousy—"

"You rushin' me, meester!" said the man, now sounding frantic.

"But—"

"I gotta think!" he screamed and then hung up.

Immediately the auxiliary phone was ringing.

"Good going, Shockley," said Nisbet. "You're taking control of the situation. And you had him on for a good couple of minutes. Hang on."

Shockley waited tensely.

"OK," Nisbet returned. "We got a make on that call. Call you back as soon as—"

The hot line began to ring again.

"It's him!" Shockley gasped.

"Let it ring," the cop warned.

"What do I do if he won't wait?" said Shockley, panic surging in him.

"He'll wait," said Nisbet. "Take control. Don't clutch!"

The phone kept ringing.

"OK. You relaxed?"

Shockley took in a deep breath and let it out slowly.

"Yes?" he said, trying to slow his racing heart. If he screwed up, she was finished. He'd never see her again. She'd never sing again. He had to be cautious. Calm. Not let this guy stampede him.

"OK," said Nisbet. "Pick up the line now."

Shockley put down the one phone and picked up the other.

"Yes?" he said, trying to sound determined.

"Professor Shockley?" asked a creaky old lady's voice, taking him by surprise. "This is Doris. Doris Rumsey."

"Doris? How'd you get through on this line?"

"I told them who I was. I'm calling about Baby," said Doris, beginning to weep despite her resolve.

"Listen, Doris, you're calling on the wrong line. And at a terrible time. The kidnappers are supposed to call back in a minute and you're tying up the phone. Please," said Shockley, rushing his words, "just hang up. I'll call you right back. I promise."

"But—"

"Please. Now!"

Doris hung up.

The auxiliary phone rang again.

Then the hot line rang.

Shockley feared he would go insane. He didn't know which to grab first.

The auxiliary phone fell silent and he picked up the hot line.

"Eight in dee mornin'. Day after Christmaas, got it?"

"Too early. We need the full day."

"Tha's all you got. Not a meenit more!"

"Where do I drop it?"

"You' find out."

"How do I know if Baby's alive and well?"

"She OK."

"I want assurances."

"You've got it, meester."

"Huh?"

"My assurances," said the man with a chilling laugh, and hung up.

The auxiliary phone rang.

"Hang on, Shockley," said Nisbet.

Shockley sat holding the receiver in his trembling hand. In the background he could hear garbled radio chatter. Tensely he waited, feeling sweat soaking through his shirt. A minute later Nisbet was back.

"Hell," he muttered disgustedly. "We almost had the son of a bitch. It was another coin box eight blocks away. Damn, that was close! Next time," he added, trying to sound optimistic. "Next time we'll nail him."

Shockley put the phone back into its cradle and stood up. He poured himself three fingers of whiskey and downed it in a single gulp. Slowly the warmth spread outward from his stomach, untying the knots in his nerves. Then, suddenly, he remembered Doris.

"Nisbet," he said, picking up the auxiliary phone.

"Yeah?"

"I'm going down to the lobby to make a call. I'll be back in a couple of minutes."

"Why don't you use the hot line? I doubt if he's going to call back. It's better you stick around here."

"OK," said Shockley and, picking up the outside line, suddenly realized that he didn't know Doris's new number. He called information in Ithaca.

Standing in the phone booth on the street, Doris put in her dime, called the Plaza and, identifying herself, asked for Shockley's room. The line, so she was informed by the switchboard, was busy. She hung up and waited.

Shockley put down his phone. Doris had no listing for her new home, which meant probably no phone. He debated calling Ruth and asking her to drive out to the trailer park, but knew that Ruth had had her fill of playing messenger and courier. He picked up the phone and, calling Ithaca information, tried to get Olive Eldridge's number. There were three Eldridges listed, none with Olive's first name. Shockley scribbled down all three.

Doris put another dime in the phone.

Shockley dialed the first listing.

Doris dialed the hotel again.

"Olive Eldridge?" said a man. "Why, that's my sister-in-law. You got the wrong Eldridge. She lives down on Third Street."

"I'm sorry, that line is still busy," said the woman on the hotel switchboard. "Do you want to hold the line?"

"I'll wait," said Doris.

Shockley depressed the button on his phone for an instant, then dialed the eleven digits that were Olive's number.

"Still busy," said the switchboard lady. "Please hold."

Olive's number in Ithaca rang. It rang three times, but no one answered. Shockley let it continue to ring.

Disgusted with waiting, Doris finally hung up.

The auxiliary phone rang.

"I just learned from our lady on the switchboard that she's been trying to get you," said Nisbet.

"Who?"

"Doris Rumsey."

"Oh, damn!" muttered Shockley. "Do you have her number?"

"Yeah. They put a trace on it. Just to be sure."

Doris swung open the door to the booth. She had used up her last dime and wasn't about to waste any more time or money trying to contact Shockley. She didn't need him, and she had been stupid to even try to call him. Picking up her bag, she moved to the corner and waited for the light to change. Enough was enough, she thought, crossing the street and heading up the avenue as the phone in the booth started to ring.

"Oh, honey," sighed Fay when Baby suddenly stopped singing, her little chest racked by a deep, painful cough. "Save your strength."

Baby coughed up a small glob of rusty sputum and tried to sing again. She forced out a few feeble notes, took a quick, wheezing gasp, and gave out a few more.

"You don't have to sing for me," said Fay tenderly to the child, who lay drooping in her arms. "I know what a good little girl you are."

"She's suffering." She cornered Sloan when he came back from his latest foray. "Just listen to her," she said, distressed as Baby was gripped by a loud, hacking spasm. Fay picked her up and patted her back until the coughing subsided—Baby lying spent in her arms, flushed and soaked with sweat.

"Sure. I hear her. And so does probably half the neighborhood. In fact, I heard her all the way down the stairs," said Sloan, preoccupied. He was thinking about the two days that that professor had wheedled out of him. Was it a trick? Were they trying to hold him off as they zeroed in? Maybe he should have taken less and split? Two days. Two long days. How would he last with this broad driving him up a tree? He must have been out of his skull to ever think he could spend the rest of his life with her.

"We've got to do something for her."

"OK," he agreed a moment later when Baby started to hack again, "we'd better get her some cough medicine." He didn't want anything happening to the baby before the payoff.

"She needs a doctor, a pediatrician, dummy, not cough medicine!"

"Hey, who are you calling a dummy, huh?"

"Myself. That's who. I must be to have ever gotten into a mess like this with you."

"Christ Almighty, will you stop harping on the same thing!"

"Harping?" she mimicked. "Listen, I'm the one they can finger. Not you. *Me*!"

"Well, you're in it. And while I'm trying to pull off a three-million-dollar deal for us, all you do is get bent out of shape on piddling little shit. It's too cold in here. It's too drafty. The kid needs baby food. The kid has a cold. The kid needs a doctor. I'm not running a fucking nursery here," he fumed.

"I think," he continued, calming himself, "that you've been listening too much to that baby's singing. It's going to your head."

"What do you know, anyhow?"

"That if this keeps up I'm going to have to go out and buy you a set of those lips to hang around your neck or stick in your twat or whatever."

"You really are disgusting!"

"Let me put this very straight to you, Fay dearest"— he spoke through gritted teeth—"I don't want you holding the kid anymore. I don't want you listening to her or talking to her or touching her."

"I'll do whatever the hell I feel like!"

"You do and you'll end up *really* wishing you had never gotten into this. Do I make myself perfectly clear?"

Shuffling northward along Fifth Avenue as it skirted the eastern rim of Central Park, Doris was struck by how much more peaceful and habitable this part of the city seemed. The tall, ornate buildings across the street were clean and orderly with their sidewalks neatly shoveled and a doorman in every entrance. On her side was the stone wall bordering the park and beyond it the small, undulating hills and sturdy, ice-encrusted trees that brought to mind the serenity of Ithaca. Though it was still noisy, the sleaziness and detritus of the terminal area had yielded to civilization as she thought of it, and slowly, as though a veil were being lifted, her mind began to clear.

Spotting in the distance a line of deserted benches, Doris pushed ahead, and when she reached the first bench, she brushed a spot free of snow and sat down on the hard wooden slats. Reaching into her bag, she extracted the remains of the sandwich the man on the bus had given her, and biting into the bread, she chewed slowly, trying to formulate a plan. Faced with the enormousness of this city, she understood that there was no earthly way she could attack the problem of finding Baby. It was hopeless, she told herself. She didn't even know where to start. Yet, since arriving in the city, she realized that she had been steadily moving in the

same direction, driven by some strange whim. Logic—
that old common sense of the librarian that craved
ordered thoughts like neatly arranged books—warned
Doris that she was just wasting her breath. Her instincts, however, kept gnawing restlessly, prodding her
to get back on her feet and stop wasting precious
time. But what instincts? she wondered. It was absurd
wandering aimlessly through the endless canyons of this
city looking for Baby. Downright ridiculous. As ridiculous as it had been for her to have gotten pregnant, carried a child, been given an infant who could sing. If she
were to worry about a logical explanation for what she
was doing now, she thought, swallowing her last bite of
sandwich, why then she'd have to go back and explain—

Doris suddenly stopped and looked up.

Above the noise of the city she thought she heard
something calling to her. She strained to hear it again,
tilting her head from side to side, but it was gone.

With a grunt she rose from the bench and looked
around. Then suddenly she heard it again. It was Baby's
voice. Faint, faint, faint. A few feeble notes. Then it
stopped.

Doris cocked her head to one side and waited. Yes,
she thought excitedly when it came back again, a short
string, barely audible. It was Baby singing, calling out
to her, the child's voice raspy and weak. And it was
coming from the distance ahead, she thought, hurrying
forward as the faint sound disappeared, lost in the jumble of city noises.

"Am I losing my mind?" she asked herself later, continuing to plod up the endless avenue. "Was it real or
just in my head?" she fretted, inching wearily ahead as
the day slowly began to wane.

"Baby, where are you?" she mumbled to herself exhaustedly, leaving the park behind her and moving through the darkening streets of Harlem, loitering men on the streets watching her through the corners of sleepy-lidded eyes, giving no more than a desultory glance to the old, broken-down shell of a white lady, a nonperson moving through their territory, a shopping-bag lady muttering to herself, drifting up along Lenox Avenue toward the Harlem River.

When Sloan saw the headlines splashed on the front page of the evening *New York Post*, he was delighted.

"Look at this!" he piped, holding up the paper for Fay, trying to shake her out of the doldrums, hoping against hope that he could still win her over and unknot their entangled situation.

"Look at this." He waved the paper in front of her eyes as she sat by the heater holding Baby pressed against her body, her coat enclosing the two of them like a cocoon. Baby's parted lips were dry and cracked, her nose running, and that telltale gurgling in her chest had gotten worse. "Look!" he said, and Fay shifted her glance just enough to catch the headline.

PUERTO RICAN TERRORISTS BEHIND
$3M BABY SNATCH

When she failed to react, he approached her cautiously.

"Don't you see? I really pulled it off."

"You're going to get an Academy Award," she said woodenly.

"Fay. Please," he began, nuzzling her ear, "let's be friends, huh?"

Her head hanging limply out of the front of Fay's coat, Baby opened her feverish eyes and rolled them languidly up toward Sloan.

"Whew!" he gasped, pulling away abruptly as a putrid odor hit his nose. "What is it that stinks like that?"

"She's got diarrhea. What do you think it is? She's dying, don't you understand? Dying! This little tiny kid is dying, and you're coming up here kissing me and trying to make nice as if nothing's wrong."

"I was just—" he began, and then stopped.

"Just what? Don't you have *any* human decency at all?"

"Aw, shit," he mumbled disgustedly and, flopping down on his mattress, opened the paper and began to read.

By the time Doris crossed the bridge into the Bronx, she had heard Baby's voice twice more. Each time the faint, short burst of notes seemed slightly closer, more urgent—reaching her at a point just as her strength began to flag. It was dark now as she reached the end of the bridge and, ahead, the traffic was light, the snow faintly cleaner, the sounds of the city falling upon her ears muted and subdued. By now, Doris reckoned to herself, people were already in their homes eagerly preparing for tomorrow's holiday. She thought about friends and families together. Mothers with their children. And she envied them.

A sharp wind gusted down the river, lifting the flaps of her coat. Shivering, she tightened her scarf and looked out. From her vantage at the end of the bridge, she could see the vast desolate miles of tenements stretching awesomely before her, and once again her determination began to wilt.

Which way now, she sighed, wondering how much more she could press on. She felt herself inexplicably drawn ahead to the left but resisted the insistent pull. She strained her ears to hear above the wind that howled through the frame structure of the bridge, but try as she might she could not discern Baby's voice.

"Baby," she called out hoarsely into the night. "Baby, Baby." She strained her ears, moving her head from side to side, but could hear only the rumble of a train, the dull throb of a distant jet.

"Baby, darling. Where are you?" she called out again. Still nothing, just that ineffable tug to the left.

"Oh, Lord." She turned her face up to the sky, afraid to trust her own feelings. "Please guide me," she prayed, continuing to gaze into the low sky, milky from the reflected lights of the city. "Give me some sign," she begged, and suddenly, as she uttered those words, Doris saw a break in the low clouds, saw the deep chasm that magically appeared leading out into space, saw the distant but bright, starlike light that moved slowly but unwaveringly across that gap, traveling across the heavens and following the identical path that her instincts had all along been urging. And then she knew, recognized that the song she had heard, the message that was in her soul had been real all along. Gaining heart, the hint of a smile forming on her frozen face, she picked up her bag and hurried off to the left, following the guiding light that was the night flight to Montreal.

The South Bronx was crawling with cops—city police drawn from precincts in all five boroughs, detectives from the state Bureau of Criminal Investigation pulled off other less-prominent cases, Feds flown in from offices all across the East. From Bruckner Boulevard in the east to the Major Deegan Expressway in the west, from the Triborough Bridge at the southern tip of the Bronx to a line running east-west through Fordham

Road, the place was thick with police of every description. There were cops in cruisers, cops in unmarked units, cops in disguises, cops in uniform, cops hanging around the South Bronx precinct house just waiting to be dispatched at a moment's notice.

"Not a living thing is going to move on those streets without our knowing about it," said Inspector Albert Heath to Special Agent Nisbet. Heath, a ranking fifteen-year veteran who headed the Philadelphia field office and was considered a specialist in kidnappings, had been brought in to coordinate the search for Baby. With public attention focused on what was being called the case of the decade, law enforcement agencies knew they had their reputations on the line and they weren't taking any chances. There were now close to one hundred and forty cops either directly or indirectly working to crack the case.

When Shockley saw the *Post* story, he immediately called Nisbet.

"Have you seen the paper?"

"I heard."

"What the hell kind of shoddy operation are you people running there, anyway?"

"Who says the leak came from this end?"

"No. It came from me!"

"That's a distinct possibility."

"Nisbet, are you accusing me?"

"No. I just said it's a possibility."

"Stop playing games with me. You know I didn't talk to anyone. The leak came from your end. And if that's the slipshod way you people are going to run this investigation, then we're never going to get her back!" he fumed, slamming down the phone with a crash.

Later, when his anger had dissipated, Shockley went back to the paper and carefully read through the articles, combing the long piece on the coordinated police search, the background on the terrorist group, even the article on the upcoming Christmas telethon. Nowhere, absolutely nowhere was there mention of the South Bronx. Then he understood: The business about the terrorists had all been pure, unadulterated bullshit. They were trying to flush out the kidnappers by lulling them into a false sense of security. Which meant they had been stringing him along as well. They had nothing, not one lousy lead to Baby except that she was somewhere in the Bronx. Maybe.

Led by her impulses, Doris had now been walking in the South Bronx for almost two hours. Cutting through back lots and over mountains of rubble, she made her way through the maze of burned-out brick shells, pressing forward in an inward-spiraling loop. Dizzy with hunger, numb with cold, her head thrust resolutely forward, Doris drove herself on. She was closing in and Baby was near, she sensed, tightening again the helix that now enclosed little more than three blocks at its widest point. At that moment Doris was so near, in fact, that had Baby's kidnappers looked out their side window they might have caught a glimpse of her as she shambled along a cross street at the far end of the block. The pair, however, had momentarily let their vigil lapse, for as Doris was steadily homing in on their hideout, Sloan was lying sprawled on his back on his mattress, snoring deeply, while Fay, holding Baby, sat dozing in her chair by the kerosene heater.

Doris's progress through this torched-out section of the city, however, was not going entirely unnoticed. Two patrolmen in an unmarked cruiser had spotted her early on, wedging her way through a hole in the mesh of a high cyclone fence. For a minute they had sat in their darkened car observing her as she picked her way through the garbage-strewn lot. Their radio had squawked, they had exchanged knowing glances, and then moved on.

Doris had been spotted twice after that. Once by another patrol car. And once by a city cop by the name of Len Alicki. Alicki, who was disguised as an aging and disheveled hippie, had been sitting on the front stoop of an abandoned building apparently catching a few drug-induced winks when Doris had come plodding by. Out of the corner of his eye he had watched as the old lady had stumbled past, weeping and jabbering to herself. Alicki, a hardened, street-wise cop, who had worked some of the toughest precincts in the city, had seen people like Doris and worse, much worse. Yet, watching her, he had been inexplicably pricked by a sense of pity. Here was this poor, old, shopping-bag lady on a dismal Christmas Eve with no place to go but the war-torn streets of the Bronx. It was a downright shame, he had thought, stung by reminiscences of his own mother, who had died almost five years ago after a long and debilitating senility. Doris had then disappeared around a corner, and Alicki had conveniently forgotten her, returning to his surveillance of the near-empty, snowy streets.

A scant minute before ten, plainclothesman Alicki pulled up his sleeve and, checking his watch, saw that it was finally time to end his shift. Rising off the cold concrete steps, he stretched himself, yawned, and began walking the six blocks to the rendezvous point where he was to be picked up for the night. He had already gone a few blocks when he spotted Doris for the second time. She was on the opposite side of the street, shuffling ahead as she wound in on her final loop, now but a few

doors away from the entrance to the building where
Baby was being held. Striding on toward the point
where he was to meet with the pickup, Alicki continued on down the street, passing an unmarked unit that
stood parked in the shadows. Exchanging a brief nod
with the men who sat in the car taking a smoke, he went
on a few more steps, came to a full stop and, suddenly
turning around on his heels, marched back down the
street. He knew that what he was doing was utterly
meaningless, but something in his head warned Alicki
that if he didn't go back to the old lady tonight, tomorrow would be a miserable Christmas—that thoughts of
the old woman would plague him all through the night
and the next day. A soft touch, he told himself as he
saw Doris come to a stop at the doorway of the abandoned tenement in front of him, that's what he was, just
an old, soft touch.

Checking his watch, Alicki picked up his pace. He
was already late for his rendezvous, and he knew the
men in his team would be getting itchy.

"Excuse me, lady," he called out, approaching
Doris from the rear.

Doris slowly turned her hunched back and looked up
at him.

"Where're you going?" asked this strange man
dressed in fringes and beads, his face covered with hair.

Doris looked at him in confusion.

"Can I help you?" he asked, as Doris stared at him
in continued bewilderment. "Are you lost? Are you
looking for someone?"

"Baby," she finally mumbled through her cracked
lips. "I'm looking for Baby," she said, exhausted, glad
for any offer of help.

"Which baby?"

"My Baby," explained Doris, wiping her runny nose with the back of her hand. "My Baby," she repeated. "The one who sings," she added for clarity.

"Oh," said Alicki, taking a second look at Doris. Though she certainly didn't seem prosperous—wisps of ice-encrusted hair stood out from under her frayed scarf, her coat looked old and worn, her body broken and decrepit—Alicki couldn't help but note the glimmer of intelligence in her face. And her speech, though halting and weak, seemed clear and educated. She was not a shopping-bag lady, he now realized, and that was what had bothered him from the first. She was just a poor, old woman, one of those nutso Babyists. Probably someone's gaga mother. But what the hell was she doing out here?

"Please, help me," she said imploringly, feeling her last vestiges of strength dwindling. "I'm close, so close."

Alicki stared at her, debating what to do. He certainly couldn't leave her around here, prey to every lousy mugger and thug. He scratched his head and tugged at his frozen beard as Doris looked up at him with her rheumy eyes. Then, reaching into his back pocket, he extracted a walkie-talkie.

In less than a minute a dark car screeched up to the curb. Seated in it were three men dressed as hoboes and derelicts.

"Come on, get in, lady," he gently urged her, taking Doris by the arm.

"No," said Doris, resisting. "I have to—" she tried to shake free his hand.

"It's OK. We're police officers," he said, flashing his badge. "We're going to help you," he tried to soothe her.

"What's this, Alicki?" complained the man in the

front seat, wearing a torn stocking cap. "We're supposed to go off duty now."

"Come on, Len. It's Christmas Eve. Give us a break," whined the other.

"We're going to find you a warm place," said Alicki to the old woman, ignoring the complaints.

"No. I can't leave. Not now! Please. Baby. She's here. I know she's here!" Doris struggled, feeling Officer Alicki's powerful hand tightening on her arm as she tried to wrestle free.

"We'll get you a good, warm Christmas meal and you can have a nice, clean—"

"Please. No. Don't! I have to—" Doris struggled with her last bit of strength.

"Come on now, lady. No one's going to hurt you."

"Oh, please." She struggled, feeling herself weaken. "Please don't take me away," she pleaded, crumbling into an exhausted heap into the man's arms.

"Chrisake, leave her!" said the cop at the wheel disgustedly, as Alicki lifted Doris into the car.

"I'll lose her! I'll lose her!" Doris objected as she felt herself being hoisted into the rear seat. "My Baby, my Baby," she sobbed, turning and looking out the back window as the car drove off with her. "She's here. I know it!"

"Those lights," said Jacobsen, dispatching one of his assistants as he stared through a monitor into the darkness of the theater. "They flare in camera two. Tell those guys they should either turn or kill them. Rolf"—he motioned for Pettersson who stood watching a line of shapely dancers going through a dry run of their routine, their choreographer snapping his fingers and counting out the beat—"who told them to put those phones there? They should be more toward center stage. Where they've got them now they're almost off into the wings," he said, referring to the technicians who had started wiring in the lines in the late evening and would probably have to work through most of the night to meet the 9:00 A.M. start of the telethon.

"I told them to put them there," injected Father Tom, coming up the aisle from the stage. "If you place the phone bank more toward the middle it'll block half the stage for the audience on that side."

"Yes, that's true," said Jacobsen as if it hadn't occurred to him. "But don't you think it would be better if the phones were always on camera?" He smiled patronizingly. He was feeling too good to argue. The show was coming together beautifully like a flower ready to bloom at the optimum moment, the telethon airing on Christmas morning just as gifts were being unwrapped

and people's hearts were most open to giving. Why mar
it with petty bickering?

"Well," Fitzgibbons deferred, "I'm hardly an expert
when it comes to putting on shows."

"True"—Jacobsen smiled, putting his arm around
Fitzgibbons—"leave it to me. I know what the priorities
are. Just keep everybody happy as you've been doing
and you'll be doing more than your share. Your contribution so far has been nothing short of spectacular."

Fitzgibbons smiled uneasily and slipped away from
Jacobsen's arm.

"Rolf, my boy" said Jacobsen later, still in an effu-
sive mood. "You're watching television history being
made."

"Yes, sir," Pettersson grinned.

"They're going to be talking about this program for
years to come. That you can count on."

Shortly thereafter, just when Jacobsen was sure the
program was in the bag, the telethon was hit by a seemingly endless barrage of calamities.

Just after eleven there was a mysterious power failure that confounded the theater crew. After forty minutes of struggling around in the darkness and trying to
unsnarl the confusion of circuitry, a young man,
proudly claiming to be a CURBist, was discovered hiding
in the theater. He had been flipping power switches in
an effort to disrupt the program. The man was arrested,
security immediately tightened, and no one was allowed
to enter or leave the premises without passing through a
phalanx of armed guards.

Soon thereafter, a man claiming to be an official
from the union representing the telephone technicians
installing the phone bank appeared on stage and announced that, according to a contract negotiated with
the phone company last fall, his men were strictly pro-

hibited from working after midnight. Anxiously, Jacobsen pulled the man aside and tried to reason with him. Weren't there exceptions to the rule? Yes, said the man. In cases of national emergency. Well, this was a national emergency! The man laughed away the notion. Jacobsen offered a cash bonus to the men on top of their double time if they continued to work. The man said he would take the suggestion under consideration and turned to leave. Jacobsen slipped something into the man's pocket. Yes, said the man stopping for an instant, maybe this telethon did, in fact, come under that emergency provision. He would ask his men to stay on the job.

"I'm sorry to call you at this hour," said Harry Terkel, sounding half asleep himself.

"What's the matter?" asked Olive groggily. She yawned, flipped on the light, and, squinting at the clock, saw that it was just about three.

"I just got a call about Mrs. Rumsey," he explained.

"Doris?" exclaimed Olive, trying to clear her head. "Where is that woman? I've been trying to get ahold of her. I went out to the trailer today, but the place was locked and her cat's gone." Olive suddenly stopped short. "Is she all right?"

"She's in New York City," said Terkel tersely. "Bellevue."

"Oh, Lord." Olive sat up in her bed alert. "You don't mean that poor soul went to the city to—"

"She was picked up somewhere wandering the streets in a state of confusion. They asked her for the name of a family member," Terkel explained, a little embarrassed, "and she apparently gave them my name and number." He paused and waited.

"What're we going to do?" asked Olive.

"We ought to get her out of there. As fast as possible."

"You want me to go down and get her?"

"I was hoping you'd say that," said Terkel, noticeably relieved. "They'd be willing to release her in your custody. All you have to do is sign for her."

"Why, of course," said Olive, preparing herself mentally for the trip.

"And Mrs. Eldridge?"

"Yes?"

"This thing. It could really hurt her custody fight."

"But—"

"I'm looking ahead, Mrs. Eldridge. So, for her sake, please don't mention this incident to anybody."

"Don't you worry none about that," said Olive, reaching for her robe. "My lips are sealed."

Fay awoke with a sudden start in the midst of a nightmare. Seated by the kerosene heater, she had been sleeping with Baby tucked under her coat. Dazed, she looked around the room trying to place herself. Though it was after daybreak, the apartment was still dark, only faint swatches of gray outside light seeping in through the plastic-covered windows. Immediately she realized something was terribly wrong. She looked down. In her lap lay Baby writhing convulsively, the child gasping for breath.

"Oh, God!" She sprang to her feet, holding the jerking child in her arms. "She's choking!" she wailed, seeing Baby's face turn blue, the child struggling for air, her arms and legs thrashing out wildly. Gripped by panic, Fay dashed with Baby to the front door of the apartment.

Sloan was already scrambling to his feet as Fay stood fumbling with the door lock.

"Stop!" he barked, shoving her roughly aside and blocking her exit.

"Sloan"—she wept hysterically—"she's dying! Let me out! Let me OUT!" she cried as his fist came flying across her face, knocking her to the ground with Baby. "Sloan. Oh, Sloan!" she pleaded, getting up on her knees and grabbing onto his leg. "Please let us out. You can still get away. I'd never tell. I swear. Please. Please!" she begged, the shadow looming above her.

Sloan kicked his leg free.

"Look," she said, holding Baby out to him, the child's pitiful body torn by convulsions as she frantically fought for each gulpful of air. "Don't you have an ounce of humanity in you?" she beseeched as he remained planted squarely in front of the door, staring tight-lipped out into the darkness, refusing to look down at the dying infant.

Seeing him standing hard and silent, immovable as stone, Fay leaped to her feet and charged to the kitchen. Laying the gasping child on the icy floor, she tried to pry open the window, and when it wouldn't budge, she picked up a chair and swung it with all her might. The glass and frame exploded into the alley in a shower of fragments that tinkled down the metal steps of the fire escape. As she bent down to take Baby, Sloan was already behind her, grabbing a fistful of hair and yanking her violently away from the shattered window.

"You bastard," she hissed, reaching out and swinging wildly at him as he held his grip. "You miserable bastard!" she snarled, lashing out in a last frenzy, catching his face with her nails and ruthlessly ripping his flesh.

"Augh!" he cried out and flung her by her hair against the wall.

Moaning, the wind knocked out of her, Fay raised

herself weakly on one arm. She looked at Baby, who lay sprawled next to her. The child now lay flaccid and barely conscious, her breath little more than a feeble, gurgling rattle. Fay stared back up at Sloan, who stood glaring down at her, clutching his torn face as he waited for her next move. She could feel the warm blood that coursed from her nose and into her mouth and seeing Sloan standing there, personifying all that was cruel and mean in life, she became an animal herself, cornered and enraged, ready to fight to the death. Slowly she raised her bruised body, sliding upward against the wall, her head throbbing, her eyes widened in rage, her bloodied mouth open and panting. With her eyes locked on Sloan as he stood ready for her, his feet spread, his fists clenched, she searched for an opening, a point of weakness, a momentary lapse. Seeing the murder in her eyes, Sloan backed up a foot and stood poised for her next assault as she circled to one side, her hands up, nails extended. Her eyes darted about the room. The vague form of an iron skillet that stood on the counter suddenly caught her attention. Still fixing Sloan with her eyes, Fay continued to circle to her right, moving steadily inch by inch toward the counter, frantically hoping she could reach the pan before he lunged for her. When she was but an arm's length away, Baby suddenly let out a loud, gasping, barklike sound. Sloan looked for an instant at the child, and in that fleeting second, Fay, in a single, coiled movement, leaped for the pan, grabbed its handle, and let it fly with all her strength.

Coming out of the dimness, the skillet caught Sloan unawares, the heavy iron slamming into the bone between his eyes in a searing white flash of pain. Crying out, he stumbled drunkenly backward, his hands going up to his eyes. In that split second Fay had Baby in her arms and, in one jump, had broken through the shattered remains of the window.

By the time Sloan realized what had happened, Fay was already out on the fire escape, clattering furiously down the stairs. Sloan flung himself through the opening, feeling the jagged edges of glass slicing into him, warm blood spurting out against his skin. Grasping the rusty railings of the fire escape, he clambered down the steps.

"Help! Help!" Fay screamed desperately, her voice shrill and breaking. "Help! Someone! The baby's dying! Help!" she cried, holding the infant under one arm as she bolted down the metal stairs, tripping and recovering her hold and seeing Sloan narrowing the gap between them. "Oh, dear Lord. Someone! Help us!" she wailed in the raw deserted dawn, her voice echoing hollowly in the narrow alley between the buildings.

Scampering down past the landing, Fay suddenly found herself dangling in the air, futiley searching for the missing rungs, the final extension that should have bridged the last twenty feet to the littered alley below. She saw Sloan closing in, his face twisted in hatred, rivulets of blood streaming down his eyes and cheeks. Fay looked back down into the darkness of the narrow alley, trying to estimate the long drop. In another second he would be within arm's length. She stared down into the dimness, pressed Baby tight against her body and, bending her legs, leaped out blindly.

Fay felt herself flying through the cold air, saw that elusive ground suddenly appear and move up at her, then felt the shock of impact reverberate through her bones as she hit the concrete, her feet crumbling under her in a bone-crunching jolt. Moaning in stunned pain, she looked up and saw Sloan dangling by his hands

from the last rungs, ready to leap after her, the bones of
her legs jutting out through her torn flesh. Desperately,
still holding Baby, she began to crawl, pulling with her
free arm and dragging her shattered legs behind her.
Reaching the end of the alley and nearly the front sidewalk, she heard Sloan land behind her with a loud
grunt.

"Please! Dear God, help me!" she called out, hoping to reach the empty street. "Help!" she cried as
Sloan stumbled to his feet and began to hobble toward
her. "Someone! Baby's dying!" she called out with her
last breath, fainting as the pain became unbearable.

The harsh bell jarred Shockley out of sleep. Stum-
bling to the phone, he picked up the receiver to the hot
line. A dial tone hummed in his ear while the other
phone continued to ring. He put down the first receiver
and picked up the second.

"We found her," said Agent Nisbet without preliminaries.

"Baby?" he asked in disbelief.

"Yes," answered Nisbet in a subdued voice.

"Thank God!" he said and then stopped short.
"What's the matter?" he asked, picking up the agent's
tone.

"She's not—not in good shape."

"She's dead!" Shockley exclaimed.

"No. No," Nisbet answered quickly. "Look, let's not
waste time. Can you be ready in a couple of minutes?"

"I've just got to throw on some clothes," said Shockley, rushing his words.

"Good. We'll pick you up at your hotel. The car'll be
waiting in front."

Shockley hung up, pulled a pair of pants over his pa-

jamas, and put on a shirt that was lying on a nearby
chair. He yanked on a pair of socks and shoes and,
grabbing his coat, bolted for the elevator.

"Come on. Come on. Come on," he fretted, repeatedly pressing the down button and watching the indica-
tor, which seemed to move with deliberate slowness. Finally the elevator arrived and Shockley rode down in
shaky silence, his hands nervously clenched at his side.

Idling in front of the main entrance to the hotel was
a late-model dark sedan with a short, telltale antenna
sticking up in front of the trunk. As he raced down the
stairs, the front door to the car swung open. Shockley
jumped in.

"You Nisbet?" he asked the youngish, dark-haired
agent as the car peeled away, its siren going.

"I'm Special Agent Howard," said the man with the
long nose and square-cut jaw.

"How's Baby?" he asked anxiously as they whizzed
eastward, flying through chains of red lights.

"I don't know. I really don't. I'd tell you if I did. I
just got a call to pick you up."

"Where are we headed?" he asked as they reached
the East Side Highway and Howard took the northbound
entrance.

"The Bronx. Bronx Hospital."

"Oh, God," uttered Shockley, his hands locked together, blocking out the gruesome images served up by
his fantasy. Sitting stonily in the car, he looked out at
the river as they raced up the near-empty highway. A
lonely tug was making its way down the ice-choked
river and he concentrated on it until it fell out of view.
Baby was alive, he told himself, hanging on to that ten-
uous thread, and that was the important thing. Overhead, the sky, which had been gray since daybreak,
turned ominously black.

"We're in for another one," said Howard, trying to ease Shockley's wait.

"Huh?"

"Snowstorm. Some pisser of a winter we're having, isn't it?"

Shockley nodded.

"What time is it?" he asked, breaking the silence a little later.

"Eight"—Howard glanced at his watch as he zig-zagged through a jumble of cars blocking both lanes—"eight fifty-seven. Hang on. We'll be there in no time."

"I appreciate your calling me," said Jacobsen.

"I only wish it had been better news," said Nisbet.

"Have your people made an announcement?" he asked, staring nervously up at the clock in the busy control room. There were scant minutes before the telethon was scheduled to start in the eastern- and central-time zones, and they were already on a countdown, the network affiliates waiting to be fed. The audience was seated and the orchestra was playing, warming them up.

"Not yet," answered Nisbet. "We want to make sure we've nabbed everyone involved. We want to hold a little longer."

"Of course. I understand," said Jacobsen, striving to sound cooperative. "Will you let me know *before* you announce it?"

"I'm not announcing anything. I'm going home to sleep. That isn't my department, anyhow."

"Then whose is it?"

"Press-liaison people."

"Can you give me a name?"

"This way," said the uniformed city cop, taking a sharp turn in the corridor as they raced through hospital halls, the pungent odor of disinfectant and drugs and sickness assaulting Shockley's nostrils.

At the far end of the hall another cop standing guard in front of a door looked up as the pair hurried toward him. A nod from the officer accompanying Shockley and he quickly opened the door and moved aside.

Shockley stepped into the room and heard the door close behind him. In the room he saw two men in white and a nurse standing around the large crib at the far side of the room. His heart thudding, Shockley looked past them, past the tangle of drip bottles and wires and monitors.

"Baby!" he whispered in anguish, spotting the little figure that lay inertly encased in a plastic tent. "Oh my God, my God, what did they do to you!" he gasped, biting his lip as tears rushed in to cloud his vision. Approaching Baby's crib he saw Baby's bluish-white body pressed cold and lifeless against the crisp sheets, her eyes sealed, her face slack. Sinking down to his knees, bitter tears searing his cheeks, he slid his hand under the tent, reaching in until he finally made contact with Baby's tiny hand. Taking her fine fingers in his, he was almost shocked to find that they were not icy, but hot, burning hot.

"I'm Dr. Martinez," said the first man, gently trying for Shockley's attention. He was brown-skinned and short and had an accent faintly reminiscent of the kidnapper's. "I'm the chief pediatric resident," he added.

Shockley stared up at him in a daze.

"We're doing all we can," the doctor said in a subdued voice. "But she's very sick."

"She's got severe pneumonia. She has had a very high fever—we don't know for how long. She's dehydrated," added the second man.

"She's been in a coma ever since she was admitted," continued Martinez, Shockley's eyes moving from one doctor to the other.

"We've got her on ampicillin, and we're trying to replace her lost fluids," said Martinez, and Shockley's eyes drifted up to the bottles and then traced the lines that ended in large needles that were taped into Baby's frail arms. He brought his head close to Baby, pressing it against the cold plastic, and stared at her. There were beads of perspiration on her face, her angel locks damp and plastered against her head. Her chest was rapidly rising and falling as though she were a wounded animal panting its last breaths. Then he heard a strange gurgling that sounded as though air were being bubbled through water. At first he thought it was a respirator or one of the machines. Then, in horror, he realized it was Baby herself, fighting for air, her lungs filling with liquid.

"We did one aspiration already, when she first came in," said the doctor as though reading his mind. "But her chest has filled up again," continued the man, who also had an accent.

Shockley looked from one man to the other, looked

searchingly at the nurse. The woman tried to give him an encouraging smile. Shockley swallowed. Wiping his eyes he tried to clear his head. He began to formulate the question that was on the tip of his tongue, but he was afraid to ask, fearing that posing it would be giving substance to his deepest dread. He stared fixedly at Baby's face, trying to match it to the little girl who had, only days earlier, cooed and sung for him, but those images refused to converge. She had moved away, he feared, her fragile body dangling over the edge of that eternal abyss.

"Will she make it?" he finally asked, the words needing to be forced out of him.

"I honestly don't know," answered Martinez. "We're doing all we can," he explained softly. "It's in God's hands," he commiserated, nodding his head sadly.

Within the next hour Baby's condition became even more acute.

"I don't like the sound of her heart," said Martinez.

"What do you mean?" asked Shockley, trying to tie him down.

"There's a frictional rub synchronous with her heartbeat," he said, as his colleague, after listening to Baby with a stethoscope, looked up and nodded.

"I don't understand," said Shockley.

What Martinez meant was that Baby's pneumonia looked as if it were becoming complicated by an acute bacterial endocarditis. There was an ominous sound in Baby's heart, and the doctors suspected that the infection had turned metastatic and was now attacking the child's aortic valve.

"If this endocarditis goes any farther," explained Martinez yet later, looking plainly worried, "there's a real danger that a rupture or perforation of the cusps might occur, or even a rupture of the aorta itself. We're going to have to monitor this *very* carefully."

Shockley looked at him blankly.

"What I'm saying is that we may have to consider surgical repair."

"Oh," said Shockley, his stomach twisting.

"Would you mind," he asked Martinez a few minutes later as Baby was wheeled in her tent together with her i.v. bottles down to the X-ray room, her police guards following on either side, "if we brought in some other specialists?" Shockley was only going through the formality. He had just made up his mind to get a second opinion.

"No. Not at all. In fact"—Martinez smiled, almost relieved—"I was going to suggest that myself."

Shockley wasn't quite sure how to go about getting a specialist in the city, but he knew that Baby required the best that money could buy. The logical person to call was Jacobsen, who seemed to know everybody.

"Yes. I just heard about Baby," said Jacobsen, shielding the receiver to blot out the music in the background. "How is she?" he inquired hastily.

"It looks bad," answered Shockley dully.

"Is there anything I can do?"

"Yes. That's why I called."

Shockley then quickly told him about Baby's condition, about the complications, about the need for specialists. For a good pediatrician. A good cardiologist.

"Consider it done," said Jacobsen.

"I've got to run," said Shockley, seeing Baby's bed being wheeled back toward the elevator.

"Keep me posted, Shockley. I'll try to get over to the hospital later."

"Is Father Tom there?" Shockley asked.

"Let me see," said Jacobsen, looking straight at Fitz-gibbons, who stood no more than a few yards away from him in front of the control room. "No. No, I don't see him. He was around earlier but—"

"As soon as you can find him, please tell him what's happened," said Shockley, his voice breaking.

"Certainly."

"Thanks," said Shockley weakly and started to hang up.

"Shockley," Jacobsen caught him in the last second.

"Huh?"

"The police don't want any announcements made about Baby's return until they're sure they've rounded up everyone involved. Please, don't break the news to the press. There'll be a joint release at the appropriate time."

"Sure," agreed Shockley. The last thing in the world he wanted to do at this point was talk to reporters.

Around eleven o'clock Shockley got a call, which he took at the nurses' station down the hall from Baby's room.

"How's it going?" asked Nisbet. The agent was calling from his home in Queens. He was getting ready to hit the sack and just couldn't go to sleep without first checking with Shockley.

"Not so good. They had her on penicillin, but she's not responding. They suspect the infection might be penicillin resistant. They're trying another antibiotic now. She's got heart trouble too."

"It's a bitch," commiserated Agent Nisbet, who had children of his own. "If it's any consolation—" he began.

"The kidnappers?"

"Yeah. I thought you'd want to know."

"Yes."

"It looks like it was a couple. A boyfriend and a girlfriend team. Just two. No one else. The woman's confessed. They weren't Babyists or CURBists or anything. Just your average greedy people. The woman's in surgery right now. She fractured both her legs trying to escape with Baby from her boyfriend. She's in pretty tough shape."

"And the man?" he asked, picking up the cue.

"One of the city stakeouts pulled up just as she was crawling to the street after jumping from the second story. Her boyfriend was right behind her. When they told him to freeze, he reached into his pocket. That's what they say, anyway. They shot him. One shot. Through the head."

Silence.

"They didn't find a gun," Nisbet added uneasily, filling the void. "Look, if there's some way I can help, just give me a call," he said and gave Shockley his home number.

"I appreciate that. I really do," said Shockley, scribbling down Nisbet's number and stuffing the slip of paper into his pocket.

Replacing the receiver, Shockley remained standing in the glass-enclosed cubicle that was the nurses' station. A nurse stepped in, reached past him to take a clipboard off a hook, and left. He watched her move down the corridor, then looked up at the clock and followed the second hand as it swept across the large face. Somewhere in the back of his mind a thought was stirring. He was thinking about Baby. About Doris. About the connection between the two of them. He knew he was probably grasping at straws, but—but—He recalled the time Baby had fallen despondent and stopped singing. Now that he thought about it, it had coincided with Doris's confinement to Willard. He wasn't positive, but it seemed that Baby had started to sing again just about the time Doris had been released.

Shockley's pulse began to quicken as he dug further back into the recesses of his memory. He then remembered the onset of Baby's elegiac song, that longing, mournful melody that began just about the time Doris had become deathly ill. And then, of course—Then there was that gruesome day that Baby had almost drowned. Looking out during the television interview, he had seen a hunched-over, snow-clad figure moving fleetingly past his window. It could only have been one person, he now realized, and the odds in his mind were now stacked against sheer coincidence. Doris had come because she knew Baby was in trouble. She had known about Baby, just as Baby had always known about her. Suddenly a multitude of small, seemingly meaningless and disconnected occurrences all jelled. As utterly absurd as it was, as much as it defied all experience, now in this moment of desperation it made perfect sense.

Shockley fumbled through his pockets for Nisbet's number. He grabbed the phone and punched out the numerals, waiting impatiently as the call wended its way sluggishly through the system. The phone on the other end began to ring. Someone picked up the line and without waiting Shockley hurriedly asked, "Nisbet?"

"Yeah," said the agent, sounding a bit startled.

"Can I take you up on that offer? Of a favor?"

"Sure."

"Baby's real mother. Doris Rumsey."

"Yeah. The lady who tried to call."

"Right."

"You want me to try and locate her?" he asked, anticipating Shockley's request.

"More than that. I want you to find her and get her here to the hospital. Quick."

"It may not be that easy. This is a big city."

"Nisbet. It's important. Urgent."

"I understand," said Nisbet.

"No, you don't. Not really," said Shockley, guessing what the cop was thinking. "I know this is going to sound nuts, but, Nisbet, I've got this feeling in my bones that she's the only one now who can really save the child."

"Shockley," said Nisbet, trying to pull him back to earth.

"Look, there isn't time for me to go into the details. You offered me a favor. I'm asking for it. Just tell me, will you do it or won't you?"

"OK," came Nisbet's slow reply. "OK."

"I know you're exhausted."

"I'm on my eighth wind." Nisbet tried to sound up.

"Thanks."

"Don't thank me yet. I haven't found her."

"Just thanks. And listen. I'm sorry about snapping at you earlier."

"You don't owe me an apology. I would have been pissed, too."

At 11:10 a team of three high-powered physicians converged on the Bronx Hospital. There was a specialist in pediatric medicine from Columbia-Presbyterian, a world-famous cardiologist who had pioneered new techniques in heart repair, and a specialist in internal medicine from the Cornell School of Medicine. Dr. Martinez and his aide stepped aside deferentially to let them take over. They reran all the tests that Martinez had performed, from sputum and spinal-fluid cultures to a complete blood and urine work-up to a fresh series of lung X rays. They listened to Baby's heart and ran an EKG. They ordered frequent alcohol rubdowns in the hope of dampening her stubborn fever. They slid long needles into her side, aspirated the thick, viscous fluid filling her chest, and instilled erythromycin—all just as their predecessor, Dr. Martinez, had done through the early morning. After they had finished, they gathered for a second huddle and then finally spoke with Shockley.

"She's got a severe pneumococcal infection that appears metastatic. There appears to be endocarditis," said the pediatric specialist from Columbia. He was an elderly man with deep furrows in his brow and a cold, professional manner that reminded Shockley of Krieger. When he spoke, he fixed Shockley with his unrelenting greenish blue eyes. "The bacteria seem to be penicillin resistant, and from the beginnings of Dr. Martinez's sensitivity study, it looks as if it might respond to erythromycin. We're going to run a second study to be sure. But we need time. Right now we're running blind."

"Will she live?" asked Shockley bluntly.

"I don't know," said the man without flinching. "Babies are not little adults. The outlook for children under a year in her condition, at least in my experience, is not good. I'd like to be more positive," he said, finally looking away, "but I don't want to raise false hopes."

"I see," murmured Shockley.

"If the new antibiotic works, you may see a remarkable turnaround," he said, trying to hold out a glimmer of hope.

"I see," repeated Shockley, lacking words. But what he saw was that money and high-powered physicians were not going to save Baby. The prognosis of these illustrious doctors was no more heartening than that of Dr. Martinez, and their treatment was merely a continuation of what the doctor had done already. Despite his lack of fancy credentials, Martinez was just as competent as they were and, Shockley was coming to understand, much more of a human being.

"What are we?" said Martinez, bringing Shockley a much-needed cup of hot coffee. Even though the other three doctors had taken charge, Martinez had stayed as if to console Shockley. "We're a bunch of technicians. That's all." He spoke with his hands, his eyes dark and alive. "We give bacteriostatic chemicals, antibiotics, but these drugs don't lick the infections. They merely hold them in check. It's the body itself that must ultimately eliminate the infection," he said, making a fist. "At times like this we become almost helpless, superfluous," he added with a sad nod.

"Do you think maybe she doesn't have the will to live?"

"Well, I—" began Martinez, taken aback by the question. "Why do you ask?"

"I was just wondering, that's all," Shockley answered vaguely, his eyes drifting back to the bed.

"She's just a baby. All babies want to live. It's built into them by creation."

"Are you religious?" Shockley asked Martinez, trying to pin down the doctor.

"I never heard her sing, if that's what you mean," he said with a smile, referring to Babyism.

"No. I meant in general." Shockley brought him back on track.

"Well"—Martinez laughed uneasily—"we're not supposed to be. Oh, nobody in med school ever said it right out. But it's something that's infused into your system by osmosis. Am I religious?" He raised his dark eyebrows and looked up at the tile ceiling. "No. Not in the conventional sense. But in my own way, I suppose—Yes. Yes, I am," said Martinez, gaining resolution as though he had not pondered the question in years. "I believe there is a God. Someone looking over us now, watching over this sick child." Martinez stopped and looked straight at Shockley. "Prayer certainly never hurt," he added as if reading Shockley's thoughts.

Nisbet called Shockley back at eleven-thirty.

"How's Baby looking?" he asked.

"No change. Did you locate Doris?"

"Yeah. She was picked up—now listen to this—of all places right in front of the building where the pair was holding Baby."

"When?" he asked tensely.

"Before. Almost *twelve hours* before we caught them."

"Then she knew!" he uttered.

"It's weird," said Nisbet, sounding baffled.

"But where's she now?"

"She was acting very disoriented and confused, so they took her to Bellevue for observation."

"She's there?"

"No. She was released a couple of hours ago. Some friend came to pick her up."

"Damn!" muttered Shockley.

"Well, that's how things stand. I thought you'd want to know."

"Please. Please, don't give up," he urged. "Keep looking for her."

"Have I given up so far? I can't give you any guarantees that I'll find her, but I'll stay on the phone and keep trying. That I promise."

"You're an angel," he said, and Nisbet laughed. "I mean it. An honest-to-goodness angel."

The hospital chaplain came by a few minutes later and offered to pray with Shockley for the health of the child. Shockley thanked him but declined.

Dr. Martinez dropped by after seeing to another case and suggested that Shockley take a few minutes off and come down to the cafeteria with him to have some breakfast. Shockley declined that offer too. He was waiting for Nisbet's call.

Finally, a couple of minutes later, it came.

"Shockley?"

"Shoot," said Shockley.

"She was released in the custody of a Mrs. Eldridge. Olive Eldridge. That ring a bell?"

"Yes. Yes, that's her friend from Ithaca."

"Well, they left in her car about two and a half hours ago—but that's only an approximation. They're in an old Volkswagen."

"Do you have the license number?"

"I'm ahead of you."

"Well?"

"This is not very kosher," said Nisbet, knowing what was coming next.

"I know. But for the child's sake. For the sake of her music. For the sake of us all, please," he pleaded.

"How in the world am I going to explain this?"

"Don't!"

"I've got superiors to deal with, Shockley. I've got a job I want to keep. Kids to support. I don't want them thinking I've gone off the deep end."

"Please, Jeff," said Shockley.

Silence.

"OK, OK. I'll alert the state police."

"If they're headed back to Ithaca they're probably somewhere on Route 17"—Shockley did a quick calculation in his head—"somewhere between, say—say—"

"Between Liberty and Binghamton," chimed in Nisbet, who had already consulted a map before calling Shockley.

As the minutes ticked by and the hunt for Doris went on, Shockley kept his vigil by Baby's crib, searching her comatose face for some small hint of consciousness. Once, for an instant, he thought he saw her eyebrows knit and nearly flew out of his skin. The brief twitch passed, however, and her features remained as dead still as ever, only her gurgling breath giving any hint of life. Hoping to penetrate the shroud of unconsciousness enveloping her, Shockley tried to rouse Baby by talking to her. When that failed he sang to her, singing in his unsteady voice a lullaby his mother had crooned to him as a child. Nothing seemed to work. Baby just lay there inert, her lifeless face cast in an eerie bluish hue. Finally, in desperation, Shockley broke down and took Martinez's advice.

"Dear God in heaven," he whispered under his breath, hoping that the nurse in the room wouldn't hear him. "Please save her. Because of my greed and selfishness, I brought this upon her. She doesn't deserve to die for my stupidity. Please, dear Lord, if you're there, save this innocent baby."

Later, as Baby's breathing became shallower, her heart showed signs of faltering, and Shockley was dispatched to the corridor as the doctors rushed into the room, he tried praying again. He prayed louder and

more fervently than before, no longer afraid that someone might overhear him. It didn't matter. All that
counted was Baby.

"Dear God, if you let her live, I promise that I'll
change all my ways. I promise that I'll never again exploit her as I've done. I'll serve *her* instead of letting
her serve my ends. I know now that she's more than
just a genetic quirk. She *is* a gift from you. If she lives
I'll dedicate my life to her and you. Please. This one
favor. Spare her."

Shockley paced the corridors waiting for the doctors
to emerge. He circled up and down the halls, repeatedly
checking the door to Baby's room. As he wandered
along one of the corridors, it suddenly dawned on him
that most of the televisions were on in the patients'
rooms. Not only that, but they all seemed to be tuned to
the same channel.

Entering one of the open rooms, he approached the
bed of an emaciated old man and looked at his set. On
the screen at that instant were Donny and Marie Os-
mond, and what Shockley saw and heard he could
hardly believe.

"The money that you call in this morning," said
Donny woodenly, obviously reading from a cue card.

"Your dollars, even quarters and dimes, however
much," chirped Marie.

"All will help gain release of Baby."

"Our operators are standing by," said Marie as the
camera panned the men and women sitting at the bank
of ringing phones.

"Minutes count," urged Donny as a toll-free number
traveled across the bottom of the screen.

"On this Christmas morning with your loved ones—"

"Think of Baby, who loves us all."

"And now while you're calling in your donation," announced Donny on an upbeat note, "here is—"

"Mr. Ray Charles!"

Applause.

Up the corridor at the nurses' station, the phone rang. It was for Shockley.

"We found her," piped Nisbet. "Got her right before Binghamton. It was close. She's already on her way back to the city."

"Get her back *fast*," said Shockley, looking at Baby's closed door.

"We're moving mountains. The state police are using a chopper."

"Hurry. Please. She doesn't have much time."

"Hang in there."

"Jeff?"

"Yeah."

"The telethon," said Shockley succinctly. "It's still running."

"Yeah. I just noticed. My kids turned on the tube."

"What's going on?"

"That's what I'd like to know. From what I understood the Mayor's office was supposed to make a joint announcement with your people hours ago. I can't figure it."

"I can," said Shockley. Then the door to Baby's room opened slowly and he hung up.

"For those of you who've just joined us," said Osgood, looking earnestly into the camera, his back to the tiers of operators feverishly answering the phones, "we're steadily moving toward Baby's freedom and our goal of three million dollars. And—"

The screen cut to the large electronic billboard on

center stage that was continually tallying up the donations.

"And, as you can now see, we're at"—Osgood sneaked on his glasses and took a squint—"at one million, two hundred and fifty-six thousand—Whoops!—fifty-eight thousand, one hundred and sixty-two dollars and seven cents!" he crowed, grabbing at the latest digits in the ever-changing display.

"And this is *your* money, *your* gift, every single penny of which is going to Baby. Somewhere in this city our precious child's life hangs in the balance. With your help we can tilt that balance in her favor. Please, don't hesitate. There is no one to save her but *you*!" He leveled a finger at the camera. "It is for you that Baby has sung and for you she will continue to sing if we can rescue her. Spare the life of this God-sent child," he said, the screen dissolving into a picture of Baby in concert, her mouth open in joyous song. At the bottom of the screen the toll-free number was urgently flashing in a hot shade of red.

As he stood in the rear of the control room, Jacobsen's eyes shifted from Osgood on the outgoing monitor back up to the series of clocks lining the wall. It was now almost twelve in New York. In a couple of minutes it would be nine o'clock for the network affiliates in the Pacific time zone, the moment at which the central control in Rockefeller Center was scheduled to start feeding the first hour of the New York tape just as they fed the mountain-time stations the first tape an hour earlier. If they could just squeak through the next hour without word leaking out that Baby had been found, thought Jacobsen nervously, they could wrap the last hour of the show in New York and keep the tapes running and the money rolling in. If only those who had agreed to keep the lid on this thing could hold out for a few more hours, they would break the three-million mark with ease.

Jacobsen stared tensely out the window of the control booth and saw Fitzgibbons standing partially hidden in the wings of the stage. Father Tom looked back up at Jacobsen, then at the electronic board and, making a sign of victory with his fingers, gave a broad smile.

"One million, two hundred and eighty-three thousand," crowed Osgood when he was cued, "six hundred and forty-two dollars and sixty-three cents!" he laughed, pretending to catch his breath. "We're getting there. We're getting there!"

"Roll the number," cued the director into his mike, and slicing across Osgood's waist there appeared in red that now familiar train of numbers: 800-555-2000.

"Our operators have been working tirelessly," said Osgood, extending his hand toward the line of people answering the phones, which continued to ring almost as fast as they could put them down. The audience burst into spontaneous applause. "And I want you people around the country, all around this great, generous nation of ours to just keep these phones ringing right off the hooks. Let's show the world on this Christmas Day that we care, care about Baby! And now to start our fourth hour—"

"OK. Camera three. Get ready. Move to the left. Little lower. That's it. Hold it!"

"It's coming up on noon," said a woman at the far side of the console into her headset. "Let's get ready to roll for Pacific. Five, four, three—"

"Our last big hour. Here's the maestro of comedy, the man who taught America how to laugh, America's own—"

"Roll tape one on Pacific."

"Mister—" said Osgood, building suspense for the next act.

"And now," issued a slick, deep voice from the monitor marked Pacific. "From New York City's Town Hall"—fanfare of trumpets—"the Christmas Benefit for Baby!" Applause. "With a star-studded cast including—"

"Welcome back to the second hour," chirped Osgood on the mountain monitor, sweat glistening on his brow as it had two hours earlier.

"Mister Jerry Lewis!" crowed Osgood live as the orchestra came on with a blast of an intro, Lewis striding across the stage to a thunderous ovation, his toothy smile flashing in the lights, his arms outstretched as though he could enfold the country in his arms.

"Rock-a-bye your baby with a Dixie melody," he crooned, coming in on beat. The music built on the insistent beat.

"A million baby kisses I'll deliver/If you would only sing—"

As Jacobsen stood in the rear of the half-darkened control room, his eyes traveled across the line of monitors. He flicked a tail of ash off the end of his cigarette, brought the cigarette to his lips, and took a long, slow drag. The end glowed brightly, then slowly faded and disappeared in a cloud of swirling smoke.

"What the hell is going on there?" asked Shockley when Pettersson picked up the phone backstage.

"A million baby kisses I'll deliver—"

"What do you mean?" asked Pettersson above the roar of the music.

"Why is that show still on the air?" asked Shockley, one eye peeled on the hospital corridor.

"Still on?"

"Baby's been found."

"Why that's just great—!"

"She was picked up hours ago!"

"Hours ago?" he repeated amidst the bustle. A team of acrobats was setting up for their high-wire act, which came right after the Lewis act and, with minutes left, they were frantically trying to reinstall a set of lines that had just come loose. "I think you'd better speak to Mr. Jacobsen," said Pettersson cautiously as a pair of twins in lavender tights edged past him. "He's in the control room. I can have you transferred," he said, looking up and seeing his boss's glasses glinting in the light of the control's and color monitors.

"No!"

"But—"

"Absolutely not! I don't want to talk to him, I want to talk to Fitzgibbons. Is he there?"

"Why, yes. He's right—"

"Let me speak to him. Now!"

Pettersson waved across to Father Tom, who stood on the other side of the stage talking to a man.

"Irwin?" asked Fitzgibbons, covering an ear as he watched Pettersson scurry off to the control booth.

"Why is that show still on the air?"

"I don't follow you."

"You didn't know about Baby either?"

"Talk sense, man!"

Shockley told him the whole story about Baby.

"Hours ago?" he said, dumbfounded.

"I spoke with Jacobsen myself. He's known all along."

"He hasn't said a word to me or anybody."

Shockley suddenly spotted Doris and Olive rushing down the hall escorted by a state trooper, the trio dashing up the corridor toward Baby's room.

"I've got to run," he said hurriedly. "Doris has just come."

"Go ahead. I'll take care of everything on this end. I'll see you at the hospital as soon as I can break away."

"Let her," Dr. Martinez urged the pediatrician from Columbia when Doris reached in below the tent to take hold of Baby. Shockley had just stepped into the room and stood with Olive by the door watching as Doris knelt down and lovingly lifted Baby's slack body into her arms.

"Be careful of i.v.s," warned the specialist with the silver-rimmed spectacles, but Martinez put a quieting hand on his arm.

All eyes in the room were fixed on Doris, who had moved in under the tent and stood hunched over the bed, rocking Baby in her arms. "Baby, Baby, Baby," she intoned in her creaky voice, fighting her tears as she pulled her child's feverish face against her own cold cheek.

Shockley watched as the old woman cradled her unconscious child and continued to rhythmically chant, her rounded shoulders swaying with each deep call to life. "Baby, Baby, Baby," Doris continued to sing, oblivious to all in the room.

The pediatrician heaved a sigh and left the room. Soon Martinez excused himself, and Olive slipped out into the corridor. Shockley remained frozen as the minutes passed, waiting expectantly, hoping for some change in Baby. But the child continued to hang limply in her mother's arms, rolling with each sway of the old lady's body.

* * *

Father Tom Fitzgibbons wasted no time. As soon as Jerry Lewis had completed his song and was taking his bows, he darted onto the stage and, grabbing the microphone from the bewildered Mr. Lewis, boldly stepped in front of the camera with the red light.

"Ladies and Gentlemen," he began, but suddenly the light went out.

The camera that stood facing Osgood in front of the phone banks unexpectedly flashed on.

Dropping his mike, Fitzgibbons made a dash for it. The stage crew looked on stunned as he raced headlong across the length of the stage.

"He's running over to camera one!" shouted Jacobsen in the control booth to the director. "Go to camera three!"

"What's he doing?" asked the director.

"He's gone nuts. Get him off! Call security!"

"That's Father Fitzgibbons," said the woman who was assistant director. "I think he wants to say something."

"Cut to camera three," ordered Jacobsen, and the director looked up at him, his face flushing.

"Ladies and Gentlemen," began Father Tom, out of breath. "I—"

"I said three!" fumed Jacobsen and, reaching across the director, pushed a button on the console. Immediately the broadcast monitor cut to the acrobats, catching them unawares as they stood in a group waiting for their cue. One of the twins in the troupe, seeing the camera light, poked her mother who, in turn, alerted the others, the whole family staring blankly into the camera.

"Get your fucking hands off my controls!" snapped the program director. "Get this man out of here!"

Father Tom was already sprinting toward the acrobats when the red light on camera three went off and the ongoing monitor displayed a startled Judson Osgood.

Quickly Osgood gathered himself.

"Well"—he forced a nervous smile, trying not to appear rattled—"we're approaching our goal of—"

Father Tom was racing back to the phone bank.

"Excuse me, Judson," he said, delicately twisting the microphone out of Osgood's hand. "Ladies and Gentlemen! I have a vital announcement," he began, blocking Osgood, who kept trying to snatch back his mike. "Baby"—he took a breath—"Baby has been *found* by the police."

For an instant, dead silence.

Osgood froze.

Then the audience broke into loud cheers and applause. Fitzgibbons, raising his hands to quiet them, shook his head. The theater fell quiet.

Jacobsen, who had been wrestling with two technicians, gave up struggling and stood passively in their grip, facing the monitor, his eyes narrowed into a pair of angry slits.

"At this moment Baby is in the hospital in grave condition. She's suffering from acute pneumonia with very serious complications." He paused. "Her life, I'm sorry to say, is in critical danger." Father Tom wet his lips and took a long breath.

In the control room, the director had just halted the tapes and was feeding Father Tom's address live to all stations across the country. His assistant was on the phone to the news department. The performers who had been in the wings began drifting onto the stage of the hushed theater and stood watching Father Tom— the women dabbing at their mascara-smeared eyes.

"This morning, by your generosity, you have shown the world how much you truly care for her. But, unfortunately, the problem facing us right now cannot be surmounted with the power of money. Nor apparently, science. The doctors caring for Baby have done all they can. Their medicine has gone as far as it can go. There is now only one power that can rescue this miraculous child. And it is the power of prayer. Ladies and Gentlemen, in your homes all around the country on this Christmas Day, I ask you to please raise up your voices as one for this child," implored Father Tom, lowering himself to his knees and bending his head as the camera tilted down to follow him. "Let us all pray together," he entreated as millions of Americans saw how the people assembled on the sides of the stage, comedians and soundmen, wardrobe workers and celebrities, grips and security men, sank to their knees.

"Our Father in heaven, save this precious child," he said, and the voices of the crew and the theater audience echoed his plea in unison, their prayer going out over the airwaves to be joined by millions of other voices, all calling Baby back to the living. "We beseech thee to forgive our sins and continue to grant us the comfort of her presence—"

When Father Tom finished, he remained kneeling, his head silently bowed as instinctively the director slowly faded to black, bringing the program to an end.

Shockley couldn't quite believe what was going on. It started in the ward rooms with televisions, the ill and their visitors responding to Father Tom's plea, clasping their hands, lowering their heads, and mumbling a few halting words. Almost immediately it began to spread, moving up and down the corridors, touching the nurses and orderlies, until even the cops who stood guard in front of Baby's door were bowing their heads uncertainly. Everyone in the hospital, it seemed to Shockley, even the doctors, had stopped what they were doing and were praying for Baby. It was uncanny, he thought, before lowering his own head to pray for the dying child, who lay in her mother's arms.

As quickly as the prayer had begun, it was over, nurses, looking a little sheepish, returning to their rounds, visitors picking up their conversations with their bedridden friends and relatives, orderlies moving hurriedly as before, pushing baskets of dirty linen or serving lunch up and down the halls. When Shockley raised his eyes, the first thing he saw was that Baby's eyelids were twitching, fluttering weakly as she tried to open her eyes.

"I don't believe it!" he gasped, turning to Olive Eldridge to confirm what he was seeing. Olive just looked at him, shaking her head in disbelief as tears of relief glistened down her cheeks.

"Doctor! Doctor!" said the nurse, racing out of the room, looking for the specialist from Columbia.

Word spread like wildfire through the hospital, and in less than a minute Baby's room was packed. They were all there: the pediatrician from Columbia, the world-renowned cardiologist, the internist from the Cornell School of Medicine, Dr. Martinez and his colleague of the earlier morning, the chief of nursing and as many of her staff who could acceptably squeeze into the room—all staring down in amazement at the child who was making her first tentative movements.

"My God!" uttered Shockley beside himself with emotion, watching as Baby wriggled in her mother's arms, her big, feverish eyes sweeping across the panoply of faces staring in at her.

"Thank you, Jesus," said Olive emphatically, clasping her hands.

"It's a miracle," said Dr. Martinez, his face aglow. "A real honest-to-goodness miracle."

"I wouldn't have believed it if I hadn't seen it with my own eyes," said the nurse who had been on duty since Baby's arrival.

"The hand of the Lord," said one of the older, more hardened nurses.

"It was the erythromycin," said the pediatric expert after conferring with his colleagues, who nodded in agreement. "Once it starts to work, you get these dramatic turnarounds," he explained to Shockley, who listened politely, but was no longer certain just what to believe.

FOUR

Over the next days, Doris and Shockley took turns
watching over Baby, the two never exchanging more
than a word, their pattern of shifts developing out of a
tacit understanding—Doris leaving when Shockley arrived and vice versa. While Shockley continued to stay
on at the Plaza in midtown, Olive had taken a nearby
motel room and made it a point of ferrying Doris in her
Volkswagen to and from the hospital.

Each shift brought new and startling improvements
in Baby's condition. Her fever plummeted, and within
two days it was only slightly above normal. Baby's periods of wakefulness began to stretch as she became progressively more alert and the phlegm that she coughed
up started to clear. Though Baby at first refused to eat,
Doris was able to coax her into accepting a few mouth-
fuls of juice. Soon that gave way to part of a bottle and
that to some spoonfuls of baby food. As Shockley also
continued to ply Baby with nourishment and liquids,
the doctors finally ordered removal of the i.v.s, and
within another three days a very debilitated but recovering Baby was eating near normally and gradually beginning to recoup some of her lost weight.

Around the clock, Doris's and Shockley's vigil continued unabated, night and day merging for the pair.

And through it all Father Tom was there, spending long hours watching over Baby, praying and waiting.

"You're worried that she won't sing again, aren't you?" asked Shockley late one evening when they were alone in Baby's room and she was sitting up for the first time, holding her own bottle and drinking busily. Though she was now breathing easily and cooed and made her usual baby sounds, nothing even faintly resembling song had yet emerged from her lips.

"My first concern was for her life," said Father Tom, brushing back a lock of white hair that had fallen over his forehead. "Now that we're over that crisis, thank God, well—Yes, I am frankly worried. I spoke with one of the doctors in our congregation, and he told me there might have been brain damage either from the high fever or oxygen deprivation."

Shockley nodded. The same fear had been running through his mind.

"But she does seem normal." Father Tom tried to look on the bright side of things. He felt Shockley had gone through enough trauma and didn't need his anxieties stoked.

"Whatever is, is," said Shockley with a fatalistic shrug. "At this point there's nothing we can do about it, is there?"

Father Tom's whole face broke into a smile. Even his eyes were smiling.

"If I believed that, Irwin, I wouldn't be here," he said.

"The power of prayer."

"Don't knock it."

"Oh, I'm certainly not knocking it." Shockley fell serious. "It's just not easy for a dyed-in-the-wool atheist to change colors this late in the game."

"Anything is possible. Even that," said Father Tom

with a laugh, and then Doris appeared. Seeing her, Shockley automatically rose from his seat and took his coat. Baby dropped her bottle, smiled, and stretched out her hands in greeting.

"Doris," he said, putting on his hat and stalling by the door as she greeted Baby with a hug. "Can't we at least talk?"

Doris shed her heavy wool coat with an audible sigh and sank down in the chair still warm from Shockley's body.

"No," she answered woodenly. "I have nothing to say to you. There's been too much talk already."

Shockley gave a hopeless shrug and, seeing his glum look, Father Tom gave him a reassuring nod.

Later that evening, as Baby lay sleeping soundly, Father Tom tried to approach Doris.

"Don't you think, perhaps," he ventured, "that the time has come for some sort of reconciliation between you and Irwin?"

Doris slowly turned her head and looked at Fitzgibbons.

"If for nothing else," he continued cautiously, "then for the sake of Baby."

Doris continued to stare at him.

"Don't you think it would be a good idea?"

"No," she answered flatly, putting an end to that. "Absolutely not!"

Yet another couple of days passed, and Baby became her old self. The color returned to her cheeks; she seemed happy at all the attention lavished on her and took an active interest in the endless parcels of toys and gifts sent by well-wishers from around the world.

"If only you'd sing," Shockley said to Baby as he held her in his lap on New Year's Day, trying to give her a spoonful of her apparently awful-tasting antibiotic as she twisted her head back and forth. "Come on, you little troublemaker," he struggled to get her to take the shimmering, red medicine balanced on the spoon. Finally, as she swung her head past, Shockley managed to target the spoon, sluicing the cherry-flavored liquid into her mouth.

Baby pulled a disgusted face.

"Ah, there," he exclaimed victoriously, only to have her spit it all out, the syrup running down her chin onto the front of her bib.

"I'll tell you what," he joked indulgently. "I'll make you a deal. If you sing," he carefully poured a fresh spoonful, "you don't have to take your medicine."

Baby looked at him in puzzlement.

"You know," he smiled. "La la la la," he gave her a quick sequence of notes reminiscent of her earliest song.

Baby cocked her head quizzically, but Shockley, intent on not spilling the full spoon, failed to notice the expression. Baby's eyebrows began knitting furiously as she held her head still. Seeing his chance, Shockley eagerly raised the spoon to her lips and just as he was about to slide it into her mouth, out came a high, tentative sound. A single, clean note.

Shockley dropped the spoon into his lap, the sticky syrup soaking his pants. Excited, he sat motionlessly waiting for the next note, but as quickly as it had appeared the tone vanished, and in its place there was nothing but the ordinary hum of the hospital. Shockley looked beseechingly at Baby, who stared back at him. He waited, but there was nothing more.

Baby began to fidget in his lap.

"Sing, darling," he whispered to her. "Come on, sing," he coaxed and gave out a few notes himself.

Baby looked at him and cocked her head again.

"Sing. Please sing."

Baby took a small breath.

"Yes," he urged. "Yes."

Then she let out three more tones, her notes this time more certain, crisper, clearer than the first. Baby stopped and looked questioningly at Shockley. He smiled reassuringly, afraid to speak.

Baby grinned, showing her two little milk teeth on the bottom row. Then she took a long, deep breath and began to sing in earnest, her voice low but steady, note after perfect note emerging from her lips. Shockley nearly went out of his mind with joy. She was singing. Baby was singing! he exulted. It was almost too good to be true. At that instant he wanted to race up and down the corridors of the hospital shouting with joy, get on the phone and call half the world, tell the reporters who had been hounding him for days, call Father Tom, alert Doris and Olive, even call Ruth. But instead he sat glued to his seat, spellbound, listening to that near-forgotten song, that heavenly melody emerging from a previous life and moving through the eons of time to reach his ears, that velvety clear song of chirping birds and water lapping a forgotten shore, of wind whistling through the trees.

"Oh, darling," he sighed when she had finished and sat in his lap looking proud and happy. "That was gorgeous. Thank you, sweetie," he said and kissed her cheek that tasted of cherry syrup. Then he remembered the spoon that lay in his lap. He looked down at the clinging mess and laughed. Picking up the spoon Shockley debated with himself.

"I'm afraid," he said to her, filling up the spoon for the third time, "that I'm a liar. But, please," he said, trying to slip her the medicine, "understand. It's for your own good." And with that he plunged the spoon into her mouth and, holding her jaw shut, waited until she finally swallowed. "Will you ever forgive me?" he asked.

On Thursday, Jacobsen finally appeared at the hospital to see how his client was faring, an entourage of new assistants in tow. He was already talking about the future, a new tour, a European swing—all as if nothing had happened.

"We could start with a big bang opening at La Scala. From Milano we could shoot up for, maybe, two nights at the Vienna Opera House. From there—"

Shockley listened speechlessly as Jacobsen rattled on, dropping names from the Gewandhaus in Leipzig to Tel Aviv's Mann Auditorium. When Jacobsen finally finished his spiel, Shockley looked him straight in the eye and answered him with one word.

"No."

"No?"

"No!" repeated Shockley emphatically—his single-worded obstinacy reminding him oddly of Doris.

"What are you talking about?" asked Jacobsen, looking genuinely surprised. He turned to his three assistants, who all shrugged their shoulders.

"I'm talking about your relationship with Baby. Consider it at an end."

Jacobsen looked at him blankly.

"You know, finished. Fini. The end. This is the last time you're going to see Baby. Say good-bye to the man," he said to Baby for effect as she looked at him with her blue eyes and grinned.

"You mean, because of the benefit?" he asked, supinating his hands in a gesture of apology. "Shockley, look. I'll be the first to admit that I got a little carried away. But after all that work and preparation, I just couldn't see—"

"It's not just that. And it's not just that you're thick-skinned and don't really give a damn about Baby. It's basically because I've decided that I'm not going to exploit her gift anymore."

Jacobsen glared at him menacingly.

"I made a promise to myself and I intend to keep it," he said, ignoring the look.

"It's those Babyists." Jacobsen's face boiled a deep red, his nostrils flaring as his temper broke loose. "Fitzgibbons and those fucking Babyists. They've gotten to you!"

"Absolutely not," he answered sharply, which made Jacobsen all the more convinced. "It's a decision I reached solely on my own. From now on anybody who wants to hear Baby can hear her for free. She doesn't belong to you or me or the Babyists or *anyone*."

"That's very noble." Jacobsen snorted. "Very lofty."

"It's not meant to be."

"But, before you go off on your little religious kick, I suggest you take a good, hard look at your contract."

"I don't have to read a contract to know what I have to do."

"For the next five years Baby belongs to me." Jacobsen leveled a threatening finger at Shockley.

"She doesn't belong to anyone!" Shockley shouted back.

"Unless she sings for me, she sings for no one!"

"That's ridiculous!"

"Oh? Is it now?" asked Jacobsen, a nasty smile dancing across his lips. "Well, we'll just have to wait and see how 'ridiculous' it is, won't we?" Then he turned with a contemptuous smile and marched off, his people trailing single file down the hall.

* * *

"Yes," said Kiely, responding to Shockley's phone inquiry. "You're most definitely bound by the terms of the duly executed contract you signed with the Jacobsen organization."

"But—But—"

"You were appointed guardian *ad litem* by the court. The court gave you authorization to make that contract. In it, you specifically agreed to make the child available for performances, granting the Jacobsen association sole agency. As far as I can see, once she is sufficiently well to perform again, that contract becomes binding upon you and the child. For the next five years she can never sing in public—that being clearly defined as more than five people—unless it's under their aegis."

"That's crazy."

"Perhaps. But that's what you get for signing an agreement without first consulting an attorney."

"Can I fight this thing?"

"Of course. I was going to bring that up. If we can prove in some way that the child, in the process of going on these concerts, was abused or subjected to—"

"What? Do you think I want to undermine my own credibility as guardian and end up losing custody of Baby?"

"Or," Kiely went on, "that the contract was misrepresented or signed under duress."

"What does it all mean?"

"It means that there are plenty of grounds for challenging that agreement. But it also means a tough battle. A knock-down drag-out court fight."

"More publicity?"

"More publicity. More accusations and counteraccusations. More expense. A lot of expense," he warned with characteristic bluntness. "Jacobsen's no small fry. He'll have the best legal minds at his disposal."

"What do I do?"

"Nothing. Nothing yet. Sit tight. Wait for him to make the first move. It might all be bluff."

"Not likely."

"No. It's not likely."

"You know what he's trying to do."

"Sure. He's trying to grab Baby from you. He might even succeed. But just remember one thing."

"What's that?"

"You set yourself up for it."

"I was thinking about all that money raised by the telethon," said Shockley to Father Tom the next day as they walked together to the subway station near the hospital. It was a bright, windless January afternoon and, as they strolled in the sun, there was a vague, springlike thaw in the air. "There must be quite a fortune there."

"I got a peek at the accounting the Jacobsen people had made, and it looks like there's just a shade under two million dollars," said Father Tom, squinting in the light.

The two walked on, passing a line of elderly people sitting in chairs against the sheltered front of a building, their faces turned up to the sun.

"What's going to happen to it?"

"I think that's partly up to you. It was intended to be used for Baby—or at least in her name. I keep getting calls and letters from people urging us to build some sort of shrine for her. Perhaps a place where people could go into retreat."

"That's a good idea," said Shockley. "But I've got an even better one," he said, brightening noticeably.

"Oh?"

A garbage truck roared by, drowning them out, and Shockley waited for it to pass.

"Let's use some of it to buy out Jacobsen's contract," he suggested excitedly. "Get rid of him once and for all."

"I'm afraid it's not going to be that easy. Yesterday, after you told me about Jacobsen's threat, I took the initiative and went and spoke with him. I brought up the notion of buying back his contract."

"And?"

"He just laughed at me. Laughed right in my face," said Fitzgibbons as they descended into the subway station, a rush of stale air rising up to greet them. "He doesn't want money, Irwin."

"Yeah, I know," said Shockley worriedly. "The bastard wants blood."

"No. Not blood." Father Tom put two tokens into the turnstile. "Just Baby."

Regrets, Shockley had long ago concluded, were like lifelong hangnails. They were always there at the corner of your life, nagging, gnawing, irritating. The more you clawed away at them, the more inflamed they became. And Shockley felt he already had more than any man's share.

He had old regrets: that he hadn't stood up to his father and protected his sister when he saw how the old man was destroying her; that he had let his mother die without ever visiting her bedside; that, at the end of the old man's life, he hadn't been big enough to forgive and forget. And now he had new regrets: that he had destroyed his marriage, broken up his home, hurt his children, misused Baby for his own ego gratification.

Between the old and the new, there lay that wasteland of mistakes, small regrets at having unnecessarily offended someone, taken unfair advantage of a friend, lied, bragged, and all the other human foibles.

The last thing that Shockley wanted was another inflamed hangnail to carry through life. So when he heard from Olive that Doris was planning on returning to Ithaca now that Baby was almost well, Shockley decided the time was ripe to attempt reconciliation once more. It was a delicate situation. He realized it was wrong for Baby to be separated from her mother. Yet, he couldn't in good conscience return Baby to Doris's sole care. To his mind came visions of Leeming's Trailer Park, the surrounding shanties and shacks and junk-piles. The thought of sending Baby out to that made him shudder. He loved Baby, cared about her deeply, and could never live with himself if he just dumped her out there. Baby was an extraordinary child who deserved something at least a little better than that. Shockley thought back to the first time he had entered Doris's house on Willow Avenue, the disorder and sloppiness of that dingy place, Baby's obvious undernourishment. He recalled Baby's state of neglect when Doris had grabbed her back after breaking out of the hospital—the bleeding diaper rash that took weeks to cure, Doris's barren refrigerator, the turd-deep boxes of unemptied kitty litter. Baby was a princess. She didn't deserve to live stifled in bleakness because of her aged mother's obsession with total control. Love was necessary, but it wasn't enough to warrant what Doris would ultimately subject Baby to. If only some reasonable settlement could be hammered out—

"Doris, please," began Shockley, arriving early for his shift at the hospital that Saturday morning. "Let's try to talk this thing over."

With Shockley was Father Tom, who had offered to come along to mediate. Olive Eldridge was also in the room.

"I know you're going back to Ithaca this afternoon and before you leave I—"

"Who told you I'm leaving?" asked Doris, looking accusingly at Olive. Olive turned and pretended to play with Baby.

"It's not important," he said, holding up a pacifying hand. "What is—is—well, there must be a way for us to work out some sort of compromise."

Doris looked at him with her rheumy eyes and then, turning and hunching over the chair holding her coat, said to Olive, "Come on, Olive. It's time to go."

Olive stalled.

"I don't want you to be separated from Baby any longer."

Doris looked over her shoulder at him through the corner of her eye, her body stooped over farther than ever, it seemed to Shockley.

"Don't you try and sweet-talk me again in this lifetime," she said, trying to control her seething resentment.

Shockley threw up his hands.

"Christ, Doris, I'm trying to undo some of the damage. Don't you understand that?"

"I understand perfectly. You want to keep Baby for you and your friends and salve your conscience at the same time. Oh, I understand perfectly."

"No, I want to return Baby to you!"

"Oh, really? Then give her to me and let me take her home this instant." She abruptly picked up Baby from the bed to call his bluff.

Shockley shook his head and turned to Fitzgibbons in frustration.

"Let me make a suggestion, Mrs. Rumsey," began Father Tom. "Please, just hear me out."

Doris gave an impatient snort.

"We've got lots of money from the telethon. We want to build a house for you and Baby. You wouldn't have to live in a trailer park any longer. You wouldn't have to worry about—"

"I don't want any handouts!"

"It's not a handout. Look, Doris," Father Tom said gently. "All Irwin wants, all anybody wants, is to ensure that Baby is well cared for, that she's not hidden from the rest of the world. She's growing, she's getting older. She's going to blossom into a wonderful human being. She—"

"You may be a priest," said Doris, interrupting him, her jaw set firmly, "but you're awfully thick."

"Doris!" scolded Olive.

"Don't Doris me! I've had enough of all this sanctimonious—" she said, searching for a shocking word, "sanctimonious crap! And that's what it is. Crap!" she repeated angrily. "You steal my very own baby from me, the child that came from my body, that I carried for—"

"You weren't able to care for her!" Shockley finally burst out. "And you're not able to properly care for her now. You don't even have the vaguest idea of what a child needs. Admit it!"

"Have you been any better?" Doris shouted back. "Look at the state she got into, thanks to you!"

"Please. Please," said Father Tom, stepping between the two adversaries. "I think we're getting somewhere," he said, trying to be positive.

"Don't fool yourself," said Doris, picking up her wool coat and pulling it over her shoulder.

"You're still blaming me for the time you were in the hospital and I deceived you," Shockley tried again. "And rightly so. But that's ancient history."

"For you, maybe," answered Doris, a blue vein bulging at the side of her forehead.

"There are lots of alternatives," said Fitzgibbons.

"There's only one," said Doris, and there were tears in her eyes as she said good-bye to Baby who clung to her neck.

"Why don't you at least listen to these folks?" said Olive, reluctantly picking up her own coat. "Try to be just a little reasonable."

"Be reasonable! Be reasonable!" Doris pressed her fist against her mouth to stifle a sob. "How many times have I heard that? I'm sick of it. Whose side are you on, anyway?"

"I'm on your side, dear. Always have been," said Olive, coming up and putting an arm around Doris's shoulders. "You know that."

Doris nodded through her tears.

"I'm sorry," she muttered feebly.

Shockley looked forlornly at Father Tom, Shockley himself verging on tears.

"I'm going," said Doris, giving Baby a long, hard hug. She kissed both her cheeks with big, wet, sloppy kisses. Baby opened her mouth and started to sing, but Doris took a finger and resting it against the child's lips silenced her.

"There isn't that much time in life," said Olive astutely. "And every day you go without Baby is a day lost. Talk to these gentlemen. Please. For your own sake."

Doris turned away from Baby.

"Come on," she said to Olive. "I've waited this long. I can wait just a little longer."

When by chance Shockley turned on the television in his hotel room that Sunday evening, he was taken completely by surprise. There, suddenly, on "On Line" was the story about Baby that had been scheduled for airing at the end of the month.

"Tonight," began Joel Webster opening the segment, sitting as he had in the Shockley living room, Baby in his arms, "we have a rather unusual story for you. Some say this little girl sings and could do so from birth. Many, including the sixty-year-old mother of this child, insist that she was the result of a virgin birth. To others, this has been one big hoax."

Shockley grabbed a chair and pulled it up close to the set as the scene cut to Webster sitting in the studio in front of a blown-up picture of Baby with production credits.

"But the story we're about to tell is not about the alleged mystical or curative powers of her singing, nor her conception. But rather, it is the tale of a power struggle, a veritable tug-of-war involving big money, fame, greed, mendacity, and a host of other human foibles. And, at the center of this maelstrom is one innocent child. A little girl. A little girl called Baby."

His heart beginning to pound in his ears, Shockley leaned forward and anxiously turned up the sound.

"Enter one Dr. Irwin Shockley, a university professor of music, Pulitzer Prize-winning composer."

Shockley watched as his own owl-eyed face stared back out at him from the screen. It looked haggard and harassed, his skin washed in hues of green on the out-of-sync color set.

WEBSTER: How did you get the child?

SHOCKLEY: She was put in our foster care by the Department of Social Services.

WEBSTER: Why?

SHOCKLEY [*Swallows uneasily.*]: *Why?* [*Shrugs and tries to appear nonchalant.*] Apparently she was being neglected in her previous home.

The screen suddenly cut to Olive Eldridge.

OLIVE: Neglected? That woman loved that baby more than anything in the world. She was her whole life. Now, I'm a retired elementary-school principal. Children have been my business for almost forty years. [*Getting feisty.*] So I know what I'm talking about. Now Doris may not have been as wealthy as those other folks or as well educated or as important, but she loved that child and in *my* book that's more important than all the fancy clothes and toys. It's love that counts, not money! Neglected? My foot!

WEBSTER [*Voice-over as Shockley sits uneasily on the sofa beside his wife.*]: Was Baby in fact neglected?

SHOCKLEY: Well, according to the people at social services and according to the courts and whoever else was involved, it was determined that she was not getting proper care. I really don't know much more about it.

WEBSTER: Come now, Dr. Shockley. You don't mean to say that you didn't know the mother well *before* the child was placed in your custody?

SHOCKLEY: If you're implying in any way that I was instrumental in her removal from her mother's custody, the answer is emphatically no! When I learned of the court decision my wife and I offered our services. Period.

WEBSTER: And not before?

SHOCKLEY [*Irritably.*]: I said *no.* If you want to know more, why don't you talk to the authorities?

WEBSTER [*Voice-over.*]: And that's exactly what we did.

As Shockley looked on in helpless dismay, cursing himself for his blunder, Andrea Cassaniti appeared on camera. She was standing on the corner of Cayuga and Green streets in front of the old brick building housing the Department of Social Services.

WEBSTER: Miss Cassaniti, what precisely made you choose the Shockleys as foster parents?

CASSANITI: The Shockleys seemed well suited to be foster parents. The home environment seemed a very positive one. And, since Dr. Shockley was very interested in her musical ability, we thought that would be of special advantage to the child.

WEBSTER: When did the Shockleys offer their services as foster parents?

CASSANITI: Let me see—[*Stalls.*]

WEBSTER: Was it *before* the family court hearing?

CASSANITI: I'm just not exactly—

WEBSTER: Surely you must know. You do have records, don't you?

CASSANITI: Well—

WEBSTER: These copies I have here—[*Produces a sheaf of papers.*] Aren't they copies of the file your department has on Baby?

CASSANITI [*Looks surprised.*]: Yes. But those are confidential and are not supposed to—

WEBSTER: And doesn't it very explicitly state here, right here, that Dr. Shockley in fact spoke with your agency well *before* Mrs. Rumsey was ever subpoenaed to appear in family court? [*Puts on glasses and reads.*] Two full weeks before?

CASSANITI: Why, I suppose it's possible. My memory is not that great and—

WEBSTER [*Zeroing in.*]: And that here, a day before the issuance of that show-cause order for the removal of the child, you've logged—and this is your handwriting, isn't it?—an interview with Dr. Shockley during which he provided you with detailed information supporting allegations of neglect?

CASSANITI [*Looking around nervously.*]: I think that's all I can say at this point.

Shockley again found himself on camera.

WEBSTER: Dr. Shockley, you launched Baby's career by first visiting a number of music schools around the country.

SHOCKLEY: Yes. That's correct.

WEBSTER: Did you have permission from the mother to take her child on that tour?

SHOCKLEY [*Taken aback and unprepared.*]: Tacitly. There were many factors involved, including the mother's health. [*Clears his throat.*] The woman was very sick and apparently dying. Yes. I would say that there was a tacit understanding.

The screen suddenly cut to Doris sitting in her trailer, stroking a cat in her lap.

DORIS: Never! I never gave any permission. When I asked to see Baby at the hospital, Mrs. Shockley tricked me by parading a bundle or something wrapped in a blanket in front of my window, trying to make me think that Baby was still in Ithaca when all along she was on that tour.

Olive returned to the screen.

OLIVE: I didn't always agree with Doris, but she had

always made it clear that she would not approve of Baby going on any tours or shows. She just didn't want that child leaving town. She was firm as a rock on that!

The screen cut back to Doris.

DORIS: I was railroaded. By the Shockleys. By the social services people. By the court. By my very own lawyer.

Shockley then watched as Kiely appeared on the screen, was introduced, and promptly raked over the coals.

WEBSTER: You represented Doris Rumsey in her custody fight?

KIELY [*Looking suspiciously at the camera.*]: That's correct.

WEBSTER: And took a very handsome retainer.

KIELY: My legal fees are purely a matter between myself and my clients.

WEBSTER: And didn't even appear at the hearing!

Shockley watched as Kiely tried to weasel his way out of Webster's tightening grip. Though Kiely was more adept than Andrea Cassaniti, it soon became apparent where the truth lay.

WEBSTER: Sending instead a neophyte assistant, fresh out of law school, with no prior trial experience, who was totally unfamiliar with the case.

KIELY [*Indignant.*]: Mr. Bennett is a perfectly competent attorney, licensed by the state bar association. I was ill that day and asked him to take my place. He was thoroughly familiar with the case from the beginning.

Doris popped on the screen.

DORIS: Ill? I was told by Mr. Bennett that he was on another case. But that doesn't really matter, does it? I hired him and he never appeared. I paid him one thousand dollars!

Kiely came back on camera.

WEBSTER: Mr. Kiely. You represented Mrs. Rumsey.

KIELY: Yes.

WEBSTER: Not long after the hearing you became the attorney responsible for managing Baby's business affairs, essentially in the employ of Dr. Shockley. Isn't that [*Looks dramatically puzzled.*], well, isn't that a conflict of interests?

KIELY [*Rising up from his chair.*]: Mr. Webster, I'm tired of sitting here and listening to your insinuations. I was kind enough to grant you this interview, and you're using my hospitality to impugn my good name. I don't believe in trial by television, and as far as I'm concerned this meeting is over. Now turn off those damn cameras!

The screen returned to Olive.

OLIVE: Doris didn't have a chance. There was big money involved. Everybody wanted a slice of Baby. There were movie contract offers. Offers to appear on television shows. Offers for interviews. She refused to cooperate, so they went after her.

Doris came on screen again. She was now walking with Webster through the snow outside her trailer, telling him about how she sold her house to pay for her court appeal, about her further determination to fight Shockley for the return of Baby.

DORIS: That man forced his way into our lives. Right from the beginning he wanted Baby for himself. He wasn't the only one, but he was the most persistent. I suppose it was my fault. I wasn't strong enough. I was tired, I was weak after the birth.

Shockley got up and poured himself a stiff drink, the glass trembling in his hand. The program rolled on.

DORIS: The facts have been twisted, have been distorted [*Chokes up, speaking haltingly but effectively.*]. They even tried to have me adjudged insane. Everybody wants a share of Baby, and they're tearing her to pieces for their own greed.

Shockley downed his drink in a single gulp and looked at the set where Father Tom was being interviewed, obviously well before the kidnapping.

FITZGIBBONS: Our main concern all along has been accessibility to this miraculous child. She is a gift from God and was not meant to be used as a trained seal. Our congregation feels that certain people are exploiting her and using this poor child in a rather immoral way.

Shockley poured himself another drink. After Fitzgibbons, on came Jacobsen, acting predictably arrogant.

JACOBSEN: Look, I'm a busy man, Mr. Webster. Let me put it to you simply. Dr. Shockley and I have an arrangement. He wants to give Baby exposure by putting her in concert. I am meeting that need. Our arrangement it sanctioned by the courts and, as far as Baby is concerned, it's an exceedingly generous one. I might add that all the child's earnings are being held in a trust for her.

WEBSTER: Do you make money under that "arrangement"?

JACOBSEN: Well, of course I do! I'm not running a church here. [*Scoffs.*]

As Shockley began to pace he floor in front of his television, Webster brought the program up-to-date, explaining over a shot of the Plaza Hotel about the woman who had wormed her way past Shockley's defenses, of the seduction and ultimate abduction.

On and on the program went, the point being hammered home: Shockley with his music, the Babyists with their religion, Jacobsen with his business, the kidnappers with their extortion, the social services with collusive interests of their own, all were trying to get their grips on Baby. It was true, thought Shockley, and yet it wasn't quite true.

Shockley felt disgusted. To all the regrets he had in life, he added a couple more. One was lying. The other was ever having let a TV camera into his house.

Shockley stared back at the set. Webster was finally winding up the segment.

"All this raises more questions than it really answers. But at the heart of it all lie some very central questions that go beyond even this fascinating tale. What constitutes neglect? Do, in fact, unusually gifted children have requirements and needs that lawfully go beyond those of normal children? To just what extent do the courts have a right to intercede within a parent-child relationship? When the appellate court finally hears Doris Rumsey's case, some of these questions may well be resolved."

Shockley reached over and snapped off the television.

On Tuesday morning, three days after Doris had departed for Ithaca, Shockley checked Baby out of the hospital. Lining the hallway were well-wishers from the hospital staff who turned out to say good-bye. There were the nurses who had seen Baby through her crisis, Dr. Martinez and his colleague from that first, frightening morning, countless orderlies and candy-stripers. Even the pediatric specialist from Columbia journeyed all the way uptown that early morning just to see Baby off.

"Godspeed," said Martinez, taking Shockley's hand in both of his and holding it tightly. "Take good care of our little girl."

Shockley tried to thank Martinez for all he had done, but somehow the words didn't quite come and all he could do was nod and smile gratefully.

Baby went from hand to hand, moving down the length of the ward corridor, getting hugged and kissed and tickled. When she finally reached Shockley's arms she opened her mouth and spontaneously burst into song. It was a short melody but clearly a new one. To the hospital staff, who listened in awed silence, it sounded like a song of expectation, a song of promise and relief. Caught in the swirling undertones of her voice they could detect the sounds of the coming spring, the sounds of icicles dripping, flowers opening into delicate blossoms, a newborn chick emerging from its shell.

When Baby finished, the staff broke into delighted applause.

"Thank you," said Shockley, addressing the throng. "Thank you one and all for everything you've done for Baby."

Then, following the two city cops who had been on the morning shift with Baby from the beginning, Shockley took the elevator down to the ground level and hurried past the throng of reporters anxiously waiting in the lobby.

"Is it true, Dr. Shockley, that Baby will no longer be performing?" asked a reporter, sticking out a mike. Deftly avoiding it, Shockley hurried toward the car that stood waiting, Father Tom holding open the rear door.

"What about the upcoming appeals hearing that could—?"

A phalanx of waiting motorcycle cops moved in and helped clear the path.

"Whew!" said Shockley when he and Baby were safely ensconced in the limousine and the motorcade was ready to roll.

But the car remained motionless.

"What are we waiting for?" asked Father Tom, leaning forward to the driver. The driver shrugged, then motioned toward a man in a brown suit that the police had let through their lines. The man approached the car and knocked on Shockley's window. Puzzled, Shockley rolled it down.

"Are you Irwin R. Shockley of Ithaca, New York?" asked the man, identifying himself as a federal marshal.

"Yes, I am," admitted Shockley warily.

The marshal then served Shockley with a document, signaled the police, and the convoy took off.

As the car sped out to the airport under escort, Shockley opened the paper and read it. It was, from what he could make out, a show-cause order from the district federal court. Shockley was to show cause within ten days why an injunction should not be granted to Jacobsen Associates, preventing Baby from singing in public.

Shockley handed it over to Father Tom.

"That's not an injunction," said Father Tom, showing anger for the first time. "It's a gag order!"

Shockley said nothing, just stared glumly out the window.

Emerging from the plane after landing in Ithaca, Shockley was immediately jolted by the arctic air engulfing them at the top of the open ramp. Bundling Baby up, Shockley rushed with her over the snow-encrusted tarmac toward the one-room terminal as around him the wind swirled, picking up funnels of snow that traveled furiously across the high, barren airstrip. Moving through a howling headwind that made Baby bury her face against his shoulder, he was suddenly struck by a sense of having been cut loose from the world. Today there would be no Ruth waiting to meet him. Nor the expectant face of one of the children who had come along for the ride. It was over. He was alone. A single man. Nevertheless, Shockley searched the waiting faces pressed up against the glass in the warm terminal, searched them only to be keenly stung by disappointment.

In the lobby was a small contingent of reporters and cameras waiting for him. There were familiar faces

from the *Ithaca Journal* and local radio stations as well
as a couple of television people who had come from
nearby Binghamton and Syracuse. Compared to the
hubbub in New York, the reporters were quiet and low
keyed. In a way it was a pleasant welcome that eased
the pain of his loneliness, and he took a few minutes to
answer their questions as patiently and honestly as possible.

No, he admitted to one reporter, he didn't know
what the future held. There were legal entanglements
that would have to be unsnarled. No, he was not afraid
of losing Baby.

"Ivar Jacobsen obviously has no further claim to Baby's services, especially in light of—"

"Dr. Shockley," interrupted the young woman from
the *Journal* who had posed the question. "I was referring to the appellate court."

"Huh?" said Shockley, a little confused. "Oh. Yes,"
he nodded, remembering Doris's petition. "I'm not too
worried about that. That's still far off and when it does
come around I think that the higher court'll sustain the
family-court decision considering the child's history. In
the meantime I'm trying and hoping to circumvent the
whole appeal process by reaching some sort of compromise with the mother that would permit her to live with
Baby while—"

"Excuse me," interjected the woman, looking surprised. "Aren't you aware of the announcement made
this morning by the appellate court?"

"No. What announcement?"

"They're scheduled to hear Mrs. Rumsey's appeal tomorrow."

Shockley looked flabbergasted.

"The program," he uttered under his breath.

"Yes," she said, picking it up. "Justice may be blind," she closed her notebook, "but apparently it does watch television."

As soon as he had taken a room in the downtown Ramada Inn, Shockley called his lawyer. Kiely was out of the office, so he left urgent word for the attorney to get back to him.

After waiting a full hour he called back and once again the secretary assured him that Mr. Kiely would promptly return his call.

For most of the afternoon Shockley sat glued by the phone in his motel room, awaiting Kiely's call. As he waited tensely, valuable time ticking away, Baby seemed oblivious to his anxiety. She spent much of the time playing on the floor with her toys, often singing happily to herself, her songs more exuberant and joyous than at any time in the seven months of her life.

Shockley, however, failed to give her singing much attention. His ear was tuned to a different sound, the sound of a ringing phone, which never materialized.

When Shockley realized that the secretary's promises were just putoffs, he took the initiative and began calling around town trying to locate the lawyer. He tried Kiely's home, the courthouse, the county clerk's office, and even some of Kiely's colleagues' offices. Finally, in the early evening, Shockley located him in Collegetown at one of his properties. It was his Eddy Street apartment house that had just been closed down by an order of the Ithaca Housing Authority during one of its sporadic crackdowns on student slum housing.

"Where have you been?" Shockley asked, his voice nearly frantic. "I've been trying to get you since the morning."

"What's the problem?" asked Kiely. In the background Shockley could hear the sound of power saws and pounding hammers. On his end Baby was belting out a happy song, and he had to cover his ear to hear.

"The problem is that the appellate division is hearing Mrs. Rumsey's appeal tomorrow. That's the problem."

"Relax. I'm fully apprised of the situation. We're on top of it."

"How?" asked Shockley, dispensing with any politeness.

Kiely gave him a thin laugh trying to embarrass him.

"We're filing an amicus brief—that's a friend of the court's brief—and we're also going to be giving input when oral arguments are heard."

"Who's *we*?"

"I sent my associate Mr. Bennett to Albany. He's already there. So just relax and take it easy."

"Your associate?" asked Shockley incredulously, suddenly realizing that Kiely was going to screw him just as he had screwed Doris. "I retained *you*, not your associate."

"Mr. Shockley," said Kiely above the whine of a saw, "I don't work for you. You're not my client. I represent Baby. I am the executor of her trust. I do what I deem to be in her interests. And, I felt that it was in her best interest to send Mr. Bennett. Discussion completed," he said and abruptly hung up.

Shockley sat stunned on the edge of the bed holding the phone as Baby continued to sing.

"Sh-sh, honey." He tried to hush her, but she just smiled cheerfully and continued to croon. Shockley pulled his hair and tried to concentrate. It was too late to get another lawyer by tomorrow morning. Damn, damn, damn! He pounded his fist into the palm of his hand until it burned. He knew what was happening. It was the rats-deserting-the-sinking-ship syndrome. And he was the ship.

Terkel drove directly out to Leeming's Trailer Park as soon as he got back from Albany.

"Our case looks very promising," he said, taking Doris's hand excitedly. Doris was dressed in new clothes that she had bought with Olive on the way back from the City, and the trailer looked neat as a pin. In the tiny kitchen and living area there were bouquets of fresh flowers wired by well-wishers who had seen the program about her plight, and the air in the trailer smelled fragantly sweet. Doris herself looked radiant. There was lipstick on her lips, and there was the hint of rouge on her cheeks. Her hair had been done up in small waves by a lady in a neighboring trailer who ran a hairdressing business. Even the cats looked as if they had been spiffed up, their coats gleaming and silky.

"I submitted our brief and the court agreed to hear oral arguments." Terkel was now pacing back and forth in the tiny enclosure and spoke as though he were in court presenting his case. Doris watched the performance with obvious pleasure. "It went beautifully, if I may say so myself. And not just because of my splendid arguments," he said with a quick, happy laugh. "There was a lawyer there from social services as well as your acquaintance Mr. Bennett. They were in such a state of disarray that they really botched it up. They couldn't have helped us more if they had tried."

Doris smiled from ear to ear. She was so excited she could barely catch her breath.

"Now, all we have to do," he said, stopping and facing her, "is sit tight and wait for the decision. I'm usually very cautious about saying anything before an opinion, but—well, I could just sense where the judges' sympathies lay. Heck, I'd almost be willing to bet my last dollar," Terkel threw off the restraint. "I really think we won. I think you're going to get Baby back."

"Oh, Mr. Terkel," exclaimed Doris, unsure whether to laugh or cry. "You don't know how happy this makes me!" She held her hand to her chest. "I'm actually going to get Baby back."

"I think so."

"I can't quite believe it."

"You deserve it. And much more. If this thing goes the way it should, I'm also going to see to it that you get your house back, as well as some sort of settlement for damages."

"I don't want anything but Baby," she said dreamily. "Nothing at all."

"Let's make this brief and to the point," said Ruth when they sat down in the Gazebo Room of the motel and Shockley suggested lunch. People kept stopping by their table to touch Baby and listen to her as she sang on to herself, and for once Shockley wished she would just be quiet. Her song actually seemed to be aggravating an already-tense situation.

"After eighteen years, a bite of lunch with me is not going to kill you," he said, ordering.

"We can either settle everything amicably or—" Ruth broke off her sentence and waited until the waitress had served them. Then she continued, "Or we can let the courts decide an equitable settlement."

"What are you talking about?"

"Property."

"Yeah. I know. But that sounds like a prepared speech."

"I've already seen a lawyer," she said ominously over Baby's song.

"Look, what do you—?" He stopped in midsentence as a fat woman stood by Baby's high chair clasping her hands in rapture as Baby sang with a mouth full of crumbs. "Please," he muttered. The woman excused herself and reluctantly moved on. He turned back to Ruth. "What do you want?"

"Whatever's fair. We've been together for many years. During a good portion of that time I worked. When I wasn't working, I was making a home for you, serving your needs, taking care of your children."

"Is that what your lawyer told you to say?" asked Shockley, his hamburger tasting of bile.

"As a matter of fact."

"Look, let's make it simple. Why don't you take it all?"

"Huh?"

"Everything. The house. The cars. The savings accounts."

"Are you kidding?" she asked, taken aback.

"No, I'm not 'kidding.' I don't want any of it. It's all yours."

Two days later the appellate division of the New York State Supreme Court handed down its opinion.

Citing what they termed manifest injustice, the judges in a unanimous decision reversed the family court's action. In its written opinion, now a matter of public record, the court held that in the case of the *Tompkins County Department of Social Services* v. *Rumsey*:

1. The presiding justice had been in error when he admitted into evidence the child's entire case file from

the county Department of Social Services since many of the entries in the file consisted of statements, reports, and even hearsay made by persons under no business duty to report to the department.

2. The defendant had no opportunity to examine said documents prior to the hearing.

3. There appeared to be some element of collusion between individuals within the Department of Social Services and the foster parents.

What it all meant, Shockley learned from Ed Lutz, the new lawyer he had retained to examine the opinion, was that the appellate division had definitely wiped the slate clean, putting the onus on the Department of Social Services to begin an action in the higher court of appeals if they so desired.

"Considering the fact that Andrea Cassaniti was swiftly discharged today," said the lawyer, looking curiously at the child, who sat on the floor of the motel room singing to herself, "I'd say that the possibility of their initiating a new action is very small."

"And the bottom line?" Shockley asked as Lutz got up to leave.

"You're going to have to return the child to her mother," he said, snapping closed his briefcase. "Immediately."

After Lutz left, Shockley stood by the door looking sadly at Baby, who now lay on her back with her feet in the air as she dreamily serenaded herself, her voice soft and lilting. Biting his lip, Shockley closed his eyes and listened to her song, listened as though for the last time, soaking in her mellifluous voice as it unraveled the knots twisting his soul.

Suddenly Baby stopped singing in midnote.

Shockley immediately opened his eyes.

The child lay on the floor, her eyes wide, her body rigid as a board. She had stopped breathing.

Shockley charged over to her. But by the time he reached her and knelt down, whatever it was that had occurred had passed and she now seemed normal again.

For a long time Shockley carefully observed her. He watched as Baby rolled over, hit a ball with her hand, and scampered repeatedly after it as it tumbled across the floor. Letting out a loud sigh of relief, he realized that it had been nothing serious, just a momentary stomach cramp. Kids got them all the time.

Shockley procrastinated. Though he expected the phone to ring at any moment or the police to come marching into the motel in search of Baby, Shockley couldn't pull himself to take Baby back to Doris yet. For a while he thought about running away with her, to another state or another country, but in his heart he knew he could never do it. He also considered trying to gum up the transfer, dragging his heels until—as Lutz had warned—the courts would cite him for contempt. He knew, however, nothing would be gained by it and in the end he would have to return Baby.

What Shockley did instead was stall a little, buying himself a few hours in which to come to grips with losing Baby. And it wasn't going to be easy, that. Not after all these months of being so close to her, he thought staring out the motel window with Baby in his lap, watching as the day began to dwindle, darkness creeping up in the late afternoon as a fresh snow started to fall.

"Well, this is the end of the road," he said as Baby remained nestled quietly against him, her head tucked under his chin, her eyes following the passing traffic. In his mind Shockley ran through the closing loop of his life with Baby, starting at the very beginning that spring evening when he had almost run into Doris with his bike, unaware that buried within her swollen body lay the fetus destined to leave its mark on him and history. He recalled his children telling him of the miraculous infant who lived down in the flats and how he had laughed at the absurd notion of a newborn child who could sing—remembered then how his skepticism had crumbled before her unearthly song, how incredulity had given way to elation and ultimately that single-minded obsession with her music. Through his mind passed those notes of her first song, and he thought back to how that music had stirred his soul, evoking feelings that he had been sure were dead, her flutelike voice catapulting him to dizzy heights of joy and ectasy, unlocking a flood of forgotten creativity. How— Shockley shook himself out of his reverie and looked at Baby. This was ridiculous, he told himself. Here he was in essence eulogizing her. But she was not dead; it was only their life together that was finished. Once returned to Doris, Baby would go on playing, singing and living, probably even happily. She didn't need him in order to exist. It was the other way around.

It was then that he was struck by the continued absence of Baby's song—her silence as hard to ignore as her recent burst of constant singing. Except for the sounds of passing traffic drifting in through the plate glass, the hush in the motel room was unsettling.

"Sing, Baby. Sing for me again," he urged her. "One last time."

Baby looked up at him, tilted her head to one side as she usually did before singing, even opened her mouth, but failed to sing.

She was hungry, he thought, checking his watch and realizing that it was well past dinnertime. Putting on her sweater, he took Baby to the restaurant and fed her. When they came back, he let her play on the floor while he continued to watch her. She played for a while, scattering her brightly colored cars and stuffed animals across the floor, and then let out a long yawn. Shockley watched and waited. Waited, but still no song.

As evening yielded to night, he picked Baby off the floor, bathed her, dressed her in her pajamas, and laid her down in the crib and waited. Leaning over the bars of her crib, he looked down at her and watched as she stared back up at him, her eyebrows knitting. She yawned again, closed her eyes, and went to sleep. The silence was deafening.

Baby's soundlessness continued to bother Shockley that night. He debated with himself, put his fears to rest, only to have them pop up again. It was silly, he told himself, to get all upset simply because she hadn't sung that afternoon and evening. There were other times besides illness that Baby had not sung for hours. Yet—Yet—Still dressed in his clothes, Shockley fell asleep on top of his bed.

When he awoke in the morning, Baby was already up, standing in her crib and waiting for him. When he looked at her, she smiled. Drawing apart the curtains he stared glumly out at the morning. The snow that had started to fall last night was still coming down and was getting deep. Remembering the court order as if recounting a bad dream, he wondered if the roads out to Doris's trailer would be passable. With the clarity of morning he knew that he was just looking for an excuse. Today, he realized without equivocation, today he would return Baby. Shockley pulled some fresh clothes out of his suitcase, showered, shaved, and dressed slowly. All the time he kept listening, hoping that Baby would at least leave him with one last song to erase that nagging worry that kept chafing at the back of his mind. He lifted Baby out of her crib, changed her diapers, dressed her, took her to breakfast and, finally, when he could stall no longer, bundled her up in her snowsuit and carried her out to the car.

Driving out along the highway that rose above the lake, Shockley skirted the edge of Cayuga Heights and then passed the shopping malls, Baby sitting in her little seat and contentedly watching the passing scenery. As he drove past the airport, the land turning into high plateau, Shockley debated making a last plea to Doris but knew it was hopeless. Baby was hers, he thought, glancing at the child who sat ever silent, and that was the end of that. From now on he would have to concentrate on picking up the pieces of his own life.

Shockley turned off the highway and onto the road that led him past all the shacks and shanties of West Dryden. Under the soft blanket of fresh snow they looked benign and peaceful, the junk piles pristine mounds of white. Even Leeming's Trailer Park seemed pretty this early morning, he thought, turning into the entrance, the road winding through the park deep and clean with fresh lines of tire tracks cut through the perfect snow, sharp and incisive. A graceful roof of snow arched over each trailer, making them look like oblong mushrooms. The trees were plastered with white, like frosting on pastry.

Shockley pulled off the road. He unfastened Baby from her seat, took her in his arms, and tramped through the hushed maze toward Doris's trailer. As he approached the door, his eye was immediately caught by Doris's two cats, who stood huddled in front, the snow deep and undisturbed except for their prints. When they saw him, they began to meow loudly, and Baby reached out toward them. Mounting the steps, Shockley knocked on the aluminum door. No response.

He knocked again and, tilting his head toward the trailer, listened for some noise. Seeming to imitate him, Baby also tilted her head. Shockley strained to detect a sound from inside, but all he could make out were the cats crying and the noise of a snowplow grinding down a distant road.

He rapped again, louder, and waited, stamping his feet to keep warm.

"She's in there. Just keep knockin'," said a voice from behind, startling him. He turned around. Mrs. Schooley was standing behind him, wearing only a thin blouse and flowery summer skirt, her bare, white legs plunged into a pair of men's high rubbers.

Shockley turned back to the door and pounded loudly.

"Are you sure she's in there?" he asked, his suspicions gaining momentum.

"She hasn't gone out. I'd know. Why, I jus' live right—" The woman continued to rattle on.

Shockley moved away from the door and, leaning over the front steps, looked into a window.

"She's been just sitting there an' waiting for—Now, I'll just bet that little girl there is Baby. Now aren't you?" she chuckled, coming closer to the child.

Blocking out the morning glare with his free hand, Shockley peered in the front window. There was not a single light on in the trailer and from what he could see, the living room was empty. The kitchen was deserted, too. Craning his neck to see through a partially opened door, Shockley then spotted something on the floor in the tiny, dim bedroom. Pushing his face hard against the icy glass, he looked closer. Suddenly his jaw fell open and he let out a gasp. It was a leg.

"You gonna sing for us, honey?" asked Mrs. Schooley, taking Baby's mittened hand in hers. "You gonna—"

"Quick!" Shockley shouted to the woman. "Get someone to open this door!" Jumping off the steps into the deep snow, Baby tucked under one arm, he plunged through the layers of snow drifted up against the side of the trailer, fighting his way to the rear bedroom window, his heart echoing loudly in his chest. "Hurry!" he cried out to the startled woman, who stood frozen in her tracks. "Get someone with some tools!"

The fat woman turned and scurried back to her home.

Around the rear of Doris's trailer the snow was crotch-deep, and by the time Shockley had broken a trail to the window, he was dizzy and spent, his lungs on fire. Forcing himself up on tiptoes, he stared into the window.

"Oh, God!" he cried, looking in and seeing Doris's inert form lying on the floor, her curved body forming an almost perfect U.

Quickly he circled back around the trailer, following his broken path. By the time he had waded back to the front, the woman's husband was standing by the door with a crowbar. Shockley nodded, and with a single fast jerk, the skinny man sprung the lock and they all bolted in.

"Sweet Jesus!" uttered the man, looking down at Doris, who was lying there as she had since the previous afternoon, her face ghostly white and contorted, her body rigid as though frozen in an agonizing cramp.

"She's dead!" cried Mrs. Schooley, horrified. "Dead!"

From the vantage of Shockley's arms Baby looked down at her mother's body, then looked at the frightened couple who stood in the trailer—the man dangling a crowbar from a limp arm, the woman weeping tears that spilled over her round cheeks. Then, slowly, she turned her head and looked at Shockley. Shockley shifted his eyes away from Doris's body and looked back at Baby. Baby tilted her head, took a breath, opened her mouth and emitted a sound, a sound that echoed like a roar through Shockley's brain.

"Mama," she said, speaking her first word. "Mama, Mama."

EPILOGUE

Baby never sang again. Though she learned to walk and talk like other children, grew and developed normally, never once did she emit so much as a single, unearthly note.

Shortly after Doris Rumsey's death, the Department of Social Services, while repeatedly denying Irwin Shockley's petitions for custody, initiated an extensive search for relatives of the deceased mother. The agency managed to uncover a second cousin in Alabama, an aging aunt in Maine, and an even-more-distant cousin in Minneapolis, all of whom expressed an interest in adopting the child. When the relatives learned, however, that Baby was no longer singing, they indicated no further interest in the orphaned child. As the search dragged on and no one was forthcoming with an offer to adopt the little girl, the agency decided it both prudent and in the best interests of the child that she remain in familiar surroundings and, upon petition, she was returned to the foster care of Ruth Shockley.

With Baby's singing at a clear and definite end, Ivar Jacobsen's request for an injunction became a moot question and was subsequently dropped. The controversy surrounding the nearly two million dollars raised for Baby's ransom, however, continued to rage. Many

Babyists were urging that the money be used to build a shrine to the mother and child. A consumer group in Washington was demanding that the money, acquired on a fraudulent basis, immediately be returned to its original donors, and there was a strong movement in Congress calling for a joint House-Senate investigation of the matter. A number of prominent clergy originally associated with the CURB movement were insisting that the money be confiscated and distributed among relief organizations and established churches around the country.

The controversy surrounding the money, however, was brought to an abrupt close when it was discovered that Mr. Ivar Jacobsen had absconded with the entire fund. Jacobsen was first spotted in his native Denmark approximately one month after his sudden departure, but when proceedings were initiated to extradite him, he conveniently dropped out of view, reported sightings having since been made in such far-flung places as Tegucigalpa, Singapore, and Johannesburg.

Two months after Doris's death, Father Tom Fitzgibbons moved to Ithaca, accepting a part-time position as chaplain at the university. He divided his time between counseling students and continuing his avid pursuit of Babyism.

As Baby's singing faded to little more than a memory, many of the people who had firmly believed in Baby's descendancy from God began to falter in their conviction. What had once been a vast congregation steadily dwindled, and soon even those who had actually heard Baby sing began to doubt. Through it all, however, Father Tom Fitzgibbons never once wavered in his faith.

The Baby who had sung, he would explain to anyone who would listen, had died when the mother died, its spirit departing from the earth. It was the soul invested in this child that he had worshiped and continued to worship, not the little girl herself. Through the child's singing, God had sent a message to the people of the earth and it was there, and continued to be there, for those who would only open their hearts and listen.

Father Tom continued to correspond with the faithful, writing and printing a monthly newsletter linking the remaining Babyists around the globe. Through friends he managed to raise enough money to purchase the Lansing field in which Doris had given birth, and after a protracted fund drive, a modest five-room building was constructed the following year at the edge of that field, the structure's large front wall of glass looking out on the jutting shale rock marking the point where Doris had lain that morning. Ultimately the A-frame-type building came to serve as the International Center and Archives for Babyism as well as a home for Father Fitzgibbons and Irwin Shockley.

That fall, following Doris Rumsey's death, Harry Terkel ran on the independent ticket for Tompkins County District Attorney. Running against his better-financed, better-organized Republican opponent, Frank Kiely, he nonetheless won by an impressive landslide, his victory due in part, it was felt, to his success in the Rumsey appeal. Upon being sworn into office he immediately launched an investigation into the activities of the Department of Social Services, his probe resulting in a number of important reforms.

A few months after Terkel's election, Ruth Shockley was quietly married to a colleague of hers in the physics department and became Ruth Goldman. She, together with her new husband, began adoption procedures, and within a short time Baby became their legal daughter. Along with the child, who had grown into a rather happy-go-lucky tomboy, went a sizable trust fund, totaling nearly three hundred thousand dollars.

Walking down Willow Avenue one morning in June just after a freak snowstorm, Olive Eldridge slipped and fell on an unshoveled walk, breaking her hip in two places. As coincidence would have it, it was the sidewalk in front of what had once been Doris's house. Olive initiated suit against the new owner for contributory negligence, and upon receiving a substantial out-of-court settlement, moved to Florida, where she now lives happily in her own condominium.

Fay Dworkin, the convicted kidnapper of Baby, is serving a life sentence in a federal women's prison in the state of New Mexico. A few months after her conviction, she wrote a long and rather touching letter to Irwin Shockley, explaining that not a day goes by without her thinking about him and Baby and how she regrets having brought about the end of Baby's singing. Could he, she concluded in her letter, ever find a way to forgive her for what she had done? Shockley promptly replied that she was not to blame herself for precipitating Baby's change. And, as far as he was concerned, she was forgiven for her part in the kidnapping, though it wasn't really for him to forgive. Thus began a continuing correspondence in which Miss Dworkin expressed her sincere desire to continue spreading the message of Baby's song while in prison. If and when she ever got paroled, she hoped to come to Ithaca in order to serve, in whatever way she could, the cause of Baby-ism.

To this very day, five years later, Irwin Shockley continues to reside in Ithaca. He lives an exceedingly simple, essentially ascetic existence. He wears the same set of worn-out clothes, eats sparingly, remains strictly celibate, and has no possessions of his own other than his violin. Shunning all modern contrivances, he gets to his lessons by walking long miles. His hair has turned snow white, and he can often be seen moving across the countryside in the scorching heat of summer or the midst of icy winter, shuffling along in his broken down shoes, his shoulders hunched over, a small pair of golden lips dangling from a chain around his neck. Some say he has gone off the deep end. Others claim that he is doing penance, begging God for forgiveness for all his sins, both real and imagined.

With the passing of time, the extraordinary story of Baby is now little more than a memory. Many of those who heard her sing, or claimed they did, are no longer sure just what it was they did hear. Controversy still surrounds this tale, though what is perhaps germane to the question is to be found in a letter recently sent to and printed by a Chicago newspaper:

"Whether the story is true or not, or to what degree, seems to be almost immaterial," said the anonymous writer. "The point really is that the world just wasn't ready for her. Or anyone like her."

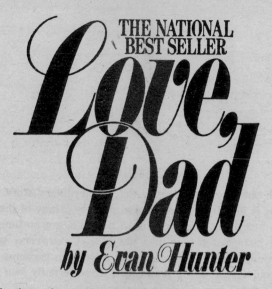

THE NATIONAL BEST SELLER
Love, Dad
by Evan Hunter

A deeply moving novel about a father and daughter reaching out to each other as changing times and changing values drive them apart. It is so moving, so true, so close to home—that it hurts. For we all have been there.

"Gripping. Moving. Enormously readable. A fine and sensitive novel that deals with an important aspect of the sixties."—Howard Fast, bestselling author of *The Immigrants*

A Dell Book $3.95   (14998-3)